P9-DDV-011
3 1524 00058 0508
FICTION
Bal Balzac, Honoré de
Lost illusions
WITHDRAWN
Woodridge Public Library
JAN 08 1991
MAY 30 1992
JUL 01 1992
JAN 2 1993
DEC 31 1992
JAN 20 1993
5/99
JUL 23 1999
SEP 03 2000
FEB 02 2001
FEB 09 2001
WOODRIDGE PUBLIC LIBRARY
WOODRIDGE, ILLINOIS 60517

HONORÉ DE BALZAC

LOST ILLUSIONS

TRANSLATED BY KATHLEEN RAINE

MODERN LIBRARY
NEW YORK

FIRST MODERN LIBRARY EDITION
1985 Printing

 Published in the United States by Random House, Inc., New York and simultaneously in Canada by Random House of Canada Limited, Toronto. This translation was originally published by John Lehmann Ltd, London in 1951 and by Random House, Inc. in 1967.

Reprinted by arrangement with Macdonald and Company Ltd., London.

Library of Congress Cataloging in Publication Data

Balzac, Honoré de, 1799-1850.
Lost illusions.
Translation of : Les illusions perdues.
I. Title.
PQ 2167.16E5 1985 843'.7 84-26159
ISBN 0-394-60523-3

Manufactured in the United States of America

CONTENTS

PART ONE

Two Poets

PART ONE

Two Poets

AT THE time when this story opens, the Stanhope press and the ink-distributing roller had not yet come into use in small provincial printing-houses; and, notwithstanding its paper industry, that linked Angoulême so closely with Paris printing, wooden presses—of the kind to which the figure of speech "to make the press groan" was literally applicable—were still in use in that town. Old-fashioned printing-houses were still using leather ink-balls, with which the printers used to ink the type by hand. The movable tables for the formes of type, set ready for the sheets of paper to be applied, were still made of stone and justly called *marbles*. The rapid spread of machine presses has swept away all this obsolete gear to which, for all its imperfections, we owe the beautiful books printed by Elzevir, Plantin, Aldus Didot, and the rest; so that some description is necessary of the old tools to which Jérôme-Nicolas Séchard was almost superstitiously attached, for they play a part in this great story of small things.

Séchard had been a journeyman printer, a "bear", according to compositor's slang. The movement to and fro, like that of a bear in a cage, of the printers coming and going from the ink-table to the press, from the press to the table, no doubt suggested the name. In revenge, the "bears" used to call the compositors "monkeys", because of those gentlemen's constant employment in picking out letters from the hundred and fifty-two compartments of the type cases. In the disastrous year of 1793 Séchard, who was about fifty at the time and a married man, was passed over in the great conscription which swept the bulk of the workmen of France into the army. The old pressman was the only hand left in the printing-house when the master (otherwise known as "the boss") died, leaving a widow but no children. The business seemed on the point of closing down altogether. The single-handed bear could not transform himself into a monkey, for, in his capacity as pressman, he had never learned to read or write. But, regardless of his incapacities, a Representative of the People who was in a hurry to spread the good tidings of the Decrees of the Convention issued a master-printer's licence to Séchard and requisitioned the press. Citizen Séchard accepted this dangerous patent, compensated his master's widow by giving her his wife's savings, and bought up the press at half its value. But that was only the beginning; he was faced with the problem of printing, quickly and without mistakes, the Decrees of the Republic. In this dilemma, Jérôme-Nicholas Séchard had the good luck to meet a nobleman from Marseilles who did not want to emigrate and lose his estate, nor, on the other hand, to be discovered and lose his head, and who in consequence had no alternative but to earn a living in some kind of manual work. M. le Comte de Maucombe accordingly donned the jacket of a provincial printer and set up, read, and corrected, single-handed, the decrees that forbade citizens to harbour nobles, on pain of death. The "bear", now "the boss", printed them off and had them posted up, so that both of them were safe and sound. By 1795 the mad fit of the Terror was over, and Nicolas Séchard had to look for another jack-of-all-trades for the job of compositor, proof-reader, and foreman; and an Abbé (he became a bishop after the Restoration), who refused to take the Oath, succeeded M. le Comte de Maucombe until the day when the First Consul restored the Catholic religion. The Count and the Bishop met later when both were sitting on the same bench in the House of Peers.

Jérôme-Nicolas Séchard could read no better in 1802 than he could in 1793; but by allowing a good margin for "materials" in his estimates he was able to pay a foreman. Their onetime easy-going mate had become a terror to his monkeys and bears. For avarice begins where poverty ends. From the day the printer saw the possibility of making a fortune self-interest brought out in him a covetous, suspicious, keen-eyed practical aptitude for business. His methods disdained theory. He had learned by experience to estimate at a glance the cost per page or per sheet, in every kind of type. He used to prove to his illiterate customers that big letters cost more to move than small; or if they wanted small type, that small letters were more difficult to handle. Compositing was the process in printing about which he knew nothing, and he was so frightened of cheating himself over that item that he always piled on the price. If his compositors were paid by the hour, he never took his eyes off them. If he knew that a manufacturer was in difficulties, he would buy up his paper stocks cheap and store them. He owned, besides, by this time, the premises in which the printing office had been housed from time immemorial. He had every kind of luck : he was left a widower, with only one son, whom he sent to the local grammar school, not so much in order to give him an education, as to provide himself with a successor. He treated him hardly, so as to prolong the time of his parental power; he made him, for example, work at the case in the holidays, and instilled into him that he must learn to earn his own living, so that he would one day to be able to repay his old father who was slaving in order to bring him up. After the departure of the Abbé, Séchard chose as overseer one of his four compositors recommended by the future Bishop as being both honest and intelligent. In this way the old man was in a position to wait until his son could take over the business, which would be sure to expand in the hands of a young man with brains.

David Séchard's career at the Angoulême grammar school was brilliant. But as a bear who had got on without any education, old Séchard had a marked contempt for book-learning and sent his son to Paris to study the higher branches of typography, but with such strong recommendations to save a round sum in the city that he described as "a workman's paradise", and warnings that he could not count on anything from the paternal purse, that he must have seen means of gaining ends of his own by his son's sojourn in the Land of Sapience. While he was learning his trade, David completed his education in Paris. Didot's foreman become a scholar. In the autumn of 1819 the old man sent for him to take charge of the business, and David Séchard left Paris without having cost his father a penny piece. Nicolas Séchard's printing establishment held at that time the monopoly of all the official printing for the Department, for the Prefecture, and for the Diocese, three connections which could not fail to make a fortune for an enterprising young man.

At this precise moment, however, the Cointet Brothers, paper-manufacturers, purchased the second printer's licence in Angoulême. Hitherto old Séchard, thanks to the military crises under the Empire, and the consequent crippling of all industrial enterprise, had reduced this licence to a dead letter. For this reason, he had not troubled to buy up the second licence, and his parsimony was to be the ruin of the old business. When he heard the news, old Séchard thought joyfully that the coming struggle with the Cointets would have to be fought out by his son and not by himself.

"I would have gone under," he thought to himself, "but a young fellow trained by the Didots will pull through."

The septuagenerian was longing for the day when he could live as he pleased. If his knowledge of the higher branches of typography was small, he made up for his ignorance of that art by his reputation in the art that workmen pleasantly call "topeography", held in such high esteem by the immortal author of *Pantagruel*, but which, persecuted by the so-called Temperance Societies, is falling, day by day, into disuse. Jérôme-Nicolas Séchard, true to the destiny of dryness conferred upon him by his name, was the victim of an insatiable thirst. For years his wife had kept within reasonable limits this passion for the juice of the grape—a taste natural to bears, as M. de Chateaubriand observed among that species in America—but philosophers have noticed that the habits of youth return with renewed force in old age. Séchard confirmed this moral hypothesis, for, the older he grew, the more he drank. His passion left its mark on his ursine features, giving them an original stamp. His nose had developed the proportions of a capital A (bold, triple-canon), and his veined cheeks, bloated with purple, violet, and mottled patches, suggested vine leaves; he reminded one of a monster truffle, surrounded by autumn vine sprays. Concealed beneath two thick eyebrows, like two brushes dipped in snow, his little grey eyes, bright with an avarice that had extinguished every other passion, even that of paternity, never lost their expression of cunning, even when he was drunk. His bald pate, fringed with bushy grizzled hair, reminded one of La Fontaine's Franciscan friars. He was short and stout, like one of those old-fashioned lamps that consume more oil than wick for all excesses exaggerate the natural physical tendencies, and drink, like study, makes the fat man fatter and the thin man thinner.

For thirty years Jérôme-Nicolas Séchard had worn the famous municipal tricorne hat that you still occasionally see on the head of the town-crier of a provincial town. His breeches and waistcoat were of greenish velvet; and he wore an old brown great-coat, grey cotton stockings, and silver-buckled shoes. This dress, in which the workman was still visible in the prosperous tradesman, suited his habits and vices so well, so completely expressed his way of life, that the old man might have come ready clad into the world; you could no more imagine him without his clothes than an onion without its skin.

If the old printer had not long since given proofs of the extent of his blind greed, his manner of retiring would have been enough to reveal his character.

In spite of the fact that his son must have learned a great deal in the great school of the Didots, he proposed to drive a bargain with him, which he had been thinking over for some time—a good bargain for the father, but a bad one for the son ; but for the old man there was no question of father and son in matters of business. If he had ever looked upon David as his only son, he had later come to regard him as the natural purchaser of the business, whose interests were opposed to his own. He was determined to sell dear ; David would want to buy cheap. His son was, therefore, an enemy to be overcome. This transformation of sentiment into self-interest, which is usually a gradual, tortuous, and hypocritical process among the educated classes, was rapid and direct with the old bear; and this only goes to show the superiority of shrewd "topeography" over expert typography.

When his son arrived the old man met him with the commercial cordiality that clever business men adopt towards their dupes. He was as attentive to him as a lover to his mistress; he took his arm, he told him where to walk to avoid the mud, he had warmed his bed, lit a fire, and prepared supper. The next day, after trying to fuddle his son in the course of a lavish dinner, Jérôme-Nicolas Séchard, well wined, began with a "Now for business", which came out so oddly between two hiccoughs that David begged him to put off business discussion until the next day. But the old bear knew too well how to turn his drunkenness to advantage to abandon the plan of battle that he had been preparing for so long. Besides, he had been dragging his chain for fifty years, and he did not want to wear it, he said, for another hour. Tomorrow his son should be the boss.

Perhaps at this point it would be as well to say a word or two about the premises. The printing-house had been established to-towards the end of the reign of Louis XIV, at the corner of the Rue de Beaulieu and the Place du Mûrier. The building had therefore been arranged to suit the needs of this craft for a long time past. The ground floor consisted of one enormous room, lighted by an old-fashioned window looking on to the street, and by a large sash-window opening on to a courtyard at the back. There was also a back passage leading to the master's office. But in the country the processes of printing are the object of such lively curiosity that customers always preferred to come in by a glass door opening on to the street, although this meant going down three steps, as the floor of the workshop was below the level of the street. Spellbound newcomers always failed to notice the dangers of the passage through the workshop. If they happened to be gazing at the sheets of paper hung in cradles made by cords suspended from the ceiling, they bumped into the rows of cases, or had their hats knocked off by the iron bars that held the presses in position. If they were intent upon the nimble movements of a compositor picking out his type from the hundred and fifty-two compartments of his case, reading his copy, reading his line over in his composing stick, and leading the lines, they were sure to stumble over a stack of damp paper weighted with slabs, or catch their hips against the corner of a bench, to the great amusement of the bears and the monkeys. No one had ever been known to reach without accident the two big cages in the depths of that room, built out into the yard at the back. In one of these miserable pavilions sat the foreman, in the other the master-printer. In the yard the walls were pleasantly decorated with vines which, in view of the owner's reputation, was an appropriate piece of local colour. At the back, against the partition wall, stood a tumbledown shed where the paper was trimmed and damped down. There, also, was the sink where the *formes*—in other words, the blocks of set-up type—were washed; from it issued an inky stream, mixed with the dirty water from the kitchen sink, so that peasants coming in on market day might have thought that the devil was taking a wash inside the house. On one side of this shed was the kitchen, on the other the woodshed. There were three rooms on the first floor of the house, and above these only two attic rooms. The first room, which ran the length of the passage, less the landing of the old wooden staircase, had a little oblong casement looking over the street and a bull's-eye window into the yard. This room served both as lobby and dining-room. It bore the stamp, from the plain whitewashed walls to the dirty brick floor, of the cynical simplicity of commercial greed. The furniture consisted of three rickety chairs, a round table, and a sideboard standing between two doors that opened into the bedroom and the living-room. Windows and doors were dingy with grime; there was usually a litter of blank or printed papers, and as often as not Jérôme-Nicolas Séchard's dirty dinner-plates and bottles were left standing about on the packages. The bedroom, with its leaded window-panes, looking out into the yard, was hung with those old tapestries that you see hanging outside houses in the provinces on Corpus-Christi day. It contained a big four-poster bed with curtains, canopy, and bedspread of crimson serge, two wormeaten armchairs, two tapestry-covered walnut chairs, an old bureau and a cartel clock on the mantelpiece. This room, with its air of homely comfort, and its warm brown tints, was just as it had been left by old Rouzeau, Jérôme-Nicolas Séchard's predecessor. The sitting-room had been modernised by the late Mme Séchard. The wainscot was painted a hideous powder-blue; the panels were decorated with a wall paper of oriental scenes, in sepia on a white ground. The furniture consisted of six lyre-backed chairs upholstered in blue leather. The two clumsy arched windows that looked out into the Place du Mûrier, were curtainless, and the mantelpiece had neither candle sconces, clock, nor mirror, for Madame Séchard had died in the midst of her projects of decoration, and the bear, who saw no use in improvements that brought in no profit, had abandoned them. It was here that, *pede titubante*, Jérôme-Nicolas Séchard led his son, pointing to an inventory of the contents of his printing establishment, drawn up by the foreman under his own direction, which lay on the round table.

"Read that, my boy," said Jérôme-Nicolas, rolling his drunken eyes from the paper to his son and back again to the paper. "You will see what a gem of a printing-business I am giving you."

" ' Three wooden presses held in position by iron bars, with cast iron plates . . . ' "

"An improvement of my own," put in old Séchard, interrupting his son.

" ' . . . together with all their implements, ink-tables, balls, benches, etc., sixteen hundred francs.' But, Father," David Séchard exclaimed, dropping the inventory, "your presses are old clogs not worth a hundred crowns, only fit for firewood ! "

" Clogs ? " cried old Séchard. " Clogs ? Bring the inventory and we will go downstairs ! You'll see whether your flimsy new-fangled stuff will work like these solid reliable old tools. And then you will not have the heart to insult honest presses that roll like post-chaises, and that will still be rolling all your time, without needing repairs of any sort. Clogs! Yes, you will find salt enough in these clogs to cook your eggs for you! Clogs that your father has been running for twenty years, that enabled him to make you what you are! "

The father negotiated the rickety staircase, slippery and worn, without mishap; he opened the door of the passage leading to the workshop and made for the nearest press, that had been surreptitiously oiled and polished; he pointed out the strong oak side-beams, rubbed up by his apprentice.

" What do you say to this for a press ? " he said. A wedding announcement was lying in the press. The old bear lowered the frisket on to the tympan, and the tympan on to the forme, which he rolled under the press; he raised the lever, let out the cord that drew out the forme, and raised the tympan and frisket again as nimbly as any young bear. Thus operated, the press creaked in such fine style that you would have thought that it was a bird that had dashed itself against a window-pane and flown off again.

" Show me an English press that can go at that pace! " said the father to his astonished son.

Old Séchard hurried in turn to the second and third presses, on each of which he performed the same manœuvre with equal dexterity. On the third, his wine-dimmed eye descried a patch overlooked by the apprentice. He swore considerably and rubbed it up with the skirt of his overcoat, like a horse-coper polishing the coat of a horse that he is trying to sell.

" With these three presses, David, you can make your thousand francs a year without a foreman. As your future partner, I am all against your replacing them with these wretched cast-iron machines that ruin the type. In Paris you made such a song and dance about that invention of some wretched Englishman, an enemy of France who wanted to put a fortune into the pockets of the iron-founders. So you have seen Stanhopes! You can keep your Stanhopes. They cost two thousand five hundred francs apiece, nearly twice the value of my three jewels put together, and they ruin your type, because there is no give in them. I'm not educated like you, but you mark my words: the life of the Stanhope is the death of the type. These three presses will give you good service, the printing will be properly done, and in Angoulême they don't ask for more. Whether you print with iron or wood, or gold or silver, come to that, they are not going to pay you a farthing more."

" ' Item '," David continued, " ' five thousand pounds' weight of type from Vaflard's foundry. . . .' "

Didot's apprentice could not suppress a smile at the name.

" All right, you can laugh! After twelve years, that type is as good as new. That is what I call a type-founder! M. Vaflard is an honest man, and he supplies good hard-wearing metal; and to my way of thinking, the best type-founder is the one you go to least often."

"Valued at ten thousand francs," David continued. "Ten thousand francs, Father, but that comes to forty sous a pound, and the Didots sell their *Cicero* at thirty-six, new. Your old nail-heads are only worth the price of scrap metal, ten sous a pound."

"So you call M. Gillé's italics, running-hand and round hand, nail-heads, M. Gillé who used to be a printer to the Emperor, type worth six francs a pound, masterpieces of engraving bought only five years ago, and some of them still as bright as when they came from the foundry—look at this!"

Old Séchard grabbed a few packets of sorts that he had never used and showed them to David.

"I'm not an educated man, I don't know how to read or write, but I know enough, all the same, to see that Gillé's characters are the fathers of your Messrs. Didot's English styles. Here's a round hand for you," he continued, taking up an unused pica type.

David saw that it was no use arguing with his father. He must take it or leave it—it was a question of yes or no. The old bear had included in his inventory the very cords on the ceiling. The smallest job-chases, wetting-boards, paste-pots, rinsing-trough and brushes, were valued with miserly exactitude. The total amounted to thirty thousand francs, including the printer's licence and the good-will. David wondered whether the thing was feasible or not. Seeing that his son remained silent about the total, old Séchard grew uneasy, for he preferred a violent argument to a silent acceptance. In dealings of this sort, bargaining proves that a customer is capable of looking after his interests. "A man who agrees to everything will pay you nothing," old Séchard was thinking. While he was trying to fathom his son's mind he went over all sorts of worthless odds and ends needed for running a country printing-house. He led David now to a glazing-press, now to a cutting-press used for the work of the town, pointing out its usefulness and good condition.

"Old tools are always the best tools," he said. "In printing you have to pay more for them than for new ones, as you have for gold-beaters' tools."

Hideous vignettes representing Hymens, Amours, and skeletons raising tombstones so as to make a V or an M, enormous borders of masks for theatre posters, became, through the bibulous eloquence of Jérôme-Nicolas, objects of immense value. He assured his son that country people's habits are so deeply rooted, that he would be wasting his pains if he tried to give them the finest examples of the printer's art. He, Jérôme-Nicolas Séchard, had tried to set them a better class of almanac than the *Double Liégeois* printed on sugar-bag paper. Very well, what had happened ? They had preferred the *Double Liégeois* to the finest almanacs obtainable. David would soon discover the value of these old things when he found that he could get a better price for them than for the most expensive novelties.

" Ah, my boy, the country is the country, and Paris is Paris. If a man from l'Houmeau comes and asks you to print his wedding-cards, and you do them without cupids and garlands, he won't think he's properly married ; he would bring them back if he found nothing but a plain M on them in the style of your Messrs. Didot—the glory of typography, no doubt, but their ideas won't come in in the country for another hundred years. So there you are."

Generous men drive bad bargains. David's nature was of the sensitive and affectionate kind that shrinks from an argument, and which gives in the moment an adversary touches his feelings. His fine feelings, and the influence that the old toper still had over him, put him still further at a disadvantage in an argument about money with his father ; especially as he credited him with the best of intentions, for he put down selfish greed to the old printer's attachment to his tools. All the same, Jérôme-Nicolas Séchard had taken everything over from the widow Rouzeau for ten thousand francs, paid in Assignats, and in its present condition thirty thousand francs was an exorbitant price.

" Father, you are cutting my throat," exclaimed the young man.

" I, who gave you your life ? " said the old toper, raising his hand to the ropes hanging from the ceiling. " But, David, consider what the licence is worth! Do you realise that the Advertising Journal alone, at ten sous a line, brought in five hundred francs last month ? Look at the books, my boy, see what the posters and registers for the prefecture are worth, and the work for the mayor's office, and the bishopric! You are a slacker who doesn't care about getting on. You are haggling over the horse that would carry you to a nice bit of property, like Marsac."

Along with the inventory there was a deed of partnership between father and son. The worthy father was to let his house to the Company for a sum of twelve hundred francs a year although he himself had bought it for only six thousand. He was to reserve one of the attic rooms for his own use. Until David Séchard should have paid back the thirty thousand francs the profits were to be shared equally ; from the day when that sum had been paid to his father he was to become the sole and only proprietor of the business. David ran over in his mind the value of the licence, the good-will, and the newspaper, without taking the plant into account ; he decided that he could pay off the debt, and he accepted the conditions. Accustomed as he was to peasant haggling over details, and knowing nothing of the wider views of Parisians, the father was astonished at this prompt conclusion.

" Has my son been making money," he wondered, " or is he scheming not to pay me ? "

So thinking, he tried to find out if he had brought any money with him, hoping to be paid something on account. His father's curiosity awakened the son's suspicions. David gave nothing away.

Next day old Séchard got the apprentice to carry upstairs into the room on the second floor the things that he planned to take to the country in some cart returning empty. He left the three rooms on the first floor empty of furniture, and left his son not a penny to pay the workmen their wages. When David asked his father, as a partner, to contribute this necessary means to their mutual profit, the old man pretended not to understand. He had not undertaken, so he said, to part with money as well as parting with his printing-house. He had paid his share. Pressed by his son, he retorted that when he had bought the business from Rouzeau's widow he had not had a penny left. If he, a poor workman without a friend in the world, had got on, a pupil of the Didots ought to be able to do even better. What was more, had not David been earning money, thanks to an education paid for by his father by the sweat of his brow ? He had better make use of that education now.

" What have you done with your wages ? " he said, returning to the charge, hoping for some light on the problem which his son's silence yesterday had left unsolved.

" But I had to live! And I had to buy my books! " David replied indignantly.

" Oh! So you bought books, did you ? You will never make a good business man. A man who buys books isn't fit to print them," the bear retorted.

David experienced the bitterest of all humiliations—that of shame for a father ; he had to listen to the stream of mean, servile, sordid, money-grubbing excuses in which the old miser framed his refusal. He crushed down his pain into his heart, realising that he was alone, that there was no one to whom he could turn ; he realised, also, that his father was trying to make money out of him, and, in a spirit of philosophic curiosity, he wondered how far the old man would go. He pointed out that he had never made any enquiries as to his mother's fortune. If that fortune would not cancel out the price of the printing-press, it would at least help towards running it for their mutual profit.

" Your mother's fortune," said old Séchard, " was her intelligence and her beauty."

David now understood his father completely and realised that his only means of obtaining money that was his by right would be an endless, expensive and humiliating lawsuit. His noble heart accepted the burden that had been laid upon him, for he knew how hard it would be to clear himself of the engagements into which he had entered with his father.

" I will work," he thought. " After all, if I have a hard time, so had the old man. Besides, after all I shall be working for myself."

" I am leaving you a treasure," said the old man, uneasy at his son's silence.

David asked what the treasure was.

"Marion," said his father.

Marion was a big country girl, indispensable to the printing establishment : she damped down the paper and trimmed it to size, did the errands, the cooking, and the washing, unloaded the paper from the carts, collected accounts and cleaned the ink-balls. If Marion had been able to read, old Séchard would have given her the type-setting into the bargain.

The old man set out on foot for the country. He was delighted by his sale, disguised as a partnership, but he was worried about how he was going to be paid, for after the anxieties of the sale come those of the payment. All passions are essentially jesuitical. This man who regarded all education as useless was trying to force himself to believe in the value of education. He was risking his thirty thousand francs on the ideas of honour that education might be supposed to have developed in his son. David had been well brought up, so he would sweat blood to pay off his engagements, and his knowledge would find means. He seemed to be full of fine sentiments—therefore he would pay up! There are many fathers who behave in this way, and who think that they have acted paternally—just as old Séchard did, as he reached his vineyard at Marsac, a little village some ten miles out of Angoulême. This property, on which the previous owner had built a pleasant house, had been added to by the old bear, year by year, ever since 1809, when he had purchased it. He now exchanged the cares of the printing-press for those of the wine-press, and he had, as he put it, " been in that line so long that he ought to know something about it ". During the first year of his country retirement old Séchard's face, over his vine-props—for he was always to be found among his vines, just as formerly he had always been in his workshop—was a worried one. Those unlooked-for thirty thousand francs went to his head more than the September vintage, and already, in imagination, he was fingering the coin. The less right he had to the money, the more anxious he was to have it safely in his purse. So that he often hurried up from Marsac to Angoulême, driven by his anxieties. He would ascend the rock-hewn steps to the town and go into the workshop to see how his son was running the business.

There were the old presses in their places. The one apprentice, in his paper cap, would be cleaning the ink-balls. The old bear would hear the press creaking over some trade circular, recognise his old type, observe his son and the foreman, each in his cage reading a book which the old bear mistook for proofs. After dining with David, he would make his way back to his Marsac estate, thinking over his worries. Avarice, like love, has a gift of second sight for future contingencies, divines them and hugs them. Far away from the workshop, from the tools to which he was so attached, because they reminded him of the days when he made his fortune, the old vine-grower could sense symptoms of inactivity in his son. The name of *Cointet Brothers* haunted him, for he saw that of *Séchard and Son* dropping into second place. In short, the old man scented trouble on the wind. And his presentiment was well founded: disaster was hovering over the house of Séchard. But there is a providence that looks after misers. By an unhoped-for chain of circumstances, this deity was, after all, to put the price of his extortionate sale into the pocket of the old toper.

And this is why the Séchard business, notwithstanding its seeds of prosperity, was falling into ruin.

Indifferent to the movement of religious reaction the Restoration produced in the Government, but equally indifferent to liberalism, David maintained a most unfortunate neutrality in political and religious matters. At that time provincial business men had to profess political opinions if they wanted to attract customers, and they had to choose between the custom of the royalists and that of the liberals. But David had another love at heart, and his scientific preoccupations and fine nature prevented him from having that commercial avarice that is the mark of the successful business man, and that would have made him pay attention to the differences that distinguish business in the country from business in Paris. The Cointet brothers came out in unison on the Royalist side, they observed Lent ostentatiously, haunted the cathedral, set out to cultivate the society of the clergy, and when devotional books came into demand they were the first to print them. Thus the Cointets were the first in a lucrative field; they slandered David Séchard with accusations of liberalism and atheism. How, they asked, could anyone employ a man whose father had been a Septembrist, a drunkard, a Bonapartist, an old miser who had piled up a small fortune? They were poor men with families to support, whereas David was a bachelor, would be a rich man one day, and had only himself to consider, and so on. Influenced by these accusations against David, the prefecture and the diocese transferred their business to the Cointets. And soon these keen competitors, emboldened by the inactivity of their rival, started a second advertising journal. The old press still had the local printing jobs, but the profits on the advertising newspaper were reduced by half. The Cointets made handsome profits on their devotional books and presently proposed to Séchard to buy up the newspaper, so as to have the advertisements and judicial announcements all in their hands. No sooner had David sent this news to his father, than the old vine-grower, who was already alarmed by the progress of the Cointets, descended from Marsac upon the Place du Mûrier with the rapidity of a raven who scents the corpses on a field of battle.

"Leave the Cointets to me, and don't you meddle with this business," he said to his son.

The old man saw through the Cointets' game and they took fright at his shrewd insight. His son was making a blunder, he said, and he had come to put a stop to it.

"What will become of our connection if he gives up the paper?" The attorneys and solicitors of l'Houmeau were liberals to a man; the Cointets had tried to discredit Séchard on the charge of liberalism and that gave old Séchard his clue—the Séchards had the liberal business in their pockets. Sell the Chronicle? They might as well sell up the business and the licence into the bargain!

Then he went on to ask the Cointets for sixty thousand francs for the printing business so as not to ruin his son. He was fond of his son, he was going to stand by his son. The vine-grower made use of his son as a bargaining-counter as peasants make use of their wives; his son would not agree to this or that, according to the propositions that he wrested one by one from the Cointets. Finally he led them, not without difficulty, to a proposal to pay the sum of twenty-two thousand francs for the *Charente Chronicle.* But David was to undertake never to publish any newspaper whatsoever, under a penalty of thirty thousand francs' damages. This sale was the suicide of the Séchard business. But that did not worry the old vine-grower. After theft comes murder. The old man counted on that sum towards the payment of his account; and to get his hands on it, he would have sold David into the bargain, the more so as that wretched son of his had the right to half this unlooked-for windfall. In compensation, the generous father gave up his share in the business, but continued to let him the house for the famous sum of twelve hundred francs.

After the sale of the paper to the Cointets the old man came seldom to the town, pleading his age. But the real reason was that he took very little interest in the business now that it was no longer his. Even so, he could not entirely repudiate his old affection for his gear. When his own affairs brought him to Angoulême, it would be hard to say whether it was affection for his wooden presses that drew him back to his old house, or the pretext of asking his son, as a mere matter of form, for his rent. His old foreman, who had gone over to the Cointets, knew exactly how much his paternal generosity was worth; in his opinion, the old fox was determined to keep the right to interfere in his sons' affairs by becoming a privileged creditor through the accumulation of rent.

David Séchard's carelessness arose from causes that throw light on that young man's character. A few days after his installation in the paternal business, he had met an old school friend, who was at this time in a state of extreme poverty. David Séchard's friend was a young man of twenty-one or thereabouts, called Lucien Chardon, the son of an ex-army surgeon who had retired from service in the Republican armies as a result of a wound. Nature had intended M. Chardon senior for a chemist; and chance had made him a chemist of Angoulême. Death overtook him in the midst of his uncompleted researches into a discovery to which he had devoted many years of scientific study and which would have made his family rich. He was looking for a specific for all kinds of gout; and gout is a disease of the rich, and the rich will pay a high price for health once they have lost it. This was why the chemist had chosen this problem among the various ones that presented themselves to his mind. As between science and empiricism, the late Chardon had seen that science alone could make his fortune: therefore he had studied the causes of the malady and based his remedy on a certain treatment, to be modified according to the patient's temperament. He died during a visit to Paris, where he had gone in order to apply for the approval of the *Académie des Sciences*, and so lost the fruits of his labours.

Anticipating that he would make his fortune, the chemist had spared nothing on the education of his son and daughter, and his family had lived up to the income derived from his chemist's shop. So that he left his children not only poor, but, what was worse, poor when they had been brought up in the expectation of a brilliant future, which died with him. The great Desplein, who attended him, saw him die in convulsions of rage. The army-surgeon's ambition was the outcome of his passionate love for his wife, the last survivor of the family of de Rubempré, saved by a miracle from the scaffold in 1793. Without the girl's knowledge or consent to the lie, he had gained time by saying that she was pregnant. Having thus, as it were, created the right to marry her, he had done so, their common poverty notwithstanding. Their children, like all children of love, inherited their mother's marvellous beauty, a heritage too often fatal when joined with poverty. These hopes, labours and despairs that Madame Chardon had had so deeply at heart had wrought inroads on her beauty, just as the gradual degradation of poverty had changed her habits; but her courage, and that of her children, had been equal to their misfortune. The poor widow had sold the chemist's business in the High Street of l'Houmeau, the chief suburb of Angoulême. The investment of the price of the business brought her an income of three hundred francs, which would not have been enough for her to live on even had she been alone. But she and her daughter accepted their situation with pride and made up their minds to earn a living. The mother went out as a midwife, and because of her superior manners she was preferred to all others in the wealthy houses, where she had her keep without costing her children a penny, and earned two francs a day. In order to spare her son the embarrassment of seeing his mother fallen so low, she had taken the name of Madame Charlotte. Those seeking her services applied to M. Postel, M. Chardon's successor. Lucien's sister worked with a very respectable woman of good standing in l'Houmeau, their neighbour Mme Prieur, a laundress, and earned fifteen sous a day. She was Madame Prieur's forewoman and had in the workroom a position of superiority that raised her a little above the general run of the working girls. Their slender earnings, together with Madame Chardon's income of three hundred francs, came to about eight hundred francs a year, with which this family of three contrived to pay for food, rent, and clothes. By strict economy, they could just manage on this sum, most of which was spent on Lucien.

Mme Chardon and her daughter Eve believed in Lucien as Mahomet's wife believed in the Prophet. Their devotion to his future knew no bounds. This poor family lived in l'Houmeau, in rooms for which they paid a very low rent to M. Chardon's successor, at the end of the yard behind the dispensary. Lucien occupied a wretched attic room. Inspired by a father whose passion for natural sciences had at first impelled him in that direction, Lucien had been one of the most brilliant boys at the Angoulême grammar school, where he was in the third form when David Séchard left.

When the two school friends chanced to meet again Lucien was tired of drinking from the harsh cup of poverty and was ready to embark upon any of those rash courses that we are liable to take at the age of twenty. The forty francs a month that David generously offered Lucien to come and learn to be a printer's foreman—although he had no need of one—saved Lucien from despair. The bonds of this schoolboy friendship, thus renewed, were soon drawn closer, no less by the similarity of their lot in life than by their dissimilarity of character. Both, with their thoughts full of dreams of a great future, possessed that high intelligence that brings men within reach of the loftiest heights; both found themselves confined to the lowest level of society. This sense of injustice was a powerful bond between them. Both, besides, had discovered poetry, though by different routes. Lucien, although destined for the highest fields of natural science, had turned with ardour towards literature; while David, whose thoughtful nature predisposed him to poetry, had become interested in the natural sciences. This reversal of roles engendered a kind of spiritual fraternity. Lucien presently confided to David the high opinions that he had heard from his father on the possible application of science to industry, and David pointed out to Lucien the new fields that he ought to open up in literature, in order to make his name and his fortune. The friendship between these two young men ripened within a few days into one of those passions known only to youth. Nor was it long before David caught a glimpse of the beautiful Eve and fell in love with her, in the way of grave and thoughtful natures.

The *Et nunc et semper et in secula seculorum* of the liturgy is the theme of those sublime unknown poets whose epics are both conceived and buried between two hearts! When the lover had divined the secret of the hopes that mother and daughter reposed in that fine poet's brow, when he had understood their blind devotion, he found it sweet to approach his mistress by sharing her sacrifices and her hopes. So that Lucien was, for David, a chosen brother. Like those extremists who try to be more royalist than the king, David outdid his mother and sister in his faith in Lucien's genius, and he spoiled him as a mother spoils a child. In the course of those conversations in which, under the stress of the lack of money that tied their hands, the two used to consider how they could possibly make a fortune quickly by shaking all the trees already stripped by previous comers, Lucien bethought him of two ideas that his father had talked of. M. Chardon had spoken of the possibility of reducing the price of sugar by half by the use of a new chemical, and of reducing the price of paper in the same way by importing from America a certain vegetable product similar to that used by the Chinese, which would effect a great saving in the price of raw materials. David, who knew the importance of this question that was already engaging the attention of the Didots, seized on this idea, in which he saw the possibility of making a fortune, and looked upon Lucien as a benefactor to whom he owed a debt that he could never repay.

Anyone can see that the ruling thoughts and inner life of these two friends rendered them quite unfit to run a printing establishment. Far from bringing in fifteen to twenty thousand francs, like the business of their rivals the Cointets, printers and publishers to the diocese, proprietors of the *Charente Courier*, now the only newspaper of the department, the younger Séchard's printing establishment brought in barely three hundred francs a month, out of which the foreman's salary had to be paid, besides Marion's wages and the rent and taxes; which reduced David's profits to a hundred francs a month. An active and industrious man would have replaced the old type, bought steel presses, and found a means of getting orders in Paris for printing books at cheap rates; but the master and the foreman, absorbed in dreams of intellectual works, made do with such orders as came in from their few remaining customers. The Cointet brothers at last came to understand David's character and mentality, and no longer slandered him; on the contrary, a shrewd sense of policy counselled them to let the old firm survive, indeed to keep it going, at a level of honest mediocrity, lest it should fall into the hands of some dangerous rival; they themselves sent David the job-printing of the town. And so it happened, without his being aware of it, that David Séchard owed his existence, commercially speaking, to the business astuteness of his rivals. Delighted with what they called his craze, the Cointets appeared to be behaving fairly and honourably towards him; but in fact they were only acting on the principle of carriers who set up a sham rival coach to scare off real competitors.

The exterior of the Séchard printing establishment was in harmony with the crass avarice that had prevailed within, for the old bear had never done any repairs. Rain and sun, the weather of all the seasons, had left their mark and given the old house the appearance of an old tree-trunk standing at the corner of the road, so cracked and knotted it was with uneven patches. The house front, badly built in brick and stone, lacked all proportion and seemed to be bending under the weight of a worm-eaten roof loaded with those carved pantiles of which all roofs in the south of France are built. The rotten window-frames were fitted with those immense shutters, held up by heavy cross-bars, that are necessary in that hot climate. It would have been hard to find in the whole of Angoulême another house in such a state of dilapidation; it seemed held together only by the plaster. Try to imagine the workshop, light at both ends, dark in the middle, its walls covered with posters, and discoloured, below, by the shoulders of all the workmen who had rubbed past them for the last thirty years; the tangle of ropes hanging from the ceiling, the stacks of paper, the old presses, the pile of slabs for weighting damped sheets, the rows of cases, and at the far end the two offices where, each in his own den, sat the master and the foreman; and you will have some idea of the daily life of the two friends.

In 1821, early in May, David and Lucien were standing by the window overlooking the yard at about two o'clock, the time when their four or five workmen knocked off for the dinner hour. When the master saw his apprentice close the street door, he led Lucien into the yard, as if he found the smell of papers, printing-ink, presses and old wood insupportable. They both seated themselves in an arbour, whence they could see if anyone should come into the workshop. The rays of sunlight that filtered through the sprays of the vine caressed the two poets and seemed to envelop them in an auriole of light. The contrast between the two faces and the two characters was brought out into clear relief. David's features were those bestowed by nature on men destined to fight hard battles, whether in the eyes of the world or in obscurity. His sturdy torso was surmounted by strong shoulders, in harmony with his powerful build. His face, dark-skinned, fleshy and highly coloured, was surmounted by a thick crop of black hair, suggesting at first glance one of Boileau's famous canons. But a closer scrutiny revealed in the line of the thick lips, in the cleft of his chin, in the turn of his square nostrils, the set of his neck and, above all, in his eyes the suppressed fire of steadfast love, the wisdom of the thinker, the ardent melancholy of a mind capable of embracing the whole scope of a subject, of penetrating all its ramifications, and which would be ready to subject all purely ideal joys to the clear light of ruthless analysis. That face might kindle with the fire of genius, but there, too, one could see the ashes of the volcano ; hope had been extinguished in it by that profound sense of social obscurity, by which humble birth and want of fortune hold back so many superior minds. Beside the poor printer, who so loathed his craft, although so nearly akin to intellectual work, beside this Silenus, wrapped up in himself, who drank such deep draughts of the cup of science and poetry that at last he became drunk and forgot the sorrows of provincial life, stood Lucien in the graceful pose in which some sculptor might have represented Indian Bacchus ; for his face had the distinguished lines of antique beauty, a Grecian nose and brow, the pale complexion of a woman, eyes of a blue so dark as to be almost black, eyes full of love, whose whites were as clear and fresh as those of a child. Those beautiful eyes were surmounted by brows traced as if by a Chinese brush, and fringed with long chestnut lashes. On his cheeks grew a soft down whose colour matched the fairness of his wavy hair. His fair temples were radiant with a divine grace. His short chin, curved but without abruptness, was of a matchless nobility. A sad, angelic smile hovered on his coral lips, that parted to reveal his perfect teeth. He had the hands of an aristocrat, elegant hands, whose gesture men must obey, hands that women love to kiss. Lucien was slender and of middle height. On looking at his feet, a man might have been tempted to think him a young girl in disguise, the more so because, like nearly all men of subtle, not to say astute, minds, the contour of his hips was womanly. This indication, which is rarely deceptive, was a true guide to Lucien's character, for his restless mind often inclined him, in analysing the present state of society, to take his stand on the grounds, characteristic of diplomacy, that success justifies any means, however shameful. One of the misfortunes to which great intelligence is subject is that of understanding everything too well, vice no less than virtue.

The standards by which these two young men judged society were all the higher, because they themselves were low on the social scale, for unknown men are apt to revenge themselves by their lofty outlook. But their despair was the more bitter since those standards themselves were a continual reminder of their present lot.

Lucien had read a great deal and made comparisons ; David had thought and reflected. In spite of his appearance of rude rustic health, the printer's genius was of a melancholy cast, prone to depression. He lacked self-confidence ; whereas Lucien, enterprising but unstable, had an audacity that contradicted his frail, almost delicate physique with its effeminate grace. Lucien had in the highest degree the Gascon character, bold, brave, adventurous, prone to exaggerate the good and belittle the bad aspects of a situation, never stopping at any crime if there is anything to be gained by it, laughing at vice when it serves as a stepping stone. These ambitious traits were still held in check by the idealism of youth, by the enthusiasm that inclined him to prefer those noble means that men who love glory try first. He was as yet in the toils only of his desires, not of the difficulties of life ; of his own powers, but not yet those of the wickedness of men, a fatal example to unstable minds. Quite under the influence of Lucien's brilliance of mind, David admired him, and at the same time rectified the errors into which his friend was betrayed by his French impetuosity. This upright man, whose timid character was in disaccord with his robust constitution, had all the tenacity of the northern races. He might see all the difficulties in his way, but he had the decision to face and overcome them ; and although he possessed a truly apostolic steadfastness of virtue, he could temper it by the graces of a boundless tolerance. In this friendship already old, one of the friends—David—was the worshipper ; and Lucien ruled him like a woman who knows herself adored. David obeyed with pleasure. His friend's physical beauty implied a superiority that he, regarding himself as coarse and common clay, willingly recognised.

" To the ox the patient plough, to the bird careless flight," the printer told himself. " I will be the ox, Lucien shall be the eagle."

So for three years the two friends had shared their destinies, so rich in promise. They read all those great works that had been appearing on the literary and scientific horizon since the peace : the works of Schiller, Goethe, Lord Byron, Walter Scott and Jean-Paul, of Berzélius, Davy, Cuvier, Lamartine and the rest. They warmed their spirits at these great fires, they attempted abortive works of their own, abandoned and recommenced with equal ardour. They worked continually, with the inexhaustible vitality of youth. Both equally poor, equally devoured with the love of art and science, they forgot their present poverty in working to lay the foundations of their fame.

"Lucien, do you know what I have just had sent from Paris?" asked the printer, drawing a little octavo volume from his pocket. "Listen to this." David read, as only poets can read, André de Chénier's *Néère*, then the *Jeune Malade,* then the *Elegy on Suicide*, the *Elegy in an Antique Mode*, and the two last *Iambes*.

"So that is André de Chénier!" Lucien repeated, over and over again. "It makes one despair," he said for the third time, while David, too moved to continue, handed him the book. "A poet discovered by a poet!" he added, looking at the signature to the preface.

"After that one volume," David continued, "Chénier never thought anything else that he wrote worth publishing."

Lucien in his turn read the fragment of an epic entitled *L'Aveugle,* and several of the elegies. When he came to the line. "If theirs be not happiness, is there such on earth?" he kissed the book, and the two friends were both moved to tears, for both were in love with Chénier, to idolatry. The vine shoots were showing colour; the old walls of the house, cracked and battered, traversed with squalid cracks, had been transformed to the fluted columns, traceries and bas-reliefs of who knows what masterpieces of architecture built with fairy hands. Fancy had scattered her flowers and gems over the little obscure yard. André de Chénier's *Camille* had become, for David, his adored Eve, and for Lucien a great lady to whom he was paying court. Poetry had spread the majestic folds of her starry robe over the workshop and the uncouth visages of the monkeys and bears of the printing-press. Five o'clock came, but the two friends knew neither hunger nor thirst; for them life was a golden dream, all the treasures of the earth lay at their feet. Their eyes were upon that blue patch on the stormy horizon of life, to which Hope points a finger, urging men on with her siren words, saying: "Come, take wing, through that golden, silver, or azure rift you shall escape from all misfortune." At this moment an apprentice called Cérizet (a Paris urchin that David had brought to Angoulême) opened the little glass door that led from the workshop into the yard and indicated the two friends to a stranger who greeted them politely.

" Sir," he said to David, drawing a fat notebook from his pocket, " this is a memoir that I wish to have printed ; can you give me an estimate ? "

" We do not undertake to print such large manuscripts," David answered without looking at the notebook. " You had better take it to the Cointets."

" All the same, we have a very pretty type that might do," Lucien remarked, taking the manuscript. " If you would be good enough to call tomorrow we will look over your manuscript and let you have an estimate of the cost of printing."

" Have I the honour to address M. Lucien Chardon ? "

" Yes, sir," said the foreman.

" I am happy to have had the opportunity of meeting a young poet destined for such great things. I was sent here by Mme de Bargeton."

On hearing that name, Lucien blushed crimson and murmured a few words to express his gratitude for the interest that Mme de Bargeton had showed towards him. David noticed his friend's embarrassment, and left him talking to the country gentleman, the author of a monograph on the breeding of silk-worms, whose vanity had inspired him with the desire to see himself in print so as to be read by his fellow-members of the Agricultural Society.

" Well, Lucien," David said when the gentleman had left, " are you in love with Mme de Bargeton ? "

" Desperately ! "

" But you are more completely cut off from her by social prejudices than if she were in Pekin and you in Greenland."

" The will of two lovers can overcome anything," said Lucien, lowering his eyes.

" You would forget all about us," said the timid lover of beautiful Eve.

" On the contrary—it may be that already I have sacrificed my mistress."

" What do you mean ? "

" In spite of my love, in spite of the many reasons for which I might desire her patronage, I have told her that I shall never go back there unless I can take with me a man whose talents are superior to mine and whose future is sure to be a great one—unless my friend and brother, David Séchard, is received as well. There should be a reply waiting at home. But although all the aristocracy have been invited this evening to hear me read my poems, if the answer is no, I shall never set foot in Bargeton House again."

David pressed Lucien's hand with fervour, as his eyes filled with tears. Six o'clock struck.

" Eve will be wondering where I am. Goodbye," said Lucien abruptly.

He hurried away, leaving David overcome by an emotion that one only feels at the age, and in the circumstances, of those two young swans whose wings had not yet been clipped by provincial life.

" Heart of gold ! " David exclaimed, watching Lucien's retreating figure as he crossed the workshop.

Lucien went down to l'Houmeau by the beautiful Promenade de Beaulieu, then by the Rue du Minage and the Porte Saint-Pierre. If he took the longest way round, you must understand that Mme de Bargeton's house lay on that route. He experienced such pleasure in passing under that lady's windows, even unknown to her, that it was two months since he had gone back to l'Houmeau by the Porte Palet.

As he walked under the trees of Beaulieu he reflected upon the distance that separates Angoulême from l'Houmeau. Country conventions raise barriers far harder to climb than the stone steps down which Lucien now made his way. This ambitious youth, who had recently effected an entry into Bargeton House, throwing glory before him like a sort of scaling-ladder, was as anxious about his mistress's decision as a favourite who, having exerted the full extent of his influence, fears disgrace. These words must seem obscure to those who are not familiar with the customs of the country cities that are divided into an Upper and a Lower Town; which makes it necessary to pause here in order to give some account of Angoulême, without which account it will not be possible to understand Mme de Bargeton, one of the principal characters in this story.

The old city of Angoulême stands on the summit of a sugar-loaf rock, commanding a view of the plain through which the Charente winds its way. This rock is joined, on the Périgord side, to a long ridge of hills that ends abruptly above the road from Paris to Bordeaux in a sort of promontory that commands a view, on three sides, over picturesque valleys. The importance of this town in the time of the religious wars is attested by its ramparts, by its gates, and by the ruins of a castle perched on the summit of the crag. By reason of its situation, it was formerly a point of vantage equally coveted by Catholics and by Calvinists; but what was once its strength is now its weakness; with no access to the Charente, and shut within its ramparts, the steepness of the rocky ascent has condemned the old city to dull stagnation.

At the time of this story the Government was making an attempt to extend the town in the direction of Périgord by building the prefecture, a naval school and barracks out along the hillside, and opening up roads. But private enterprise had forestalled them elsewhere. For a long time the mushroom growth of the suburb of l'Houmeau had been spreading at the foot of the rock, and along by the river, beside the main road from Paris to Bordeaux. Everybody has heard of the great paper mills of Angoulême, which were established three hundred years ago on the Charente and its tributaries, that supply the necessary water power. The State Marine Ordnance factory was founded at Ruelle. Carriers, post-houses, inns and wheelwrights, all kinds of trades to do with public conveyance, and depending upon the road and the river for their livelihood, grew up in Lower Angoulême, in order to avoid the difficulties of the steep hill. Tanneries, laundries and other trades depending on water, were also, naturally, established within reach of the Charente; and there were also warehouses for brandy and for all the other goods carried by water—in fact transport depots of every kind had sprung up along the river. Thus the suburb of l'Houmeau had become a wealthy industrial town, a second Angoulême rivalling the Upper Town, seat of the prefecture, the cathedral, the courts of justice, and the aristocracy. But l'Houmeau, in spite of its active and growing industry, remained a mere suburb of Angoulême. Above was aristocracy and power; below, trade and money: two social groups perpetually at war everywhere, and it would be difficult to say which of the two factions hated the other more heartily. For the past nine years the Restoration had exaggerated this state of affairs, after a period of relative calm under the Empire. Most of the houses of Upper Angoulême are occupied by noble families, or by old middle-class families living on private incomes, and constituting a kind of autochthonous nation that admits no strangers. It occasionally happened that after two hundred years' residence, and a marriage into one of the aboriginal families, some family from a neighbouring district would be adopted; but they were still, in the eyes of the natives, regarded as newcomers of yesterday. Prefects, receivers-general, and the various administrations that have come and gone during the last forty years, have attempted to tame this race of aborigines, perched on their rock like defiant ravens. The aborigines have always accepted invitations to dinners and social functions, but, as to admitting newcomers to their own houses, they were adamant. Scornful, disparaging, jealous, mean in their money dealings, these families have intermarried among themselves until they constitute a serried battalion whose closed ranks keep out intruders, and at the same time prevent any of their own members from straying. The innovations of modern luxury are unknown to them; for them, to send a son to Paris is to send him to his ruin. This instance of their wisdom reveals the habits of thought and out-of-date attitudes of these families, afflicted with unintelligent royalism, bigoted rather than religious, for whom everything remains for ever unchanged, like their old town on its rock. In spite of this Angoulême enjoyed a great reputation in neighbouring districts for its educational advantages. Neighbouring towns sent their daughters to its boarding schools and convents. It is easy to imagine the effect of class sentiment on the feeling that divided Angoulême and l'Houmeau.

Commerce is wealthy, aristocracy is nearly always poor. Each revenges itself on the other by a contempt that is equal on both sides. The middle classes of Angoulême are allies in the feud, and a tradesman of the Upper Town will say of a lawyer of the Lower, in an accent of indescribable contempt! " He is a l'Houmeau man! " By recognising the status of the French nobility, and at the same time holding out hopes to them which could not possibly be realised short of a complete unheaval of society, the Restoration increased the social distance—so much wider than the physical distance between the Upper and the Lower Town—between Angoulême and l'Houmeau. Aristocratic society, now backed by the Government, became in this town more exclusive than in any other part of France. A resident of l'Houmeau was little better than a pariah. From this proceeded the deep and bitter hatred that was to give such terrible unanimity to the insurrection of 1830 and to destroy the elements of a stable social system in France. The haughtiness of the nobility at court alienated the provincial nobility from the Throne, just as the latter themselves alienated the middle classes by galling their vanity in every possible way. For a young man from l'Houmeau, the son of a chemist, to be received by Mme de Bargeton was in the nature of a minor revolution. Who, then, were responsible? Lamartine and Victor Hugo, Casimir Delavigne and Canalis, Béranger and Chateaubriand, Villemain and M. Aignan, Soumet and Tissot ; Étienne and Davigny, Benjamin Constant and Lamennais, Cousin and Michaud ; in short, the great ones of literature young and old, liberal and royalist alike. Mme de Bargeton loved literature and the arts, an outrageous taste, highly disapproved of in Angoulême, which must be accounted for in telling the story of the life of this woman, a born celebrity, whom unlucky circumstances had kept in obscurity, and whose influence was to decide Lucien's fate.

M. de Bargeton was the great-grandson of a mayor of Bordeaux named Mirault, who was given titles of nobility under Louis XIII for long tenure of office. Under Louis XIV his son, bearing the name of Mirault de Bargeton, was an officer in the Royal Guards, and made such a wealthy marriage that his son was able to call himself purely and simply M. de Bargeton. This M. de Bargeton, grandson of M. Mirault, the mayor, made such strenuous efforts to behave like a real gentleman that he ran through all the family money and brought its fortunes to a standstill. Two of his brothers, great-uncles of the present Bargeton, went back to commerce and that is why the name of Mirault is to be found among the tradespeople of Bordeaux. As there was an entail on the Bargeton estate at Angoumois, on the lands of the de la Rochefoucauld family, and also on the Angoulême house—called Bargeton House—the grandson of M. de Bargeton the waster inherited these two properties. In 1789 he lost all his rights and was left with only the income from his land, which amounted to something in the region of ten thousand francs a year. If only his grandfather had followed the glorious examples of Bargeton I and Bargeton II, Bargeton V, whom we may call Bargeton the Silent, might have been a Marquis; he might have married into some great family, might have become a duke and a peer of France, as others have done; whereas, as things were, he thought himself highly honoured when, in 1805, he married Mlle Marie-Louise-Anaïs de Nègrepelisse, daughter of a gentleman long forgotten among his peers, although he belonged to the younger branch of one of the most ancient families of the south of France. There had been a Nègrepelisse among the hostages of St. Louis; but the head of the elder branch bears the illustrious name of d'Espard, acquired in the reign of Henri IV by a marriage with the heiress of that family. This gentleman, the younger son of a younger son, lived on his wife's property, a small estate near Barbezieux, that he farmed with great success, marketing his own corn, distilling his own brandy, regardless of ridicule, so long as he was able to pile up gold pieces and add to his property from time to time.

A combination of circumstances rarely met with in the depths of the country had inspired Mme de Bargeton with a love of music and literature. During the Revolution a certain Abbé Niollant, who had been Abbé Roze's best pupil, went into hiding in the little manor-house of Escarbas, bringing with him his music, for he was a composer. He had abundantly repaid the old gentleman's hospitality in undertaking the education of his daughter Anaïs (called Naïs for short), and who, but for this accident, would have been left to her own devices, or, which would have been worse, to be brought up by servants. The Abbé was not only a musician, but had also a very wide knowledge of literature, and read German and Italian. He therefore taught these two languages, as well as counterpoint, to Mlle de Nègrepelisse; he expounded to her the great works of French, Italian, and German literature, and deciphered with her the music of all the masters. Finally, to combat the idleness of the complete solitude to which political events had condemned him, he taught her Greek and Latin, and gave her some smattering of the natural sciences. No mother's influence modified this masculine education of a young girl in whom rustic habits had already fostered a spirit of independence. The Abbé Niollant, who was of a poetic and enthusiastic turn of mind, was chiefly remarkable for the artistic temperament, a temperament characterised indeed by many estimable qualities, but one that by the freedom of its judgments and the breadth of its views soars high above middle-class ideas. In the great world such temperaments may be forgiven for their disregard of conventions, because their eccentricities arise from profound motives, but in private life there is much to be said against this disposition, which invariably leads to deviations from the established order of things. The Abbé was by no means without goodness of heart, which made his ideas all the more contagious to a young girl, in whom the native wilfulness of youth had been fostered by the solitude of country life. Abbé Niollant communicated to his pupil his own fearless criticism and boldness of judgment, never dreaming that these qualities, so necessary to a man, might become faults in a woman destined for the humble station of a homemaker. Although the Abbé constantly impressed it upon his pupil that she must be the more gracious and modest in proportion to her attainments, Mlle de Nègrepelisse formed a very good opinion of herself and a hearty contempt for the rest of humanity. Surrounded only by inferiors, anxious to do her bidding, she had all the haughtiness of a great lady without any of the mollifying urbanity that generally accompanies it. Flattered in all her vanities by the poor Abbé, who admired her, as an author always admires his own work, she had the misfortune never to meet anyone against whom she could measure herself. Lack of society is one of the greatest drawbacks of country life. Without any inducements to take trouble about dress and appearance, one gets out of the habit of making even the smallest personal sacrifices for the sake of other people. Everything in us is affected—both mind and outward appearance are changed for the worse. Uncurbed by the intercourse of society, Mlle de Nègrepelisse's bold ideas passed into her manners and expression; she had that cavalier air whose originality strikes us at first, but that only really suits women living a life of adventure. And so this education, whose asperities would have been softened in high society, was only calculated to make her appear ridiculous in Angoulême as soon as her admirers should cease to worship in her faults that are only charming in the very young. As for M. de Nègrepelisse, he would have given all his daughter's books to save the life of a sick bullock; he was so mean that he would never have allowed her a pound more than the income to which she was entitled, even for the smallest trifle necessary for her education.

The Abbé died in 1802, before the marriage of his dear child—a marriage which he would certainly never have advised. The old squire found his daughter a great burden now that the Abbé was dead. He felt himself unequal to the struggle that was about to break out between his avarice and a daughter of independent mind with nothing to do. Like all young girls who leave the beaten track laid down for women, Naïs had her own views on marriage and held it in low regard. The idea of submitting her intelligence and her person to any of the commonplace and undistinguished men that she had happened to meet was hateful to her. She wished to rule, and must obey. Between the alternatives of submitting to the stupid whims of some fool with no understanding of her tastes, and flying with a lover after her own heart, she would not have hesitated. But M. de Nègrepelisse was still gentleman enough to dread a *mésalliance*. Like many another father, he made up his mind to marry his daughter, not so much for her own sake, as for his own peace of mind. What he wanted was a member of a noble family or a country squire, of no great intelligence, who would not think of arguing over the account of his daughter's trust that he proposed to produce; sufficient of a nonentity in intelligence and character for Naïs to have her own way, and disinterested enough to marry her without a dowry.

But where to find a son-in-law to suit both father and daughter? Such a man must be a very phoenix of sons-in-law. M. de Nègrepelisse considered all the eligible men of the neighbourhood, with this double requirement in mind, and came to the conclusion that M. de Bargeton was the only one who met the case. M. de Bargeton, aged forty, and considerably shattered by the amorous dissipations of his youth, passed for a man of remarkably feeble intelligence; but he had just enough common sense to manage his affairs and sufficient breeding to live in Angoulême society without blunders or indiscretions. M. de Nègrepelisse bluntly pointed out to his daughter the negative advantages of the model husband that he proposed for her and made her see how she might turn the situation to her own happiness. So she married a coat-of-arms already two hundred years old, the Bargeton quarterings: *Three stag's heads gules, on or; three ox's heads cabossed two and one, sable; One and two party per fesse, azure and argent; in the first, six shells or, three, two and one.* Provided with a chaperon, she could live as she pleased in the shelter of social status and with the help of whatever connections her intelligence and beauty could provide for her in Paris. Naïs could not resist the prospect of such liberty. M. de Bargeton was of the opinion that he was making a brilliant marriage, calculating, as he did, that it would not be long before his father-in-law would leave him the estate that he was rounding out with so much love; but at that time it seemed more likely that M. de Nègrepelisse would write his son-in-law's epitaph.

Mme de Bargeton was now thirty-six and her husband fifty-eight. This difference was the more striking because M. de Bargeton looked seventy, while his wife could still have passed as a young girl, worn pink, and let her hair down. Although their income was not more than twelve thousand francs, they passed as one of the six wealthiest families in the Old Town, not, of course, counting trade and officials. The necessity of remaining on good terms with her father, whose fortune they needed before they could go to Paris (and who kept her waiting so long that his son-in-law predeceased him),

Member of a noble family or country squire of no great intelligence

compelled M. and Mme de Bargeton to live in Angoulême; there Naïs's brilliant intellectual gifts, and the riches of her nature, that lay like undiscovered ore, were doomed to stagnate and in course of time were transformed into absurdities. For really our absurdities are for the most part the product of some good quality, of some virtue or ability carried to extreme. Pride that is not tempered by intercourse with the great, and exercised only on petty things, instead of expanding in an environment of noble sentiments, becomes rigid. Enthusiasm, that virtue within a virtue that produces saints, the inspiration alike of hidden devotion, and of the dazzling manifestation of poetry, becomes mere exaggeration when it is exercised upon provincial trivialities. Far from the centre, where great minds cast their light, where the very atmosphere is charged with ideas, where everything is perpetually renewed, knowledge becomes out of date, and taste grows as stale as stagnant water. For want of scope, through making much of petty things, passions dwindle. And herein lies the reason for the meanness and cliquishness that poisons provincial life. In time the contagion of narrow-mindedness and petty behaviour must infect even the most naturally distinguished character; and here perish men born to be great, and women who, under the influence of superior minds, and in a less narrow world, might have been charming.

Mme de Bargeton went into raptures over every trifle, making no distinction between private and public emotions. Sensations that are not likely to be understood are best kept to ourselves. To be sure, a sunset is highly poetic, but what is more ridiculous than a woman describing it in long words for the benefit of matter-of-fact people? There are delights that can only be savoured when two kindred spirits meet, poet with poet, heart with heart. She was in the habit of using those high-sounding phrases, larded with adjectives, so well described in journalistic slang as *tartines*—a commodity that is meted out every morning to the public, who consume it in vast quantities, difficult as it is to swallow. Her conversation abounded in superlatives, and the smallest trifles took on vast proportions. At about this time she was beginning to individualise, synthesise, dramatise, superiorise, analyse, poetise, prosify, typify, colossify, angelicise, neologise and tragify—for one must violate the language to describe those novel whims in which some women indulge. Her mind and her language was all on fire. Her heart and her speech alike moved to dithyrambic measures. She palpitated, swooned, and went into raptures over everything : over the devotion of a Sister of Charity, over the execution of the Fauchet brothers, over M. d' Arlincourt's *Ipsiboé*, and Lewis' *Anaconda*, the escape of la Valette, and over a woman friend who had frightened away burglars by putting on a deep voice. Everything, for her, was sublime, extraordinary, amazing, divine, marvellous. She would work herself up into a state of excitement, rage or melancholy, soar in rapture and sink in gloom, gaze at the heavens, or, with downcast looks, on the earth ; her eyes filled readily with tears. She wore herself out with perpetual admirations, and burned with strange disdains. She dreamed of the Pasha of Janina, and would fain have matched herself with him in his seraglio ; and she thought that it would be a fine thing to be sewn up in a sack and thrown into a river. She envied Lady Hester Stanhope ; she longed to be a sister of Saint-Camilla and die of yellow fever in Barcelona, tending the sick. That would be a high, a noble destiny! In fact, she thirsted for everything but the limpid stream of her own life, hidden among flowers. She adored Lord Byron, Jean-Jacques Rousseau, all poetic and dramatic existences. She had ready tears for all misfortunes, paeans for all triumphs. She sympathised with Napoleon in his defeat, she sympathised with Mahomet Ali, massacring the Egyptian tyrants. In fact, her fancy invested all men of genius with haloes, and she imagined that such lofty souls must live on incense and light.

Most people regarded her as a kind of harmless eccentric, but a more profound observer might well have seen all these peculiarities as the ruins of a wonderful edifice of love, for ever crumbling away as fast as it was built, the ruins of a New Jerusalem—in short, love without a lover. And this was the truth. The story of the first eighteen years of Mme de Bargeton's marriage can be told in few words. For some time she lived upon herself and upon distant hopes. Then, realising that she was debarred by the mediocrity of her fortune from the life in Paris to which she aspired, she began to examine the people amongst whom she lived and was appalled at her solitude. There was not a single man in her circle who could conceivably have inspired one of those follies to which women are apt to abandon themselves under the pressure of despair at the futility of a life that is dull, uneventful, meaningless. When the Empire was in the full radiance of its glory, at the time when Napoleon was throwing the flower of his troops into the Prussian campaign, all her hopes, hitherto deceived, revived again. Natural curiosity impelled her to try to see those heroes who in obedience to a word in the Orders of the Day were conquering Europe, who were performing, in the present, the legendary feats of chivalry. Even the most avaricious and refractory towns were obliged to entertain the Imperial Guard, and mayors and prefects went out to meet them, with prepared speeches, as if they had been royalty. Mme de Bargeton, at a party given to the town by a regiment, fell in love with an officer, a simple sub-lieutenant to whom the crafty Napoleon had allowed a glimpse of the baton of a Marshal of France. This unspoken passion, noble and great, and unlike many passions lightly entered into and as lightly abandoned in those days, was chastely consecrated by the hand of death. A shell on the field of Wagram shattered the only record of Mme de Bargeton's youthful beauty—the picture of her that the Marquis de Cante-Croix carried next his heart. For a long time she wept for the handsome young soldier who in two campaigns, fired as he was by glory and love, had risen to the rank of colonel and who valued a letter from Naïs above imperial favour. Pain drew a veil of sadness over her face, and that veil did not lift again until that terrible age when a woman begins to regret the years of her beauty that have slipped away without her having had any joy in them, when she sees that her roses are fading and when the longings of love revive with the desire to prolong the last smiling hours of youth. All her noble qualities were so many wounds in her heart, when the chill of provincial life seized upon her. She would have died of grief like the ermine if, by any chance, she had been soiled by contact with men who had no thoughts beyond spending their evenings playing cards for small stakes after a good dinner. Her pride preserved her from petty provincial love affairs. Between the emptiness of the men of her circle and the emptiness of her own solitude, a superior woman has but one choice. Marriage and society were, for her, a monastery. She lived in poetry, as a Carmelite lives in religion. The works of distinguished foreign writers hitherto unknown, that were appearing between 1815 and 1821, the great essays of M. de Bonald and M. de Maistre, those two eagles of the intellect, besides all the lesser works of French literature whose first branches were sprouting with such vigour, made her solitude sweet to her, but did not give flexibility to her mind or to her person. She remained rigid and erect, like a tree struck by lightning that still has not fallen. Her dignity was stilted, her autocratic position made her precious and over-refined. Like all those who allow themselves to be adored by their courtiers, she queened it with her faults. Such was the past life of Mme de Bargeton, a frigid story that must be told in order to explain her relationship with Lucien, who was introduced to her in the strangest manner.

During the winter a newcomer to the town had brought a little interest into the monotony of Mme de Bargeton's life. The post of Controller of Excise had become vacant, and M. de Barante sent to fill it a man whose adventurous life served as a passport that pleaded sufficiently in his favour to arouse the curiosity of the local queen and to gain his admittance into her court.

M. du Châtelet—he began life as plain Sixte Châtelet, but since 1806 he had thought fit to qualify himself with the particle—was one of those agreeable young men who, under Napoleon, always managed to escape conscription by remaining very close to the Imperial sun. He began his career as private secretary to an Imperial Princess. M. du Châtelet possessed all the disqualifications that fit a man for a position of this kind—a good figure, good-looking, a good dancer, an excellent billiard-player, good at games and a passable amateur actor and singer of drawing-room ballads. He applauded everybody's jokes; accommodating, envious, he was never at a loss. He knew everything—and knew nothing. With no real knowledge of music, he could play a piano accompaniment well enough for a lady who had consented, after much pressing, to sing a song that she had been rehearsing with infinite pains for the past month. He had no feeling for poetry, but would boldly ask permission to retire for ten minutes in order to compose an impromptu verse, some quatrain as flat as a pancake, in which rhyme replaced reason. M. du Châtelet had, besides, a talent for filling in the tapestry round the flowers that had been begun by the Princess. With infinite charm, he used to hold the skeins of silk for her, entertaining her with sweet nothings, salacities concealed by the most transparent of veils. Ignorant of painting, he could sketch a landscape, draw a profile, make a dress design and colour it. In fact he possessed all those minor talents that could be turned to such good account as a means to success at a period when women had more influence in affairs than is generally imagined. He posed as an expert in diplomacy—the science of the ignorant, whose emptiness alone is deep; a very useful science all the same, in so far as it is demonstrated by the exercise of the following lofty functions: as it requires discreet men, it enables the ignorant to say nothing and to retire with mysterious head-shakings; and above all, the man who is best at this science is the one who can swim with his head well above the stream of events so that he seems to be leading it—a question of specific gravity—or rather of specific lightness. Here, as in the arts, one meets a thousand mediocrities for one man of genius. But in spite of his services—ordinary and extraordinary—the influence of his Imperial protectress had not been able to procure him a seat on the Privy Council; not but that he would have made a delightful Master of Requests, like plenty of others—but the Princess was of the opinion that he was better placed near her than anywhere else in the world. All the same, he was made a Baron, went to Cassel as Envoy-Extraordinary—and was in fact a very extraordinary envoy indeed. On another occasion Napoleon made use of him as a diplomatic courier in the middle of a crisis. Baron du Châtelet had been promised a nomination as Minister to Jerome in Westphalia. When the Empire fell, and thus cheated him of what he called his family ambassadorship, he went off in despair to Egypt with General Armand de Montriveau. Separated from his companion by a strange misadventure, he had wandered for two years from desert to desert, from tribe to tribe, as a prisoner of the Arabs who sold him to one another, but who were never able to make the least use of his talents. At last he reached the territory of the Imam of Mascate, at the time when Montriveau was advancing on Tangier; but he had the good luck to find an English ship at Mascate just about to sail and managed to get back to Paris a whole year before his travelling companion. His recent misfortunes, some old connections, and services rendered to personages then in favour, obtained him a recommendation to the President of the Council, who found him a place with M. de Barante until some vacancy should occur. The part that M. du Châtelet had played in the life of an imperial princess, his reputation as a ladies' man, the strange story of his travels and his sufferings, served to excite the curiosity of the ladies of Angoulême. After making himself acquainted with the customs of the Old Town, Baron Sixte du Châtelet adapted his behaviour accordingly. He posed as a broken man, disillusioned, disgusted with the world.

On every occasion he would clasp his head as if his suffering never gave him a moment's respite—a little manœuvre which suggested his travels and made him interesting. He was on visiting terms with all the authorities—the General, the Prefect, the Receiver-General, and the Bishop; but he always behaved with distant politeness, cold, a little supercilious, like a man not in his proper place and waiting the favours of power. He allowed his social talents to be guessed at, and these had everything to gain by remaining unknown; then, when he had succeeded in arousing interest, while still keeping curiosity active, having realised the nonentity of the men, and examined the women with an expert eye, for a few Sundays at the cathedral, he decided that Madame de Bargeton was the person with whom it would be most useful for him to be on terms of intimacy. He counted on music to open the doors of a house that no stranger could hope to penetrate. Surreptitiously he procured a Mass by Miroir and practised it on the piano; then, one fine Sunday when all Angoulême society was at Mass, he sent the ignorant into raptures by playing the organ and revived the interest that already attached to his person by allowing his name to leak out among the lower clergy. After Mass Mme de Bargeton complimented him, and expressed regret at having had no opportunity of playing duets with him; and in the course of that well-planned encounter he was offered, in the most natural way, the passport that he would never have obtained if he had asked for it. The adroit Baron visited the queen of Angoulême, to whom he rendered services designed to compromise her. This elderly beau—for he was forty-five—recognised in her a latent youth waiting to burst into flower, a treasure to be turned to account, perhaps a marriageable widow with expectations—in short, an alliance with the Nègrepelisse family, which would mean, in Paris, an introduction to the Marquis d'Espard, whose influence might again open the way to a political career. In spite of the thick and sombre mistletoe that marred that fair tree, he made up his mind to cultivate it, to devote himself to it, to tend it, to gather its fruits.

All the gentry of Angoulême were loud in protest against the introduction of a giaour into the holy of holies—for Mme de Bargeton's drawing-room was the sanctuary of a society unspotted from the world. The Bishop alone was a regular visitor; the Prefect was not received there more than two or three times a year; the Receiver-General had never set foot there—Mme de Bargeton went to his receptions and concerts, but never dined with him. Not to admit the Receiver-General and to be accessible to a simple Controller of Excise—such a reversal of the heirarchy seemed monstrous in the eyes of those authorities upon whom she looked down.

Those who can, by an effort of imagination, enter into these pettinesses—which, for that matter, are to be found in every social sphere—will understand the awe in which Bargeton House was held by the middle classes of Angoulême. For the inhabitants of l'Houmeau, the grandeurs of this miniature Louvre, the glory of this local Rambouillet, shone at a solar distance. Those who assembled there were of the meanest intelligence, all the bores among the decayed gentry within a radius of twenty leagues. Political views were aired in heated and long-winded banalities; the *Quotidienne* was luke-warm, and Louis XVIII was looked upon

The adroit Baron visited the queen of Angoulême

as little better than a Jacobin. As for the women, the majority were plain and stupid, badly dressed, and all had some defect that spoiled them ; in dress and conversation alike they lacked finish. But for his designs on Mme de Bargeton, Châtelet would never have endured them. Nevertheless, the manners and consciousness of their class, the air of gentility, the pride of the nobleman in his small manor-house and a knowledge of the rules of good breeding, covered this void. Nobility of feeling was, moreover, far more real here than in the sphere of Parisian grandeur ; one could not but respect their attachment to the House of Bourbon, *right or wrong.* This society might be compared, if the image may be permitted, to antique plate, tarnished, but weighty. The very immobility of their political opinions was a kind of fidelity. The distance that they set between themselves and the middle class, their exclusiveness, gave a semblance of elevation and conferred upon them such worth as convention can bestow. Each of these nobles had a certain value in the eyes of the townspeople, rather as cowries represent money among the Bambara negroes.

Several of the women, flattered by M. du Châtelet and recognising in him superior qualities lacking among the men of their own set, proceeded to calm the insurrection of self-esteem : each hoped to inherit the succession to the Imperial Highness. Purists were of the opinion that you might see the intruder at Mme de Bargeton's, but that he was not to be received in any other house. Du Châtelet had to put up with a fair number of slights, but he held his ground by cultivating the clergy. Then he set about to flatter the faults which her native soil had bred in the queen of Angoulême, brought her all the new books, and read her poems as they appeared. They went into ecstasies together over the works of the young poets, she in good faith, he bored, but patiently enduring the romantics whom, as a man of the Empire School, he understood very imperfectly. Mme de Bargeton, full of enthusiasm for the renaissance that followed the restoration of the Bourbon lilies, loved M. de Chateaubriand for calling Victor Hugo a *sublime child.* Sad to think that she knew genius only from a distance, she sighed for Paris, where great men lived. So M. du Châtelet hit upon the brilliant idea of telling her that there was, in Angoulême, another *sublime child*, a young poet who, unknown to himself, surpassed in brilliance all the rising stars of the Parisian firmament. A great man of the future had been born in l'Houmeau! The headmaster of the school had shown the Baron some wonderful pieces of verse. Poor and modest, this child was a Chatterton without political guile, without the bitter hatred against society that drove the English poet to write pamphlets against his benefactors. In her little circle of five or six people who shared her taste for literature and the arts, this one because he scraped a fiddle, that because he daubed white paper with sepia, another in his capacity as president of the Agricultural Society, and a fourth by virtue of a bass voice which enabled him to sing *Se fiato in corpo avete* like a war-whoop; among these fantastic figures Mme de Bargeton was like a starving man at a stage dinner in which all the dishes are made of cardboard; so that no words can describe her joy when she heard this news. She must see this poet, this angel! She was in raptures, she raved about him, and talked of nothing else for hours on end. Two days later the ex-diplomatic courier had arranged, through the headmaster, to introduce Lucien to Mme de Bargeton.

You alone, poor provincial helots, you for whom social distances take longer to travel than they do for Parisians (in whose eyes they are daily growing less), you upon whom weigh so heavily the bars between which each of the world's different worlds anathematise one another, each crying *Raca!*—you and you alone will comprehend the ferment that worked in the mind and in the heart of Lucien Chardon when no less a person than his headmaster told him that the doors of Bargeton House were about to open to receive him! Glory had made them turn on their hinges! He would be well received in this house, at whose old-fashioned gables he had often gazed as he walked along Beaulieu in the evenings with David, thinking how their names would perhaps never reach those ears deaf to knowledge when it comes from below.

Only his sister was let into this secret. Like a good housewife, Eve, the divine diviner, brought out a few sovereigns that she had been saving to buy Lucien some thin shoes from the best shoemaker in Angoulême and a new suit from the town's most celebrated tailor. She trimmed his best shirt with a frill that she washed and ironed herself. What joy when she saw him dressed! How proud she was of her brother! And what a quantity of advice she gave him! She thought of a thousand small details. Because of his habit of meditating, Lucien had got into the way of leaning his elbows on the table; he would even pull a table towards him in order to lean on it; Eve forbade him to give way in the sanctuary of aristocracy to this form of bad manners. She accompanied him as far as the gate of Saint-Pierre and remained, almost opposite the cathedral, watching him as he went down the Rue de Beaulieu in the direction of the Promenade, where M. du Châtelet was waiting for him. For a long time the poor girl stood there, deeply moved, for all the world as if some great event had taken place. That Lucien should visit Mme de Bargeton was, for Eve, the dawn of success. Little did this heavenly creature know that where ambition begins innocent affections end.

When he reached the Rue du Minage, the externals failed to impress Lucien. This Louvre, so much exaggerated in his thoughts, was a house built of the soft stone of the district and mellowed by time. Its external aspect was dismal, and the interior was of the utmost simplicity, built round the usual provincial courtyard, trim and cold; severe, almost monastic architecture, well preserved. Lucien ascended the old staircase with chestnut wood balustrades, only the two first steps of which were of stone. Having crossed a shabby anteroom and a large, dark drawing-room, he found the sovereign lady in a small wainscoted boudoir; the carved woodwork, in the taste of the eighteenth century, was painted grey. The upper panels of the doors were decorated with paintings in camaien; old red damask, with meagre trimmings, decorated the walls. The old-fashioned furniture took refuge pathetically under red and white check covers. The poet saw Mme de Bargeton seated on a sofa with a thin quilted mattress. He beheld her by the light of two wax candles on a screened sconce that stood in front of her on a round table covered with a green cloth.

The queen did not rise, but twisted round very agreeably on her throne, smiling at the poet, who was much moved by these serpentine contortions—they seemed to him distinguished. Lucien's extraordinary beauty, his shyness, his voice, in fact everything about him, made a great impression on Mme de Bargeton. The poet quickly became the poem. The young man made a stealthy examination of this woman, who seemed to him worthy of her renown; she disappointed none of his ideas of what a great lady should be. Mme de Bargeton was wearing, according to a new fashion, a slashed cap of black velvet. This headdress carried a suggestion of the middle ages, which impressed the young man by enlarging, as it were, the idea of woman; from it escaped her wild red-gold hair, gilded in the light, red in the shadow of her curls. The noble lady had the dazzling white skin that redeems the supposed disadvantages of that ardent colouring. A white clearcut massive brow nobly surmounted her sparkling grey eyes, encircled by a margin of mother-of-pearl, a delicate setting enhanced by two blue veins on either side of her nose. Her nose had the Bourbon curve, which enhanced her long ardent face, presenting, as it were, a central feature that bespoke the royal temper of the house of Condé. Her neck was not entirely hidden by her hair. Her dress, negligently crossed, revealed a snowy bosom from which rose her white and shapely throat. With a friendly gesture of her finely tapered fingers, well groomed but a little too dry, Mme de Bargeton indicated to the young poet a chair close to her. M. du Châtelet took an easy-chair and Lucien then realised that no one else was present. Mme de Bargeton's conversation intoxicated the poet of l'Houmeau. The three hours that he spent with her were, for Lucien, like a dream that one longs to continue for ever. For him, she was not thin, but slender; in love, but without a lover, delicate, for all her strength; her faults, exaggerated by her mannerisms, delighted him, for young people always begin by loving exaggeration, that infirmity of noble minds. He did not notice her faded cheeks, or the brick-red blotches on her cheek-bones, the result of boredom and a certain amount of ill-health. His imagination seized, first of all, on those ardent eyes, those elegant curls that caught the candlelight, that dazzling whiteness—so many points of light that drew him like a moth to a candle-flame. Besides, how could he judge dispassionately a woman whose soul spoke so intimately to his own ? Her feminine exaltation, the ardour of the rather dated phrases that Mme de Bargeton had been repeating for a long time past, but which were new to Lucien, fascinated him the more because he was in a state of mind to admire everything. He had not brought any poems with him to read. But there was no question of reading poems ; he had purposely forgotten them so as to have the right to come again ; and Mme de Bargeton did not mention them either, so that she would be able to ask him to read on a future occasion. Was not this already a first understanding ?

M. Sixte du Châtelet was not too well pleased with this reception. Too late, he perceived a rival in this handsome youth whom he escorted back as far as the first ramp of stone stairs below Beaulieu in order to try the effect of a little diplomacy. Lucien was not a little astonished as he listened to the Controller of Excise boasting that he had introduced him, and, in that capacity, giving Lucien some pieces of advice.

M. du Châtelet hoped to Heaven that Lucien would be treated better than he had been ; the Court itself was less insolent than this pack of rustic bores ; you were expected to put up with deadly insults : their snobbery was something abominable. We would have the Revolution of 1789 over again if these people went on as they did. For his part, the only reason why he ever set foot in that house was because he liked Mme de Bargeton, the only woman in Angoulême worth a second thought. He had paid court to her because he had nothing better to do, and had ended by falling madly in love with her. He would soon possess her, she loved him, he was pretty sure of that. The subjection of that proud queen should be his sole vengeance on that stupid collection of country bumpkins.

Châtelet spoke of his passion in the tones of a man prepared to kill a rival if he should meet one. The old Imperial butterfly came down with all his weight on the poor poet, in an attempt to obliterate him with a display of his own importance, and to frighten him off. He expatiated on the much-vaunted perils of his famous travels ;

he may possibly have imposed on the poet's imagination, but the lover felt no alarm.

After that evening, the old coxcomb notwithstanding, with his threats and his air of a respectable brigand, Lucien continued to visit Mme de Bargeton ; at first, indeed, with the discretion that was proper in a resident of l'Houmeau, but soon he came to take for granted what had at first seemed to him such a tremendous favour and went to see her more and more frequently. The son of a chemist was regarded, in that world, as a being of no consequence. At first, if any of the local gentry or their wives happened to visit Naïs when Lucien was there they treated him with the overwhelming politeness that well-bred people use towards their inferiors. At first Lucien thought them very kind, but later he recognised the motive from which proceeded that appearance of consideration. It was not long before he detected a patronising tone that stirred his gall and confirmed him in his bitter republicanism—a phase through which not a few of these aspiring aristocrats pass as a prelude to their entry into high society. But what sufferings would he not have endured for Naïs—for so he heard her named, since among themselves the members of that set, like the grandees of Spain, and the élite of the Austrian nobility, called one another, men and woman alike, by their Christian names—a last shade of social distinction that marked off the inner circle of the aristocracy of Angoulême. Lucien loved Naïs as all young men love the first woman who flatters them ; for Naïs prophesied a brilliant future for him and untold glory. Mme de Bargeton did everything in her power to bind her poet to her. Not only did she flatter him out of all measure, but she pictured him as a penniless boy whom she was anxious to give a start in life ; she treated him like a child, in order to keep him ; she made him read to her, treated him as her secretary ; but she was more fond of him than she would have thought possible, after the great sorrow that had befallen her.

She was very hard on herself in her own mind and told herself what folly it would be to love a young man of twenty, so far removed from her, besides, in social position. Her familiar treatment of him was capriciously interspersed with fits of pride, the outcome of her scruples. She was in turn patronising and haughty, tender and flattering. Intimidated at first by her high rank, Lucien experienced all the hopes and fears, all the despairs that forge a first love and drive it so deep into the heart with alternate blows of anguish and delight. For two months he saw her as a benefactress whose interest in him was maternal. But then she began to confide in him. Mme de Bargeton addressed her poet as " my dear Lucien ", and then simply as " my dear ". The poet, gaining courage, ventured to address that great lady as Naïs. On hearing him use that name, she flew into one of those rages that impress the very young; she reproached him for calling her by a name by which everybody else called her. This proud high-born daughter of the house of Nègrepelisse offered this handsome angel her other name, that was still new, and desired to be, for him, Louise. Lucien was in the third heaven of love.

One evening Lucien came in to find Louise studying a portrait, which she promptly covered up; he wanted to see it. To quiet the despair of a first access of jealousy, Louise showed him the portrait of the young Cante-Croix and told him, not without fears, the sad story of their love, so pure and so cruelly extinguished. Was she contemplating some infidelity to her dead lover, or had she hit upon the notion of producing the portrait as a rival to Lucien? Lucien was too young to analyse his mistress; he naïvely despaired —for she had begun that phase of the campaign during which women entrench themselves behind scruples, thought up with more or less ingenuity. When women discuss duties, or conventions, or religion, these things are really so many fortified positions that they love to have taken by storm. But Lucien was too innocent for these strategies; he would have conducted the campaign quite straightforwardly.

" I shall not die for you, I shall live for you," said the audacious Lucien one evening, anxious to dispose of M. de Cante-Croix once and for all; and he turned upon Louise a look of full-fledged passion.

Alarmed at the progress that this new love was making in herself and in her poet, she asked him for the poem he had promised for the first page of her album, looking for a pretext to quarrel with him because he had taken so long to produce it. What, then, must her feelings have been when she read the two following stanzas, which, naturally, she considered better than anything by Canalis, the finest poet of the aristocracy.

Not always the deceptive muse
Or fancy's brush shall decorate my leaves,
These pages pure:
The secret pencil of my fair mistress
Confides to me at times a secret happiness,
Or hidden care.

Ah! when her fingers turn my yellowing leaves
And record of a rich fulfilment trace,
Undreamed as yet:
Then, ah then, may Love's sweet memories rise,
to recollection sweet,
A radiant vision of unclouded skies.

"Was it really I who inspired these lines?" she asked.

This doubt, suggested by the coquetry of a woman who enjoys playing with fire, brought tears to Lucien's eyes; she comforted him, kissing for the first time his brow. There could be no doubt that Lucien was a great man, and she intended to form him; it occurred to her that she might teach him Italian and German, and improve his manners; this gave her a pretext for having him always with her, under the very eyes of her tiresome entourage. What an interest in her life! She began practising her piano again for her poet, to whom she revealed the world of music. She played him wonderful pieces of Beethoven that sent him into raptures; happy in his delight, and seeing him almost transported, she said to him, hypocritically:

"Is not this happiness enough?"

And the poor poet was fool enough to answer: "Yes!"

Finally, things had reached such a point that Louise had invited

Lucien to dine with her the previous week, with M. de Bargeton as a third. But in spite of that precaution, the whole town talked of nothing else; the thing seemed so fantastic that everybody was asking if it was really true. The outcry was terrific. There were those who saw in it a sign that society was on the eve of another revolution. Others exclaimed:

"That is what comes of liberal doctrines!"

The jealous du Châtelet then discovered that Mme Charlotte, the midwife, was Mme Chardon, mother of the Chateaubriand of l'Houmeau, as he put it. Mme de Chandour was the first to hasten to Mme de Bargeton.

"Do you know, dear Naïs, what everybody in Angoulême is talking about?" she began. "That little poet's mother is Mme Charlotte, the midwife who attended my sister-in-law at her confinement two months ago!"

"My dear," said Mme de Bargeton, assuming her most regal air, "what is there extraordinary in that? Is she not an apothecary's widow? A hard destiny for a de Rubempré! What should we do if we were suddenly to find ourselves penniless? What could you or I do to make a living? How would you bring up your children?"

Mme de Bargeton's calm put an end to the loud lamentations of the gentry. Great minds always tend to see virtue in misfortune. And, besides, there is something irresistibly attractive about doing a good deed for which we are spoken ill of—it lends innocence all the piquancy of vice. That evening Mme de Bargeton's drawing-room was full of friends who had come to remonstrate with her. She used her caustic wit to good purpose; she said that as the best families did not seem able to produce men like Molière, Racine, Rousseau, Voltaire, Massillon, Beaumarchais and Diderot, we must accept tapestry-weavers and clock-makers and cutlers as the parents of great men. She said that genius is always aristocratic. She railed at the poor country bumpkins for having such a narrow view of their own best interests. In short, she said a great many very stupid things that would have been seen through at once by auditors less dense, but her originality left them speechless with admiration. Thus she silenced the storm by letting off her heavy artillery. When

Lucien, at her command, set foot for the first time in the old faded drawing-room where four whist-tables were set out, she received him graciously and introduced him like a queen who means to be obeyed. She addressed the controller of excise as *Monsieur Châtelet* and left him petrified by this revelation that she knew about the illegal superfoetation of his particle. Lucien was, from this evening, introduced by main force into Mme de Bargeton's circle ; but he was accepted among them as a poisonous substance which each of them inwardly vowed to expel by the antidote of insolence.

But in spite of this victory, Naïs had lost her supremacy : there were dissidents who attempted to emigrate. On M. Châtelet's advice, Amélie (Mme de Chandour) decided to raise a rival shrine and receive at her house on Wednesdays. Mme de Bargeton was at home to her friends every evening, and her circle were such creatures of habit, so long accustomed to meeting at the same tables, to sitting down to the same game of backgammon, to seeing the same faces, the same candle-sconces, to hanging up their coats, leaving their overshoes and hats in the same corridor, that they were as much attached to the treads of the staircase as to the mistress of the house. "All resigned themselves to endure the songster (chardonneret) of the sacred grove," said Alexandre de Brébian—another witticism. And finally the President of the Agricultural Society put down the seditious faction with a magisterial pronouncement.

" Before the Revolution," he said, " the greatest houses received Duclos, Grimm and Crébillon, who were all nobodies, like this little poet from l'Houmeau ; but they did not receive tax-collectors, like that fellow Châtelet."

So du Châtelet suffered for Chardon, and everybody cut him. Feeling himself threatened, the Controller of Excise, who, from the moment when she had called him *Châtelet* had vowed to himself to possess Mme de Bargeton, took the part of the mistress of the house ; he stood up for the young poet and declared himself his friend.

In order to launch the poet, he gave a dinner to which were invited the Prefect, the Receiver-General, the Colonel of the Garrison, the Director of the Naval College, the President of the Court—in fact all the heads of the administration. The poor poet was fêted so splendidly that anyone but a young man of twenty would have had very strong suspicions that all this praise was some kind of practical joke played at his expense. After dinner Châtelet made his rival recite an ode entitled *The Dying Sardanapolis*, the masterpiece of the moment. This performance moved the headmaster of the school, a man phlegmatic by nature, to clap loudly and to declare that "Jean-Baptiste Rousseau had written nothing finer". Baron Sixte du Châtelet was of the opinion that the little rhymer would succumb, sooner or later, in the hot house atmosphere of applause; or perhaps that, intoxicated with the prospect of future glory, he would commit some impertinence that would consign him again to his original obscurity. While awaiting the decease of the young genius, he pretended to immolate his own aspirations at Mme de Bargeton's feet; but with the subtlety of the confirmed rake, he held his hand and followed the progress of the lovers with diplomatic attention, waiting for his opportunity to exterminate Lucien.

About this time it began to be rumoured in Angoulême and the surrounding district that there was a great man living in the town. Mme de Bargeton was everywhere praised for her exertions on behalf of this young eagle. Her conduct thus approved, she was determined to obtain a general sanction. She proclaimed to the whole Department an evening with ices, cakes, and tea—a great innovation in a town where tea was still sold at the chemist's as a drug to cure indigestion. The flower of the local aristocracy was summoned to hear Lucien read a great work. Louise had concealed from her young friend the difficulties that she had had to surmount, but she dropped a hint of the hardening of opinion against him in her set; for she did not wish him to be ignorant of the dangers that men of genius must encounter in the course of their career—obstacles that only men of supreme courage can overcome. She drew a lesson from this victory; with her white hands she pointed out to him the glory that can be bought only at the price of continual sacrifice, she spoke of martyrs burned at the stake, she buttered some of her finest *tartines* for him and spread them thickly with all the adjectives at her command. It was a parody of the purple passages that disfigure the pages of *Corinne*. But Louise was so delighted with her own eloquence that she loved all the more the darling boy who inspired her to such rhapsodies ; she counselled him to be bold, to abandon his father's name and to take the noble name of de Rubempré, without regard for the outcry that would be the result of this change which, for that matter, the King would authorise. She was related to the Marquise d'Espard, who was a Blaumont-Chauvry before her marriage and had influence at Court ; she would undertake to make use of that influence. These magic words *the King, the Marquise d'Espard, Court,* were so many fireworks that dazzled Lucien, and the necessity of this baptism became very clear to him.

" Dear child," said Louise in a tone of tender mockery, " the sooner it is done the sooner it will be sanctioned."

She went through each of the successive social strata and made the poet realise how many rungs higher he would immediately be placed by this able decision. At the same time, she persuaded Lucien to abjure his chimerical notions of the popular equality of 1793 and awakened in him that thirst for fame that David's cool reason had calmed ; she proved to him that high society was the only stage for his talent. The rabid liberal became a monarchist there and then. Lucien bit the apple of aristocratic luxury and glory. He vowed to lay a crown at the feet of his lady, even though that crown should be stained with blood ; he would win it at all costs, *quibuscumque viis*. In order to prove his courage, he described his present hardships that he had hitherto concealed from Louise with the instinct of that indefinable modesty that characterises the sentiments of youth and which restrains a young man from displaying his merits, much as he may like to have his mind appreciated through its incognito. He described the constrictions of poverty, endured with pride, his work with David, his evenings spent in study. That youthful ardour reminded Mme de Bargeton of the colonel of twenty-six, and her expression softened. Seeing how his imposing mistress was weakening, Lucien took the hand that she did not attempt to withdraw, and kissed it with all the ardour of a poet, a young man, and a lover. Louise went so far as to permit the apothecary's son to press his quivering lips upon her brow.

"Child, child! If anyone were to see us I should look very ridiculous!" she exclaimed, shaking off an ecstatic torpor.

In the course of that evening Mme de Bargeton's wit made great ravages in what she described as Lucien's prejudices. According to her, men of genius had neither brother nor sister, father nor mother; the great works that it is their task to create impose upon them what seems like egoism, oblige them to sacrifice everything to their own greatness. If at first the family must suffer from the exalting absorption of a great brain, later it will reap a hundredfold reward for the many and various sacrifices demanded by the first struggles of shackled nobility and share in the fruits of victory. Genius is answerable only to itself; it is the sole judge of the means, since it alone knows the end: thus genius must consider itself as above the law, for it is the task of genius to remake the law; moreover, the man who frees himself from his time and place may take everything, hazard everything, for everything is his by right. She quoted the early life of Bernard Palissy, of Louis XI, Fox, Napoleon, Christopher Columbus, Caesar, all those illustrious gamblers who started life crippled with debts, or as poor men, not understood, regarded as mad, bad sons, bad fathers, bad brothers, but who later became the pride of their family, of their country, of the world. These reasonings fell on the fertile soil of Lucien's secret weaknesses and hastened on the corruption of his heart; for, to the ardour of his desires, all means were permissible. But not to succeed is high treason against society. For has not the defeated man flung to the winds all the conventional virtues upon which society is built—and society drives away in horror Marius seated among the ruins. Lucien, all unconscious of the fact that he was standing between the infamy of the hulks on the one hand and the palm of genius on the other, soared above the Sinai of the prophets, without seeing at its base the Dead Sea, the loathsome pall of Gomorrha.

So effectively did Louise loosen the swaddling-bands of provincial prejudice from the heart and mind of her poet that Lucien resolved to sound Mme de Bargeton in order to discover, without encountering the humiliation of a refusal, whether he could hope to achieve the conquest of this noble prey. The forthcoming party gave him the opportunity of making this test. There was an element of ambition in his love. He loved, but he also wanted to rise, a double desire natural enough in any young man who has a heart to satisfy and poverty to combat. Society today, by throwing open the same banquet to all her children, arouses their ambitions in the very morning of life. She deprives youth of its graces, and vitiates most of its generous sentiments by an admixture of calculation. Poetry would have it otherwise; but fact too often gives the lie to the fiction in which we would like to believe; we cannot allow ourselves to represent youth otherwise than as it was in the nineteenth century. But Lucien's calculation seemed to himself to be prompted by a feeling entirely noble, his friendship for David.

Lucien wrote a long letter to his Louise, for he had more courage on paper than in person. In a twelve-page letter, copied out three times, he told of his father's genius and shattered hopes and of the terrible poverty of which he was now the victim. He described his dear sister as an angel, David as a future Cuvier, who, besides being a great man, was both father, brother, and friend to Lucien; he would consider himself unworthy of his greatest glory, that of being loved by Louise, were he not to ask her to do for David what she was doing for himself. He would renounce everything rather than betray David Séchard; he would like David to be present on his great evening. He wrote one of those wild letters in which the young point a pistol at a refusal, a letter full of childish casuistry and of highminded irrational reasoning, enchanting verbiage, embroidered with those naïve declarations, spoken unawares from the heart, that women love so much. After giving this letter to the maid, Lucien had proceeded to spend the day reading proofs, supervising various pieces of work, and setting in order the small affairs of the printing-press, without saying a word to David. In the days when the heart is still childlike, the young are capable of sublime discretion. Or perhaps Lucien was already beginning to fear the Phocion's axe that David knew so well how to wield; perhaps he feared to have his soul exposed to one of David's searching looks. But after reading the Chénier, at the sting of a reproach that touched him to the quick, as when a doctor lays his finger on a wound, his secret had risen from his heart to his lips.

Now try to imagine the thoughts that must have troubled Lucien's mind as he went down from Angoulême to l'Houmeau. Was his great lady angry ? Would she receive David at her house ? Or would he be thrown back, with all his ambitions, into his obscure corner, back to l'Houmeau ? Before he had kissed Louise on the brow Lucien had had occasion to measure the distance that divides a queen from her favourite, so that he did not imagine that David would be able to cross overnight a barrier that it had taken him five months to overcome. But, not knowing the extent to which the lower classes were regarded as social outcasts, he did not realise that a second experiment would mean ruin to Mme de Bargeton. Accused and convicted on the charge of a liking for the lower orders, Louise would have to leave the town, where she would be shunned by her own class like a leper in the Middle Ages. The flower of the aristocracy, and the clergy into the bargain, would have stood by Naïs if she had been guilty of a moral lapse; but the crime of knowing the wrong people would never be forgiven her; for we may excuse the faults of those in power, but we condemn them after the abdication. And to receive David, would not that be to abdicate? But if Lucien did not appreciate that aspect of the question, his aristocratic instinct presented to him plenty of other difficulties that caused him no small anxiety. Nobility of mind does not always go with elegance of manners. Racine may have had the manner of a courtier, but Corneille behaved more like a cattle-dealer. Descartes might have been taken for some worthy Dutch merchant. Visitors to La Brède, meeting Montesquieu in his nightcap, a rake over his shoulder, often mistook him for one of the gardeners. Worldly good manners, when they are not the birthright of aristocracy, a knowledge imbibed with our mother's milk, or something innate, must be learned, and opportunity must be seconded by a certain natural elegance, grace of features, and a cultured voice. All these important trifles, with which nature had endowed his friend, David altogether lacked. Lucien was nobly born, on his mother's side, and was every inch a Frank, even to his high-arched instep; whereas David had inherited his physique from his father, the printer, and was as flat-footed as a Welshman. Lucien could already hear the jokes that would be made at David's expense and he could almost see Mme de Bargeton's suppressed smile. And finally, without exactly being ashamed of his comrade, he decided in his own mind not to act again on a first impulse and to think twice next time. And so, for Lucien, the hour of poetry and loyalty, the reading that had so recently revealed to the two friends the wide fields of literature shining in the light of a newly risen sun, was followed by the hour of policy and calculation. As he reached l'Houmeau, he was already regretting his letter and wishing that he could recall it; for he had divined something of the inexorable laws of the world.

As he reflected that nothing succeeds like success, it cost him a pang to withdraw his foot from the first rung of the ladder by which he must climb to attack the heights of fame. Then pictures of his simple, peaceful life rose before his mind, beautiful with the brightest flowers of affection; David, with his genius, who had so nobly come to his aid, who would lay down his life for him if need be; his mother, so dignified in her humiliation, who believed him to be as good as he was brilliant; his sister, so generous in her self-effacement, his innocent childhood, his conscience, still unsullied; his hopes, whose buds no rough winds had yet shaken—all these things broke into flower once more in his memory. He reflected that it was a finer thing to penetrate the ranks of the aristocracy, or the middle classes for that matter, by hard-earned success, than to succeed through the favours of a woman. Sooner or later his genius would shine, like that of many other great men before him, who had got the better of society; and then women would love him! The example of Napoleon—the bane of the nineteenth century, because of the vain ambitions it inspired in so many nonentities—rose before Lucien's mind, and he threw his calculations to the wind, despising himself for them. For Lucien was made so; he would pass from evil to good, or good to evil, with equal facility.

Instead of feeling the scholar's love for his retreat, Lucien, for the past month, had felt a sort of shame whenever he caught sight of the shop, over which, in yellow letters on a green ground, was written:

POSTEL (LATE CHARDON) PHARMACEUTICAL CHEMIST

It hurt him to see his father's name written up in that way, in sight of all the passing traffic. When he went through that vulgar iron-barred gate of an evening on his way to Beaulieu, to give his arm to Mme de Bargeton among the smart set of the Upper Town, he bitterly resented the disparity between this dwelling and his present fortune.

"To be in love with Mme de Bargeton, soon perhaps to possess her, and to live in a hole like this!" Lucien thought to himself as he went down the alley into the little yard where bundles of all kinds of boiled herbs were hung along the walls, where the apprentice was scouring the dispensary cauldrons, and where M. Postel, in his dispenser's overall, retort in hand, was examining some chemical product and at the same time keeping an eye on the shop; and however attentively his eye might be on his drug, he was always listening for the bell.

The scent of camomile, peppermint, and all kinds of distilled herbs pervaded the yard of the humble dwelling, reached by a flight of steps with a rope on either side instead of a handrail. Lucien's room was the attic above.

"Evening, *son*," said M. Postel, who was the very type of a country shopkeeper. "How is the world treating you? I have been trying an experiment with treacle, but it would need a man like your father to find out what I am looking for. A great man, your father! If I had known his gout remedy you and I would have kept our own carriages today."

A week never passed but the chemist, whose denseness was only equalled by his kindness of heart, turned the knife in Lucien's wound by reminding him of the fatal discretion with which his father had kept the secret of his discovery.

"It is a great pity," said Lucien shortly. He was beginning to realise that his father's pupil was fearfully common, although he had often had reason to bless him ; for honest Postel had come to the aid of the widow and children on more occasions than one.

" What's the matter with you ? " asked M. Postel, setting down his test-tube on the laboratory bench.

" Are there any letters for me ? "

" Yes, one that smells like balm! It is on the counter, just by my desk."

Mme de Bargeton's letter lying among the bottles of the pharmacy! Lucien dashed into the shop.

"Hurry up, Lucien! Your dinner has been waiting for an hour, it will be cold! " a sweet voice called gently through a half-open window. But Lucien did not hear.

" He's gone crazy, your brother, miss," said Postel, raising his head.

The little bachelor, who looked for all the world like a small brandy flask upon which some artist had amused himself by painting a fat red face, pitted with smallpox, always looked at Eve with a civil and agreeable expression from which it was evident that he had thoughts of marrying the daughter of his predecessor, but could not put an end to the conflict in his heart between love and caution. And he often used to say to Lucien with a smile, as he did on this occasion as the young man passed him again :

" She's remarkably pretty, your sister! You're not so bad-looking, either! Your father did everything well! "

Eve was tall and dark-skinned, with black hair and blue eyes. Although there was something masculine in her appearance, she was gentle, tender-hearted and affectionate. Her frankness, her simplicity, her quiet acceptance of her life of hard work, her irreproachable goodness, could not have failed to win the heart of David Séchard. So, from their first meeting, an unspoken, single-hearted passion had sprung up between them, in the German style, undemonstrative and without any ardent protestations. Each thought, in secret, of the other, for all the world as if they were divided by some jealous husband to whom this love might have given offence. Both concealed it from Lucien, thinking perhaps that his feelings would in some way be hurt. David's great fear was that he was not good enough for Eve, who, on her side, gave way to fears on the grounds of her poverty. A real working-girl would have been bolder ; but as a well-bred girl who had come down in the world she resigned herself to her dreary lot. Diffident as she seemed to be, she was, in reality, proud ; and Eve would not for the world have pursued the son of a man who was said to be rich. Those who knew the rising value of land estimated the present value of the Marsac estate at eighty thousand francs, not counting the additions that old Séchard, rich in savings, lucky in his harvests, good at driving a bargain, must by this time have added, as occasion offered. David was probably the only man in Angoulême who had no idea of his father's wealth. In his eyes, Marsac was a tumbledown place bought in 1810 for fifteen or sixteen thousand francs, to which he had gone once a year, at harvest time, and where his father used to lead him up and down the rows of vines boasting of vintages about which David knew nothing and cared less. The love of a student, accustomed to solitude, a love that grows all the greater by dwelling upon imaginary difficulties, has to be encouraged ; for to David Eve was a woman more awe-inspiring than a great lady to a simple clerk. He was awkward and ill at ease in the presence of his idol, always as anxious to escape from her presence as he had lately been to find himself in it. Instead of declaring his passion, he stifled it. Often of an evening, having invented some pretext of consulting Lucien, he would walk down from the Place du Mûrier to l'Houmeau, by the Porte Palet ; but at the iron-barred gate his courage would fail and he would go away again, afraid of calling too late, or of disturbing Eve, who had probably gone to bed. Although this great love only revealed itself in small things, Eve had guessed it ; she was flattered, but without being proud, to find herself the object of the profound respect expressed in David's looks, behaviour and words ; but it was the printer's enthusiastic faith in Lucien that was his greatest merit in her eyes : he had discovered the best way to Eve's heart. The mute delights of this love differed from tumultuous passion as wild flowers do from garden blooms : glances as sweet and delicate as blue lotus-flowers floating on the stream ; looks as fugitive as the delicate scent of honeysuckle, melancholy as soft as velvet moss; such were the flowers of two rare natures, deeply rooted upon rich, fertile soil. On many occasions already Eve had divined the strength concealed beneath that diffidence; she understood so well all that David had not dared to say, that the smallest incident now might lead to the closest union of their souls.

Lucien found that Eve had already opened the door, and he sat down without a word at the little trestle table, without a cloth, where his dinner was laid. This poor little household possessed only three silver spoons and forks, and Eve had laid them all for her adored brother.

" What are you reading?" she asked, after she had placed a dish on the table and put out her portable stove by covering it with the extinguisher.

Lucien did not answer. Eve took a little plate, prettily arranged with vine-leaves, and put it on the table with a jug of cream.

" Look, Lucien, I've got you some strawberries."

Lucien was so absorbed in reading that he did not hear. So Eve came and sat beside him without a murmur, for one of the greatest pleasures in a sister's love for a brother is to be treated without ceremony.

" But what is it, Lucien?" she exclaimed, seeing tears shining in her brother's eyes.

" Nothing, nothing at all, Eve," he said, putting his arm round her, drawing her to him and kissing her brow, her hair, and finally her neck, with surprising warmth.

" Are you keeping something from me?"

" Well, then—she loves me!"

" I knew quite well that it was not me you were kissing," replied his poor sister in a sulky tone, flushing crimson.

" We shall all be happy!" exclaimed Lucien, gulping down his soup in great spoonfuls.

" We?" Eve echoed.

Inspired by the same presentiment that had occurred to David, she added:

" You will not care so much for us now!"

" How can you think that, if you know me ? " Eve held out her hand and pressed his ; then she took away the empty plate and the brown earthenware soup tureen and brought the dish that she had cooked for him. Instead of eating it, Lucien re-read Mme de Bargeton's letter ; Eve discreetly refrained from asking to see it, out of respect for her brother. If he wanted her to know what was in it, she would have to wait until he told her ; and if he did not, was it for her to ask him ? She waited. Here is the letter :

" My dear, why should I refuse to your companion in learning the help that I have given to you ? In my eyes, all talents have equal rights. But you don't know the prejudices of the circle in which I live. We cannot hope to make this aristocracy of ignorance recognise intellectual greatness. If I have not enough influence to impose M. David Séchard on them, I will gladly sacrifice these poor creatures for your sake. It would be like an antique hecatomb! But, my dear, naturally you cannot expect me to accept someone whom I might not like, or with whose ideas I might be out of sympathy. From the way you flatter me, I know how blind friendship can be! If I agree may I be allowed to make just one condition ? I would like to meet your friend, so that I can know and judge for myself, in the interests of your own future, whether you are right about him. Is not that one of the motherly duties that I must undertake on behalf of my poet ?

Louise de Nègrepelisse."

Lucien had no idea of how, in society, one says yes as a more tactful way of saying no, and how a no can lead to a yes. In his eyes that letter was a triumph. David would visit Mme de Bargeton and shine there in the splendour of genius. Intoxicated by a victory that made him believe in the power of his ascendancy over others, such pride, so many hopes shone in his face, that he became positively radiant. His sister could not resist telling him how handsome he was.

" If she has any sense, how can she help loving you! And won't she be jealous tonight, because all the women will fall in love with you. You will be wonderful when you read your *St. John on Patmos*. I wish I could turn into a mouse and slip in to see you! You must go and change—I have laid out your clothes in Mother's room."

This room expressed a self-respecting poverty. There was a walnut bedstead with white hangings, and a strip of thin green carpet at the foot; a chest of drawers with a wooden top, fitted with a mirror, and a few walnut chairs completed the furniture. On the mantelpiece a clock served to recall the old vanished days of prosperity. There were white curtains in the window and on the walls a grey flowered paper. The tiled floor, coloured and polished by Eve, shone with care. In the middle of this room stood a small round table on which three cups and a sugar-basin in Limoges porcelain were set out on a red tray with a pattern of gilt roses. Eve slept in a small adjoining closet, which contained a narrow bed, an old easy-chair, and a work-table by the window. This ship's-cabin was so small that the glass door always stood open, for the sake of air. But in spite of the evidence of poverty, there was an atmosphere of quietness and study. To those who knew the mother and her two children, this setting seemed touchingly fitting.

Lucien was tying his cravat when David's step was heard in the little yard, and the printer presently appeared with the air of a man in a hurry.

" Well, David," exclaimed the ambitious poet, " we have won! She loves me! You shall come, too."

" No," said the printer, with an air of embarrassment. " In fact I have come to thank you for that proof of friendship, but I have been thinking it over seriously. My life is cut out for me, Lucien. I am David Séchard, printer to His Majesty in Angoulême, and you can read my name on every wall, in the corner of the posters. For people of that world, I am a workman—a tradesman if you like, but, even so, an artisan established in a shop in the Rue de Beaulieu, at the corner of the Place du Mûrier. I have neither the wealth of a Keller nor the fame of a Desplein, both of which kinds of power the nobility still try to ignore, but which—and I agree with them there—are useless without the polish and manners of a gentleman. What have I done to justify such a sudden elevation?

I should be laughed at just as much by the townspeople as by the gentry. It is different for you. A foreman is not committed to anything. You are working in order to gain useful experience, you can explain your present occupation by your future. Besides, you could throw up your present job tomorrow and study law, or diplomacy, go into the Civil Service. In fact, you are not labelled, or pigeonholed. Take advantage of your social virginity, go on alone, and grasp your honours! Enjoy all the pleasures you can, even the most frivolous ones. Enjoy it all—I shall be happy watching your success, you shall be my second self. Yes, I shall live your life in my own thoughts. You shall go to the parties and have the quick success that comes from knowing people. I shall stick to the dull, hard-working routine of a tradesman and the slow plodding of scientific research. You shall be our aristocracy," he added, with a glance at Eve. " If you slip, I shall be there to support you. If you find the world treacherous, you can take refuge in our affections, where you will always find unchanging love. Protection, favour, the good-will of the world, divided between two, would be bound to come to nothing, and we should stand in each other's way. You go ahead—you can take me in tow, for that matter. Far from envying you, I am devoted to you. What you have just done for me, in running the risk of losing your benefactress, perhaps your mistress, rather than desert me, or disown me—that little thing meant a great deal—and, you see, Lucien, it would have bound me to you for ever, if we had not been like brothers already. Do not have any remorse or be afraid to take what looks like the better part. This one-sided bargain suits me admirably. And after all, if you do sometimes cause me a pang, I daresay it will be all for my good."

So saying, he cast a shy glance in the direction of Eve, in whose eyes there were tears, for she had understood everything.

" The fact is," he said to the astonished Lucien, " you are tall, handsome, wear your clothes well, and look every inch a gentleman in that blue coat with yellow buttons and those plain nankeen trousers ; but as for me, I would look like a workman among all these people ; I would be clumsy and do the wrong thing ; I would make a fool of myself, or say nothing at all ; besides, you can overcome their prejudice about names by calling yourself Lucien de Rubempré ; I am, and always shall be, plain David Séchard. In those surroundings everything is in your favour, but everything would tell against me. You are cut out to get on in that world. The women will all adore your god-like beauty, won't they, Eve ? "

Lucien flung his arms round David and embraced him warmly. David's modesty had cut short many doubts and no end of difficulties. How could he fail to feel an access of affection for a man who had reached through friendship the same conclusions that he had reached through ambition ? The aspiring poet and lover in him saw the way clear ; and all his youth and friendship went out to David. It was one of those rare moments in life when all our powers are in tune, when every cord vibrates and adds its full sound to the harmony. But the goodness of that noble mind had already begun to foster in Lucien a tendency to regard himself as the centre of everything. We are all more or less inclined to say, like Louis XIV : " L'État, c'est moi ! " The adoration of his mother and his sister, and David's devotion, of which he was the sole object, the habit of seeing himself made the centre of the secret efforts of these three, had developed in Lucien all the faults of a spoilt child, and produced in him that egoism that devours nobility—an egoism fostered, moreover, by Mme de Bargeton who encouraged him to forget his obligations to his sister, his mother, and to David. He had not done so as yet ; but was there not reason to fear that, as the circle of his ambition widened, he would come to think only of himself and of how to maintain himself in it ?

When this emotion had subsided, David suggested to Lucien that perhaps *St. John on Patmos* might be too biblical to read to an audience who would probably not be familiar with apocalyptic poetry. Lucien, about to appear before the most exacting audience in the Charente, looked worried. David advised him to take André de Chénier, and to forgo a doubtful for a certain pleasure. Lucien read beautifully, and he would be sure to please, and at the same time would show a modesty that would certainly be all to his advantage. Like most young people, these two attributed to the world their own intelligence and virtues. Youth that has not yet known failure has no mercy on the faults of other people; but it has also a sublime faith in them. Indeed, we must have learned a great deal about life before we can recognise that, according to Raphael's epigram, to understand is to equal. The faculty necessary for the understanding of poetry is on the whole rare in France, where intellect and wit soon dry up the source of the sacred tears of ecstasy and where nobody takes the trouble to decipher the sublime or to sound its depths in the desire to perceive the infinite. Lucien was about to have his first experience of the ignorance and indifference of the world! He called in at the Rue du Mûrier on the way to pick up the volume of poems.

When the two lovers were alone, David felt more embarrassed than ever in his life before, the prey of a thousand terrors; he both hoped and feared that Eve would praise him; he wanted to escape, for diffidence has a coquetry of its own. The poor lover did not venture to utter a word that might seem to imply a desire to be thanked; anything he might have said seemed to him compromising, so he remained silent and looked guilty. Eve, divining the tortures of his shyness, enjoyed the pleasures of this silence; but when David twisted his hat and made as if to go, she smiled.

"Monsieur David," she said, "if you are not spending the evening at Mme de Bargeton's we might spend it together. It is fine; would you like to come for a walk by the Charente? Then we can talk about Lucien."

David longed to throw himself at the feet of this adorable girl. The manner of Eve's reply was a reward beyond his wildest hopes. She had, by the tenderness of her tone of voice, resolved the difficulties of the situation; her proposal was more than praise, it was the first favour of love.

"But you must give me a few minutes to dress!" she added at David's gesture of assent.

David, who had never in his life known one tune from another, went out humming to himself, much to the surprise of honest Postel, who conceived a violent suspicion of the state of affairs between Eve and the young printer.

Every detail of that evening was to make a deep impression on Lucien, who was by nature inclined to be influenced by first impressions. Like all inexperienced lovers, he arrived so early that Louise was not yet in the drawing-room. M. de Bargeton was there alone. Lucien had already begun his apprenticeship in small deceits with which the lover of a married woman pays for his happiness and from which women discover how much they can demand ; but he had never before found himself alone, face to face with M. de Bargeton.

This gentleman's intellect was nicely poised between an inoffensive vacancy with some glimmerings of sense and a proud stupidity that will neither accept an idea nor yield an inch. He was fully alive to his social duties, and in the effort to be agreeable he had adopted, as his sole means of expression, a dancer's smile. Whether he was pleased or displeased, he smiled. He smiled at bad news and good. This smile was made to suit all situations by the slight modifications of expression that M. de Bargeton imparted to it. When absolutely obliged to give direct approval, he would reinforce the smile with a pleasant laugh, but never vouchsafed a word except in the last extremity. A tête-à-tête made him suffer the only embarrassment that complicated his vegetative existence, for then he was compelled to search in the immense void of his inner vacancy for something to say. As a rule he got out of the difficulty by reverting to the simplicity of his childhood : he thought aloud ; he told you the most intimate details of his life ; he confided to you his needs, the little sensations that, for him, took the place of ideas. He did not talk about the weather, nor did he make use of any of the conversational commonplaces invented for the self-protection of weak intellects, but plunged into the most personal topics : " Just to please Mme de Bargeton, I ate veal for lunch—she is very fond of it, but my stomach can't stand it. I knew it would not agree with me, it's always the same. How do you explain it ? " Or : " I am just going to ring for a glass of *eau-sucrée*—would you like one, too ? " Or : " I am going to ride over to see my father-in-law tomorrow."

These little phrases, which did not open the way to any discussion, drew a yes or a no from the other party, and conversation languished. Then M. de Bargeton would implore the assistance of his visitor, by turning westward his old broken-winded pug-dog's muzzle and looking at you with big bloodshot eyes as much as to say : " You were saying ? " The bores who wanted to talk about themselves were those he liked best ; he appreciated them ; he listened to them with an unfeigned and delicate attention that endeared him to them ; so that all the twaddlers of Angoulême credited him with having more intelligence than he chose to show, and declared that he was misunderstood. For when nobody else would listen to them these people always turned to him to finish their stories or their arguments, sure in advance of M. de Bargeton's approving smile. As his wife's drawing-room was usually full, he was, as a rule, quite at his ease. The smallest details were enough to interest him ; he noticed who came in, bowed and smiled, and led the new arrival to his wife ; he watched for those who were leaving and escorted them to the door, taking leave of them with that eternal smile of his. When the evening was in full swing, and he saw everybody happily occupied, he was perfectly content to stand there on his two long legs like a swan balanced on both feet, with the air of a man listening to a conversation on politics ; or he would go and study the hand of one of the card-players, without its conveying anything to him, for he did not play any games. Or he would walk about taking snuff to aid his digestion. Naïs was the bright side of his life, a source of boundless happiness to him. When she was playing the hostess he would stretch himself in an armchair and admire her, for she did the talking for him ; besides, it was a pleasure to him to try to see the point of her remarks ; and as often he did not do so quite at once, his smiles penetrated the conversation like the explosion of a series of timed fuses. His respect for her, besides, amounted almost to adoration. And is not such an adoration a sufficient happiness in life ? Intelligent and generous by nature, Naïs had never taken advantage of her husband, recognising in him a childlike nature that asked only to be told what to do. She had taken care of him, as one takes care of a coat ; she saw that he was well groomed, brushed, and cared-for ; she managed him ; and M. de Bargeton repaid his wife with a dog-like devotion. It is easy to give a pleasure that costs us nothing! Mme de Bargeton, knowing that her husband's only pleasure consisted in good food, saw that he had excellent dinners; she had pity on him; never did she utter a word of complaint, and many people, not understanding the silence of her pride, attributed to M. de Bargeton hidden good qualities. She had, besides, drilled him into military obedience, and his wife's wishes were law to him. She would say to him: "Go and call on this or that person," and he would go like a soldier at the word of command. And, in her presence, he would stand, in perfect silence, awaiting her orders.

Just now there was some talk of nominating this mute gentleman as a deputy. Lucien had not frequented the house for long enough to have lifted the veil beneath which this unfathomable character was hidden. He was prodigiously in awe of M. de Bargeton, who, ensconced in his easy-chair, always seemed to observe and to understand everything, whose silence lent him the greater dignity. Far from regarding him as a granite block, Lucien saw him as a redoubtable sphinx, according to the natural tendency of imaginative people to elevate everything, to attribute souls to all existing forms; and he thought it necessary to conciliate him.

"I am the first arrival," he said, bowing with rather more respect than people usually showed to this worthy gentleman.

"That's quite natural," replied M. de Bargeton.

Lucien took this remark as the epigram of a jealous husband, blushed, and looked at himself in the mirror in an attempt to regain his composure.

"You live in l'Houmeau," said M. de Bargeton. "The people who have the farthest to come are always the first to arrive."

"How do you explain that?" said Lucien, assuming an agreeable manner.

"I don't know," replied M. de Bargeton, relapsing into immobility.

"You have not tried to discover the reason," Lucien went on. "A man capable of making an observation is capable of finding the cause."

"Ah!" said M. de Bargeton. "Final causes, what?" The

conversation came to a full stop. Lucien racked his brains to think of some way of reviving it.

" Mme de Bargeton is no doubt dressing ? " he proceeded, trembling at the silliness of the question.

" Yes, she is dressing," the husband naturally replied.

Lucien raised his eyes to the two beams of the ceiling, painted grey, and scanned the plastered space between them, without being able to think of anything else to say ; but with deep alarm he saw that the gauze had been removed from the little chandelier with pendant crystals and that it was filled with candles. The chair-covers had been removed, and the faded flowers of the red silk were exposed to view. These preparations announced a party of no ordinary kind. The poet began to fear that his clothes were not right, for he was wearing boots. Paralysed with terror, he tried to concentrate on a Japanese vase standing on a garlanded console table of the Louis Quinze period ; then, afraid of offending the husband by not being attentive to him, he decided to find out whether the old gentleman had any hobby on which one could draw him out.

" You very seldom go out of town, sir ? " he said, turning to M. de Bargeton.

" Very seldom."

Another silence. M. de Bargeton watched Lucien's slightest movements like a cat watching a mouse, which upset him considerably. Each was terrified by the other.

" Has he any suspicions of my attentions ? " Lucien wondered. " He seems to be most unfriendly."

Fortunately for Lucien, who was suffering tortures of embarrassment under the uneasy glances that M. de Bargeton directed upon him as he walked up and down the room, the old manservant, who was dressed in livery for the occasion, announced du Châtelet. The Baron came in, quite at his ease, greeted his friend Bargeton, and gave Lucien the little nod that was then in fashion but which the poet registered mentally as purse-proud insolence. Sixte du Châtelet appeared in trousers of dazzling whiteness, with straps under the soles of his shoes, that held them in position without a wrinkle. He was wearing thin slippers and fine worsted stockings. Over his white waistcoat floated the black ribbon of his eyeglass. Parisian cut and style was written in every line of his black coat. He looked every inch the beau that his reputation might lead one to expect, in spite of the fact that age had already bestowed upon him a small round corporation that could not entirely be restrained within the bounds of elegance. He dyed his hair and whiskers (greyed by the sufferings of his travels), which made his face look hard. His complexion, once so fine, had now the copper-red tan characteristic of men returned from the tropics, but for all that, and in spite of his absurd pretentions to youthfulness, you could still recognise in him the charming and accommodating secretary of an Imperial Highness. He raised his eyeglass and scrutinised Lucien's nankeen trousers, the boots, his waistcoat, and the blue coat made by the Angoulême tailor—in short, looked his rival over from top to toe ; then he coolly replaced his eyeglass in his waistcoat pocket, with a look that meant : " I am satisfied." Crushed for the moment by the elegance of Customs and Excise, Lucien reflected that he would have his revenge when the assembly should see his face, lit up by poetry ; all the same, the unformulated distress occasioned by M. de Bargeton's supposed hostility was succeeded by an acute pang. The Baron seemed to be bringing to bear on Lucien the full weight of his fortune in order to humiliate that penniless upstart. M. de Bargeton, who had counted upon having no more to say, was dismayed by the silence maintained by the rivals as they examined each other, but whenever he found himself at his wit's end he had a question, that he kept like a pear in case of thirst, and he decided that it was now necessary to launch it. He assumed an important air.

" Well, sir," he said, addressing Châtelet, " what's the latest news ? What are people talking about these days ? "

" Oh," replied the Controller of Excise, " but M. Chardon is the latest news. You must ask him. Have you brought a beautiful poem to read to us ? " asked the gay Baron, adjusting one of his principal side-curls that had become disarranged.

" To know that, I shall have to ask you," Lucien replied. " You have been writing poetry longer that I have."

" Pooh! Only a few little trifles, good enough in their way, written to oblige—but occasional verse, ballads that are nothing without the music, and my longer *Letter to a sister of Buonaparte* (the ungrateful wretch!) will not ensure my fame with posterity."

At this moment Mme de Bargeton appeared in the full glory of a studied toilette. She was wearing a Jewish turban, adorned with an oriental brooch. Beneath a gauze scarf, gracefully wound about her throat, the stones of her necklace glittered. The short sleeves of her printed muslin dress allowed her to display a series of bracelets on her fine white arms. This theatrical get-up Lucien thought enchanting. M. du Châtelet addressed himself gallantly to his queen in a series of fulsome compliments that made her smile with pleasure, so delighted was she to be praised in Lucien's hearing. She only exchanged a glance with her beloved poet, and mortified the Customs official by the cold civility of her reply, with its implication that he was excluded from any degree of intimacy with her.

Meanwhile the guests were beginning to arrive. Among the first were the Bishop and his Vicar-General, both solemn and impressive figures, but in violent contrast, for his Lordship was tall and thin, his acolyte short and fat. The eyes of both churchmen were bright, but the Bishop's face was pale, that of his vicar ruddy with the rudest health. Both were impassive, and sparing in their gestures. Both had a responsible air, and their silence and reserve were intimidating. Both had the reputation of being men of great intelligence.

The two ecclesiastics were followed by Mme de Chandour and her husband, a couple so extraordinary that, for those unfamiliar with country life, they would have to be seen to be believed. M. de Chandour—better known as Stanislas—the husband of that Amélie who aspired to be Mme de Bargeton's rival, still thought himself a young man at forty-five. He was slim, and had a face like a sieve. His cravat was always tied so as to present two menacing points—one level with the right ear, the other pointing downwards in the direction of the red ribbon of his decoration. His coat-tails were violently upturned. From his cut-away waistcoat protruded a stiffly starched shirt fastened by massive studs. In short, his whole dress was so exaggerated that he looked like a caricature, so that at a first encounter strangers could never refrain from smiling. Stanislas was for ever looking himself up and down with an air of satisfaction, verifying the number of his shirt-buttons, following the undulating curves that traced his tight-fitting trousers ; running over his legs a caressing glance ending at the points of his boots. When he had finished looking over himself in this way, his eyes would wander in search of a mirror, in which he would examine his hair, to see if it was keeping in curl ; he would then turn his questioning glance upon the women, with a delighted expression, one finger in his waistcoat pocket, leaning backwards and turning three-quarters view—all which airs served him very well in his role of cock of this aristocratic poultry-yard. For the most part, his conversation was limited to coarse remarks that were, according to himself, in the eighteenth-century manner. This detestable form of conversation gained him a certain popularity with women—he made them laugh. He was beginning to be a little worried on account of M. du Châtelet. And with good reason—for the air of disdain assumed by that foolish individual, enhanced by his pose of a man whose boredom nothing can alleviate, had begun to intrigue the women of Angoulême. His manner of a jaded sultan was a challenge to them ; and since Mme du Bargeton had taken up the Byron of Angoulême he was all the more in demand. Amélie, a little plump fair-complexioned woman, with dark hair, was for ever acting a part, and acting it badly. Everything about her was exaggerated. Her voice was loud, and she always went out wearing feather hats in summer, flowered hats in winter. She had a fine flow of conversation, but she could never finish a sentence without getting quite out of breath, owing to a tendency to asthma, to which she would never confess.

M. de Saintot, better known as Astolphe, the President of the Agricultural Society, was a large stout man of high complexion. He arrived in the wake of his wife, a lady whose face reminded one of a dried fern—Lili (short for Elisa). This name, with its suggestion of childishness, was quite out of keeping with Mme de Saintot's character and manners, for she was a solemn woman, extremely pious, and a most trying partner at cards. Astolphe passed for a scientific man of the first rank. He was as ignorant as a carp, but he had written the articles on *Sugar* and *Brandy* for a Dictionary of Agriculture, every detail of which he had lifted piecemeal from the newspapers or from certain out-of-date works dealing with those two products. The whole department believed that he was engaged on a work on modern agriculture. But although he shut himself up in his study every morning, he had not written two pages in the last twelve years. If anyone came to see him, he always contrived to be found searching through his papers, looking for a lost note, or mending his pen ; but he trifled away all the time in his study, reading the newspaper from cover to cover, cutting figures out of corks with his penknife, or doodling on his blotting-pad. He sometimes skimmed through his Cicero hoping that some phrase or passage applicable to the events of the day would catch his eye ; then, in the evening, he would bring round the conversation to a subject that would give him an opportunity of saying " There is a passage in Cicero that might have been written about our own times " ; then he would recite his passage, to the great astonishment of his auditors, who would say to one another, " Really, Astolphe is a mine of information." This remarkable fact would be reported by everyone in the town, and served to maintain M. de Saintot's flattering reputation.

After this couple, came M. de Bartas, known as Adrien, who sang bass tunes, and who had enormous musical pretentions. His amour-propre had taken its stand upon solfeggio : to begin with, he had admired himself singing, then he went on to talking music, and finally it had become his sole preoccupation. The art of music was his monomania ; he became animated only when he was talking about music, and a party was a penance to him, until he was asked to sing. But when he had bellowed one of his airs, life began for him. He strutted up and down, rested on his heels, and assumed a modest air as he received compliments. All the same, he always moved round from group to group to collect his due of praise ; then, when there was no more to be said, he would revert to music, and open up a discussion of the difficulties of his song, or the merits of its composer.

With M. de Bartas was Alexandre de Brebian, that hero of sepia, the artist whose crude productions infested the houses of his friends, and disfigured all the albums of the Department. They came in together, each with the other's wife on his arm. According to gossip, this exchange was complete. The two wives, Lolotte (Mme Charlotte de Brebian) and Fifine (Mme Joséphine de Bartas), were both passionately interested in scarves and trimmings, and in matching unusual colours; both were consumed by the desire to appear Parisian, and neglected their homes, where everything went wrong. If these two women, dressed like dolls, in tight-fitting dresses run up at home, presented in their persons an object-lesson in bizarre and outrageous colours, the husbands, on the other hand, permitted themselves, in the quality of artists, a provincial carelessness strange to behold. Their threadbare coats gave them the air of those extras in a provincial play, who come on to represent high society at a wedding.

Among the faces that made their appearance in the drawing-room, one of the most original was that of M. le Comte de Senonches, better known by the aristocratic name of Jacques, a great huntsman, haughty, lean, and sunburned, about as amiable as a wild boar, suspicious as a Venetian, jealous as a Moor, who lived on terms of the friendliest intimacy with M. du Hautoy, otherwise Francis, the friend of the family.

Mme de Senonches (Zéphirine) was tall and beautiful, but for the fact that her complexion was already marred by a liver complaint, on account of which she was said to be extremely exacting. Her slender figure and delicate proportions, permitted her to adopt a languorous manner that savoured a good deal of affectation, but which revealed the capriciousness of a woman who is loved, and whose every whim is satisfied.

Francis was a rather distinguished-looking man, who had left the Consulate at Valencia and his hopes in the Diplomatic Service in order to live at Angoulême near Zéphirine (also known as Zizine). The ex-consul ran the household, took charge of the children's education, taught them foreign languages, and managed the finances of M. and Mme de Senonches with single-minded devotion.

The gentry, the administration, and the townspeople of Angoulême had for a long time looked askance on the perfect unity of this three-cornered relationship, but in the end this mystery of conjugal trinity struck them as such a rare and beautiful thing that they would have thought M. de Hautoy prodigiously immoral if he had thought of marrying. All the same, things were beginning to be said about Mme de Senonche's excessive attachment to a young girl called Mlle de la Haye, her companion, and there were rumours of shocking mysteries ; in spite of the patent impossibilities presented by dates, people noticed a striking resemblance between Francoise de la Haye and Francis du Hautoy. When Jacques was hunting in the neighbourhood, friends always asked after Francis, and he would give an account of the trifling indispositions of his voluntary steward, and only mentioned his wife in the second place. This blindness seemed so strange in a jealous man that his best friends could not resist drawing him out and propounding the mystery for the benefit and amusement of those who did not know it. M. de Hautoy was a fastidious dandy whose preoccupation with personal details had degenerated into childish fussiness. He was for ever thinking about his cough, whether he had slept well, his digestion and his diet. Zéphirine had succeeded in making a valetudinarian of her factotum ; she kept him in cotton wool, coddled him, and doctored him ; she cosseted him with special diet, like a lady's lap-dog; she prescribed this food, and forbade that; she embroidered his waistcoats, his cravats, and his handkerchiefs ; she had got him into the habit of wearing such beautiful things that he looked like a sort of Japanese idol. Their understanding was perfect. Zizine consulted Francis over everything, and Francis seemed to take his ideas from Zizine's eyes. They frowned together, they smiled together, and seemed to consult together before saying the simplest good morning or good afternoon.

The richest landowner of the neighbourhood was the Marquis de Pimentel, who had driven in from the country with his wife and their neighbours the Baron and Baroness de Rastignac, their two daughters, and the Baroness' aunt. The combined income of the Marquis and his wife amounted to forty thousand francs a year, and they spent the winters in Paris. The two young girls were both charming, well bred, but penniless, and dressed with the simplicity that is so becoming to natural beauty. This party, who were certainly the most distinguished persons present this evening, were received in chilly silence, indicative of jealous respect—the more so as everyone observed the particular distinction with which Mme de Bargeton received them. These two families belonged to that very small number of people who, in the country, are above familiar intimacies, who do not mix with any society, and who live apart, maintaining an impressive dignity. M. de Pimental and M. de Rastignac were addressed by their titles ; no length of acquaintance had drawn their wives or their daughters into the social world of Angoulême ; they were too closely connected with the court to involve themselves in provincial follies.

The last to arrive were the Prefect and the General ; they came in with the same country gentleman who that morning had brought his monograph on silkworms to David. He was no doubt the mayor of some canton, and a fine estate must have made up for everything ; because his dress and behaviour betrayed a complete ignorance of society. He looked uncomfortable in his clothes, he did not know what to do with his hands, he fidgeted all the time when he was speaking, and got up and sat down again when anybody spoke to him. He always looked as if he was just going to perform some domestic office ; he was obsequious, restless, and worried in turn ; he hastened to laugh at any joke ; he listened in the most servile manner, but sometimes, when he thought that he was being laughed at, he assumed a sly expression. Several times that evening, his memoir on his mind, he tried to bring silk into the conversation ; but the unfortunate M. de Séverac picked, of all people, first on de Bartas, who replied with music, and then on M. de Saintot, who quoted Cicero at him. Half way through the evening, the poor mayor was lucky enough to find sympathetic listeners in a widow and her daughter, Mme and Mlle du Brossard—by no means the least interesting members of this society. Their story may be briefly told : they were as poor as they were noble. There was in their bearing that hint of pretentiousness that reveals concealed penury. Mme du Brossard was always boasting, very clumsily and on all occasions, of her great lump of a daughter, aged twenty-seven, who was supposed to play the piano very well. She was willing to declare that her daughter shared the tastes of any eligible man, and in her anxiety to see her dear Camille settled, she had been known, on the same evening, to expatiate on how Camille adored the wandering life of a garrison, and the peaceful life of a country farmer who never left his estate. Both had the rather pinched, acid dignity of those with whom everyone is only too pleased to sympathise, in whom people take an interest out of vanity, and who have sounded the empty depths of those consoling phrases with which the world takes so much pleasure in comforting the unfortunate. M. de Séverac was fifty-nine, a widower with no children ; so mother and daughter listened with devout admiration to the details he gave them on the subject of his silk-worm nurseries.

"My daughter has always loved animals," said the mother. "And as the silk that these little creatures produce is so interesting to women, I shall ask your permission to come to Séverac so that my Camille can see how it is harvested. Camille is so intelligent that she understands what you say immediately. She actually understood, the other day, the inverse ratio of squares of distances!"

This remark brought to a glorious close the conversation between M. de Séverac and Mme du Brossard, after Lucien's reading.

A few regular visitors had slipped uninvited into the assembly, as well as two or three eldest sons, shy, silent, dressed up like enshrined saints, delighted at having been brought to this literary function. The bravest of them overcame his shyness to the point of talking a great deal to Mlle de la Haye. All the women seated themselves solemnly in a circle, and the men stood behind. This assembly of oddities, of heterogeneous costumes, and lined faces, was imposing enough in Lucien's eyes. For all his assurance, it was all he could do to endure that first trial, the encouragements of his mistress notwithstanding, as she lavished all her airs and graces on her welcome to the illustrious of Angoulême.

The sense of uneasiness to which he was a prey was increased by a circumstance not hard to foresee but which was bound to come as a shock to a young man, still but little accustomed to worldly tactics. Lucien, all eyes and all ears, heard himself called M. de Rubempré by Louise, M. de Bargeton, the Bishop, and by a few guests who wished to please the mistress of the house; and M. Chardon by the majority of that redoubtable gathering. Taking fright under the scrutiny of so many curious eyes, he could read his plebeian name in the very movements of their lips; he divined in advance the judgments that they were passing on him with that rustic bluntness that so often borders on downright rudeness. These continual, unlooked-for pinpricks made him more ill at ease than ever. He waited impatiently for the time to begin his reading, so that he could strike an attitude and bring his mental martyrdom to an end, but Jacques was describing the recent hunt to Mme de Pimentel; Adrien was holding forth to Mlle Laure de Rastignac on the latest musical star, Rossini; Astolphe, who had learned by heart a newspaper paragraph on a new plough, was describing it to the Baron. Lucien was quite unaware, poor poet that he was, that not one of these people, with the exception of Mme de Bargeton, had any understanding of poetry. They were all of them quite devoid of feeling, and had come on a complete misunderstanding of the nature of the entertainment that was in store for them. There are certain words that, like trumpets, like cymbals, like the mountebank's big drum, always draw a crowd. The words beauty, glory, and poetry have a magic that bewitches the coarsest minds.

When everybody had arrived, and the murmurs of conversation had died down—not before M. de Bargeton had repeatedly asked for silence, sent round by his wife like a beadle in church, tapping his stick on the pavement—Lucien took his place at the round table, beside Mme de Bargeton, experiencing as he did so a thrill of terror. He announced, in a shaky voice, that, so that no one should be disappointed, he was going to read the recent work of a great poet, as yet unknown. Although André de Chénier's poems were published in 1819, no one in Angoulême had heard of him. Everyone interpreted this announcement as a device of Mme de Bargeton intended to save the poet from embarrassment and put his auditors at ease.

Lucien began by reading *Le Jeune Malade*, which was greeted with murmurs of applause ; then *l'Aveugle*, which to these commonplace intelligences seemed too long. As he read, Lucien suffered diabolical tortures, of a kind only to be understood by great artists, or by those with enough sympathy and intelligence to put themselves in their place. If poetry is to be spoken aloud in such a way as to be understood, absolute concentration is necessary. There must be complete sympathy between the reader and the audience, in the absence of which no electrical communication of emotion can take place. If this sympathetic atmosphere is lacking, the poet finds himself rather in the position of an angel attempting to sing heavenly music against a background of the mocking laughter of hell. Now, in their particular spheres, men of intelligence have their eyes on stalks, like snails, noses like dogs, and ears like moles : they see, feel, and hear everything that goes on round them. The musician and the poet know instantly whether they are appreciated or misunderstood, like plants that wilt or revive as conditions are favourable or unfavourable. The subdued conversation of the men, who had only come to please their wives, was amplified in Lucien's ears by the laws of that peculiar kind of acoustics. In the same way, he observed the violent workings of jaws, whose teeth seemed to grin at him. When, like the dove in the flood, he looked for some kindly spot on which his eyes might rest, he encountered the impatient glances of people who had evidently come to this party only in order to discuss practical affairs. With the exception of Laure de Rastignac, the Bishop, and one or two others, everyone was bored. Those who would understand poetry must allow the germ that the author has put in his verses to unfold in their own minds : but these indifferent auditors, far from aspiring to understand the soul of poetry, could barely understand the words. Lucien experienced such profound discouragement that cold sweat broke out on his brow. Only an ardent glance from Louise, to whom he turned in his distress, gave him the courage to finish ; but his poet's heart was bleeding with a thousand wounds.

" Do you find this very amusing, Fifine ? " the dried-up Lili asked her neighbour. Perhaps she had been expecting something wonderful.

" Don't ask me, my dear! I can never keep my eyes open when anyone begins to read aloud."

" I hope Naïs won't make a habit of giving us poems in the evenings," said Francis. " When I have to listen to reading after dinner the concentration of attending upsets my digestion."

" Poor darling! " Zéphirine whispered. " You had better take a glass of *eau sucrée*."

" It was very well read," said Alexandre, "but I prefer whist myself."

On hearing his verdict, which was considered very witty, because of the pun on the word *whist*, several card-players suggested that the reader needed a rest. On this pretext, one or two couples slipped away into the boudoir. Lucien, at the request of Louise, the charming Laure de Rastignac, and the Bishop, caught their attention again with the stirring counter-revolutionary *Iambes*, which a number of people applauded, carried away by the impassioned delivery, but without understanding a word. People of this kind can be moved by declamation, as gross palates can be excited by spirits. During the interval for ices, Zéphirine sent Francis to look at the book and told her neighbour Amélie that the poems that Lucien had read were printed.

" Well," replied Amélie, delighted with her acuteness, " that is very simple, M. de Rubempré works at a printer's. It's just the same," she said, with a glance at Lolotte, " as when a pretty woman makes her own dresses."

" He printed his poems himself," the woman said to one another.

" Then why does he call himself M. de Rubempré ? " asked Jacques. " When he works with his hands, a noble ought to give up his name."

" So he has," said Zizine, " but his was plebeian and he has taken his mother's which is noble."

" If his verses are printed why can't we read them for ourselves ? " said Astolphe.

This inane remark complicated the discussion, until Sixte du Châtelet deigned to inform that ignorant assembly that the announcement had not been a rhetorical device, and that these fine poems were the work of a royalist brother of Marie-Joseph Chénier the revolutionary. All Angoulême society, with the exception of the Bishop, Mme de Rastignac, and her two daughters, thought that a trick had been played on them, and took offence at this hoax. A low murmur arose ; but Lucien did not hear it. Isolated from that odious world, he was intoxicated by the inner melody that he was endeavouring to render, and saw these faces only through a mist. He read the sombre elegy on suicide, the *Elegy in an Antique Mode*, filled with such sublime melancholy ; then the ode in which occurs the line " Thy poems are sweet, I love to say them over ". He concluded with the graceful idyll *Néère*.

Sunk in a delicious reverie, one hand among her curls, heedless of their disorder, the other hanging idle, with unseeing eyes, alone in the centre of her own drawing-room, Mme de Bargeton felt herself for the first time in her life transported into her native sphere. Judge, then, of her disagreeable descent to earth when Amélie, who had been asked to express the general wish, broke in upon her thoughts :

" Naïs, we came to hear M. Chardon's poems, and you have given us poetry that has been published. Although these pieces were very pretty, these ladies are patriotic enough to prefer the local vintage."

" The French language does not lend itself very well to poetry, don't you agree ? " said Astolphe to the Director of Excise. " To my mind there is more poetry in Cicero's prose."

" The true poetry of France is light verse, the song-lyric," replied Châtelet.

" The song is the proof that our language lends itself to music," said Adrien.

" I would very much like to hear the poems that have been Naïs's downfall," said Zéphirine ; " but, judging by the way she received Amélie's request, she is not disposed to give us a sample."

" She owes it to herself to have them recited," said Francis, " for that little fellow's genius is his only justification."

" You have been a diplomat, can't you manage it for us ? " said Amélie to M. du Châtelet.

" Nothing easier," said the Baron.

The ex-Private Secretary, who was an old hand at manœuvres of this kind, went off in search of the Bishop and managed to bring him forward. At his lordship's request, Naïs could not refuse to ask Lucien for some poem that he knew by heart. The Baron's prompt success in this negotiation won him a languishing smile from Amélie.

" Really, the Baron is a very clever man," she said to Lolotte.

Lolotte had not forgotten the cattish remark about women who make their own dresses.

" Since when did you recognise Empire Barons ? " she asked smiling.

Lucien had essayed to deify his mistress in an ode which he had addressed to her under a title dear to all youths who have just left school. This ode, so fondly cherished, adorned with all the love that he felt in his heart, seemed to him the only poem worthy to stand beside Chénier's verse. He gave Mme de Bargeton a decidedly fatuous glance, and announced the title : " To Her! " Then he struck a confident pose, preparatory to reciting this ambitious work, for his author's self-esteem felt safe behind Mme de Bargeton's petticoat. At this moment, Naïs betrayed her secret to the eyes of the women. Accustomed though she was to dominating all these people from the heights of her superior intelligence, she could not help trembling for Lucien. She looked distressed, and her expression was one of mute appeal for indulgence ; after that she was obliged to lower her eyes, in order to conceal her growing delight as these stanzas proceeded.

TO HER

From the heart of those torrents of glory and light
Where at Jehovah's feet angels attendant sit,
And on their sistrums of gold repeat
  The prayers of our plaintive stars,

Oft some cherub with golden tresses aglow
Veiling the divine glory of a lofty brow,
His silver pinions leaves in the precincts of heaven
   And descends to earth below

Obedient to God's compassionate command
Of genius in distress the sufferings they assuage,
In guise of some beloved maid, the staff of age
   With childhood's flowers they bind

The wretch's tardy cry for mercy swift to hear,
To the mother's anxious heart fair dreams of hope they bear
And, full of heavenly joy, they mark the sigh
   Bestowed on poverty.

But of these eternal messages one there is
That earth, grown amorous, bids tarry still,
The angel weeps, and ever with sad sweet gaze
   Aspires again to realms celestial

Not that fair brow of dazzling radiance sublime
Nor those bright eyes, nor yet the kindling fire
Of heavenly virtue has to me betrayed
   An origin divine

But by excess of light, my love grown blind
To mingle with her heavenly substance long in vain has striven
The archangelic arms in vain assailed
   Of a terrible angel of the hosts of heaven

Mortal, beware, beware, lest love again behold
The brilliant seraph to her heaven ascend
Too soon the angel must obey the magic word
   Whispered at eventide.

Then shall you see afar, piercing the veils of night
A brightening gleam of dawn ascending to the stars in kindred flight
And the wakeful mariner, watching for a sign
Shall mark the track of these illustrious feet
 For an eternal beacon of ethereal light.

" Can you guess the riddle ? " said Amélie to M. du Châtelet with a roguish glance.

" That's the kind of stuff we all wrote more or less when we left school," replied the Baron with an air of boredom, in keeping with his role of an arbiter of taste whom nothing could surprise. " In my day we used to go in for Ossianic mists, Malvinas and Fingals, cloudy apparitions, knights rising from their tombs with stars above their heads. Nowadays these poetic trimmings have been replaced by Jehovah, sistrums, angels, seraphic pinions, and all the rest of the wardrobe of paradise, brought up to date by a sprinkling of words like vast, infinite, solitude, and eternal. You have ethereal distances and divine commands, a sort of christianised pantheism, helped out with rare and unlikely rhymes like *appalled* and *emerald*, or *age* and *assuage*, and so on. And we have changed latitude, of course ; instead of being in the North, we are now in the East ; but the darkness is just as deep as ever."

" The ode may be obscure," Zéphirine remarked, " but the declaration seems to me very clear."

" And the armour of the archangel is a tolerably thin muslin dress," added Francis.

As politeness demanded that for Mme de Bargeton's sake the ode should be declared ravishing, the women, furious because they themselves had no poet at their service to treat them as angels, rose with an air of boredom, murmuring a chilly " Charming! " " Beautiful! " or " Perfect! "

" If you love me, you will compliment neither the author nor his angel! " said Lolotte to her dear Adrien in despotic tones that brooked no denial.

" After all, what are words ? " said Zéphirine to Francis. " Love is a poem that we live."

" You have just said the very thing that I was thinking, Zizine, but I could never have expressed so neatly," said Stanislas, scanning himself from top to toe with a caressing look.

" I would give a great deal," said Amélie to Châtelet, " to see Naïs's pride taken down. She poses as an archangel, as if she were better than the rest of us, and then asks us to meet the son of a chemist and a nurse, who works at a printer's, and whose sister is a laundress."

" If the father sold worm-powders,[1] he ought to have given some to his son," Jacques remarked.

" He has followed in his father's footsteps, because what he has just administered is a powerful soporific," said Stanislas, taking one of his most irresistible poses. " Drug for drug, I would rather have the other sort."

In a moment everyone seemed to have united in order to humiliate Lucien, with some genteel irony or other. Lili, that pious lady, was of the opinion that it would be an act of charity to open Naïs's eyes, for she seemed in great danger of committing a folly. Francis, the diplomat, undertook to manage this foolish conspiracy, in which all these petty-minded people became as interested as in the last act of a play. It would make a good story for the next day. The ex-consul, who was far from wishing to have to engage in a duel with a young poet who, in the presence of his mistress, would fly into a rage at a word of insult, realised that Lucien must be assassinated with sacred fire against which vengeance would be impossible. He imitated the example set by du Châtelet when it had been a question of getting Lucien to read his poems. He went over and talked to the Bishop, and pretended to share his lordship's enthusiasm for Lucien's ode ; then he proceeded to mystify the Bishop by telling him that Lucien's mother was a remarkable woman, of excessive modesty, who found for her son the subjects of all his compositions. Lucien's greatest pleasure was to hear his mother recognised, for he adored her. Having impressed this idea upon the Bishop, Francis left it to the hazards of conversation to bring up the wounding word that he had planned should be

[1] There is a pun here on *vers*—which means both *worms* and *verses.*

spoken by his Lordship. When Francis and the Bishop returned to the circle of which Lucien was the centre, and where he was being made to drink the hemlock in small doses, everybody was on the alert. Ignorant as he was of the ways of drawing-rooms, the poor poet could do nothing but gaze at Mme de Bargeton, and reply stupidly to the stupid questions addressed to him. He did not know the names or ranks of most of those present, nor how to talk to women the silliness of whose conversation put him to shame. He felt, besides, how very far removed he was from these divinities of Angoulême as he heard himself addressed sometimes as M. Chardon, sometimes as M. de Rubempré, while they called one another Lolotte, Adrien, Astolphe, Lili, Fifine. His confusion reached a climax when, having mistaken Lili for a man's name, he addressed the brutal M. de Senonches as *Monsieur Lili.* This Nimrod interrupted Lucien with " *Monsieur Lulu?* "—and Madame de Bargeton turned crimson.

" She must be very blind to let this little fellow visit her, and introduce him to us! " he muttered.

" *Madame la Marquise*," said Zéphirine in a stage whisper to Mme de Pimentel, " don't you see a striking resemblance between M. Chardon and M. de Cante-Croix ? "

" The likeness is ideal," replied Mme de Pimentel with a smile.

" One must admit that glory has great attractions," said Mme de Bargeton to the Marquise. " There are actually some women who are as strongly attracted by greatness as others are by littleness," she added, with a glance in the direction of Francis.

Zéphirine did not understand, for she thought her consul very great ; but the Marquise laughed, and this ranged her on Naïs's side.

" You are very lucky, sir," said M. de Pimentel, addressing Lucien, in order to call him M. de Rubempré, having first called him Chardon ; " you can never be bored."

" Are you a quick worker ? " Lolotte asked him much as she might have asked a carpenter if he would take long to make a box.

Lucien was utterly abashed by this knock-out blow ; but he raised his head when he heard Mme de Bargeton reply, smiling :

" My dear, poetry does not grow in M. de Rubempré's head like grass in our courtyards."

" We cannot show too much respect, madame," said the Bishop to Lolotte, " to those noble souls in whom God has placed something of the divine Spirit. Yes, indeed, poetry is a holy thing. Whoever says poetry, says suffering. How many silent nights those verses that you admire must have cost! We should greet the poet with love, for he nearly always lives a life of suffering, and God has doubtless reserved a place in heaven for him among his prophets. This young man is a poet," he added, placing his hand on Lucien's head; " do you not see the mark that Fate has set on that fine brow ? "

Grateful at finding so noble an ally, Lucien acknowledged the Bishop's defence with a look of gratitude, little knowing that the worthy prelate was about to deal his death blow.

Mme de Bargeton looked triumphantly round the enemy circle, and her looks, like so many arrows, pierced the hearts of her rivals and redoubled their fury.

" Oh, my Lord," the poet replied, hoping to knock these thick heads with his golden sceptre, " but ordinary people have neither your intelligence nor your charity. Our sorrows are ignored, and nobody knows our labours. It is easier for the miner to dig gold from the rocks then to draw poetic images from the entrails of the most unrewarding of languages. If it is the function of poetry to state ideas so that everybody can feel and understand them, the poet must constantly run the gamut of every type of human mind, so as to be capable of satisfying all; he must conceal logic and feeling, those conflicting powers, under the brightest colours; he must condense a whole world of thought into a single word, sum up whole philosophies in an image; indeed, his poems are the seed whose flowers must blossom in all hearts, growing there in soil made receptive by personal experience. How can you state everything unless you have felt everything ? And to feel deeply, is not that to suffer ? Poems are born only after difficult explorations of the vast regions of the mind, and of the world as well. Are there not immortal works in which we find characters whose life is more real to us than that of human beings who have really lived—characters like Richardson's Clarissa, or Chénier's Camille, Tibullus's Delia, or Ariosto's Angelica, Dante's Francesca, Molière's Alceste, Beaumarchais's Figaro, or Scott's Rebecca, or Cervantes' Don Quixote ? "

" And what are you going to create for us ? " asked du Châtelet.

" If I were to promise such conceptions as these," said Lucien, " I should be giving myself out as a man of genius, should I not ? Besides, these sublime births come only after a long experience of life and a study of human motives and passions that I could not possibly have made. But I have made a beginning! " he said with some bitterness, with a vengeful glance round the circle. " The pregnancy of the mind is a long one."

" Then your childbirth will be difficult," interposed M. du Hautoy. " But your excellent mother will be able to assist you."

This epigram, so successfully prepared, this revenge that they had been waiting for, brought the light of joy into all eyes. On all lips there hovered a smile of aristocratic triumph, to which M. de Bargeton's imbecility further contributed, when he burst into a belated laugh.

" My Lord, you are talking a little above our heads ; these ladies do not understand you," said Mme de Bargeton, and at her words the laughter died and everybody looked at her in astonishment. " A poet who takes all his inspiration from the Bible has indeed a true mother in the Church. M. de Rubempré, won't you recite for us your *St. John on Patmos*, or *Belshazzar's Feast*, so that his Lordship may see that Rome is still the *magna parens* of Virgil ? "

The women exchanged a smile on hearing Naïs bring out these two Latin words.

At the outset of life, the proudest courage is not above defeat. Lucien had sunk into the depths at the blow ; but his foot found a bottom, and he rose again to the surface, vowing to conquer this world. Like a bull pricked by the matadors, he rose in fury, and hastened to obey the voice of Louise, by declaiming *St. John on Patmos* ; but most of the card-tables were already made up, as the players slipped back into the groove of habit, in which they found a pleasure that no poetry could give them. Besides, they felt that the revenge of so many wounded vanities would not have been complete without the negative indifference to local talent expressed in this desertion of Lucien and Mme de Bargeton. Everyone appeared to be otherwise occupied ; one was discussing a local road with the Prefect ; another was suggesting that a little music would add variety to the pleasures of the evening. The high society of Angoulême felt that it was no judge of poetry and was therefore the more anxious to discover what the Rastignacs and the Pimentels thought of Lucien, and a number of people had gathered round them. The great influence exercised in the Department by these two families could always be observed on important occasions ; everyone was jealous of them, but everyone paid court to them, for they could all foresee circumstances in which they might have need of their protection.

" What do you think of our poet and his poems ? " Jacques asked the Marquise, over whose land he hunted.

" Why, for provincial poetry," she said with a smile, " they are not bad. Besides, such a very handsome poet could do nothing badly."

Everyone was delighted with this dictum, and hastened to repeat it, with a malicious turn that the Marquise had not intended. Châtelet was then asked to accompany M. de Bartas, who proceeded to massacre Figaro's great solo. The door once open to music, there was nothing for it but to listen to a chivalrous romance written by Chateaubriand under the Empire, rendered by Châtelet. Then came some schoolroom piano duets, rescued from oblivion by Mme du Brossard, eager to display the talent of her dear Camille for the benefit of M. de Séverac.

Mme de Bargeton, hurt by the contempt with which everyone was treating her poet, returned scorn for scorn by retiring into her boudoir while the music was in progress. There she was followed by the Bishop, to whom his Vicar-General had explained the profound irony of his involuntary epigram, and who was anxious to atone for it. Mlle de Rastignac, who had been enchanted by the

"What do you think of our poet and his poems?"

poetry, also slipped away to the boudoir, unknown to her mother. Louise led Lucien to her mattress-cushioned sofa and made him sit by her. There, unseen and unheard, she whispered in his ear.

" Dear angel, they did not understand you! But ' your poems are sweet, I love to say them over '." Lucien, comforted by this flattering speech, forgot his troubles for a while.

" Glory cannot be purchased cheaply," said Mme de Bargeton, taking his hand and pressing it. " Suffer, my dear, suffer and you will be great ; your sorrows will purchase your immortality. I wish that I had the trials of such a struggle before me! Heaven preserve you from a life of monotony, without any battles to fight, where your eagles's wings have no room to soar. I envy you your sufferings, because at least you are alive! You will exert your powers, you will aspire to victory! Your struggle will be a glorious one. When you have arrived in the sphere of the great, your native kingdom, will you remember those poor souls disinherited by fate, whose minds are stifled under the oppressive atmosphere of conventions, and who go to their graves, knowing what life is, yet never having been able to live it, whose vision is clear, but who have had nothing to see, keen scent, but only festering flowers to smell. Sing, then, of the tender plant that fades in the darkness of a forest, smothered by briars, by dense rank vegetation, that dies without ever having flowered! That would be a terribly sad poem, would it not—an improbable story! What a theme for a poet would be the story of a young girl, born under Eastern skies, or some daughter of the desert, transported to a cold Western land, calling ever upon her beloved sun, dying of sorrows none could comprehend, overcome by cold, and by longings unfulfilled! That would be the true story of many loves."

" That is the story of the soul that remembers heaven," said the Bishop. " A poem that must have been written many times. I like to think that there is a fragment of it in the Song of Songs."

" You must write that story," said Laure de Rastignac, expressing a naïve faith in Lucien's genius.

" France has no great sacred poem," said the Bishop. " Believe me, glory and fame await the man of genius who devotes his talents to religion."

" That task shall be his," said Mme de Bargeton eagerly. " Do you not see the idea of that poem kindling already like a fiery sunrise in his eyes ? "

" Naïs is treating us very badly," said Fifine. " What can she be doing ? "

" Don't you hear ? " Stanislas replied. " She's off on her hobby-horse, using long words that nobody can make head or tail of."

Amélie, Fifine, Adrien and Francis appeared at the door of the boudoir, along with Mme de Rastignac, who was looking for her daughter, in preparation for leaving.

" Naïs," the two women began, delighted at the prospect of disturbing the little group in the boudoir, " won't you come and play something for us ? "

" My dear child, M. de Rubempré is just going to read us his *St. John on Patmos*, a magnificent biblical poem," Mme de Bargeton replied.

" Biblical ! " Fifine repeated in astonishment.

Amélie and Fifine returned to the drawing-room with this piece of news, as new food for mirth. Lucien excused himself from reciting the poem on the pretext that he could not remember it. When he reappeared nobody was interested in him any longer. Everyone was talking or playing cards. The poet had been shorn of all his glory ; the country squires had no use for him ; those with intellectual pretensions feared him, as a power inimical to their ignorance ; the women were jealous of Mme de Bargeton, the Beatrix of this new Dante, as the Vicar-General remarked, and looked at him with cold scorn.

" So that is society ! " Lucien thought to himself as he went down to l'Houmeau by the steps of Beaulieu, for there are occasions when we like to take the longest way round, walking to maintain the flow of some important train of thought to which we wish to devote ourselves.

Far from discouraging him, Lucien's rage and the repulse to his ambition, served only to give him new strength. Like all those whose instinct leads them into a higher social sphere, but who reach it before they can hold their own there, he vowed that at all costs he would remain in society. As he walked, he drew out one by one the poisoned darts that had wounded him, and demolished in his own mind the fools with whom he had had to deal; he thought of witty repartees to the stupid questions that they had asked him, and was in despair to think that these brilliant replies had only occurred to him after the event. When he reached the Bordeaux road that passes along the foot of the cliff and follows the windings of the Charente, he thought he could see Eve and David sitting on a joist of timber by the river, near a warehouse, and he went down the footpath towards them.

While Lucien was hastening to his torture in Bargeton House, his sister changed into a pink cotton dress with fine stripes, a straw hat, and a little silk shawl. In that simple costume she gave the impression of being elegantly dressed, as women can whose natural dignity sets off the most simple accessories. So that David was quite overcome with shyness, now that she had changed out of her working-dress. The young printer had made up his mind to speak to her of himself; but now that he had actually given Eve his arm to walk through l'Houmeau, he was speechless. These terrors of respect, akin to the awe that the faithful experience in the presence of the glory of God, are among the delights of love. The two lovers walked in silence towards the bridge of Saint Anne, which they would have to cross to reach the left bank of the Charente. Eve, who found this silence embarrassing, stopped in the middle of the bridge to look at the river, which, from that point as far as the newly built powder-works, stretched in a long sheet of water, kindled by the joyous rays of the setting sun.

"What a beautiful evening!" she said, looking for a subject of conversation. "The air is warm and fresh, there is a scent of flowers, and how beautiful the sky is."

"Everything speaks to the heart," David replied, endeavouring to reach the subject of love by analogy. For those in love there is an infinite pleasure in finding in the details of a landscape, the brightness of the air, in the scents of the earth, the poetry that is in their own souls. Nature speaks for them.

" And loosens the tongue as well," said Eve, smiling. " You were very silent as we came through l'Houmeau. Do you know, I felt quite embarrassed! "

" You looked so beautiful that I was speechless," David replied simply.

" So I am not so beautiful now ? " she asked.

" It is not that, but I am so happy to be walking alone with you that. . . "

He stopped short and looked across at the hills where the road crosses from Saintes.

" If this walk is giving you any pleasure, I am delighted, because I felt that I must give you an evening in exchange for the one you have sacrificed for me. It was just as generous of you to refuse to go to Mme de Bargeton's party as it was of Lucien to risk offending her by his request."

" Not generous at all, only sensible," David replied. " Since we are alone under the sky, without any other witnesses except the reeds and the bushes along the Charente, I should like to tell you, dear Eve, that I am very worried about the way Lucien is going on. After what I have just said to him, I hope that you will understand that my anxiety is only a refinement of my love. You and your mother have done everything in your power to raise him above his social position ; by exciting his ambition, have you not unwittingly condemned him to great unhappiness ? How will he hold his own in the world into which his inclinations are carrying him ? I know Lucien! He wants the harvests without the toil—that is his nature. Social duties will eat up his time, and time is the capital of those whose intelligence is their only fortune ; he loves to shine, and the world will only stimulate tastes that no amount of money will ever satisfy. He will spend money without earning any ; in short, you have encouraged him to think himself a great man ; but before the world recognises superiority of any kind it demands brilliant achievement. Now literary success can only be won in solitude, by persevering labour. What can Mme de Bargeton give your brother in return for so many days passed at her feet? Lucien is too proud to accept help from her, and we know that he is still too poor to continue to move in her circle—which is doubly ruinous. Sooner or later she will abandon your dear brother, but not before she has made him lose the habit of work, not before she has developed in him a taste for luxury, a contempt for our quiet way of life; a love of pleasure and his natural tendency to idleness—the bane of poetic souls. Yes, I am terribly afraid that the great lady is only playing with Lucien. Either she really loves him and will make him forget everything else, or she does not love him and will make him unhappy, for he is madly in love with her."

"You frighten me," said Eve, stopping at the weir. "But so long as mother has the strength for her exhausting work, and so long as I am alive, our earnings will perhaps be enough for Lucien's expenses, so that he can wait until his success comes. I shall never lose heart, because the thought of working for someone we love"—Eve kindled to her theme—"takes all the bitterness and hardship from work. I am happy whenever I think who it is I am working so hard for, if it *is* so hard. Oh, don't be afraid, we will earn enough money to enable Lucien to go into society. That is where he will find success."

"That is where he will also find disaster," said David. "Listen, dear Eve. A great work takes a long time to produce, and a man must either have ample private means or the sublime cynicism of poverty. Believe me, Lucien has such a horror of the privations of poverty, he has already developed such a taste for the scent of banquets, the incense of success, he has developed such a high opinion of himself in Mme de Bargeton's drawing-room, that he will risk everything rather than failure; and what you can earn will never keep pace with his needs."

"You are not a true friend after all!" Eve cried in despair, "or you would not discourage us like this!"

"Eve! Eve!" David replied. "I would like to be a brother to Lucien. Only you can give me that right, which would enable him to accept anything from me, which would give me the right to devote myself to him with the same love that you put into your heavenly sacrifices, but with a certain amount of worldly wisdom. Eve, my darling girl, make it possible for Lucien to have a source on which he can draw without feeling any sense of shame! A brother's purse is like one's own. If you could only know how much I have thought about Lucien's new position! If he is taken up by Mme de Bargeton, he cannot go on being my foreman, he cannot go on living in l'Houmeau, it will never do for you to go out to work, and your mother must give up her nursing. If you would consent to be my wife, everything would be simple: Lucien could have the second floor at the Place du Mûrier until I can build a room above the shed at the end of the yard, that is unless my father refuses to do it. So we could arrange a life of complete freedom and independence for him. My wish to keep Lucien would give me the necessary courage to make a fortune and that I should never have simply for my own sake; but only you can give me the right to devote myself to him. Perhaps one day he will go to Paris, the only place where he can make his way and where his talents will be appreciated and rewarded. The cost of living in Paris is high, and it will need all three of us to support him there. And then would not you and your mother need someone to lean on? Dearest Eve, marry me for Lucien's sake. Later you might come to love me, when you see what efforts I will make to help him and to make you happy. We have both simple tastes, we do not need a great deal; Lucien's welfare shall be our great work in life, and his heart shall be the treasury of our wealth, affections, experiences, everything!"

"But our positions are too far apart," said Eve, moved to see how this great love made little of itself. "You are rich and I am poor. It would need a great deal of love to overcome such a difficulty."

"Then you don't love me enough!" cried David, utterly crushed.

"But your father might object."

"That's all right," said David; "if it is only a matter of my father, you shall be my wife. Eve, dearest Eve, you have made life's burdens very light for me, all in a moment. For my heart has been heavy with things I could tell no one. Things I did not know how to say. Only tell me that you love me a little and I shall have courage to say all the rest."

" Indeed," she said, " you put me to shame ; but, since we are telling one another all our thoughts, I must tell you that never in my life have I thought of any other man except you. I have always thought of you as a man to whom a woman would be proud to belong, but I never dared to hope such a wonderful thing for myself, a poor working girl with no prospects."

" Don't say any more! " he cried, sitting down on the wooden beam of the lock-gates, for they had been walking up and down the same stretch of path like two mad things.

" What is it ? " she asked him, revealing for the first time that sweet solicitude that a woman feels for the man who belongs to her.

" Nothing but good," he answered. " In seeing in prospect a whole lifetime of happiness, I am dazzled. My heart is overwhelmed. But why should I be happier than you ? " he asked a little sadly. " But, of course, I know why."

Eve looked at David with a mischievous questioning expression that demanded an explanation.

"Dearest Eve, because I receive more than I can give. And because I shall always love you more than you will love me, because I have more reason to love you ; you are an angel, and I am only a man."

" I am not so sure of that," Eve answered, smiling. " I love you very much. . . . "

" As much as you love Lucien ? " he interrupted.

" Enough to be your wife, to devote myself to you, and to try never in my life to give you any pain—and we shall have some difficulties, at first."

" Did you know, dearest Eve, that I have loved you ever since the first time I saw you ? "

" Was there ever a woman who did not know when she was loved ? " she asked.

" Now allow me to dissipate your scruples on account of my supposed wealth. I am a poor man, my dear Eve. Yes, my father has had the pleasure of ruining me ; he has made a speculation of me, like so many so-called benefactors. If I become rich, it will be thanks to you. That is not a lover's speech, but a very sober reflection. I must not conceal my faults from you—and they are enormous in a man who is obliged to make his own way. My character, my tastes, and all my interests make me totally unfit for everything to do with business and making money, and we can only hope to make money by some kind of business. I might be able to discover a gold-mine, but no one could be more incapable of exploiting it. But you, who out of love for your brother have learned to watch the most trifling details, with your genius for economy, the careful watchfulness of a born business-woman, you shall reap the harvest that I shall sow. Our situation—for I have considered myself as a member of your family for a long time past—has been so much on my mind that I have thought of nothing else, day or night, but how to discover some means of making a fortune. My knowledge of chemistry, and my experience of the needs of the trade, have put me on the track of a discovery that would certainly make us rich. I cannot say anything about it yet, I foresee too many delays. It might mean several years of hardship ; but in the end it would be an important industrial invention. Many others are already on the track of it, and if I am the first in the field it will mean a fortune. I have said nothing to Lucien, because in his enthusiasm he would wreck everything ; he would convert my hopes into realities and live in grand style and probably run into debt. So you must keep my secret. Your sweet and dear companionship must be my only consolation during the long research that will be involved, and the desire to make you rich, you and Lucien, will give me perseverance and single-mindedness."

" I had also guessed," said Eve, interrupting him, " that you were one of those inventors, like my poor father, who need a woman to look after them."

" Then you really love me! Ah! Do not be afraid to tell me so, for your very name has been the symbol of my love. Eve was the only woman in the world, and what was a material fact for Adam is a spiritual reality for me! Heavens! Do you love me ? "

" Yes," she said, prolonging that one word, as if to make it cover the full extent of her feelings.

" Then let us sit here," he said, as he led Eve by the hand towards a great joist of timber below the wheels of a paper-mill. " Let me breath the air of the evening, and hear the croaking of the frogs, and admire the moonlight trembling on the water ; let me take all this world of nature into myself, for I see my happiness written on everything. I see the earth for the first time in its full splendour, illumined by love, made beautiful by your presence ; Eve, my beloved, this is the first moment of unclouded joy that I have ever experienced! I do not think that Lucien can be as happy as I am."

Feeling the hand of Eve, moist and trembling, in his own, tears came into David's eyes.

" May I know the secret?" she pleaded gently.

" You have every right, because your father was interested in the problem, which will soon be a serious one. I will tell you why. Since the Empire fell, cotton has come more and more into use, because it is cheaper than linen. At present paper is still made of a mixture of hemp and linen rags ; but linen is dear, and its expense is holding back the great expansion that is bound to come about in the publishing trade. Of course, one cannot increase the output of rags. Rags depend upon the use of linen, and the quantity produced by a given population is bound to remain constant. This quantity can only be increased by a rise in the birth-rate. To bring about any marked change in the birth-rate, a country needs a quarter of a century and a complete change in its way of living, either in industry or in agriculture. So that if the requirements of French paper manufacture rise to twice or three times the production of linen rags some new method will have to be discovered of manufacturing cheap paper. This conclusion is based on a fact well known in Angoulême. The paper manufacturers—the last to use pure linen rags—are alarmed at the increased proportion of cotton in the pulp."

In reply to a question from the young girl, who did not know what *pulp* was, David gave her an account of paper manufacture that will not be out of place in a work that owes its concrete existence no less to the existence of paper than to the printing-press ; but this long digression between a lover and his mistress had better be abridged.

Paper, an invention no less remarkable than printing, which

"Then you really love me!"

indeed depends upon it, has long been known in China, from which country, by the underground channels of commerce, it was introduced into Asia Minor, where according to some traditions, paper was already being made out of cotton pounded to pulp in about the year 750. The necessity of finding a substitute for parchment, an excessively expensive material, led to the invention of an imitation of the so-called *bombycine paper* of the East. This was a rag paper and, according to some authorities, was first made at Basle in 1170 by Greek refugees ; according to others, at Padua in 1301 by an Italian named Pax. The manufacture of paper was perfected slowly and obscurely ; but this much is certain, that in the reign of Charles VI paper for playing-cards was already being manufactured in Paris. While Faust, Coster, and Gutenburg, of immortal memory, were inventing the printed book, craftsmen, anonymous, like so many great artists of the same period, were adapting paper to the requirements of typography.

During that century, characterised no less by its simplicity than by its energy, the names given to type-faces, and also those given to the different formats of paper, bear the imprint of the naïvety of the times. So we have *le raisin*, *le jesus*, *le colombier*, *le papierpot*, *l'écu*, *la coquille*, *la couronne*, so-called from the grapes, the image of our Lord, the tankard, the crown, or other water-mark imprinted in the middle of the sheet, just as later, under Napoleon, *grand-aigle* paper was introduced, so named from the imperial eagle of the watermark. In the same way, there were Cicero, Augustine, and Canon type-faces, so named from the classical or theological works for which they were first used. Italics were invented by the Aldus family ; in Venice—hence the name. Before the invention of machine-made paper, which can be of any length, the largest formats were the *grand jesus* and the *grand colombier*. The latter is now no longer used except for atlases and engravings. The size of printing paper was dependent on the size of the impression-stone. In David's time paper in lengths was almost undreamed of in France, although already Denis Robert d'Essonne had, in 1799, invented a machine for its manufacture that had been further perfected by Didot–Saint-Leger. Vellum paper, invented by Ambroise Didot, dates only from 1780. This rapid survey goes to show how very slowly great advances in industry and thought come about—by almost imperceptible degrees, like nature itself. In process of perfection, writing, perhaps language itself, has gone through the same groping advances, as have typography and paper manufacture.

"Rag pickers scour the whole of Europe for old linen rags, and buy up any kind of cloth," the printer concluded. "These rags are sorted by the wholesale rag merchants, who in turn supply the paper manufacturers. To give you some idea of the scale of this trade, you must know that in 1814 Cardon the banker, who owns the pulping-vats of Buges and Langlée, where Leorier de l'Isle was working, in 1776, on the problem that occupied your father, had a lawsuit with a certain Proust, over an error of two million pounds' weight of rags in a total of ten million, involving a cost of about four million francs. The manufacturer washes the rags and reduces them to a thin pulp that is sieved, exactly as a cook sieves a sauce, through a metal-lined mould, in which is the water-mark that gives its name to the paper. During the time that I spent at Messrs. Didot a great deal of thought was already being given to this question, and still is, for the invention for which your father was looking is one of the most pressing needs of the present time, for a very good reason. Although linen wears much better than cotton and is therefore in the end cheaper, the poorer classes prefer, as always, to pay less than more, and, by the law of *Vae victis*, really spend far more in the end. The middle classes behave in much the same way. So that there is a shortage of linen thread. In England, where three-quarters of the population are using cotton instead of linen, only cotton paper is being made. This paper tears and creases easily, and, what is worse, it is so soluble that a book made of cotton paper will turn to pulp in a quarter of an hour if it is left standing in water, while an old book can be left in water for two hours without being spoilt. One can dry an old book, and although it may be yellow and faded, the print can still be read, and the book is not destroyed. The time has come when the policy of equalisation is diminishing fortunes, so that everything will have to be of poorer quality. There will be a demand for cheap clothes and cheap books, just as pictures today are small because no one now has the space for large ones. Well, neither clothes nor books will last, that is all. One sees it everywhere—the quality of goods is deteriorating. So the problem to be solved is of the greatest importance to literature, to science—and to economics. There was a lively discussion in my office one day on the ingredients used by the Chinese for paper-making. There, thanks to the raw materials, paper has, from the first, been of a finer quality than ours. A great deal was said on the subject of Chinese paper, which is lighter and finer than ours and yet of a strong texture; and however thin it may be, it is not transparent. A proof-reader who knows a good deal about such things (for in Paris you often find scholars among proof-readers: Fourrier and Pierre Leroux are proof-reading for Lachevardière at this moment!)—well, the Comte de Saint-Simon, who was proof-reading at the time, came in in the middle of the discussion. And he told us that, according to Kempfer and du Halde, the *Broussonetia* provides the raw material for Chinese paper, which is a vegetable product, just as ours is. Another reader maintained that Chinese paper is made principally of an animal product that is plentiful in China—silk, in fact. They actually made a bet on it in my presence. As Messrs. Didot are printers to the Institute, naturally the question was submitted to members of that learned body. M. Marcel, one-time Director of the Imperial printing establishment, was asked to arbitrate, and he sent the two proof-readers to consult the Abbé Grozier, Librarian to the Arsenal. According to the Abbé's verdict, both the proof-readers lost their bets. Chinese paper is made neither of silk nor of *Broussonetia*; the pulp is made from triturated bamboo fibres. Abbé Grozier had in his possession a Chinese book, of both iconographical and technical interest, in which there were a number of illustrations representing the manufacture of paper in all its stages, and in one charming drawing he pointed out to us the bundles of bamboo lying in a pile in the corner of a paper-workshop. When Lucien told me that your father, with the infallible instinct of an experimenter, had had the idea of finding a substitute for linen rags in some very common vegetable substance, to be found on the spot, like the fibrous stems used by the Chinese, I collected all the material on the work that has hitherto been done, and then I began to study the subject on my own. Bamboo is a kind of reed, so naturally I thought at once of the common reeds of our own country. Labour is cheap in China, where a workman earns about three halfpence a day, so that when the paper is taken out of the mould the Chinese can afford to handle each leaf separately, pressing it between heated porcelain plates ; this gives it the fine surface, the consistency and texture, that satin smoothness that makes it the best paper in the world. Well, the Chinese process could be carried out by a machine. Machinery solves the problem of production at a low cost, that in China is solved by cheap labour. If we can succeed in finding a cheap way of manufacturing paper of a quality comparable to the Chinese, the weight and size of books could be reduced by at least half. A set of Voltaire, which weighs two hundred and fifty pounds printed on our woven papers, would weigh less than fifty on Chinese paper. And that would be a triumph indeed. The space available in libraries will be a growing problem in a period when everything is becoming smaller—men as well as things, and houses in particular. In Paris the great houses will sooner or later be pulled down, for there will soon be no fortunes to match the constructions of our fathers. What a disgrace to our time if we produce books that will not last! In another ten years Dutch paper—that is, paper made of linen rags—will be quite unobtainable. Now it was your brother who told me the idea that your father had of using certain fibrous plants in the manufacture of paper, so you see that, if I succeed, you have a right to. . . . "

Lucien came up at this moment and interrupted David's generous proposition.

" I don't know whether you have enjoyed this evening, but it has been an ordeal for me."

" My poor Lucien, what has happened ? " Eve asked, seeing her brother's excited face. The angry poet told the story of his agonies, pouring into those friendly hearts the flood of thoughts that tormented him. Eve and David listened to him in silence, grieved at the spectacle of that torrent of grief, revealing as it did a strange blend of greatness and pettiness.

" M. de Bargeton," Lucien concluded, " is an old man, who was no doubt suffering from indigestion ; well, I intend to master that proud world ; I shall marry Mme de Bargeton! In her eyes I have read a love equal to my own. Yes, she felt all my wounds ; she poured balm on my sufferings ; she is as great and noble as she is beautiful and gracious! No, *she* will never fail me! "

" Is it not time that we made his life easier for him ? " David whispered to Eve.

Eve pressed David's arm without speaking ; and, reading her thoughts, David hastened to tell Lucien his own plan. The two lovers were just as full of themselves as was Lucien, so much so that Eve and David, eager to have Lucien's approval of their happiness, did not notice that Mme de Bargeton's lover started at the mention of his sister's marriage to David. Lucien, who had just been dreaming about some great match for his sister, which he would arrange when he himself had grasped some high position, a match that would secure his own status by the interest of a powerful family, was desolated to see, in this marriage, one more obstacle to his worldly success.

" If Mme de Bargeton agrees to become Mme de Rubempré, she will never consent to being David Séchard's sister-in-law! "

This phrase sums up, in a few words, the tenuous ideas that passed through Lucien's mind.

" Louise is right! Men with a future are never understood by their families," he reflected bitterly.

If this news had not been broken to him at the very moment when he had, in imagination, just killed M. de Bargeton, he would certainly have greeted it with heartfelt pleasure. If he had considered the facts of the situation, and asked himself what was likely to be the future of that beautiful but penniless girl, Eve Chardon, he would have seen this marriage as an unhoped-for piece of good fortune. But he was living in one of those golden dreams in which the young, on the wings of an *if*, surmount all barriers. He had just been imagining himself with society at his feet ; and it was painful to the poet to be precipitated so suddenly into reality. Eve and David thought that their brother was silent because he was overcome at the thought of so much generosity. For these two noble characters, silent acceptance was the proof of true friendship. The printer proceeded to paint, with the warm eloquence of generosity and happiness, the prospects that awaited all four of them. In spite of Eve's protests, he furnished the first floor for her with all the luxury of a lover ; with simple good will, he built the second floor for Lucien, and a room above the shed for Mme Chardon, for whom he was all eagerness to show a son's solicitude. In fact he made the whole family so happy, and his brother-in-law so independent, that Lucien, charmed by David's words and Eve's endearments, forgot, among the shadows of the path, by the long stretch of the Charente, calm and moonlit, under the starry vault, and in the warmth of the night, the wounding crown of thorns that society had pressed upon his brow. " M. de Rubempré ", in fact, recognised David's worth. The instability of his character now swung him back into the pure, hard-working, obscure life that he had lived hitherto ; he saw it, but beautified and free from care. The clamour of the aristocratic world died away in the distance. And when, on the pavement of l'Houmeau, the ambitious poet pressed his brother's hand, he shared wholeheartedly the lovers' happiness.

" So long as your father does not raise any objections to the marriage," he said to David.

" You know how much he cares about me! The old man is only interested in himself; but I shall go to Marsac tomorrow and see him, if only to get his permission to do the building that we shall need."

David accompanied the brother and sister to their house, where he asked Mme Chardon's consent to his marriage with Eve, with all the haste of a man who can brook no delay. The mother took her daughter's hand and laid it in David's with joy ; the bold lover kissed his beautiful betrothed on the brow, and she smiled at him, blushing.

" The betrothals of the poor," said the mother, raising her eyes as if to implore God's blessing on them. "You have courage, my child," she said to David, "for we are unfortunate, and I only hope that our misfortunes are not contagious."

" We shall be rich and happy," said David seriously. " To begin with, you must give up your nursing and come and live with your daughter, and Lucien, in Angoulême."

The three young people made haste to tell their astonished mother the wonderful plan, in one of those wild family discussions, in which we delight to store our unsown harvests, enjoying our pleasures in advance. They had to turn David out at last; he would have liked that evening to last for ever. One o'clock struck as Lucien walked back to the Porte Palet with his future brother-in-law.

The worthy Postel, alarmed by these unusual activities, got up, opened the window and peered through his shutters. On seeing a light in Eve's room at this hour, he wondered what could possibly be happening in the Chardon household. "Anything the matter, son?" he called down to Lucien, as he came in again. "Is there anything I can do?"

"No," the poet replied; "but as you are a friend of the family, I will tell you. My mother has just given her consent to my sister's engagement to David Séchard."

Postel's only reply was to close the window with a bang, in despair because he had not asked for the hand of Mlle Chardon.

Instead of returning to Angoulême, David set out at once for Marsac. He walked the whole way to his father's, and as he turned along by the close beside the house the sun was rising. The lover caught sight of the head of the old bear under an almond tree overhanging the hedge.

"Good day, Father," said David.

"Why, is that you, my boy? What are you doing here on the road at this hour? Come in this way," added the vinegrower, pointing to a little wicket gate. "My vines have all flowered, and not a shoot frosted. There should be more than twenty casks to the acre this year; but then look at the manure I have put on!"

"Father, I have come to talk to you about something important."

"Very well. How are our presses doing? You should be making heaps of money as big as yourself?"

"So I shall, father, but I am not rich yet."

"They all say round here that I over-manure," the father replied. "All the gentry—M. le Marquis, and M. de Comte, and *Monsieur* this and *Monsieur* that, say that I am spoiling the quality of the wine. What's the use of education? It muddles your head, that's all. You listen to me! These gentry harvest seven, sometimes eight casks to the acre, and they sell at sixty francs a cask, in a good year. Very well, I harvest twenty casks, and sell at thirty, total six hundred francs! Haven't they got any sense? Quality? Quality? What's that to me? They can keep their quality! For me, money is quality! What were you saying?"

"Father, I am going to get married, and I have come to ask you . . ."

"Ask me! What's that? Not a penny, my boy! Get married if you want to, I won't stop you; but as for giving you anything, I haven't got a penny myself. It's all these top-dressings that have ruined me! For the last two years I have been paying out money on fertilisers, taxes, all kinds of expenses; the government takes it all, every penny of profit goes to the government! The vine-growers have made nothing for the last two years. This year promises well, but there you are, the wretched casks have gone up to eleven francs already! We work to put money into the pockets of the coopers. What do you want to get married for before the vintage?"

"Father, I did not come to ask you for anything but your consent."

"Ah! That's another matter. Who is the victim, may I ask?"

"I am going to marry Mlle Eve Chardon."

"And who is she? How much will she spend?"

"She is the daughter of the late M. Chardon, the chemist in l'Houmeau."

"So you are going to marry a Houmeau girl, you, proprietor of a business, the King's printer in Angoulême! That's what comes of education! Send your children to school! Well, then, she must have a lot of money, my boy?" said the old vine-grower, edging up to his son in a cajoling manner; "because you would not be marrying a girl from l'Houmeau unless she had a tidy pile! Very well, you can pay the arrears of rent. Do you realise, my boy, that there is two years and three months' rent due, which comes to two thousand seven hundred francs, which I could do with to pay for my casks.

If you were not my son, I would have every right to ask for interest, because, when all is said and done, business is business. Well, how much is she worth ? "

" Her fortune is the same as my mother's was."

The old man was on the point of saying, " Then she has only ten thousand francs! " but he remembered just in time that he had refused to give an account of his wife's fortune to his son, and exclaimed :

" She has nothing! "

" My mother's fortune was her intelligence and her beauty."

" Just you go to the market and you'll see how much that will fetch! Upon my word, fathers don't have much luck with their children! When I married, David, a paper hat and a pair of hands was all the fortune I had! I was just a poor bear! But with the fine printing establishment I *gave* you, with your industry and education, you could marry a girl of the town with thirty or forty thousand francs! Give up your romantic notions, and I'll find a wife for you myself! There's a rich miller's widow not far from here, thirty-two, worth forty thousand francs in real estate—that's your party! You could join that property on to Marsac, for they are adjoining! Ah! We should have a nice little estate then, I'd make it pay! They say she's going to marry Courtois, her foreman, but you're worth more than he is! I would run the mill, and she could live like a lady in Angoulême!"

" But, Father, I'm engaged! "

" David, you have no head at all for business ; you'll ruin yourself, I can see. Yes, if you marry this girl from l'Houmeau, I shall settle up my accounts with you, I shall sue you for the rent, for I can see that no good will come of this. Oh, my poor presses, my presses! It needed money to keep you oiled and in working order, and keep you rolling. Nothing but a good harvest can comfort me after this!"

" But, Father, it does not seem to me that so far I have given you any cause for pain! "

" And mighty little rent! " retorted the countryman.

" I came to ask you, besides your consent to the marriage, if you would consider building a second floor on your house, and rooms over the shed in the yard?"

"The deuce I will—I haven't a sou, as you know very well. Besides, it would be money thrown away, because what should I get out of it? So you get up first thing in the morning to come and ask me to undertake reconstructions that would ruin a king. Although I called you David, I have not the treasures of a Solomon! But you are mad! You must be a changeling, you're no son of mine. There's one that will have some grapes on it!" he exclaimed, interrupting himself to point out a shoot to David. "Those are the children that do not disappoint their parents: you manure them, and they repay you. Whereas I sent you to the grammar school; I laid out a small fortune to make a scholar of you! I sent you to the Didots to learn your trade, and all this fancy education ends in your giving me a girl from l'Houmeau for a daughter-in-law, without a penny to her name! If you had not read all those books, if I had kept you under my eye, you would have done what I wanted, and you would at this moment have been marrying a rich miller's widow worth a hundred thousand francs, not counting the mill. And so your cleverness leads you to imagine that I am going to reward you for your fine sentiment by helping you to build palaces? Really, anyone might think that the house has been no better than a pigsty for the last two hundred years, not good enough for your girl from l'Houmeau to sleep in! What next! I suppose she's the Queen of France?"

"Very well, Father, I will build the second floor at my own expense; the son will enrich the father. The opposite is more usual, but it does sometimes happen."

"So that's how it is, my boy: you have the money for building, but not to pay your rent? You're a sly one, trying to get round your father!"

The question, stated in this way, was difficult to answer, for the old man was delighted to have forced his son into a position which enabled him to give him nothing, while at the same time posing as a good father. So that all David was able to get out of his father was his bare consent to the marriage, and permission to build, at his own expense, in his father's house, whatever improvements he liked. The old bear, that model of an economical parent, was generous enough to agree not to press his son for the rent, and not to deprive him of the savings to which he had been imprudent enough to confess. David returned in low spirits; he saw that he would never be able to count on any help from his father, in misfortune.

In Angoulême everybody was talking about the Bishop's epigram and Mme de Bargeton's reply. The smallest details were so completely misrepresented, exaggerated, and embellished, that the poet became the hero of the day. As this storm in a teacup raged on high, a few drops fell on the town below. As Lucien went along Beaulieu on his way to visit Mme de Bargeton, he noticed the envious looks with which quite a number of young men observed him, and overheard chance remarks that made him more conceited than ever.

"That's a lucky young fellow," said a lawyer's clerk, a very plain youth called Petit-Claud, a schoolfellow of Lucien's, who had formerly treated him with small patronising airs.

"Yes, that's a fact. He is handsome, and very talented, and Mme de Bargeton is mad about him," replied one of the eldest sons who had been present at the reading.

He had been waiting impatiently for the hour when he was sure of finding Louise alone; he would have to reconcile her to his sister's marriage—for she had become the arbiter of his destiny. After the party of the previous evening, he hoped that Louise might be a little softened, and that this might lead to a moment of happiness. Nor was he mistaken! Mme de Bargeton received him in a demonstrative manner that this novice in love took as a touching progress in passion. She abandoned her beautiful golden hair, her hands, and her head, to the burning kisses of the poet who had suffered so much on the previous evening.

"If only you could have seen your face while you were reading!" she said, using the intimate *tu,* that caress of language—they had reached this point of intimacy the night before, when Louise, on her sofa, had with her white hand wiped away the beads of sweat that had pearled the brow on which she now placed a crown. "There were sparks of fire in those beautiful eyes! I could see falling from your mouth, as you spoke, those chains of gold that suspend all hearts to a poet's lips! You shall read me the whole of Chénier, for he is the poet of lovers. You shall not suffer any longer, I will not allow it! Yes, dear angel, I will be for you an oasis where you shall live all your poetic life, active or languid, indolent or at work, or thoughtful, each in turn ; but you must never forget that you will owe your laurels to me, that they must be the noble guerdon of the sufferings that I must endure. Poor darling, society will not spare me any more than it has spared you ; it must always be revenged on all happiness that it does not share. Yes, I shall always be envied—did you not see that yesterday? Those bloodthirsty insects came thick and fast to drink blood from the wounds that they pierced! But I was happy! I was alive! It is so long since all the strings of my heart have sounded! "

Tears flowed down Louise's cheeks ; Lucien took her hand and kissed it long and tenderly—his sole reply. So the vanities of the young poet were flattered by this lady, just as they had been by his mother, and sister, and by David. All his little circle conspired to raise the imaginary pedestal on which he had set himself. Encouraged by everyone, by the fury of his enemies no less than by his friends, in his ambitious credulity, he lived in a world of illusion. Youthful fantasies so naturally lend themselves to such flatteries and such notions. Everything seems to conspire to serve a handsome young man, with the future at his feet, and it needs more than one hard and bitter lesson to dissipate the spell.

" So will you really, my beautiful Louise, be my Beatrix, a Beatrix who allows herself to love ? "

She had lowered her beautiful eyes, but now she raised them to him and said with an angelic smile that belied her words :

" If you deserve it—some day! Are you not happy ? To possess a heart entirely! To be able to say everything, certain of being understood, is that not happiness indeed ? "

"Yes," he said, with the pout of a frustrated lover.

" Child! " she exclaimed, mocking him. " Come, you have something you want to tell me, have you not ? You look quite worried, dear Lucien."

Lucien timidly confided to his beloved the news of David's love for his sister, and the projected marriage.

" Poor Lucien! " she said. " He is so frightened of being beaten and scolded! Just as if it were you yourself who are going to be married! But what does it matter ? " she went on, running her hand through Lucien's hair. " What is your family to me, for you are an exception! Supposing my father were to marry his housekeeper, would that trouble you much ? Dear child, lovers are in themselves all their family. What other interest have I in the world besides my Lucien ? To be great, to conquer fame, that is our concern! "

Lucien was the happiest man in the world at this selfish reply. While he was listening to the foolish reasons by which Louise was proving to him that they alone existed in the world, M. de Bargeton came in. Lucien frowned and looked upset ; but Louise made him a sign, and asked him to stay to dinner with them, and to read her André Chénier until the people arrived for their nightly game of cards.

" You will not only give pleasure to my wife," said M. de Bargeton, " but also to me. I like nothing better than to be read to after dinner."

Made much of by M. de Bargeton, petted by Louise, treated with deference by the servants, who always show respect to those in favour with their masters, Lucien remained at Bargeton House, already regarding as his due the full enjoyment of the fortune whose fruits were already his to use. When the drawing-room was full of people, he felt, what with M. de Bargeton's stupidity and Louise's love, that his position was so strong that he adopted a lordly air, and this his mistress encouraged. He enjoyed all the advantages of the despotism that Naïs had won for herself, and that it was her pleasure to share with him. So all that evening he tried to live up to the part of a small-town hero. Noticing this change in Lucien's attitude, some people concluded that he had, according to the old phrase, already tried conclusions with Mme de Bargeton. Amélie, who came with M. de Châtelet, was proclaiming this deplorable fact in a corner of the drawing-room where the jealous and the envious had gathered.

" Don't hold Naïs responsible for the vanity of a young upstart who is as proud as he can be to find himself in society in which he never thought it possible to set foot," said Châtelet. " Don't you see that Chardon mistakes the graciousness of a society woman for advances? He is too young to know the difference between the silence that conceals a real passion, and the protective flatteries that he owes to his good looks, his youth and his talent! Women would have too much to complain of if they were to be blamed for every passion that they inspire. He is obviously in love, but as for Naïs . . . "

" Oh, Naïs," echoed the perfidious Amélie, " Naïs is delighted with that passion. At her age a young man's love offers so many attractions! A woman becomes young again in his company, acts the young girl, and all the scruples and hesitations, and never dreams how ridiculous she is! Just look! Imagine the son of a chemist giving himself such airs in Mme de Bargeton's house! "

" What recks love of high or low degree? " hummed Adrien.

Next day there was not a house in Angoulême in which the degree of intimacy between M. Chardon, *alias* de Rubempré, and Mme de Bargeton was not discussed. They had exchanged only a few kisses at most; the world already believed them guilty of the most criminal happiness. Mme de Bargeton was paying the penalty of her autocracy. Among the peculiarities of society, have you not noticed the capriciousness of its judgments and the inconsistency of its demands? There are people to whom everything is permitted. They can be guilty of the most outrageous things, and nothing they do is wrong; people hasten to find excuses for their conduct. But there are others on whom the world is inexplicably severe: such people must always do everything well, never make a mistake, never show any weakness, not even permit themselves a foolish action; they are like statues that everyone admires, but which are taken down from their pedestals the moment that winter chips off a finger or cracks a nose; no human weakness is permitted them, they are obliged to remain for ever divine and faultless. A single look exchanged by Mme de Bargeton and Lucien outweighed Zizine and Francis's twelve years of illicit happiness. One pressure of the hand between the two lovers had brought down upon them all the thunders of Charente.

David had brought back from Paris a secret hoard, which he devoted to the expenses involved by his marriage and by the addition of a second floor to his father's house. But was not this enlargement of the house work undertaken in his own interest? Sooner or later he would inherit it—his father was seventy-eight. So the printer had rooms built for Lucien in timber, so as not to overweight the dilapidated walls of the tumbledown old house. He took pleasure in repainting and furnishing handsomely the first-floor rooms where his lovely Eve was to spend her days. This was a time of light-hearted and unclouded happiness for the two friends. Bored as he was with the triviality of provincial life, and tired of that sordid economical mentality that looked upon a five-franc piece as a large sum of money, Lucien endured the petty calculations of poverty and his own hardships without grumbling. His deep melancholy had given place to the radiance of hope. He saw a star shining above his head; he dreamed of an unclouded future, for he built his hopes on M. de Bargeton's grave, for the latter suffered, from time to time, from attacks of indigestion, and also from a providential illusion that a good dinner was the best cure for an attack brought on by lunch.

By the beginning of September Lucien was no longer a foreman, but M. de Rubempré living in rooms splendid in comparison with the wretched attic with the dormer window where the boy Chardon had lived at l'Houmeau. He was no longer branded as an inhabitant of l'Houmeau; he was a resident of the Upper Town of Angoulême, and dined as often as four times a week with Mme de Bargeton. The Bishop treated him as a friend, and he was admitted to the palace. His occupations placed him amongst people of the highest rank. And one day he would surely take his place among the illustrious names of France. To be sure, as he came and went in his pretty sitting-room, his charming bedroom, and his tasteful study, he could console himself for accepting thirty francs a month out of the wages earned with such difficulty by his mother and sister; for he could see the day when *The Archer of Charles IX,* the historical novel that he had been working on for two years, and a volume of poems entitled *Marguerites,* would make his name famous in the world of letters and bring him in enough money to repay his mother, his sister, and David. So, thinking of his future greatness, listening to the echoes of his future name, he could accept these sacrifices for the time being with noble assurance: he smiled at his distress, and enjoyed these last days of penury.

Eve and David had set their brother's happiness before their own. Their marriage had been delayed because of the time still needed by the workmen to complete the furnishing, painting, and papering of the first floor—for Lucien's needs had come first. No one who knew Lucien would have been surprised at such devotion; he had such charm, he had such engaging ways! He gave vent to his impatience, uttered his wishes, with so much grace! He had always won his case before he had opened his mouth. This fatal gift may be a blessing to a few, but it is the ruin of many more. Accustomed to having every wish anticipated, good-looking young men enjoy the advantages of the selfish generosity that the world accords to those who amuse it, as one gives money to a beggar who appeals to sentiment and stirs the facile emotions. Many of these grown-up children bask in that favour instead of making use of it. They mistake the significance and the fickleness of social relations, they imagine that they will always encounter these deceptive smiles; but the moment comes when the world closes its doors to them, or leaves them neglected in a corner, like old flirts, shorn of their glory, without money or reputation.

But Eve herself had wished for this delay; she was anxious to be economical in the outlay necessary for setting up their home. But what could two lovers refuse a brother who, seeing his sister at work, would exclaim with such heartfelt feeling, "How I wish I could sew!" And besides, the grave and observant David had been her partner in devotion. All the same, since Lucien's triumph with Mme de Bargeton he had been alarmed at the change that was taking place in his friend; he was afraid that Lucien would come to look down on their homely way of life. In his desire to test his friend, David would sometimes make him choose between the patriarchal joys of the family and the pleasures of society; and, when Lucien sacrificed the pleasures of his vanity for their sake, he would say to himself, " They will not corrupt him for us! " Often the three friends and Mme Chardon went on outings together, in country fashion. They went walking in the woods by the Charente, beyond Angoulême; they picnicked on the grass, on provisions brought to a certain spot at a prearranged time by David's apprentice; then in the evening they would return, a little tired, but without the excursion having cost them three francs. On special occasions, when they dined at what is called a *restaurat*, a country inn something between the provincial *bouchon* and the Parisian *guignette*, they spent as much as five francs, shared between David and the Chardons. David felt infinitely grateful to Lucien for setting aside, on these country expeditions, the pleasures of Mme de Bargeton's society and the grand dinner-parties. So that they were all anxious to give pleasure to the great poet of Angoulême.

At this stage, just when everything was almost ready for the new home, and David had gone to Marsac to try to persuade his father to come to the wedding, hoping that the old man might relent on seeing his daughter-in-law and contribute to the heavy expenses that had been incurred by the alterations of the house, an event occurred of a kind that, in a small town, entirely changes the face of things.

Lucien and Louise had in Châtelet a spy ever at hand, who watched them with all the persistence of hate, a blend of passion and avarice, for the opportunity to make a scandal. Sixte wanted Mme de Bargeton to compromise herself with Lucien in such a way that she should be what is generally called *lost*. He posed as Mme de Bargeton's humble confidant; but, although he praised Lucien in the Rue du Minage, he pulled him to pieces everywhere else. Little by little he had acquired the right of dropping in on Naïs at any time, for she no longer felt any suspicions of her old admirer. But he had taken too much for granted as to the degree of intimacy existing between the two lovers, for their relationship remained platonic, to the great despair of both of them. There are, to be sure, love affairs that begin badly—or well, according to the way one looks at it. Two people embark on the tactics of sentiment, talk instead of acting, and skirmish in the open instead of laying a determined siege. And so they often become bored with one another and their desires evaporate into the void. For two lovers then have time to reflect, to become critical of one another. It often happens that passions that have entered the field with colours flying, in battle array, violent enough to carry all before them, end by returning home without victory, put to shame, crestfallen, cutting a sorry figure after so much sound and fury. These mishaps are sometimes to be explained by the timidity of youth, sometimes by the temporisations of an inexperienced woman ; for mutual frustrations of this kind never happen to old fops who know the game, nor to coquettes experienced in conducting love-affairs.

Besides, provincial life is singularly ill adapted to the ends of love, and favours only the intellectual encounters of passion. All the same, the obstacles that it opposes to that sweet interchange that binds so many lovers drives ardent souls to extreme measures. For country life is based on a system of meticulous espionage ; in the country everyone lives in glass houses ; so little opportunity is there for that intimacy that consoles love without offending virtue, so outrageously scandalous are the constructions placed on the purest relationships, that many women's reputations are blackened although they are perfectly innocent. There are even some who regret that they have not enjoyed all the felicities of a fault, for which they suffer all the punishment. Society, that praises or blames, without looking behind the apparent facts that are the termination of some long internal struggle, is thus to blame in the first place for bringing about these scandals ; but most of those whose voices are loudest against supposed lapses on the part of this or that woman, calumniated without reason, have never reflected upon the causes that may have driven her to commit herself publicly. Mme de Bargeton was now about to find herself in this ridiculous situation, as a result of which so many women only fall after they have already been unjustly accused.

At the beginning of a love affair the obstacles are alarming to the inexperienced ; and those encountered by the two lovers were like those cords with which the Lilliputians bound Gulliver hand and foot. They consisted of a multitude of trifles that combined to render all movement impossible and brought to nothing the most violent desires. Mme de Bargeton, for instance, must always be visible. Had her door been closed at the times of Lucien's visits, the worst would have been said; she might just as well have run away with him. It is true that she received him in the little boudoir that he knew so well and in which he felt he was master; but the doors were always left scrupulously open, and everything was done with the strictest propriety. M. de Bargeton buzzed about his house like a cockchafer, never dreaming that his wife wished to be alone with Lucien. If he had been the only obstacle, Naïs could easily have sent him away, or found something for him to do; but visitors flocked to the house, the more so as curiosity grew. Country people are born teases, they love to thwart growing passions. The servants came and went in the house without being summoned or giving notice of their arrival, a habit that they had gradually acquired in the house of a mistress who had nothing to conceal. A change in the interior arrangements of the house would have been tantamount to a confession of a relationship about which Angoulême still remained in doubt. Mme de Bargeton could not set foot outside her own house without the whole town knowing where she was going. To go for a walk alone with Lucien outside the town would have been proof positive; it would have been less dangerous to shut herself up with him in her own house. If Lucien had remained after midnight with Mme de Bargeton, unless other company was present, it would have been talked of the next day. So that, indoors and out, Mme de Bargeton lived always in public. These details are an accurate description of life in the provinces: an intrigue is either acknowledged or impossible.

Louise, like all inexperienced women who are carried away by passion, became aware, one by one, of the difficulties of her situation; she became frightened. Her fear was presently reflected in those amorous conversations in which lovers pass the sweetest hours when they find themselves alone. Mme de Bargeton had no country estate whither she could lead her beloved poet, as some women do, finding some clever pretext or other for burying themseves in the depths of the country. Weary of leading her life in public, driven to desperation by that tyranny whose heavy yoke was compensated by few pleasures, she thought of l'Escarbas and considered going there to visit her father, so irritated was she by all these petty hindrances.

Châtelet did not believe in any such innocence. He would lie in wait for the times when Lucien went to the house, and arrive a few minutes later, always accompanied by M. de Chandour, the most indiscreet man in Angoulême. He always made M. de Chandour go in first, hoping to take the lovers by surprise, by this stubborn persistence in pursuit of chance. His part, and the carrying out of his project, were the more difficult as he had to remain neutral, so as to be able to direct all the actors in the drama that he was anxious to produce. So, to lull the suspicions of Lucien, whom he flattered, and of Mme de Bargeton, who was no fool, he had given himself face by attaching himself to the jealous Amélie. The better to spy on Louise and Lucien, he had succeeded, during the last few days, in establishing between himself and M. de Chandour a controversy on the subject of the two lovers. Châtelet maintained that Mme de Bargeton was only amusing himself at Lucien's expense, that she was too proud, too well-born to stoop to the son of a chemist. This pose of incredulity fitted in well with the plan that he had outlined, for he wished to appear in the role of Mme de Bargeton's defender. Stanislas was of the opinion that Lucien was no unhappy lover. Amélie urged on the discussion in the hope of discovering the truth. Each produced his arguments. As always happens in small towns, friends of the Chandour family would arrive in the middle of a discussion in which Châtelet and Stanislas were ably defending their opinions, each bringing forward arguments of extreme acuteness. What more likely then than that each of the adversaries should seek to enlist supporters, turning to a neighbour with the remark "And what do *you* think?" This controversy kept Mme de Bargeton and Lucien constantly before the public eye.

At last, one day, Châtelet called attention to the fact that whenever M. de Chandour and himself arrived at Mme de Bargeton's and found Lucien there there was never the slightest trace of a suspect relationship : the door of the little drawing-room was open, the servants were always in and out, nothing mysterious suggested the sweet crimes of love, and so on. Stanislas, whom nature had endowed with a marked strain of stupidity, made up his mind to arrive the following day on tiptoe, to which exploit the treacherous Amélie urged him on.

That fatal morrow was, for Lucien, one of those days when a young man tears his hair and vows to play no longer the part of a sighing lover. He had grown accustomed to his situation. The poet who had so timidly taken a chair in the sacred bower of the queen of Angoulême had been transformed into an urgent lover. In six months he had come to regard himself as the equal of Louise, and now he wanted to be her master. He left home, promising himself to be thoroughly unreasonable, to hazard his life, to employ all the resources of burning eloquence, to say that he was no longer able to work, could no longer think, or write a line. Some women have a horror of contracts that does honour to their delicacy ; they would rather submit to a living impulse than to a dead convention. Scarcely anyone indeed, has a taste for obligatory pleasures. Mme de Bargeton observed on Lucien's brow, in his eyes, in his face and behaviour, that distraught expression that betrays a frustrated resolve : she made up her mind to cross him, partly out of a spirit of contradiction, but also from a noble conception of love. Given to exaggeration in all things, she also set an exaggerated value on her person. In her eyes, Mme de Bargeton was a sovereign queen, a Beatrix, a Laura. She had seated herself, in the manner of the Middle Ages, on the dais of the literary tournament, and Lucien must win his right to her after repeated victories ; he must first surpass " the sublime child ", Lamartine, Walter Scott, and Byron. The noble creature thought of her love as a creative principle ; the desires that she had inspired in Lucien should be the motive to urge him on to glory. This feminine quixotry is a sentiment that dedicates love to a worthy purpose ; it makes use of it, exalts it, crowns it with honour. Mme de Bargeton had made up her mind to play the part of Dulcinea in Lucien's life for the next seven or eight years, and she wished, like many provincial ladies, to set a price on her person, in the form of a prolonged period of service, a time of constancy that would enable her to judge her lover.

When Lucien opened fire with one of those fits of violent petulance that women laugh at when they themselves are still free, and which sadden them only when they have given their love, Louise assumed an air of dignity and embarked upon one of her long speeches, adorned with rhetorical phrases.

" Is this your promise to me, Lucien ? " she concluded. " Do not poison so sweet a present with remorse that will embitter the rest of my life. Do not spoil the future! And, I say it with pride, do not spoil the present! Have you not my whole heart ? What more would you have ? Is it, then, that your love is influenced by the senses, when it is the highest privilege of a woman who is loved to impose silence upon them ? For whom do you take me ? Am I no longer your Beatrix ? If I am not, for you, something more than a woman, then I am indeed less than a woman."

" You would say exactly the same thing to a man whom you did not love," exclaimed Lucien, furious.

" If you do not feel all the true worth of love in my thoughts, you will never be worthy of me."

" You are calling my love in question so as not to have to answer," Lucien cried, flinging himself at her feet and bursting into tears.

The poor boy cried in earnest at the prospect of having to wait so long at the gate of paradise. They were the tears of a poet who feels all his powers humbled, of a child crying in despair because he has been refused a toy.

" You have never loved me! " he cried.

" You don't believe what you are saying," she replied, flattered by all this violence.

" Then give me some proof that you are mine," begged Lucien, distraught.

At this point Stanislas arrived, unheard, saw Lucien quite overcome, in tears, his head in Mme de Bargeton's lap. This tableau was sufficiently suspect to satisfy Stanislas, who stepped back almost on top of Châtelet, who was waiting outside the door. Mme de Bargeton sprang to her feet, but she did not catch the two spies, who, as intruders, had retreated in haste.

"Who came in just now?" she asked the servants.

"M. de Chandour and M. du Châtelet," said Gentil, her old footman.

She returned to her boudoir, pale and trembling.

"If they saw you just now, I am lost!" she said to Lucien.

"So much the better!" exclaimed the poet.

She smiled at that exclamation of selfish love.

In the country an incident of this kind is exaggerated in the telling. In no time at all everybody knew that Lucien had been surprised kneeling at Naïs's feet. M. de Chandour, full of self-importance, went first of all to tell this great piece of news at the club, then he went from house to house. Châtelet hastened to make it known everywhere that he had seen nothing; but by putting himself in this way, as it were, out of the picture, he egged Stanislas on to talk and to add fresh details; and Stanislas, thinking himself very clever, added new ones every time he repeated the story. That evening Amélie's house was full of visitors; for by the evening the most exaggerated versions were circulating in the high society of Angoulême, for everyone who had passed on the story had imitated Stanislas's example. Men and women alike were all agog to hear the true version. The women who hid their faces in their hands and cried scandal the loudest were none other, paradoxically enough, than Amélie, Zéphirine, Fifine and Lolotte, all of whom stood more or less convicted of illicit love affairs. The cruel theme was repeated with variations in every key.

"Well," said one lady, "poor dear Naïs, have you heard? Of course, I don't believe it; she has an irreproachable life behind her; she is much too proud to be anything more than a patroness to M. Chardon. But if it is true, I am really sorry for her."

"She is all the more to be pitied, because she is making herself frightfully ridiculous; she is old enough to be the mother of M. Lulu, as Jacques called him. The little poet cannot be more than twenty-two, and Naïs, between ourselves, cannot be a day less than forty."

" For my part," said Châtelet, " I believe that the very situation in which M. de Rubempré was found is the proof of Naïs's innocence. A man does not go down on his knees to ask a second time for what he has had already."

" That all depends! " said Francis with an air of levity that brought upon him a disapproving look from Zéphirine.

" But do tell us just what really happened," they begged Stanislas, gathering round for a private session in the corner of the drawing-room.

Stanislas had finally put together a little story, full of innuendos, which he accompanied by dumb show which made the whole thing prodigiously incriminating.

" It is incredible! " they all said to each other.

" In the middle of the day ? " said one.

" Naïs is the last person I should ever have suspected."

" What will she do now ? "

Then followed comments and guesses without end. Du Châtelet defended Mme de Bargeton ; but he defended her so ill that he only fanned the fire of gossip instead of extinguishing it. Lili, deploring the fall of the fairest angel of the firmament of Angoulême, went off tearfully to break the news to the Bishop. When the whole town was well and truly agog, Châtelet, in high delight, went off to Mme de Bargeton's where, alas, there was only one table of whist ; he diplomatically asked Naïs if he might speak to her in private, in her boudoir. They both seated themselves on the sofa.

" Of course you know what everybody in Angoulême is talking about ? " Châtelet began in a low voice.

" No," she said.

" Well," he replied, " I am too much your friend to allow you to remain in ignorance. And it is my duty to put you in a position to silence the slanders that have no doubt been invented by Amélie, who has the overweening audacity to consider herself your rival. I called this morning with that stupid ape Stanislas, who was a few steps in front of me, and when he got as far as there," he said, indicating the door, " he says that he saw you and M. de Rubempré in a situation that made it impossible for him to enter ; he turned round on me—I was quite bewildered—and hurried me off without giving me time to collect my thoughts ; and we were in Beaulieu before he told me the reason for his rapid retreat. Had I known, nothing would have induced me to leave your house until the matter had been cleared up, to your advantage ; but to have gone back after leaving in that way would not have done any good. And now, whether Stanislas's eyes deceived him or whether he is right, *he must have been mistaken.* Dear Naïs, do not let that ass play with your life, your honour, your future ; he must be silenced at once. You know my position here. Although I have to see all these people, I am entirely devoted to you. Although you have repulsed my advances, my heart will always be yours. I am ready to prove my devotion to you at any time, in any way. Yes, I will watch over you like a faithful servant, without hope of reward, for the sole pleasure of serving you, even unknown to you. This morning I said everywhere that I was at the door of the drawing-room and that I saw nothing. If you are asked who has told you what is being said about you, you may use my name. I shall be very proud to be your acknowledged defender ; but, between ourselves, M. de Bargeton is the only person who can call Stanislas to account. Little Rubempré may have made a fool of himself, but that is no reason why a woman's honour should be at the mercy of the first boy who throws himself at her feet. That's what I have been saying."

Naïs thanked du Châtelet with a bow and remained thoughtful. She was utterly weary, to the point of disgust, of provincial life. When Châtelet had begun to speak her first thought had been Paris. Mme de Bargeton's silence put her wily adorer in an awkward situation.

"I repeat, I am at your service," he said.

" Thank you," she replied.

" What are you going to do ? "

" I shall see."

A prolonged silence.

"Are you so much in love with that little Rubempré?"

She permitted herself a proud smile, folded her arms, and looked at her drawing-room curtains. Châtelet left, without having fathomed the heart of that haughty queen. After the departure of Lucien and the four old gentlemen who had come for their game of whist, without troubling themselves about vague rumours, Mme de Bargeton called back her husband, who was on the point of going to bed and who had just opened his mouth in order to say good night to his wife.

"Come here, my dear; there is something I want to say to you," she said with some seriousness.

M. de Bargeton followed his wife into the boudoir.

"I have perhaps been to blame," she said, "for allowing too much warmth to appear in my protective interest in M. de Rubempré, which the stupid people of this town, and he himself, have misunderstood. This morning Lucien threw himself at my feet, here, and made a declaration of love. Stanislas came in just as I was telling the child to get up. In utter disregard of the rules that courtesy imposes on a gentleman towards a woman in any circumstances whatever, he has been saying that he surprised me in an equivocal situation with this boy, whom as a matter of fact I was treating as he deserved. If the young scatterbrain knew the scandal to which his folly has given rise, he would go, I am quite convinced of it, and insult Stanislas and challenge him to fight. I do not need to assure you that your wife is innocent; but you will realise that it would be dishonourable both for you and for me if M. de Rubempré were to champion me. Go at once at Stanislas and ask him to give you satisfaction for the insulting insinuations that he has made about me; tell him that you cannot let the affair rest unless he is prepared to retract what he said in the presence of several witnesses of credit. In this way you will earn the respect of all right-thinking people; you will be acting as a man of spirit, and a gentleman, and you will have earned my esteem. I will send Gentil on horseback to l'Escarbas, my father must be your second; in spite of his age, I know he is a man to trample underfoot this puppet who has blackened the reputation of a Nègrepelisse. The choice of weapons rests with you ; so fight with pistols, because you are a marvellous shot."

"I will go," said M. de Bargeton, picking up his hat and stick.

"Thank you, my dear," said his wife, touched by his conduct. "That is how I like to see men behave. You are a gentleman."

She offered her brow, and the old man kissed it, proud and happy. His wife, who felt a kind of maternal affection for this grown-up child, could not suppress a tear as she heard the carriage gate shut with a bang behind him.

"He really loves me!" she thought to herself. "The poor man clings to life, but for me he would lay it down without a thought."

M. de Bargeton was not at all troubled by the thought that the next day he would have to face his man and coolly look into the muzzle of a pistol directed point blank upon him ; no, he was troubled only by one thought, and he quaked inwardly all the way to M. de Chandour's house.

"What shall I say?" he was thinking. "Naïs really ought to have told me what to say!" And he racked his brains to find phrases that would not sound utterly ridiculous.

But men who live, like M. de Bargeton, in a silence imposed by a limited intelligence, exercised only within narrow limits, have, in the great circumstances of life, a dignity already to hand. As they say little, it follows that they say very few foolish things ; and besides, as they think a great deal before saying anything at all, their extreme mistrust of themselves induces them to weigh their words so carefully that they speak marvellously to the point—a phenomenon comparable to the loosing of the tongue of Balaam's ass. So that M. de Bargeton acquitted himself like a man of superior qualities. He justified the opinion of those who regarded him as a philosopher of the school of Pythagoras. He called at Stanislas's house at eleven o'clock at night, and there he found a large company present. He bowed to Amélie in silence, and greeted the others with that simple smile of his which, under the circumstances, gave the impression of profound irony. Then there was a deep silence, as before an approaching storm. Châtelet, who had returned, looked significantly, first at M. de Bargeton, and then at Stanislas, whom the injured husband greeted politely.

Châtelet realised the meaning of a visit at this hour, when the old man was always in bed : Naïs must have set this weak arm in motion ; and, as his relationship to Amélie gave him the right to interfere in the affairs of the family, he rose, and, taking M. de Bargeton aside, said to him :

" You wish to speak to Stanislas ? "

" Yes," said the old man, glad to have a go-between who would perhaps do the talking for him.

" Very well, go into Amélie's bedroom," replied the Director of Taxes, delighted at the prospect of this duel, that might make Mme de Bargeton a widow, at the same time making it impossible for her to marry Lucien, the cause of the scandal.

" Stanislas," said Châtelet to M. de Chandour, " Bargeton has no doubt come to ask for an explanation of the things that you have been saying about Naïs. Go into your wife's room, and mind you both behave like gentlemen. Don't make a scene, be very polite, and in fact assume all the coldness of British dignity."

A moment later, Stanislas and Châtelet joined Bargeton.

" Sir," said the injured husband, " you say that you found Mme de Bargeton in an equivocal situation with M. de Rubempré."

" With M. Chardon," Stanislas replied ironically, for he did not think that Bargeton was a man to be reckoned with.

" Very good," continued the husband. " Unless you are prepared to take back that statement in the presence of the company in your house at this moment, I must ask you to choose your second. My father-in-law, M. de Nègrepelisse, will call on you at four in the morning. We had both of us better make our final arrangements, because there is no alternative other than those I have put to you. I choose pistols, as I am the injured party."

M. de Bargeton had thought out this speech, the longest he had ever made, on the way, and he delivered it without heat, in the simplest way in the world. Stanislas turned pale and asked himself :

" After all, what *did* I see ? "

But, between the alternatives of taking back his words before everybody in Angoulême, in the presence of this mute gentleman who appeared to mean business, and the fear, the hideous fear which caught him by the throat with its burning fingers, he chose the more distant peril.

" Very well. Tomorrow morning," he said to M. de Bargeton, reflecting as he did so that the affair could probably be settled in some way.

The three men re-entered, and everyone examined their faces carefully : Châtelet was smiling, M. de Bargeton was exactly as he was in his own house ; but Stanislas was deathly pale. On seeing this, several women guessed the purpose of the conference. The words " They are going to fight! " were whispered from one to another. Half of those present decided that Stanislas was in the wrong and that the paleness of his countenance convicted him of a lie ; the other half admired M. de Bargeton's conduct. Châtelet was grave and mysterious. M. de Bargeton stayed for a few moments to examine their faces, then took his leave.

" Have you pistols ? " Châtelet whispered to Stanislas, who was shaking from head to foot.

Amélie realised what was happening ; she turned faint, and the women pressed round to carry her to her bedroom. There was a terrific sensation, and everybody began talking at once. The gentlemen stayed in the drawing-room and declared with one voice that M. de Bargeton was within his right.

" Would you ever have thought that the old man had it in him to act like this ? " said M. de Saintot.

" But," said the pitiless Jacques, " in his young days he was a crack shot. My father often used to tell me about Bargeton's exploits."

"Nonsense! Put them twenty paces apart, and they'll miss each other if you give them cavalry pistols," said Francis to Châtelet.

When everyone had gone, Châtelet reassured Stanislas and his wife, and explained to them that all would be well, and that in a duel between a man of sixty and a man of thirty-six the latter must have the advantage.

Next morning, while Lucien was at breakfast with David, who had returned from Marsac without his father, Madame Chardon came in in great agitation.

"Well, Lucien, do you know what everyone is talking about this morning, even the people in the market? M. de Bargeton almost killed M. de Chandour at five o'clock this morning in M. Tulloye's field; people are making puns on the name.[1] It seems that M. de Chandour said yesterday that he had surprised you with Mme de Bargeton."

"It is not true! Mme de Bargeton is innocent!" Lucien exclaimed.

"I heard the whole story from a countryman who saw the whole thing, standing on his cart. M. de Nègrepelisse arrived at about three in the morning to second M. de Bargeton; he told M. de Chandour that if anything happened to his son-in-law he would avenge him. An officer of the cavalry regiment lent his pistols and M. de Nègrepelisse tested them in every possible way. M. du Châtelet wanted to stop them from practising with the pistols, but the officer that they had chosen as referee said that if they were not going to behave like children, they ought to make sure that their arms were in working order. The seconds placed the opponents at twenty-five paces. M. de Bargeton, who arrived as coolly as if he had been going for a walk, fired first; the ball lodged in M. de Chandour's neck, and he fell without being able to return the shot. The surgeon at the hospital has just said that M. de Chandour's neck will be crooked for the rest of his life. I came at once to tell you what had happened so that you should not go to Mme de Bargeton's, or show yourself in Angoulême, because some of M. de Chandour's friends might challenge you."

As she was speaking, the workshop apprentice brought in Gentil, Mme de Bargeton's footman, who handed Lucien a letter from Louise: "My dear, you have doubtless heard the outcome of the duel between Chandour and my husband. We are not receiving anyone today. Be careful, and don't be seen in town—I ask this in the name of your affection for me. Do you not think that this sad day would best be spent in coming to listen to your Beatrix, whose

[1] *Tue l'oie.*

whole life has been changed by this event, and who has a thousand things to say to you ? "

" Luckily," said David, " my wedding is arranged for the day after tomorrow ; you will have an excuse for not going to see Mme de Bargeton so often."

" My dear David," said Lucien, " she asks me to go and see her today. I think I had better go, she will know better than we how I ought to behave in the present circumstances."

" Then is everything ready here ? " asked Mme Chardon.

" Come and see," said David, delighted to show the transformation that the first floor had undergone, where everything was now fresh and new.

These rooms breathed the sweet spirit that reigns in early married days, when the orange blossoms and the bridal veil still crown the inner life, and the spring of love is reflected in every object ; when everything is white and spotless, and decked with flowers.

" Eve will be like a princess," said her mother, " but you have spent too much money, you have been extravagant! "

David smiled, but did not answer, for Mme Chardon had put her finger on a sore spot that was causing this poor lover cruel pangs ; the expenses had so far exceeded his estimate, that he could not now afford to build above the shed. It would be a long time before he would be able to give his mother-in-law the home that he had planned for her. Generous hearts suffer keenly when they have to break promises of that kind, promises that are, as it were, the little vanities of affection. David scrupulously concealed his anxiety, so as to spare Lucien's feelings, who might otherwise have been quite overcome by the sacrifices made for him.

" Eve and her friends have been working hard, as well," said Mme Chardon. " The trousseau, the household linen, everything is ready. Those girls are so fond of her that without her knowing anything about it they have covered the mattresses with white twill with rose-coloured piping. So pretty! It makes one wish one was going to be married! "

Mother and daughter had spent all their savings on buying for David's house all those things that young men never think of. They knew that he was furnishing in great luxury, for there was mention of a service of Limoges china, and so they had attempted to make their contributions match David's purchases. This little rivalry of love and generosity would mean that the two young people would have to be very economical in the early days of their marriage, in the midst of all these evidences of homely comfort that might indeed pass for luxury in an old-fashioned town, as Angoulême was in those days.

As soon as Lucien saw his mother and David go into the blue-and-white bedroom, which he had already seen, he slipped away to Mme de Bargeton. He found Naïs with her husband, whose early morning adventure had given him an appetite, and who was eating his breakfast quite unmoved by what had just taken place. The old country gentleman, M. de Négrepelisse, an imposing figure, a relic of the old French nobility, was with his daughter. When Gentil announced M. de Rubempré, the old gentleman with white hair turned on him the inquisitive look of a father who is anxious to form an opinion of the man whom his daughter has singled out. Lucien's extraordinary beauty struck him so much that he could not restrain an approving glance; but he seemed to regard this affair of his daughter's as a flirtation, a passing fancy rather than a lasting love. Breakfast over, Louise was able to leave her father with M. de Bargeton; she beckoned Lucien to follow her.

"My dear," she began, and her voice was sad and happy at the same time, "I am going to Paris, and my father is taking my husband back with him to l'Escarbas, where he will stay while I am away. Mme d'Espard, who was a Blamont-Chauvry, a relation by marriage through the d'Espards, who are the older branch of the Nègrepelisse family, is at present very influential and has influential relations. If she deigns to recognise us, I shall cultivate her acquaintance: she might be able to use her influence to obtain a place for Bargeton. I may be successful in using my influence in order to have him asked for by the Court as Deputy for Charente, which would be a step towards his nomination here. If he were made Deputy, that might lead later on to other things that I should like to do in Paris. It is you, dear child, who have inspired me with the wish to change my life. This morning's duel makes it necessary for me to close my house for a time, because there will be some people who will take the Chandours' side against us. In a situation like ours, and in a small town, an absence is always necessary to give enmities time to die down. But either I shall succeed, and shall never set foot in Angoulême again, or I shall fail, and then I shall wait in Paris until the time comes when I shall be able to spend all the summers at l'Escarbas and the winters in Paris. It is the only possible life for a woman of quality, and I have delayed too long already in living it. One day will be long enough for all our preparations, and I shall leave tomorrow night, and you will come with me, will you not? You must set out first. Between Mansle and Ruffec, I will pick you up in my carriage, and we shall soon be in Paris. There, my dear, is the only life for superior people. We are only at ease among our peers; in any other society one suffers. Besides, Paris is the intellectual capital of the world, the stage of your success; cover quickly the distance that divides you from it. Do not let your ideas stagnate in a country town, get in touch at once with the great men who represent the nineteenth century. Approach the Court, and power. Neither distinctions nor honours come in search of talent whose star shines only in a little town. Tell me the great works that have been written in the provinces! Think, on the other hand, of the sublime and poor Jean-Jacques, irresistibly attracted by that mental sun, that creates glories, setting minds on fire by the friction of rivalries. Is it not your duty to make haste to take your place among those pleiades that repeat themselves in every age? You cannot imagine how helpful it is to young talent to be placed in the limelight of high society! I will get an introduction for you to Mme d'Espard; no one has ever found it easy to get an entrée into her drawing-room, where you will meet all the great: ministers, ambassadors, orators of the Chamber, the most influential peers, wealthy and famous people of every kind. You could scarcely fail to arouse their interest, handsome as you are, and young, and talented. Men of genius are not petty-minded; they will give you what help they can. When you are known to be highly placed, your works will acquire immense prestige. For artists, the great problem is to attract notice. And there you will find a thousand openings, sinecures, perhaps a pension from the civil list. For the Bourbons love to favour the arts and letters! So be at the same time a religious and a royalist poet. Not only would that be a good thing in itself, but it will make your fortune. Has Opposition, has liberalism places and rewards at its disposal that will make a fortune for a writer? So take the wise choice, and go the way of all men of genius. I have told you my secret, keep it absolutely, and get ready to follow me. Do you not want to?" she added, astonished to find that her lover remained silent.

Lucien, bewildered by the sudden vision of Paris called up by this speech, hearing these seductive words, felt that hitherto he had only been making use of half his mind; he seemed suddenly to have discovered the other half, so rapidly did his ideas expand: he saw himself, in Angoulême, like a frog under a stone at the bottom of a swamp. Paris and its splendours, Paris, that in all provincial imaginations figures as an Eldorado, appeared before him robed in gold, her head crowned with royal jewels, her arms open to embrace talent. Famous men were ready to accord him fraternal welcome. There, all things smiled on genius. There, no jealous booby squires humiliated writers with wounding words; there, poetry was not heard with stupid indifference. There the works of poets poured from the fountain-head; there they were paid for and brought into the light. The publishers would only have to read the first few pages of *The Archer of Charles IX* to open their cash-boxes, and ask him how much he wanted. He understood, besides, that after a journey during which circumstances would throw them together that Mme de Bargeton would be entirely his, that they would live together.

On hearing these words, "Do you not want to?" tears came into his eyes, he took Louise in his arms, drew her to his heart, and marbled her throat with impassioned kisses. Then he stopped suddenly, as if a memory had struck him, and exclaimed:

"Good heavens! My sister's wedding is the day after tomorrow!"

It was the expiring cry of pure and noble boyhood. Those powerful ties that bind young hearts to their families, to their first friend, to all the affections of early life, were about to be severed at one terrible blow.

" Indeed! " exclaimed the haughty Nègrepelisse. " How can you compare your sister's marriage with the progress of our love ? Does it mean so much to you to be best man at a wedding of tradespeople and workmen that you cannot sacrifice for my sake such noble joys ? A fine sacrifice! " she cried with scorn. " This morning I sent my husband to fight a duel on your account! Go, sir, leave me! I have been mistaken! "

She fell swooning on the sofa. Lucien went over to her, begged her pardon, calling down execrations on his family, David, and his sister.

" I had such faith in you! " she said. " M. de Cante-Croix had a mother whom he adored, but, in order to win a letter from me in which I wrote '*I am satisfied*' he died in the thick of the battle. And you, when it is a question of travelling with me, you cannot even forgo a wedding-breakfast! "

Lucien would gladly have killed himself, and so acute, so deep was his despair, that Louise forgave him, but making it clear at the same time that he must atone for this fault.

"Go, then," she said at last, "be discreet, and tomorrow at midnight be waiting a hundred yards beyond Mansle."

The earth seemed small beneath Lucien's feet, and he returned to David's house pursued by his hopes, as Orestes was pursued by his furies, for he could foresee a thousand difficulties, all summed up in that terrible phrase : *where is the money to come from ?* He feared David's perspicacity so much that he shut himself up in his charming study in order to recover a little from the bewilderment of his new position. So he must leave this room, so dearly bought, furnished at such a cost, render useless so many sacrifices! Then it occurred to Lucien that his mother could occupy it, and thus save David the expense of building at the end of the yard as he had planned. This departure would be a convenience to the family ; he found a thousand urgent reasons for his flight, for there is nothing more Jesuitical than desire. He hurried at once to l'Houmeau, to see his sister, to tell her his new destiny and to confer with her. When he arrived at the door of Postel's shop it struck him that if all other means were to fail, he could borrow from his father's successor enough money to live on for a year.

" If I live with Louise, three francs a day will be wealth to me, and that only comes to a thousand francs for a year," he reflected. " And in six months' time I shall be rich! "

Lucien took Eve and his mother into his confidence, under promise of absolute secrecy. Both of them wept as they listened to his ambitious projects ; and when he asked them the reason for their grief, they told him that every penny they possessed had been spent on table linen for the new house, on Eve's trousseau, on all the multitude of small purchases that David had overlooked, and that they were glad to have been able to provide, as the printer had made over to Eve a marriage settlement of ten thousand francs. Lucien then told them of his idea of a loan, and Mme Chardon undertook to ask M. Posten for a thousand francs, for a year.

" But, Lucien," said Eve, whose heart suddenly contracted, " then you won't be able to come to our wedding ? Oh! Do come back! I can postpone it for a few days! Surely she will let you come back in a fortnight, if you go with her now! She can surely spare you for a week for us—after all, we brought you up for her. Our marriage will never go right if you are not at the wedding!—But will a thousand francs be enough for you ? " she said, breaking off suddenly. " Your coat suits you divinely, but you only have one! You have only two thin shirts, the other six are coarse linen, and three lawn cravats, the other three are common muslin. And you have no good handkerchiefs. You won't have a sister in Paris to wash your things for you the same day when you need them quickly! You will need much more! You have only the one pair of nankeen trousers made this year, the old ones are too small for you ; you will have to buy new clothes in Paris, and Paris prices are very different from prices in Angoulême. You have only two wearable white waistcoats ; I have had to mend the others already. Really, I advise you to take two thousand francs! "

David came in at this moment, and he must have heard Eve's last words, for he looked at the brother and sister in silence.

"Don't hide anything from me," he said at last.

"Very well," said Eve. "He is going away with her."

"Postel has agreed to lend you the thousand francs, but only for six months," said Mme Chardon, who came in, without seeing David, "and he wants a receipt from you, endorsed by your brother-in-law, for he says that you can offer no securities."

The mother turned round, saw her son-in-law, and all four remained silent. The Chardon family felt that they had taken advantage of David's goodness. All three felt ashamed. Tears came into the printer's eyes.

"Then you won't be coming to my wedding?" he said. "You are not going to live with us, then? And here have I been spending everything I had! Ah! Lucien, as I came here, bringing Eve her few bits of wedding jewellery, little did I think that I should regret having bought them," he said, drying his eyes and pulling the little cases out of his pocket.

He laid the morocco-covered boxes on the table in front of his mother-in-law.

"You should not think so much of me!" said Eve, with a heavenly smile that belied her words.

"Mother dear," said the printer, "go and say to M. Postel that I agree to endorse the receipt, for I see by your face, Lucien, that you have quite made up your mind to go."

Lucien bowed his head, slowly and sadly; then after a pause he said:

"Don't think too hardly of me, my dear, good angels."

He put his arms round Eve and David, and drew them to him, holding them close. "Wait until you see what will come of it, and then you will know how much I love you. David, what is the use of all our high thinking, if it does not enable us to be above those little ceremonies in which the law ensnares our affections? In spite of the distance, shall I not be with you in thought? Have I not a destiny to fulfil? Are the publishers going to come here and look for my *Archer of Charles IX* and *Marguerites*? Sooner or later, must we not always do what I am doing today? Does not my whole success in life depend upon my going to Paris and my being received by the Marquise d'Espard ? "

" He is right," said Eve. " Did you not say to me yourself that he ought to go to Paris as soon as possible ? "

David took Eve's hand and led her into the little closet that had been her bedroom for seven years and whispered to her :

" Did you say that he needed two thousand francs, my love ? Postel is only lending him a thousand."

Eve looked at her future husband with an expression of anguish that revealed all that she was suffering.

" Listen, my beloved Eve, we are going to have a bad start in life. Yes, my expenses have absorbed everything I had. I have only two thousand francs, and half of that I need, in order to keep the business going. If I give a thousand to your brother it will mean giving away our bread, our peace of mind. If I had only myself to consider, I know what I would do. But we are two. You must decide."

Eve, quite overcome, threw herself into her lover's arms, kissed him tenderly and whispered in his ear, weeping as she did so.

" Do as you would do if you were alone. I will work to make it up! "

In spite of the most ardent kiss that lovers ever exchanged, David left Eve quite overcome, and returned to Lucien.

" Don't worry," he said, " you shall have your two thousand francs."

" Go and see Postel," said Mme Chardon, " for you will both have to sign the receipt."

When the two friends returned, they found Eve and her mother on their knees, praying. Although they knew how many hopes the return would be sure to realise, at that moment they felt only how much they were losing by this parting ; for they felt that future happiness was too dearly bought by an absence that would break up their lives, and fill them with a thousand fears for Lucien's future.

" If you ever forget that sight," said David in Lucien's ear, " you will be the worst of men."

The printer no doubt felt that those grave words were necessary ; the influence of Mme de Bargeton was no less alarming to him than the deplorable instability of Lucien's character, that would as easily precipitate him into an evil way of life as into a good.

Eve had soon packed Lucien's clothes. This Fernando Cortez of literature carried little with him. He wore his best overcoat, his best waistcoat, and one of his two fine shirts. All his linen, his famous coat, a few odds and ends, and his manuscripts made up such a small parcel that, so that Mme de Bargeton should not see it, David suggested sending it on by coach to the house of an acquaintance of his, a paper merchant, to whom he would write and ask him to keep it until Lucien called for it.

In spite of the precautions that Mme de Bargeton had taken to conceal her departure, Châtelet heard about it, and was anxious to know whether she was travelling alone or with Lucien. He sent his valet to Ruffec, with instructions to examine all the carriages that changed horses at the stage.

" If she is taking her poet," he thought to himself, " she is mine."

Lucien set out the next morning at daybreak, accompanied by David, who hired a horse and trap on the pretext that he was going to discuss business with his father, a white lie that was very plausible under the circumstances. The two friends arrived at Marsac, where they spent part of the day with the old bear ; then, in the evening, they went on to beyond Mansle to wait for Mme de Bargeton, who arrived just before dawn. When he saw the sixty-year-old carriage that he had so often seen in the coach-house, Lucien experienced one of the most powerful emotions of his life, and flung himself into David's arms.

" God grant that this may be for your good ! " David said.

The printer climbed back into his shabby trap and disappeared, his heart torn, for he had terrible presentiments of Lucien's fate in Paris.

PART TWO

A Provincial Celebrity In Paris

The arrival in Paris

PART TWO

I

A Provincial Celebrity In Paris

NEVER thereafter did Lucien, nor Mme de Bargeton, nor Gentil, nor Albertine, the maid, make any reference to what happened on that journey; but it is easy to imagine that the constant presence of the servants must have been decidedly irksome to a lover who had been living in expectation of all the pleasures of an elopement. Lucien, travelling post for the first time in his life, was appalled to see almost the entire sum on which he had proposed to live for a year in Paris melt away in the course of the journey. In the way of all those in whom the charm of childhood is united with great talent, he made the mistake of giving expression to his naïve astonishment at the sight of so many new things. A man must be very sure of a woman before he allows her to see his emotions and his thoughts as they arise. A mistress whose heart is as tender as her mind is great may smile at such childishness and understand it; but let her have even the smallest trace of vanity, and she will never forgive her lover for exposing himself as childish, vain, or petty. Some women carry their devotion to such lengths that they must always see their idol as a god; and only those who love a man for his own sake, rather than for their own, love his weaknesses no less than what is great in him. Lucien had not yet come to realise that Mme de Bargeton's love was rooted in her pride. He failed to ask himself the meaning of certain smiles that Louise failed to repress from time to time in the course of that journey, and he overflowed with all the abandon of a puppy let off the lead for the first time.

The travellers arrived at the Hôtel Gaillard-Bois, in the Rue de l'Echelle, just before daybreak. Both the lovers were so tired that Louise's one desire was to go to bed, and go to bed she did, telling Lucien to ask for a room above her own. Lucien slept until four in the afternoon. Madame de Bargeton sent a servant to call him for dinner; he dressed hurriedly when he heard the time, and found Louise in one of those dreary rooms, the shame of Paris, where, for all that city's pretentions to elegance, there is not a single hotel where a rich traveller can take a room of the kind to which he is accustomed at home. Even though his eyes were still dimmed with the sleep from which he had been so hastily wakened, he hardly recognised his Louise in that cold, sunless chamber, with its faded curtains, bleak polished floorboards, and ugly second-hand furniture, shabby with wear. And indeed there are certain types who have neither the same appearance, nor the same value, when we see them apart from the faces, the things, the surroundings that serve to frame them. There is a certain atmosphere that suits living faces, just as the light and shade of Flemish pictures bring to life the faces that the painter's genius places in that setting. Country people are nearly all like this. And besides, Mme de Bargeton was looking more serious, more thoughtful than she should have been, on the threshold of a life of unhindered happiness. Lucien could not protest, for Gentil and Albertine were waiting on them.

The dinner had none of that abundance, that quality of essential hospitality, that distinguishes provincial life. The dishes, which were sent in from a neighbouring restaurant, were so vigorously cut down, with an eye to profit, that there was hardly enough. Paris is not a pleasant place in little things of this kind for travellers of moderate means. An inexplicable change seemed to have come over Louise, and Lucien waited until the end of the meal to question her.

Nor was he mistaken. A momentous event—for thoughts are events of the inner life—had taken place while he slept.

At two o'clock that afternoon Sixte du Châtelet had called at the hotel, had Albertine roused from her sleep, and expressed a wish to speak to her mistress; he had returned almost before Mme de

Bargeton had had time to dress. Naïs's curiosity was aroused by this unexpected appearance on the scene of M. du Châtelet, for she had imagined that her movements were a profound secret. She received him at three o'clock.

" I have risked a reprimand from my Ministry in order to follow you," he said as he greeted her, " because I foresaw what was likely to happen to you. But I would rather lose my job than see *you* lost! "

" What do you mean ? " exclaimed Mme de Bargeton.

" I can see plainly that you must be in love with Lucien," he went on, with an air of tender resignation, " because you must love a man very much to throw all caution to the winds, to disregard all the conventions—you, who know them so well! Do you really imagine, my adored Naïs, that Mme d'Espard, or anyone else in Paris for that matter, will receive you the moment it is known that you have virtually fled from Angoulême with a young man, especially after the duel between M. de Bargeton and M. de Chandour ? Your husband's visit to l'Escarbas looks like a separation. In a situation of that kind a gentleman always fights for his wife first, and then leaves her at liberty. Love M. de Rubempré by all means, give him your protection, do whatever you like, but don't live under the same roof! If anyone here were to know that you had travelled in the same carriage you would be put on the index by the very people you want to meet. And besides, Naïs, don't make all these sacrifices for a young man that you have had no opportunity of comparing with others, who has not, as yet, undergone any test, and who may very well forget you here for some little Parisienne whom he thinks may be useful to his ambitions. I do not wish to cast a slur on anyone whom you love, but you must allow me to place your interests before his, and to say to you, ' Consider him well! Think carefully of all the implications of any step you decide to take! ' If you find doors closed, if women refuse to receive you, at least be sure that you will not regret all that you have sacrificed, be certain at least that the man for whom you will have sacrificed so much will always be worthy of everything that you have given up for him ; and that he will understand how much that is! Mme d'Espard is all the more prudish and strict in these matters because she herself is separated from her husband, although nobody has ever been able to discover the reason for their separation, but the Navarriens, the Blamont-Chauvrys, the Lenoncourts, all his relations have stood by her, the most strait-laced women have called on her and receive her with respect, so that the Marquis d'Espard has been put in the wrong. You will see that I am right the very first time you call on her. Indeed, knowing Paris as I do, I can tell you beforehand that the moment you set foot in the Marquise's drawing-room you will pray that she will never know that you are staying at the Gaillard-Bois with the son of a chemist, even if he does call himself M. de Rubempré. You will find very different rivals in Paris from Amélie—clever and experienced rivals, who will not fail to find out who you are, where you are staying, where you come from. You have counted on being incognito, I can see; but for people of your class there is no such thing as an incognito. You will encounter Angoulême everywhere. There are the Charente deputies, who are coming up for the opening of Parliament; there is the General, who is on leave in Paris; but you only need be seen by one single inhabitant of Angoulême for your career to be cut short for no apparent reason: you would simply be Lucien's mistress. If you should need me at any time, I shall be staying with the Receiver-General, in the Rue du Faubourg-Saint-Honoré, practically next door to Mme d'Espard. I know the Maréchale de Carigliano, Mme de Sérizy and the President of the Council well enough to introduce you to them; but you will meet so many people at Mme d'Espard's that you will not need me. You will not be in need of any introductions, because everybody will be wanting to meet you."

Châtelet talked on, and Mme de Bargeton made no attempt to interrupt him: she was impressed by the truth of his observations. For the queen of Angoulême had, in fact, counted on remaining incognito.

"You are right, my dear friend," she said, "but what am I to do?"

"Allow me," said Châtelet, "to find you suitable furnished

rooms ; there you will be able to live less expensively than in hotels, and you will have a home of your own ; and, if you will take my advice, you will sleep there tonight."

"But how did you know my address ?" she asked.

"Your carriage was easy to recognise, and, besides, I was following you. At Sèvres the postillion who had driven you gave mine your address. But will you allow me to be your house agent ? I will send you a note presently to tell you where I am installing you."

"Very well, do so," she said.

In those words, seemingly insignificant, all was said. Baron du Châtelet had spoken the language of the world to a woman of the world. He had made his appearance in full Parisian elegance, and a smart carriage was waiting for him at the door. And as it happened, Mme de Bargeton went over to the window to think over her situation, and saw the old dandy depart. A few moments later Lucien, hastily wakened, hastily dressed, made his appearance in his last-year's nankeen trousers and his shabby jacket, too small for him. He was handsome, but his clothes were ridiculous. Dress the Apollo Belvedere, or Antinous, in a porter's overalls, and who would recognise the divine creation of the Greek or Roman chisel ? The eyes will make a comparison before the heart has time to rectify that rapid, mechanical judgment. The contrast between Lucien and Châtelet was too abrupt for Louise not to be struck by it. When at about six o'clock dinner was over Mme de Bargeton beckoned to Lucien to come and sit by her on a wretched sofa, covered with a red calico material with a design of yellow flowers.

"Lucien, my dear," she said, "don't you think that even if we have done a stupid thing, fatal for both of us, we ought to try to put it right ? My dear child, we must not either live in Paris together, nor allow anyone to guess that we travelled together from the country. Your future depends to a very great extent on my position, and I must not do anything to spoil it in any way. Therefore, from this evening, I shall take lodgings not far from here ; but you must stay in this hotel, and we can see one another every day without giving anyone cause to criticise us."

Louise expounded the conventions to Lucien, who opened his eyes in astonishment. Even without realising that women who go back on their follies go back on their love, he understood that he was no longer the Lucien of Angoulême. Louise spoke only of herself, of her interests, of her reputation, of the world; and in order to excuse her egoism, she tried to make him think that she was acting on his behalf. He had no claims upon Louise, who had so suddenly become Mme de Bargeton once more, and, what was worse, he had no power! He could not keep back the tears that filled his eyes.

"I may be your glory, but you are more than that to me! You are my only hope, my whole future. I imagined that if you made my successes yours you would surely stand by me in my misfortunes, and now we are going to part already!"

"You are judging my conduct," she said, "you do not love me."

Lucien looked at her with an expression of such grief that she could not but say to him:

"Dear child, I will stay if you want me to; we shall be lost and have nowhere to turn. But when we are both equally wretched, both ostracised, when failure (for one must face every possibility) has driven us both back to l'Escarbas, remember, darling, that I foresaw what would happen, and that I advised you from the first to proceed according to the rules of the world, and to submit to the conventions."

"Louise," he replied, taking her in his arms, "your wisdom terrifies me. Remember that I am a child, that I have put myself entirely in your dear hands. For my part, I would rather overcome men and obstacles by my own exertions. But if I can succeed more quickly with your help than alone, I shall be very happy to owe everything to you. Forgive me! You mean so much to me that I cannot help being afraid. For me, separation is half-way to desertion, and if you desert me that will be death to me."

"But, dearest child, the world does not ask very much of you," she replied. "It only means sleeping here, and you can spend the whole day at my house without anybody being able to say a word."

A few caresses sufficed to calm Lucien. An hour later Gentil brought word from Châtelet that he had found rooms in the Rue Neuve-de-Luxembourg. She made enquiries as to the whereabouts of this road, which was not very far from the Rue de l'Echelle. " We shall be neighbours," she said to Lucien.

Two hours later Louise got into the cab that Châtelet sent for her and went off to her new home. The flat was one of those that upholsterers take and furnish, and let to wealthy deputies and important people staying in Paris for short periods—luxurious, but uncomfortable. Lucien returned to the little Hôtel du Gaillard-Bois, still having seen nothing of Paris except the part of the Rue Saint-Honoré between the Rue Neuve-de-Luxembourg and the Rue de l'Echelle. He went to bed in his wretched little room, which he could not refrain from comparing with Louise's splendid apartment.

Just as he was leaving Mme de Bargeton, Baron du Châtelet had arrived, on his way from a ball given by the Minister of Foreign Affairs, in all the splendour of his evening dress. He had come to enquire about all the arrangements he had made for Mme de Bargeton. Louise was worried ; so much luxury alarmed her. Provincial ways had, after all, left their mark on her. She was meticulously careful in her accounts ; her strict economy would have been considered miserly in Paris. She had brought nearly twenty thousand francs in the form of a draft on the Receiver-General, and she intended that sum to cover, amply, her expenses for the next four years ; she was already beginning to fear that she would not have enough and that she would get into debt. Châtelet informed her that her flat would only cost her six hundred francs a month.

" Dirt-cheap," he said, seeing Naïs start. " You can hire your own carriage for five hundred francs a month, which only comes to fifty *louis*. And, besides that, you will only have to think of your clothes. A woman moving in good society could not live on less. If you want to have M. de Bargeton made a Receiver-General, or to get him an appointment in the royal household, you must not look poverty-stricken. Here they only give to the rich. It is fortunate," he added, " that you have Gentil to accompany you, and

Albertine to dress you, because servants cost a fortune in Paris. You will not often need to eat at home, with the introductions you will have."

Mme de Bargeton and the Baron chatted about Paris. Châtelet recounted the gossip of the day, all those trifles that one has to know, on pain of being an outsider in Paris. Then he gave Naïs advice about the right shops to go to : Herbault for toques, Juliette for hats and bonnets. He gave her the address of a dressmaker who was almost certainly going to supersede Victorine ; in short, he made her feel how necessary it was for her to shed Angoulême. He left on a parting inspiration that he luckily thought of.

"Tomorrow," he remarked carelessly, "I shall probably have a box at one of the theatres ; I will come and call for you and M. de Rubempré, for you must allow me to do the honours of Paris to both of you."

"He has a more generous nature than I gave him credit for," Mme de Bargeton reflected, on finding that Lucien was included in the invitation.

In June ministers hardly know what to do with their boxes at the theatres ; their deputies and their constituents are busy in their vineyards or ensuring their crops, and their more exacting acquaintances are in the country or abroad ; so that at this time even the best boxes in Paris are filled with the most heterogeneous occupants, never seen again by the regular theatre-goers. The audiences at such times give the theatre the appearance of being upholstered with shabby tapestry.

Châtelet had already reflected that, this being so, he could offer Naïs those amusements that provincials long for most, without having to spend very much money.

The next day, the first time Lucien called, he found that Louise was not at home. Mme de Bargeton had gone out to do some indispensable shopping. She had gone to take council with the most weighty and illustrious authorities (those cited by Châtelet) on the matter of feminine toilet, for she had written to inform Mme d'Espard of her arrival. Although Mme de Bargeton had all the self-confidence bred of a long habit of domination, she was desperately afraid of appearing provincial. She had sufficient tact to realise how much relations between women depend upon first impressions; and, although she felt confident that she could very quickly take her place in the distinguished circles of women like Mme d'Espard, she realised that she would need their good-will at first; and she was determined, above all, not to overlook any detail that might help to ensure success. She therefore felt infinitely grateful to Châtelet for having indicated to her the means of putting herself into line with the world of fashion.

By a singular chance, the Marquise was in a situation in which she was delighted to be of service to a member of her husband's family. For no apparent reason, the Marquis d'Espard had withdrawn from society; he had ceased to pay any attention either to his own affairs or to politics, to his family or to his wife. Left in this way her own mistress, the Marquise felt herself in need of the approval of public opinion; and she was glad, therefore, to act on behalf of the Marquis on the present occasion, and to give her protection to a member of her husband's family. She meant to be ostentatiously kind, so as to put her husband the more in the wrong. So that very day she wrote to Mme de Bargeton, née Nègrepelisse, one of those charming notes, so elegantly phrased that it takes some time to realise that they mean nothing:

"She was happy that circumstances should have brought a member of the family of whom she had heard so much, and had long wished to know, for the friendships of Paris are so very superficial, and she longed to have one more real friend in the world; and if this was not to be, it would be but one more lost illusion to bury with the rest. She placed herself entirely at her cousin's disposal, and would have called on her, but for an indisposition that kept her at home; but she already regarded herself as under an obligation to the cousin who had remembered her."

During the course of his first aimless walk across the boulevards and along the Rue de la Paix, Lucien, like all newcomers, was much more interested in things than in people. In Paris the scale of everything is the first thing that strikes one ; the luxury of the shops, the height of the houses, the affluence of the carriages, the contrast, everywhere seen, between great wealth and extreme poverty. Astonished at that crowd, in which he himself was a stranger, that man of inspiration felt himself immensely diminished. People who have a measure of local celebrity in a provincial town, and who at every step encounter some proof of their own importance, can never reconcile themselves to this sudden and total extinction of the basis of their self-esteem. To be somebody in one's own town, and nobody in Paris—these are two conditions that call for gradual adjustment ; and those who pass too abruptly from the one state to the other fall into a kind of annihilation. For a young poet, who had always found a response to all his moods, a companion to listen to all his ideas, a friend in whom to confide his smallest experiences, Paris could only be a terrible desert. Lucien had not yet been to collect his best blue suit, so that he was acutely conscious of the shabbiness (to say the least of it) of his clothes, as he once more approached Mme de Bargeton's door, at the time at which she was expected back ; here he found Baron de Châtelet, who carried them both off to dinner at the Rocher de Cancale. Lucien was stunned by the whirl of Paris, and could say nothing to Louise, for there were three in the cab ; but he squeezed her hand, and she responded in friendly fashion to all the thoughts that he expressed in this way. After dinner Châtelet conducted his two guests to the Vaudeville. Lucien felt a secret dissatisfaction at this reappearance of Châtelet, and cursed the chance that had brought him to Paris. The Director of Taxes put down his journey to his ambition : he hoped for an appointment as Secretary-General of a Department and to enter the Council of State as Master of Requests ; he had come to ask that the promises that had been made him should be honoured, for a man of his stamp could not be expected to remain a Director of Taxes ; he would rather be nothing at all, go into Parliament, or into the Diplomatic Service. He had grown in stature ; Lucien vaguely recognised in the old beau the superiority of the man of the world who knows his Paris ; above all, he was ashamed of being indebted to him for his pleasures. But if the poet was humiliated and unhappy, the ex-private secretary was quite in his element. Châtelet smiled at the hesitations, the surprises, the questions, the little mistakes that his rival, in his ignorance, made, like an old salt who laughs at a young midshipman who has not yet got his sea legs. Lucien's delight in seeing the spectacle of Paris for the first time made up, however, for the annoyance of these small embarrassments.

It was on this memorable evening that Lucien secretly repudiated a number of provincial ideas of life. The horizon had widened, society took on new proportions. The proximity of so many pretty women of Paris, so elegantly and daintily dressed, made him notice how dowdy Mme de Bargeton's clothes were in comparison, although she had done her best. Neither the material, the cut, nor the colours were fashionable. The hair-style that had made such an impression in Angoulême here looked in strikingly bad taste in comparison with the delicious inventions that he saw on all sides.

" Will she always look like this ? " he wondered, not knowing that the day had been spent in planning a transformation.

In the provinces there is no question of choice or comparison ; one is used to seeing faces, and they come to seem beautiful through familiarity. Transported to Paris, a woman who passes for pretty in the country will not be worth a glance, for she is only beautiful by the application of the proverb : " In the kingdom of the blind, the one-eyed man is king." Lucien's eyes made the same comparison that Mme de Bargeton's had made on the previous evening between himself and Châtelet.

On her side, Mme de Bargeton gave way to strange reflexions on the subject of her lover. For all his striking beauty, the poor poet cut a sorry figure. His coat too short at the cuffs ; his country gloves and his waistcoat, that was too small for him, made him look prodigiously silly beside the young men in the balcony. Mme de Bargeton thought he looked positively pitiable. Châtelet, unobtrusively attentive, looked after her with a consideration that betrayed a deep passion ; Châtelet, elegant and at his ease like an actor back once more on the boards of his theatre, regained in two days all the ground that he had lost during the past six months. Although the vulgar will not have it that sentiments can change so suddenly, it is nevertheless a fact that two lovers often separate more quickly than they were drawn together. In Mme de Bargeton and Lucien a secret process of disillusionment was at work, and the cause was Paris. The poet's view of life had widened, just as society had taken on a new aspect for Louise. For both of them some small accident would be enough to sever the bonds that united them. Nor was that blow, so terrible for Lucien, long delayed.

Mme de Bargeton set the poet down at his hotel, and M. du Châtelet accompanied her home—to the immense annoyance of her wretched lover.

" I wonder what they are saying about me ? " he wondered as he climbed up to his dismal room.

" That poor boy is uncommonly dull," said Châtelet with a smile, as the door of the cab was closed again.

" It is always so with those who have a world of thoughts in their hearts, in their minds. Men who have so many things to express in the form of works of art, the product of years of reflection, profess a certain contempt for conversation, a commerce in which ideas are frittered away in small change," said the proud Nègrepelisse, who still had enough courage to defend Lucien, less for Lucien's sake than for her own.

" I willingly grant you that," replied the Baron, " but we live with people, not with their books. Listen, dear Naïs, I can see that there is still nothing between you and him, and I am delighted. If you do decide to add to your life an interest that it has not had hitherto, I beg you, do not let it be this so-called genius. What if you were mistaken! If, in a few days, after comparing him with men of real talent, with men who really are remarkable, whom you will meet, you realise, dear lovely mermaid, that you have carried to the shore on your dazzling white shoulders not a man with a lyre but a little ape with no manners, no idea how to behave, stupid and scheming, who may be an intellectual by the standard of l'Houmeau but who in Paris will turn out to be a very commonplace youth indeed! After all, there are volumes of verse published here every week, the least of which is worth all M. Chardon's poetry! I do beg of you, wait, and compare! Tomorrow—Friday—is the opera," he said, as the cab turned into the Rue Neuve-de-Luxembourg; "Mme d'Espard has the box of the first Gentleman of the Chamber, and no doubt she will take you with her. To see you in your glory, I shall go to Mme de Sérizy's box. They are playing *Les Danaïdes*."

"Good night," she said.

Next day Mme de Bargeton made an attempt to dress herself suitably for calling on her cousin, Mme d'Espard. It was a trifle cold, and in her old rag-bag from Angoulême she could find nothing better than a certain green velvet dress, trimmed fantastically enough. Lucien, for his part, felt that it was time to go and fetch his famous blue suit, for he had taken a great dislike to his tight jacket, and was anxious always to look well dressed, thinking that he might meet Mme d'Espard unexpectedly, or be sent for to visit her at short notice. He got into a cab in order to fetch his parcel immediately. Two hours later, he had spent three or four francs, which gave him cause to reflect on the financial proportions of Paris life. Having dressed to the best of his ability, he set out for the Rue Neuve-de-Luxembourg, where he encountered Gentil on the doorstep, accompanied by a footman in full feather.

"I was just on my way to you, sir. Madame has just given me this little note for you," said Gentil, who, accustomed to the more homely ways of the provinces, was innocent of the Parisian formulae of respect. The footman mistook the poet for a servant.

Lucien unsealed the note, in which he read that Mme de Bargeton was spending the day with the Marquise d'Espard and going to the opera in the evening; but she told Lucien to meet her there; her cousin had kindly allowed her to offer a place in her box to a young poet, for whom the Marquise was delighted to be able to procure that pleasure.

"Then she does love me! My fears were quite absurd!" Lucien though to himself. "She is going to introduce me to her cousin this evening."

He jumped for joy and thought only of how to pass pleasurably the time that separated him from that happy evening. He dashed off in the direction of the Tuileries with the idea of strolling there until it should be time to dine at Véry's. There was Lucien, bounding and prancing, walking on air, making his way to the Terrasse des Feullants, to watch the fashionable crowd, the lovely women with their admirers, men of fashion, walking in couples, arm in arm, greeting one another with glances as they passed. What a difference between this terrace and Beaulieu! The birds on this gilded perch were different indeed from those of Angoulême! Here was all the wealth of colour, the exotic plumage of the Indes or America, compared with the grey colours of the birds of Europe. Lucien passed two hours of torture in the Tuileries : a violent revulsion overcame him as he examined himself. In the first place, among all these elegant young men, he did not see a single cutaway coat. The only cutaway coats he saw were worn by a few shabby old outcasts, a pensioner from the Marais, or an underclerk. Having thus made the discovery that there is a difference between morning and evening dress, that poet of violent emotions, of subtle perceptions, realised the ugliness of his costume, whose cut was old-fashioned, whose blue was the wrong shade, whose collar was beyond everything, and whose tails, through long wear, overlapped each other ; the buttons were tarnished, there were fatal white lines along the creases. What was more, his waistcoat was too short, and of grotesquely provincial cut. In order to hide it, he hastily buttoned up his coat. And, finally, he noticed that only common people wore nankeen trousers. The better people all wore either exquisite fancy materials or immaculate white! What is more, all the trousers were worn with straps under the soles, while his scarcely came down to the heels of his boots from which the trouser-hems rolled back as if in violent antipathy. He was wearing a white cravat with embroidered ends ; his sister, who had seen similar ones worn by M. du Hautoy and M. de Chandour, had made haste to copy them for her brother. Nobody, except a few elderly business men, and one or two sedate civil-servants, seemed to wear white cravats in the morning ; but what was worse, there was a grocer's errand-boy with a basket on his head on the other side of the railings on the pavement of the Rue de Rivoli, about whose neck the young man from Angoulême noticed the two ends of a cravat, embroidered by the hands of some adored shop-girl. This sight stabbed Lucien's breast, wounding that organ, as yet uncertainly defined, that is the seat of our feelings, towards which, ever since feelings have existed, men have always carried their hands, in any excess of joy or sorrow. Do not say that this is a childish narration. For the rich, to be sure, who have never known sufferings of this kind, such feelings must seem unbelievably petty; but the sufferings of the unfortunate are as deserving of our attention as the crises that shake the lives of the great and privileged ones of the earth. And is not the pain as great in the one as in the other? Suffering dignifies all things. And we only have to change the terms: for a suit, more or less good, let us substitute a ribbon, a decoration, a title. Have not these seemingly small things been the torment of brilliant lives? And besides, the question of dress is enormously important to those who wish to seem to have what in fact they have not; for it is often the best means of obtaining it later on. Lucien broke out into a cold sweat as he reflected that he was to appear that very evening in these clothes before the Marquise d'Espard, a relative of a First Gentleman of the Bedchamber, before a woman at whose house were gathered the most distinguished men in every field, the élite of the élite.

"I look like the son of a chemist, like a shop assistant!" he said to himself, raging as he watched the elegant, the smart, the fashionable sons of the best families of the Faubourg Saint-Germain, who passed him. They all had a certain distinction of contour, a certain style, the same carriage, the same expression of face; and yet every one had selected a different setting to bring out his individuality to the best advantage. Each one had emphasised his good features by a kind of display that young men in Paris understand as well as women. Lucien had inherited from his mother that rare physical distinction that so dazzled him in these sons of the aristocracy. But the metal was still in the ore, not refined. His hair was badly cut. Instead of carrying himself well, with the aid of an elastic corset, he felt himself smothered inside a clumsy shirt-collar; and his limp cravat offered no support to his bowed and dejected head. What woman would have guessed at the elegance of his feet, encased in the cheap boots that he had brought with him from Angoulême? What young man would have envied him his graceful figure, disguised in that blue sack that he had until now mistaken for a coat? He noticed ravishing studs on shirts whose dazzling whiteness made his own look yellow in comparison! All these elegant gentlemen wore the most marvellous gloves, while his were only fit for a policeman. One toyed with an exquisitely mounted cane; another wore a shirt with delicious gold cuff-links. One, as he chatted with a woman, twisted an elegant riding crop. There were a few specks of mud on the full folds of his breeches, and from his clanking spurs and his tight-fitting jacket it was evident that he was about to remount one of the two horses held by a diminutive *tiger*. Another drew out of a waistcoat pocket a watch no thicker than a five-franc piece, and looked at the time with the air of a man who is either too early or too late for an appointment. As he noticed these charming trifles, whose very existence he had never even suspected, he became aware of a whole world of necessary superfluities, and he shuddered as he reflected that one must have enormous capital in order to play the part of a young man about town. The more he admired those young men, with their air of gay irresponsibility, the more he became conscious that he looked a stranger, like a man who has no idea where the road he is following leads to, who doesn't know his way to the Palais-Royal when he is just beside it, and who asks the way to the Louvre from a passer-by, who replies: "This is it." Lucien realised that a great gulf divided him from this world, and he asked himself how he was ever going to cross it, for he was determined to be like these graceful and elegant young men of Paris. All these sons of the aristocracy greeted divinely dressed, divinely lovely women; Lucien would gladly have gone to the scaffold like Countess Koenigsmark's page for a single kiss from one of them. In the background of his memory, Louise, beside these princesses, seemed like an old woman. He saw not a few of those women whose names will be remembered in the history of the nineteenth century, whose wit, whose beauty, and whose loves will be no less illustrious than are those of the queens of former days.

He noticed an exquisite young girl, Mademoiselle des Touches, the celebrated writer, better known under the name of Camille Maupin, no less remarkable for her great beauty than for her distinction of mind. Her name was whispered by the strollers and their ladies as she passed.

"Ah!" he thought to himself. "There is poetry." What was Mme de Bargeton beside that angel radiant with youth, hope, and the future, with her wonderful smile, her great dark eyes that seemed as deep as the sky, as brilliant as the sun? She was smiling and chatting with Mme Firmiani, one of the most charming women in Paris. A voice in him said: "Intellect is the lever with which a man can move the world." But another voice replied that money is the fulcrum of intellect. He could no longer bear to remain in the midst of his ruins, on the scene of his defeat, and he went in the direction of the Palais-Royal, having first asked the way, for he did not yet know the topography of his district. He went to Véry's and ordered (by way of initiating himself into the pleasures of Paris) a dinner that consoled him in his despair. A bottle of Bordeaux, Ostend oysters, a fish, a partridge, macaroni, and fruit, were all that his heart could desire. He gave himself up to this little enjoyment, reflecting that he would give Mme d'Espard proof of his superior intelligence that evening and make up for the absurdities of his deplorable clothes by a display of his intellectual riches. He was rudely awakened from his dreams by the bill, which left him the poorer by fifty of the francs with which he had meant to go so far in Paris. He could have lived for a month in Angoulême on what that dinner cost him. He therefore closed the door of that palace with respect, reflecting that he was never likely to set foot in it again. "Eve was right," he thought to himself as he went back under the stone arcade to fetch some more money. "Everything is much more expensive in Paris than in l'Houmeau."

As he went he gazed at the tailors' windows, and thought of the wonderful suits he had seen that morning.

"No," he exclaimed, "I cannot appear before Mme d'Espard looking like a scarecrow."

He sped like a deer to his hotel, climbed up to his room, extracted a hundred crowns, and made his way back to the Palais-Royal in order to dress himself from top to toe. He had taken note of the shoemakers, the shirtmakers, the tailors and the hairdressers of the Palais-Royal, where his future elegance was scattered in a dozen shops. At the first tailor's establishment he went into the tailor let him try on as many coats as he had a mind to, assuring him that they were all of the very latest fashion. Lucien left, the possessor of a green coat, white trousers, and a fancy waistcoat, all for the sum of two hundred francs. He next found a pair of very elegant ready-made boots. Then, having bought everything he needed, he sent for a hairdresser at his hotel, to which his various purchases were also delivered. At seven in the evening he hailed a cab and drove to the opera, his hair curled like a waxwork saint in a procession, satisfied with his waistcoat and his cravat, but feeling a little awkward in this sheath that he was wearing for the first time. He enquired for the box of the First Gentleman of the Bedchamber, as Mme de Bargeton had told him to do. At the sight of a man whose borrowed elegance suggesting nothing so much as the best man at a wedding, the man at the box-office asked to see his ticket.

" I have not got one."

" In that case you cannot go in," the man at the box-office replied dryly.

"But I am with Mme d'Espard's party," he said.

" That's no affair of ours," said the man, exchanging a scarcely perceptible smile with his colleagues in the box-office.

At this very moment a carriage drew up under the peristyle. A footman in a livery that Lucien did not recognise lowered the step and two ladies in evening dress descended from the brougham. Lucien did not want to expose himself to an impertinent request from the man in the box-office to get out of the way, so he stood aside to allow the two ladies to pass.

" But that is the Marquise d'Espard, whom you say you know, sir," said the box-office man ironically.

Lucien was all the more abashed, as Mme de Bargeton seemed not to recognise him in his new plumage ; but when he went up to her, she smiled at him and said :

" But this is splendid, come along! "

The men in the box-office became serious again. Lucien followed Mme de Bargeton, who introduced her Rubempré to her cousin as they went up the great staircase of the opera. The box of the First Gentleman is in one of the two angles at the end of the house, from which one can see and be seen from all sides. Lucien took his place behind Mme de Bargeton, on a chair, glad to be in the shadow.

" M. de Rubempré," said the Marquise in honeyed tones, " since this is your first visit to the opera, you must have a good view. Take this chair, sit in the front ; you have our permission."

Lucien obeyed, as the first act of the opera came to an end.

" You have made good use of your time," Louise whispered in his ear, in her first surprise at Lucien's transformation.

Louise was still the same. The proximity of a woman of fashion, of that Mme de Bargeton of Paris, the Marquise d'Espard, eclipsed her ; in contrast with the brilliant woman of Paris, her provincial imperfections were so clearly visible that Lucien, doubly enlightened by the spectacle of the dazzling audience of that ornate chamber, and of the great lady, saw at length poor Anaïs de Nègrepelisse as she really was, the woman that all Paris saw : a tall, thin, withered woman with a blotched complexion, red hair, angular, stiff and affected in her manner, precious in her tastes, provincial in her speech, and, above all, badly dressed! The fact is that the very creases of an old Paris dress still bear witness to good taste, they are expressive, and one can see what the dress must have been once. But an old country dress is meaningless, laughable. Both the dress and the woman lacked grace and freshness, both velvet and the complexion were worn. Lucien, ashamed to think that he had ever loved this cuttle-bone, made up his mind to make Louise's next access of virtue an excuse for leaving her. His excellent view of the house enabled him to see lorgnettes directed upon this most aristocratic of boxes. These elegant women must undoubtedly be scrutinising Mme de Bargeton, for they were all smiling as they chatted to one another. If Mme d'Espard realised, from these feminine smiles and gestures, the reason of their sarcasms, she remained entirely unruffled. In the first place, anybody would be bound to recognise in her companion the poor relation from the provinces, an affliction from which every family in Paris suffers. And in the second place, her cousin had raised the subject of dress, with some anxiety; she had reassured her, for she had seen that Anaïs, once she was properly dressed, would very quickly learn the ways of Paris. Mme de Bargeton may have lacked experience, but she had the native haughtiness of a well-born woman, and that indefinable quality that one may describe as *race*. The following Monday would see her revenge. And, besides, once people had realised that this lady was her cousin, the Marquise knew very well that they would think twice before criticising her, until they had looked again. Lucien could not foresee the change that was soon to be wrought in Louise's appearance by a scarf to soften the line of her neck, a well-cut dress, a different hairstyle, and Mme d'Espard's advice. As they had walked up the staircase, the Marquise had already whispered to her cousin not to dangle her handkerchief unfolded in her hand. Good and bad taste have so many fine shades of this kind, which an intelligent woman will quickly learn, and that some women can never learn. Mme de Bargeton, already full of good will, had more than enough good sense to recognise her shortcomings. Mme d'Espard, sure that her pupil would do her credit, was very willing to form her. So that there was a kind of pact between these two women, cemented by their mutual interests. Mme de Bargeton had promptly become a votary of the idol of the day, whose manners, brilliance, and social world she found enchanting, enthralling, fascinating. She had recognised in Mme d'Espard the secret power of the ambitious *grande dame*, and she had decided that her own success could be be achieved by making herself the satellite of this star; and therefore she did not disguise her admiration. The Marquise was pleased by this naïve conquest, and she decided to help this cousin, who was, she discovered, poor and helpless. Besides, it suited her very well to have a pupil, to found a school, and she asked nothing better than to have Mme de Bargeton as a sort of lady-in-waiting, a slave to sing her praises—a treasure that is as rare among the women of Paris as is a devoted critic in the world of letters. All the same, the symphony of curiosity became too obvious for the new arrival to fail to notice it, and Mme

"Since this is your first visit to the opera, you must have a good view"

d'Espard endeavoured politely to put her on the wrong scent about this stir in the house.

" If anyone comes to visit us," she said, "we shall perhaps discover to what we owe the honour of the interest that these ladies are taking in us."

" I strongly suspect that it is my old velvet dress and my Angoulême face that Parisian ladies find amusing," said Mme de Bargeton with a smile.

" No, it is not you; it is quite inexplicable to me," she replied, turning towards the poet, at whom she now looked for the first time, and it seemed to strike her that he was singularly dressed.

" There is M. du Châtelet! " Lucien exclaimed at this moment, pointing with his finger to Mme de Sérizy's box, that the renovated beau had just entered.

Seeing him point, Mme de Bargeton bit her lips for shame, for the Marquise could not cover up a look of astonishment, and a contemptuous smile, that clearly meant: " Where does this young man come from ? " Louise felt humiliated in her love—the most acute pain known to a Frenchwoman, and one that she will never forgive the lover who has occasioned it. In that world where little things have great importance, a gesture, a phrase, is enough to ruin a newcomer. The principal merit of beautiful manners and the tone of high society is that it presents a harmonious whole, in which everything is so subtly blended that nothing jars. Even those who do not, either from ignorance or because they are carried away by some impulse, observe the laws of this science will understand that a single false note is, as in music, a complete negation of the art itself, all of whose conditions must be observed down to the smallest details, or that art cannot even exist.

" Who is that gentleman ? " the Marquise asked, indicating Châtelet. "Have you met Mme de Sérizy already, then ? "

" Oh! So that is the famous Mme de Sérizy who has had so many love affairs and who is nevertheless received everywhere ? "

" It is quite incredible, my dear," said the Marquise, " explicable, but unexplained! The most powerful men are her friends, and why ?

Nobody dares to enquire into that mystery! So is that gentleman the lion of Angoulême ? "

" But the Baron du Châtelet," said Naïs, who, out of vanity, gave her adorer the particle whose validity she had called in question, " is a man who has been talked about a great deal. He is M. de Montriveau's colleague."

"Ah! " said the Marquise. " I can never hear that name without thinking of the poor Duchess of Langeais, who vanished like a star from the firmament—there is M. de Rastignac," she added, indicating a box, " and Mme de Nucingen, the wife of a merchant banker, business-man and broker, powerful in the city, a man who has imposed himself on Paris society by his wealth, and who is said to have very few scruples in his methods of augmenting it ; he goes to fantastic lengths to make people believe in his devotion to the Bourbons ; he has already tried to get an introduction to me. His wife evidently thinks that by taking Mme de Langeais's box she will acquire her charm, her wit, and her social success! The old fable of the jay who borrowed the peacock's feathers."

" How do M. and Mme de Rastignac, who, as we know, have an income of less than a thousand crowns, manage to support their son in Paris ? " Lucien enquired of Mme de Bargeton in his astonishment at that young man's elegant and expensive clothes.

" It is evident that you come from Angoulême," remarked the Marquise with some irony and without lowering her lorgnette.

Lucien missed the point of her remark ; he was entirely absorbed in what was going on in the boxes, where he could read the judgments that were being passed on Mme de Bargeton and the curiosity of which he was the object.

Louise, on her side, was deeply mortified by the small regard that the Marquise showed for Lucien's beauty.

" He cannot be as handsome as I imagined! " she thought to herself.

From that to thinking him also less brilliant was but a step. The curtain had fallen. Châtelet, who had come to pay a visit to the Duchess de Carigliano, whose box was next to that of Mme d'Espard, greeted Mme de Bargeton from it, and she replied with an inclination of the head. A woman of the world sees everything, and the Marquise noticed du Châtelet's beautiful manners. At the same moment, four persons of distinction entered Mme d'Espard's box one after the other.

The first was M. de Marsay, a man famous for the passions that he inspired and chiefly remarkable for his effeminate beauty, soft and delicate, but contradicted by his look which was calm, cruel, and unflinching as a tiger's : he was loved and feared. Lucien was handsome, too ; but his expression was so gentle, his blue eyes so limpid, that one might have thought that he lacked the vitality that many women find so attractive. Besides, nothing had so far brought out the poet's qualities, whereas de Marsay, with his ready wit, the certain knowledge of his own attractions, and the right clothes, eclipsed all rivals within his range. Judge, then, of the effect of his presence on Lucien, stiff, starched and wooden, and as green as his coat! De Marsay had acquired for himself the right to say the most outrageous things by the wit and charm of manner with which he delivered them. From the way in which the Marquise greeted him, Mme de Bargeton immediately realised that he was a person of importance.

The second was one of the Vandenesse brothers, the one who had caused a scandal with Lady Dudley, a quiet, intelligent, modest young man who owed his success to qualities quite the opposite of those by which de Marsay shone ; he had been warmly recommended to the Marquise by Mme de Martsauf, her cousin. The third was General de Montriveau, who had occasioned the fall of the Duchess de Langeais. The fourth was M. de Canalis, one of the most distinguished poets of the moment, a young man still in the early days of his glory ; he prided himself more on his breeding than on his talent, and paid court to Mme d'Espard as a screen for his passion for the Duchesse de Chaulieu. In spite of his charming affected manner, one could divine the immense ambition that was later to drive him into the stormy career of politics. His almost pretty features, his caressing manners, thinly disguised a profound egoism, and the perpetual calculations of a man still not secure in his career ; but his choice of Mme de Chaulieu (who was over forty) had already brought him interest at court, the applause of the Faubourg Saint-Germain, and abuse of the liberals, who called him a *poet of the sacristy*.

As she watched these four remarkable men, Mme de Bargeton understood why the Marquise paid so little attention to Lucien ; and when conversation became general, when each of these fine subtle minds came into play with sallies that contained more good sense, more profundity than Naïs had ever heard in a whole month of talk in the country ; and, above all, when the famous poet gave utterance in sonorous phrase, expressive of all the energy and attack of the day, and yet gilded with poetry, Louise understood what Châtelet had said to her the previous evening ; Lucien no longer counted. Everyone looked at the poor unknown with such cruel indifference, he was so much like a foreigner who does not speak the language, that the Marquise took pity on him.

" Allow me to introduce M. de Rubempré," she said to Canalis. " Your own position is so high in the world of letters that I know you will not refuse to befriend a beginner. M. de Rubempré has just arrived from Angoulême, and he will certainly need your influence with those people who discover genius. He has no enemies as yet who can make his fortune by attacking him. Don't you think it would be an orginal idea to obtain for him through friendship what you yourself owe to enmity ? "

The four gentlemen turned to look at Lucien as the Marquise spoke. Although he was only two feet away from the newcomer, de Marsay raised his eye-glass in order to see him; his glance went from Mme de Bargeton to Lucien, and he coupled them in an unspoken thought that they both found cruelly mortifying ; he examined them as if they had been animals of some strange species, and he smiled. That smile was like a sword-thrust to the provincial celebrity. Felix de Vandenesse assumed a charitable expression. Montriveau turned on Lucien a glance that searched him to the core.

" Madame," said M. de Canalis with a bow, " I shall obey you, notwithstanding the personal interest that we have in showing no favour to our rivals ; but you have accustomed us to miracles."

" Very well, give me the pleasure of coming to dinner at my house on Monday with M. de Rubempré, where you will be able to talk more easily than here, about literary matters; I shall endeavour to enlist some of the tyrants of literature and the celebrities who protect her, the author of *Ourika* and some of the more reputable of the young poets."

" Madame la Marquise," said de Marsay, " you patronise this gentleman for his talent, but I will take him up on account of his good looks ; I will give him advice that will make him the most popular dandy in Paris. After that, he can please himself about being a poet."

Mme de Bargeton thanked her cousin with a look full of gratitude.

" Since when were you jealous of men of genius ? " Montriveau enquired of de Marsay. " Happiness is the death of poets."

" Is that why you want to get married ? " retorted the dandy, addressing Canalis in order to see whether Mme d'Espard would show any emotion at that remark.

Canalis shrugged his shoulders, and Mme d'Espard (Mme de Chaulieu's niece) laughed.

Lucien, who in his clothes felt like an Egyptian mummy in its sheath, to his great shame could think of nothing to say. Finally he said to the Marquise in his gentle voice :

" After your kindness, Madame, I must have no failures."

Châtelet entered at this moment and took advantage of the chance to be introduced to the Marquis by Montriveau, who was one of the lions of Paris. He greeted Mme de Barton, and begged Mme d'Espard to pardon him for the liberty he had taken in thus invading her box : he had been parted for so long from his travelling companion! He and Montriveau now beheld each other for the first time since they had parted in the middle of the desert!

" Part in the desert and meet again at the opera! " exclaimed Lucien.

" A theatrical meeting, to be sure! " said Canalis.

Montriveau introduced Baron du Châtelet to the Marquise, and the Marquise received the one-time ex-personal secretary who had obeyed the commands of the Imperial Princess the more warmly because she had already seen him well received in three boxes; because Mme de Sérizy only knew the right people; and because he had been Montriveau's companion. This third qualification had so much weight that Mme de Bargeton did not fail to remark in the tone of voice, in the looks and in the behaviour of the four eminent personages, that they accepted Châtelet as one of themselves without question. Châtelet's sultanesque behaviour in the provinces was suddenly explained to Naïs. Finally Châtelet noticed Lucien, and gave him one of those dry little nods by which a man indicates the small regard in which he holds another man and that indicates to men of the world the insignificant position that he occupies in the social scale. He accompanied his greeting with a sardonic look that meant: "By what extraordinary chance do you come to be here?" Châtelet was perfectly understood, for de Marsay leaned over to Montriveau in order to whisper, audibly enough for the Baron to hear:

"Do ask him who is this extraordinary young man who looks like a tailor's dummy?"

Châtelet whispered something in his comrade's ear, under the cover of renewing his acquaintance, and no doubt he cut his rival to pieces. Astonished by the ready wit, by the adroitness with which these gentlemen formulated their replies, Lucien was stunned by the flash of epigram and repartee, by their unhesitating responses, their easy manners. The wealth that had overwhelmed him that morning in things he now discovered in ideas. He asked himself by what mysterious operation of the mind these men found such brilliant things to say on the spur of the moment, replies that he would never have thought of except after hours of reflection. Not only were these five men of the world at ease in their conversation, but in their clothes as well; these looked neither new nor old, nothing in them was striking, and yet everything attracted the eye. Their style of today was that of yesterday, would be that of tomorrow. Lucien divined that he looked like a man wearing evening dress for the first time in his life.

"My dear," said de Marsay to Félix de Vandenesse, "that

young Rastignac is rising like a kite! There he is with the Marquise de Listomère! He is coming on, he is quizzing us! He knows you, of course," added the dandy, addressing Lucien, but without looking at him.

"It would be surprising," said Mme de Bargeton, "if he had not heard the name of a great man of whom we are all proud. His sister heard M. de Rubempré read us some very beautiful poetry not long ago."

Félix de Vandenesse and de Marsay took their leave of the Marquise and went off to pay their respects to Mme de Listomère, Vandenesse's sister. The second act was about to begin, and everyone went away, leaving Mme d'Espard, her cousin, and Lucien alone in the box. Some went off to explain Mme de Bargeton to the women who were so greatly intrigued by her presence, others to announce the arrival of the poet, and to laugh at his clothes. Canalis returned to the Duchess de Chaulieu's box and did not reappear. Lucien was glad of the respite afforded by the second act. All Mme de Bargeton's fears on Lucien's account were increased by the attention that her cousin had shown to the Baron du Châtelet, so different from the patronising civility that she accorded to Lucien. During the second act Mme de Listomère's box was full, and a conversation was going on, whose subject appeared to be Mme de Bargeton and Lucien. It was plain that young de Rastignac was entertaining the party; it was he who was setting off the peals of that Parisian laughter that needs fresh fuel every day, quickly exhausts every new topic and makes anything stale and threadbare in a moment. Mme d'Espard was troubled; she knew that those whom it will wound never remain long in ignorance of what is said about them, and she waited for the end of the second act.

When there is a revulsion of the feelings, like that which was taking place in Lucien and in Mme de Bargeton, strange things happen in a very short time: moral revolutions take place according to laws that operate very rapidly. Louise had present in her memory the wise and politic words that Châtelet had spoken on the subject of Lucien on the way back from the Vaudeville. Every phrase was prophetic, and Lucien seemed to have set himself the task of fulfilling all of them. As his illusions about Mme de Bargeton faded, as hers about himself were also fading, the unhappy boy, whose fate bears a certain resemblance to that of Rousseau, followed the example of his predecessor; under the spell of Mme d'Espard, he fell in love with her on the spot. Young men, or men who remember the emotions of their youth, will realise that this passion was only to be expected and very natural. With her elegant manners, her charming accent, her refined voice, that fragile woman, so nobly born, so highly placed, so greatly envied—this queen seemed to the poet all that Mme de Bargeton had seemed to him in Angoulême. The instability of his character impelled him forthwith to covet her high protection; the surest way to this was to possess the woman, and then he would have everything! He had succeeded in Angoulême; why should he not succeed in Paris? Involuntarily, and in spite of all the magic of the opera, new to him as it was, his eyes were drawn towards this Célimène, and returned to her again and again; and the more he looked at her the more he desired to look at her! Mme de Bargeton observed one of those eager looks, and perceived that he was more interested in the Marquise than in the stage. She would gladly have resigned herself to being forgotten for the Fifty Daughters of Danaus; but when another glance, yet more ambitious, more ardent, revealed to her what was taking place in Lucien's heart, she became jealous, but not so much for the future as for the past.

"He has never looked at me like that," she thought. "Good heavens, how right Châtelet was!"

She now saw that her love had been a mistake. When a woman comes to the point of repenting of her weaknesses she passes a sponge, as it were, over her life, in order to efface everything. Although each of these glances of Lucien increased her rage, she remained calm. De Marsay returned during the interval, bringing with him M. de Listomère. This serious personage, and the young wit, soon informed the haughty Marquise that the best man in his Sunday suit whom she had had the misfortune to admit to her box had no more right to the name of M. de Rubempré than a Jew has a baptismal name. Lucien was the son of a chemist named Chardon. M. de Rastignac, who knew all about Angoulême affairs, had already sent two boxes into fits of laughter at the expense of the desiccated mummy that the Marquise called her cousin, and at the precautions taken by that lady in having with her a chemist, no doubt in order to sustain her artificial life by means of drugs. Now de Marsay recounted a selection from the thousand witticisms that Parisians can compose in an instant and that are forgotten as soon as spoken; but behind all of them was Châtelet, the real author of this Carthaginian treachery.

"My dear," said Mme d'Espard behind her fan to Mme de Bargeton, "for heaven's sake tell me, is your protégé really M. de Rubempré?"

"He has taken his mother's name," said Naïs, embarrassed.

"But what is his father's name?"

"Chardon."

"And what was this Chardon?"

"He was a chemist."

"I was quite sure, my dear, that the whole of Paris could not be laughing at a woman whom I have taken under my protection. I never thought to see these wits coming in such high glee because I have a chemist's son in my box; if you will follow my advice, we will both leave, and at once."

Mme d'Espard's expression became not a little insulting, without Lucien being able to divine the cause that had given rise to this change of expression. He thought that his waistcoat must be in bad taste, which it was. He realised, with secret bitterness, that he would have to get himself dressed by a really good tailor, and he made up his mind to go the very next day to the best tailor in Paris, so that on the following Monday he would be able to hold his own with the men whom he would meet at Mme d'Espard's house. While he was lost in these reflections, his eyes were at the same time following the third act, and never left the stage. As he watched the splendours of that matchless spectacle, he gave himself up to dreaming about Mme d'Espard. He was in despair at that sudden coldness, in such striking contrast with the imagined ardour with which he was embarking upon this new love, regardless of the immense difficulties that he foresaw, and which he vowed to overcome. He emerged from his reverie to look again at his new idol; but on turning his head, he saw that he was alone; he had heard a slight sound—the door had closed, as Mme d'Espard led away her cousin. Lucien was utterly astonished by this abrupt desertion, but he did not think about it for long, for the very good reason that he found it inexplicable.

When the two ladies were seated in their carriage, that was by now rolling along the Rue de Richelieu towards the Faubourg-Saint-Honoré, the Marquise began, in a voice of veiled annoyance:

"My dear child, what were you thinking of? You must wait until the son of a chemist is really a celebrity before you take him up. The Duchess de Chaulieu still does not acknowledge Canalis, and he is famous, and a gentleman. This boy is neither your son nor your lover, I suppose?" said that haughty woman, directing on her cousin a glance of penetrating curiosity.

"How fortunate for me that I have kept that little fellow at a distance, and given him nothing!" Mme de Bargeton reflected.

"Good," the Marquise continued—for she took the expression in her cousin's eyes for a reply; "leave it at that, I do beg of you. To assume an illustrious name!—But society will punish him for his audacity. I grant you it is his mother's name; but consider for a moment, my dear, only the King has the right to confer, by a special ordinance, the name of Rubempré on the son of a daughter of that family; if she made a misalliance, it would be an enormous favour, and it would cost an immense sum to obtain it, or services rendered, or the most powerful influence. That get-up of a shop assistant in his Sunday best proves that the boy is neither rich nor a gentleman. He has a beautiful face, but he looks very foolish to me; he does not know how to behave or what to say; in fact, he is not well-bred. How did you come to take him up?"

Mme de Bargeton, renouncing Lucien as Lucien had already renounced her, in his own mind, was overcome by a sudden fear lest her cousin should discover the truth about her journey.

"My dear cousin, I am so very sorry to have compromised you."

" People do not compromise me," replied Mme d'Espard with a smile ; " I am thinking only of you."

" But you have invited him to dine with you on Monday."

" I shall be indisposed," replied the Marquise instantly. " You can tell him so, and I shall say that he is to be shown the door, under either name."

Lucien hit upon the idea of walking in the foyer during the interval, noticing that this was where everyone went. But none of the people who had visited Mme d'Espard's box greeted him, or paid him the slightest attention, which seemed quite extraordinary to the provincial poet. Châtelet, moreover, to whom he tried to attach himself, watched him out of the corner of his eye and avoided him. Having convinced himself, as he watched the throng of men who were strolling in the foyer, that his clothes were impossible, Lucien ensconced himself in the corner of the box, and stayed there for the rest of the performance, absorbed now by the ornate spectacle of the fifth act of the ballet, the famous *Inferno* scene, now by the great opera house itself, his eyes travelling from box to box, now by his own reflections; the sight of Paris society had stirred him to the depths.

" This is my kingdom! " he thought to himself. " This is the world that I must conquer! "

He walked back to his hotel, thinking over all that had been said by the distinguished men who had come to pay their court to Mme d'Espard ; their manners, their expressions, the way they entered and took their leave—all these details his memory reproduced with extraordinary fidelity. At noon the following day his first thought was to pay a visit to Staub, the best tailor of the day. He persuaded him, by dint of pleading, and ready cash, to have his clothes ready for the famous Monday. Staub went so far as to give his word that he should have an exquisite coat, waistcoat and trousers for the great day. Lucien ordered shirts and handkerchiefs, in fact a little outfit, at a shirt-makers, and was measured for shoes by a famous shoe-maker. He purchased an elegant stick at Verdier's, gloves and studs at Madame Irlande's ; in short, he did his best to come up to the standard set by the dandies. When he had satisfied all his fancies, he went to the Rue Neuve-de-Luxembourg, to find that Louise was not at home.

" She is dining with Madame la Marquise d'Espard, and will not be in until late," Albertine told him.

Lucien dined at a cheap restaurant near the Palais-Royal and went to bed early. On Sunday he called on Louise at about eleven ; she was not yet dressed. At two, he returned.

" Madame cannot see anybody yet," Albertine told him, " but she has left this note for you."

" Cannot see anybody ? " Lucien repeated. " But I am not just anybody."

" I don't know, I'm sure," said Albertine very rudely.

Lucien was less surprised at Albertine's retort than at receiving a letter from Mme de Bargeton ; he took the letter and in the road read these depressing lines :

" Mme d'Espard is indisposed, and she will not be able to see you on Monday ; I am a little unwell myself, but even so I shall have to dress presently to go and keep her company. I am so sorry about this little disappointment, but your talent reassures me, and you will succeed without charlatanism."

"—And no signature! " Lucien said to himself ; he found himself in the Tuileries without realising where he had been walking.

The gift of second sight, that all men of talent possess, suggested to Lucien that this cold note was the precursor of catastrophe. He walked on, lost in thought, gazing at the monuments in the Place Louis XV. It was a fine afternoon. A stream of fine carriages passed him as he made his way towards the Champs-Elysées. He moved with the crowd of strollers and saw the three or four thousand carriages that stream into that great avenue on a Sunday, converting it into a kind of Longchamp. Stunned by the luxury of the horses, the clothes, and the liveries, he walked on and on, until he reached the still unfinished Arc de Triomphe. What were his thoughts when, returning, he saw coming towards him Mme d'Espard and Mme de Bargeton in a beautifully appointed calèche, behind which waved the plumes of a footman whose green livery embroidered with gold was unmistakable? The stream of traffic was held up for a moment, and Lucien was able to see Louise, transformed out of all recognition. The shades of her clothes were selected in such a way as to set off her colouring; her dress was adorable; her hair, softly waved, became her; and her hat, in exquisite taste, was striking even beside Mme d'Espard, one of the leaders of fashion. There is an indefinable art in wearing a hat: wear it too far back, and it gives you a bold expression; too far forward, it has a sinister air; too far to the side, it gives you a jaunty look; but well-dressed women can put a nat on just as they like, and yet it will always look right. Mme de Bargeton had instantly mastered that curious problem. A charming belt emphasised her slim waist. She had adopted her cousin's gestures and mannerisms. Seated beside her, she toyed with an elegant scent-bottle which hung from one of the fingers of her right hand by a little chain, so as to display her slender, beautifully gloved hand without appearing to do so deliberately. In short, she had modelled herself on Mme d'Espard, but without apeing her; she was worthy to be the cousin of the Marquise, who seemed to be well pleased with her pupil. The pedestrians on the side-walk gazed at the shining carriage whose panels were adorned with the arms of d'Espards and the Blamont-Chauvrys. Lucien was astonished at the number of people who greeted the two cousins; he did not realise that the whole of Paris (which consists of perhaps twenty *salons*) already knew of the relationship between Mme de Bargeton and Mme d'Espard. A group of young men on horseback —Lucien noticed de Marsay and Rastignac among them—rode up alongside the calèche, to accompany the two ladies to the Bois. Lucien could plainly see from their expressions that the two gallants were complimenting Mme de Bargeton on her metamorphosis. Mme d'Espard was radiant with health and charm: so her indisposition had been only a pretext for not receiving Lucien, for there was nothing said about any other day! The poet, furious, approached the calèche, walked slowly, and, when he was in full view of the two ladies, he bowed. Mme de Bargeton pretended not to see him; the Marquise raised her lorgnette and deliberately cut him.

A group of young men on horseback rode up alongside the calèche

It was one thing to be despised by the county families of Angoulême, quite another by the aristocracy of Paris; by going out of their way to insult Lucien, the booby-squires had admitted his importance and treated him as a man; but for Mme d'Espard he simply did not exist. This was not a sentence, it was a refusal of justice. A deadly chill seized the poor poet when he saw that de Marsay was eyeing him through his glass; this lion of Paris let his eyeglass drop in such a way that to Lucien it suggested the blade of the guillotine. The carriage drove on.

Rage, the desire for vengeance, took possession of the scorned man. If Mme de Bargeton had been in his power he would gladly have cut her throat; he would have liked to be Fouquier-Tinville if only to enjoy the exquisite pleasure of sending Mme d'Espard to the scaffold; he would have liked to be able to subject de Marsay to one of those refined forms of torture that savages invent. He saw Canalis riding past, elegant, as befitted the most suave of poets, bowing to all the prettiest women.

"My God, I must have money at all costs!" Lucien said to himself. "Money is the only power that brings the world to its knees." ("No!" cried his conscience. "Not money but fame, and fame means work! Work! That is what David said.") "Oh, God, what am I doing here? But I will triumph! I will ride along this avenue in a calèche with a footman! I will possess a Marquise d'Espard!" And flinging out these words of rage, he went to dine at Hurbains for forty sous.

Next morning at nine o'clock he set out to call on Louise, with the intention of reproaching her for her cruelty. Mme de Bargeton was not at home to him, and, what was worse, the porter would not allow him to go upstairs; so he waited in the road, watching her house, until noon. At noon Châtelet came out of Mme de Bargeton's door, saw the poet out of the tail of his eye, and avoided him. Lucien, cut to the quick, pursued his rival; Châtelet, realising that he was cornered, turned and bowed, evidently intending to shake him off by this civility.

"I beg you, sir," Lucien exclaimed, "give me just one moment; there is something I must say to you. You have been a friend to me, and in the name of the friendship you have shown me I must ask you to do me a very small favour. You have just come from Mme de Bargeton—can you explain to me the reason why I have fallen into disgrace with her and with Mme d'Espard ? "

" M. Chardon," Châtelet replied with false affability, " do you know why these ladies left the opera ? "

" No," said the poor poet.

" Well, it was M. de Rastignac who spoke against you from the start. That young dandy, when he was questioned about you, simply said that your name was Chardon and not de Rubempré ; that your mother is a monthly nurse ; that your father, when he was alive, was the chemist at l'Houmeau, a suburb of Angoulême ; that your sister is a charming girl who launders shirts to perfection, and that she has just married a printer of Angoulême called Séchard. Such is the world! You no sooner show yourself but you are talked about! M. de Marsay came to laugh about you with Mme d'Espard, and the two ladies left at once, realising that your presence compromised them. Do not try to see either of them. Mme de Bargeton would not be received by her cousin if she were to continue to see you. You have genius ; try to have your revenge. The world despises you—despise the world. Take refuge in some attic and write masterpieces, make yourself powerful in any way you will, and you will soon see the world at your feet ; then for every wound that you have received you can give back a wound in return. The more friendship Mme de Bargeton has shown you, the more anxious she will be not to see you. That is the way with women. But there is no question at present of regaining Naïs's friendship—the question now is not to incur her enmity, and I don't mind giving you a piece of advice. She has written letters to you : return them all to her. That is the gentlemanly thing to do and she will appreciate it. Then, later on, if you have occasion to ask her to do you a service, she will not be hostile. For my part, I have such a high opinion of your future that I have defended you everywhere ; and if I can be of any assistance to you here, you will always find me at your service."

Lucien was so dejected, so white-faced and woebegone that he did not return the bow of cold civility with which the old beau, rejuvenated by the air of Paris, took leave of him.

He returned to his hotel, where he found Staub in person—he had come, not so much to try on the clothes, which he did, as to discover from the hostess at the Gaillard-Bois the financial position of his unknown customer. Lucien had arrived by post, Mme de Bargeton had brought him back from the Vaudeville on the previous Tuesday in her carriage. These reports were satisfactory. Staub addressed Lucien as " Monsieur le Comte " and pointed out to him the skill with which he had brought out the elegant lines of his figure.

" A young man in these clothes," he remarked, " has only to go and walk in the Tuileries and he will have married an English heiress within a fortnight."

Lucien was a little cheered by the German tailor's joke, by the perfection of his new clothes, the fineness of the cloth, and his own handsome figure when he surveyed himself in the mirror. He told himself vaguely that Paris is a city of luck, and for the moment these trifles made him feel that luck was on his side. Had he not a volume of poems and the manuscript of a magnificent novel, *An Archer of Charles IX*?

He had faith in his destiny. Staub promised him the coat and the rest of the clothes for the following day. Next day the shoemaker, the shirt-maker, and the tailor all returned, armed with their bills ; and Lucien, who had not mastered the art of getting rid of creditors, Lucien, still under the spell of provincial customs—paid them ; but having done so, only three hundred and sixty francs remained of the two thousand that he had brought with him to Paris ; and he had only been there a week! All the same, he dressed and went for a stroll on the Terrasse des Feullants. There he had his revenge. He was so well-dressed, so graceful, so handsome, that quite a number of women looked at him, and two or three were so taken with his good looks that they turned round. Lucien studied the carriage and deportment of the young men and took a lesson in good manners, as he thought about his three hundred and sixty francs.

That evening, alone in his room, it occurred to him that he had better discover how he stood with the Gaillard-Bois, where he always had the simplest breakfast, thinking to economise in this way. He asked for his account, as if he intended to leave, and he discovered that he owed a hundred francs. Next day he set off to the Latin Quarter that David had recommended to him for its cheapness. After a long search, he at last discovered a miserable furnished house at the corner of the Rue de Cluny, near the Sorbonne, where there was a room at a price that he could afford to pay. He settled his account at the Gaillard-Bois immediately and moved to the Rue de Cluny that very day. His move cost him only a cab-fare.

Having taken possession of his poor room, he made a packet of all Mme de Bargeton's letters and laid them on the table; before writing to her, he thought over the events of that disastrous week. He did not reflect that he himself, in his ignorance of what Paris would do for his Louise, had been the first to go back on his love; he did not think about his mistakes, but only about his present situation; he blamed Mme de Bargeton. Instead of her lighting his way, she had ruined him. He worked himself up into a rage of pride and indignation and proceeded to write the following letter:

" What would you say, Madame, of a woman who takes a fancy to a poor, timid child, full of that noble faith that men later call illusions, and who used all her feminine graces, all her arts, and a fine display of maternal love, to lead that child away? The rosy promises, the card-houses that so enchanted him, cost her nothing; she leads him away, she takes possession of him, now scolding him for his want of confidence, now flattering him; when the child finally leaves his family, and follows her blindly, she leads him to the shore of a vast sea, persuades him, with a smile, to set foot in a frail skiff, and sends him forth alone, without succour, to face the storm; then, from the rock where she remains, she laughs, and wishes him good luck. You are that woman, I am that child.

"That child has in his possession a keepsake, that might betray the crimes of your favour, and the favour of your desertion. Perhaps you would have cause to blush if you were ever to encounter that child, striving with the waves, if you were to remember that once you had held him in your arms. When you read this letter, that keepsake will be in your possession. You are free to forget everything. After those fair hopes that your finger pointed out to me in the sky, I now perceive the realities of poverty, in the gutters of Paris. While you go, brilliant and adored, across the stage of that great world on whose threshold you deserted me, I shall be shivering in the wretched garret whither you have discarded me. But perhaps some remorse may seize upon you in the midst of your round of parties and pleasures, perhaps you will think of the child whom you have plunged into the abyss. Think of him, Madame, without remorse! From the depths of his misery, that child proffers you the one thing that remains to him—his forgiveness, in a last look. Yes, indeed, thanks to you, I have nothing left in the world. Nothing?—did not that suffice for the creation of the world? Genius is godlike—I begin by emulating the divine forgiveness, but whether I possess the divine creative powers, I still do not know. You need only tremble if I go astray—for you will be responsible for my errors. Alas! I regret for your sake that you will no longer have any share in the glory to which I aspire, whither work shall lead me."

After writing this letter, firm, but full of that sombre dignity that the artist of twenty-one is inclined rather to overdo, Lucien's thoughts turned towards his family: he thought of the rooms that David had decorated so prettily for him, sacrificing part of his own savings to do so; he remembered vividly the tranquil happiness, the modest and humble joys that he had known; images of his mother, his sister, and David rose before his mind; he remembered afresh the tears that they had shed at his departure, and alone in Paris, without friends, with no one to whom he could turn, he, too, wept.

A few days later, Lucien wrote to his sister:

" My dear Eve,

" It is the sad privilege of sisters to partake in more troubles than joys if they share in the experiences of brothers dedicated to the arts, and I am beginning to fear that I shall be a great burden to you. Indeed have I not already abused your goodness, all of you who have sacrificed so much for my sake? Thoughts of the old days, happy memories of home, help me to bear the solitude of my present lot. My thoughts cross the distance between us with the swiftness of an eagle returning to its eyrie, to feel myself in the midst of true affection—for I have tasted the first miseries, the first deceptions, of the world of Paris! Were there sparks in your candle? Did a coal fall out of the fire? Have your ears been burning? Did mother say: 'Lucien is thinking of us'? and did David reply: 'He is battling with difficulties, and people'? Eve, my dear, I am writing this letter to you in confidence. You are the only person in the world to whom I can tell all the good and the bad that has happened to me, and I blush equally for both, because good here is as rare as evil ought to be. You will understand a great deal from a few words when I tell you that Mme de Bargeton was ashamed of me, disowned me, would not see me, and sent me away within nine days of my arrival. She saw me and looked the other way, and in order to follow her in the world into which she was going to introduce me, I have spent seventeen hundred of the two thousand francs I brought from Angoulême, the money raised with such difficulty! 'On what?' you will ask. My poor dear sister, Paris is a bottomless gulf: you can get a meal for eighteen sous, and yet the simplest dinner at a smart restaurant costs fifty francs; there are waistcoats for four francs and trousers for forty sous; but a fashionable tailor will never charge you less than a hundred francs. It costs a sou to cross the gutters in the street when it rains; and to go the shortest distance in a cab costs thirty-two sous. I lived at first in an expensive district, but my present address is Hotel de Cluny, Rue de Cluny, in one of the poorest and darkest side-streets in Paris, shut in between three old churches and the old buildings of the Sorbonne. I am living in a furnished room on the fourth floor, it is very dirty and has practically no furniture, and even so I am paying fifteen francs a month. I breakfast on a roll (two sous) and milk (one sou), but I dine extremely well at a restaurant called Flicoteaux, in the Place de la Sorbonne itself. Until the winter, I shall not need to spend more than sixty francs a month for everything, less I hope. So that my two hundred and forty francs will be enough for the first four months. By that time I shall no doubt have sold *An Archer of Charles IX* and *Marguerites*. So don't worry about me. The present may be cold, bare, and shabby, but the future is blue, rich, and splendid. Nearly all great men have gone through the same vicissitudes that depress, but do not overwhelm me. Plautus, the great comic poet, was a miller's son. Machiavelli wrote *The Prince* in the evenings, and worked as a labourer during the day. And the great Cervantes himself, who lost an arm at the battle of Lepanto, helping to win that famous victory, was called a 'shabby old sleeve' by the scribblers of his day; there was an interval of ten years between the first and second part of his sublime *Don Quixote* because he could not find a publisher. It is not so bad as that nowadays. Poverty and neglect only affect unknown talents; but once a writer is known, he becomes rich, and I shall be rich. And besides, I spend my whole time thinking—I spend half my days at the library of Sainte-Geneviève, where I am trying to make up for the shortcomings in my education, without which I shall get nowhere. So today I am feeling almost happy. In a few days I have settled down very cheerfully to my new life. I am free all day to devote myself to the work I love; the necessities of my life are assured; I think a great deal, I study, and I do not see in what way I can be hurt, since I have renounced the world, where my vanity would have been continually open to injury. The great men of any period are destined to live apart. They are like forest birds—they sing, all nature falls under the spell of their charm, but nobody ever sees them. That is what I shall do, if I am able to carry out my ambitions. I have no regrets on account of Mme de Bargeton. A woman who can behave as she did is not worth remembering. I do not regret leaving Angoulême either. She was right to fling me into the sea of Paris and leave me to my own devices. This is the place for writers, and thinkers, and poets. This is the only soil in which fame can flourish, and I know what fine harvests are being reaped these days. Only here can writers find, in the museums and exhibitions, the living works of the genius of the past, that fire and inspire the imagination. Only here are there great libraries, always open, offering to the mind inspiration and nourishment. In Paris, in fact, there is in the air, in the smallest details, a spirit that breathes and expresses itself in literary creations. One learns more in conversation in a café, or at the theatre, than in ten years in the provinces. Here, it really is true to say that everything is pageantry, one learns, one compares. Everything is either extremely cheap or extremely dear, that is Paris; every bee finds its own cell, every mind can find the nourishment that it needs. I may be suffering for the time being, but I have no regrets. On the contrary, a fair future is unfolding, its joy already cheers my heart, saddened though it is for the moment. Goodbye, my dearest sister. Don't expect me to write regularly—it is one of the peculiarities of Paris that one does not notice the passage of time. It is terrifying how the days fly past. My love to Mother, David, and yourself—you are more to me than ever."

The name of Flicoteaux is inscribed on many memories. There were few students living in the Latin Quarter during the first twelve years of the Restoration who did not frequent that temple sacred to hunger and lack of money. A three-course dinner cost eighteen sous, including a quarter-bottle of wine or a bottle of beer, and twenty-two sous with a bottle of wine. That friend of the young would doubtless have made a fortune but for an item in his menu, that rival establishments printed in large type: BREAD AT DISCRETION—that is to say, " at indiscretion ". Flicoteaux has been the nursing-father of many a famous name. And indeed the heart of more than one great man ought to feel a glow of pleasure from a thousand nameless memories at the sight of the small leaded panes that look on to the Place de la Sorbonne and the Rue Neuve-de-Richelieu. Flicoteau II or III still kept then, until the July Revolution, respecting their dingy glass, their air of old-fashioned respectability, disdaining the charlatanry of shop fronts, a kind of advertisement by which most restaurants please the eye at the expense of the stomach. Instead of all the trussed game, never destined to be cooked, instead of those immense fish that have given rise to the music-hall joke " I have just seen a fine carp, I expect I shall buy it today week " ; instead of those greens (long past their salad-days), deceptively displayed to lure young corporals and their girls, at Flicoteaux the eye of the customer was delighted by great well-worn salad bowls, or dishes of stewed prunes, whose presence assured him that the word *dessert*—used far too loosely on so many menus—was not intended to mislead. Six-pound loaves, cut in four, were reassuring as to the meaning of BREAD AT DISCRETION. Such was the luxury of an establishment that Molière would no doubt have immortalised in an epigram, had it existed in his day, so apt is its name. Flicoteaux still exists—it will continue to do so as long as students have a mind to remain alive. You get enough to eat there—neither more nor less ; but you eat as you work, eating is a task to be performed, cheerfully or gloomily as the case may be. That famous establishment consisted in those days of two rooms, at right angles to each other, long, low and narrow, one looking on to the Place de la Sorbonne, the other on the Rue Neuve-de-Richelieu ; both are furnished with tables that must have come from the refectory of some abbey, for there was something monastic in their length ; the places were laid ready, with the serviettes of regular customers in numbered shiny tin serviette-rings. Flicoteau I only changed the serviettes on Sundays ; but Flicoteau II was said to change them twice a week, because his empire was threatened by competitors.

This restaurant is no festive place where one looks for elegance and pleasure, but a work-shop, provided with its proper tools ; everybody leaves as soon as he has finished. The service is rapid. Waiters come and go without dawdling ; they are understaffed and always busy. The dishes are not very varied. There is the everlasting potato ; when there is not a single potato left in Ireland, when potatoes have vanished from the rest of the world, you will still find them at Flicoteaux. Any day in the past thirty years you might have seen them there, their pale yellow (the colour Titian was so fond of) sprinkled with chopped verdure. They enjoy a privilege that all women covet

That temple sacred to hunger and lack of money

—for in 1840 they are still exactly as they were in 1814. Mutton cutlets and beefsteaks are what ptarmigan or sturgeon are at Vérys—dishes not on the menu that you have to order in the morning. The meat of the cow there prevails ; and the young of the the bovine species abound in many ingenious disguises. When whiting and mackerel are plentiful on our coast, they are abundant also at Flicoteaux. There, everything reflects the vicissitudes of French agriculture, and the caprices of the harvest. There one learns many things of which the rich, the idle, those people who pay no attention to the course of nature, have no suspicion. The student, shut away in the Latin Quarter, has nevertheless the most exact knowledge of the seasons ; he knows when there has been a bumper crop of beans or green peas, when the market is glutted with cabbages, when lettuces are plentiful, when the beetroot crop has failed. An old libel, that was revived at about the time of Lucien's appearance there, connected the sudden appearance of beef-steaks with mortality among horses.

Few restaurants in Paris are so well worth seeing. There, you see youth and hope on all sides, poverty cheerfully endured, although, to be sure, there are plenty of earnest and grave faces, and some gloomy and anxious ones. Very little attention is paid to dress ; but occasionally regular customers will appear well dressed. Everybody knows what this unusual occurrence signifies ; a meeting with a mistress, a visit to a theatre, or a party in higher spheres. It is said that friendships have been formed there between students who have since become famous, as will be seen in the course of this narrative. But for all that, except for young men from the same town who form little groups at the end of a table, the diners as a rule preserve a seriousness that is not often relaxed ; perhaps this gravity is due to the catholicity of the wine, that does not encourage expansiveness. Those who have frequented Flicoteaux can all remember gloomy, mysterious figures, enveloped in the shadows of the chilliest penury, who have managed to dine there for a year or two, and who have disappeared, without the most regular frequenters having the slightest clue to the subsequent history of these spectres of Paris. Friendships initiated at Flicoteaux are usually sealed in the neighbouring cafés over the fumes of heady punch, or by the warmth of a small cup of coffee with a lashing of something stronger.

In the early days of his residence at the Hotel de Cluny, Lucien, like all novices, was timid and regular in his habits. After the sad experience of fashionable life that had absorbed nearly all his capital, he threw himself into work with the kind of pristine enthusiasm that is so quickly discouraged by difficulties, or frittered away by the amusements that Paris offers to rich and poor alike; an enthusiasm which, if it is to succeed, must be reinforced by the fierce energy of real talent or the grim determination of ambition.

Lucien used to drop into Flicoteaux at about half-past four, for he had observed the advantages of going there early; there was a greater choice of dishes, and still some chance of getting the one you ordered. Like all imaginative people, he had taken a fancy to a particular place, and his choice showed considerable good sense. The very first time he had gone there he had noticed, near the counter, a table where the faces of the diners, and the snatches of conversation that he overheard, convinced him that these were fellow-writers. A sort of instinct, besides, suggested to him that if he sat near the counter he would be able to get on to friendly terms with the management. Sooner or later they would get to know him, and then, in times of financial distress, he would no doubt be able to obtain the necessary credit. He therefore sat at a little square table near the desk, where there were only two places laid, with clean serviettes without rings, intended, no doubt, for casual customers.

Opposite Lucien there was a pale thin young man, evidently as poor as himself, whose handsome face, already haggard, suggested that disappointed hopes had lined his brow, and ploughed in his soul deep furrows in which no seed had ripened. Lucien felt drawn to the stranger by these vestiges of poetry, and by an irresistible impulse of sympathy.

After a week of small civilities and brief observations, the poet from Angoulême at last succeeded in entering into conversation with this young man, whose name was Étienne Lousteau. Étienne, like Lucien, had left his native town, in Berri, two years before. His nervous gestures, feverish looks, and the occasional curtness of his speech, betrayed the bitterness of his experience of the world of letters. Étienne had left Sancerre, a tragedy in his pocket, drawn to Paris by the same desires as had impelled Lucien : fame, power, and money. At first this young man dined at Flicoteaux several days in succession, but later he only appeared there occasionally. After an interval of five or six days, he would reappear, and Lucien would hope to see him the next day ; but on the following evening there would be a stranger in his place. With young men, the warmth of the discussion of the previous evening is reflected in the next day's conversation ; but these interruptions obliged Lucien to break the ice afresh each time, and retarded the growth of an acquaintance that made but little progress during the first few weeks.

Lucien asked the girl at the cash-desk about him, and learned that his future friend was on the staff of a small newspaper, for which he wrote book-reviews, and theatre notices on the Ambigu-Comique, the Gaieté, and the Panorama-Dramatique. The young man instantly became a great figure in Lucien's eyes, and he became most anxious to get on to closer terms with him ; he was prepared to go out of his way to make a friendship that would be so useful to a beginner.

The journalist did not appear for a fortnight. Lucien had not yet discovered that Étienne only dined at Flicoteaux when he had run out of money, which was the reason for that gloomy, bitter expression, that coldness that Lucien tried to overcome with flattering smiles and soft words. All the same, this was not a friendship to be entered into hastily, for this obscure journalist seemed to lead an expensive existence, punctuated with brandies, cups of coffee, bowls of punch, theatres, and suppers. And in the early days of his residence in the Latin Quarter Lucien behaved like a poor child, stunned by his first experience of Paris life. And, after studying prices and considering his financial position, he did not dare venture on Étienne's way of life ; he was afraid of embarking on another series of blunders, like those he was still repenting. And always (for he was still hampered by the yoke of provincial prejudices) the thought of his two guardian angels, Eve and David, would rise and reproach him at the first evil thought, reminding him of the high hopes they had of him, his responsibility for the happiness of his old mother, and all the promise of his genius.

He spent his mornings at the library of Sainte-Geneviève reading history.

His first researches had already revealed to him some frightful mistakes in his novel *An Archer of Charles IX.* When the library closed, he returned to his cold damp little room and worked on the corrections of his manuscript, revising it, suppressing whole chapters. After dining at Flicoteaux, he used to walk down to the Passage du Commerce and read the new books, the newspapers and reviews and latest poetry, in Blosse's reading-room, so as to keep abreast of the latest literary movements. Then he would return to his miserable hotel at midnight, having used neither fuel nor light.

This reading changed his ideas so completely that he set about revising his collections of sonnets on flowers, his beloved *Marguerites* ; and he rewrote them to such purpose that less than a hundred lines of the original version remained.

At first, therefore, Lucien lived the innocent, pure life of the poor provincials, for whom Flicoteaux is luxury in comparison with what they are accustomed to at home, whose only recreation consists in strolling slowly under the trees in the Luxembourg, watching the pretty women out of the corner of their eyes, their hearts beating fast ; young men who never go beyond the Quarter, and who devote themselves entirely to work, thinking only of their future. But Lucien, a born poet, was soon beset with immense longings and could not long resist the seductions of the theatre-bills. The Théâtre-Français, the Vaudeville, the Variétés, the Opéra-Comique, although he went in the pit, accounted for sixty francs. What student could resist the opportunity of seeing Talma in the parts that he has made famous ? The theatre, that first love of all poetic souls, fascinated Lucien. The actors and actresses seemed to him awe-inspiring figures ; he never dreamed of the possibility of crossing the footlights and conversing with them as ordinary people. Those able to give so much pleasure seemed to him marvellous beings, treated by the newspapers on an equal footing with affairs of state. To be a playwright, to be acted—that was a dream to be cherished ! Yet a few ambitious ones, like Casimir Delavigne, succeeded in realising that dream ! These fertile thoughts, these alterations of self-confidence and despair, agitated Lucien, and kept him in the narrow path of work and economy, in spite of the distant rumblings of stormy desires. In an excess of caution, he did not allow himself to go anywhere near the Palais-Royal, that place of perdition, where, in a single day, he had spent fifty francs at Vérys, and nearly five hundred francs on clothes. And when he did succumb to the temptation of seeing Fleury, Talma, the two Baptistes, or Michot, he did not venture beyond the gallery, for which one has to queue from half-past five, and where those coming late have to pay ten sous for a seat near the ticket-office. Often, after standing in the queue for two hours, the words " All seats sold " would ring in the ears of more than one disappointed student. After the performance, Lucien went home with his eyes downcast, looking neither to the right nor to the left, through the streets, thronged, at that hour, with living seductions. It may be that a few of those very elementary adventures befell him that loom so immensely large in the timid imaginations of youth.

One day, alarmed at the rate at which his capital was melting, Lucien counted his money. He broke out in a cold sweat, as he realised that the time had come for him to find a publisher, and to look for some work for which he would be paid. The young journalist with whom he had made a one-sided friendship no longer came to Flicoteaux. Lucien waited for some lucky chance that did not occur. There is no such thing as luck in Paris, except for people with a wide circle of acquaintances ; the number of connections increases the number of openings of all kinds, and so even chance is on the side of the big battalions. Lucien still retained some provincial foresight and he did not want to wait until he found himself down to his last crown: he made up his mind to tackle the publishers.

On a cold September morning he set off down the Rue de la Harpe, his two manuscripts under his arm. When he reached the Quai des Augustins, he walked along the pavement, looking at the waters of the Seine, and at the bookshops, as if a good genius was counselling him to take a plunge into the water rather than into literature. After agonising hesitations, after deep consideration of the various faces, more or less good-natured, encouraging, scowling, cheerful, or sad, that he could see through the windows or at the doors, he decided upon a house where packers were busy parcelling up books. Goods were being despatched, the walls were covered with posters :

NOW ON SALE

Le Solitaire by M. le Vicomte d'Arlincourt.
Third edition.

Léonide, by Victor Ducagne, five volumes
12 mo, printed on
fine paper. 12 francs.

Inductions Morales by Kératy.

" Lucky people ! " Lucien exclaimed.

The poster, a new and original creation of the famous Ladvocat, was now blossoming for the first time on walls. Paris was soon to be a patch-work of the imitations of this form of announcement, an important source of public funds. At last, his heart beating with anxiety, Lucien, lately such a great figure in Angoulême, now so insignificant in Paris, walked the length of the pavement, summoned up his courage, and entered that shop, full of salesmen, customers, and books—" and perhaps authors ! " Lucien thought.

" I would like to speak to M. Vidal or M. Porchon," he said to a salesman.

He had read on a sign the names " VIDAL and PORCHON, *French and Foreign Wholesale Booksellers* ".

" Both these gentlemen are busy," replied the shopman.

" I will wait."

Left to himself, the poet examined the packages ; he waited for two hours, looking at titles, opening books, reading a page here and there. At last, he leaned his shoulder against a glass partition, for it crossed his mind that the little green curtains concealed either Vidal or Porchon, and he overheard the following conversation :

" Will you take five hundred copies ? If you do I will let you have them at five francs, and give you fourteen to the dozen."

" How much does that come to ? "

" Sixteen sous discount."

" Four francs four sous," said Vidal or Porchon to whoever was trying to sell his books.

" Done," replied the vendor.

" On account ? " asked the purchaser.

" Old humbug! And then you would pay me eighteen months from now with bills post-dated a year ! "

" No, we can arrange it at once," replied Vidal or Porchon.

" How long a term ? Nine months ? " asked the publisher or author who was evidently selling a book.

" No, my dear fellow, a year," replied one of the wholesale booksellers.

There was a short pause.

" You are cutting my throat! " exclaimed the unknown.

" But do you imagine we shall have sold five hundred copies of *Léonide* in a year ? " replied the wholesale bookseller to Victor Ducagne's publisher. " If books sold according to the fancies of the publishers we should be millionaires, my dear sir ; but they sell according to the fancies of the public. Walter Scott's novels are on sale at eighteen sous a volume, three livres twelve sous the set ; do you expect me to ask more for your trash ? If you want me to push this novel you must make it worth my while. . . . Vidal! "

A fat man with a pen behind his ear came over from his desk.

" How many Ducagnes did you dispose of on your last journey?" Porchon enquired.

" I got rid of two hundred *Petit Vieillard de Calais* ; but to do so I had to cry down two other books that pay us a smaller percentage and a nice pair of nightingales they are now."

Later, Lucien was to learn that the name " nightingale " is used by booksellers to describe those works that remain unsold, perched out of sight on the obscurest shelves of their shops.

" And as I expect you know," Vidal went on, " Picard has some novels coming out. He has promised us twenty per cent on the published price, on condition we push them for him."

"Very well, a year," the publisher replied in piteous tones, overwhelmed by this last confidential observation of Vidal to Porchon.

"Is that agreed?" Porchon asked curtly.

"Yes."

The editor went out. Lucien heard Porchon remarking to Vidal:

"We have three hundred copies on order now; we will keep him waiting for his settlement, and sell *Léonide* for five francs net, settlement in six months, and——"

"And that is fifteen hundred francs into our pockets," Vidal concluded.

"Oh! I could see that he was in a fix."

"He was bluffing! He is paying Ducagne four thousand francs for an edition of two thousand."

Lucien interrupted Vidal by opening the little door of that den.

"Sirs," he said, addressing both partners, "I have the honour to wish you good-day."

The booksellers barely acknowledged his greeting.

"I am the author of a romance on the history of France, in the style of Walter Scott, entitled *An Archer of Charles IX*, and I have come to offer it to you."

Porchon glanced at Lucien indifferently and laid his pen down on his desk, while Vidal glared at the author and replied:

"We are not publishers, we are wholesale booksellers. When we do take on books ourselves, we only touch established reputations. Besides, we only consider serious literature, historical books, and summaries——"

"But my book is a serious work; it is an attempt to describe the truth about the struggle between the Catholics, who stood for absolute monarchy, and the Protestants, who wished to establish a republic."

One of the salesmen called: "Monsieur Vidal!" Vidal slipped away.

" I am not saying that your book is not a masterpiece," said Porchon, with an insolent shrug, " but we only deal in printed books. Go and see somebody who is interested in manuscripts. Old Doguereau, Rue du Coq, by the Louvre—he is in the novel line. If you had only spoken sooner, you might have seen Pollet, who is in competition with Doguereau, and the publishers in the Wooden Galleries."

" I have a volume of poems——"

Somebody called : " Monsieur Porchon! "

" Poetry! " exclaimed Porchon indignantly. " What do you take me for ? " he added, laughing in Lucien's face, and he disappeared into the back regions of his shop.

Lucien crossed the Pont Neuf, lost in thought. From what he had understood of that commercial jargon, he had begun to realise that books are to publishers what cotton nightcaps are to drapers, goods to be bought cheap and sold dear.

" I have made a mistake," he reflected, but he was struck, nevertheless, by the brutal and material aspect that literature had suddenly taken on.

He found a modest establishment in the Rue du Coq that he had not noticed the first time he passed it, over which was painted, in yellow letters on a green ground, " DOGUEREAU, PUBLISHER ". He now recollected that he had seen those same words at the bottom of the title-page of more than one of the novels that he had read in Blosse's reading-rooms. He entered, with that inward trepidation that all imaginative men feel at the certain prospect of a struggle. In the office, he discovered an odd-looking old man, one of those eccentric figures associated with publishing in the days of the Empire. Doguereau was wearing a black coat with enormous square skirts, although the fashion of the day demanded swallow-tails. His waistcoat was of some cheap material, in a check pattern of several colours, and from his fob hung a steel chain from which a copper key dangled over his vast black breeches. His watch must have been the size of an onion. Dark-grey ribbed stockings and shoes with silver buckles completed his costume. The old man's head was bare and adorned with greying hair,

One of those eccentric figures associated with publishing

poetically scanty. Old Doguereau, as Porchon had called him, might, to judge by his coat, trousers, and shoes, have been a teacher of literature ; but the business-man was discernible in the waistcoat, the watch, and the stockings. His face bore out this singular combination ; he had the magisterial and dogmatic manner, the lined face of a teacher of grammar, and the sharp eyes, suspicious mouth, and vague uneasiness of a bookseller.

" M. Doguereau ? " Lucien enquired.

" That is my name, sir."

" I am the author of a novel," said Lucien.

" You are very young," said the publisher.

" But my age has nothing to do with it."

" Very true," said the old publisher, taking the manuscript. " Ah, by Jove! *An Archer of Charles IX*—a good title. Now, young man, tell me briefly what is it about."

" It is an historical work, sir, in the style of Walter Scott, in which the issue at stake in the conflict between Protestants and Catholics is presented as a struggle between two systems of government, in which the Throne was seriously threatened. I have taken the part of the Catholics."

" Dear me, young man, you have ideas! Very well, I will promise to read your book ; I would rather have had a romance in the style of Mrs. Radcliffe ; but if you are a hard worker, if you have style, and ideas, a grasp of your subject, the art of telling a story, I ask nothing better than to be of service to you. That is just what we publishers want—good manuscripts."

" When shall I come back ? "

" Well, this evening I am going down into the country ; I shall be back the day after tomorrow. By then I shall have read your manuscript, and if it is what I want we can discuss terms at once."

Lucien, finding him so friendly, had the fatal idea of producing the manuscript of *Marguerites*.

" I have also a collection of poems, sir——"

" Oh! You are a poet! Then I don't want your novel," said the old man, handing him back the manuscript. " Versifiers can never write prose. In prose it is no use using fine meaningless phrases; prose absolutely must say something."

"But, sir, Walter Scott wrote poetry as well——"

"That is true," said Doguereau, relenting; he guessed that the young man was poor, and he kept the manuscript. "Where are you living? I will come and see you."

Lucien gave his address, without for a moment suspecting the old man of any ulterior motive; he did not recognise in him a publisher of the old school, a man of the days when publishers expected to be able to keep Voltaires and Montesquieus locked up in garrets to die of starvation.

"The Latin Quarter—that is on my way," said the old publisher, reading the address.

"What a decent old fellow!" thought Lucien, as he took leave of the publisher. "I have really discovered a friend of young writers, a man of taste, who knows something. That is the kind of man for me! That is what I always said to David—talent makes its way easily in Paris."

Lucien went home with a light heart, dreaming of success. He had already forgotten the sinister conversation that he had overheard in Vidal and Porchon's office; he saw himself already rich, to the extent of twelve hundred francs at least. Twelve hundred francs represented a whole year in Paris, a year during which he would be able to write other books. What plans he built upon these hopes! What day-dreams, what visions of a life based on hard work! He planned where he would live, settled himself in his new quarters, and it would have taken very little to set him day-dreaming about things he would buy. The only way of controlling his impatience was by constant reading in Blosse's reading-room.

Two days later old Doguereau, impressed by the style of Lucien's first book, delighted with the exaggeration of character (sanctioned by the period of the drama), struck by the impetuosity of imagination with which all young authors develop their first plots (old Doguereau was not too particular)—he called at the house where this budding Walter Scott was living. He had decided to offer a thousand francs for the outright purchase of *An Archer of Charles IX* and to bind Lucien by contract for future works. But when he saw the house, he thought better of it.

" A young man who lives here must have simple tastes, he is a lover of study, a hard worker; I could probably offer him only eight hundred."

" Fourth floor," answered the landlady, whom he asked for M. Lucien de Rubempré.

The publisher, peering up, saw nothing but the sky above the fourth floor.

" This young man," he reflected, " is a good-looking lad, one might almost say very handsome; if he has too much money, he will waste his time, he won't do any more work. For both our sakes, I shall offer him six hundred—but cash down, not on publication."

He climbed the stair and gave three raps on Lucien's door. Lucien let him in. The room was dismally bare. There was a bowl of milk and a penny roll on the table. Old Doguereau was struck by the poverty of genius.

" I hope he will keep these simple tastes," he thought, " this economy, these modest needs. . . . I am delighted to see you " he said aloud. " This was how Jean-Jacques lived—you have much in common with him. It is in rooms like these that the fires of genius burn, where masterpieces are written. This is how authors ought to live, instead of idling away their days in cafés, and restaurants, wasting their time, talent, and money."

He sat down.

" Young man, your novel is not bad. I was once a professor of rhetoric, I know a little about the history of France; there are some fine things here; and you have a future."

" Oh, sir! "

" No, I really mean it; we can come to an arrangement. I will buy your novel. . . ."

Lucien's heart beat fast, palpitated with delight; he was about to enter the world of literature, he was going to be published at last.

" I will pay you four hundred francs," said Doguereau in honeyed tones, looking at Lucien with an expression that implied that this was a great concession of generosity.

"The volume?" said Lucien.

"For the novel," said Doguereau, seeming not to notice Lucien's surprise. "But on acceptance," he added, "you will undertake to write two novels a year for me for six years. If the first sells out in six months, I will pay you six hundred francs for the subsequent books; your income will be assured, you will be well off; I have authors to whom I pay only three hundred francs for a novel. I give two hundred for a translation from English. These would have been unheard-of rates in the old days."

"Sir, we cannot agree on these terms; I must ask you to give me back my manuscript," said Lucien, chilled to the marrow.

"Here it is," said the old publisher. "You don't understand business, my friend. A publisher is risking sixteen hundred francs in bringing out an author's first novel—the cost of printing and paper. It is easier to write a novel than to find that sum. I have a hundred manuscript novels in my office, but I have not sixteen hundred francs in my cashbox! Alas, I have never made that amount of money in the twenty years I have been a publisher. Fortunes are not made by publishing novels. Vidal and Porchon will only take them off our hands on conditions that become harder for us from one day to the next. You are only risking your time, but I, for my part, have to part with two thousand francs. If we don't succeed—*habent sua fata libelli*, you know—I shall have lost two thousand francs. But all you have to do is to write an ode against the stupidity of the public. When you have thought over what I have said to you, come and see me again—you will come back to me," the publisher repeated with conviction, in response to an expression of scorn that Lucien did not attempt to conceal. "Far from finding a publisher willing to risk two thousand francs on an unknown young author, you will not even find a publisher's clerk who will take the trouble to read your screed. I have read it—and I could point out plenty of faults in your French; you have written *observer* for *faire observer*, and *malgré que*: *malgré* is followed by a direct object."

Lucien looked ashamed.

"When I see you again, I shall offer you a hundred francs less," he added; "I shall not offer you a penny more than a hundred crowns."

He rose and took his leave; but at the door he said:

"If you had not talent, and a future, if it were not that I take an interest in young intellectuals, I would not have offered you such favourable terms. A hundred francs a month! Think it over! After all, a novel in a drawer is not like a horse in a stable—it does not eat bread. But it won't provide you with any either, and that's a fact."

Lucien seized his manuscript and flung it to the ground.

"Sir, I would rather burn it!" he exclaimed.

"Just like a poet!" said the older man.

Lucien devoured his roll, gulped down his milk, and went downstairs. His room was too small to hold him; he was walking up and down it like a lion in a cage at the Jardin des Plantes. At the Library of Sainte-Geneviève, whither Lucien now made his way, he had always noticed a young man, of about twenty-five, who always worked in one particular corner, with that studious application that nothing could distract or disturb, by which one can always recognise a real writer. This young man had evidently been using the library for a long time, because the assistants, and even the librarian himself, treated him with special consideration; the librarian allowed him to take books home, and Lucien noticed that this unknown student always brought them back the next day; from these signs, our poet had recognised him as a brother in poverty and hope. Small, slight, and pale, this toiler's fine brow was concealed under a mass of thick black hair, to which he paid little attention; he had fine hands and people used to turn to look at him because of a vague resemblance to Robert Lefebvre's portrait of Bonaparte. That engraving is a poem of melancholy intensity, of latent ambition, of hidden energy. Examine it well: for in it you will discern genius combined with caution, subtlety with greatness. The eyes are as expressive as a woman's; the glance is eager for scope, craves difficulties to be overcome. If the name of Bonaparte were not written below it, you would look at it none the less attentively.

The young man who resembled this engraving usually wore long trousers, thick-soled shoes, a coat of poor quality cloth, a black cravat, a grey-and-white waistcoat buttoned up to the chin, and a cheap hat. He obviously had a contempt for excessive attention to dress. This mysterious unknown, marked with the seal that genius stamps upon the brow of her slaves, was, Lucien had noticed, one of the most regular of Flicoteaux' customers ; he ate there in order to live, without paying the slightest attention to the food, to which he seemed to have grown accustomed, and he drank water. Whether at the library or at Flicoteaux, he displayed in everything he did a sort of dignity that comes, no doubt, from a man's knowledge that his life is occupied in some great work, a dignity that made him unapproachable. He had the expression of a thinker. Meditation inhabited his noble, finely moulded brow. His dark, brilliant eyes, clear-sighted and quick, revealed a habit of probing to the bottom of things. His manner was quiet, his expression serious. Lucien felt an instinctive respect for him. Already on more than one occasion they had looked at one another as if they were about to speak, going in or out of the library or the restaurant, but neither of them had ventured to do so. This silent young man always sat at the farthest end of the room, in the part at right angles to the Place de la Sorbonne, so that Lucien had not so far made his acquaintance although he felt drawn to this hard-working young student, who bore all the indefinable marks of superiority. Both, as they later came to realise, were inexperienced and timid, a prey to all those fears which the emotions amuse themselves by arousing in solitary men. If they had not suddenly happened to meet at the time of the disaster that had just befallen Lucien, perhaps they would never have spoken to each other at all. But, as he turned into the Rue des Grès, Lucien saw this young man coming towards him from the direction of Sainte-Geneviève.

" The library is closed, I don't know why," he said to Lucien.

Lucien had tears in his eyes at that moment. He expressed his thanks by one of those gestures that are more eloquent than words, and which, between young men, immediately unlock hearts. They walked back together along the Rue des Grès in the direction of the Rue de la Harpe.

" Then I shall go for a walk in the Luxembourg," said Lucien. " Once one has gone out, it is difficult to go back and start work again."

" The train of thought is broken," said the stranger. " You seem upset," he added.

" An extraordinary thing has just happened to me," said Lucien.

He told the story of his visit to the Quai, and then to the old publisher, and the proposition that had just been made to him ; he added his name, and a few facts about his present situation. In the last month he had spent sixty francs on board, thirty for his room, twenty on theatres, ten at the reading-room—a hundred francs in all, and he had only a hundred and twenty francs left.

" Your story is my own," said the stranger, " and that of the ten or twelve hundred young men who come to Paris every year from the provinces. And we are by no means the worst off. Do you see that theatre ? " he said, pointing to the turrets of the Odéon. " One day a man of talent came to lodge in one of the houses in the square —a man who had known the depths of poverty ; he was married—an added misfortune from which we are both free—to a woman whom he loved ; the richer, or the poorer, as you like to look at it, by two children, with a mountain of debts, but with faith in his talent. He offered a five-act comedy to the Odéon, and it was accepted, it was put into production, the actors had learned their parts, and the rehearsals were in full swing. These five pieces of good fortune were five dramas far harder to accomplish than the five acts of the comedy had been to write. The poor author, whose lodgings were in an attic just over there, had spent his last resources in order to live until his play came on, his wife had pawned her clothes, the family was living on bread. On the day of the last rehearsal, the day before the play was to have come on, they were owing fifty francs to the butcher, the baker, and the porter. The poet possessed only the barest necessities : a coat, a shirt, a pair of trousers, a waistcoat and a pair of boots. Sure of success, he had just kissed his wife and told her that they had come to the end of their misfortunes. ' Nothing can stand in our way now! ' he exclaimed. ' There is a fire,' said his wife. ' Look, the Odéon is on fire! ' My friend, the Odéon *was* on fire! Don't complain of your misfortunes. You have clothes, you have neither a wife nor children, you have a hundred and twenty francs in your pocket for emergencies, and you have no debts. That play ran for a hundred and fifty performances at the Louvois. The King gave the author a pension. As Buffon says, genius is patience. Patience is, in fact, the quality in man that most resembles the process that nature employs in her creations. And what is art but the quintessence of nature ? "

The two young men were by now striding along by the Luxembourg. Lucien had now learned the name, that has since become famous, of the individual who was attempting to console him. This young man was Daniel d'Arthez, today one of the greatest writers of the age, a man of whom it may be said that he possesses, as a poet has put it, the rare combination of " a character no less noble than his mind ".

" One can only become great at a price," Daniel said to him in his gentle voice. " The works of genius are watered with tears. Talent is a mortal creature that has, like all other living beings, a childhood subject to maladies. Society discourages imperfect talents, just as nature eliminates feeble or misshapen creatures. Whoever wishes to rise above the common run of men must be prepared to fight a battle and not retreat at the first difficulty. A great writer is nothing less than a martyr who does not die. You bear the mark of genius on your brow," said d'Arthez to Lucien, with a look that seemed to take him in completely. " If you have not determination in your heart, if you have not the patience of an angel, if, no matter how far the freaks of fortune have placed you from your goal, you are not prepared to find the way to your infinite, as turtles, wherever they may be, will make their way back to the ocean, you had better give up at once."

" Then do you yourself expect these ordeals ? " said Lucien.

" Trials of all kinds, calumny, treachery, the injustice of rivals ; insults, deceptions, and commercial greed," the young man replied in tones of resignation. " If your work is good, what do initial defeats matter ? "

" Would you read mine and give me your opinion of it ? " said Lucien.

" To be sure," d'Arthez responded. " I live in the Rue des Quatre-Vents, in the very house where one of the greatest men, one of the most remarkable men of genius of our time, the scientist Desplein, the greatest surgeon who has ever lived, suffered his early hardships, and struggled with the first difficulties of life and his glorious career. I think of that every evening, and that gives me the dose of courage that I need every morning. I am living in the very room where he used to eat bread and cherries, like Rousseau—but without a Thérèse. Come round in about an hour—I shall be in."

The two poets clasped one another's hands as they took leave of each other, with an inexpressible emotion of melancholy tenderness. Lucien went off to fetch his manuscript, Daniel d'Arthez to pawn his watch in order to buy two faggots so that his new friend should not be cold. Lucien was punctual. He noticed at once that this house was even shabbier than his own lodgings. He could not at first see the gloomy staircase at the end of a dark passage. Daniel d'Arthez's room was on the fifth floor. Between two small windows there was a bookcase filled with labelled boxes. At the other end of the room was a narrow painted wooden bedstead of the kind one sees in school dormitories, an old washstand, picked up somewhere, and two horsehair armchairs. The wallpaper, a tartan plaid pattern, was glazed with age and smoke. Between the fireplace and the windows stood a long table littered with papers; and opposite the fireplace stood a dilapidated mahogany chest of drawers. A second-hand carpet entirely covered the floor. This necessary luxury saved fuel. At the table stood a common office chair covered in leather, once red, but now grey with age; and six other rickety chairs completed the furniture. On the mantelpiece Lucien noticed an old candle-sconce with an eye-screen, of the kind used for card-tables, in which stood four wax candles. Lucien, recognising the marks of the direst poverty in everything, asked about the candles, and d'Arthez explained that he could not bear the smell of tallow—a circumstance that denoted great delicacy of the senses, a sign of correspondingly exquisite sensibility of mind.

The reading lasted for seven hours. Daniel listened conscientiously without saying a word or making any comment—one of the rarest proofs of good taste in an auditor.

"Well?" said Lucien to Daniel, laying the manuscript on the mantelpiece.

"You have made a very good start on the right lines," replied the young man seriously; "but you will have to re-cast your book. If you do not want simply to ape Walter Scott, you must develop an individual style—at present you have merely imitated him. For instance, you begin, as he does, with long conversations to introduce your characters; when they have finished talking, they proceed to action; and the conflict, that is essential in any dramatic work, comes last of all. I would like to see the terms of the problem reversed. Replace those diffuse conversations, magnificent in Scott, but colourless in your work, by description, to which our language lends itself so well. The dialogue ought to arise out of the events that have led up to it; plunge at once into action. Approach your subject from different angles; in fact, you must vary your plot, if you are to avoid monotony. You can adapt the Scottish novelist's form of dramatic dialogue to the history of France and still be original. There is no passion in Walter Scott; either he himself is without it, or it is forbidden by the hypocritical laws of his country. For him woman is duty incarnate. With one or two exceptions, his heroines are all exactly alike; he has drawn them all from the same model, as painters say—they all derive from Clarissa Harlowe; and since he has reduced them all to a single idea, all he can do is to give different examples of the same type, painted in more or less vivid colours. But woman brings disorder into society, through passion. Therefore you must portray the passions—then you will have at your disposal immense resources that the great Scottish novelist had to forgo in order to provide family reading for the prudish English. In France you have the contrast between Catholicism, with its charming sins and brilliant manners, and the sombre figures of Calvinism, during the most passionate years of our history. Every authentic reign, from Charlemagne onwards, calls for at least one novel, some for four or five, like the reigns of Louis XIV, Henry IV, and François I. You would give us, in that way, a picturesque history of France, in which you could describe costumes, and furniture, houses and interiors, and everyday life, while at the same time giving the spirit of the period, and not simply a laborious narration of known facts. You have scope for great originality, in rectifying the popular errors that disfigure most of our kings. Have the courage, in your first book, to re-establish the great, magnificent figure of Catherine, that you have sacrificed to the prejudices that still cloud her name. And, above all, paint Charles IX as he really was, and not as protestant writers have made him. Ten years of perseverance, and you will have fame and success."

By this time it was nine o'clock. Lucien followed the example of his future friend's secret hospitality by inviting him to dinner at Edon's, where he spent twelve francs. During that dinner, Daniel confided to Lucien the secret of his hopes and his studies. D'Arthez believed that no writer could be outstanding without a profound knowledge of metaphysics. He was at that time engaged in ransacking the riches of ancient and modern philosophy, which he had set himself to assimilate. Like Molière, he was determined to be a profound philosopher before writing comedies. He was a student of the world of books, and of the real world—of thought and of life. His friends were students of science, young doctors, political writers and painters, a society of studious, serious young men, full of promise. He earned enough to live on by writing conscientious and badly paid articles for encyclopaedias and dictionaries of biography and natural science; he wrote neither more nor less than he needed in order to live and pursue his studies. D'Arthez was also working on a piece of imaginative writing that he had undertaken for the purpose of studying the resources of the language. This book, that was still unfinished, he took up from time to time, keeping it for days of great distress. It was a highly serious psychological work, in the form of a novel.

Although Daniel talked about himself with great modesty, he seemed a giant to Lucien. By the time they left the restaurant at eleven o'clock Lucien had developed a warm affection for that unassuming merit, that nature unconscious of its own sublimity.

The poet accepted Daniel's advice without question, and followed it to the letter. That rare talent, already matured by thought and by a critical habit of mind, a talent developed in solitude, not for publication, but for himself alone and for no other, had suddenly opened for the poet from the provinces a door into the most magnificent palaces of imagination. His lips had been touched by a burning coal, and the words of the laborious student of Paris had fallen on fertile soil in the brain of the young man from Angoulême. Lucien set to work to rewrite his novel.

In his delight at having found, in the desert of Paris, a heart full of generous sentiments, in harmony with his own, our distinguished provincial did what young men starved of affection always do—he attached himself to d'Arthez like a chronic disease. He called for him on the way to the library, he walked beside him in the Luxembourg on fine days, he saw him back as far as his poor lodgings every evening, after dining by his side at Flicoteaux ; in fact he kept as close to him as a soldier pressing close to his comrade on the frozen plains of Russia. In the early days of their acquaintance Lucien realised, not without mortification, that his presence always created a certain restraint among the circle of Daniel's close friends. The conversations of these superior beings, of whom d'Arthez had talked with such concentrated enthusiasm, kept within the bounds of a reserve that accorded ill with the obvious signs of their close friendship. Lucien used to slip discreetly away, pained by the ostracism of which he was the object, and also by the curiosity he felt about these unknown individuals who all called one another by their Christian names, and every one of whom bore on his brow, like d'Arthez, the mark of outstanding genius.

When Daniel had overcome, on his behalf, certain secret oppositions, Lucien was at last judged worthy to become a member of this circle of great intellects. Lucien was henceforth to know these men, united by the warmest affection, and by the seriousness of their intellectual life, who met nearly every evening in d'Arthez's room. In d'Arthez they all divined the future great writer ; and now that they had lost one of their number, one of the most remarkable minds of the age, a mystical genius, who had been their first leader, they regarded him as their chief. For reasons that it would serve no useful purpose to describe, the young man whom Lucien often heard spoken of as Louis, had returned to his province. How this group must have aroused the interest and curiosity of a poet it is easy to understand when we consider those of them who have since, like d'Arthez, become famous—for some fell by the way.

One member of the group who is still living was Horace Bianchon, at that time a house-physician at the Hôtel-Dieu ; his appearance, his personality, and the nature of his mind, are at present too well known for any description to be necessary. Next came Léon Giraud, the philosopher, whose bold and deep speculations have shaken all systems, criticising, expounding, formulating, and laying them all at the foot of his idol—Humanity ; great even in his errors, that are ennobled by his sincerity. An intrepid worker, a conscientious scholar, he has become the leader of a school of ethical and political thought on whose merits history alone can pronounce. But if his convictions have led him into spheres remote from those in which his comrades have found their destiny, he has, none the less, remained their loyal friend.

Art was represented by Joseph Bridau, one of the finest painters of the younger school. But for the inner misfortunes brought upon him by a too impressionable nature, Joseph might have continued the great tradition of the Italian masters—and indeed the last word has not yet been said about him. He has the Roman gift for design, the colour of the Venetian school ; but love has been his undoing, for it not only makes inroads into his heart—it shoots its arrows into his brain, and upsets his life, precipitating him into the most erratic courses. If the mistress of the moment is making him either too happy or too miserable, Joseph will either exhibit drawings in which colour entirely obliterates the design, or pictures that he has forced himself to finish, under the stress of imaginary woes, in which he has been so preoccupied with the composition that colour has been left to take care of itself, and is entirely lacking. He is a perpetual disappointment to his friends and to the public. Hoffman had an enormous admiration for his bold experiments in the field of art, for his flights of fancy, for his caprices. At his best, he arouses admiration, and as he loves praise, he becomes furious when he does not receive eulogies for his failures, in which his own imagination sees all the merits that they lack in the eyes of the public. He is capricious to a degree. His friends have known him to destroy a picture because he thought it looked too highly finished. "It is too laboured," he will say, "art-school work."

At once eccentric and sublime, he suffers from all the misfortunes, and enjoys all the delights of a highly strung temperament, whose very perfection may turn to malady. His mind is of the same cast as Sterne's, although he is not a man of letters. His sayings, his witticisms, have a flavour all their own. He is eloquent, he knows how to love, but in his feelings he is no less capricious than in his behaviour. The group of friends loved him for just those qualities that the bourgeois world would have called his faults.

Lastly, there was Fulgence Ridal. No author of our day has more of the true spirit of comedy than this poet, so indifferent to fame, who flings only his most commonplace productions to the theatre managers, keeping the best scenes in the privacy of his own brain, for himself and his friends; all he asks from the public is enough money to enable him to be independent, and refuses to do anything more. Lazy and prolific as Rossini, his nature compels him, like those great comic poets, Molière and Rabelais, to see both sides of every question. He was, therefore, sceptical, and could laugh or smile at everything. Fulgence Ridal is a great practical philosopher. His knowledge of the world, his genius for observation, his indifference to fame (*show*, as he calls it), have not dried up the kindness of his heart. He is as active on behalf of others as he is indifferent to his own interests, and if he exerts himself it is for a friend. Living up to his truly rabelaisian countenance, he is no enemy of good cheer, but he does not go out of his way to find it. He is at once melancholy and gay. His friends used to call him "the dog of the regiment", and no nickname could have suited him better.

Three others, no less remarkable than the four already described, were destined, one by one, to fall by the way. Meyraux was the first to go. He died soon after he had started the famous controversy between Cuvier and Geoffrey Saint-Hilaire, an important issue that was to divide the scientific world between these two men of genius, equal in stature. It was Meyraux who, only a few months before his death, had made a plea for an exact and analytical science, against the pantheist who is still living and who has a great following in Germany. Meyraux was a close friend of that Louis whose premature death was so soon to remove him from the intellectual world. With these two men, both singled out by death, both forgotten today, the scope of their learning and their genius notwithstanding, must be joined the name of Michel Chrestien, a republican idealist, who dreamed of a federation of Europe, and who in 1830 played an important part in the Saint-Simonian movement. A politician whose energy was comparable with that of Saint-Just or Danton, he was yet as simple and as gentle as a young girl, affectionate, full of illusions and gifted with a voice that would have delighted Mozart, Weber, or Rossini. When he used to sing some of Béranger's songs he could melt the heart with poetry, or love, or hope. Michel Chrestien, who was as poor as Lucien, or Daniel, or any of his friends, earned his living with stoic indifference. He indexed lengthy works, he drew up catalogues for publishers, keeping as silent as the grave on the subject of his political doctrines. This gay, clever Bohemian, this born statesman who might have changed the course of history, died in the cloister of Saint-Merri as a simple soldier. Some tradesman's bullet shot down one of the noblest spirits that ever trod French soil, and Michel Chrestien died for doctrines not his own. His federation plan was a far graver menace to the aristocracy of Europe than any Republican propaganda; for it was more reasonable and less hysterical than those lamentably ill-defined notions of liberty proclaimed by the young fools who regard themselves as the heirs of the Convention. This great man of the people was lamented by all those who knew him; not one of them but thinks often of that great unknown political theorist.

These nine men formed a group where esteem and affection kept the peace among the most incompatible doctrines and ideas. Daniel d'Arthez came from a good family in Picardy. His belief in the monarchy was no less staunch than was Michel Chrestien's faith in his European federation. Fulgence Ridal made fun of the philosophical doctrines of Léon Giraud; who in turn predicted to d'Arthez the end of Christianity and the family. Michel Chrestien, who believed in the religion of Christ, the divine legislator of equality, defended the immortality of the soul against the analysis of Bianchon's scalpel. They discussed, but did not dispute. They were all without vanity, for they were their own audience. They discussed the work they were doing, and consulted one another with the delightful openness of youth. If any serious matter arose, the opponent would set aside his own opinion and enter into his friend's point of view, all the better able to help him by reason of his impartiality in a cause or a work outside the scope of his own intellectual activities. Nearly all of them were kindly and tolerant, two qualities that bore witness to their superiority. Envy, that hideous treasure of our disappointed hopes, of our abortive talents, of our failures, and our mortified pretensions, was unknown among them. All of them, besides, were working in different fields. Those, therefore, who were admitted, as Lucien was, into their society, felt at their ease. True talent is always straightforward, simple, and open, and never formal; epigrams, in that circle, stimulated the mind, but were never aimed at self-respect.

Once the first emotion caused by respect had worn off, it was infinitely pleasant to be one of that elect society of young men. Familiarity did not diminish the sense that each one had of his own value, and each felt the deepest respect for the others; since each one took it for granted that he might at any time find it necessary either to ask for help or to give it, no one felt any embarrassment about accepting. Discussions were full of charm, and never boring; they ranged over a wide variety of subjects. Light as arrows, their words sped to the heart of things. The contrast between their great material poverty and the splendour of their intellectual riches was remarkable. No one among them ever thought of the practical problems of life except as a subject for friendly jokes. One cold day at the beginning of winter five of d'Arthez's friends arrived, each one having had the same idea of bringing a bundle of firewood under his coat, for all the world like one of those picnics at which everyone brings something, when every one of the guests has had the same happy inspiration of bringing a pie.

All of them were gifted with that moral beauty that stamps the features and which imparts to young faces a golden radiance, as does also work and vigils. Purity of life and the fire of thought had formed and refined their rather worn faces. Their brows were remarkable for their poetic amplitude ; their bright, sparkling eyes bore witness to the purity of their lives. The hardships of poverty, when they made themselves felt, were borne so cheerfully, embraced with so much enthusiasm by one and all, that they did not disturb the serenity that characterises the faces of young men still innocent of any serious faults, men who have not yet descended to any of those base compromises to which we are driven by impatience with poverty, and the desire to succeed regardless of means ; or to that easy complaisance with which the literary world accepts or overlooks betrayals.

Friendship has one quality that renders it indissoluble and doubles its delight, a quality that love itself does not possess : certainty. These young men were sure of themselves : the enemy of one became forthwith the enemy of all. They would have set aside their most pressing interests, if these had clashed with the sacred solidarity of their friendship. As all were alike incapable of baseness, they could meet any accusation with a formidable denial, and defend each other with absolute conviction. Alike in nobility of heart, alike in depth of feeling, there was nothing that they could not think and say to one another in the spheres of science and speculation ; hence the innocence of their dealings with one another, the gaiety of their conversation. Certain of being understood, they unfolded their thoughts freely ; they stood upon no ceremony, confided their joys and sorrows to one another, thought and suffered with absolute openness. The charming delicacy of feeling that makes the story of the *Deux Amis* such a treasury for great souls was customary among them. So that it is easy to imagine that they would hesitate before admitting a new member to their circle ; they were too much aware of their own greatness and their happiness to disturb it by allowing any new and unknown element to enter their lives.

This community of interests and affections was to last without clashes or disappointments for twenty years. Death alone, that took Louis Lambert, Meyraux, and Michel Chrestien, could diminish the number of that noble galaxy. When Chrestien fell, in 1832, Horace Bianchon, Daniel d'Arthez, Léon Giraud, Joseph Bridau, and Fulgence Ridal all went, regardless of the danger they ran, to bring back his body from Saint-Merri and to pay the last honours to their friend in the face of political violence. They took his precious remains to the Père Lachaise cemetery by night. It was Horace Bianchon who, undaunted by the difficulties of this undertaking, made this possible : he pleaded with ministers, confessing his long-standing friendship with the dead federalist. It was a moving scene engraved for ever on the memories of the few friends who accompanied the five famous men. As you walk in that elegant cemetery, you may see a plot, purchased in perpetuity, where there is a grass mound surmounted by a black wooden cross, on which is carved, in red letters, the two words : Michel Chrestien. There is no other monument like it. The five friends considered that this simplicity was the only fitting tribute to the simplicity of the man.

So in that cold attic the fairest dreams of friendship were realised. There, the brotherhood, all equally able in their different fields of knowledge, told everything to one another without reserve, withholding nothing, not even their unworthy thoughts ; all were men of great knowledge, all tried in the crucible of poverty. When he was admitted among that elect society, Lucien represented, for them, poetry and beauty. He read them his sonnets, and they admired them. They would ask him for a sonnet as they asked Michel Chrestien for a song. So that in the desert of Paris Lucien found an oasis in the Rue des Quatre-Vents.

By the beginning of October Lucien, having spent the rest of his money on buying a little firewood, found himself almost penniless, in the midst of the strenuous task of revising his book. Daniel d'Arthez burned peat and supported poverty heroically ; he never complained ; his life was as ordered as an old maid's, as methodical as a miser's. His courage fired Lucien to emulation. A new member of the circle, he did not like to speak of his hardships. One morning he went to the Rue du Coq to sell *An Archer of Charles IX* to Dogereau, but the old publisher was not there.

Lucien did not know how indulgent great natures can be. Every one of his friends had some idea of the weaknesses peculiar to poets, the fits of depression that follow the efforts of a spirit, over-excited by the contemplation of that nature which it is the poet's mission to reproduce. These men, so strong to withstand their own hardships, had pity on Lucien's sufferings. They had guessed that his money was giving out. And to those delightful evenings of talk, of deep thought, of poetry, of confidences, of fearless speculations in the realms of intellect, on the future of nations, in domains of history, they added a crowning trait that was to show how little Lucien had understood his new friends.

" Lucien, my dear fellow," Daniel said to him, " you did not dine at Flicoteaux last night, and we know why."

Lucien could not keep back the tears that ran down his cheeks.

" You ought to have trusted us," said Michel Chrestien ; " we shall chalk up a cross over the fireplace, and when there are ten . . ."

" We have all of us been doing a little extra work," said Bianchon. " I have been looking after a rich patient for Desplein ; d'Arthez has written an article for the *Revue Encyclopedique* ; Chrestien had just decided to go and sing at the Champs-Elysées one evening with a handkerchief and four candles when he was given a pamphlet to write for a man who wants to be a politician, and he has given him six hundred francs' worth of Machiavelli. Léon Giraud has borrowed fifty francs from his publisher, Joseph has sold some sketches, and Fulgence's play was performed last Sunday, and there was a full house."

" Here are two hundred francs," said Daniel, " and let us say no more about it."

" Why, if he isn't going to hug us all as if we had done something extraordinary ! " said Chrestien.

Lucien meanwhile had written a letter home, a masterpiece of sensibility and good intentions, a terrible cry wrung from him by his distress. The replies that he received on the following day will give some idea of the delights that Lucien enjoyed, in the company of that living encyclopaedia of angelic spirits, of those young men marked by the diverse traits stamped upon each by his particular art or science.

David Séchard to Lucien

" My dear Lucien,

" You will find enclosed a cheque for two hundred francs, made out in your name, and payable in ninety days. You can cash it with M. Métivier, the paper-merchant, our Paris agent, in Rue Serpente. My dear Lucien, we have absolutely nothing. My wife has taken over the printing business, and she is performing her task with so much devotion, patience, and energy that I bless Heaven for having given me such an angel for a wife. She herself assures me that it is impossible to send you the least help. But, my dear friend, I can see that you are on such a promising way in the company of such noble minds, that you cannot fail to fulfil your highest destiny when you have the companionship of such almost divine intelligences as Daniel d'Arthez, Michel Chrestien and Léon Giraud to help you, and Meynaux, Bianchon and Ridal to give you good advice, as you tell us in your welcome letter. So I have made out this cheque without Eve's knowledge, and I shall manage to meet it somehow when the time comes. Keep on as you are living now; the way is hard, but it will be glorious. I would rather suffer any misfortune than think of your sinking into the sloughs of Paris, of which I saw quite enough. Have the courage to go on avoiding, as you are doing now, scrapes and bad company, do not waste your time with fools, and writers of a certain type that I learned to know at their just valuation during my stay in Paris. In fact, imitate worthily those heavenly spirits whom I love for your sake. Your efforts will be rewarded in time. Goodbye, my dear friend and brother; you have given me great happiness—I did not think you would have so much courage.

" David."

Eve Séchard to Lucien

" My dear,

" Your letter made us all cry. I should like those noble hearts to whom your good angel has led you to know that a mother and an unfortunate young wife pray for them morning and evening. And if the most fervent prayers ascend to the throne of God, they will bring some blessings upon you all. Indeed, my dear brother, their names are engraved upon my heart. Oh! I shall see them some day. I would go all the way barefoot, if necessary, to thank them for their friendship towards you which has been to me as a balm to my open wounds. Here, my dear, we are working like poor labourers. My husband, that great man unknown to the world whom I love more every day (every minute I discover new riches in his heart), is neglecting his printing business, and I can guess why : your poverty, ours, mother's, is breaking his heart. Our adored David is like Prometheus devoured by a vulture, a grief with a sharp yellow beak. He is hoping to make a fortune, but not for himself—he never gives a thought to himself, noble man that he is. He spends all his days making experiments on the manufacture of paper ; so he has asked me to look after the business for him, and he helps me when he can. Alas! I am pregnant. This fact, which ought to make me so very happy, saddens me in our present circumstances. My poor mother has grown young again ; she has summoned up her strength and gone back to her exhausting work as a nurse. We should be happy but for these money worries. David's old father will not give his son a penny ; David went to see him to try and borrow a few pounds for you, for he was in despair over your letter. 'I know Lucien,' he said ; 'he will lose his head and make a fool of himself.' I gave him a good scolding : 'My brother fail us in any way ?' I said. 'Lucien knows that I would die of grief.' Mother and I have pawned a few things, without David having any suspicion of it ; mother can redeem them when she has earned a little money. In this way we have managed to raise a hundred francs, which I am posting to you. If I did not answer your first letter, don't be too hard on me, dear Lucien. We were working far into the night, I was working like a man. I really would never have believed how strong I am! Mme de Bargeton is a heartless soulless woman ; even if she does not love you any more, at least she owed it to herself to protect you and help you after having torn you from our arms to fling you into the terrible ocean of Paris where it is only by the grace of God that one can expect to find true friends among these whirlpools of people and interests. She is not worth a regret. I would like to think that you had some devoted woman to stand by you—somebody like me! but so long as I know that you have friends who care for you as we do, I am quite satisfied. Spread your wings, my dear handsome genius! We will all be as proud of you some day as we love you now.

"Eve."

" My darling boy, I have nothing to add to what your sister has written except my blessing, and my assurance that you are more in my prayers and my thoughts (alas!) than those I have always with me ; for some hearts, the absent can do no wrong, and it is so with the heart of

" Your loving mother."

And so, two days later, Lucien was able to repay to his friends the loan that they had offered so graciously. Never, perhaps, did life seem sweeter to him, but the trace of self-love in his action did not escape the penetrating eyes and delicate sensibilities of his friends.

" Anyone would think that you were afraid to be indebted to us," Fulgence exclaimed.

" Oh, I take a very grave view indeed of his obvious pleasure," said Michel Chrestien ; " it confirms what I have already observed: Lucien is vain."

" He is a poet," said d'Arthez.

" Do you hold such a very natural feeling against me ? "

" We must give him credit for not attempting to hide it," said Léon Giraud. " He is still frank with us ; but I have an idea that he will be afraid of us some day."

" Why ? " Lucien asked.

" We can read your thoughts," said Joseph Bridau.

" There is a diabolical strain in you," Michel Chrestien said to him, " with which you will justify in your own eyes things absolutely opposed to our principles ; you may not be a sophist in theory, but you will be a sophist in practice."

" That is just what I am afraid of," said d'Arthez. " Lucien, you will carry on wonderful arguments with yourself, in which you will appear in the noblest light, but the outcome will be ignoble actions . . . You will never be at one with yourself."

" On what grounds, may I ask, do you make these charges ? " Lucien asked.

" Your vanity, my dear poet, is so great that it enters even into your friendship ! " said Fulgence. " All vanity of that sort is a symptom of an appalling egoism, and egoism poisons friendship."

" Oh dear! " exclaimed Lucien. " You cannot have any idea how much I love you all! "

" If you had loved us as we love one another, would you have been in such a hurry and made such a point of returning the money it gave us so much pleasure to give you ? "

" We don't lend here—we give," said Joseph Bridau brutally.

" Don't think us unkind, my dear boy," said Michel Chrestien. " We are thinking of the future. We are afraid of seeing you one day preferring the joys of a petty revenge to the joys of our simple friendship. Read Goethe's *Tasso*, the greatest work of that wonderful genius, and you will see there how the poet loves brilliant clothes, feasts and triumphs, applause ; very well : be a Tasso without the folly. If the world and its pleasures tempt you, transpose into the realm of ideas all that your vanities suggest to you. Stay here. . . . Transpose your folly—put virtue into your actions, and vice into your ideas, instead of thinking nobly and acting badly, as d'Arthez said just now."

Lucien hung his head : his friends were right.

" I admit that I am not as strong as the rest of you," he said with an adorable look. " I have not the back and shoulders to bear the weight of Paris, to struggle on bravely. Nature has given us different temperaments, different gifts, and nobody knows better than you do that vices and virtues are reversible. I am tired already, I confess."

" We will stand by you," said d'Arthez ; " that is just what real friends are for."

" The help that I have just received is precarious and we are all as poor as one another. I shall soon be in want again. Chrestien, who works for whoever will give him a job, has no influence with the publishers. Bianchon is quite outside that world. D'Arthez only deals with publishers of scientific and learned books, who have nothing to do with the publication of new literature. Horace, Fulgence Ridal and Bridau work in worlds miles away from that of publishing. I must do something! "

" Follow our example, and go on enduring! " said Bianchon. " Endure courageously, and put your trust in hard work! "

" But what is only enduring for you is death to me," said Lucien feelingly.

" Before the cock crows thrice," said Léon Giraud with a smile, " this man will have betrayed the cause of hard work for that of the idleness and vices of Paris."

" Where has work got you ? " said Lucien with a laugh.

" When one sets out for Italy from Paris one does not find Rome half-way," said Joseph Bridau. " As for you, you would like your green peas to grow ready buttered."

" They only grow like that for the eldest sons of peers of France," said Michel Chrestien. " But it is men like us who sow them and water them, and we enjoy them all the more for it."

The conversation was turned to a joke, and they changed the subject. His friends, with their perspicacity and delicacy, did their best to make Lucien forget this little quarrel ; from now on he realised that it was not easy to deceive them. But before very long he fell into a state of deep depression, that he did his best to conceal from his friends, whom he had come to regard as stern mentors. His Mediterranean temperament, that ran so easily through the whole gamut of feelings, set him making the most contradictory resolutions.

More than once he spoke of writing for the newspapers, and always his friends replied : " Don't do it on any account."

" That would be the end of the beautiful, charming Lucien that we know and love," said d'Arthez.

" You would not be able to resist the perpetual extremes of work and pleasure of the journalist's life ; and resisting those extremes is the very basis of virtue. You would be so carried away by the sense of power, of being able to exercise the right of life and death over works of intellect, that in two months you would be a journalist. And to be a journalist is to be a dictator in the republic of letters. Those who can say anything will sooner or later stick at nothing. Napoleon used to say that, and it is very understandable."

"But you would be by my side, would you not?" said Lucien.

"We would no longer be there," said Fulgence; "once you were a journalist, you would think no more about us than an opera-singer, brilliant and admired, in her silk-upholstered carriage, thinks of the village and the cows and the sabots of her early days. There is too much of the journalist in you as it is; your thought comes in brilliant flashes. You could never resist being clever, however deeply you might be hurting a friend. I see journalists in the foyers of the theatres, and they appal me. Journalism is a hell, a sink of iniquity, lies, and betrayals that no one can pass through, or emerge from uncorrupted, unless they are protected, like Dante, by Virgil's sacred laurel."

The more the group opposed this career, the more Lucien desired to find out about its dangers for himself, and he began to argue with himself as follows: would it not be ridiculous to allow himself to run out of money again without taking any steps about it? In view of the small success of his attempts to place his first novel, Lucien felt very little inclination to write a second. Besides, how would he live while he was writing it? He had exhausted his store of patience in a month of privation. Why should he not do honourably what other journalists did without conscience or dignity? His friends' lack of faith in him was insulting; he would prove to them his strength of character. Perhaps one day he would be in a position to help them, to be the herald of their fame!

"Besides, what sort of friendship is it that shrinks from standing by a friend?" he asked Michel Chrestien one evening when he and Léon Giraud had walked home with him.

"We do not shrink from anything," Michel Chrestien replied. "If you had the misfortune to kill your mistress, I would help you to conceal your crime, and I would still be able to respect you; but if you were to become a spy, I should avoid you in abhorrence, because you would be deliberately committed to base and shameful actions. And that is journalism. Friendship can pardon a mistake, or the unthinking impulse of passion; but it must be firm when it comes to selling your soul, your intellect, and your opinions."

"Why should I not become a journalist until I have sold my collection of poems and my novel and then give it up at once?"

"Machiavelli might do that, but not Lucien de Rubempré," said Léon Giraud.

"Oh! Now you've done it!" Michel exclaimed as he took leave of Léon. "Lucien," he said, "you have three hundred francs, enough to live on comfortably for three months; very well, work hard, write a second novel, d'Arthez and Fulgence will help you to plan it; you will improve, you will be a novelist. And I, meanwhile, will enter one of those intellectual leper-colonies. I will be a journalist for three months, and I will sell your books to some publisher by attacking his publications; I shall write articles, and I will get some for you. We will organise your success, you shall be a great man and remain our Lucien."

"You must despise me very much if you think that I should perish where you would survive!" said the poet.

"Oh, heaven forgive him, what a child he is!" said Michel Chrestien.

When his wit had been stimulated in the course of evenings spent in d'Arthez's room, Lucien had sometimes looked at the jokes and articles of some of the smaller newspapers. He felt sure that he could do at least as well as the wittiest contributors, and he made some experiments, in secret, in mental gymnastics of this type. One morning he set out with the triumphant idea of offering his services to some colonel of this light-infantry of the press. He put on his best suit, and crossed the bridges, thinking that authors, journalists and writers—in fact his future comrades—would be a little more sympathetic and disinterested than the two kinds of publisher who had dashed his hopes. He would be sure to find friends, and the same kindly and generous affection as he had found among the circle of the Rue des Quatre-Vents. The prey of those forebodings that so many men of imagination are apt at one moment to listen to, the next to combat, he arrived at the Rue Saint-Fiacre, off the Boulevard Montmartre. He stopped outside the house where a small newspaper had its offices, and at the sight of which his heart began to beat like that of a young man about to enter some evil haunt. All the same, he went upstairs to the offices, which were on the first landing. In the first room, which was divided into two equal parts by a partition, half of timber and half of wire netting up to the ceiling, he found a one-armed pensioner who was holding several reams of paper on his head by means of his one hand, and between his teeth the pass-book demanded by the Inland Revenue Department. This poor fellow, whose yellow face, covered with red swellings, had earned for him the name of " the Coconut ", indicated to Lucien the cerberus of the newspaper, seated behind the grill. This personage was an old officer, wearing a medal, his nose wreathed in his grey moustaches, a black silk skull-cap on his head, and enveloped in an ample blue overcoat, like a tortoise in its carapace.

" From what date do you want your subscription to commence, sir ? " this officer of the Empire enquired.

" I have not come about a subscription," said Lucien.

The poet was looking at a notice on the door next to the one by which he had entered, on which appeared the words " Editorial Office " and below, in smaller letters, " No admittance."

" A complaint, I suppose ? " the veteran went on. " Ah, yes, we were hard on Mariette. But there you are! I still do not know why. But if you want satisfaction, I am ready," he added, indicating a collection of foils and pistols, stacked in a corner, the armoury of a modern warrior.

" Not that either, sir. I have come to see the chief editor."

" There is never anybody here before four."

" Look here, Giroudeau, old chap, I make it eleven columns, which at a hundred sous a column comes to fifty-five francs ; I have only been paid forty—therefore you still owe me fifteen francs, as I have been telling you."

These words proceeded from a little weasel-face as pallid as an underdone white of egg, with a pair of eyes, soft blue in colour, but appalling in their malice; the owner, an insignificant young man, was concealed behind the dense mass of the old soldier. The voice came as a shock to Lucien, for it was something between a caterwaul and the asthmatic cough of a hyena.

"No doubt, my little militiaman," replied the retired officer, "but you have counted the crossheadings and the spaces, and I have Finot's orders to count the total number of lines and to divide by the average number for each column. Having performed that ruthless operation on your copy, it comes to three columns less."

"He won't pay for the spaces, the old Jew, but he counts them in all right when he sends his estimate for the whole paper in to his director! I shall go and see Étienne Lousteau and Vernou."

"I cannot go beyond my instructions, my boy," said the officer. "What! You cry out against your foster-mother over a matter of fifteen francs? And you write articles as easily as I smoke a cigar! All right, just stand your friends one bowl of punch less, or win one more game of billiards, and there's no more to be said."

"Finot's economy is going to cost him dear!" said the newspaper man as he took his departure.

"Anyone would think he was Voltaire and Rousseau!" the cashier remarked to himself, as he looked at the provincial poet.

"I will come back at four, then," said Lucien.

During the argument, Lucien had noticed on the walls portraits of Benjamin Constant, General Foy, the seventeen illustrious orators of the Liberal party, together with caricatures of members of the Government. He had noticed above all the door of the editor's private sanctuary, where, as he guessed, the witty newspaper that amused him every day, that enjoyed the privilege of ridiculing kings and the gravest events, in fact of undermining anything and everything with some smart catchphrase, was made up. He went and strolled on the boulevards, a pleasure quite new to him, but so pleasant that he saw the hands of the clocks in the clockmakers' pointing to four o'clock without having noticed that he had had no lunch. The poet hurried back forthwith to the Rue Saint-Fiacre, climbed the stairs and opened the door of the office. The veteran was no longer to be seen, but the old pensioner was seated on a pile of stamped papers eating a hunk of bread and keeping guard with an air of resignation. The paper he took for granted just as he had fatigue-duty in the old days, and he understood no more about it than he had known the reason for the forced marches ordered by the Emperor. Lucien was struck with the brilliant idea of deceiving this redoubtable official ; he pulled his hat down firmly on his head, and opened the door of the sanctuary as if he was one of the staff.

The editorial office presented to his eager eyes a round table covered with a green cloth, and six cherry-wood chairs with straw seats, still new. The floor of coloured tiles had not been polished ; but it was clean, which suggested that the public did not often set foot in that room. On the mantelpiece there stood a mirror, a cheap clock covered with dust, two candlesticks into which two tallow candles had been clumsily thrust, and a few visiting cards. On the table a few old newspapers grimaced round an inkwell, whose dry ink looked like lacquer and about which lay a few quill pens, bent into circles. He read one or two articles illegible as hieroglyphics on old scraps of paper that had been torn across the top by the compositors as they checked off the sheets as they were set up. He admired a few quite clever caricatures, drawn on brown paper, evidently by somebody trying to kill time by killing something else, to keep his hand in. Nine pen-and-ink caricature sketches at the expense of *Le Solitaire* (the journalists seemed to have got tired of this book of enormous European popularity) were pinned up on the cheap sea-green wallpaper : " *Le Solitaire* arrives in the provinces : sensation among the women." " Scene in a château—reading *Le Solitaire*." " Effect of *Le Solitaire* among domestic animals." " *Le Solitaire* explained to savages, with brilliant results." " The Chinese translation of *Le Solitaire* presented to the Emperor at Pekin, by the author." " The Mont Sauvage—Rape of Élodie." (This drawing struck Lucien as very indecent, but it made him laugh all the same.) " *Le Solitaire* on a dais, carried in procession by the newspapers." " *Le Solitaire* smashes a printing-press and defeats the *bears*." " The professors are struck by the unusual beauty of *Le Solitaire*, read backwards." Lucien noticed in the margin of one newspaper a drawing of a contributor, hat in hand, beneath which was written: " Finot, my hundred francs! " signed with a name that has since become widely known but which will never be glorious.

Between the fireplace and the window stood a writing-table, a mahogany armchair, a waste-paper basket, and an oblong hearthrug —all thickly coated with dust. There were only half-curtains on the windows. On the desk were piled some twenty books that had evidently been deposited there in the course of the day, together with engravings, music, " Chamber " snuff-boxes, a copy of the ninth edition of *Le Solitaire*, still the great joke of the moment, and about a dozen unopened letters.

By the time Lucien had made a mental inventory of this unusual furnishing, and had reflected deeply upon it, five o'clock had struck, and he went back to question the pensioner. The Coconut had finished his hunk of bread, and was waiting with the patience of a sentry for the decorated military gentleman, who was perhaps taking a stroll along the boulevard. At this moment the rustle of a skirt, and an unmistakably light feminine tread was heard on the staircase, and a moment later a woman appeared at the door. She was rather pretty.

" Sir," she said to Lucien, " I know why you are always giving Mademoiselle Virginie's hats so much publicity and I have come to ask, first of all, for a year's subscription; but I want to know your terms. . . ."

" I am not on the staff."

" Ah! "

" A subscription from the first of October? " asked the pensioner.

" What does the lady want? " said the veteran, reappearing.

The old officer entered into a discussion with the pretty milliner. When Lucien, tired of waiting, came back into the outer room, he heard the end of the conversation:

" But I shall be only too delighted! Mademoiselle Florentine is welcome to come to my shop and choose whatever she likes. I specialise in ribbons. So everything is settled: you won't mention

Virginie again—a clumsy creature who could no more invent a new shape . . . but I have ideas! "

Lucien heard a number of coins drop into the cash-box. After that, the old soldier set to work on the day's accounts.

" I have been waiting here for an hour, sir," said the poet in considerable annoyance.

" And *they* have not come ? " said the veteran of the Empire, in tones of polite concern. " I am not surprised. It is a long time since I have seen them, either. It's the middle of the month, you see. These fellows only turn up on pay-days, the 29th and the 30th."

" And M. Finot ? " Lucien asked. He had remembered the name of the editor.

" He is at home, in the Rue Feydeau. Coconut, my boy, call round with everything that has come in today as you take the paper to the printers."

" Then where is the paper made up ? " said Lucien, speaking his thought aloud.

" The paper ? " said the official, as the Coconut handed over to him the rest of the stamp money. " The paper—*broum! broum!* (My boy, mind you are at the printers at six o'clock tomorrow morning to send out the porters)—the paper, sir, is written in the street, at the authors' houses, and at the printers, between eleven o'clock and midnight. In the Emperor's time, sir, these shops for spoiled paper were unknown. Oh, he would have made short work of them with four men and a corporal—he would not have let himself be rattled by their talk, like this lot. But I must not start talking. If my nephew manages to make a living out of it, and so long as they are writing for the son of the *Other—broum! broum!*—after all, there is something to be said for it. But subscribers do not seem to be pouring in in serried ranks by the looks of things. I shall give up this job."

" You seem to know all about the newspaper, sir ? "

" Only on the financial side, *broum ! broum !* " said the old soldier, clearing his throat. " From a hundred sous to three francs a column according to talent—fifty lines to a column, forty letters to the line, without blanks—there you are! As for the contributors, they are a rum lot, little fellows I wouldn't have taken on for the commissariat, and who, because they can scrawl like flies on white paper, think they have the right to look down on an old Captain of Dragoons in the Imperial Guard, retired as a Major, after entering every capital in Europe with Napoleon."

Lucien was being driven towards the door by the soldier of Napoleon, who was brushing his coat and making as if to go out. But Lucien found the courage to stand his ground.

"I came as a contributor," he said, "and I assure you that I am full of respect for a Captain of the Imperial Guard, those men of bronze . . ."

"Very nicely put, my little civilian," said the officer, "but what kind of contributor do you wish to become?" The trooper swept past Lucien and descended the stairs. He paused to get a light for his cigar at the porter's lodge.

"If any subscriptions come in, take them and make a note of them, Mère Chollet—subscriptions, I only deal with subscriptions," he went on, turning to Lucien, who had followed him. "Finot is my nephew, the only member of my family who has ever lifted a finger to help me. And anyone who wants to pick a quarrel with Finot will have to reckon with old Giroudeau, Captain in the Dragoons of the Guard. Began as a private in a cavalry regiment in the army of Sambre-et-Meuse, five years fencing-master to the First Hussars, in the Italian army! One, two—and the plaintiff would be among the shades!" he added, making a lunge. "Now, my boy, we have various writing-corps: there is the contributor who writes and draws his pay; the contributor who writes and gets nothing, what we call a volunteer; and, last of all, there is the contributor who writes nothing, and he is by no means the biggest fool, for he makes no mistakes; he sets himself up as an author, he is on the editorial board, he stands us dinners and swanks about the theatres, keeps an actress and has a good time. What do you want to be?"

"Why, a contributor who works hard and is therefore paid well."

"You are like all those recruits who want to be a Marshal of

France! Take old Giroudeau's advice, turn right about, double quick, and go and pick up nails in the gutter, like that good fellow over there who has done service, you can see it by the look of him. Isn't it a shame that an old soldier who has walked any number of times into the jaws of death should be picking up nails in Paris? Well, upon my soul, you are only a poor beggar, but you did not stand by the Emperor! Well, my boy, that civilian you saw this morning has earned forty francs for a month's work. Do you expect to do any better?—and, according to Finot, he is the cleverest of our contributors."

"When you enlisted in the Sambre-et-Meuse, did they tell you it was dangerous?"

"Yes, by Jove!"

"Well?"

"All right, go and see my nephew Finot, he's a good fellow, the best fellow you can hope to meet, if you ever manage to meet him; for he is like a fish, always on the move. His job is not to write, you see, but to see that others do the writing. These customers seem to like having a good time with the actresses better than scribbling on sheets of paper. Oh, they are a funny lot! Hope I may have the honour of seeing you again!"

The cashier strode off, swinging his redoubtable leaded walking-stick (a method of defence dating from Germanicus), and left Lucien on the pavement, no less astonished by this picture of a newspaper office than he had been by the practical aspects of literature that he had encountered at the offices of Vidal and Porchon. Lucien called ten times at the house of Andoche Finot, the editor, in Rue Feydeau, but never found him in. First thing in the morning Finot had not come in yet; at noon he was out—breakfasting at a certain café, so they told him. Lucien went to the café, and, surmounting his unspeakable repugnance, asked the waitress for Finot; Finot had just left. Lucien came at last to the conclusion that Finot was a fabulous apocryphal creature, and he decided that it would be simpler to lie in wait for Étienne Lousteau at Flicoteaux. That young journalist would no doubt explain the mystery that surrounded the newspaper to which he was attached.

Ever since the day, a hundred times blessed, when Lucien had made the acquaintance of Daniel d'Arthez, he had changed his place at Flicoteaux. The two friends always dined side by side, talking in low voices about high literary matters, possible subjects, and ways of presenting, opening up, and developing them. Daniel d'Arthez was, at the present time, revising the manuscript of *An Archer of Charles IX*; he had re-cast whole chapters, and it was he who wrote the fine passages that there are in that book, and he added the magnificent preface—probably the best thing in the book—that throws so much light on the younger literary school. One day, as Lucien was about to sit down beside Daniel, who had been waiting for him, and who had already held out his hand to him he saw Étienne Lousteau just coming in at the door. Lucien abruptly let go of Daniel's hand and told the waiter that he would be dining in his old place, near the counter. D'Arthez gave Lucien a look in which reproach was wrapped in angelic forgiveness. This look went straight to Lucien's heart, so that he took Daniel's hand again and pressed it warmly.

"It is about something very important for me; I will tell you later," he said.

Lucien was in his old place by the time Lousteau reached his; as the first comer, he greeted him, and they soon fell into a conversation that made such progress that Lucien went off to fetch the manuscript of *Marguerites* while Lousteau finished his dinner. The journalist had consented to look at his sonnets, and Lucien was already counting on his merely polite expressions of interest, to find an editor, or to get him a job on a newspaper. When he came back, Lucien saw Daniel in the corner of the restaurant, leaning sadly on his elbow watching him thoughtfully; but he pretended not to see his friend; driven by poverty, and led on by ambition, he followed Lousteau.

In the late afternoon the journalist and the novice went and sat under the trees in the Luxembourg, in that part of the gardens which leads from the broad Avenue de l'Observatoire to the Rue de l'Ouest. The Rue de l'Ouest was at that time a long stretch of mud bordered with planks and market-gardens; there were houses only at the end nearest the Rue de Vaugirard, and this footpath was so little frequented that at the hour when all Paris dines, two lovers could quarrel, or exchange the pledges of a reconciliation, without fear of being seen. The only possible spoil-sport was the old veteran night-watchman at the little gate of the Rue de l'Ouest, if that venerable pensioner should take it into his head to increase the number of paces of his monotonous beat. It was here, on a bench between two lime trees, that Étienne listened to the sonnets, chosen at random from *Marguerites*. Étienne Lousteau, who after two years' apprenticeship was firmly in the saddle as a newspaper man, and who counted several celebrities of the moment among his friends, was a person of consequence in Lucien's eyes. Therefore, as he untied the manuscript of *Marguerites*, our provincial poet judged it necessary to make some introductory remaıks.

" The sonnet," he began, " is one of the most difficult of verse-forms, and this little poem has been generally abandoned. No French writer has equalled Petrarch, whose language is infinitely more supple than ours, and makes possible plays of thought that our positivism (if I may use the word) does not permit. It seemed to me, therefore, that a sequence of sonnets would have the merit of originality. Victor Hugo has appropriated the ode, Canalis specialises in light verse, Beranger has monopolised the lyric, Casimir Delavigne has taken tragedy and Lamartine meditative verse."

" Are you a classic or a romantic ? " inquired Lousteau.

Lucien's look of astonishment revealed such a complete ignorance of the state of affairs in the republic of letters that Lousteau judged it necessary to enlighten him.

" My dear fellow, you have arrived in the middle of a pitched battle, and you must take sides immediately. Literature, at first sight, might seem to be divided into several zones ; but our great men all belong to one of two camps. The royalists are romantics, the liberals are classics. Difference of literary opinion goes with difference of political opinion, and the result is a war between the rising and the waning glories, in which all weapons are employed, torrents of ink, double-edged witticisms, deadly calumnies, and epithets to the death. By a strange coincidence, the royalist romantics demand freedom in literature, and the revocation of the laws that have established our accepted literary forms ; while the liberals are all for maintaining the unities, the alexandrine, and classical themes. Literary opinions, therefore, are in direct opposition to the political opinions of the respective camps. If you are eclectic, you will have no one for you. Which side do you intend to take ? "

" Which is the winning side ? "

" The sales of the Liberal papers are much bigger than those of the Royalist and Ministerial journals ; all the same, Canalis is read, in spite of being a Catholic and a Monarchist, and favoured by the Court and the clergy. Sonnets!—why, they date back to before Boileau," said Étienne, seeing Lucien's dismay at the prospect of choosing between two banners. " Be a romantic. The romantics are all young men, and the classicists are all old periwigs. The romantics will win the day."

The word periwig was the latest epithet that had been taken up by romantic journalism for the purpose of pinning on to the classicists.

" *The Easter Daisy*," Lucien began, choosing the first of the two title sonnets that served as an introduction to the series.

Not blossoming only for the eyes' delight,
Daisies, your varied colours you display,
For, eloquent, your wordless poetry
Unfolds to man the riches of his heart.

Your golden stamens, set in silver bright
Those gods we fondly worship signify,
And in your petals' tips, that crimson die,
Our glory's grievous price, is eloquent.

Is it because you flowered upon that morn
When from His risen pinions, heavenward bent,
Jesus shook virtues down from wings unfurled

That in our autumn fields you bloom forlorn ?
Do you recall our faithless treasures spent,
Or the wasted morning of our springtime world ?

Lucien felt piqued to see that Lousteau remained quite unmoved as he listened to this sonnet ; he had not yet encountered the disconcerting impassibility of the professional critic, so characteristic of journalists who have become bored with a surfeit of prose, drama, and verse. The poet, accustomed as he was to applause, swallowed his disappointment ; he read the sonnet that Mme de Bargeton, and some of his friends in d'Arthez's circle, liked best.

The Marguerite

I am the marguerite that fairest grew
Of all the flowers that star the grassy path ;
Happy when sought for my own beauty's worth,
I thought my morning ever would be new.

Alas for my fond hopes—one more virtue
Fate has bestowed on me—the gift of truth!
I suffer, and I die! knowledge brings death,
Whose fatal brightness shines upon my brow.

I know no quiet now, no sweet repose,
Love plucks the future from my living shrine,
To read there whom I love, my heart he bares,
And from my brow tears its bright diadem.
My flower discarded, then, without regret,
Its secret known, he tramples underfoot.

At the end, the poet looked at his Aristarchus ; Étienne Lousteau was contemplating the trees in the nursery garden.

" Well ? " said Lucien.

" Well, my dear fellow, go on! I am listening, am I not ? In Paris, to listen without saying anything is already high praise! "

" Have you had enough ? " said Lucien.

" Go on," said the journalist curtly.

Lucien read the following sonnet; but he read it with death in his heart, for Lousteau's impenetrable indifference froze his eloquence. If he had been less of a novice in the literary world, he would have realised that, among authors, silence and curtness under such circumstances are the signs of jealousy; whereas outspoken admiration is merely an expression of the pleasure that mediocre work gives to their self-esteem.

The Camellia (thirtieth sonnet)

Flowers are the words of nature's poetry:
The rose is love, to beauty dedicate;
A soul's pure essence breathes the violet,
Unsullied innocence the radiant lily.

Lily not sweet, rose without majesty,
This hothouse bloom, this false immaculate
Camellia-blossom opes her frozen heart
For weariness of her own virginity.

Yet in the boxes of the theatre
I love to see those waxen bells unfold,
Crown of cold hearts, snowy camellias,

Pale gleaming in some woman's shadowy hair
Whose cunning can inspire a love as cold
As marble carved by Grecian Phidias.

" What do you think of my poor sonnets?" Lucien asked, point-blank.

" Do you want to know the truth?" said Lousteau.

" I am young enough to love the truth, and I am so determined to succeed that I can hear it without taking offence, if not without pain," said Lucien.

" Very well, my dear fellow ; from the involved style of the first sonnet, I should judge it to be a work of your Angoulême period, that no doubt cost you so much trouble that you cannot bear to part with it ; the second and third already bear the marks of Paris ; but do read me one more ! " he added, in tones that charmed our provincial celebrity.

Encouraged by this request, Lucien read with more confidence the sonnet that d'Arthez and Bridau (perhaps because of its colour) thought his best.

The Tulip (fiftieth sonnet)

The tulip I, the flower of fair Holland ;
Such my renown, the Flemish merchant pays
For but a single bulb, a diamond's price
So pure my stock, so tall am I, and grand.

Feudal my port, like some antique Yolande
With ample skirts ; in rich embroideries
Upon my gown is blazoned my device :
Gules with fesse azure, or on purple ground.

And with his hand, the gardener divine
Upon my robe of texture smooth and fine
Has woven purple of kings, rays of the sun.

No garden flower in equal splendour stands,
But nature no essential sweetness lends
To fill my cup of orient porcelain.

" Well ? " said Lucien, after a pause that seemed to him far too long.

" My dear fellow," said Étienne Lousteau, looking at the toes of Lucien's boots (they were the pair he had brought from Angoulême, and he was wearing them out), " I strongly recommend you to black your boots with ink to save blacking, to turn your pens into tooth-picks so that when you take a walk in this picturesque alley after eating at Flicoteaux people will think that you have dined well, and to take any job you can get. Become a bailiff's under-clerk if you have a weak heart, or a shop assistant if you have a strong back, or a soldier if you like military music. You have the makings of three poets ; but before you become known you will have had time to die of starvation six times over, if you are hoping to live on your poetry. Now I gather from your highly unsophisticated discourse, that you are hoping to earn a living by writing. I am not criticising your poems—they are a good deal better than all those volumes of verses that are taking up shelf-space in the booksellers'. The elegant nightingales that are sold for a little more than the rest because they are printed on hand-made paper generally end up on the bookstalls beside the Seine, where you can go and study their verses if you ever feel inclined to make an instructive pilgrimage to the Quais between old Jérome's bookstall on the Pont Notre-Dame and the Pont Royal. There you will find all those *Essais poetiques* and *Inspirations* and *Elevations*, all the *Hymnes* and *Chants* and *Ballades* and *Odes*, in fact the entire brood hatched during the last seven years. There are all those muses, covered with dust, spattered with mud from the passing cabs, violated by every passer-by who only wants to look at the vignette on the title-page. You know nobody ; you have no influence with any newspaper—your *Marguerites* will remain as chastely closed as they are at this moment ; they will never expand in the sun of publicity, on pages with wide margins, decorated with all those daring little flowerets that the illustrious Dauriat, King of the Wooden Galleries, who publishes all the well-known poets, scatters so liberally. My poor young poet, I came to Paris, like you, full of illusions, impelled by the love of art, and by an unconquerable desire for glory ; I discovered the realities of the literary world, the difficulties of publication, and the hard facts of poverty. My lofty ideals—which I now have well under control—my first youthful enthusiasm—prevented me from seeing the workings of the social machinery ; I was compelled to see it in the end by bumping against its wheels, knocking into its shafts, getting covered with its grease, and hearing the constant clatter of its chains and fly-wheels. You will have to learn, as I did, that behind all those fine things we once dreamed of there are human intrigues, and passions, and necessities. You will find yourself involved, willy-nilly, in the horrible struggle of book against book, man against man, party against party, and you must fight your way systematically unless you want to find yourself deserted by your own party. These mean contests are disillusioning. They leave you exhausted and depraved, and all to no purpose, because more often than not you will have expended your efforts to crown a man whom you dislike, a writer of second-rate talent whom you are obliged to put forward as a genius whether you like it or not.

" A great deal goes on behind the scenes in the literary world. Success—whether it comes as a result of chance or of merit—that is what the public applauds. But the preparations—and they are always ugly, what with the minor actors in the drama, the hired claque, and the scene-shifting—all that goes on behind the scenes. You are still in the front of the house. There is still time—turn back before you set your foot on the first step that leads to the throne of fame, for which so many ambitions are contending, and do not dishonour yourself as I have had to do in order to live "—and there were tears in Étienne Lousteau's eyes as he spoke.

" Do you know how I make a living ? " he went on in passionate tones. " The small sum of money that my family could afford to give me was soon used up. I had just had a play accepted by the Théâtre-Français when I found myself without a penny. At the Théâtre-Français you may have the influence of a prince, or a First Gentleman of the Bedchamber, but that will get you nowhere ; the actors will not lift a finger for you unless you are in a position to damage their reputations. If you have the power to spread a rumour that the leading actor has asthma, or that the leading lady has a fistula wherever you please, or that the soubrette has foul breath, your play will be put on tomorrow. I do not know whether in two years' time your humble servant will be in a position to exert such power : one needs too many friends. Where, and how, and by what means, meanwhile, am I to earn enough to live on ?—that was the question I often asked myself, under the stress of hunger. Well, after trying a number of things—I wrote an anonymous novel for which I was paid two hundred francs by Doguereau, who did not make much out of it either—I came to the conclusion that journalism was the only means of livelihood open to me. But how was I going to get into that shop? I will not bore you with an account of all my vain attempts, all the snubs I encountered, and of the six months I spent as a free-lance on a paper, where I was told that I scared subscribers away, when as a matter of fact I sent the sales up. We will pass over these insults. At this moment I am being paid almost nothing for doing the plays at the Boulevard theatres for Finot's paper—Finot is that big fellow who still lunches two or three times a month at the Café Voltaire (but you never go there). Finot is the chief editor. I live by selling the free tickets that the management of these theatres give me to secure my good will (for what it is worth) on the paper, and by selling the review copies sent me by the publishers. And lastly, I do a trade in the gifts in kind from tradesmen (when Finot has taken all he wants) for whom, or against whom, Finot permits me to write paragraphs. *Eau Carminative* and *Pâte des Sultanes* and *Huile Céphalique* and *Mixture Brèsilienne* are willing to pay twenty or thirty francs for a facetious article.

"It is my business to run down publishers who don't send in enough review copies—the paper likes to have two, that Finot sells and I need two, which I sell. A publisher who is stingy with review copies may bring out a masterpiece, but he will still get bad notices. It is a low trade, but I manage to make a living by it, like plenty of others! And you needn't imagine that political journalism is any better—everything in these two spheres is corrupt; there is not a man in that world who does not either offer bribes or receive them.

"If a publisher is bringing out a work of some importance, he pays me, so that I shall not attack it. So that my income varies according to the publishing lists. When the prospectuses burst out like a rash, money pours into my pocket, and I can buy drinks for my friends. When nothing is coming out, I dine at Flicoteaux.

"The actresses will pay you for good notices, too, but the clever ones pay for criticism; what they fear most is silence. The best thing, from their point of view, is a notice that starts a discussion; it is worth more to them, and they will pay more for it, than for a simple puff that is forgotten the next day. Controversy, my dear fellow—that is the pedestal of all celebrities. I make fifty crowns a month as a hired gangster, trading in commercial, literary, and theatrical reputations ; I could get five hundred francs for a novel, and I am beginning to have the reputation of being a man to be reckoned with. Some day, instead of living with Florine at the expense of a druggist who fancies himself as a milord, I shall have a place of my own, and a column in a big newspaper ; and then, my boy, Florine will become a great actress. What I shall become I don't know ; a minister or even an honest man—all things are still possible ! "

He raised his humiliated head and looked up at the leaves with an expression of despairing self-contempt terrible to see.

" And once I had a tragedy accepted! And among my papers I have a poem that will not live! And I was a good fellow! My love was pure, once—and now I have an actress at the Panorama-Dramatique for my mistress—I, who once dreamed of noble loves, for distinguished women of the great world! And now, if a publisher refuses to send a copy of it to my newspaper, I am prepared to run down a book that I think is good."

Lucien was moved to tears, and clasped Étienne's hand in his.

The journalist rose to his feet and walked in the direction of the wide Avenue de l'Observatoire, where the two poets walked up and down, as if to breathe more freely.

" Outside the literary world," Lousteau continued, " there is no one who has the slightest idea of the terrible Odyssey by which writers reach what is called vogue, or fashion, or reputation, fame, celebrity, public favour—all these are different rungs on the ladder that leads to glory—for which, however, they are a poor substitute. This moral phenomenon, brilliant as it is, is the product of a thousand accidents that vary perpetually, so that two men have never been known to arrive by the same route. Take Canalis and Nathan, their stories are utterly dissimilar, and neither of them will ever be repeated. D'Arthez who wears himself out with work, will become famous by some chance or other.

"And once I had a tragedy accepted!"

"This fine thing reputation that is so much desired, is nearly always crowned prostitution. Yes, the lowest forms of writing are like those poor creatures who freeze at street-corners; second-rate writing is the kept woman who has managed to get away from the evil haunts of journalism and lives at *my* expense; and successful literature is the brilliant insolent courtesan who has her own property and pays income-tax, who entertains lords, treating or ill-treating them as she pleases, who has her carriage and her livery, and can afford to keep her thirsty creditors waiting. Ah! Those who see her as I once did, and as you still do at this moment, as an angel with diaphanous wings, clad in immaculate white, with a palm of virtue in one hand and a flaming sword in the other—a sort of cross between the mythological abstraction who lives at the bottom of a well, and the virtuous poor girl of the suburbs, who refuses to grow rich at the expense of chastity, and who makes her way by the efforts of a noble courage, reascending to the skies without a stain on her character (always supposing she does not end her days soiled, despoiled, polluted, and forgotten on a pauper's bier)—men like that, whose brains are helmeted in bronze, whose hearts remain still warm under the snows of experience, are seldom met with in the country that now lies at our feet," he said, indicating the great city, with its smoke rising into the evening sky.

A vision of the circle of the Rue de Quatre-Vents passed rapidly before Lucien's eyes, and he was moved at the thought of them; but he was carried away by Lousteau, who continued his appalling lamentation.

"They are few and far between in that great fermenting vat, as rare as true lovers in the amorous world, or as fortunes honestly come by in the financial world, or as men with clean hands in journalism. The experience of the first man who said to me what I have just said to you was thrown away on me, as no doubt mine will be on you. It is the same story, year after year—the same eager rush to Paris of ambitious young fellows from the provinces, who arrive —more of them every year—their heads erect, their hearts full of high hopes, to take Fashion by storm—Fashion! She is like Princess Tourandot in the *Mille et un Jours*, and they all hope to be her Prince Calaf. But not one of them guesses the riddle. They all tumble into the slough of misfortune, into the filth of journalism, into the mire of publishing.

" Poor beggars, they pick up a living by writing biographical articles, Paris news items, odds and ends, or books commissioned by those astute dealers in blackened paper, who would rather publish trash that sells out in a fortnight than a work of genius that will take some time to make its way. These caterpillars are crushed to death before they ever turn into butterflies. They live by shame and dishonour, equally ready to tear to pieces or cry up a budding talent at a word from a Pasha on the *Constitutionnel* or the *Quotidienne* or the *Débats*, at a hint from the publishers, or at the request of a jealous rival, often just for the sake of a dinner. Those who surmount these obstacles forget the struggles of their early days. Take myself, for example—for six months I put my best ideas into a series of articles for a scoundrel who passed them off as his own, and who on the strength of these samples has been given a job as sub-editor ; he has not taken me on, he has not given me so much as a hundred sous, and yet I cannot afford to refuse to shake hands with him whenever we meet."

" Why not ? " Lucien asked indignantly.

" Because I might want to put a dozen lines into his newspaper one day," Lousteau replied coolly. " In fact, my dear boy, hard work is not the secret of success as a writer, but knowing how to exploit the hard work of others. The newspaper proprietors are the contractors, we are the bricklayers. And the more second-rate you are the sooner you will succeed ; for you have to swallow insults, to be utterly thick-skinned, to play up to all the little base passions of these sultans of literature—like Hector Merlin, who came from Limoges a little while ago. He is already the political correspondent of a Right Centre newspaper, and he writes on our little paper as well. And I have seen that man pick up the hat that a chief editor had dropped! By never giving offence, that fellow will always manage to slip between rival ambitions, leaving them to fight it out.

" You are sorry for me. I see in you myself as I was, and there is nothing more sure than that, two years from now, you will be what

I am now. You think there is some secret jealousy, some personal motive, behind this bitter counsel. But it is dictated by the despair of the damned who can never again leave hell. Nobody will dare to tell you these things that I have spoken out of the bitterness of my soul, like Job among the ashes, showing his sores! "

" But whether I fight in this field or elsewhere, fight I must! " said Lucien.

" Then be sure of this! " Lousteau continued. " If you have talent, it will be a fight to the death, for your best chance is to have none. At this moment your conscience is clear, but it will give way before those who hold your success in their hands; when a word from one of them is a matter of life and death to you, and he will not say that word. Believe me, the successful writer is more insolent, more hard-hearted towards newcomers than the most ruthless publisher. The publisher is only afraid of losing money, but the author is afraid of a possible rival ; the publisher shows you the door, but the author will crush the life out of you. To write good books, my poor boy, you must draw tenderness, vitality, the sap of life, from your own heart's blood at every dip of the pen, and put your very soul into the passions, sentiments, and phrases of your work. Yes supposing you write instead of acting, sing instead of battling with the world, and put all your loves and hates into your books ; supposing you keep your wealth for your style, your money and fine clothes for your characters, while you walk about the streets of Paris in rags, happy to think that you have rivalled the Registrar of Births by bringing into existence an individual called Adolphe, or Corinna, or Clarissa, or René or Manon ; when you have ruined your life and your digestion in order to give life to this creation of yours, you will see it condemned, betrayed, sold, and swept into the back waters of oblivion by the journalists, and disregarded by your best friends. Will you be able to wait for the day when your work will emerge again into the light of day ? Who will resurrect it, and when and how ? There is a magnificent book, the very heart-cry of unbelief, *Obermann,* lost in the wilderness of the bookshops, shelved among the nightingales, as the publishers so ironically call them : when will its Easter come ? Who knows! For a start, just try and find a publisher who will venture to print the *Marguerites*—not pay you anything for them, mind you, but simply print them. If you do, you will see some curious things."

This brutal tirade, uttered in the accents of all the diverse passions that it expressed, descended like an avalanche of snow upon Lucien's heart, leaving a sense of glacial cold. He remained standing in silence for a while ; and then, as if inspired by the horrible poetry of difficulties, his spirit caught fire. Lucien grasped Lousteau's hand.

"I will triumph!" he exclaimed.

"Good!" said the journalist. "One more Christian going down to the arena to offer himself to the lions. Well, my dear fellow, there is a first performance tonight at the Panorama-Dramatique ; it doesn't begin until eight, and it is six o'clock now. Go and put on your coat, make yourself presentable, in fact. Then come and pick me up. I live in the Rue de la Harpe, above the Café Servel, on the fourth floor. We will look in at Dauriat's on the way. You are determined to go ahead, I suppose ? Very well, I will introduce you this evening to one of the kings of the publishing world, and to one or two journalists. After the theatre, we will go on to supper at my mistress's flat, with some friends, for the dinner we have just had cannot be called a meal. You will meet Finot there, the chief editor and proprietor of my paper. You remember what Minette says in the Vaudeville—*Time is an old skinflint,* very well, chance is a skinflint, too, for the likes of you and me, and must be tempted."

"I shall never forget this day," said Lucien.

"Bring your manuscript with you, and mind you are decently dressed, not on Florine's account, but because of the publisher."

This comradely familiarity which succeeded the violent outburst of a poet describing the battlefield of letters, touched Lucien no less than he had previously been touched, in those same gardens, by d'Arthez's grave words of faith. Inexperienced as he was, excited by the prospect of an imminent battle between himself and the world, Lucien had no conception of the reality of the moral evils that the journalist had denounced to him. Nor did he know that he stood at the parting of two ways—the one, represented by the circle at the Rue de Quatre-Vents, long, honourable, and sure ; the other—that of journalism—beset with hidden dangers, a perilous path, among muddy ditches where his conscience, inevitably, must be spattered with mire. His character impelled him to take the shortest, and, to all appearances, the more pleasant way, to snatch at the quick and decisive means. Nor did he see, at that moment, any difference between d'Arthez's noble friendship and the facile camaraderie of Lousteau. His unstable mind saw journalism as a weapon ready to hand, he felt himself capable of wielding it, and he was resolved to take it up.

He was dazzled by the offers of his new friend, who had shaken his hand with an easy affability that he mistook for graciousness ; for how was he to know that in the ranks of the press everybody needs friends, just as generals need soldiers ? Lousteau, seeing Lucien's resolution, was recruiting him in the hope of attaching him to himself. The journalist was at the stage of needing a first recruit, just as Lucien needed his first protector : the one was about to be promoted to the rank of corporal, the other to that of a private.

The novice returned to his hotel in high spirits, where he took as much care over his toilet as on that unlucky day when he had presented himself at the Marquise d'Espard's box at the opera ; but already he had learned to wear his clothes better, and they looked as if they belonged to him. He wore his beautiful tight-fitting, light-coloured trousers, his elegant tasselled boots that had cost him forty francs, and his evening coat. His fine thick golden hair, curled and perfumed, rippled in shining waves. Self-confidence and faith in his future lit up his brow. His effeminate hands were carefully tended, their almond nails spotless and rose-pink. The white contours of his chin were set off by his black satin stock. Never did a more handsome young man come down from the heights of the Latin Quarter.

Beautiful as a Greek god, Lucien took a cab, and reached the door of the Café Servel at a quarter to seven. The portress gave him some decidedly complicated instructions on the topography of the fourth floor, and armed with these directions he found, not without difficulty, an open door at the end of a long dark passage, and recognised the typical room of the Latin Quarter.

Here, as in the Rue de Cluny, in d'Arthez's room, in Chrestien's, everywhere he went, Lucien recognised the signs of youthful poverty. But in each case this poverty bore the stamp of the particular character of the victim. Here the aspect of poverty was sinister. A shabby secondhand carpet lay crumpled at the foot of a walnut-wood bedstead, without hangings; the window curtains were stained yellow with cigar-smoke and smoke from the chimney, which did not draw; on the mantelpiece stood a Carcel lamp, a present from Florine that had hitherto escaped the pawn-shop; a lustreless mahogany chest of drawers, a table strewn with papers, upon which lay two or three dishevelled quill pens, and no books other than those that had arrived during the last twenty-four hours —such was the furniture of that room, in which there was not one single object of any value. An ignoble display of shabby boots gaped in one corner, and old socks worn to ribbons; in another corner, crushed cigar-ends, dirty handkerchiefs, shirts that had done double duty, and waistcoats that had reached a third edition. It was, in fact, a journalist's bivouac, containing things whose only character was negative, the most strangely denuded room that it would be possible to imagine.

On the bedside-table, strewn with books read that morning, glowed a tinder-box. On the mantelpiece a razor, a brace of pistols, and a box of cigars had been carelessly flung down, and a pair of foils, crossed under a wire mask, hung on a panel. Three upright and two armchairs, almost too shabby for the shabbiest house in the street, completed the furniture. That room, dirty and cheerless, told of a restless life, devoid of self-respect: it was a room used to sleep in, to scramble through hurried work, a room in which its occupant obviously stayed for as short a time as possible and got out of as soon as he could. What a difference between this cynical disorder, and the orderly, self-respecting poverty of d'Arthez! But this warning in the form of a memory Lucien did not heed, for Étienne greeted him with a joke that covered up this nudity of vice.

"This is my kennel!" he said. "My public appearances are made in the Rue de Bondy, in the new flat that our druggist has furnished for Florine, where we are having a housewarming this evening."

Étienne Lousteau was wearing black trousers, well-polished boots and a coat buttoned up to the neck; his shirt, which he no doubt intended to change at Florine's, was concealed by a velvet stock, and he was brushing his hat in the hopes of making it look new.

"Let us go," said Lucien.

"Not yet; I am waiting for a bookseller to bring me some money. There may be play, and I haven't a sou; besides, I must have some gloves."

At this moment the two new friends heard a man's step in the passage.

"Here he is," said Lousteau. "You shall see, my dear chap, the form that Providence takes when she appears to poets. Before you contemplate Dauriat, the fashionable publisher, in all his glory, you are about to see the bookseller of the Quai des Augustins, the cut-price bookseller, the street-vendor of the trade, the Norman ex-greengrocer. Come on in, old Tartar!" Lousteau shouted.

"Here I am," said a voice as crazy as a cracked bell.

"With the money?"

"Money? There isn't any money in the book trade any more," said a young man who eyed Lucien curiously as he came in.

"You owe me fifty francs for a start," Lousteau went on. "And here are two copies of *Voyage en Egypte*—a first class book they say, swarming with wood-cuts, sure to sell: Finot has been paid for two articles that I am to write on it. *Item* two copies of the latest novel of Victor Ducagne an author highly thought of in Marais. *Item* two copies of the second novel of a new author, Paul de Kock, in the same style. *Item* two *Yseult de Dôles*, a charming provincial work. Total, a hundred francs, and dear at that. In other words, you owe me one hundred francs, Barbet old chap."

Barbet looked at the books and examined the edges and bindings carefully.

"Oh, they are in a perfect state of preservation," said Lousteau. "*The Voyage* is uncut, and so is the Paul de Kock, the Ducagne, and that one over there on the mantelpiece, *Considerations sur la Symbolique*—I will throw that one in as well. Myths are so boring that I will let you have it so that I shall not have to see millions of bookworms coming out of it."

" Then how are you going to write your reviews ? " Lucien enquired.

Barbet looked at Lucien in profound astonishment, then back to Étienne! He chuckled.

" One can see that this gentleman has not the misfortune of being a literary man."

" No, Barbet, no. He is a poet, a great poet who will put Canalis, Béranger and Delavigne in the shade. He will go far, unless he throws himself into the river, and even so he will be washed down as far as Saint-Cloud."

" If the gentleman would like to hear my advice," said Barbet, " it is to give up poetry and to take up prose. They don't want any more poetry on the Quais."

Barbet was wearing a shabby overcoat held by a single button ; his stock was greasy. He kept his hat on all the time. He wore slippers, and his unbuttoned waistcoat revealed a good strong hard-wearing shirt. His round face with its pair of greedy eyes was affable enough ; but he had that look of vague uneasiness peculiar to men who have money and are constantly being asked to part with it. He looked open and easy-going, for his business shrewdness was well wadded with fat. He had started as a shop-assistant, and two years later he had taken a poor little shop on the Quai, and from there he travelled round among journalists, authors, and printers, buying their free copies at low prices, and making a profit of twenty or thirty francs a day in this way. He had money saved, and he had a gift for divining everybody's needs, and a keen eye for business. He would cash publishers' promissory notes for hard-pressed authors at fifteen or twenty per cent discount, and, armed with these, he would go off the next day to the publishers, buy books that were in demand at trade rates, and then offer the publisher his own note by way of payment. He had educated himself well enough to know better than to have anything to do with poetry or modern novels. He liked small transactions best. He would buy up the whole stock of some useful handbook outright for a thousand francs, and then exploit it in his own good time—books like *A Child's History of France*, or *Bookkeeping in Twenty Lessons*, or *Botany for Young*

Ladies. Two or three times already he had let a good book slip through his fingers, after having made the author come and see him a score of times, unable to make up him mind to buy his manuscripts. When anyone reproached him for his want of courage, he would point out that the account of a famous lawsuit that had appeared in the newspapers, and that had not cost him a penny, had brought him in two or three thousand francs.

Barbet was the type of bookseller who lives precariously on bread and walnuts, who signs few cheques, who picks up small profits on invoices, sells at a discount, and hawks his own books Heaven knows where, but who manages to sell them and to get paid for them. He was the terror of printers, who did not know what to make of him ; he paid cash down, and cut down their invoices when he knew they were pressed for money ; and he never went back to firms he had fleeced in case they should set some trap to catch him.

" Well," said Lousteau, " shall we get back to business ? "

" Well now, my lad," said Barbet in familiar tones, " I have six thousand volumes of stock in my shop. And *livres* are not *francs* as the old bookseller used to say. Business is slow just now."

" If you go into his shop, my dear Lucien," said Étienne, "you will see an oak counter, bought at the sale of some bankrupt wine merchant, a tallow candle that is never snuffed, because it burns more slowly that way. Dimly lit by that dubious light, you will perceive shelves—all empty. To guard this nothingness there is a little boy in a blue suit, who sits blowing his fingers, slapping his chest, or stamping his feet like a cabman on his seat. Take a look round! No more books to be seen than I have here! Nobody could guess what business is carried on there! "

" Here is a bill for a hundred francs, payable in three months," said Barbet, who could not restrain a smile as he drew a stamped paper from his pocket, "and I will take your books off your hands. You see, I'm not paying cash any longer, sales are too slow. I said to myself that you would be wanting to see me, and I hadn't a sou, so I signed a bill, just to oblige you, because I don't like signing anything."

" So you want my thanks and esteem into the bargain ? " said Lousteau.

" You cannot pay bills with sentiments, but I will accept your esteem all the same," said Barbet.

" But I must have a pair of gloves, and the perfumers will be wicked enough to refuse your note," said Lousteau. "Wait a bit— I have a superb engraving, there, in the top drawer of the chest of drawers—it is worth eighty francs, it is proof before *letter*, but after *press*, for I wrote a pretty scathing article on it. The subject lent itself to satire—*Hippocrates refusing the presents of Artaxerxes*—just the thing for all the doctors who refuse the excessive gifts of the satraps of Paris, eh ? You will find twenty or thirty novels underneath it. Come now, take the lot, and give me forty francs! "

" Forty francs! " exclaimed the bookseller, in the voice of a startled hen. " Twenty at most. Even then I may never get my money back," Barbet added.

" Where are the twenty francs ? " said Lousteau.

" Upon my word, I'm not sure that I have it on me," said Barbet, fumbling in his pockets. " Here we are. You'll have me bankrupt, you know how to get round me."

" Come along, let us go," said Lousteau. He took Lucien's manuscript and drew a line of ink under the string.

" Is that all you've got ? " Barbet enquired.

" That's the lot, Shylock. I am going to put you in the way of doing a good piece of business (in which you will lose a thousand francs, to teach you to rob me like this)," he added under his breath to Lucien.

" And what about your reviews ? " said Lucien, as they drove along towards the Palais-Royal.

" Good Lord! You don't know how reviews are knocked up! As to the *Voyage en Egypte*, I opened the book in one or two places, without cutting the pages, and I found eleven mistakes in grammar. I shall devote a paragraph to saying that the author may have learned the duck-language on those Egyptian pebbles called Obelisks, but he does not know his own, and I shall prove it. I shall say that instead of telling us about natural history and antiquities, he ought to have written about the future of Egypt, the progress of civilisation, the means of strengthening the bond between Egypt and France, who, after having conquered and lost that country, might still form links by gaining a moral ascendency. There you are—a patriotic *tartine*, interlarded with tirades against Marseilles, the Levant, and foreign trade."

" But if he had done so, what would you have said ? "

" Well, I would have said that instead of boring us with politics, he ought to have devoted himself to art and given an account of the scenery and the picturesque aspects of the country. The critic always complains. We are inundated with politics (I would say), we are bored with politics, we can never get away from them. I should regret all those charming travel books, where the author explains to us the difficulties of navigation, the charms of disemboguing, the delights of crossing the line, in fact all the things that those who have never been on a voyage ought to know about. While approving them, one makes at the same time a little fun of those travellers who make a great event of a bird flying over, a flying-fish, or a good haul, or well-known geographical facts,—shallow waters that everybody knows about. Why do we never have, nowadays, those absolutely unintelligible scientific facts that have the fascination that characterises all that is profound, mysterious, incomprehensible ? The reader laughs, and what more does he want. As for the novels, Florine is the world's greatest novel-reader ; she tells me the plots and I base my reviews on her opinion, When she is bored by what she calls ' author's long-windedness ' I take the book into consideration and ask the publishers for another copy, which they send, delighted to have a favourable review."

" Good God! But criticism, and the critic's sacred office ? " cried Lucien, imbued with the doctrines of his circle.

" My dear chap," said Lousteau, " criticism is too stiff a brush to apply to flimsy stuff ; it carries the whole thing away with it. Let us stop talking shop. Listen, do you see this mark ? " he said, holding out the manuscript of *Marguerites* for Lucien to see. " I have put an ink mark on the paper where the string goes. If Dauriat reads your manuscript, he will certainly not put the string back in exactly the same place. So your manuscript is, as it were, sealed. This will be useful for the experiment you want to make. And what is more, may I point out that you are not arriving alone and without a sponsor in this shop, like all those poor lads who call at ten publishers before anyone even offers them a seat."

Lucien had already proved by experience the truth of this detail. Lousteau paid the cabby, handing him three francs, to Lucien's great astonishment that such prodigality should follow so close upon such impecuniosity. The two friends then entered the Wooden Galleries, which at that time was the headquarters of what was called the New Literature.

II

The Wooden Galleries were at that time one of the most notable sights of Paris. A description of this squalid bazaar will not be out of place, for it played a very important rôle in Paris life for thirty-six years, and most men of forty will still enjoy a description which to the young will seem quite incredible. Instead of the high, cold, Galerie d'Orleans, that vast greenhouse without flowers, there used to be booths, or, to be more precise, small wooden huts, far from weather-proof, and badly lit through small apertures overlooking the court and the garden, by courtesy called windows, but as dirty as those dingy orifices that keep the daylight out of wineshops on the shabby outskirts of Paris. Three rows of booths about twelve feet high formed two galleries. The centre row opened into both galleries, whose foul atmosphere pervaded them; they were lit by skylights whose glass was invariably dirty and allowed little light to penetrate. But by reason of the crowds that thronged this busy hive their rent was anything up to a thousand crowns for a cell measuring barely six feet by eight or ten. The booths that looked onto the garden and the court were flanked by green trellis-work intended perhaps to protect the cheap plastered walls at the back of the shops from the contact of the crowd, and there, in the two or three feet of earth at the back, flourished the strange freaks of a vegetation unknown to science, together with those of various no less flourishing trades. There you might see a rosebush capped with proof-sheets, whose flowers of rhetoric were perfumed by the abortive blooms of that neglected garden, evil-smelling from the foul slops with which it was liberally watered. Ribbons of all colours, or handbills, flourished among the leaves. The litter of fashion stifled the vegetation. You were liable to find a knot of ribbons on a clump of grass, and you were apt to be mistaken in your ideas of a flower, and find that you were about to admire, not a dahlia, but a satin rosette. From the side opening onto the court also this fantastic palace presented all the odd freaks that Paris squalor could produce—daubed whitewash, patched plaster, blistering paintwork, fantastic posters; and the green trellises were equally befouled by the Paris crowds on the garden side, and on the side opening on the court. So that, from both sides, the disreputable and nauseating approaches might have been designed expressly to warn off sensitive people from approaching the galleries; but sensitive people no more thought of turning back from these horrors than do princes in fairy-tales before the dragons and other obstacles interposed by the wicked fairy between themselves and the princesses.

There was a passage down the centre of these galleries, just as there is today, and you entered it, then as now, through the two existing peristyles, commenced before the Revolution and then abandoned for lack of funds. The handsome stone gallery that leads to the Théâtre-Français was at that time a narrow alley of disproportionate height and so badly roofed that the rain often came through. It was called the Glass Gallery, to distinguish it from the Wooden Galleries. The roofs of these dens were all, indeed, in such bad condition that on one occasion a well-known silk-mercer brought a case against the House of Orleans, because his stocks had been extensively damaged during the night. The merchant won his case. A double thickness of tarpaulin was the only covering in some places. The floor of the Glass Gallery, where Chevet laid the foundations of his fortune, as well as that of the Wooden Galleries, was the natural Paris earth, with some addition of alien soil brought in on the boots and shoes of the crowds. Feet were continually stumbling over mountains and valleys of hardened mud, daily swept there by the tradesmen, and newcomers needed practice before they acquired the art of walking there.

That sinister mass of mud-heaps, those windows encrusted with dust and rain, the mean huts all in tatters outside, the grimy unfinished walls, and a general air of something between a gypsy encampment, the booths of a fair, and those temporary constructions which in Paris we erect around public buildings that remain unbuilt—the grotesque aspect of the market accorded well with the different kinds of commerce that swarmed and seethed in those obscene shacks. In this shameless, unblushing haunt, amid a babel of talk and the screams of wild mirth, an immense amount of business was transacted in the years between the revolutions of 1789 and 1830. For twenty years the Bourse was just opposite, on the ground-floor of the Palais, and public opinion and reputations, as well as political and financial transactions, were made and unmade there. People used to meet in the Galleries before and after the Bourse. Bankers and capitalists often overflowed the court of the Palais Royal and sheltered in the alleys on wet days. The buildings that had sprung up there, no one knows how, were strangely resonant. Peals of laughter re-echoed. Every word of a quarrel at one end could be overheard at the other. Booksellers dealing in poetry, politics, and prose, and the clothing trade, enjoyed a monopoly of the place, except for the prostitutes, who arrived only towards evening. There novels flourished, and works both classical and modern, and so did political conspiracies and all the trickeries of the publishing trade. There all the latest works were on sale to the public, who resolutely declined to buy them anywhere else. There, in a single evening, several thousand copies would be sold of a pamphlet by Paul-Louis Courier, or the *Adventures de la fille d'un roi*, the first shot fired by the Orleanists against the Charter of Louis XVIII. At the time when Lucien first made his appearance there, several booths had shop-fronts, and quite elegant glass windows, but these belonged only to those booths that looked out on the garden or the court. Until the day when this strange encampment perished under the hammer of Fontaine, the architect, the booths situated between the two galleries were entirely open, supported on props like the stalls at a country fair, and you could look right through the two galleries between the piles of merchandise or through the glass doors. As it was impossible to have fires here, the tradesmen had to make do with chafing-dishes, and themselves acted as unofficial fire-watchers, for a careless act might have burned down in a quarter of an hour that republic of timbered booths, dried by the sun, and rendered the more inflammable, so

The different kinds of commerce that swarmed and seethed in those obscene shacks

to say, by the prevalence of prostitutes, along with the gauze, muslin, and paper, fanned at times by draughts of air.

The milliners' booths were crammed with the most inconceivable hats, which seemed to be there not so much for sale as for advertisement, perched by hundreds on wire holders terminating in a mushroom-shaped knob, and decking out the galleries in all the colours of the rainbow. For twenty years passers-by used to wonder on what heads these dusty hats would end their careers. Saleswomen, generally very ugly but loud-mouthed, accosted the women with importunate phrases, according to the custom and parlance of the market-place. A shop-girl, whose tongue was as quick as her eyes were sharp, would sit on a stool haranguing the strollers with " Buy a pretty hat, *madame* ? Won't you let me sell you something! " Their rich and colourful vocabulary was enhanced by inflexions of the voice, by bold looks and free comments on the passers-by. The booksellers and the clothing trade lived together in good understanding.

In the passage so luxuriously named the Glass Gallery were plied the strangest trades of all. There were established ventriloquists, mountebanks, and charlatans of all sorts, side-shows where you see nothing at all and others that show you the whole world. A man who has since made seven or eight thousand francs by travelling round the fairs, began his career there. His sign consisted of a sun revolving in a black frame, around which shone these words, written in red : " Here man can see what God can never see : Admission two sous." The showman never admitted anyone alone, and never more than two customers at a time. Once you were inside you found yourself face to face with a huge mirror. Suddenly a voice that might have terrified Hoffmann of Berlin, would begin speaking like a machine whose spring has been touched : " You see here, gentlemen, something that God can never see in all eternity—your like. For God has not his like! " You left, ashamed, but not daring to own up to your stupidity.

From all the little doors came sinister voices, extolling the merits of Cosmoramas, views of Constantinople, marionette shows, a chess-playing automaton, a dog who could pick out the prettiest woman in the room. Fitz-James, the ventriloquist, flourished there, in the Café Borel, before he went off to fight at Montmartre, there to lose his life, among the crowd of students from the Polytechnic. Here, too, were fruit stalls and flower stalls, and a famous tailor, whose embroidered uniforms shone like suns in the evenings when the shops were lighted.

In the mornings, up to two o'clock, the wooden galleries were silent, sombre, and deserted. The tradesmen chatted among themselves. The populace of Paris did not reckon to arrive there before three o'clock, when the Bourse opened. As soon as the crowds arrived, penniless youths, thirsting for knowledge, availed themselves of the opportunity to read, gratis, the books on the booksellers' stalls. The salesmen in charge of the books displayed charitably allowed these impecunious ones to turn their pages. A two-hundred page duodecimo volume like *Smarra, Peter Schlehmihl, Jean Sbogar,* or *Jocko,* could be devoured at two sessions. In those days there were no reading-rooms and you had to buy a book in order to read it, so that novels were sold in numbers that seem incredible nowadays. There was something very French in this charity shown to youthful intelligence, poor and thirsting for knowledge.

The poetry of this terrible bazaar burst forth at nightfall. Prostitutes from the adjacent streets came and went unhindered. Thither all the street-walkers of Paris flocked to " do the Palais ". The stone galleries belonged to privileged houses, who paid for the right of exposing there, between the archways and in the corresponding sites on the garden side, creatures dressed like princesses, but the wooden galleries were the public ground common to all prostitutes, *the* Palais—a word that signifies, in fact, the temple of prostitution. A woman could go there and leave, accompanied by her prey, leading him whither she pleased. These women drew, in the evenings, such large crowds to the Wooden Galleries that one had to walk in step, as if in a procession or at a masked ball. This slow motion nobody minded, for it gave time for examination. The women were dressed in a way that is no longer seen ; they wore their gowns cut extremely low back and front ; their fantastic head-gear was designed to attract the eye. Some arranged their hair *à la Caucheois*, others wore Spanish mantillas; some had their hair curled like poodles, others wore it in smooth bands. Their legs, in tight-fitting white stockings, were displayed, somehow or other, always at the right moment; but now all that poetry of vice has vanished. The licence of solicitation and response, the public cynicism, in keeping with the place, is no longer to be found, at masks, or even at those famous public balls that are given nowadays. It was horrible and gay. The dazzling skin of necks and shoulders glistened among the darker vesture of the men, producing magnificent contrasts. The hubbub of voices and the shuffling of feet produced a hum of sound that could be heard in the middle of the gardens like a thorough bass, accompanied by peals of laughter and the shouts of an occasional dispute. You might have seen gentlemen and celebrities side by side with men with faces like gaol-birds. These monstrous assemblies had something indescribably exciting about them, and even the most insensible of men felt the charm of the place; so that all Paris continued to frequent the galleries until the very last moment, and walked up and down on the wooden planks that the builders laid over the cellars while they were being built. Deep and unanimous regret accompanied the fall of these squalid wooden erections.

Ladvocat's bookshop had opened only a few days before at the corner of the passage that divided the galleries down the centre, opposite Dauriat's—a young bookseller now forgotten, but whose enterprise blazed the trail for his competitor. Dauriat's bookshop was in the row of booths giving on to the garden; Ladvocat's looked onto the court. Dauriat's shop was divided into two parts, a large public shop for his publications, and the smaller portion as his private office. Lucien, who set foot in the galleries for the first time that evening, was bewildered by a sight that all young men, and provincials especially, found irresistible. He soon lost his guide and mentor.

"If you were as handsome as that young fellow I would give you your money's worth," said one of the local harpies to an old man, indicating Lucien.

Lucien slunk through the throng like a blind man's dog, in a state of excitement difficult to describe. Importuned by glances, solicited by white curves, dazzled by necks audaciously exposed, he hung on to his manuscript like grim death in case anyone should steal it from him, poor innocent that he was!

" Well, sir, what is it ? " he exclaimed as someone took him by the arm, thinking that his poetry had proved too great a temptation for some envious author. He recognised Lousteau. " I knew that you would find your way here sooner or later! " said his friend.

The poet was at the doorway of a shop into which Lousteau led him, where quite a crowd of people were waiting their turn to speak to the sultan of the trade. Printers, paper merchants and designers clustered round the assistants, asking them about affairs in progress, or in prospect.

" Look, there's Finot, the editor of my paper ; talking to a young man who has talent, Félicien Vernou—a little fellow as dangerous as a hidden disease."

" By the way, old chap, you have a first-night, haven't you ? " said Finot, coming over to Lousteau with Vernou. " I have disposed of the box."

" Sold it to Braulard ? "

" Well, so what ? You will get a seat. What do you want out of Dauriat ? . . . By the way, we had better push Paul de Kock ; Dauriat has taken two hundred copies and Victor Ducagne has refused him his next novel. Dauriat say he wants to build up another author in the same style. So you must say that Paul de Kock is better than Ducagne."

" But I have a play on at the Gaieté that I wrote in collaboration with Ducagne," said Lousteau.

" All right, you can say I wrote the article ; I wrote a slashing review and you toned it down—tell him that, and he will thank you for it."

" Could you possibly get Dauriat's cashier to cash this little cheque for a hundred francs ? Don't forget we are both going to Florine's housewarming party."

" Oh, of course, you are standing us all treat," said Finot, as if with a great effort of memory. " I say, Gabusson," said Finot, taking

Barbet's cheque over to the cashier, " give ninety francs to that man over there for me, will you ? Endorse the cheque, old boy."

Lousteau took the pen from the cashier and signed the cheque, while the latter counted out the money. Lucien, all eyes and ears, did not lose a syllable of that conversation.

" There's one other thing, dear friend," Étienne continued. " I won't thank you, it's life and death between us, you know. I want to introduce this gentleman to Dauriat, and I want you to make him listen to us."

" What is it about ? " asked Finot.

" A volume of poems," replied Lucien.

" Oh! " said Finot with a shrug of the shoulders.

" Your friend cannot have had much experience of publishers," said Vernou, looking at Lucien, " or he would have hidden his manuscript in the most desolate corner of his dwelling."

At this moment Emile Blondet, a handsome young man, who had just written a very important series of articles for the *Journal des Débats* came in, shook hands with Finot and Lousteau, and nodded to Vernou.

" Come to supper with us at midnight at Florine's," said Lousteau.

" I should like to," said the newcomer. " Who is going to be there ? "

" Oh, there will be Florine," said Lousteau, " and Matifat, the druggist ; du Bruel, the author who has given Florine her part ; a little old fellow called Cardot and his son-in-law, Camusot ; and Finot. . . . "

" Does your druggist do things well ? "

" He is not going to give us drugs," said Lucien.

" You are very witty," said Blondet seriously, looking at Lucien. " Is he going to be there, Lousteau ? "

" Yes."

" Then we shall have a good laugh."

Lucien blushed to the tips of his ears.

" Are you going to be long, Dauriat ? " said Blondet, tapping the glass partition of Dauriat's office.

" My friend, I am at your service."

" Good," said Lousteau to his protégé. " That young man, who is almost as young as you are, is on the *Débats*. He is one of the princes of criticism. He is to be reckoned with ; Dauriat will come out and make up to him, and so we shall be able to put in a word with the pasha of vignettes and typography. Otherwise we should still have been waiting our turn at eleven o'clock. The audience is getting larger every minute."

Lucien and Lousteau accordingly went over to Blondet, Finot and Vernou, and formed a little knot at the back of the shop.

" What is he doing? " Blondet asked Gabusson, the head salesman, who rose to greet him.

" He is buying a weekly newspaper that he wants to work up in opposition to the *Minerva,* which is too much at the service of Eymery, and the *Conservateur* which is too blindly romantic."

" Is he going to pay well ? "

" Too well—as usual."

A young man came in at this moment, who had just brought out a first-rate novel, that had quickly been crowned by success of the first order—Dauriat was printing a second edition. This young man was remarkable for that extraordinary and freakish appearance that is the mark of the artistic temperament. He made a great impression on Lucien.

" That's Nathan," Lousteau whispered to the provincial poet.

Nathan, for all the fierce pride of his features—he was still young at the time—came up to the journalists hat in hand, and his approach to Blondet, whom he still knew only by sight, was almost servile. Blondet and Finot did not remove their hats.

" I am delighted, sir, that good luck has given me the happy chance——"

" He is so worried that he has committed a pleonasm," said Félicien aside to Lousteau.

"—of expressing my gratitude for the very fine article you were so kind as to write about me in the *Journal des Débats*. Half the success of my book I owe to you."

" Not at all, my dear fellow," said Blondet—and the note of

patronage was barely concealed by his affability. " You have talent, by Jove, and I am delighted to meet you."

" As your article has already appeared, I shall no longer seem to be courting favour : so that we can meet perfectly naturally. Will you do me the honour and the pleasure of dining with me tomorrow? Finot will be there—Lousteau, old boy, you will not refuse me, will you ? " Nathan added, offering his hand to Étienne.

" You have a great future before you, sir," he continued, addressing Blondet. " You are in the tradition of Dussault and Fievée, and Geoffroi! Hoffmann was talking about you to Claude Vignon, his pupil, a friend of mine, and he said that now he would die happy, because the *Journal des Débats* would live for ever. They ought to pay you tremendously well ? "

" A hundred francs a column," said Blondet. " But what is that considering the books one has to read—one has to read a hundred before finding one that is worth serious consideration, like yours. Your book gave me real pleasure, I really mean it."

" And brought him in fifteen hundred francs," Lousteau whispered to Lucien.

" But you write political articles, don't you ? " Nathan went on.

" Yes, now and again," said Blondet.

Lucien felt like an embryo in this company. He had admired Nathan's book, and revered its author as a kind of god, and he was appalled at this display of servility towards a critic whose name and importance were equally unknown to him.

" Shall I ever behave like that ? Must one really sacrifice one's dignity ? " he thought. " Put on your hat, Nathan! You have written a fine book, and this critic has only written an article! "

These thoughts made his blood boil. He saw first one timid young man, and then another—penurious authors, wanting to speak to Dauriat. Seeing that the shop was crowded, they went off, saying, " I will come back later on ", despairing of being able to have a word with him. Two or three politicians, surrounded by a group of political celebrities, were talking about the convocation of the Chambers and public affairs. The weekly for which Dauriat was negotiating had the right to speak on political matters, and at that time newspaper licences were becoming rare. A newspaper was a privilege as much sought after as a theatre. One of the largest shareholders in the *Constitutionnel* was among the political group. Lousteau performed the part of cicerone admirably; and with every phrase, Dauriat rose in Lucien's estimation, as he saw how politics and literature converged upon that shop. There he had seen a distinguished poet prostituting his muse to journalism, there he had seen him humiliate his art, as womanhood was humiliated and prostituted in these ignoble galleries; the great man of the provinces had taken to heart the terrible lesson: money! That was the answer to all riddles.

Lucien felt how utterly alone he was, unknown, attached only by the thread of a doubtful friendship to success and fortune. He blamed his real, affectionate friends of the Rue de Quatre-Vents for having painted the world in false colours, for having prevented him from leaping, pen in hand, into the arena. "I shall be a Blondet yet!" he vowed to himself.

Lousteau, whose cry of a wounded eagle had re-echoed on the heights of the Luxembourg, and who had seemed such a great figure, had now dwindled to negligible proportions. There, the important figure was the fashionable publisher, on whom all these existences depended. The poet, manuscript in hand, experienced a trepidation akin to fear. In the middle of this shop he noticed some busts on wooden pedestals, painted to look like marble—Byron and Goethe were among them, and M. de Canalis, from whom Dauriat was hoping to get a book, and who might see, on the day when he set foot inside that shop, the high estimation in which he was held by the publishing trade. Lucien, in spite of himself, felt his self-esteem ebbing from him, and his courage failed as he realised the extent of Dauriat's influence over his destiny. He waited impatiently for him to appear.

"Well, my children." The speaker was a little stout man with a fat face that suggested a Roman proconsul, toned down by an expression of affability that deceived superficial observers. "I am now the proprietor of the only weekly paper on sale, a paper with two thousand subscribers."

" Nonsense! The registered number is seven hundred, and that is a liberal estimate," said Blondet.

" Twelve hundred, on my most sacred word of honour. I said two thousand," he added, lowering his voice, " for the benefit of the paper merchants and printers present. I thought you had more tact, my boy," he finished, again raising his voice.

" Are you taking on any partners ? " Finot enquired.

" That depends," said Dauriat. " Would you like a third of the shares for forty thousand francs ? "

" I might think about it if you will take on as contributors Emil Blondet here, Claude Vignon, Scribe, Théodore Leclercq, Félicien Vernou, Jay, Jouy, and Lousteau——"

" And why not Lucien de Rubempré ? " said our provincial poet, with great daring, interrupting Finot.

" And Nathan," Finot finished.

" And why not all those people outside ? " said the publisher, scowling. " Whom have I the honour of addressing ? " he asked, looking at Lucien with an insolent air.

" One moment, Dauriat," Lousteau broke in. " I brought this gentleman. While Finot is thinking over your proposal, listen to me."

Lucien's shirt was wet with perspiration at the look of cold annoyance that this formidable tyrant of publishers—this man who called Finot *tu*, while Finot addressed him as *vous*, who called the redoubtable Blondet " my boy " and who had so royally held out his hand to Nathan, with an air of easy familiarity—now assumed.

" Another book, my boy ? " Dauriat exclaimed. " I have eleven hundred manuscripts already! . . . Yes, my friends," he said raising his voice, "I have had eleven hundred manuscripts submitted to me—ask Gabusson! In fact I shall soon need a staff for looking after the manuscript files and a department for reading them ; there will be committees for deciding on their merits, with counters to vote with, and a full-time secretary to present me with the reports. It will be a special department of the Academie Française, and the academicians will be paid better in the Wooden Galleries than at the Institute."

"It's an idea," said Blondet.

"A bad idea," said Dauriat. "It is not my business to take stock of the lucubrations of those among you who take to literature because they can't manage to be either capitalists, or bootmakers, or corporals, or lackeys, or civil servants, or bailiffs! No one sets foot here who has not an established reputation! Become famous, and you will find streams of gold here. I have made three great men in the last two years—three instances of ingratitude! Nathan wants six thousand francs for the second edition of his book, which has cost me three thousand francs in advertising, and on which I have not made a thousand francs. For Blondet's two articles I had to spend a thousand francs on admirers, and five hundred francs——"

"But, sir, if all the publishers talked like you, where could anyone publish a first book?" Lucien enquired—Blondet had vastly diminished in his eyes when he heard the sum that Dauriat had spent on the articles in the *Débats*.

"What's that to me?" said Dauriat, looking daggers at the handsome Lucien, who was smiling pleasantly at him. "I do not find it amusing to risk two thousand francs on publishing a book in the hope of making two thousand; I speculate in literature: I publish forty volumes at ten thousand copies each, so does Panckoucke, and so do the Beaudouins. With my influence and the articles that I secure, I handle affairs worth a hundred thousand crowns, not little volumes worth two thousand francs. It is just as much trouble to sell a new name—the author and his book—as to make a success with *Théâtres étrangers*, *Victoires et Conquêtes*, or *Mémoires sur la Revolution*—books worth a fortune. I am not here to serve as a stepping-stone to future fame, but to make money, and to make it for men with distinguished names. A manuscript for which I pay a hundred thousand francs costs me less than the one for which I pay six hundred francs to any unknown author! I may not be a Maecenas, but literature owes me some recognition: I have already sent up the price of manuscripts to more than double. I tell you all this because you are a friend of Lousteau's, my boy," said Dauriat, patting the poet on the shoulder with an air of revolting familiarity. "If I spent my time talking to all the authors who want me to be their publisher, I should have to close my shop, because I would spend my time in conversations which would be extremely agreeable but much too expensive. I am not yet rich enough to listen to all the monologues of self-conceit. Nobody does, except at the theatre ; in classical tragedies."

The terrible Dauriat was dressed in clothes whose expensive quality added weight, in the mind of the provincial poet, to this ruthless logic.

" What is it, anyway ? " he asked Lousteau.

" A magnificent volume of verse."

On hearing this, Dauriat turned to Gabusson with a gesture worthy of Talma.

"Gabusson, my friend, from today anyone who comes here to submit manuscripts . . . Do you hear, all of you ? " he said, addressing his three salesmen who emerged from behind the bookcases on hearing their employer's angry voice. Dauriat examined his nails and his well-groomed hand. " Anyone who brings in a manuscript, ask him whether it is verse or prose. If he says verse, show him the door instantly. Verses mean reverses in publishing."

" Bravo! That's very neat, Dauriat! " cried the journalists.

"It is true," said the publisher, striding about his shop with Lucien's manuscript in his hand. " You have no idea, any of you, of the harm that has been done by the success of Lord Byron, Lamartine, Victor Hugo, Casimir Delavigne, Canalis and Béranger. Their fame has brought us an invasion of barbarians. There must be at this moment a thousand manuscripts of verse going the round of the publishers, broken off stories that nobody can make head or tale of, in imitation of the *Corsairs* and *Lara*. On the pretext of originality, the young poets go in for these incomprehensible stanzas, and in their descriptive poems they think they are being original by discovering Delille! For the last two years poets have been swarming like black-beetles. I lost twenty thousand francs on poetry last year —ask Gabusson! There may be immortal poets in the world--I know some that are fresh and rosy cheeked and have no beards as yet"—addressing Lucien—" but for the publishing trade, young man, there are only four poets : Béranger, Casimir Delavigne,

Lamartine, and Victor Hugo. As for Canalis, his reputation has only been built up by publicity! "

Lucien lacked the courage to reply, and to make a demonstration of pride in the presence of all these influential people who were laughing heartily. He realised that he would only look ridiculous, but he felt a violent desire to take the insolent publisher by the throat, and spoil the insulting composure of his cravat, to break the gold chain that shone on his chest, to stamp on his watch and smash it. Injured self-esteem opened the door to vengeance, and he vowed undying hatred for the publisher, at whom he smiled.

" Poetry is like the sun," said Blondet, " that makes the eternal forest grow, and also breed sants, and flies, and mosquitoes. There is no virtue that is not counterbalanced by a vice. Literature breeds publishers."

" And journalists! " added Lousteau.

Dauriat burst into a laugh.

" What is this, anyway ? " he asked, indicating the manuscript.

" A collection of sonnets that would have put Petrarch to shame," said Lousteau.

" What do you mean ? " asked Dauriat.

" Just what I say," said Lousteau, seeing a knowing smile on every face.

Lucien could not take offence, but he raged inwardly.

" Very well, I will read it," said Dauriat, with a regal gesture that revealed the full extent of this concession. " If your sonnets are up to the standard of the nineteenth century, I will make you a great poet, my boy."

" If his talent is equal to his good looks, you won't be running any great risk," said a famous orator of the Chamber who was chatting with one of the proprietors of the *Constitutionnel* and the editor of the *Minerva.*

" Glory," said Dauriat, " is twelve thousand francs on articles and a thousand crowns on dinners, General. Ask the author of *Le Solitaire.* If M. Benjamin de Constant would care to write an article on this young poet I shall not take long to conclude the deal."

At the word *General,* and on hearing the illustrious name of

Benjamin Constant, the bookshop assumed, in the eyes of the great man from the provinces, the proportions of Olympus.

" Lousteau, I want to talk to you," said Finot, " but I shall see you later at the theatre. Dauriat, I will accept your offer, but conditionally. Let us go into your office."

" Come in, my boy! " said Dauriat, allowing Finot to go in front of him, and assuming, for the benefit of ten persons who were waiting to speak to him, the manner of a man engaged on important business.

He was about to disappear when Lucien, all impatience, stopped him.

" You are keeping my manuscript ; when can I have your decision ? "

" Come back in three or four days, my little poet, and we shall see."

Lucien was led off by Lousteau, who did not stop to take leave of Vernou, Blondet, Raoul Nathan, General Foy, or Benjamin Constant, whose book on the Hundred Days was just about to appear. Lucien had a glimpse of that fine fair head, the oval face, the intelligent eyes, and the pleasant mouth—in short, of the man who for twenty years had played the part of Potemkin to Mme de Staël, and who made war first on Napoleon and then the Bourbons, but who was to die, stricken down by his victory.

" What a shop! " exclaimed Lucien as he seated himself in the cab beside Lousteau.

" To the Panorama-Dramatique, and as fast as you can. Thirty sous if you hurry," said Étienne to the cabby. " Dauriat is a scoundrel who sells something like fifteen or sixteen thousand francs' worth of books in a year, and is a kind of Minister of Literature," said Lousteau, whose self-esteem was pleasantly flattered ; he was showing off to Lucien. " He is just as grasping as Barbet, but on a wholesale scale. Dauriat knows how to behave ; he is generous but he is vain ; as for his wit, he has a faculty for picking up everything that he hears other people saying. His shop is a very good place to go to ; you can talk to all the great men of the day there. There, my dear fellow, a young man can learn more in an hour than by growing pale over books for ten years. People discuss articles, and concoct subjects, and get to know famous and influential people who may be useful. To succeed today one must get to know people. It is all a matter of luck, you see. There is nothing more fatal than to be an intellectual all alone in your corner."

" But what insolence! " said Lucien.

" Oh, we all laugh at Dauriat! " said Étienne. " You need him, and he tramples on you; he needs the *Journal des Débats*, and so Emile Blondet can twist him round his little finger. Oh, you will find plenty more like him if you go in for literature. Well, what did I tell you? "

" Yes, you are right," said Lucien. " I suffered in that shop even more than I expected, according to your programme."

" And why give way to suffering? The thing that we have spent our very life on, the theme that we have racked our brains over for many a sleepless night; all these flights across the fields of thought, the monument built with our own blood—for the publishers is simply a good or bad piece of business. Will your book sell, or will it not? That is the whole question, so far as the publishers are concerned. For them, a book represents a risk of so much capital. The better a book is, the less likely it is to sell. Every man of superior mind is above the level of the masses, and the time needed for his success will be in direct ratio with the time needed for his work to be appreciated. No publisher wants to wait. The book of today must be sold tomorrow. Acting on that system, publishers refuse important books that will win great, but slow, fame."

" D'Arthez is right! " Lucien exclaimed.

" Do you know d'Arthez? " said Lousteau. " I know nothing more dangerous than these solitary spirits who think, like that fellow, that they will be able to make the world come to them. These men of posthumous glory excite youthful imaginations by a faith that flatters the immense self-confidence that we all have to start with, and they prevent the young from taking action at the age when action is still possible and profitable. I am all for Mahomet's system—since the mountain would not come to him, he would go to the mountain! "

This witticism, giving point to the arguments of reason, was calculated to make Lucien hesitate between the theory of patient poverty preached at the Rue des Quatre-Vents and Lousteau's militant doctrine. And so the poet from Angoulême remained silent all the way to the Boulevard du Temple.

The Panorama-Dramatique no longer exists. A house stands on the site of the charming theatre that used to be situated opposite the Rue Charlot, on the Boulevard du Temple. Two successive managements collapsed without making a single success, even though Vignol, who has inherited a share of Potier's popularity, made his first appearance there, and so did Florine, the actress who five years later was to become so famous. Theatres, like men, are subject to chance. The Panorama-Dramatique was in competition with the Ambigu, the Gaieté, the Pont-Saint-Martin, and the vaudeville theatres; it was unable to survive their intrigues, coupled with too many restrictions, and too few good plays. Authors were unwilling to break with theatres whose existence was assured for one whose existence was, to all appearances, problematical. All the same, the management was counting on the success of this new play, a sort of comic melodrama, by a young playwright, named du Bruel, who had been helped by the collaboration of several well-known authors, but who gave out that the play was entirely his own. This play had been specially written for Florine's first appearance. This young actress had begun her career as an extra at the Gaieté, and during the past year had been promoted to small parts, in which she had attracted notice; but as she had not succeeded in being offered a part there, the Panorama had carried her off from the rival theatre. Another actress, Coralie, was also making her first appearance.

When the two friends arrived Lucien was amazed at the power of the press. "This gentleman is with me," said Étienne, and all the box-office clerks bowed with one accord.

"You will find it very difficult to get in," said the head clerk. "There are no seats left except the stage box."

Étienne and Lucien wasted some time in wandering up and down the corridors parleying with the box-openers.

" Come round to the back and we will have a word with the manager—he will let us go into the stage-box. And I will introduce you to Florine, the heroine of the evening."

At a sign from Lousteau, the doorkeeper of the orchestra took a little key and opened a door, concealed in the thickness of the wall. Lucien followed his friend, and passed suddenly from the brightly lit corridor into the dark hole that, in nearly all theatres, leads from the house to the wings. Presently, after ascending a short flight of damp steps, the provincial poet emerged into the wings, where he beheld the strangest sight. The flimsiness of the props, the height of the theatre, the ladders hung with Argand lamps, the scenery, hideous when seen close up, the actors with their make-up, and their extraordinary costumes, made of such coarse material, the scene-shifters in greasy overalls, the hanging ropes, the stage-manager walking about with his hat on, the extras sitting about, the hanging back-cloths, the firemen—all that ludicrous medley of things, sordid, dirty, hideous, and gaudy, was utterly unlike anything that Lucien had seen from the front of the house. His astonishment knew no bounds. The curtain was just about to fall on a full-blooded melodrama entitled *Bertram*, a play adapted from a tragedy by Maturin, which had been a failure in Paris although it was much admired by Nodier, Lord Byron and Walter Scott.

" Hold on to my arm unless you want to fall through a trap-door or bring down a forest on your head, or upset a palace or get caught on a cottage," Étienne warned Lucien. " Is Florine in her dressing-room, my angel ? " he asked an actress who was waiting for her cue and listening to the actors on the stage.

" Yes, darling! Thank you for the nice things you said about me. You have been much kinder since Florine came here."

" Nonsense! Don't spoil your entry, pretty one," said Lousteau. " Run along, get cracking, say ' Stop! wretched man! ' nicely, because there are two-thousand-franc takings."

Lucien was thunderstruck when he saw the actress's whole aspect change, as she shrieked " Stop! wretched man! " in a voice fit to freeze you with terror. She was a different woman.

" So this is the theatre! " he exclaimed to Lousteau.

" It is just what a newspaper, or the Wooden Galleries, are for literature—a kitchen," his new friend replied.

Nathan appeared at this moment.

" What are you doing here ? " Lousteau asked him.

" As a matter of fact I am doing the smaller theatres for the *Gazette* until something better turns up," said Nathan.

" Well—come to supper with us this evening, and mind you are kind to Florine, or I shall have my revenge! " said Lousteau.

" At your service! " Nathan replied.

" She is living in the Rue de Bondy now, you know."

" Who is that handsome young man with you, my little Lousteau ? " said the actress, who had returned from the stage to the wings.

" A great poet, my beautiful, who will be famous one day. As you will be meeting M. Nathan at supper, allow me to introduce M. Lucien de Rubempré."

" Yours is an illustrious name, sir," said Raoul to Lucien.

" Lucien, M. Raoul Nathan," said Étienne to his new friend.

" I read your book two days ago, and upon my soul, I cannot conceive how a man who has written two books like your novel and your collection of poems could have been so humble to a journalist."

" Wait till your first book comes out," said Nathan with a bitter smile.

" Well well well! Ultras and liberals shaking hands! " exclaimed Vernou, catching sight of the trio.

" In the mornings my views are those of my newspaper," said Nathan, " but in the evenings I think what I please ; at night all journalists see double."

" Étienne," said Félicien to Lousteau, " I came here with Finot, and he is looking for you—ah, there he is."

" You don't mean to say there is not a place anywhere ? "

" You have one always in our hearts! " said the actress, turning on him the sweetest of smiles.

" Really, my little Florville, have you recovered so quickly from

"Stop! wretched man!"

your love, then ? I thought you had been carried off by a Russian prince! "

" Who carries women off nowadays ? " said Florville—the actress who cried " Stop! Wretched man! " " We stayed for ten days at Saint-Mandé, and my prince got out of it by paying compensation to the management. The director is praying for more Russian princes, because their compensations are clear profit! " she added with a laugh.

" And you, little one," said Finot to a pretty peasant-girl who was listening to this conversation, " where did you steal those diamond earrings ? Have you been making an Indian prince ? "

" No—a blacking-manufacturer, an Englishman. He's gone already. We can't all have millionaire shopkeepers bored with family life, like Florine and Coralie! "

" You will miss your cue, Florville," exclaimed Lousteau, " your friend's blacking has gone to your head! "

" If you want a success," Nathan said to her, " instead of screaming ' He is saved! ' like a fury, go in quite quietly, walk to the front of the stage, and say ' He is saved ' in a chest-voice, like Pasta's, *O patria!* in *Tancred*. . . . Run along! " he added, pushing her towards the stage.

" Too late, she has spoiled her effect! " said Vernou.

" What has she done, the house is applauding like mad! " said Lousteau.

" She bared her breast as she flung herself on her knees—it is her great resource," said the blacking-maker's widow.

" The manager is letting us have his box—you will find me there," said Finot to Étienne.

Lousteau then led Lucien behind the stage, through a labyrinth of passages, gangways, staircases. They reached a little room on the third floor, Nathan and Félicien Vernou following them.

" Good day—or good night," said Florine. " These gentlemen are the arbiters of my destiny," she said to a little fat man standing in a corner ; " my future is in their hands ; but I hope that they will be under our table tomorrow morning, if M. Lousteau has remembered everything. . . ."

" Remembered! You are going to have Blondet of the *Débats*," said Étienne, " the one and only Blondet, Blondet, no less—in fact, Blondet in person."

" Oh, my dear little Lousteau, I must give you a kiss! " she exclaimed, and she threw her arms round his neck.

At this demonstration, Matifat, the fat man, looked serious.

At sixteen, Florine was thin. Her beauty, like a bud full of promise, could only have pleased those artists who prefer the sketch to the finished painting. All the quick subtlety of her character was visible in her features, and at that time she reminded one of Goethe's Mignon. Matifat, the rich druggist of the Rue des Lombards, had thought that a little boulevard actress would not be very expensive ; but in eleven months, Florine had cost him sixteen thousand francs. It struck Lucien as a most extraordinary thing to see that worthy honest shopkeeper standing there like the god Terminus, in the corner of this tiny dressing-room, with its pretty wallpaper, furnished with a cheval-glass, a divan, two chairs, a carpet, a fire-place, and ample cupboards. A maid was completing the actress's Spanish costume, for the play was an imbroglio in which Florine was to play the part of a countess.

" In five years that girl will be the most beautiful actress in Paris," said Nathan to Félicien.

" I say, darlings," said Florine turning to the three journalists again, " you will take care of me tomorrow, won't you ? Meanwhile I have ordered cabs for tonight, because you are going home as drunk as lords. Matifat has ordered wines—wines worthy of Louis XVIII I do assure you, and he has hired the Prussian Ambassador's cook! "

" We expect big things from the gentleman's appearance."

" And he is quite aware that he is giving a party for the most dangerous men in Paris," retorted Florine.

Matifat looked at Lucien uneasily, for the young man's great beauty aroused his jealousy.

" But here is somebody I don't know," said Florine, looking Lucien over. " Which of you has brought the Apollo Belvedere from Florence ? He is as attractive as a painting by Girodet."

"This gentleman is a poet from the country whom I forgot to introduce to you. You are looking so beautiful this evening that it is impossible to think about mere commonplace civility."

"I suppose he is rich, as he writes poetry?" said Florine.

"Poor as Job," Lucien replied.

"A great temptation for the likes of us," said the actress.

Du Bruel, the author of the play, suddenly appeared. He was a young man in an overcoat, small and slightly built, who looked like a cross between a bureaucrat, a landlord, and a stock-broker.

"Well, my little Florine, you know your part, eh? No lapses of memory! And be very careful about that scene in the second act—bring out the irony, the subtlety! And be sure you say 'I do not love you' in the way we agreed upon."

"Why do you accept parts with sentences like that in them!" said Matifat to Florine.

This observation from the druggist was greeted by a general laugh.

"What does that matter," she said, "so long as I don't say it to you, great stupid? . . . Oh! the silly things he says are my daily delight!" she added, looking at the authors. "On the word of an honest girl, I would pay him so much a blunder, only it would ruin me!"

"Yes, but you will look at me when you say it, like you do when you are learning your part, and it gives me quite a turn," retorted the chemist.

"Very well, I will look at my little Lousteau," she said. A bell rang along the passage.

"Run along, all of you," said Florine; "just let me read my part over again and try to understand it."

Lucien and Lousteau were the last to leave. Lousteau pressed Florine's shoulders, and Lucien heard the actress say, "Tonight is absolutely impossible. That old fool has told his wife that he is going into the country."

"Isn't she charming?" said Étienne to Lucien.

"Yes, but, my dear fellow, that Matifat——"

"My dear boy, you don't know Paris life yet!" said Lousteau.

"There are necessities to which one has to submit! It's just the same as if you loved a married woman. It all depends on how you look at it."

Étienne and Lucien entered a box on the ground floor where the manager and Finot were already seated. In the opposite box was Matifat, with a friend of his, a silk-mercer named Camusot, Coralie's protector, and a respectable little old man, Camusot's father-in-law. These three business men were polishing their opera-glasses, and anxiously scanning the house, plainly troubled by sundry disturbances in the pit. The oddly assorted audience of a first-night filled the boxes, journalists with their mistresses, kept women with their lovers, a few of those regular playgoers who never miss a first night, and a sprinkling of society people with a taste for sensational melodrama. In the first box was a company director and his family, who had fixed up du Bruel in a directorship with all the advantages of a sinecure.

Since dinner-time Lucien had passed from astonishment to astonishment. For two months he had seen the literary career as a life of poverty and want; he had encountered its full horrors in Lousteau's room; in the Wooden Galleries he had seen its contrasts of humility and insolence; its strange glories and unexpected manifestations had unfolded before him. The contrasts of heights and depths, power and want of principle, compromises with conscience, glories and dependences, left him stupefied. He seemed to be the spectator of some strange drama.

"Do you think that du Bruel's play will pay?" Finot enquired.

"It is an intrigue—du Bruel has tried to write in the style of Beaumarchais. Boulevard audiences don't like that sort of thing, what they want is to be harrowed with emotions. They don't appreciate wit. Tonight depends entirely on Florine and Coralie, who are ravishingly pretty and charming. These two girls—they wear very short skirts, and do a Spanish dance—they might make a hit with the public. It's a gamble. If I get one or two clever notices, and it's a success, I might make a thousand crowns."

"I see—you are not expecting a big success, then?"

"A scheme has been organised by the three neighbouring

theatres to hiss the play; but I have made arrangements to cope with that. I have squared the claque they have sent to hiss the play, and they are going to make a muddle of it. And those two business men over there, who are out to arrange a triumph for Coralie and Florine, have each bought a hundred tickets and given them to friends of ours who will, if necessary, act as chuckers-out. As they have been paid twice, the claque will go quietly, and that kind of thing always wins the sympathy of the house."

"Two hundred tickets! What useful men!"

"Yes, with two more actresses as well backed as Florine and Coralie, I could pull through."

For the past two hours Lucien had been hearing every problem reduced to terms of money. Neither in the theatre nor in publishing, neither in bookselling nor in journalism, had there been any mention of art, or of glory. The beat of that great pendulum, money, struck like a hammer blow after blow on his mind and heart. While the orchestra was playing the overture, he could not refrain from contrasting the noisy bursts of applause and hisses that filled the pit, with the quiet, pure poetry that he had known with David, in the old printing-house, when together they had contemplated the wonders of art, the noble triumphs of genius, dreams of glory with her white pinions. And as he remembered evenings with d'Arthez and his friends, the poet's eyes were bright with tears.

"What is the matter?" asked Étienne Lousteau.

"I see poetry dragged in the gutter."

"Ah, my dear fellow, you have still some illusions left."

"But is it really necessary in the theatre to put up with these gross Matifats and Camusots, and actresses bowing down to journalists, as we ourselves bow down to publishers?"

"My dear boy," Étienne whispered, indicating Finot. "You see that great lout, who has neither brains nor talent, only greed, and a desire to succeed at any price, and a talent for business deals? Did you notice how in Dauriat's shop he did me out of forty per cent as if he was doing me a favour? Well, he gets letters from plenty of budding geniuses, who will go on their knees to him for a hundred francs."

A spasm of disgust contracted Lucien's heart, as he remembered the words: " Finot, my hundred francs "—the drawing left on the green baize table of the editorial office.

" I would rather die," he said.

" Rather live," Étienne retorted.

The curtain now rose, and the manager went out into the corridors to give certain instructions.

Finot turned to Étienne. " I have Dauriat's promise, old boy, of a third share in his weekly. I agreed to pay thirty thousand francs on condition that I was made chief editor and director. It's a first-class deal. Blondet tells me that there are going to be restrictions on the press—the bill is going through—and no new papers will be allowed. Six months from now it will cost a million to start a new newspaper. So I accepted, even though I have only a few thousand francs myself. Listen to me: if you can sell half my shares—a sixth—to Matifat for thirty thousand francs, I will make over to you the chief editorship of my little paper, at two hundred and fifty francs a month. Your name will appear as editor, but I still want to control the paper, and keep my interest in it, only I would rather it wasn't known that I still have anything to do with it. You will be paid for all articles at the rate of five francs a column; you need only pay contributors three francs, so you will make a bonus of fifteen francs a day, and get the editorial contributions free. That brings it up to four hundred and fifty francs a month. But I want to retain the power to attack or defend men and affairs in the newspaper as I wish—always allowing you to indulge in private likes and dislikes that don't interfere with my politics. I may be a Ministerialist or an Ultra, I haven't made up my mind; but I want to keep up my connection with the Liberals. I am being perfectly frank with you, because I know I can trust you. I might perhaps let you report the Chambers for another paper for which I write them up, because I shall not be able to keep the job on as things are. So do get Florine to work this little scheme, and tell her to put the screw on her druggist, because I only have forty-eight hours in which to conclude the deal. Dauriat has sold the other third share of thirty thousand francs to his printer and his paper merchant. He gets his third for nothing and makes ten thousand profit, because the whole thing cost him only fifty thousand. And in another year it will cost the court two hundred thousand francs to buy it up, if they have the good sense to suppress the newspapers, as they are saying."

"You are lucky," Lousteau remarked.

"If you had passed your days in the poverty that I have known you would not say that. I had more than my share of misfortune in those days, you see. My father is a hatter—he is still selling hats in the Rue du Coq. It would need a revolution to bring me success—or failing that, millions—and I'm not sure that the revolution is not the easier of the two. If I had a name like your friend's it would be a different matter. Quiet, here comes the manager.

"Goodbye," Finot concluded, as he rose to his feet. "I am going on to the Opéra; I may be fighting a duel tomorrow, because I have written an article and signed it F, attacking dancers who have Generals as protectors—I am giving it them hot and strong at the Opéra!"

"That so?" said the manager.

"Yes, they are all being very stingy with me," said Finot. "One is cutting down my press tickets, another refusing me fifty subscriptions. I have given my ultimatum at the Opéra—I'm asking for a hundred subscriptions now, and four boxes a month. If they accept, my paper will have eight hundred readers and a thousand subscribers. I know how to get hold of another two hundred subscriptions: we shall have twelve thousand by January."

"You will be the ruin of us," said the manager.

"You can't complain, with your ten subscriptions! I gave you two favourable notices in the *Constitutionnel*."

"Oh, I am not complaining of you!" said the manager.

"Goodbye, until tomorrow evening, Lousteau," said Finot. "You can give me an answer at the Français, where there is a first night; as I shan't be able to do the notice, you can have my press tickets. I am giving you the first chance: you have worked like a black for me, and I'm grateful. Félicien Vernou offered me twenty thousand francs for a third share in the paper, and to work for a year without a salary, but I want to keep complete control. Goodbye."

" That fellow is not called Finot for nothing," said Lucien to Lousteau.

" Oh, he'll live to be hanged," said Étienne, not caring whether or not he was overheard by the astute individual who was just closing the door of the box.

" Him ? He will be a millionaire," said the manager, " and be universally esteemed, and perhaps even have friends. . . ."

" Good God! " said Lucien. " What a set-up! And are you going to make that delightful girl put through a deal like that ? " he asked, indicating Florine, who was darting glances at them from the stage.

" And she will succeed. You don't know the devotion and the cunning of these dear girls," said Lousteau.

" They redeem all their faults, they wipe out all their sins by the infinity of their love, when they love," said the manager. " An actress's love is all the more beautiful because it is in such violent contrast with her surroundings."

" It is like finding in the mud a diamond worthy to adorn the proudest crown," said Lousteau.

" But Coralie's mind is not on her part," said the manager. " I suppose Coralie has fallen for our friend, and so she is going to throw away all her lines. She is not attending to her cues ; that's twice she has not heard the prompter. Do you mind sitting in the corner, sir ? " he said to Lucien. " If Coralie has fallen in love with you, I shall go and tell her that you have left the house."

" No! Don't do that! " said Lousteau. " Tell her that he's coming to supper, and that then she can do what she likes with him, and she will play like Mademoiselle Mars."

The manager went out.

" But do you mean to say that you won't scruple to ask that druggist, through Florine, to pay thirty thousand francs for half the share that Finot has just bought for the same price ? "

Lousteau did not give Lucien time to finish his expostulation.

" What part of the world do you come from, for heaven's sake, my dear boy! That druggist is not a man, he is simply a cash-box, handed over by love."

" But your conscience! "

" Conscience, my friend, is a stick we all keep to beat our neighbours with, but never apply to ourselves. Come now, what have you to complain of? In a single day chance has worked a miracle for you that I had to wait two years for, and now you are not satisfied with the means! Really I thought you had more sense —you seemed well on the way to that broadmindedness that intellectual adventurers must have in this world; and now you are indulging in scruples worthy of a nun who blames herself for eating an egg with concupiscence! If Florine succeeds, I shall become an editor, with a fixed salary of two hundred and fifty francs; I shall do the big theatres myself, give Vernou the Vaudeville, and you can get a foot on the ladder by taking over the boulevard theatres from me. You will be paid three francs a column, and if you write one a day that will bring you in ninety francs a month; you shall have sixty francs' worth of books to sell to Barbet, and you will be able to ask your theatres for ten tickets a month, forty altogether, which you can sell for forty francs to the Barbet of the theatre world. I can give you an introduction to him. So you can make two hundred francs a month. If you make yourself useful to Finot, you might be able to place an article in his new weekly, for a hundred francs, in which case you must put all your talent into it, because articles there are signed, and you cannot get away with slipshod work, as you can for the little papers. In that case you would have a hundred crowns a month. My dear boy, there are men of talent, like poor d'Arthez, who dine every day at Flicoteaux and who don't earn a hundred crowns in ten years. You can earn four thousand francs a year with your pen, not counting what you get from the publishers, if you write for them.

" A sub-prefect's salary, you know, is only a thousand crowns, and there he is stuck in his own district like a post. I say nothing of the pleasure of going to the theatres free, because that pleasure is apt to become a bore; but you can go behind the scenes of four theatres. If you are hard and witty for a couple of months or so, you will be flooded with invitations to parties to meet actresses. Their lovers will make up to you; you will never dine at Flicoteaux except on days when you have only thirty sous in your pocket and no dinner date. At five o'clock, in the Luxembourg, you did not know which way to turn, and now you are well on the way to becoming one of the hundred privileged men who impose their views on the French public. Three days from now, if we are successful, you will be in a position to make any man's life a misery to him, just by publishing a series of thirty jokes against him, at the rate of three a day ; and you will be able to take your percentage of amusement from all the actresses in your theatres ; you will be able to ruin a good play and send all Paris to see a bad one. If Dauriat refuses to print the *Marguerites* unless you pay him, you will be able to make him come to you on bended knees, begging you to accept two thousand francs for them. If you are clever enough to write three articles in three different papers that threaten to kill one of Dauriat's speculations, or a book upon which he is counting, you will see him climbing the stairs to your attic, and hanging round your house like a clematis.

" As for your novel, all the publishers who at the moment show you the door more or less politely will queue up outside your house, and the manuscript that old Doguereau valued at four hundred francs will rise in price to four thousand! Such are the advantages of the journalist's profession. And we can keep all new comers out! Immense talent won't get you in without a great piece of luck as well—and here you are finding fault with your good fortune! Listen, if we had not met today at Flicoteaux, you might have kicked your heels for another three years, or died of starvation in an attic, like d'Arthez. When d'Arthez has become as learned as Bayle and as great a writer as Rousseau, we shall have made our fortune, and we shall be the masters of his, and of his glory. Finot will be a Deputy, and owner of a big newspaper ; and you and I will be whatever we have it in us to become—peers of France, or inmates of the debtor's prison at Sainte-Pélagie."

" And Finot will sell his big newspaper to the Ministers who pay him the highest price, just as he sells write-ups to Madame Bastienne at the expense of Mademoiselle Virginie, and proves that her hats are better than the ones the paper praised in the first place! " Lucien exclaimed, recalling the scene that he had witnessed.

"You are very green, my dear fellow," said Lousteau dryly. "Finot was walking on the uppers of his boots, and dining at Tabars for eighteen sous. He was writing advertisements for ten francs, and how his clothes held together is a mystery as obscure as the Immaculate Conception; and now Finot has his own paper, worth a hundred thousand francs. What with subscribers who pay and don't take copies, and real subscribers, and indirect contributions levied by his uncle, he makes twenty thousand francs a year; he dines like a lord every day, and for the last month he has kept a carriage; and now from tomorrow he is in control of a weekly newspaper, with a sixth share that will have cost him nothing, a salary of five hundred francs a month, and added to that he will make a thousand francs out of copy that he will get for nothing and for which he will make his colleagues pay. You yourself, if Finot agrees to pay you fifty francs a page, will be only too glad to write him two or three articles free. Wait till you are in the same situation—that will be the time to judge Finot. A man can only be judged by his peers. Think of the future you will have if you serve blindly the hates of the powers that be, if you attack when Finot says 'attack!' and praise when Finot says 'praise!'! If you want to work off a grudge against anyone, you will be able to knock your friend or enemy to pieces by a sentence in our newspaper every morning, just by saying, 'Lousteau, let us kill so and so!' You can demolish your enemy again with a long article in the weekly. In fact, if the thing is very important to you, Finot, if you make yourself useful to him meanwhile, would no doubt deal the death-blow in one of the big dailies with a circulation of ten or twelve thousand."

"Then you think that Florine will be able to persuade her druggist to buy?" said Lucien, overwhelmed.

"I am quite sure of it! This is the interval. If I go straight away and have a word with her the deal will be put through this very night. Once she has been told just what to do, Florine will have the benefit of my intelligence and her own as well."

"And there sits that honest shopkeeper, watching Florine openmouthed with admiration, all unsuspecting that he is about to be touched for thirty thousand francs!"

"There you go again! Anyone would think that the man was going to be robbed!" Lousteau exclaimed. "But, my dear fellow, if the court buys up the paper in six months the druggist will get back something like fifty thousand francs for his thirty thousand! Besides, Matifat won't think about the paper, but about Florine's interests. When it is known that Matifat and Camusot (they will go shares) own a newspaper, there will be favourable notices for Florine and Coralie in all the papers. Florine will be famous, she will perhaps get an engagement at twelve thousand francs in another theatre. And then Matifat will be able to save the thousand francs a month that he spends now on presents and entertaining to journalists. You know nothing about men, or about how things are done."

"Poor man!" said Lucien. "He is looking forward to a pleasant evening!"

"And he will be sawn in two by a thousand arguments until he has shown Florine the receipt for the sixth share he has bought from Finot! And the day after that—I shall be a chief editor, and making a thousand francs a month. And that will be the end of my troubles," Florine's lover concluded.

Lousteau went out, leaving Lucien utterly dazed, lost in thought, soaring high above this workaday world. The poet had seen the kitchen of fame, the wires that can be pulled in the publishing trade; he had gone behind the scenes in the theatre, and he had seen, what was more, the seamy side of consciences, the machinery at work behind Parisian life, the mechanism of it all. Watching Florine on the stage, he had envied Lousteau's happiness. Already, for a few moments, he had forgotten Matifat. This reverie lasted only a short time, five minutes at most. But it seemed an eternity. Ardent thoughts fired his soul; his senses were inflamed by the sight of these actresses with their wanton eyes, with their rouge, their dazzling bosoms, the seductive folds of short *basquinas* revealing legs clad in red stockings with green clocks, a costume calculated to make a sensation in the pit. Two temptations ran together, like two pools that in a flood flow into each other; they devoured the poet, as he leaned on his elbow in the corner of the box, his arm resting on the red plush, his hand hanging idle, and his eyes fixed on the curtain. He was all the more open to the enchantments of that life of bright gleams and dark shadows, because it had kindled suddenly, like a rocket, against the dark gloom of his hard-working, obscure, and monotonous existence.

Suddenly Lucien's idle glance met the amorous gleam of a bright eye through a hole in the drop-curtain. The poet, waking abruptly from his lethargy, recognised that ardent eye as Coralie's. He lowered his head and looked across at Camusot, who was just entering the box opposite.

That amateur was a worthy silk-merchant of the Rue des Bourdonnais, a big fat man, a Judge in the Commercial Court, father of four children, married for the second time, and worth eighty thousand francs a year. His grey hair was like a cap that fitted on his head, and he had the self-satisfied expression of a man who considers himself entitled, after swallowing the numberless insults of a tradesman's life, to make the most of his remaining years, and who is determined not to leave this world without his share of enjoyment. His brow, the colour of fresh butter, his rosy cheeks, like those of a jolly monk, seemed not large enough to contain the expansiveness of his superlative jubilation. Camusot's wife was not with him, and the applause for Coralie was bringing the house down.

Coralie represented the sum of all this rich tradesman's vanities, and he lorded it in her flat like a nobleman of bygone days. At this moment he was congratulating himself on being responsible for half the young actress's success, a belief further justified by the fact that he had paid for it. Camusot's conduct was sanctioned by the presence of his father-in-law, a little old fellow with powdered hair and leering eyes, but highly respectable for all that. Lucien felt a sense of disgust, and he remembered the pure and exalted love which for a year he had felt for Mme de Bargeton. And with this memory, poetic love spread its white wings, and a thousand memories encircled the great man of Angoulême with their blue horizons. He sank once again into his reverie. The curtain rose. Coralie and Florine were on the stage.

" He's no more thinking about you, my girl, than the Grand Turk," said Florine in an aside, while Coralie was making a speech.

Lucien could not help laughing, and looked at Coralie.

She was one of the most charming and fascinating actresses in Paris, rivalling Mme Perrin and Mlle Fleuriet, whom she resembled also in her fate. She was one of those women who exercise at will the power of attracting men. Coralie was the finest type of Jewess, her face a long oval, ivory-pale, her mouth as red as a pomegranate, her chin as finely formed as the rim of a porcelain cup. Her jet-black eyes burned under her eyelids with their long curved lashes, and their languishing or flashing fires suggested the scorching suns of the desert. Those eyes of hers were underlined by dark shadows, and surmounted by arched eyebrows, heavily marked. Her olive brow, crowned by two bands of hair, black as ebony, in which lights shone as if from a polished surface, seemed the seat of lofty thought, of genius, one might have said. But like so many actresses, Coralie, in spite of her back-stage repartee, had no brains, and was utterly ignorant, for all her green-room experience. She possessed only the instinctive intelligence and the generosity of a woman born to love. And who, besides, could give a thought to qualities of mind when she dazzled the eyes with her round smooth arms, her tapering fingers, her golden shoulders, her legs so adorably elegant in her red silk stockings ? Hers was the bosom, the flexible curved neck, praised in the *Song of Songs*.

These beauties of a truly oriental poetry were further set off by the Spanish costume favoured by our theatres. Coralie was the delight of the pit ; all eyes were fastened on the outlines of her figure, so well set off in her basquina, and appraised the Andalusian contours of her hips, that swayed her skirts with such wanton motions. And soon Lucien, watching this lovely creature acting for his eyes alone, gave no more thought to Camusot than the street urchins in the gods give to the peel of an apple. Sensual passion seemed more desirable than pure love, present joy better than hopes deferred, and the demon of lust stirred in him shameful thoughts.

" I know nothing of the kind of love that thrives on luxury, and wine, and material pleasures," he thought to himself. " I have so far lived more in imagination than in reality. A man who intends to paint all sides of life should experience them, too. This is my first luxurious supper, my first orgy in a world strange to me. Why should I not taste, just for once, these famous pleasures of licentiousness to which the nobility of the eighteenth century abandoned themselves with so much zest ? If only to transpose them into the higher regions of true love, ought one not to learn the joys, the raptures, the perfections, the resources and the arts of the love of courtesans and actresses ? Is not such love, after all, the poetry of the senses ? For the last two months I have thought of women like these as divinities guarded by impassable dragons, and now here is one, more beautiful than Florine, whom I envied Lousteau ; why should I not take advantage of her fancy, when great lords would spend their richest treasure for the sake of a night with a woman like her ? Ambassadors, when they set foot in these depths, give no thought to past or future. I should be a fool to be more fastidious than princes, especially as I am not yet in love with anyone."

Lucien did not give another thought to Camusot. He had expressed, to Lousteau, the deepest disgust for the most base of all partnerships, but now he was falling into that same ditch, swept off his feet by desire, carried away by the jesuitry of passion.

" Coralie is raving about you," said Lousteau as he came in. " Your beauty, rivalling the most illustrious sculptures of Greece, has wrought unparalleled havoc behind the scenes. You are in luck, my boy. Coralie is eighteen, and she might be making sixty thousand francs a year by her beauty any day. She is still a good girl. Her mother sold her three years ago for sixty thousand francs ; she has had nothing but troubles ever since, and now she is looking for happiness. She took up acting in despair because she loathed de Marsay, her first purchaser ; and when she had served that sentence —for the king of the dandies soon deserted her—she found this worthy Camusot, whom she does not love at all ; but he is like a father to her, and so she lets him love her. She has already turned down a number of rich proposals, and is faithful to Camusot, who is not exacting ; so you are her first love. Yes, you went to her heart like a pistol shot the moment she set eyes on you, and Florine is trying to reason with her in her dressing-room, where she is crying because you are so cold. The play will be a failure, Coralie has forgotten her part, and so it is goodbye to the engagement at the Gymnase that Camusot was arranging for her! "

" No, really ? Poor girl! " said Lucien, all his vanity flattered by these words, and his heart swelling with conceit. " My dear fellow, more things have happened to me this evening than in the first eighteen years of my life."

And Lucien proceeded to recount the story of his love for Mme de Bargeton, and his hatred for the Baron du Châtelet.

" That's an idea—the paper needs a butt—we will attack him. Your Baron is an Empire Beau, and he is a Ministerialist—he'll do nicely. I have often seen him at the Opéra. I have seen your great lady as close as I am sitting to you now—she is often in the Marquise d'Espard's box. The Baron is paying court to your ex-mistress, who is a cuttle-bone. Listen! Finot has just sent me an urgent message to say that the paper is short of copy, he's been let down by a contributor, Hector Merlin, because he refused to pay for blank spaces. Finot, in despair, is knocking off an article against the Opéra. Well, my boy, you write a notice on this play—listen to it and be thinking about it. And I shall go into the manager's office and think up three columns on your man, and your fair scorner, who won't be very happy tomorrow."

" So this is how and where the newspaper is written ? " said Lucien.

" It's always like this," said Lousteau. " In all the ten months I've been on the paper, they have always been short of copy at eight o'clock in the evening."

In printer's slang, the manuscript to be set up in type is called copy, perhaps because authors send only a copy of their work. Or perhaps it is an ironical derivation from the Latin word *copia* (abundance) because there is always a scarcity of *copy*.

" There is always a great plan to have several numbers read in advance," Lousteau went on, "but that will never happen. It is ten now, and there is not a line. I am going to tell Vernou and Nathan to think up twenty epigrams on the Deputies for us, on Chancellor

Crusoe and the Ministers, and on our friends if necessary, to make it a brilliant number. In a situation like this a man would libel his own father, just as a pirate will load his cannon with the gold pieces he has captured rather than lose his life. If you write a witty article, you will go up in Finot's estimation ; his generosity is calculated—and that is the most solid form of generosity there is, always excepting the pawnbrokers'."

" Journalists must be extraordinary men! Do you mean to say that I must sit down at a table and be witty to order ? "

" Just as you light an Argand lamp—so long as there is any oil left! "

As Lousteau left the box, du Bruel and the manager came in.

" Sir, allow me to take a message to Coralie from you," said the author of the play, " to say that you will go home with her after supper, or my play will be a failure. The poor girl no longer knows what she is doing or saying ; she is ready to cry when she ought to laugh, and to laugh when she ought to cry. She has been hissed already. You could still save the play—after all, it would not be a misfortune, but a pleasure for you."

" Sir, I am not in the habit of tolerating rivals," said Lucien.

" Don't tell her that! " exclaimed the manager, looking at the author. " Coralie is just the sort of girl who would throw Camusot out of the window and ruin herself in good earnest. The worthy proprietor of the Golden Cocoon allows Coralie two thousand francs a month, and pays for all her clothes, and her publicity."

" As your promise commits me to nothing, go and save your play," said Lucien with the air of a sultan.

" But don't give the impression that you mean to snub that charming girl," pleaded du Bruel.

" Very well, if I must write an article on your play and be kind to your leading lady, I suppose I must," said the poet.

The author made a sign to Coralie and vanished. From that moment she acted superbly. Vignol, who played the part of the old Alcalde, in which he showed for the first time his talent for playing old men, came forward, in the midst of a thunder of applause, and said :

" Gentlemen, the play that we have the honour of acting before you tonight is the work of Messieurs Raoul and de Cursy."

" So Nathan helped to write it! " said Lousteau. " Now I understand why he is here."

" Coralie! Coralie! " shouted the audience, and the house rose to its feet.

" And Florine," came a voice of thunder from the box where the two business men were sitting.

A few voices shouted, " Florine and Coralie! " The curtain rose, and Vignol reappeared with the two actresses, to whom Matifat and Camusot each threw a wreath. Coralie picked up hers and held it out towards Lucien.

For Lucien, these two hours at the theatre had seemed like a dream. The fascination had begun, for all the horrors of that world, behind the scenes. The poet, still innocent, had breathed there the atmosphere of dissoluteness, the contagious air of depravity. In these dirty passages, encumbered with stage machinery, smoky with greasy Argand lamps, lurked an infection that attacks the soul. Life's values no longer seem real there. There serious things are laughed at, and impossible things seem true. It affected Lucien like a narcotic, and Coralie completed the work. He was plunged in a delicious intoxication.

The chandelier was extinguished. The only people left in the theatre were the box-openers, who were making a tremendous clatter removing chairs and shutting doors. The footlights, extinguished like a single candle, gave off a foul reek of smoke. The curtain rose again, a lamp was lowered from the roof, and the firemen and scene-shifters started on their round. The fairy-like enchantment of the stage, the boxes filled with pretty women, the brilliant lights, and the magic of the new scenery and costumes, had vanished, leaving only a cold, eerie, empty darkness. It was hideous. Lucien sat on in unutterable surprise.

" Well, are you coming, dear boy ? " Lousteau called from the stage. " Jump down here."

At a bound, Lucien joined him. He scarcely recognised Florine and Coralie without their costumes, wrapped in their coats and cheap quilted cloaks, their heads concealed by their black veiled hats, for all the world like butterflies returned to their chrysalis cases.

" Will you do me the honour of letting me take your arm ? " Coralie asked him tremulously.

" With pleasure," said Lucien. He felt the actress's heart beating close to his like the heart of a captured bird.

The actress pressed close to the poet's side as deliciously as a cat rubbing herself against her master's leg, with soft ardour.

" So we are supping together! " she said to him.

The four of them went out together and got into two cabs that were waiting at the stage door in the Rue des Fossés du Temple. Coralie made Lucien come into her cab, where Camusot and his father-in-law, old Cardot, were already seated. She offered the other seat to du Bruel. The manager drove off with Florine, Matifat, and Lousteau.

" These cabs are a disgrace! " said Coralie.

" Why don't you keep a carriage? " asked du Bruel.

" Why ? " she retorted, in a pet. " I don't like to say in front of M. Cardot, because no doubt he has trained his son-in-law. Would you believe it, and him so old and little, M. Cardot only allows Florentine five hundred francs a month—just enough to pay her rent, and her grub, and her shoes and stockings ? The old Marquis de Rochegude, who has six hundred thousand francs a month, has been offering me a coupé for the last two months. But I am an artist. not a common hussy."

" You shall have a carriage the day after tomorrow, Mademoiselle," said Camusot graciously ; " but you never asked me for one."

" One doesn't *ask* for these things! Why, when a man loves a woman he surely doesn't let her paddle in the mud, and risk breaking her legs, going on foot ? It's only these tape-measure knights who like to see skirts with mud on the hem! "

As she spoke these sharp words that cut Camusot to the quick, Coralie felt for Lucien's leg, and pressed it between hers ; she took his hand and squeezed it. Then she was silent, and seemed lost in one of those moments of infinite delight that recompense poor girls like herself for all their past troubles, all their sufferings, and that in their hearts take on a poetry unknown to other women, to whom these violent contrasts are, happily, unknown.

"At the end you were acting as well as Mademoiselle Mars," said du Bruel.

"Yes," said Camusot, "something seemed to be upsetting her at first, but from half-way through the second act she was marvellous. You owe half your success to her."

"And she owes half hers to me," said du Bruel.

"You are fighting over the Bishop's cope," she said in an altered voice. The actress took advantage of the darkness to raise Lucien's hand to her lips; her tears fell upon it as she kissed it. Lucien was thrilled to the very core of his being. In the humility of a courtesan's love there is a magnificence that raises it to the level of the angels.

"This gentleman is writing a notice," said du Bruel, addressing Lucien. "You must write a charming paragraph about our dear Coralie."

"Oh, do us that little favour!" said Camusot, in the tones of a man going on his knees to Lucien, "and you will always find me ready to be at your service at any time."

"But you must not try to influence him!" exclaimed the actress indignantly. "He must write what he likes. Buy me a carriage, Papa Camusot, not praises."

"You shall have them for nothing," replied Lucien politely; "I have never written for the newspapers before, and I don't know their ways, but my virgin pen is at your disposal."

"That will be amusing," said du Bruel.

"Here we are at the Rue de Bondy," said Cardot, who had been quite crushed by Coralie's sally.

"If I am to have the first-fruits of your pen, you shall have my first love," Coralie whispered, during the brief moment she was alone with Lucien in the cab.

Coralie followed Florine into her bedroom, to change into the dress that she had sent on beforehand.

Lucien had no idea of the luxury in which a wealthy tradesman who has made money and who wants to enjoy life will keep an actress or a mistress. Matifat was not such a wealthy man as his friend Camusot, and he had done things rather shabbily; but Lucien was surprised when he saw a dining-room artistically decorated and lighted by handsome lamps. The walls were covered with green cloth, fastened with gilt-headed nails. There were flower-stands filled with flowers, and the drawing-room, hung with yellow silk with brown trimmings, was resplendent with the furniture fashionable at that time, a Thomire chandelier, and a carpet with a Persian design. The clock, candle-sconces and fireplace were all in good taste. Matifat had left everything to Grindot, a young architect who was building a house for him, and who, knowing the purpose of these rooms, had taken special pains over them. Matifat, a shopkeeper to the backbone, was careful about touching the smallest thing. He seemed to be thinking about his bills all the time, and to look upon all these magnificences as so many jewels imprudently taken out of their case.

" And this is what I shall be forced to do for Florentine! " was the thought to be read in old Cardot's eyes.

Lucien suddenly realised why the state of Lousteau's own room did not worry the journalist lover in the least. As secret lord of these banquets, Étienne enjoyed all these good things. He was standing with his back to the fireplace, like the master of the house, talking to the manager, who was congratulating du Bruel.

" Copy! Copy! " exclaimed Finot, who came in at this moment. " There's nothing in the box for the paper. The compositors are working on my article and they will have finished it soon."

" We won't be long," said Étienne. " There is a fire and a table in Florine's dressing-room. If M. Matifat will give us ink and paper, we will knock off the newspaper while Florine and Coralie are changing."

Cardot, Camusot, and Matifat went off in search of pens, penknives, and everything that the two writers needed. No sooner had they gone than Tullia, one of the prettiest dancers of the day, flew into the room.

" My dear," she said to Finot, " they have agreed to take your hundred copies! They will cost the management nothing, because the orchestra and the chorus and the *corps de ballet* are being made to take them. But your paper is so witty that nobody has complained. You are going to have your boxes. And here is the first quarter's subscription," she concluded, handing him two banknotes, " so don't pull me to pieces! "

" I am lost! " Finot exclaimed. " I shall have to suppress my infamous diatribe and I have not another idea in my head for this issue."

" What a wonderful inspiration, my divine Laïs! " said Blondet, who came in after the dancer with Nathan and Vernou. He had brought Claude Vignon with him. " You must stay to supper with us, dear angel, or I shall crush you like the butterfly that you are. As a dancer, you will arouse no passions of rivalry. And as for beauty, you are all much too sensible to be jealous in public."

" Oh Lord! Du Bruel, Nathan, Blondet, all of you, save me! " Finot begged. " I need five columns! "

" I can write two on the play," said Lucien.

" My subject will run to one column," said Lousteau.

" Very well, Nathan, Vernou and du Bruel, you must fill up the rest with jokes. If Blondet will graciously vouchsafe two short columns for the front page, I will go to the printer's. It is a good thing you brought your carriage, Tullia."

" Yes, but the Duke is waiting in it, with a German Minister," she said.

" Ask the Duke and the Minister to come up," said Nathan.

" Germans are hard drinkers, he will be expensive, and we shall commit a great many indiscretions, and he will remember them all," said Blondet.

" Who is the most serious and weighty member of our company, to go down and talk to them ? " said Finot. " Du Bruel, you are a bureaucrat, you go down and bring up the Duc de Rhétoré, and the Minister, and give your arm to Tullia. My word, isn't Tullia looking lovely tonight! "

" We shall be thirteen at table! " said Matifat, turning pale.

" No, fourteen! " exclaimed Florentine, appearing at this

moment. " I have come to keep an eye on *Milord Cardot*, " she said in a mock English accent.

" Besides, " said Lousteau, " Blondet has brought Claude Vignon."

" I brought him here for the drink, " retorted Blondet, picking up an inkstand. " Come on, show your brilliance in return for the fifty-six bottles of wine we are going to drink, " he said to Nathan and Vernou. " Above all, stimulate du Bruel. He writes for the music halls, and he is capable of producing one or two bad jokes if he is driven to it."

Lucien, eager to show all these remarkable personages what he could do, wrote his first article at a little round table in Florine's dressing-room by the light of rose-coloured candles lighted by Matifat:

The Panorama-Dramatique. First performance of *The Alcalde's Dilemma*, an imbroglio in three acts. First appearance of Mademoiselle Florine. Mademoiselle Coralie, Vignol.

" People come in, go out, talk, and stride up and down looking for something and finding nothing. Everything is in an uproar. The Alcalde has lost his daughter and found a cap, but the cap does not fit him—it must belong to the thief! Where is the thief? People come in, go out, talk, stride up and down, and search harder than ever. The Alcalde at last discovers a man without a daughter, and a daughter without a man, which is satisfactory for the magistrate, but not for the audience. Quiet is restored, and the Alcalde sets about questioning the man. This old Alcalde sits in a great Alcalde's armchair and arranges the sleeves of his Alcalde's gown. Spain is the only country where Alcaldes favour wide sleeves, and where you see round Alcaldes' necks those ruffles the wearing of which is in Paris theatres a good half of their function. This Alcalde who has done so much running to and fro with the tottering steps of asthmatic old age is Vignol—Vignol, a second Potier. This young actor plays old men well enough to make the oldest of the old laugh. He has a future of a hundred old ages before him, with that bald forehead of his, that quavering voice, those thin shanks trembling under a decrepit frame. He is so old, this young actor, that it is quite alarming, one wonders whether his old age is contagious. And what an Alcalde! What a charming anxious smile! What inane dignity! What self-important folly! What judicial hesitancy! How well he knows that you can never believe anything that you hear! And yet, on the other hand, that nothing is too impossible to be true! How truly well fitted he is to be the Minister of a Constitutional monarch! To every enquiry of the Alcalde's the unknown man replies with a question; Vignol answers in such a way that the unknown elicits the whole truth from the Alcalde. This scene is eminently funny, with a touch of Molière, and captivated the audience completely; but do not ask me what the mystery was, or why—although this seemed perfectly clear to the characters on the stage. For there was the Alcalde's daughter, a real Andalusian, a Spaniard with Spanish eyes, Spanish complexion, a Spanish figure, Spanish gait, in fact a Spaniard from top to toe, with a dagger in her garter, love in her heart, and a cross on a ribbon tied round her neck. At the end of the first act someone asked me how the play was going, and I said: ' She has red stockings with green clocks, a foot no bigger than that, patent-leather slippers, and the most beautiful legs in Andalusia! ' Ah! that Alcalde's daughter! You are on the point of declaring your love, she arouses fearful desires in you, you want to jump on to the stage and offer to her your humble cottage and your heart, or to place at her disposal your thirty thousand a year, or your pen. This Andalusian is the most beautiful actress in Paris. Coralie, since we must reveal her name, can be a countess or a *grisette*, and it would be hard to say under which disguise she is most enchanting. She can be whatever she likes, she is born to play all parts, and what more can one say of a boulevard actress?

" In the second act a Parisian Spaniard appears, with cameo features and deadly glances. I asked where she came from, and I was told that she had come in from the wings, and that her name was Mademoiselle Florine; but upon my word, I found it difficult to believe, there was so much passion in her movements, and frenzy in her love. This rival to the Alcalde's daughter is the wife of a lord, made from a cut from Almaviva's cloak, in which, to be sure, there is enough stuff for a hundred boulevard grandees. Florine has not red stockings with green clocks, or patent-leather shoes, but she has a mantilla, and a veil which she uses to good purpose, great lady that she is! She showed how well the tigeress may play the pussy-cat. I began to realise, from the sharp words that these two Spanish damsels exchanged, that some drama of jealousy was in progress; and just as all was going well, the Alcalde's foolishness upset everything again. All the torchbearers, grandees, valets, Figaros, courtiers, ladies and ladies'-maids began again to search, come in, go out, and stride up and down as before. The plot again thickened, and I will leave it to thicken; for the jealous Florine and the fortunate Coralie were once more entangled in the folds of basquina and mantilla, and my eyes were dazzled by the twinkling of their little feet.

"I managed to reach the third act without making a scene, or the police having to be called in, or scandalising the house, and I therefore begin to believe in the strength of your public and private morality, about which the Chamber has been so concerned lately that anyone might think that there were no morals left in France. I gathered that a man was in love with two women, neither of whom loved him; or that he was loved by both but did not love them in return; and that either he did not love Alcaldes or that Alcaldes did not love him; but that he was a fine fellow all the same, and certainly did love someone, himself, or even God as a last resort, because he was going off to be a monk. If you want to know any more, go to the Panorama-Dramatique. You have been warned already that you will have to go at once for the sake of those triumphant red stockings with green clocks, that little foot, so full of promise, those eyes with the sunlight shining through them; for the sake of that Parisian finesse disguised as an Andalusian, and the Andalusian disguised as a Parisian actress. You will have to go a second time to enjoy the play, to die with laughter personified as the old Alcalde, and melancholy in the shape of the love-sick lord. The play is an all-round success. The author who, it is said, worked in collaboration with one of the greatest poets, was called before our curtain with a love-sick damsel on each arm—which fairly brought down the house. These girls' legs seemed to be cleverer than the author, but when the two rivals left the stage, the dialogue seemed witty enough; than which there could be no more abundant proof of the excellence of the play. The calls for the author, and the thunderous applause, caused some anxiety to the architect of the theatre; but the author, accustomed to the eruptions of the frenzied Vesuvius that break out beneath the great chandelier, did not tremble—for he is M. de Cursy. As for the two actresses, they danced the famous bolero of Seville, that found favour in the eyes of a council of reverend fathers of olden times, and which managed to get past the censor, in spite of the dangerous seductions of its motions. This bolero in itself would be enough to draw all elderly men in whose hearts the fires of love are not yet utterly extinct; and out of charity I warn all such to see that the lenses of their opera-glasses are well polished."

While Lucien was writing this page, that was to bring about a revolution in journalism, by opening up a new and original vein, Lousteau was writing an article—a so-called social column—entitled " The Ex-Beau ", which began as follows:

" The Empire beau is invariably tall, thin, and well-preserved. He wears a corset and the Cross of the Legion of Honour. His name is something like Potelet; and in order to move with the times, the Empire Baron has conferred upon himself the particle du—he is *du* Potelet, but ready to become Potelet again if there is another revolution. A man of two worlds, as his name implies, he is paying court in the Faubourg Saint-Germain, after having once been the illustrious, serviceable, and accommodating train-bearer of a sister of that man whom shame forbids me to name. Although du Potelet denies his services to an Imperial Highness, he still sings the songs composed for the benefactress who took such a tender interest in his career . . ." and so on. The article was a tissue of these silly personalities that were the fashion at that time, for the style has been brought to a fine perfection since, by the *Figaro* in particular. Lousteau thought up an absurd comparison between Mme de Bargeton, to whom the Baron was paying court, and the cuttle-bone—a comparison that amused people who had no occasion to know anything about the two people they were laughing at.

Châtelet was compared to a heron. The story of the heron's love for the cuttle-bone that he could not swallow, and that broke in three when he dropped it, was irresistibly funny. This joke, which ran to several articles, had, as everyone knows, enormous repercussions in the Faubourg Saint-Germain, and was one of the thousand and one causes for the subsequent vigorous legislation against the Press. An hour later, Blondet, Lousteau, and Lucien returned to the drawing-room, where the poets, the Duke, the Minister, the four women, the three shopkeepers, Finot and the manager were all talking. An apprentice in his paper cap had already arrived to collect copy for the paper.

" The men will go if I don't take them something," he said.

" Here are ten francs, tell them to wait," said Finot.

" If I give it to them, they will take to topeography, and goodbye to the paper."

" The brilliance of that child is appalling! " said Finot.

The Minister was busy predicting a great future for this boy when the three authors came in. Blondet read out a very witty article against the romantics. Lousteau's article made everybody laugh. The Duke de Rhétoré suggested that it would be as well, so as not to arouse too much indignation in the Faubourg Saint-Germain, to slip in a word or two in praise of Mme d'Espard.

" Now read us what you have written," said Finot to Lucien.

Lucien read out his article, in fear and trembling, but when he had finished the room rang with applause, the actresses embraced the novice, and the three shopkeepers nearly squeezed the life out of him. Du Bruel shook hands with him, with tears in his eyes, and last of all the manager invited him to dinner.

" There are no more children in the world," said Blondet. " As M. de Chateaubriand has already used the epithet 'sublime child' for Victor Hugo, I am obliged to tell you, quite simply, that you have great talent, feeling, and style."

" He's on the paper," said Finot, and thanked Étienne with a shrewd glance.

" What have you managed to think up?" Lousteau asked Blondet and du Bruel.

" Here are du Bruel's," said Nathan.

*** " Now that the public is so occupied with Vicomte A . . ." Viscount Demosthenes was heard to say yesterday, " perhaps they will let *me* alone."

*** " An Ultra was condemning M. Pasquier's speech as a mere continuation of Decaze's policy. 'Yes,' said a lady, ' but he has beautiful Royalist legs.' "

" If it begins like that, it's good enough, it will do," said Finot. " Run and give them that," he said to the apprentice. " The paper may not be the genuine article, but it's our best number," he said, turning to the group of writers, who were already looking at Lucien and trying to take his measure.

" He has talent, that boy," said Blondet.

" His article is good," said Claude Vignon.

" Supper! " cried Matifat.

The Duke gave his arm to Florine, Coralie took Lucien's, and the dancer had Blondet on one side and the German Minister on the other.

" I do not understand why you should attack Mme de Bargeton and Baron du Châtelet, who I hear, has been nominated Préfect of the Charente and a Master of Requests."

" Mme de Bargeton showed Lucien the door as if he was a scoundrel."

" A handsome young man like that! " said the Minister.

The supper served from a new plate, on a Sèvres dinner service, on a table spread with a damask cloth, was the most sumptuous that money could buy. Chevet had planned the supper, the wines had been selected by the most famous wine merchants of the Quai Saint-Bernard, a friend of Camusot, Matifat, and Cardot. Lucien was seeing for the first time the opulence of Paris at first hand ; he went from one surprise to the next, but he concealed his astonishment like the man of talent, feeling and style, that Blondet had said he was.

As they crossed the drawing-room, Coralie whispered in Florine's ear :

" Make Camusot so drunk for me that he will have to spend the night here."

"Have you *made* your journalist, then?" Florine replied, using a word current in their world.

"No, my dear, I love him!" Coralie replied with a graceful little shrug of her shoulders.

These words rang in Lucien's ears, carried thither by the Fifth Deadly Sin. Coralie was admirably well dressed, and her dress brought out cleverly her special beauties, for every woman has good features that are peculiar to herself. Her dress, like Florine's, was made of a wonderful material, not yet on sale to the public, called *mousseline de soie*, the first pieces of which had reached Camusot as proprietor of the Golden Cocoon a few days before from the factories of Lyons. Love, and beautiful clothes, that are like make-up and scent to a woman, enhanced Coralie's seductions. She was happy. A pleasure that we have anticipated, and that cannot now escape us, has immense power over young hearts. Perhaps certainty is, in the eyes of the young, the great attraction of brothels; perhaps many a long fidelity is attributable to the same cause. Pure, sincere love—in fact, first love—combined with one of those strange violent fancies to which poor girls like Coralie are prone; all this, and her great admiration for Lucien's beauty, inspired Coralie with the wisdom of love.

"I would love you even if you were ugly and ill!" she whispered to Lucien as they sat down at table.

What words for a poet to hear! Camusot no longer counted; and Lucien, when he looked at Coralie, thought of him no more. What young man, made for enjoyment, a creature of sensation, bored by the tameness of provincial life, tired of poverty, harassed by enforced continence, weary of his monastic existence in the Rue de Cluny, of his labours to no purpose, and drawn towards the depths of Paris life—what young man would have withdrawn from this brilliant banquet? Lucien already had one foot in Coralie's bed and the other in the bird-lime of journalism, that he had pursued so hard without having been able to overtake it. After watching so often in vain in the Rue du Sentier, he had found the newspaper, at a table spread with meat and drink, gay and companionable. He was about to be avenged for all his sufferings by an article which, the

"Supper!" cried Matifat

very next morning, would infallibly pierce two hearts into which he had longed in vain to pour all the bitterness of rage and sorrow that he had had to drink. Looking at Lousteau, he thought, " Here is a real friend! " without for a moment suspecting that Lousteau was already beginning to fear him as a dangerous rival. Lucien had made the mistake of showing his talent : a colourless article would have done just as well. Blondet counter-balanced the envy that was devouring Lousteau by remarking to Finot that one ought to come to terms with talent of such an order as his. This hint dictated Lousteau's conduct, and he resolved to remain Lucien's friend and to come to an understanding with Finot in order to exploit a newcomer so dangerous by keeping him poor. This was a decision reached quickly and settled in all its implications between these two men in two whispered phrases.

" He has talent."

" He will expect to be paid for it."

" Oh! "

" Right! "

" I am always nervous when I sup with French journalists," said the German diplomat, with calm, good-natured urbanity, as he looked at Blondet, whom he had met at the house of the Countess de Montcornet. " There is a prophecy by Blücher that it is incumbent upon you to fulfil."

" What prophecy is that ? " Nathan asked.

" When Blücher came to the heights of Montmartre with Saaken, in 1814—forgive me for referring to that day that for you was so fatal—and Saaken, who was a brute, said, ' Now let us set fire to Paris! ' ' Mark my words, France cannot be destroyed except by *that*,' said Blücher, pointing to the great malignant growth that lay spread at their feet, glowing and smiling in the valley of the Seine. Heaven be praised, there are no newspapers in my country," the Minister added, after a pause. " I still have not recovered from the fright I got from that little fellow in the paper cap, who at the age of ten has all the astuteness of an old diplomat. And this evening I feel as if I were sitting down to supper with lions and panthers who have done me the honour of sheathing their claws."

" It is obvious," said Blondet, " that we could say, and prove to the whole of Europe, that a serpent issued from your Excellency's mouth this evening, and that Mademoiselle Tullia, the prettiest of our dancers, failed to charm it; and from that we might go on to comment on the story of Eve, the Bible, and the first and last sins. But don't worry, you are our guest."

" It would be amusing," said Finot.

" We could publish a scientific dissertation on all the serpents to be found in the human heart and body, and proceed to the diplomatic *corps*," said Lousteau.

" We might exhibit a specimen serpent in this bottle of cherries in brandy," said Vernou.

" You would end by believing the story yourself," said Vignon to the diplomat.

" Gentlemen," exclaimed the Duc de Rhétoré, " let sleeping claws lie."

" The influence and power of the press is only beginning to dawn," said Finot; " journalism is in its infancy, but it will grow. Ten years from now everything will be publicised. Public opinion will be turned upon all questions, ideas——"

". . . will blight everything," said Blondet, interrupting Finot.

" That's a saying worth remembering," said Claude Vignon.

" And make kings," said Lousteau.

". . . and bring down monarchies," said the Diplomat.

" And what is more," said Blondet, " if the press did not exist, it would be necessary to invent it; but it does, and we live by it."

" You will die of it," said the Diplomat. " Don't you see that the power of the masses, who will suppose that you have enlightened them, will make individual greatness more and more difficult? That if you sow ideas in the hearts of the lower classes, you will reap revolution, and that you will be the first victims? What do they smash first in Paris when there is a riot? "

" The street lamps," said Nathan; " but we are too insignificant to fear for ourselves, we shall only be cracked."

" As a nation you are too intelligent to allow any government whatever to have its own way," said the German Minister.

" Otherwise you would begin a second conquest of Europe with your pens, and win back all that you could not hold with the sword."

" Newspapers are an evil," said Claude Vignon. " The evil could be made use of, but the Government prefers to fight it. There will be a struggle. Who will give way? That is the question."

" Blondet! Blondet! " said Finot. " You are going too far! There are subscribers present! "

" You are the proprietors of one of those poison-shops, you have every reason to be frightened; but I don't give a damn for the whole business, although I live by it! "

" Blondet is right," said Claude Vignon. " Journalism, instead of being a priestly order, became first a party weapon, and then a money-making business. Like all business enterprises, it knows neither laws nor good faith. Every newspaper is, just as Blondet says, a shop where words are sold to the public, of whatever colour they like. If there was a paper for hunchbacks, it would prove morning and evening the beauty, the privilege, and the necessity of humps. A newspaper no longer exists in order to enlighten but to flatter opinions. And so all newspapers will become, in due course, unscrupulous, hypocritical, shameless and treacherous; they will kill ideas, systems and men, and thrive by doing so. All the resources of intelligence will be at their disposal. Evil will be done, and yet no one will be responsible. I—Vignon; you, Lousteau; you, Blondet; you, Finot—will be so many Aristides, Platos, and Catos —men after Plutarch's own heart; we shall all be innocent, we shall be able to wash our hands of all the infamy. Napoleon gave the reason of this moral phenomenon—or immoral phenomenon, if you prefer it—in a brilliant epigram suggested to him by his study of the Convention: ' No one is responsible for collective crimes.' A newspaper may permit itself the most atrocious behaviour; but no one feels that any personal blame attaches to himself."

" But the authorities are going to introduce repressive legislation," said du Bruel; " it is under discussion now."

" Pooh! " said Nathan. " What can the law do against French public opinion, the most subtle of all solvents? "

" Ideas can only be neutralised by ideas," Vignon continued.

"Only terror and despotism can stifle the French genius, whose language lends itself admirably to allusion and ambiguity. The more repressive the law, the more wit will flourish, like steam in an engine without a safety-valve. So the King is quite right: if the press is against him, the Ministry is responsible, and vice versa. If the newspapers invent some infamous calumny, someone has misinformed them. If the individual in question complains, the paper escapes by asking pardon for taking so great a liberty. If the case is taken to court, the editor pleads that nobody asked him to make any correction, but if he is asked to do so, he refuses, smiling, and makes his crime seem a trifle. He scoffs at his victim, if the latter wins his case. If he is punished, and has heavy damages to pay, he will stigmatise the plaintiff as an enemy of freedom, the country, and enlightenment.

"The press will write an article purporting to say that so-and-so is the most honest man in the country and manage to imply that he is a thief. In fact, the crimes of the press are mere trifles, the enemies of the press, monsters! And before very long it can make those who read it every day believe whatever it likes. Besides, everything that it dislikes is unpatriotic, and it can never be wrong. It makes use of religion against religion, the Constitution against the King; it cries out against the magistracy when the magistracy offends it; it cries it up when it serves the cause of popular passions. It invents sensational stories to send up its circulation, and thumps its tub like any mountebank. A newspaper would serve up its own father salted with its own wit rather than fail to keep its public interested and amused—like the actor who put his own son's ashes in the urn so as to weep convincingly, or the mistress who sacrifices everything to her lover."

"In fact, it is the nation in folio form," Blondet put in, interrupting Vignon.

"The nation with hypocrisy added and generosity lacking," Vignon continued. "Journalism will banish all talent from its midst, as Aristides was banished from Athens. We shall see newspapers that originally were directed by men of honour fall sooner or later into the hands of mediocrities who have the toughness and the flexibility of indiarubber—qualities that minds of fine genius never possess—or of tradesmen with money enough to buy their pens. These things are happening already! But ten years from now every youngster who has just left school will think himself a great man, ascend the column of some newspaper, insult his predecessors, and pull them down by the heels in order to have their place. Napoleon was right to muzzle the press. I am prepared to lay a wager that under a Government that they themselves had put in power, the Opposition newspapers would lead the attack, for the same reasons, and with the very same articles that they use today against the King and the present Government, the moment anything was refused them. The more concessions are made to the journalists, the more exacting the press becomes. The successful journalist will be succeeded by the poor and starving journalist. The ulcer is incurable, it will become more and more malignant, more and more insolvent; and the greater the evil grows, the more it will be tolerated, until the day comes when the newspapers have so proliferated that confusion will overthrow them, like the Tower of Babel. We all know—fools that we are—that the press will outdo any king in ingratitude, and the most dishonest business methods are not so unscrupulous and calculating; they eat up our brains in order to sell their intellectual dope; but we all write for it, like men who work a quicksilver mine, although they know that they will die as a result. Do you see that young man sitting beside Coralie?—what is his name? Lucien!—he is handsome, he is a poet, he is witty—which is worth more to him than all the rest. Well, he will enter one of those intellectual brothels called newspapers, and he will use up all his best ideas, drain his mind dry, corrupt his heart, and commit all those anonymous dishonesties, which, in the war of ideas, take the place of the stratagems, fire, looting, and betrayals of gangster warfare. When he—like hundreds more—has squandered a fine talent for the profit of the shareholders, these poison-mongers will leave him to die of hunger if he is thirsty, or of thirst if he is starving."

"Thank you," said Finot.

"But, good Lord! I knew all that, and yet here I am in the

galleys," said Claude Vignon, " and the arrival of a new convict gives me pleasure. Blondet and I have more ability than Mr. This and Mr. That who exploit our talent, and yet they will always exploit us. We have hearts, somewhere under our intellects, and we have not the ferocity of the born exploiter. We are lazy and thoughtful and critical and detached. They will drink up our talents, and then accuse us of improvidence! "

" I thought you were going to be more amusing," exclaimed Florine.

" Florine is quite right," said Blondet ; " let us leave the cure of public ills to charlatans and politicians. ' Spit in your own glass ? Never! '—as Charlet says."

" Do you know what Vignon reminds me off ? " said Lousteau to Lucien. " One of those fat women in the Rue du Pélican saying to a schoolboy, ' My boy, you are too young to come here '! "

This sally produced a general laugh, but it pleased Coralie. The shopkeepers ate and drank steadily as they listened.

" What a country this is ; you meet so much good and so much evil! " said the Minister to the Duc de Rhétoré. " You are prodigals, gentlemen, who will never fall on evil days."

And so, by a blessed chance, Lucien was warned from all sides, as he stood on the edge of the precipice over which he was about to fall. D'Arthez had set him on the noble way of hard work, awakening in him the spirit before which obstacles vanish. Lousteau himself had tried to warn him away—from selfish motives to be sure—by painting journalism and the literary world in their true colours. Lucien had been unwilling to believe in so many hidden corruptions ; but now he heard the journalists themselves bewailing their lot, he saw them at work, he saw them reading the omens in the entrails of their foster-mother. This evening he had seen things as they are. And instead of being seized with horror at the spectacle of that cancer in the very heart of Paris that Blücher had so well defined, he was intoxicated with the pleasure of being in such intellectually brilliant society. These remarkable men, with their dazzling armour of vice, and the brilliant helmets of their cynical analysis, seemed to him superior to the earnest and sincere members of d'Arthez's circle. Besides, he was savouring, for the first time, the pleasures of wealth. He was captivated by luxury, and under the influence of good cheer; his capricious instincts were awakened, and for the first time he was drinking the best wines, and making the acquaintance of masterpieces of the art of cookery. He saw a Minister, and a Duke and his dancer hobnobbing with journalists and doing homage to their infamous power; he experienced a horrible longing to dominate the kings of this world, and he felt within himself the power to vanquish them. And, last of all, there was this Coralie; a few words of his had made her happy. He had examined her by the light of the festive candles, across the fumes of dishes and through a haze of drunkenness, and she seemed to him sublime, made beautiful by her love. She was the loveliest, the most beautiful actress in Paris. The circle of the Rue des Quatre-Vents, the horizons of noble thought, were bound to give way before a temptation so complete. His author's vanity had been flattered by the experts, he had been praised by his future rivals. The success of his article and the conquest of Coralie were two triumphs to turn an older head than his.

During this conversation everyone had supped remarkably well and drunk to good purpose. Lousteau, sitting next to Camusot, had three or four times poured kirsch into his wine without anybody paying the slightest attention; he played on his vanity so as to make him drink. This manœuvre was managed so well that the good shopkeeper did not notice it; he considered himself, in his own way, a match for any journalist. Jokes became more sharp-edged over dessert, as the wines began to circulate more freely. The Diplomat, an intelligent man, made a sign to the Duke and the dancer, as soon as he detected the first symptoms of the loud-voiced nonsense that, among intellectuals, precedes the grotesque scenes of the final stages of a wild party, and the three of them disappeared. As soon as Camusot was thoroughly fuddled, Coralie and Lucien, who had behaved all through supper like lovers of fifteen, slipped away down the stairs and jumped into a cab. As Camusot was under the table, Matifat naturally concluded that he had left with the actress; he left his guests smoking, drinking, laughing, and arguing, and followed Florine when she went to bed. Day dawned on the disputants—or rather on Blondet, that intrepid drinker, who alone was capable of speech, and who proposed to the sleepers the toast of rosy-fingered Aurora.

Lucien was not accustomed to Paris parties; he was still perfectly clear-headed as he went downstairs, but the fresh air was too much for him. He was fearfully drunk. Coralie and her maid had to carry the poet up to the first floor of the charming house in the Rue de Vendôme where the actress lived. Lucien almost passed out on the staircase and was horribly sick.

"Quick, Bérénice," Coralie cried. "Some tea! Make some tea!"

"It's nothing, it's only the air," Lucien managed to say, "and I have never drunk so much before."

"Poor child, he's as innocent as a lamb!" said Bérénice, a stout Norman peasant girl, as plain as Coralie was beautiful.

At last Lucien was laid, quite unconscious of where he was, in Coralie's bed. With the help of Bérénice, the actress had undressed her poet with the care and love of a mother for her child. He kept repeating, "It's nothing. Only the air. Thank you, Mother."

"How charmingly he says 'Mother'!" Coralie exclaimed, kissing his hair.

"What a pleasure to love such an angel, Mademoiselle! Where did you hook him? I never thought there could be a man handsome enough to be a match for you," said Bérénice.

Lucien wanted to go to sleep. He had no idea where he was, and saw nothing. Coralie made him drink several cups of tea, and then she left him to sleep.

"Did the porter or anybody else see us?" Coralie asked.

"No, I was waiting up for you."

"Does Victoire know anything?"

"You bet he doesn't!" said Bérénice.

Ten hours later, about midday, Lucien awoke to meet Coralie's eyes. She had been watching him while he slept. He realised that—being a poet. The actress was still wearing her beautiful dress, horribly stained. She intended to keep it as a relic. Lucien recognised the devotion, the delicacy of true love, longing for its recompense: he looked at Coralie. She was undressed in a moment, and slipped in beside Lucien like a serpent.

At five o'clock the poet was sleeping, lulled in voluptuous delight. He had caught a glimpse of the actress's bedroom, a ravishing creation of luxury, all in white and rose, a world of exquisite things, of dainty ingenuity, that far surpassed anything that Lucien had admired at Florine's flat. Coralie had dressed. She had to be at the theatre at seven o'clock to play her part as the Andalusian. She had come back to gaze once more at her poet, sleeping in divine bliss. She was intoxicated, unable to drink deeply enough of this noble love, in which the senses were at one with the heart, and the heart with the senses, so that both were exalted to ecstasy. This apotheosis, that makes one heavenly being, by love, from two, who on earth are divided in order that they may feel love—this mystery absolved her. And besides, would not the more than mortal beauty of Lucien in itself have served as an excuse? Kneeling beside that bed, happy in the love within her, the actress felt herself sanctified.

These raptures were interrupted by Bérénice.

"Here comes the Camusot—and he knows you are here!" she exclaimed.

Lucien jumped up, his innate generosity making him anxious not to do Coralie any harm. Bérénice drew back a curtain, and Lucien slipped into a charming dressing-room while Bérénice and her mistress hurriedly brought his clothes. Just as the shopkeeper arrived, Coralie noticed the poet's boots: Bérénice had put them in front of the fire to dry and had polished them in secret. Maid and mistress had both forgotten those tell-tale boots. Bérénice exchanged a look of alarm with her mistress and went out. Coralie sank on to her settee and made Camusot sit in a *gondola* armchair opposite. That worthy man, who adored Coralie, looked at the boots without daring to look at his mistress.

"Ought I to take offence over that pair of boots and leave Coralie? That would be making a fuss over a trifle. There is always a pair of boots. This pair would be better in a shop-window, or on the boulevards, taking a walk on some man's feet. Because here,

"What a pleasure to love such an angel!"

with no feet in them, they say a lot of things contrary to fidelity. I am fifty, it is true; I ought to be as blind as Cupid."

There was little excuse for this cowardly monologue, for the boots in question were not those half-boots now in fashion and which a worried man might at least half overlook; they were made according to the fashion of the day, a full-length, very elegant pair of those boots, with tassels, that shone, nearly always, over tight-fitting trousers of a light colour, and reflected objects as in a mirror. So that these boots stared the good silk merchant full in the face, and, we must add, his heart was likewise full to overflowing.

"What's the matter?" asked Coralie.

"Nothing," he said.

"Ring the bell," said Coralie, smiling at Camusot's lack of courage. "Bérénice," she said to the Norman maid when she came in, "do get me a button-hook so that I can try on these damned boots again. Don't forget to bring them to my dressing-room this evening."

"What!... Your boots?" said Camusot, breathing more freely.

"Why? Whose did you think they were?" she asked, with a scornful air. "Big silly, what were you beginning to think?—Yes, he really did think so!" she said to Bérénice. "I am playing a man's part in What's-his-name's play, and I have never worn men's clothes before. The theatre bootmaker lent me these boots to practise walking in them while a pair is being made to fit me; he tried these on me—they were so painful that I had to take them off, but I must put them on again."

"Don't put them on if they hurt you," said Camusot, whom the boots had hurt very much.

"Mademoiselle ought really, instead of martyring herself, as she was doing just now—she was crying, sir!—and if I was a man I wouldn't let a woman that I love cry!—ought really to wear a pair made of thin morocco. But the management are so mean! You ought to order a pair for her, sir."

"Yes, yes," said the shopkeeper. "You have just got up?" he asked Coralie.

"Just this moment. I did not get back until six o'clock, after looking for you everywhere—you made me keep my cab waiting for seven hours! That's how you take care of me! Forgetting me for the bottle! I shall have to look after myself, now that I am acting every evening, so long as the *Alcalde* pays. I don't want to let down the play after that young man's article! "

" He's a good-looking boy, that," said Camusot.

" Do you think so ? He's not my type, he is too effeminate ; and men like that don't know how to make love like you stupid old business men. You get so bored with yourselves! "

" Are you dining with madame, sir ? " Bérénice enquired.

" No, my mouth is as dry as dust."

" You were beautifully fuddled last night, weren't you ? Ah! Papa Camusot, let me tell you I don't like men who drink . . ."

" You must give that young man a present," interrupted the shopkeeper.

" Oh yes! I would rather repay him like that than do what Florine does! Now, run along, my dear old good-for-nothing, or give me a carriage so that I shall not be so rushed for time."

" You shall have one tomorrow, to go to dinner with your manager at the Rocher de Cancale. There won't be a performance of the new play on Sunday."

" You must go now, I am just going to dine," said Coralie, showing Camusot out of the flat.

An hour later Lucien was released by Bérénice, Coralie's companion since her childhood. Bérénice's mind was as keen and subtle as her body was gross and corpulent.

" Stay here. Coralie will come back alone—she wants to get rid of Camusot altogether, if he worries you," said Bérénice to Lucien; " but you are too much of an angel to ruin her, and you her heart's delight! She said to me that she has made up her mind to give him the slip and leave this paradise to go and live in your garret. Oh, there are those who are jealous and envious, and you may be sure they have told her that you haven't a sou, and that all you have wouldn't fill a suitcase, and that you live in the Latin Quarter! I would come with you, of course, to do your housekeeping. But I have just been comforting her, poor lamb! It's true, isn't it, sir, that you are too clever to do anything so silly? Oh, you will soon see that the other old fool only has her body, and that you are the man she loves, her darling, and the god to whom she offers her soul. If you knew how sweet she is when I hear her say her parts over! She is the dearest girl! Well, she deserves that God should send her one of his angels, because she was sick of life. She was so unhappy with her mother, who used to beat her, and then sold her! Yes, sir, think of a mother selling her own child! If I had a daughter I should treat her like I do my little Coralie; she's like my own child to me. This is the first good time she's had since I knew her, the first time she has really been applauded. I hear that after what you wrote about her they have got up a real good applause for the second performance. Braulard came to arrange everything with her while you were asleep."

"Who? Braulard?" Lucien asked; he seemed to have heard that name before.

"The chief of the claque—he has been going through the play with her to arrange where she is to be looked after. Florine might try to play her a mean trick and get all the applause for herself, for all she calls herself her friend. They are all talking about your article on the Boulevards. Isn't this a bed fit for a prince?" she added, as she put on the lace bed-spread.

She lit the candles. Lucien, quite bewildered, thought himself transported, in real life, into a fairy palace. Camusot had chosen the richest materials from the Golden Cocoon for the hangings and window curtains. The poet trod on a carpet fit for a king. The soft light glinted from the carvings of the rosewood furniture that caught its gleams. The white marble fireplace was adorned with all sorts of precious trifles. The bedside rug was of swansdown bordered with sable. Black velvet slippers, lined with purple silk were eloquent of the happiness awaiting the poet of the *Marguerites*. A dainty lamp hung from the silk-draped ceiling. There were exquisite flower-stands filled with choice flowers, beautiful white heaths and scentless camellias. On all sides were images of innocence. How could one imagine an actress here, and the morals of the theatre?

" Isn't it lovely ? " she went on in a coaxing voice. " Wouldn't you be happier with her here than in a garret ? You will stop her from doing anything rash, won't you ? " The maid led Lucien towards a magnificent stand on which there were dishes taken from his mistress's dinner, so that the cook should not suspect the presence of a lover.

Lucien sat down to an excellent dinner, served by Bérénice on wrought silver, dishes and painted plates worth a louis apiece. This luxury assailed his mind exactly as a girl of the streets, with her naked flesh and her neat white stockings tempts a schoolboy.

" This Camusot is very lucky! " he exclaimed.

" Lucky ? " said Bérénice. " Why, he would give his whole fortune to be in your place; he would gladly exchange his old grey hairs for your young gold ones." She served Lucien with the finest wine that Bordeaux can produce for the wealthiest Englishman, and then she persuaded Lucien to go back to bed while he waited for Coralie and snatch a little sleep; and Lucien, to tell the truth, was very willing to lie down on the bed he had been admiring. Bérénice, who had read that wish in the young poet's eyes, was glad for her mistress's sake. At half-past ten Lucien awoke under a gaze overflowing with love. Coralie was there, in the most ravishing nightdress. Lucien had been asleep; he was drunk no longer with wine but with love. Bérénice left the room, asking, " What time breakfast tomorrow ? "

" Eleven; you are to bring us our breakfast in bed. I shall not be at home to anyone before two."

At two o'clock the following day the actress and her lover were dressed and sitting together just as if the poet had called to pay a visit to his protectress. Coralie had bathed him, combed him, curled him and dressed him; she had sent him out to buy a dozen beautiful shirts, a dozen cravats and a dozen handkerchiefs at Colliau's and a dozen pairs of gloves in a cedar-wood box. When she heard the sound of a carriage at her door, she flew to the window with Lucien. The two of them watched Camusot getting down from a magnificent coupé.

" I could never have believed that one could hate a man and luxury so much," she said.

"I am too poor to allow you to ruin yourself," said Lucien; and with these words he passed under the Caudine forks.

" Poor little lamb," she said, pressing Lucien to her heart, " do you love me so much, then ?—I asked this gentleman to call on me this morning," she said, indicating Lucien to Camusot, " thinking that we might all go for a drive in the Champs-Elysées to try the carriage."

" You go without me," said Camusot sadly. " I cannot dine with you tonight ; it is my wife's birthday, I had forgotten."

" Poor Musot, how bored you will be! " she said, throwing her arms round the silk merchant's neck.

She was wild with delight at the thought that she was going to drive out alone with Lucien in this beautiful coupé, that she would be alone with him in the Bois ; and in her access of joy, she seemed to love Camusot and lavished caresses upon him.

" I wish I could give you a carriage every day! " said the poor man.

" Come, sir, it is two o'clock," said the actress. She noticed that Lucien looked ashamed, and consoled him with an adorable look.

Coralie raced down the stairs, dragging Lucien after her. He heard the shopkeeper puffing after them like a seal, unable to keep up with them. The poet experienced the most intoxicating of all pleasures : happiness had made Coralie radiantly beautiful, and she appeared before the admiring eyes of all Paris, elegantly dressed in the most exquisite taste. Everybody in the Champs-Elysées admired these two lovers. In an avenue in the Bois de Boulogne their carriage met a coach in which were seated Mme d'Espard and Mme de Bargeton, who looked at Lucien in astonishment ; but he merely glanced in their direction with all the scorn of a poet who foresees his future glory and who is about to make his power felt. He was able to put into the glance that he exchanged with these two women some of the thoughts of vengeance that they had planted in his heart and that so long had gnawed it. That moment was one of the

"I wish I could give you a carriage every day!"

sweetest of his life, and perhaps decided his destiny. Lucien was again assailed by all the furies of pride ; he would appear again in the world, take a brilliant revenge, and all the social pettinesses, lately trampled underfoot by the hard worker, the friend of d'Arthez and his circle, once more entered his heart. He realised in that moment the full force of the attack made on his behalf by Lousteau : Lousteau had served his passions ; whereas the circle at the Rue de Quatre Vents, that collective Mentor, seemed only to mortify them in the cause of boring virtues and hard work that Lucien was beginning to think was useless. Work! What is it but death to souls eager for pleasure ? And with what facility writers slip into idle ways, into social life and its pleasures and the luxurious ways of actresses and women of easy virtue! Lucien felt an irresistible desire to continue the reckless life of the last two days.

The dinner at the Rocher de Cancale was exquisite. All Florine's guests were there, except the Minister, the Duke, and the dancer, and Camusot. There were, besides, two famous actors, and Hector Merlin and his mistress, a charming woman who called herself Mme de Val-Noble, the most beautiful and elegant of the women who made up, at that time, the less reputable Paris society, one of those women who are nowadays euphemistically called *Lorettes*. Lucien, who had been living in paradise for the last forty-eight hours, now heard of the success of his article. Finding himself fêted, and envied, the poet gained confidence. His wit scintillated, and he was that Lucien de Rubempré who shone for a few months in literary and artistic circles. Finot, who had an undoubted flair for discovering talent, scenting it out as an ogre smells human flesh, made much of Lucien, hoping to enlist him in the regiment of journalists under his command. Lucien nibbled at the bait of his flatteries. Coralie saw what that consumer of human talent was after and tried to put Lucien on his guard against him.

" Don't promise anything, my sweet," she whispered to her poet. " Wait ; he wants to exploit you. We will talk about it tonight."

" Nonsense! " replied Lucien. " I consider myself perfectly capable of being quite as clever and smart as they can ever be."

Finot, who had not, it seems, broken with Hector Merlin over the blank spaces, introduced Merlin to Lucien, and Lucien to Merlin. Coralie and Madame de Val-Noble made friends and made a great fuss of one another. Mme de Val-Noble invited Lucien and Coralie to dinner. Hector Merlin, the most dangerous of all the journalists present at that dinner, was a little dry, tight-lipped man, who nursed a boundless ambition and infinite jealousy; he was delighted by all the misfortunes of those around him, and took advantage of quarrels, which he fomented. He had a great deal of intelligence, but very little force of character; but the instinct that attracts upstarts towards money and power served him just as well. Lucien and he took a dislike to one another, for obvious reasons. Merlin made the mistake of voicing his thoughts, while Lucien kept his to himself.

Over dessert these men, each of whom secretly thought himself superior to the rest, seemed to be united by bonds of the most touching friendship. Lucien, as the newcomer, was made much of. They talked freely and unreservedly. Only Hector Merlin did not join in the laughter. Lucien asked him the reason for his reserve.

" Why, I see that you are entering the world of literature and journalism with illusions! You believe in friendship. We are all friends or enemies according to circumstances. We use first against one another the weapon that we ought only to use against enemies. You will discover before long that lofty sentiments will get you nowhere. If you are good-natured, learn to be ill-natured—be deliberately bad-tempered. If no one has taught you that first rule, I tell you now—and it is a secret worth knowing. If you want to be loved, never leave your mistress without making her cry a little; if you hope to make your fortune in literature, wound everybody all the time, even your friends, injure their self-respect; then everybody will court your favour."

Hector Merlin was delighted to observe from Lucien's expression that his words had stabbed the novice to the heart.

There was play, and Lucien lost all his money. Coralie carried him off, and the delights of love made him forget the terrible excitement of gambling, to which he was later to fall a victim.

The next day, when he left her and was on his way back to the

Latin Quarter, he found in his purse the money he had lost. This solicitude troubled him at first, and he had half a mind to go back to the actress and return a gift that humiliated him; but he was already in the Rue de la Harpe, so he went on towards the Hotel de Cluny. As he walked, he thought over Coralie's generous act, and he saw in it a proof of the maternal love that is so often united with an actress's passion. For women like Coralie, passion brings with it all other kinds of love. Lucien's train of thought led him at last to find a reason for accepting the gift, for he said to himself: "I love her; we will live together like husband and wife, and I shall never leave her!"

Who but Diogenes himself could fail to understand what Lucien felt as he went up the squalid ill-smelling staircase to his room, as his key grated in the lock, and he saw again the dirty floor, the wretched fireplace, repulsive in its poverty and bareness? On the table he found the manuscript of his novel, and a note from Daniel d'Arthez:

"My dear poet,

"Our friends are almost satisfied with your book. You will be able to show it with more confidence now, they say, both to friends and enemies. We all read your charming article on the Panorama-Dramatique, and you will certainly excite no less envy in literary circles than regret amongst us.

"Daniel."

"Regret! What on earth does he mean!" Lucien exclaimed, surprised at the tone of formal politeness in this note.

Was he, then, a stranger to the circle? Since he had devoured the delicious fruits that the Eve of the green-room had offered him, he had learned to set a higher value upon the good opinion and friendship of the friends at the Rue des Quatre-Vents. He stood lost in thought for a while, reflecting upon his present in this room, and his future in Coralie's. He was beset at one moment by honourable hesitations, at another by temptations. He sat down and began to look through his manuscript, to see in what state his friends had returned it to him. Great was his astonishment when he found that, in chapter after chapter, the skill and devotion of those as yet unknown great men had changed his poverty into riches. Full, closely packed, concise, energetic dialogue, replaced his conversations, that were, he now realised, mere chatter in comparison with these passages, charged with the spirit of the time. His portraits, uncertainly drawn, had been vigorously brought out, in colour and contour ; every character had been brought to life, by psychological observations, due, no doubt, to Bianchon, subtly relating each to the strange phenomena of human life. A number of wordy descriptions were now condensed and living. He had given them a misshapen, ill-clad child, and now he found a delightful young girl in a dress of spotless white, trim girdle, and rosy veil, an exquisite creature. Night came on him unawares, his eyes full of tears, humbled by so much greatness, feeling the value of such a lesson, full of admiration for corrections that taught him more about literature and art than his four years of reading, comparison, and study had done. The correction of an ill-executed sketch, a master's line on a drawing, teaches more than any amount of theory and criticism in the abstract.

" What friends! What hearts! How lucky I am! " he exclaimed, grasping the manuscript.

Carried away by the enthusiasm of his unstable and poetic nature, he rushed off to find Daniel. But as he went upstairs to Daniel's room, he felt himself less worthy of those hearts whom nothing could induce to deviate from the path of honour. A voice told him that if Daniel had loved Coralie he would not have accepted her unless she had broken with Camusot. He knew, besides, the abhorrence in which the friends held journalists, and he knew that already he had begun to be a journalist. He found his friends, all except Meyraux, who had just gone out, and on all their faces he read expressions of grief and despair.

" What is the matter ? " Lucien asked.

" We have just heard terrible news ; the greatest mind of our time, our dearest friend, who was our light for two years . . ."

" Louis Lambert ? " said Lucien.

" He has had a cataleptic stroke, and there is no hope for him," said Bianchon.

" He will die, with his body unconscious and his mind in heaven," Michel Chrestien added gravely.

" He will die as he lived," said d'Arthez.

" Love, thrown like a firebrand into the vast empire of his brain, has burned it up," said Léon Giraud.

" Yes," said Joseph Bridau, " he has risen so high that he has vanished from our sight."

" It is we who are to be pitied," said Fulgence.

" Perhaps he will recover," said Lucien.

" From what Meyraux has just told us, recovery is impossible," said Bianchon. " Medicine has no power over the phenomena that are taking place in his brain."

" But there are drugs," said d'Arthez.

" Yes," said Bianchon, " he is suffering from catalepsy now, but we might destroy his mind altogether."

" If only we could offer some other head to the spirit of evil! I would gladly give mine! " exclaimed Michel Chrestien.

" And then what would become of European federation ? " said d'Arthez.

" Yes, that is true," said Michel Chrestien. " One belongs to humanity before everything, before any individual."

" I came here with my heart full of gratitude to all of you," Lucien said. " You have changed my base metal into gold."

" Gratitude ? What do you take us for! " said Bianchon.

" The pleasure was on our side," Fulgence added.

" Well, so now you are a journalist, are you ? " Léon Giraud asked. " The stir of your first appearance has even reached the Latin Quarter."

" Not yet," said Lucien.

" Oh! So much the better! " said Michel Chrestien.

" What did I tell you ? " said d'Arthez.

" Lucien knows the value of a clear conscience, of being able to lay your head on your pillow every evening and say, ' I have not passed judgment on the work of others ; I have given pain to no one ; the keen sword of my intellect has wounded no innocent soul ; my wit has destroyed no one's happiness, not even disturbed happy stupidity, nor has it unjustly added to the burden of genius. I have disdained the facile triumphs of the epigram; in short, I have never acted against my convictions'—that is a viaticum that gives one strength."

"But," said Lucien, "I am sure one can say all that and at the same time work on a newspaper. If I had absolutely no other way of earning a living, I should have to do it."

"Oh! Oh! Oh!" said Fulgence, his voice rising a tone at each exclamation. "We are capitulating!"

"He will be a journalist," said Léon Giraud gravely. "Ah, Lucien, if only you would stay and work with us! We are going to bring out a paper in which neither truth nor justice will ever be outraged, in which we will spread doctrines that will be for the good of humanity, then perhaps . . ."

"You will not have a single subscriber," Lucien broke in with Machiavellian wisdom.

"There will be five hundred, but they will be worth five hundred thousand," said Michel Chrestien.

"You will need a great deal of capital," Lucien retorted.

"No," said d'Arthez, "a great deal of devotion."

"Anyone might take him for a perfumer's assistant," exclaimed Michel Chrestien, sniffing Lucien's head with a comic gesture. "You were seen in a very expensive carriage, drawn by a dandified pair of horses, with a mistress fit for a prince, none other than Coralie."

"Well," said Lucien, "is there any harm in that?"

"You say that as if there were," retorted Bianchon.

"I would have liked Lucien to find a Beatrix, a noble woman who would have stood by him all his life."

"But, Daniel, love is love, everywhere and always," said the poet.

"Ah!" said the republican. "In that respect I am an aristocrat. I could never love a woman kissed every night by an actor in public, a woman called by her Christian name in the wings, who plays to the gallery and smiles at the pit, who lifts up her skirts when she dances, and dresses up in men's clothes in order to display what ought to be seen by myself alone. Or if I did love such a woman, she should leave the stage, and I would purify her by my love."

"And what if she could not leave the stage?"

"I should die of vexation, jealousy, and a thousand ills. You cannot draw love out of the soul as you draw out a tooth."

Lucien became gloomy and thoughtful.

"When they know that I am tolerating Camusot they will despise me," he thought.

"The fact is," said the fierce republican with terrible good nature, "that you might be a great writer, but you will never be anything but a little good-for-nothing." He took his hat and left.

"He is very hard, Michel Chrestien," said the poet.

"Hard and salutary as the dentist's forceps," said Bianchon. "Michel is concerned for your future, and at this very moment I dare say he is thinking of you in the street with tears in his eyes."

D'Arthez was gentle and consoling, and tried to cheer Lucien. At the end of an hour the poet left, tormented by his conscience, that told him, "You will be a journalist!" as the witches told Macbeth, "You shall be king!" In the street, he looked up at the dimly lit windows of his patient friend, d'Arthez, and he returned home with a sad heart and an unquiet mind. A sort of presentiment told him that he had been among his true friends for the last time.

As he turned into the Rue de Cluny from the Place de la Sorbonne, he recognised Coralie's carriage. In order to see her poet for a moment, just to say good night to him, the actress had come all the way from the Boulevard du Temple to the Sorbonne. Lucien found his mistress in tears at the sight of his garret. She wanted to be as poor as her lover, and she was crying as she arranged his shirts and gloves and cravats and handkerchiefs in the wretched chest of drawers. Her despair was so unfeigned, so great, expressive of so much love, that Lucien, who had lately been reproached for having an actress, saw Coralie as a saint, ready to put on the hair-shirt of poverty. In order to come, this adorable girl had invented the excuse of telling her lover that the partnership of Coralie, Camusot and Lucien was returning the invitation of the partnership of Matifat, Florine and Lousteau, and inviting them to dinner, and to ask Lucien if there was anyone who might be useful to him that he would like to ask; Lucien said he would discuss it with Lousteau. The actress hurried away a few moments later, not telling Lucien that Camusot was waiting for her in the carriage.

At eight o'clock the next morning Lucien went to Étienne's room, but, not finding him there, hurried off to Florine's flat. The journalist and the actress received their friend in the pretty bedroom where they were installed like a married couple, and there the three of them breakfasted in splendour.

"Well, my boy, I advise you to come with me and call on Félicien Vernou," Lousteau said to him, when they were seated at breakfast, and Lucien had told him about the supper that Coralie was going to give. "Invite him, and try to keep in with him as much as anyone can keep in with a fellow like that. Félicien might introduce you to the political newspaper for which he does a supplement, and you could blossom to your heart's content in long articles in that eminent paper. It is a Liberal newspaper, like ours—you must be a Liberal, it's the popular party; and, besides, if you want to go over to the Ministerial side, you will go over with many more advantages if you can give them reason to be afraid of you. Did not Hector Merlin and his Mme de Val-Noble ask you and Coralie to dinner?—quite a number of important people go there, dukes and dandies and millionaires."

"Yes," said Lucien, "they are inviting you and Florine."

In the course of Friday's debauch and Sunday's dinner, Lucien and Lousteau had got onto terms of using one another's Christian names.

"Well, we shall see Merlin at the newspaper; that fellow follows close on Finot's heels, you would be wise to cultivate him, and to invite him and his mistress to supper; he might be useful to you one of these days, because venomous characters need all the friends they can get, and he might do you a good turn so as to have your pen at his service."

"Your first appearance has made such a sensation that you will have no difficulty," said Florine, "but strike while the iron is hot, or you will soon be forgotten."

" The deal," said Lousteau, " the big deal has been concluded! That fellow Finot, a man without a grain of talent, is editor and chief director of Dauriat's weekly, owning a sixth share that has cost him nothing, with a salary of six hundred francs a month. And from this morning, my boy, I am chief editor of our little paper. Everything has happened just as I foresaw the other evening. Florine has been wonderful, she could give points to Talleyrand."

" We have a hold on men through their pleasures," said Florine. " Diplomats can only play upon their self-esteem ; diplomats see men playing a part, but we see them playing the fool, so we have more power."

" In conclusion," said Lousteau, " Matifat has made the one joke of his whole druggist's career. ' This business,' he said, ' is quite in my line! ' "

" I suspect Florine of having put him up to it! " said Lucien.

" And so, dear boy, your foot is in the stirrup," said Lousteau.

" You were born with a silver spoon in your mouth," said Florine. " How many young men haven't we seen hawking their *drugs* in Paris for years without managing to get a single article into a newspaper! You will be another Emile Blondet—six months from now won't you just be giving yourself airs! " she said in the slang of her class, giving him a mocking smile.

" Haven't I been in Paris for three years," said Lousteau, " and it is only since yesterday that Finot has given me a fixed salary of three hundred francs a month as chief editor, with a hundred sous a column and a hundred francs a page for his weekly ? "

" Well, haven't you anything to say ? " Florine exclaimed, looking at Lucien.

" We shall see," said Lucien.

" My dear fellow," retorted Lousteau, piqued, " I have fixed everything up for you as if you had been my brother; but I can't answer for Finot. Finot will have any number of bright lads after him during the next two days, offering to write for him at cut rates. I promised for you, but you can refuse if you like. You may think yourself lucky," the journalist went on after a pause. " You will belong to a group whose members attack their enemies in quite a number of papers and make themselves generally useful to one another."

"Let us go and see Félicien Vernou first," said Lucien, all impatience to ally himself with those redoubtable birds of prey.

Lucien sent for a cab, and the two friends drove to Rue Mandar, where Vernou lived up an alley, in the second-floor flat. Lucien was greatly astonished to find that scathing contemptuous critic, fond of good living, in a dining-room vulgar to the last degree. The walls were covered with a cheap marbled wallpaper, with a shapeless pattern repeated at equal intervals, and adorned with aquatint engravings in gilt frames; he was seated at table with a woman too ugly not to be his legal wife, and two small children perched on high chairs with bars in front to prevent the little dears from tumbling out. Taken by surprise in a dressing-gown made up from an Indian cotton dress of his wife's, Félicien was none too friendly.

"Have you had breakfast, Lousteau?" he asked, and offered Lucien a chair.

"We have just come from Florine's," said Étienne, "and we have had breakfast."

Lucien could not take his eyes from Mme Vernou, who was for all the world like an honest fat cook, reasonably clean, but superlatively common. Mme Vernou wore a handkerchief over her night-cap, whose strings were tied so tightly that her cheeks stood out in rolls of fat. Her ill-fitting dressing-gown, without a girdle, was fastened at the neck by a button, and hung down in great shapeless folds, so that she looked like nothing so much as a milestone. She enjoyed very poor health; her cheeks were almost purple, and her fingers looked like sausages. Lucien suddenly realised that this woman was the explanation of Vernou's evident discontent in company. Wretched in his marriage, unable to bring himself to abandon his wife and family, but poet enough to suffer continually, this born actor could never forgive any man for being successful, and he was dissatisfied with himself. Lucien understood the bitter expression that froze his envious face, the harshness of the epigrams with which that journalist punctuated his conversation, the acerbity of his phrases, always pointed and sharp as a stiletto.

" Come into my study," said Félicien, getting up. " You have come to discuss literary matters, no doubt."

" Yes and no," replied Lousteau. " We have come about a supper, old boy."

" I have come with an invitation from Coralie," said Lucien. At this name Mme Vernou looked up. " To a supper at her flat today week," Lucien went on. " The same people will be there as you met at Florine's, and Mme Val-Noble, Merlin, and one or two others. There will be play."

" But, my dear that is the day we are supposed to be going to Mme Mahoudeau's," said his wife.

" Well, what does that matter ? " said Vernou.

" If we don't go she will take offence, and you are glad of her when you want her to cash your post-dated booksellers' cheques."

" This wife of mine, my dear fellow, can never be made to understand that a supper that begins at midnight does not prevent anyone from going to the party that ends at eleven. She is always near me while I am working."

" You have a wonderful imagination," said Lucien, who made a mortal enemy of Vernou by that one phrase.

" Well, then," said Lousteau, " you will come ; but that is not all. M. de Rubempré is joining us, so you must push him in your paper ; tell them he is a young man who will make a name for himself in literature, and that he ought to be given at least two articles a month."

" Certainly, if he will be one of us, attack our enemies if we attack his, and defend our friends ; I will mention him tonight at the Opéra," Vernou replied.

" Until tomorrow, then, old boy," said Lousteau, shaking hands with Vernou with every mark of the warmest friendship. " When is your book coming out ? "

" Why that depends on Dauriat," the father of the family replied. " I have finished it."

" Are you pleased with it ? "

" Yes and no."

"We will make it a success," said Lousteau, getting up and taking leave of his colleague's wife.

This abrupt departure was hastened by the squalling of the two children, who were quarrelling, fighting with their spoons, and throwing bread and milk in one another's faces.

"You have just seen, dear boy," said Étienne to Lucien, "a woman who, all unawares, will work great havoc in the literary world. We ought to get rid of her for him—in the public interest, I mean. It would spare us a deluge of scathing articles, epigrams against every kind of success or good fortune. What can you expect with a wife like that and those two abominable brats? You have seen Rigaudin in Picard's play, *La Maison en Loterie*? Well, Vernou is like Rigaudin, he will not fight himself, but he will make others fight; if he could put out both his best friends' eyes by putting out one of his own he would willingly do so; he likes to trample on every corpse, laughs at every misfortune, attacks princes, dukes, marquises, all the nobility, because he is not a gentleman; he attacks well-known celibates because of his wife, while at the same time everlastingly preaching morality, the joys of domestic life, and the duties of the citizen. All the same, his moral preaching has no good to say of anyone, not even of children. He lives in Rue Mandar with a wife who might be the Mamamouche of the *Bourgeois gentilhomme*, and two little Vernous as ugly as maggots; so he sneers at the Faubourg Saint-Germain, where he will never set foot, and makes his duchesses talk as his wife does. That is the man who is out for the blood of the Jesuits, hurls insults at the Court, that he credits with the intention of re-establishing feudal privileges and the rights of primogeniture. He is for ever crusading in favour of equality—a man who feels himself inferior to everyone. If he were a bachelor, he would go into society, if he had the charm of the Royalist poets who have been given pensions and decorated with the cross of the Legion of Honour, he would be an optimist. Motives like his dictate a great deal of journalism. The press is a great catapult set in motion by small hates. Do you still want to marry? Vernou has become absolutely heartless; everything has turned to gall for him. And that is the typical journalist—a two-handed tiger who tears everything to pieces, as if his pens had rabies."

"He is a woman-hater," said Lucien. "Has he talent?"

"He is witty, he's a columnist. Vernou breeds articles, articles, nothing but articles. No amount of labour would ever graft a book onto his prose. Félicien is incapable of conceiving a work on a larger scale, of disposing the different parts, combining the characters harmoniously according to a plot that has a beginning, and develops and unfolds to a climax; he has ideas, but he has no knowledge of actualities; his heroes would always be philosophic or liberal utopian theories personified. His style strains after originality, but his inflated phrases collapse at the first pinprick of criticism. So that he is in mortal terror of the newspapers, like all writers who can only keep their heads above water with the help of inflated bladders of criticism."

"What an article you are composing!" Lucien exclaimed.

"That kind, dear boy, may be spoken, but must never be written."

"You are becoming a chief editor," said Lucien.

"Where shall I put you down?" Lousteau asked him.

"At Coralie's."

"Ah! So we are lovers!" said Lousteau. "A mistake! Treat Coralie as I do Florine, as a housekeeper, but be free as the air on the mountain!"

"You would damn a saint!" said Lucien with a laugh.

"You can't damn a devil," retorted Lousteau.

The light, brilliant style of his new friend, his way of life, his combination of paradoxes, and the shrewd maxims of Parisian Macchiavelism, made an impression on Lucien unawares. In theory, the poet recognised the danger of these ideas, but he found them useful in practice. The two friends parted at the Boulevard du Temple, arranging to meet between four and five at the office of the newspaper, where Hector Merlin was sure to be.

Lucien was, as Lousteau had divined, swayed by the passions of the authentic love of courtesans, who attach their silken cords in the soul's most vulnerable parts, and sway a man to their desires with incredible subtlety by complying with all the weaknesses of his nature; for in those weaknesses lie the courtesan's strength. He was already thirsting for the pleasures of Paris; he was in love with the easy, expensive and luxurious life that the actress lived.

He found Coralie and Camusot in high delight; the Gymnase had offered Coralie an engagement for the following Easter, whose conditions, clearly set forth, surpassed her wildest hopes.

"We owe this triumph to you," said Camusot.

"Yes, there is no doubt of it, without him the *Alcalde* would have fallen flat," said Coralie; "but for that article I should have been in the Boulevard theatres for the next six years."

She flung her arms round Camusot's neck. The actress's delight, posed and yet ecstatic, had in it at once a sweetness and an exaltation. She was in love! As all men do in moments of great sorrow, Camusot lowered his eyes; and as he did so, he recognised, in the seam of Lucien's boots, the coloured thread used at that time by the best bootmakers, its deep yellow contrasting with the shining black leather of the leg. The unusual colour had preoccupied him during his recent unspoken monologue on the inexplicable presence of a pair of boots in front of Coralie's fireplace. He had read, in black letters printed on the soft white leather of the lining, the address of one of the best bootmakers of the day, "Gay, Rue de la Michodière".

"Sir," he said to Lucien, "you have a very beautiful pair of boots."

"Everything about him is beautiful," said Coralie.

"I would be glad if you could give me your bootmaker's address."

"Oh!" said Coralie. "How like the Rue des Bourdonnais to ask the address of a shop! Are you going to wear a young man's boots? A nice young fellow you would make! No, you stick to your top-boots—they are more suitable for a solid man with a wife and family and a mistresss!"

"All the same, if this gentleman would do me the favour of removing one of his boots I would be very much obliged," said Camusot obstinately.

"I cannot put them on again without a button-hook," said Lucien, blushing.

"Bérénice will find one—they are needed in this house," said the merchant with heavy irony.

"Papa Camusot," said Coralie, turning on him a look of bitter contempt, "have the courage of your meanness! Come, say what you really think! You are thinking that this gentleman's boots are very like mine. . . . I forbid you to take off your boots!" she said to Lucien. "Yes, Monsieur Camusot, yes, these boots are absolutely the same as the pair that were standing in front of my fire the other day, and this gentleman was hiding in my dressing-room, waiting for them. He had spent the night here. That is what you were thinking, is it not? Very well, think it—I want you to think it—it is the simple truth. I am deceiving you. And what if I am? I do so because I choose to do so!"

She sat down, without a trace of anger, with an air of perfect indifference, and looked at Camusot and Lucien, neither of whom dared to look at one another.

"I shall believe nothing that you do not want me to believe," said Camusot. "Don't joke, Coralie; I was wrong."

"I may be a shameless dissolute creature who has taken a sudden fancy to this gentleman, or I may be a poor unhappy girl who has felt true love for the first time—the love that all women long for—but you must take me or leave me as I am," she said, with a queenly gesture that crushed the business man.

"Can it be true?" said Camusot, who saw from Lucien's expression that Coralie was not joking, but yet begged to be deceived.

"I love her," said Lucien.

When she heard that word spoken, in feeling tones, Coralie flung her arms round her poet's neck and clasped him to her. She turned and looked at the silk merchant, as if to show him what a beautiful pair she and Lucien made together.

"Poor Musot! Take back all that you have given me; I don't want anything from you. I am madly in love with this adorable child, not for his brilliance, but for his beauty. I would rather starve with him than have millions with you."

Camusot dropped into an armchair, buried his face in his hands, and remained silent.

" Would you like us to go away ? " she asked him. There was an incredible ferocity in her voice.

Lucien's blood ran cold on finding himself with a woman,—an actress at that—and a household on his hands.

" Stay here, keep everything, Coralie," said the shopkeeper in a dull weak voice that came from his very heart. " I don't want anything back. There is sixty thousand francs' worth of furniture here, but I could not bear to think of my Coralie in want. All the same, you will be in want in a very short time. However great this gentleman's talents may be, he will not be able to keep you. We old fellows must expect this sort of thing! But let me still come and see you sometimes, Coralie! I might be able to help you. And the truth is, I don't know how I shall be able to live without you."

The poor man's gentleness, stripped as he was of all his happiness at the very moment when he thought himself the most fortunate of men, touched Lucien deeply, but not Coralie.

" Come by all means, my poor Musot, come as often as you like. I shall like you better when I am not deceiving you."

Camusot seemed satisfied not to be driven out of his earthly paradise, where doubtless he would suffer, but where he might still hope to return with full rights, he put his trust in the various chances of Paris life and on the many temptations that would be sure to assail Lucien. The shrewd old business man reflected that sooner or later this handsome young man would be guilty of infidelities, and in order to keep his eye on him, and to undermine Coralie's belief in him, he would remain their friend. This passion that would stoop to such humiliation frightened Lucien. Camusot invited them to dinner at Véry's, in the Palais-Royal, and they accepted.

" Isn't it wonderful ? " Coralie exclaimed when Camusot had left. " No more garrets in the Latin Quarter. You shall live here, and we will be together always. For the sake of appearances you can take a little room in the Rue Charlot—and come what may! "

She began to dance her Spanish dance with all the abandon of a boundless passion.

" I can earn five hundred francs a month if I work hard," said Lucien.

" I shall make as much again at the theatre, not counting extras. Camusot will pay for my clothes—he still loves me! We can live like lords on fifteen hundred francs a month! "

" What about the horses and the coachman and the butler ? " said Bérénice.

" I shall run up debts," said Coralie, and she began to dance a *gigue* with Lucien.

" I must accept Finot's offer, after this," Lucien exclaimed.

" Come," said Coralie, " I must dress, and take you to your newspaper ; I shall wait for you with the carriage on the Boulevard."

Lucien sat down on a sofa and gave way to very sober reflections as he watched the actress dressing. He would rather have left Coralie her freedom than have found himself thus precipitated into the responsibilities of what was virtually a marriage ; but she was so beautiful, so graceful, so attractive, as he watched her, that he saw only the picturesque aspects of this Bohemian existence, and he flung his gauntlet in the face of fortune.

Bérénice was instructed to take charge of Lucien's removal and installation. And the triumphant, the lovely, the happy Coralie, went off with her lover, her poet, and drove all over Paris on the way to the Rue Saint-Fiacre.

Lucien bounded up the stairs and walked into the newspaper office as if he owned it. The Coconut, with his paper cap still perched on his head, and old Giroudeau, told him as usual, hypocritically enough, that there was nobody there.

" But the editorial staff must meet somewhere to make up the paper! " he said.

" Very likely, but I have nothing to do with the editorial side," said the Captain of the Imperial Guard, resuming his occupation of checking wrappers, with his eternal *broum! broum!*

At this moment, by a lucky chance—or was it an unlucky chance? —Finot came in to tell Giroudeau about his nominal abdication and to ask him to watch over his interests.

" And no nonsense with this gentleman, he is on the paper," Finot told his uncle, shaking hands with Lucien.

" Oh, the gentleman is on the paper ? " Giroudeau exclaimed, astonished at the warmth of his nephew's greeting. "Well, sir, you didn't have much difficulty in getting on the paper! "

" I want to arrange things for you so that Étienne won't do you down," said Finot, looking at Lucien with a knowing expression. " This gentleman will be paid three francs a column for everything he writes, including theatre notices."

" You have never paid as much as that to anyone," said Giroudeau, looking at Lucien in astonishment.

" He will have the four Boulevard theatres, and I reply upon you to see that his boxes are not pinched, and that he gets all his tickets. All the same, I should advise you to have them sent to your private address," he added, turning to Lucien. " This gentleman is undertaking to write, besides his reviews, ten feature articles of about two columns at fifty francs a month, for a year. Does that suit you ? "

" Yes," said Lucien, whose hand was being forced by circumstances.

" Make out the contract, Uncle, and we will sign it when we come down," said Finot.

" Who is the gentleman ? " asked Giroudeau, taking off his black silk skull-cap and putting it on again.

"M. Lucien de Rubempré, who wrote that article on the *Alcalde*," Finot told him.

" Young man," exclaimed the old soldier, tapping Lucien's brow, " you have a gold-mine there. I'm not a literary man myself, but I read your article, and I enjoyed it. That's the stuff! Gay and lively! And I said to myself, ' That will bring us in some subscriptions'—and it has. We have sold fifty extra copies."

" Is my agreement with Étienne Lousteau ready for signing, in duplicate ? " Finot asked his uncle.

" Yes," said Giroudeau.

" Make out this gentleman's contract as from yesterday, so that Lousteau will be bound by the agreement."

Finot took his new contributor's arm with an appearance of friendliness that quite charmed the poet. As he led him towards the staircase he said :

" In this way your position is secure. I will introduce you myself to *my* staff. And this evening Lousteau can introduce you to the theatres. You can earn a hundred and fifty francs a month on our little newspaper that Lousteau is going to edit ; so try to get on with him. The fellow owes me a grudge, as it is, for having tied his hands so far as you are concerned, but you have talent, and I should not like to see you at the mercy of the caprices of a chief editor. Between ourselves, you can let me have two pages a month for my weekly, and I will pay you two hundred francs for them. Don't say a word to anyone about this arrangement, or I should be exposed to the vengeance of all the vanities wounded by the good luck of a newcomer. You can make four articles of your two pages, and sign two with your own name, two with a pseudonym, so that you will not seem to be taking the bread out of anybody else's mouth. You owe your position to Blondet and Vignon, who both think you have a future. So don't disgrace yourself, and, above all, don't trust your friends. And as for you and me, we must always stick together. Make yourself useful to me, and I will make myself useful to you. You will have about forty francs' worth of tickets and boxes to dispose of and sixty francs' worth of books to sell. That and your salary will bring you in round about four hundred and fifty francs a month. If you are clever, you ought to be able to pick up at least another two hundred francs from the publishers, who will pay you for reviews and notices. But you are mine, are you not ? Can I count on you ? "

Lucien pressed Finot's hand in a transport of inexpressible joy.

" Don't look as if there is any understanding between us," Finot said in his ear as he opened the door of an attic room on the fifth floor at the end of a long passage.

There Lucien saw Lousteau, Félicien Vernou, Hector Merlin and two other members of the editorial staff whom he did not know all seated round a table covered with a green cloth, in front of a good fire, laughing and smoking in armchairs. The table was littered with papers, and there was a real inkstand, filled with ink, and pens for the journalists, not too good, but adequate. It instantly became clear to the new journalist that this was where the great work was carried on.

" Gentlemen," said Finot, " the object of this meeting is the installation of our good friend Lousteau in my place as editor in chief of this newspaper, which I am obliged to leave. But whatever transformation my opinions may have to undergo in my capacity of editor of the review whose policy you all know, my convictions remain unchanged, and we will remain friends. You can all depend upon me, as I shall depend on you. Circumstances vary, principles do not change. Principles are the pivot upon which turns the pointer of the political barometer."

All the journalists laughed heartily.

" Where did you get that from ? " called Lousteau.

" Blondet," said Finot.

" Wind, rain, storm, settled fair," said Merlin, " we will stick together."

" In short," Finot concluded, " not to embark on any more metaphors, any of you who have any articles to bring along will always find Finot. This gentleman is on the staff," he added, introducing Lucien ; " I have arranged everything with him, Lousteau."

Everybody congratulated Finot on his promotion and on his new prospects.

" So here you are mounted on the shoulders of us and the rest," said one of the journalists whom Lucien did not know. " You will be a Janus——"

" Never mind so long as he is not a Janot," said Vernou.

" You will let us attack our *bêtes noires* ? "

" As much as you like! " said Finot.

" That's all very well," said Lousteau, " but the paper must pursue its policy. M. Châtelet is very annoyed ; we shall not let him off for another week."

" What has he done ? " Lucien asked.

" He has been to ask for an explanation," said Vernou. " The ex-Empire beau found old Giroudeau, who with the greatest coolness assured him that Philippe Bridau wrote the article ; Philippe asked the Baron to name his time and his weapons ; and there the matter ended. We are engaged at this moment in formulating our excuses to the Baron in tomorrow's issue. Every phrase is a home-thrust."

" Keep your teeth in him—then he will come and see me," said Finot. " I shall seem to be doing him a service by appeasing you ; he is at the Ministry, and we shall be able to get hold of something or other there—an assistant schoolmaster's place or a tobacconist's licence. It's lucky for us that he has played into our hands. Which of you would like to write an article on Nathan for my new paper ? "

" Give it to Lucien," said Lousteau. " Hector and Vernou are writing articles for their respective papers."

"Well, I must be going. We shall meet face to face at Barbin's," said Finot with a laugh.

Lucien received sundry congratulations on his admission into the redoubtable ranks of journalism, and Lousteau assured the others that they could all count on him.

" Lucien invites you all to supper at the flat of his mistress, the fair Coralie."

" Coralie is going to the Gymnase," Lucien told Étienne.

" Very well, it is understood, then, that we push Coralie ? In all your newspapers, put in a few lines on her engagement and say a word about her talent. You can credit the management of the Gymnase with tact and good sense—would it be going too far to say intelligence ? "

" We will allow them intelligence," said Merlin. " Scribe is reading Frédéric's play."

" Oh! In that case the manager of the Gymnase is the most far-seeing and perspicacious of speculators," said Vernou.

" Oh, by the way, don't write your articles on Nathan's book until we have come to an arrangement—I will explain why presently," said Lousteau. " We ought to do something to help our new comrade. Lucien has two books that he wants to place, a collection of sonnets and a novel. If there is any power in the short paragraph, he ought to be a great poet three months from now. We can use his *Marguerites* to run down odes, ballads, meditations, and romantic poetry in general."

" That would be a nice thing if his sonnets are no good! " said Vernou. " What is your opinion of your own sonnets, Lucien ? "

" Yes, what do you think of them yourself ? " said one of the unknown journalists.

" They are first-class, on my word of honour! " said Lousteau.

" Very well, I will take your word for it," said Vernou, " and I will fling them in the faces of the poets of the sacristy, who make me sick."

" If Dauriat refuses to take the *Marguerites* this evening, we will goad him with a series of articles against Nathan."

" And what will Nathan have to say ? " Lucien exclaimed.

The five journalists laughed aloud.

" He will be delighted," said Vernou. " You shall see how we manage these things."

" Then is he one of us ? " asked one of the two journalists whom Lucien did not know.

" Yes, yes, Frédéric ; stop being difficult. . . . You see, Lucien," said Étienne to the novice, " what we are doing for you, and you must not refuse to do the same for us on occasion. We all like Nathan and we are going to attack him. Meanwhile, let us divide the empire of Alexander—Frédéric, will you take the Français and the Odéon?"

" If nobody else has any objection," said Frédéric.

They all signified agreement, but Lucien noticed some envious looks.

" I shall keep the Opéra, the Italiens and the Opéra-Comique," said Vernou.

" Very well ; Hector will do the vaudeville theatres," said Lousteau.

" And what about me ? Am I not to have any theatres ? " broke in the other journalist who did not know Lucien.

" Very well, Hector will let you have the Variétés and Lucien the Porte-Saint-Martin—he is wild about Fanny Beaupré," Lousteau explained to Lucien. " You can take the Cirque-Olympique in exchange. I shall have Bobino, the Funambules, and Madame Saqui. What have we for tomorrow's issue ? "

" Nothing."

" Nothing ? "

" Nothing! "

" I would like you all to be brilliant for my first number. Baron du Châtelet and the cuttle-bone will not last out the week—the author of *Le Solitaire* is wearing very thin."

" Sosthenes–Demosthenes is stale, too," said Vernou ; " everybody has taken it up."

" The fact is, we need some new victims," said Frédéric.

" What do you say to poking a little fun at the virtuous representatives of the Right ? We might say that M. de Bonald's feet smell," Lousteau suggested.

" We could start a series of portraits of the Ministerial orators," said Hector Merlin.

" Do that, my boy," said Lousteau ; " you know them, they belong to your own party, and you can play off a few personal scores at the same time. Pitch into Beugnot, Syrieys de Mayrinhac, and the others. The articles can be written in advance, and then the paper will have some copy in hand."

" Why not invent some story of refusal of burial, with or without aggravating circumstances ? " said Hector.

" We don't want to follow in the footsteps of the big Constitutional papers, who have their files full of anti-clerical canards," Vernou objected.

" Canards ? " Lucien repeated.

" We call a canard," Hector said to him, "a statement that might very well be true, but which is invented in order to enliven the Paris gossip columns when there is nothing else to put in. Franklin is responsible for the idea—he is the inventor of the lightning-conductor, the Republic, and the canard. That journalist deceived the compilers of encyclopaedias so well with his overseas canards that Raynal has recorded two of his canards as facts in his *Histoire Philosophique des Indes*."

" I didn't know that," said Vernou ; " what were the two canards ? "

" The story of the Englishman who sold the negress who had saved his life, after getting her with child so that she would fetch a higher price ; and the moving speech in which the young unmarried mother pleaded her cause. When Franklin was in Paris, he admitted to Necker that these were canards, to the great confusion of French philosophers. So you see the New World has corrupted the Old on two occasions."

" In journalism whatever is probable is true," said Lousteau. " That is our point of departure."

" Criminal justice proceeds in the same way," said Vernou.

" Very well, we meet here this evening at nine o'clock," said Merlin.

Everybody got up and shook hands, and the meeting closed with numerous proofs of the warmest intimacy.

" How did you manage to get round Finot ? " Étienne asked Lucien as they went downstairs, " to induce him to come to an agreement with you? He has never bound himself by contract with anyone else."

" I ? Nothing ; he suggested it himself," said Lucien.

" In any case, I am delighted if you have an agreement with him —that strengthens both our hands."

On the ground floor Étienne and Lucien found Finot, who took Lousteau aside into the ostensible editorial office.

" Sign your contract so that the new editor will think the agreement was made yesterday," said Giroudeau, as he handed Lucien two stamped papers.

While he was reading his contract, Lucien overheard a heated discussion between Étienne and Finot that seemed to turn on the policy and profits of the paper. Étienne wanted his rake-off on the levies raised by Giroudeau. Finot and Lousteau must have come to an agreement, for the two friends came out together on the best of terms.

" Eight o'clock in the Wooden Galleries, at Dauriat's," Étienne said to Lucien.

A young man appeared, looking for a job, with all the timid anxiety that Lucien had so lately shown. Lucien watched with secret pleasure how Giroudeau practised on this novice all the tactics with which the old soldier had deceived him ; self-interest now made him understand perfectly the necessity of these manœuvres, which raised almost insurmountable barriers between newcomers and the attic where only the elect set foot.

" Contributors are not paid enough as it is," he said to Giroudeau.

" And if there were more of you, you would each have a little less," said the Captain, " so there you are! "

The old soldier twirled his leaded walking-stick and went out *broum-broum*-ing. He stared in amazement as he saw Lucien climb into the beautiful coupé that was waiting on the Boulevard.

" You are the army nowadays, and we are the civilians! " he said.

" Upon my word, these young men seem to me the best fellows in the world," Lucien said to Coralie. " Here am I a journalist, certain of being able to earn six hundred francs a month, if I work like a black ; but I shall find publishers for my two books, and write others, for my friends are organising a success for me! And so I say the same as you, Coralie, ' come what may '! "

" You will succeed, dear child! But don't be as kind as you are handsome or you will be lost. Be unpleasant with other people—it's the done thing."

Coralie and Lucien drove in the Bois de Boulogne, and there they again met the Marquise d'Espard, Mme de Bargeton and Baron du Châtelet. Mme de Bargeton gave Lucien a charming look that might have passed for a greeting.

Camusot had ordered the best dinner that Paris could produce. Coralie, knowing herself rid of him, was so charming to the poor silk merchant that he could not remember a single occasion during the fourteen months of their liaison on which he had seen her so gracious or so attractive.

" Come," he thought, " I will stick around, anyway."

Camusot secretly offered Coralie to settle on her an income of six thousand francs from some stock about which his wife knew nothing if she would remain his mistress, promising if she did so to shut his eyes to her relationship with Lucien.

" Deceive such an angel ?—Just look at him, you old fossil, and then look at yourself! " she said, pointing to the poet, who was a little hazy, for Camusot had plied him with drink.

Camusot made up his mind to wait until poverty restored this woman to him for a second time, as it had once already.

" Then I will just be your friend," he said and kissed her on the brow.

Lucien left Coralie with Camusot and made his way to the Wooden Galleries. What a change his initiation into journalism had wrought in his attitude! He rubbed shoulders fearlessly in the crowd that surged through the galleries ; he had an air of bold confidence, because he had a mistress, and he walked into Dauriat's with a careless swagger because he was a journalist. There he found a distinguished gathering ; he shook hands with Blondet, Nathan, and Finot, and all the literary people with whom he had been associating for the last week ; he felt himself to be somebody, and he flattered himself that he would be able to surpass his comrades ; the flush of wine suited him admirably ; he was witty, he showed that he could howl with the wolves.

All the same, the tacit approbation, silent or spoken, on which he had counted, was not forthcoming ; he divined the first stirrings of jealousy among these men, who were not so much disturbed as curious, perhaps, to know what place this able newcomer would make for himself, and what share he would gobble up of the sum total of the profits of the press. Only Finot, who regarded Lucien as a gold mine to be exploited, and Lousteau, who felt that he had claims on him, greeted him in a friendly way. Lousteau, who had already begun to assume the airs of a chief editor, tapped impatiently at the window of Dauriat's private office.

" Just a moment, my friend," the bookseller replied, looking over the top of the green curtains and recognising him.

The moment lasted an hour, and then Lucien and his companion entered the sanctuary.

" Well, have you thought over our friend's proposal ? " said the new chief editor.

" Yes, indeed," said Dauriat, leaning back in his armchair with the air of a Sultan. " I have looked through the collection, and I gave it to a reader, a man of taste, and an excellent judge, because I do not pretend to understand these things myself. For my part, my friend, I buy glory as an Englishman buys love. . . . Well, my boy, you are as great a poet as you are a handsome fellow," Dauriat went on. " On the word of an honest man (I am not speaking as a publisher, mind you), your sonnets are magnificent, they seem effortless, which is only natural in a poet who has inspiration and vitality. And what is more, your rhymes are good—that is one thing to be said in favour of the new school. Your *Marguerites* are a very fine volume, but they would not pay me, and I can only take on large ventures. I could not conscientiously take on your sonnets ; I could not possibly undertake to push them, there is not enough to be made out of them to be worth the expense of organising a success. Besides, you won't go on writing poetry ; your book will be an isolated volume. You are very young, young man! You bring me the everlasting volume of early poems that all young writers produce after they leave school ; they think a lot of it at the time, and laugh at it later. Your friend, Lousteau, I'll be bound, has a poem hidden away somewhere among his old socks—haven't you a poem that you once thought a lot of, Lousteau ? " Dauriat asked, looking at Lousteau as one man of the world looks at another.

" Why else do you suppose I am writing prose ? " said Lousteau.

" There you are, and he has never even mentioned it to me ; our friend, you see, understands the publishing trade," Dauriat continued. " The problem for me is not," he went on, in flattering tones, " that there is any doubt in my mind that you are a remarkable poet—you have great talent, very great talent ; when I was just beginning as a publisher I should no doubt have made the mistake of publishing your book. But in the first place, at the present moment my shareholders and my partners are cutting down my expenses ; the fact that I lost twenty thousand francs on poetry last year is enough for them ; they will not consider any more poetry for the moment, and I am in their hands. Even so, that is not the question. Admitting that you are a good poet, are you a prolific one ? Do you produce sonnets regularly ? Will you even run to ten volumes ? Would you be a profitable enterprise ? Of course not.

You will be a charming writer of prose; you have too much sense to spoil your prose with poetic tags, when you can earn thirty thousand francs a year by writing for the newspapers, and you are not going to exchange that for the three thousand francs that your hemistichs and strophes and all the rest of it will bring you in, and that only with the greatest difficulty."

"You know he's on the paper, Dauriat?" Lousteau put in.

"Yes," said Dauriat, "I read his article; and in his own interests, mind you, I must turn down the *Marguerites*. Yes, I shall have paid you in six months more money for the articles that I shall ask you to write than for your unsaleable poems!"

"And what about fame!" said Lucien.

Dauriat and Lousteau laughed outright.

"Bless my soul!" said Lousteau. "How that boy clings to his illusions!"

"Fame," said Dauriat, "means ten years of hard work and a hundred thousand francs either made or lost by the publishing trade. If you find anybody mad enough to print your poems, a year from now you will respect me, when you see the result of the transaction."

"Have you the manuscript there?" Lucien asked coldly.

"Here it is, my friend," said Dauriat, whose manner towards Lucien had already sweetened quite remarkably.

Lucien took the packet without looking at the string, for it seemed evident to him that Dauriat had read the *Marguerites*. He left with Lousteau, without seeming either disconcerted or depressed. Dauriat accompanied the two friends into the shop, talking about his weekly and about Lousteau's paper. Lucien played negligently with the manuscript of the *Marguerites*.

"You think that Dauriat has read your sonnets or sent them to a reader?" Étienne whispered to him.

"Yes," said Lucien.

"Look at the string."

Lucien saw that the blot of ink and the mark on the string coincided perfectly.

" Which sonnet did you like best ? " Lucien asked the publisher ; he had turned pale with rage and indignation.

" They are all quite remarkable, my friend, but the one on the marguerite is particularly delightful ; it ends with such a very fine and subtle reflection. From that poem I formed my opinion of the success that you are certain to attain as a writer of prose. I recommended you to Finot on the strength of it. If you will write some articles for us, we will pay you well. You know, glory is all very well, but there is nothing like solid success, and you should take every chance that offers. When you are rich, you can write poems."

The poet left the shop hurriedly so as not to lose his temper on the spot. He was furious.

" Well, dear child," said Lousteau, following him, " keep calm, for Heaven's sake ; take men for what they are—means. Do you want your revenge ? "

" At any price," said the poet.

" Here is a copy of Nathan's book that Dauriat has just given me ; the second edition is coming out tomorrow ; read this book again, and knock up an article demolishing it. Félicien Vernou cannot stand Nathan, whose success damages the chances, so he imagines, of his own book that is shortly to appear. Petty minds have the insane idea that there is not room under the sun for two successes. And so he will publish your article in the big newspaper he works for."

" But what is there to say against this book ? It is really first class ! " said Lucien.

" Oh! Go along! You must learn your trade, dear boy," said Lousteau, laughing. " This book may be a masterpiece, but under your pen it must turn into stupid trash, a dangerous and immoral work."

" But how ? "

" You must turn its beauties into faults."

" I am not capable of such a *tour de force*."

" My dear fellow, a journalist is a juggler, and he must accustom himself to the difficulties of his profession. Now listen! I am not a bad fellow, and this is how I should set about it. In the first place, you begin by saying that you consider the book a fine piece of work, and you can amuse yourself by writing what you really think about it. The reader will think to himself, ' This critic is not jealous, he must be impartial.' From that point the reader will believe that your criticism is conscientious. Having thus won the confidence of your reader, you will regret that you must condemn a system by which such books are given to the public. ' Does not France, by her intellectual supremacy, rule the whole world? Until the present day, century by century French writers have upheld in Europe the tradition of analysis, of philosophic examination, by virtue of their style, and by the originality with which they formulate their ideas.' Here you digress, for the benefit of the bourgeois reader, into a eulogy of Voltaire, Rousseau, Diderot, Montesquieu, and Buffon. You go on to explain that the French language is ruthlessly exacting and prove that it is like a varnish spread over thought. You let fall a few axioms like, ' a great writer in France is always a great man, for he is held within bounds by a language that compels him to think ; this is not so in other countries '—and so on. You demonstrate your proposition by comparing Rabener, a German moral satirist, with la Bruyère. There is nothing that sets up a critic so much as quoting an unknown foreign author. Kant is Cousin's pedestal.

" Once on that ground you can put in a brief summary, for the benefit of the ignorant, of the principles of our men of genius during the last century, and call their works the ' literature of ideas '. Armed with that phrase, you hurl all the illustrious dead at the heads of living authors. And then you explain that nowadays a new literature is growing up that relies upon dialogue (the easiest of all literary forms) and descriptions, that dispense with the necessity for thought. You contrast the novels of Voltaire, Diderot, Sterne and Le Sage, so trenchant, so compact, with the modern novel that consists of nothing but descriptions, so dear to Walter Scott. In such a *genre* there is scope for invention, but for little else. ' The novels of Walter Scott are a literary fashion, but not a literary style,' you will say. You proceed to fulminate against this lamentable fashion, in which ideas are diluted, and beaten thin, a style easily imitated by anyone, a style in which any writer can win facile success—a fashion that you describe as the ' literature of images '.

" Then you allow the weight of this argument to descend upon Nathan, showing that he is an imitator, who has only an appearance of talent. The grand, concise style of the eighteenth century is not to be found in his book, and you proceed to prove that instead of giving us ideas the author has given us events. Action is not life, and pictures are not ideas! Be liberal with phrases like that, and the public will repeat them.

" In spite of the merit of this work, then, it appears to you to reveal a dangerous, nay, a fatal tendency ; it opens the gates of the Temple of Fame to the rank and file, and you can already perceive, in the distance, a host of petty scribblers hastening to imitate this new and facile style. At this point you can give way to resounding lamentations on the decadence of taste and slip in a word of praise for Étienne, Jouy, Tissot, Gosse, Duval, Jay, Benjamin Constant, Aignan, Baour-Lormian, Villemain and the rest, the supporters of the Liberal Bonapartist party, under whose auspices Vernou's newspaper is published. You will point out how that glorious phalanx has withstood the invasion of romanticism, adhering to style and the Idea as against the Image and verbiage, continuing the tradition of Voltaire and withstanding the impact of the English school and the German school, just as the seventeen orators of the Left are defending the cause of the nation against the Ultras of the Right. Under the cover of these names revered by the immense majority of the French public, who are always on the side of the Left and the Opposition, you can demolish Nathan, whose book, although it contains fine things, opens the door to a bourgeois taste for literature without ideas. And from that point there is no longer any question of Nathan and his book, don't you see, but of the glory of France. It is the duty of all honest and courageous writers to oppose strenuously these foreign importations. Then flatter your readers—you say that the shrewd French public is not easily taken in. If the publishers have, for reasons that you do not choose to discuss, stolen a success, the real reading public has already rectified the errors created by the five hundred imbeciles who make up the modern literary world. You will then say that, having had the good fortune to sell out one edition of this book, the publisher has been foolhardy enough to print a second, and that you regret that such an able publisher should have so misjudged the instincts of the nation. Those are the general lines. Spice those arguments with a little wit, and a dash of vinegar, and you will have Dauriat on toast. But don't forget to say in conclusion that you regret that Nathan, a writer from whom contemporary literature may expect great things if he mends his ways, should have fallen into this mistake."

Lucien was dumbfounded as he listened to Lousteau ; as the journalist talked, the scales fell from his eyes, and he realised literary truths that he had not so much as suspected.

" But everything that you have just said is full of good sense and perfectly true! " he said.

" If it were not, how could you hope to batter a breach in Nathan's book ? " said Lousteau. " Listen to me, my boy ; that is the first type of article that is used for the purpose of demolishing a book—the pick-axe method. But there are plenty of other formulae —you will learn them in time. When you are absolutely obliged to write about a man whom you do not like, for sometimes a newspaper proprietor or chief editor has his hand forced—you employ the negative method : what we call an article based on first principles. At the head of the article you put the title of the book you are supposed to be reviewing ; you begin with general considerations—talk about the Greeks and the Romans if you like—and then at the end you write, ' . . . and this brings me to Mr. So-and-So's book, which will be the subject of a second article '—and the second article never appears. In this way the book is stifled between two promises. In the present instance you are not writing an article against Nathan, but against Dauriat ; you need the pick-axe method. The pick-axe does not damage a good book, but it goes right to the core if the book is bad. In the former case, it hurts only the publisher ; and in the latter it does service to the public. These forms of criticism are equally suitable for political criticism."

Étienne's cruel lesson opened vistas in Lucien's imagination; he understood this craft admirably.

"Let us go along to the office," said Lousteau; "we will find our friends there, and we will organise the hell of an attack on Nathan. They will laugh like anything, you will see."

Arrived at the Rue Saint-Fiacre, they went up together to the attic where the paper was made up, and Lucien was no less surprised than delighted to see the pleasure with which his colleagues agreed to demolish Nathan's book. Hector Merlin took a sheet of paper and wrote the following lines, for insertion in his own newspaper:

"A second edition of M. Nathan's book is announced. We had intended to keep silence on the subject of that work, but its apparent success obliges us to publish an article, not so much on the book itself, but on the tendency of the new school of literature."

At the head of the gossip column for the next day's issue, Lousteau inserted the following short paragraph:

⁂ "Dauriat is bringing out a second edition of M. Nathan's book. Evidently he does not know the legal maxim: *Non bis in idem.* All honour to rash courage!"

Étienne's words had fired Lucien, for whom the desire to be revenged on Dauriat displaced both conscience and inspiration. Three days later—during which time he never left Coralie's flat, where he worked beside the fire, waited on by Bérénice and soothed in his moments of fatigue by the silent and attentive Coralie—Lucien had completed a critical article, running to three columns, and a very brilliant piece of work it was. He rushed off to the newspaper—it was about nine in the evening—where he found the journalists assembled, and read them his work. They listened attentively. Félicien seized the manuscript without a word and dashed downstairs.

"What has come over him?" Lucien asked.

"He is taking the article to the printer's," said Hector Merlin; "it is a masterpiece—there is not a word to alter, not a line to be added."

" One only needs to show you the way! " said Lousteau.

" I should like to see Nathan's face tomorrow when he reads that," said the other journalist, whose own expression was one of radiant satisfaction.

" It is just as well to have you for a friend," said Hector Merlin.

" Is it really all right ? " Lucien asked eagerly.

" Blondet and Vignon won't be very long," said Lousteau.

" Here is a short article that I have knocked together for you," Lucien resumed ; " if it is a success, I could do a series on the same lines."

" Read it to us," said Lousteau.

Lucien then read one of those delightful articles that made the fortune of the little newspaper, a series of two-column sketches of Paris life, a portrait, a type, some ordinary event, or curiosity of the great city. This specimen, entitled " A Stroller in Paris ", was written in that new and original style in which evocative combinations of words, fresh and musical adverbs and adjectives, caught the attention. This article was as different as possible from the serious and profound article on Nathan, as different as the *Lettres Persanes* from the *Esprit des Lois*.

" You are a born journalist," said Lousteau. " That will appear in tomorrow's issue—write as many as you like."

" And by the way," said Merlin, " Dauriat is furious about those two bombshells we have hurled into his shop. I have just seen him ; he was thundering imprecations, and he pitched into Finot, who said that he had sold his newspaper to you. So I took him on one side and said a word in his ear. I told him that the *Marguerites* would cost him dear ; ' A man of talent comes to you,' I said ; ' you show him the door, but the newspapers welcome him with open arms! ' "

" The article we have just heard will be a knock-out for Dauriat," Lousteau said to Lucien. " Now do you see, dear boy, what the power of the press means ? Your revenge is going forward. Baron Châtelet came in this morning to ask for your address ; there was a slashing article on him this morning, and the simple-minded ex-beau is in despair. Have you seen the paper ? It is a most amusing article. Here it is: ' Funeral of a Heron, and the Cuttle-bone's lament '—Mme de Bargeton is known as the Cuttle-bone everywhere, and nobody calls Châtelet anything but Baron Heron."

Lucien took the newspaper and could not help laughing as he read this little masterpiece of Vernou's wit.

" They will capitulate," said Hector Merlin.

Lucien threw himself with enthusiasm into inventing the epigrammes used as fill-ups for the newspaper; the journalists smoked and chatted, exchanging the news of the day, picking their colleagues to pieces, and handing on pieces of personal gossip. This conversation, eminently witty, malicious and flippant, put Lucien *au courant* with the current situation in the literary world.

" I will go round with you while they are making up the paper," said Lousteau, " introduce you to the management at your theatres, and take you behind the scenes; then we will go and pick up Florine and Coralie at the Panorama-Dramatique and cast care aside in their dressing-rooms."

So the two of them went off, arm in arm, from theatre to theatre, and Lucien was installed as a dramatic critic; the managers paid him compliments, and the actresses gave him lingering looks, for they had all realised what with a single article he had done for Coralie and Florine. Coralie had been offered an engagement by the Gymnase at twelve thousand francs a year, and Florine offered eight thousand by the Panorama. All these little ovations exalted Lucien in his own eyes and gave him the measure of his power. At eleven the two friends reached the Panorama-Dramatique, where Lucien's air of indifference worked wonders. Nathan was there and held out his hand to Lucien, who shook it warmly.

" By the way, I hear that you two are out for my blood," he said, looking from one to the other.

" Just wait until tomorrow, my dear fellow, and you will see how Lucien has pitched into you! You will be pleased, on my word of honour. Serious criticism always does a book good."

Lucien blushed for shame.

" Is it severe?" Nathan asked.

" It is serious," said Lousteau.

" Then it will do no harm," said Nathan. " Hector Merlin told me just now at the Vaudeville bar that I had been cut to pieces."

" Let him say what he likes, and just wait and see," said Lucien, retreating hastily into Coralie's dressing-room. He followed the actress, who had just left the stage wearing her attractive costume.

The next morning, as Lucien was sitting at breakfast with Coralie, he heard the noise of wheels, whose crisp sound in the empty street announced an elegant carriage. The horse had that smart trot, that brisk way of pulling up that is the mark of a thoroughbred. From his window Lucien saw, sure enough, Dauriat's magnificent English horse, and Dauriat himself, who handed the reins to his groom as he got down.

" It is the publisher! " Lucien exclaimed to his mistress.

" Make him wait," said Coralie instantly to Bérénice.

Lucien smiled at the presence of mind of the young girl, so quick to identify herself with his interests. He came back and took her in his arms with heartfelt tenderness. It had been an inspiration on her part. The arrogant publisher's prompt appearance, the sudden collapse of that prince of charlatans, was occasioned by circumstances almost entirely forgotten, so completely has the publishing business been revolutionised during the last fifteen years.

Between 1816 and 1827 the reading-rooms, which were opened originally for the reading of newspapers, were beginning to lend new books for a small fee ; the increase of taxes on periodicals had not yet created the advertisement ; and publishers had no other means of publicity than articles in the newspapers or newspaper supplements. Before 1822 French newspapers were so small that the biggest papers of that time were scarcely larger than the smallest of today. Dauriat and Ladvocat were the first to make a stand against the tyranny of the journalists by means of posters by which they captured the attention of Paris, by the use of fancy type, striking colours, vignettes, and later on by lithograph illustrations which made these posters a delight for the eyes of the amateur, and often a snare for his purse. Posters became so original that one of those lunatics known as *collectors* has a complete set of Paris posters. This means of announcement, at first confined to the shop windows of Paris and stalls on the boulevards, but which later spread all over France, has since been abandoned in favour of advertisements inserted in the newspapers. Nevertheless posters, that still strike the eyes when the advertisement, and often the book itself, has long been forgotten, have come to stay, especially now that the practice of plastering walls with them has become general.

Advertisements, which can be paid for by those who can afford them, and which have transformed the back pages of our newspapers into a source of income no less fertile for the Inland Revenue Department than for the speculator, are the offspring of heavy stamp duties, newspaper licences and caution money. These restrictions were introduced under M. de Villèle, who might at that time have killed the newspapers by popularising them, but who, on the contrary, created all kinds of privileges, by making it all but impossible to start a new newspaper. In 1821, therefore, the press had the power of life and death over the works of intellect and the enterprises of the publishing trade. A short paragraph in the Paris news column cost a pretty penny. There were cross-currents of intrigue behind the scenes of the newspaper offices, and on the eve of publication when the paper was made up a pitched battle always took place to decide whether this or that item was to be put in or left out. So that the bigger publishing houses kept writers in their pay to insert those short paragraphs in which a great deal is said in few words. These obscure journalists, paid only for material actually published, would often stay all night at the printers' to make sure that their copy—sometimes long articles, obtained Heaven knows how, sometimes only short notices—actually went to press. Today the world of journalism and publishing has changed so much that many people can no longer believe the lengths to which publishers and authors would go to obtain these puffs. The martyrs of fame, and all those condemned to the penal servitude of perpetual success, had recourse to all kinds of bribery, corruption and intrigue. Dinners, flattery and presents to journalists were all customary. The following anecdote will explain better than any mere assertions the close alliance between critics and publishers.

There was once a man of great talent, who aspired to become a Member of Parliament, and who was at that time young, fond of pleasure, and the editor of a big newspaper ; and this man became the favourite of a famous publishing house. One day—it was a Sunday —in the country, where the wealthy publisher made a practice of entertaining some of the most important journalists of the day, the hostess, who was young and pretty at that time, took the illustrious writer for a walk in the park. The chief clerk of the firm, a phlegmatic, serious-minded and methodical German, whose only thought was for business, also strolled out, with one of the journalists under his wing, to discuss a matter on which he needed his advice. The consultation led them out of the park into the neighbouring wood. At the end of an avenue the German saw a figure that looked rather like his hostess ; he raised his eyeglass, made a sign to the young journalist to keep quiet and go away, and presently followed him, taking every care not to make a noise.

The young writer asked him what he had seen.

" Nothing much," he replied. " Our big article will go in. We shall have at least three columns in tomorrow's *Débats*."

Another true story will demonstrate the power of these articles.

A book by M. de Chateaubriand on the last of the Stuarts was a nightingale in the book-shops. As a result of a single article by a young writer in the *Journal des Débats* the book sold out in a week. At a time when if you wanted to read a book you could not borrow it but had to buy it, ten thousand copies of books by Liberal writers would be sold if these were given publicity in the Opposition newspapers ; but it is true that Belgian pirated editions had not yet come into being.

The preliminary attacks by Lucien's friends, followed by his article, had had the effect of arresting the sales of Nathan's book. Nathan suffered only a blow to his pride ; he had nothing to lose, for he had been paid in advance ; but Dauriat stood to lose thirty thousand francs. The business aspect of that department of the book trade that deals with new works, can in fact, be summed up as follows ; a ream of blank paper is worth fifteen francs ; printed, its value may be a hundred sous or a hundred crowns, depending on whether the book is a success or a failure. A favourable or an unfavourable review at the time of publication often decides that financial question. Dauriat, who had five hundred reams to sell, therefore made haste to come to terms with Lucien. The publisher was no longer a sultan but a slave.

After waiting for some time, grumbling and making as much noise as possible as he parleyed with Bérénice, he was admitted to Lucien's presence; and that proud publisher was all smiles, like a courtier admitted to a royal audience, but at the same time affable and self-satisfied.

"Don't disturb yourselves, dear children!" he said. "How charming they look, just like a pair of turtle-doves! Would you believe, mademoiselle, that this young man, who looks like a young girl, is a tiger with claws of steel, that will tear up a reputation as he would tear up one of your dressing-gowns, if you were too slow in taking it off?" He laughed, but left his joke in mid-air.

"My dear boy. . ." he went on, turning to Lucien. "I am Dauriat, mademoiselle," he added, addressing Coralie. (The publisher judged it opportune to drop the bombshell of his name, for Coralie, he thought, was less cordial than she should have been.)

"Have you breakfasted, or will you join us?" the actress asked him.

"Why, yes, we can talk better at table," said Dauriat. "I shall consider myself at liberty to invite you to dinner with my friend Lucien, because we are going to be friends—we shall be hand in glove very soon."

"Bérénice! Bring oysters and lemons and fresh butter," said Coralie, "and champagne."

"You are much too clever not to guess why I have come," said Dauriat, looking at Lucien.

"You have come to buy my collection of sonnets?"

"Precisely," said Dauriat. "First of all, let us both put our cards on the table." He drew an elegant note-case from his pocket, drew out three thousand-franc notes, put them on a plate, and handed them to Lucien with the air of a suppliant.

"Are you satisfied?" he asked.

" Yes," said the poet ; a sense of indescribable beatitude flooded his soul at the sight of such an undreamed-of amount of money.

Lucien controlled himself, but he wanted to sing and leap ; he believed in Aladdin's lamp, in magic—in short, he believed in his own genius.

" And so the *Marguerites* are mine," said the publisher. " But you won't attack any more of my publications ? "

" The *Marguerites* are yours ; but I cannot pledge my pen ; it is at the service of my friends, as theirs are at mine."

" But after all, you will be one of my authors. All my authors are my friends. So you will not spoil my business without warning me in advance, so that I can take steps to meet any attacks ? "

" I agree to that."

" To your fame! " said Dauriat, raising his glass.

" I can see that you have read the *Marguerites,*" said Lucien.

Dauriat was not in the least disconcerted.

" My dear boy, a publisher cannot pay you a greater compliment than to buy your *Marguerites* unread. Six months from now you will be a famous poet ; you will have good notices ; people are afraid of you, and I shall have no difficulty in selling your book. I am the same man of business that I was four days ago. I have not changed, but you have. Last week your sonnets, so far as I was concerned, were so many cabbage-leaves ; today your position places them in the same class as the *Méssenіennes.*"

" I see," said Lucien, made bold by the sultanesque pleasure of possessing a beautiful mistress and the certainty of success, " that if you did not read my sonnets, you did read my article."

" Yes, my friend, otherwise would I have come round in such a hurry ? Unhappily it is very good, that dreadful article. Ah! You have tremendous talent, my boy. I should advise you to take full advantage of your vogue," he said, with an air of friendliness that concealed the profoundly insulting implication of his speech. " But have you had a copy of the newspaper ? Have you read it ? "

" Not yet," said Lucien. " And it is the first time that I have published a long article; but Hector will have sent me a copy to my address in the Rue Charlot."

"Here it is—read it!" said Dauriat, in the manner of Talma playing *Manlius*.

Lucien took the paper, but Coralie snatched it from him.

"The first-fruits of your pen belong to me, you know," she said, laughing.

Dauriat was unwontedly flattering and courteous; he was afraid of Lucien, and so he invited him and Coralie to a big dinner that he was giving to journalists later in the week. He took the manuscript of the *Marguerites* away with him, telling *his* poet to look in whenever he liked at the Wooden Galleries to sign the contract, which he would have ready. Faithful to his habit of impressing superficial people with his regal airs—for he liked to be thought of rather as a Maecenas than as a publisher—he would not take the receipt that Lucien offered him for the three thousand francs, brushing it aside with a careless gesture, and kissed Coralie's hand as he took his leave.

"Well, my love, you would not have seen many of these little bits of paper if you had stayed in that hole in the Rue de Cluny, prowling about the bookshelves in the Bibliothèque de Saint-Geneviève!" said Coralie—for Lucien had told her the story of his life. "Really, your little friends in the Rue des Quatre-Vents seem to me to be very great ninnies!"

His friends in d'Arthez's circle were ninnies!—and Lucien could hear that verdict and laugh. He had read his article in print, and savoured the ineffable joy of authorship, that first gratification of pride that comes only once. Reading and re-reading his article, its scope and implications became clearer than ever to him. Print is to manuscripts what the stage is to an actress—it brings to light both beauties and defects; it may kill, or it may bring to life; a flaw leaps to the eye, and so does a finely expressed idea. Lucien, quite intoxicated, gave not another thought to Nathan; Nathan was only his stepping-stone; he floated in joy, and he was rich! To the youth who not long ago had so humbly descended the steps of Beaulieu in Angoulême on his way home to Postel's attic in l'Houmeau, where his whole family lived on twelve hundred francs a year, the sum that Dauriat had brought was undreamed-of riches. A memory—still vivid, but which was soon to be effaced by the round of pleasures of

Paris life—took him back to the Place du Mûrier. He remembered his beautiful, noble sister Eve, his friend David and his poor mother; and at once he sent Bérénice to change one of the notes, and while she was away he wrote a little note to his family; then he sent Bérénice off to the post office, afraid that if he delayed he would no longer have the strength of mind to part with the five hundred francs that he addressed to his mother. In his own eyes, and Coralie's, this repayment seemed a very noble action. The actress flung her arms round Lucien, for he seemed to her the paragon of sons and brothers; she overwhelmed him with her love, because generosity is a thing that these warm-hearted girls love, for they always carry their hearts in their hands.

"Now we have an invitation to dinner for every day this week," she said. "We will celebrate; you have worked hard for quite long enough."

Coralie, eager to enjoy the good looks of a man whom all other women would envy her, took him back to Staub, for she did not consider Lucien sufficiently well dressed. From there, the two lovers made their way to the Bois de Boulogne, and returned to dine with Mme de Val-Noble, where Lucien met Rastignac, Bixiou, des Lupeaux, Finot, Blondet, Vignon, Baron de Nucingen, Beaudenord, Philippe Bridau, Conti the great musician—all the artists and speculators who need to relax from arduous work in violent sensations, and they all welcomed Lucien warmly. Lucien, full of self-confidence, was prodigal of his wit, for all the world as if he had not to live by it, and was acclaimed as a "first-rate fellow"—in the slang of this world of semi-comrades.

"Oh, we must wait and see what he has in him," said Théodore Gaillard to one of the poets protected by the Court, who was thinking of starting a small Royalist paper, later known as *Le Réveil.*

After dinner the two journalists accompanied their mistresses to the Opéra, where Merlin had a box, whither the whole party adjourned. And so Lucien reappeared in triumph on the scene that a few months before had witnessed his great fall. He strolled in the foyer arm in arm with Merlin and Blondet, staring in the faces of the dandies who had made him feel so foolish on that occasion. He had trampled Châtelet underfoot! De Marsay, Vandenesse and Manerville, the lions of the day, exchanged some insolent looks with him. There was undoubtedly some talk of the handsome, elegant Lucien in Madame d'Espard's box, to which Rastignac paid a lengthy visit, for the Marquise and Mme de Bargeton examined Coralie through their lorgnettes. Did the sight of Lucien stir any regret in Mme de Bargeton's bosom ? The poet wondered ; and seeing again the Corinna of Angoulême, the desire for revenge stirred in his heart as it had on the day when he had sustained the scorn of that lady and her cousin in the Champs-Elysées.

" Did you bring a magic charm with you from the provinces ? " Blondet asked Lucien a few days later. He had called at about eleven o'clock, and Lucien was not yet up. " His good looks," he said, indicating Lucien as he kissed Coralie on the brow, " are making havoc from cellar to attic, high and low—I have come to requisition you, my dear fellow," he said, shaking hands with the poet. " At the Italiens yesterday Countess Montcornet asked me to introduce you to her. You will not refuse a young and charming lady, at whose house you will meet people of the best society ? "

" If Lucien is good," said Coralie, " he will not go to see your Countess. Why should he drag himself into high society ? He will only be bored."

" Do you want a monopoly of him ? " said Blondet. " Are you jealous of fine ladies."

" Yes," said Coralie, " they are worse than we are."

" How do you know that, my little puss ? " said Blondet.

" From their husbands," she replied. " You forget that I had de Marsay for six months."

" You don't suppose, dear child," said Blondet, " that I am particularly eager to introduce such a good-looking fellow as your Lucien to Mme de Montcornet ? If you object, we will say no more about it. But I fancy that it is not so much a matter of the ladies, as of a poor devil who has been made the butt of his newspaper and who wants to make his peace. Baron de Châtelet was foolish enough to take some articles seriously. The Marquise d'Espard, Mme de Bargeton, and all Countess Montcornet's circle take an interest in the

Heron, and I promised to reconcile Laura and her Petrarch—Mme de Bargeton and Lucien."

" Ah! " Lucien exclaimed—and his blood seemed to sing in his veins, in an access of the wild joy of revenge satisfied. " So my foot is on their necks! You make me in love with my pen, with my friends, with the fatal power of the press! I have not written a single article as yet on the Cuttle-bone and the Heron! I will go, my dear fellow!" he said, putting his arm round Blondet's shoulders. " Yes, I will go, but not before those two have felt the weight of this light weapon! " He took up the pen with which he had written the article on Nathan and brandished it.

" Tomorrow I shall hurl two columns at their heads! After that, we shall see! Don't you worry, Coralie, there is no question of love, only revenge—and I want it to be complete! "

" What a man! " said Blondet. "If you but knew, Lucien, how seldom there is such a stir in the bored world of Paris you might appreciate yourself. You will be a fine rascal! (his actual expression was rather stronger). You are on the highroad to power! "

" He will arrive! " said Coralie.

" Well, he has come on a good way in six weeks."

" And if he is within reach of a sceptre that he can only attain by stepping over a corpse, he is welcome to use Coralie's body as a stepping-stone! "

" Your love belongs to the golden age! " said Blondet. " My compliments on your famous article," he continued, looking at Lucien ; " it is full of new ideas. You are a past master."

Lousteau appeared with Hector Merlin and Vernou to see Lucien, who was prodigiously flattered at finding himself the object of their attentions. Félicien brought Lucien a hundred francs for his article. The newspaper had felt it necessary to mark its recognition of a first-class piece of work, so as to attach him to the paper. Coralie, on seeing this flock of journalists arrive, had sent out to the Cadran Bleu, the nearest restaurant, to order lunch ; Bérénice came in to say that everything was ready, and Coralie invited them all to come through into her pretty dining-room. Half-way through the meal, when the champagne had gone to all their heads, the reason for his colleagues' visit to Lucien came out.

"You do not mean to make an enemy of Nathan, do you?" Lousteau asked him. "Nathan is a journalist, and he has friends, and he might play you a dirty trick when your first book comes out. You have *An Archer of Charles IX* to dispose of, haven't you? We saw Nathan this morning, and he is in despair; but you can write another article singing his praises to his face."

"What! After my article against his book, do you expect me to . . . ?" Lucien began.

Emile Blondet, Hector Merlin, Étienne Lousteau and Félicien Vernou cut him short with a burst of laughter.

"Did you ask him to supper here the day after tomorrow?" Blondet asked.

"Your article wasn't signed," said Lousteau. "Félicien is not so green as you are, and he only signed it with a C. at the bottom—you can always sign your articles for that paper in the same way—it is extreme Left. We are all on the side of the Opposition. Félicien had the tact not to compromise your future opinions. In Hector's paper, that is Right Centre, you can sign yourself with an L. Always attack anonymously, but sign favourable reviews in full."

"Signatures don't worry me," said Lucien, "but I don't see what there is to be said in favour of the book."

"Then you do really believe what you wrote?" Hector asked Lucien.

"Yes."

"My dear boy," said Blondet, "I thought you had more sense! On my word of honour, looking at that brow of yours, I fancied you had the omnipotence of those exalted minds that are great enough to be able to consider everything from opposite points of view. My dear boy, every idea is reversible; nobody can take it upon himself to say which is the right, which is the wrong side. Everything has two aspects in the realms of thought. Ideas are bi-polar. Janus is the archetype of the critic and the symbol of genius. Only God is triangular! What is it that makes Molière and Corneille so outstandingly great unless it be their ability to affirm one point of view in the character of Alcestes and its opposite in Philinte, or Octave, or Cinna? Rousseau in *La Nouvelle Héloise* has written a letter in support of duelling, and a letter against duelling—would you take it upon yourself to say which is his true opinion? Which of us could venture to decide between Clarissa and Lovelace, or Hector and Achilles? Who is Homer's hero? What did Richardson mean? Criticism must consider a work from every side. In other words, we are great recorders."

"So you believe what you write!" said Vernou in tones of irony. "But we trade in phrases, and we live by our trade. When you write a great and beautiful work—a book in fact—you can put your ideas into it, your soul, identify yourself with it, stand by it; but articles read today and forgotten tomorrow—in my opinion these are worth neither more nor less than what we are paid for them. If you set any store by stupidities of that sort, you had better make the sign of the cross and invoke the Holy Ghost whenever you write a trade circular!"

They all seemed astonished to discover that Lucien had scruples; but they had little difficulty in tearing off him the last shreds of his boyish conscience and investing him with the *toga virilis* of journalism.

"Do you know how Nathan consoled himself after reading your article?" said Lousteau.

"How should I know?"

"Nathan said, 'Little articles pass, but great works remain!' But he will come to supper here two days from now, and he will be sure to go on his knees to you, kiss your claws, and tell you that you are a great man."

"That would be amusing," said Lucien.

"Amusing!" said Blondet. "It cannot be otherwise!"

"My friends, I should be delighted," said Lucien, who was a little tipsy, "but how is it to be done?"

"Well," said Lousteau, "write three good columns for Merlin's newspaper in which you refute yourself. We have been enjoying the spectacle of Nathan's wrath, and we have been telling him that he will thank us presently for starting a brisk controversy that will sell out his book in a week. At the present moment you are a traitor, a scoundrel, a swine in his eyes; the day after tomorrow you will be a first-rate man, a brilliant intellect, straight from Plutarch! Nathan will be treating you as his best friend! Dauriat has been to see you, you have three thousand-franc notes, and the plot has worked. Now you want Nathan's friendship and esteem. We don't want anyone to suffer except the publisher. We ought not to demolish and persecute anyone except our enemies. If this was a question of some outsider who had made a reputation without us, and who ought to be put down, we would not be talking like this; but Nathan is a friend of ours; Blondet arranged for an attack on him in the *Mercure* just for the sake of being able to reply in the *Débats*—that was how the first edition was sold out!"

"But for the life of me I could not write two lines in favour of that book!"

"You will get another hundred francs," said Merlin. "Nathan has already been worth two hundred francs to you, and counting the article that you can write for Finot's paper, Dauriat will pay you a hundred francs for it, and the paper another hundred—total, four hundred francs."

"But what shall I say?"

"You can get round it this way," said Blondet, after a moment's reflection. "Envy attacks all great works, as grubs attack the finest fruit, you will say, and has attempted to demolish this work. In order to find fault with it, the critic has been driven to invent a theory of two schools of literature—a literature of Ideas and a literature of Images—and to apply the theory to the book in question. Then, dear boy, you will say that the highest form of art is the expression of the Idea by means of the Image. You then set about proving that the Image is the essence of poetry—and lament that our literature is deficient in poetry. You can mention the fact that foreign writers always criticise us for the *positivism* of our style, and proceed to eulogise M. de Canalis and Nathan for the services that they are rendering France by infusing a less prosaic spirit into the language. Demolish your previous arguments by pointing out that we have made progress since the eighteenth century. Work the word *progress* hard—it is a beautiful vague word to impress the bourgeois reader. Say that the new school of literature proceeds by way of pictures in which all styles are concentrated—comedy, drama, description, character-study and dialogue, linked together by the brilliant handling of plot. The novel, which comprises sentiment, style, and images, is the major achievement of contemporary literature. It supersedes comedy, which, under modern conditions, is no longer possible according to the old formulae. Both facts and ideas come within the scope of the novel. The novelist must have the intellect of an incisive moralist like la Bruyère, the ability to handle characters as Molière knew how to handle them, Shakespeare's power in developing a situation, and besides all that the gift of depicting the most delicate shades of feeling—the one field that has not been exploited by our predecessors. The modern novel is, therefore, infinitely superior to the cold and logical discussion, the arid analysis, of the eighteenth century. ' The novel,' you will say sententiously, ' is an entertaining epic.' Mention *Corinne*, and bring in Mme de Staël. ' The eighteenth century questioned everything, it is for the nineteenth to find answers '—and the answers that it finds are realities—but realities that live and move ; in fact, passions are brought into play—an element unknown to Voltaire. Here follows a diatribe against Voltaire, and as for Rousseau, his characters are nothing but theories and systems dressed up. Julie and Claire are entelechies, not women of flesh and blood.

" You can expatiate on that theme and say that we owe to the peace and to the Bourbons a new and original school of literature—because you will be writing for a Centre Right paper. Ridicule the theorists. And in conclusion, you can come out with a fine enthusiastic peroration : ' Our colleague's article is full of misapprehensions and misleading statements—and to what end ? In order to depreciate a fine work, to deceive the public and to reach the illogical conclusion that a readable book should not be read! *Proh pudor*!—(mind you put in *Proh pudor*—it is a good resounding expletive, and it wakes up the reader)—and then you proclaim the decadence of criticism. Conclusion : There is only one kind of literature—books that give pleasure. Nathan has broken new ground, he has understood his period and its special problems. What this time demands is drama. Drama is the literary form proper to an age whose politics is a perpetual melodrama! Have we not seen during the last twenty years (you will say) the four dramas of the Revolution, the Directorate, the Empire, and the Restoration? And then you will strike up the dithyramb of eulogy, and the second edition will be sold out. That is how to do it.

" Then you can write a full-page article for our review to appear next Saturday and sign it DE RUBEMPRÉ in full. In this second article you can say, ' It is the mark of the best books that they always arouse abundant controversy. This week, such-and-such a newspaper said this and that about Nathan's book, and such-and-such another newspaper replied as follows.' You then criticise the two criticisms signed L and C, and pay me an incidental compliment on my first article in the *Débats*, and conclude by saying that Nathan's book is the greatest work of this century. That means nothing—it is said of every book. You will have earned four hundred francs in a week, to say nothing of the pleasure of writing the truth, up to a point. Intelligent people will agree with C or with L or with de Rubempré—some with all three! Mythology, which is certainly one of the greatest of human inventions, has placed Truth at the bottom of a well, and don't we need buckets to draw her up? You will have provided the public with three. There you are, my boy—go ahead! "

Lucien was amazed. Blondet kissed him on both cheeks. " I must go to my shop," he said.

And they all went to their shops. For these first-rate men, a newspaper was nothing but a shop. They were all meeting that evening at the Wooden Galleries, where Lucien was to go and sign his contract with Dauriat. Florine and Lousteau, Lucien and Coralie, Blondet and Finot were all dining in the Palais Royal; du Bruel was giving a dinner for the manager of the Panorama-Dramatique.

" They are right! " said Lucien, alone with Coralie. " Other people should be used simply as means by first-rate men. Four hundred francs for four articles! Doguereau offered me less than that for a book that cost me two years of work."

"Write criticism," said Coralie, "enjoy yourself! Don't I appear this evening as an Andalusian, and tomorrow as a gypsy, and the next day dressed as a man? Do as I do, give them a good performance for their money, and let us live happily."

Lucien, who always fell for paradox, mounted his muse on that capricious mule, a hybrid bred from Pegasus and Balaam's ass. He set off at a gallop in the fields of thought, as he drove in the Bois, and discovered new beauties in Blondet's thesis. He dined as happy men dine, and signed a contract with Dauriat by which he made over to him all rights in the manuscript of the *Marguerites*, without suspecting that there might be a trap; then he looked in at the office, where he knocked off two columns, and came back to the Rue de Vendôme.

Next morning he discovered that yesterday's ideas had germinated in his brain, as always happens to men of vigorous mind, whose vital sap is still rising, and whose talents have not yet been put to strenuous use. Lucien enjoyed thinking over this new article, and he set to work with enthusiasm. From his pen emerged all the beauties of contradiction. He was witty and ironical, he even developed original lines of thought on Sentiment and on the Idea and the Image in literature. In order to praise Nathan he was ingenious and subtle enough to revert to his first impressions on reading Nathan's novel at the reading-room in the Cour de Commerce. He was no longer the ruthless and carping critic, making fun of his subject; in a few concluding phrases that rose and fell with the majestic rhythm of a censer charged with incense, swung before the altar, he ascended into the sphere of poetry.

"A hundred francs, Coralie!" he cried, brandishing the eight sheets that he had covered while she dressed.

He was in the writing vein that morning. Phrase by phrase, he penned the terrible article against Châtelet and Mme de Bargeton that he had promised Blondet. He savoured one of the secret and the keenest pleasures known to the journalist—that of sharpening his epigrams, whetting the cold blade that will find its mark in the heart of the victim, and decorating the pommel for the benefit of the reader. The public admires the clever workmanship of that sword and has no conception of its malice ; the reader does not know what havoc is wrought by the steel of an epigram, barbed with revenge, and plunged with deadly aim into the victim's self-respect, that it wounds in a thousand ways. This horrible pleasure, joyless and savoured in solitude, relished unseen, is like a duel fought in absence and kills at a distance with the quill of a pen, as if journalists had the fantastic power accorded to the possessors of talismans in the *Arabian Nights*, of having all their wishes granted. The epigram is distilled from hate, the quintessence of a rancour composed of all mankind's worst passions, just as love is the distillation of all his best qualities. The man who cannot be witty to avenge himself is as rare as the man to whom love brings no pleasure. But for all the facility—not to say vulgarity—of this kind of wit, it is always well received in France. Lucien's article was to break all the newspaper's previous records for venomous spite, and two people were wounded deeply by it—Mme de Bargeton, who had once been his Laura, as well as the Baron du Châtelet, his rival.

" Well, let us go for a drive in the Bois ; the horses are harnessed, and they are beginning to fidget," said Coralie. " You must not kill yourself."

" We will take the article on Nathan to Hector. The press really is Achilles' lance, that cures the wounds it has made," said Lucien, as he completed one or two small corrections.

The lovers drove off and appeared in all their splendour before that Paris which had so lately rejected Lucien, and which was now beginning to notice him. To have Paris talking about him after having learned by bitter experience the difficulty of being someone in that great city, turned Lucien's head with delight.

" My dear, let us call at your tailor's on the way and ask him to hurry up with your suits, or to fit them, if they are ready. If you are going to meet all these great ladies, I am determined that you shall eclipse that monster de Marsay, and little Rastignac, and Ajuda-Pinto, and Maxime des Trailles, and Vandenesse, and all the rest of them. Remember that Coralie is your mistress! But you will not deceive me, will you?"

Two days later, on the eve of the supper Lucien and Coralie were giving to their friends, a new play was being put on at the Ambigu, and Lucien was to write the dramatic criticism. After dinner, Lucien and Coralie walked from the Rue de Vendôme to the Panorama-Dramatique, by the Boulevard du Temple, past the Café Turc—a fashionable walk at that time. Lucien overheard sundry comments on his good fortune and on his mistress's beauty. Several people remarked that Coralie was the most beautiful woman in Paris; others said that Lucien was worthy of her. This was a life after his own heart! The poet was in his element. He scarcely gave a thought to d'Arthez and his friends. He had admired these great spirits so much, two months ago, and now he wondered whether they were not perhaps a trifle ridiculous with their ideals and their puritanical notions. The word "ninnies", so lightly dropped by Coralie, had taken root in Lucien's mind, and had already borne its fruits. He saw Coralie to her dressing-room, strolled about behind the scenes of the theatre like a sultan, while all the actresses received him with melting glances and flattering words.

"I must go to the Ambigu to do my evening's work," he said.

At the Ambigu the house was full. There was not a seat for Lucien. He went behind the scenes and complained bitterly that no seat had been reserved for him. The box-office attendant, who did not yet know him, replied that tickets for two boxes had been sent to his paper, and sent him about his business.

"I shall write about this play as I find it," said Lucien in tones of annoyance.

"Are you mad?" the leading lady said to the box-office attendant. "This is Coralie's lover!"

The attendant instantly came back to Lucien. "I will have a word with the management, sir," he said.

And so every detail conspired to give Lucien proof of the immense power of the press and to flatter his vanity. The manager went and asked the Duc de Rhétoré and Tullia, the *prima ballerina*, who were in the stage box, whether they had any objection to allowing Lucien to share their box. The Duke agreed ; he remembered Lucien.

"You have reduced two people to despair," the young man said to him, naming Baron du Châtelet and Mme de Bargeton.

"Just let them wait until tomorrow!" said Lucien. "So far my friends have confined themselves to bird-bolts, but I have let off some red-hot cannon-bullets tonight. Tomorrow you will see why we have been making a butt of Potelet. The title of the article is 'From Potelet 1811 to Potelet 1821'. Châtelet is castigated as the type who has renounced his benefactor and rallied to the Bourbons. When I have done my worst with him, I shall go to Mme de Montcornet's."

Lucien's talk with the young Duke sparkled with wit ; he was anxious to prove to this illustrious gentleman what a great mistake Mmes d'Espard and de Bargeton had made in despising him ; but he showed his hand when he tried to justify his right, when the Duke maliciously addressed him as Chardon, to use the name of de Rubempré.

"You ought to become a Royalist. You have proved yourself to be brilliant ; show that you are also a man of good sense. The only way in which you can obtain a patent of nobility from the King allowing you to use the name of your maternal ancestors is to ask it in return for services rendered to the Palace. The Liberals will never make you a Count! Take my word for it, the Restoration will get the better of the press in the long run. It is the only power they have reason to fear ; they have waited quite long enough, and it is high time the press was muzzled. Make use of the last days of its freedom to make yourself a man to be reckoned with. A few years from now, a name and a title will be worth more than talent. Then you will have everything—talent, nobility, and good looks ; you will have the world at your feet. If you are a Liberal, let it be only for the moment, in order to sell your allegiance to the Royalists to better advantage."

The Duke asked Lucien, personally, to accept an invitation to dinner that was going to be sent to him by the Minister whom he had met at supper with Florine. Lucien was seduced on the spot by the noble peer's arguments, and enchanted to see the doors of drawing-rooms from which he had thought himself a few months ago banished for ever, opening to him. He marvelled at the power of ideas. So the press, and intelligence, really were the moving powers of present-day society! Lucien guessed that Lousteau might very well regret having opened the doors of the temple to him; he was already beginning to feel, on his own account, the importance of erecting barriers that could not easily be crossed by ambitious young men coming up to Paris from the provinces. He did not dare to ask himself what kind of reception he himself would give a poet coming to him as he had flung himself upon Étienne's mercy.

The young Duke saw that Lucien was deep in thought, and made a pretty good guess at the subject of his meditations; he had revealed to that ambitious soul, of no fixed purpose, but with boundless ambition, the whole political horizon—just as the journalists had shown him, as the devil showed Jesus from the pinnacle of the Temple, the kingdom of literature and its riches.

Lucien had no suspicion that a little conspiracy was being woven around him by the small group of people who were at that moment being victimised by the newspaper; still less that M. de Rhétoré had a hand in it. The young Duke had spread alarm in Mme d'Espard's circle by telling them how brilliant Lucien was. Mme de Bargeton had asked him to sound the journalist, and he had come to the Ambigu-Comique in the hope of meeting Lucien. Neither the social world nor the journalists are very profound. There is never any question of deep-laid plots. Neither side thinks far ahead, and their machiavellism is, so to speak, from hand to mouth, and consists in little more than being always on the spot, ready for anything, ready to take advantage of whatever turns up, of being constantly on the watch for those moments of weakness when a man plays into their hands. In the course of the supper at Florine's the Duke had taken the measure of Lucien's character, and now he had successfully laid a snare for his vanities by way of practising his diplomacy on him.

After the performance Lucien dashed off to the Rue Saint-Fiacre to write his review of the play. His notice was designedly bitter and sarcastic, written purely for the pleasure of exercising his power. The melodrama was better than *The Alcalde*, but he was eager to know whether it was true that a dramatic critic could, as he had been told, make a bad play a success and kill a good one. The next morning at breakfast he opened the newspaper, telling Coralie as he did so that he had torn the play at the Ambigu-Comique to pieces. Lucien was not a little surprised to read, below his article on Mme de Bargeton and Châtelet, a much modified account of the Ambigu; the article had been so much sweetened overnight that, while preserving his witty account, the verdict was a favourable one. The play would be a box-office success. No words can describe his wrath, and he made up his mind to ask Lousteau for an explanation. He had already come to think himself indispensable, and he said to himself that he would not put up with being tyrannised over and treated like a fool. To establish his power beyond all question, he wrote an article for Dauriat and Finot's weekly, summing up and comparing all the opinions hitherto expressed on Nathan's book; and while he was in the mood, he threw off another of his Paris sketches for the little newspaper. In the first flush of enthusiasm, young journalists deliver themselves of articles with parental love, and unwisely commit to them all their best ideas.

The manager of the Panorama-Dramatique was putting on a first performance of a vaudeville show that night, so that Florine and Coralie could have their evening free. There was to be play before supper. Lucien had written a notice in advance, after seeing the dress-rehearsal and Lousteau came to fetch it, so that the paper would be off his mind. Lucien read over to him one of those charming little essays on the by-ways of Paris that made the paper's fortune, and Étienne shook hands with him warmly and told him that he was a godsend to journalism.

"Then why do you amuse yourself with turning my articles inside out?" said Lucien who had written this brilliant sketch with the express purpose of giving more force to his grievance.

"I?" said Lousteau.

"Well then, who did change my article?"

" My dear fellow," said Étienne, " you don't know everything yet. The Ambigu subscribes for twenty copies, of which only nine are actually sent—to the manager, the leader of the orchestra, the business manager, their mistresses, and the three proprietors of the theatre. Each of the boulevard theatres is therefore paying the newspaper eight hundred francs per annum, and as much again in boxes given to Finot, not to mention subscriptions from the actors and authors. So we make a cool eight thousand on the Boulevards. These are the small theatres, so you may imagine what the big ones pay! Now do you understand? We are bound to show a certain amount of indulgence."

" By which you mean that I am not free to write as I think? "

" What does that matter, for heaven's sake, so long as it pays for your bread and butter! " said Lousteau. " And in any case, my dear fellow, what have you against the theatre? You must have had some reason for tearing the play to pieces. If you slash for the sake of slashing, the paper will get a bad name, and when the paper attacks in good earnest, it won't have any effect. Did the management annoy you? "

" They did not keep me a seat."

" In that case," said Loustea, "I will let the manager see what you wrote and tell him that I toned it down; that will do more good, you will find, than if your article had appeared. If you ask him for some tickets tomorrow, he will give you forty a month for any part of the house. I will take you to a man who will take them off your hands—he will buy them all from you at the full price less fifteen per cent. We deal in theatre tickets just as we do in books. You shall see the second Barbet, the chief of the hired claque—he lives quite near here. We may as well go round now, there is time."

" But my dear fellow, it is really scandalous that Finot should trade in bribery and corruption in intellectual fields. Sooner or later——"

" Oh! Go along! Where *do* you come from? " said Lousteau. " What do you take Finot for? Underneath his affable manner, and his ignorance and his stupidity, he is as astute a business man as his father the hatter. Haven't you seen Finot's uncle, the old soldier of the Empire in his den at the newspaper office? That uncle is not only a gentlemanly figure, he has also the good fortune of passing for a fool. He is the only one who is compromised in all these financial transactions. In Paris any man who can find a willing scapegoat is extremely well off. In politics, and in journalism, there are any number of situations in which the chiefs must not appear. If Finot were to go into politics, his uncle would become his secretary and receive the contributions levied in various Departments over big deals. Giroudeau, whom at first sight anyone would take for a fool, has just the necessary amount of shrewdness to be an inscrutable old card. He mounts guard to see that we are not pestered with all the complaints and people who want jobs, and advertisements, and I doubt if you will find his equal on any paper."

"He plays his part well," said Lucien; "I have seen him at work."

Étienne and Lucien had reached the Faubourg-du-Temple and the chief editor stopped at a pleasant-looking house.

" Is M. Braulard in ? " he asked the porter.

" *Monsieur*—then is the chief of the hired claque *monsieur* ? " said Lucien.

" My dear fellow, Braulard makes twenty thousand francs a year and he has all the Boulevard playwrights in his clutches. They all have current accounts with him as if he were a banker. He does a trade in authors' and complimentary tickets. Braulard disposes of them. You can work it out for yourself—the science of statistics has its use when you don't overdo it. Fifty complimentary tickets an evening for every show in Paris comes to two hundred and fifty tickets a day; if on an average these tickets are worth forty sous each, Braulard pays out a hundred and twenty-five francs a day for them, and takes a chance of getting back as much again. So that complimentary tickets alone must bring him in nearly four thousand francs a month, which comes to forty-eight thousand francs a year. Allow twenty thousand for losses, because he cannot always dispose of his tickets."

" Why not ? "

" Well, people who book their seats at the box-office may be sold the same seats—the places are not reserved for complimentary tickets. The theatre reserves its rights over all seats. Then there are spells of fine weather, and bad plays. So that Braulard makes perhaps thirty thousand francs a year on tickets. Then he has his hired claque—that is another of his lines. Florine and Coralie both contribute; if they did not subsidise him they would get no applause at their exits and entrances."

Lousteau gave this explanation in a low voice as the two young men went upstairs.

" Paris is a strange place," said Lucien, who found self-interest crouching in every corner.

A neat servant-girl opened the door to the two journalists. The dealer in tickets was sitting in an office armchair before an enormous cylindrical desk, but he got up when he saw Lousteau. Braulard was wearing a grey molleton coat, footed trousers and red slippers, for all the world like a doctor or a lawyer. Lucien guessed him to be a self-made man; he had a vulgar face, cunning grey eyes, hands that might have been made for hired clapping, and a complexion over which dissolute living seemed to have passed like rain over the roofs, greying hair, and a rather husky voice.

" I suppose you have come about Mlle Florine and Mlle Coralie?" he said. " I know you by sight," he said to Lucien. " But you needn't worry, I shall square the people at the Gymnase; I am looking after your mistress, and I will see that she hears of any tricks they may try to play on her."

" We won't say no to that, Braulard old man," said Lousteau, " but we have come about the press tickets for all the Boulevard theatres—I as the editor, and this gentleman as dramatic critic."

" Yes, of course, Finot has sold his paper! I heard about it. Finot is getting on. He is having dinner with me at the end of the week. If you will do me the honour and pleasure of coming as well, you may bring your ladies, and we'll make a jolly evening of it; there will be Adèle Dupuis, Ducange, Frédéric du Polet-Méré, and my mistress, Mlle Mollot—we shall have plenty of fun, and more to drink! "

" Ducange must be in difficulties; he lost his case."

" I have lent him ten thousand francs, and if the *Calas* is a success he can pay me back—so I have been boosting it for him. Ducange has talent, he'll be all right."

Lucien thought he must be dreaming when he heard a hired applauder expressing appreciation of an author's talent.

" Coralie is coming on," said Braulard with the air of a judge who knows what he is talking about. " If she is a good girl, I will take her side on the quiet—they have got up a plot against her at the Gymnase. I'll tell you what I'll do—I will put some well-dressed men in the gallery, who will smile and whisper approvingly, and that will fetch the applause. That dodge is a great help to an actress. I like Coralie, and you ought to be pleased with her, because she has feelings. Ah! I can hiss them off the stage when I want to."

" But let us settle this matter of the tickets," said Lousteau.

" Very well, I will call and collect them at this gentleman's house at the beginning of each month. He is a friend of yours, and I will give him the same terms as I do you. You have five theatres, and they will give you thirty tickets—that will be round about seventy-five francs a month. Perhaps you would like an advance...? " and Braulard went over to his desk and took out a cash-box full of money.

" No, no," said Lousteau, " we will fall back on that when we are hard up."

" I am coming round to have a talk with Coralie one of these days—we will come to an understanding."

Lucien was looking round Braulard's office in profound astonishment. He noticed bookshelves, engravings, and good furniture. They went out through the drawing-room, and he noticed that the furniture was neither cheap nor over-expensive. The dining-room seemed to him the best room in the flat, and he remarked on this jokingly.

" But Braulard is a gourmet," said Lousteau. " His dinners are mentioned in plays—they are just what you would expect from his cash-box."

" I have some good wines," said Braulard modestly. " But here are my lamp-lighters," he said, as the sound of raucous voices and shuffling feet was heard on the stairs.

As they left, Lucien watched the ill-smelling squad of the claque and the ticket vendors file past, gaol-birds in caps, old trousers and threadbare overcoats. Their faces were bluish or greenish in hue, dirty, unhealthy, and unshaven, their eyes at once savage and servile. They belonged to that horrible population that lives and swarms on the Paris boulevards; in the morning they sell watch-chains and gold brooches for twenty-five sous, and in the evenings applaud under the chandeliers, always ready to do all the dirty work of Paris.

"These are the Romans!" said Lousteau with a laugh. "There goes the fame of actresses and playwrights! Seen at close quarters, they are no pleasanter to look at than our own."

"It is difficult," said Lucien, as they got back to his flat, "to keep any illusions on any subject in Paris. Everything is taxed, everything is for sale, and everything is manufactured, even success!"

Lucien's guests were Dauriat, the manager of the Panorama, Matifat and Florine, Camusot, Lousteau, Finot, Nathan, Hector Merlin and Mme du Val-Noble, Félicien Vernou, Blondet, Vignon, Philippe Bridau, Mariette, Giroudeau, Cardot and Florentine, and Bixiou. He had invited his friends of the Rue des Quatre-Vents. Tullia the dancer, who, according to rumour, was not unkind to du Bruel, was also there, but without her Duke; and the proprietors of the newspapers on which Nathan, Merlin, Vignon and Vernou worked. There were thirty guests altogether—Coralie's dining-room would hold no more.

At eight o'clock the candles were lit, and the furniture, the curtains, and the flowers in that flat took on that festive air that lends to Parisian luxury the magic of a dream. Lucien felt an unspeakable access of happiness, of satisfied vanity and hope, in seeing himself master of these rooms; and he no longer asked himself how, nor through whom, the magic wand had been waved. Florine and Coralie, dressed with the fantastic extravagance and theatrical effect that actresses love, smiled on the provincial poet like two angels about to open to him the doors of the Palace of Dreams. Lucien was living, almost, in a dream. In a few months his life had changed so suddenly, he had passed with such rapidity from the extreme of poverty to the extreme of luxury, that sometimes he felt somehow anxious, like a man who is dreaming, and yet knows that he is asleep. But the expression with which he now beheld that fair reality was nevertheless so full of confidence that the envious might have given it the name of fatuity.

Lucien himself had changed. He had grown paler during these days of perpetual pleasure. There was a look of soft languor about him—in fact, to use Mme d'Espard's expression, he had the look of a man who is loved. His beauty had increased. Consciousness of his power and his strength was written on his face, enlightened by love and by experience. Now he could look the literary and social world in the face; he believed in his power to enter it as a master. To this poet, who was only capable of serious reflection under the weight of adversity, the present seemed cloudless. Success had filled the sails of his light skiff, and all the instruments necessary to his projects were at his command—a well-furnished flat, a mistress all Paris envied him, a carriage, and incalculable sums in his inkwell. Heart and soul and brain had all been metamorphosed; he no longer thought of questioning the means when he contemplated results so desirable.

As this way of life is bound—and rightly—to seem suspect to economists who have had any experience of Paris, it may be as well to point out the basis, however insecure, upon which reposed the material well-being of the actress and her poet. Camusot had, without revealing the fact, instructed the tradesmen to give Coralie at least three months' credit. So that the horses, the servants, everything, seemed to be there, as if by enchantment, at the beck and call of these two children, thirsting for happiness, and who enjoyed it all to their hearts' content. Coralie came and led Lucien by the hand into the dining-room, and showed him the magical transformation, the table laid out in splendour, with forty wax candles, the royal luxury of the dessert, and the menu, prepared by Chevet. Lucien kissed Coralie's brow and clasped her in his arms.

"I shall succeed, dear child," he said, "and then I shall repay you for all this love and devotion."

"Nonsense," said Coralie. "Are you happy?"

"It would be strange if I were not."

"Well, that smile repays everything," she replied, and with a serpentine movement she raised her lips to Lucien's.

When they went back they found Florine, Lousteau, Matifat and Camusot busy arranging the card-tables. Lucien's friends began to arrive—for all these people already called themselves Lucien's friends. They played cards from nine-o'clock until midnight. Luckily for himself, Lucien could not play cards ; but Lousteau lost a thousand francs and borrowed that sum from Lucien, who did not see how he could very well refuse to lend it when his friend asked him for it. At about ten o'clock Michel, Fulgence and Joseph arrived. Lucien, who went and talked to them in a corner, noticed that they looked sober and serious, not to say ill at ease. D'Arthez had not been able to come, because he was just finishing his book. Léon Giraud was busy with the publication of the first number of his review. The friends had sent the three artists, thinking that they would feel less out of place than the others at a wild party.

" Well, my dear fellows," said Lucien, assuming a slightly patronising manner, " you see that the ' little good-for-nothing ' may become a public figure."

" I ask nothing better than to be proved wrong," said Michel.

" Are you living with Coralie until something better turns up ? " Fulgence asked.

" Yes," said Lucien, trying to seem unconcerned, " Coralie had a poor old shopkeeper who adored her, and she has shown him the door. I am luckier than your brother Philippe, who doesn't know how to manage Mariette," he added, looking at Joseph Bridau.

" In other words," said Fulgence, " you are a man now, like all the rest—you are making your way! "

" A man who will never change towards you, under any circumstances," said Lucien.

Michel and Fulgence looked at one another and exchanged an ironical smile ; Lucien noticed it and suddenly realised the absurdity of his remark.

" Coralie really is marvellously beautiful," said Joseph Bridau. " What a wonderful portrait she would make."

" And good as well," said Lucien. " On my honour, she is an angel. Of course you shall paint her ; if you like she will sit for you as your Venetian courtesan, brought to a Senator by an old woman."

" All women in love are angelic," said Michel Chrestien.

At this moment Raoul Nathan rushed up to Lucien in an access of friendship, seized both his hands, and exclaimed :

" My dear friend, not only are you a great writer, but you have feeling, which in these days is rarer than genius. You are devoted to your friends. And you may count on me through thick and thin—I shall never forget what you have done for me this week."

Lucien's joy was at its height. He was being fawned on by a man whose fame had reached the highest circles, and he looked at his three old friends with an air of superiority. Nathan's dramatic entry was thanks to Merlin, who had sent him the proof-sheets of the article in praise of his book, which was to appear in the next day's issue.

" I only consented to write the attack," Lucien whispered to Nathan, " on condition that I was to be allowed to reply to it myself. I am one of you, you know."

He turned again to his three friends, delighted because circumstances had justified the phrase that had amused Fulgence so much.

" D'Arthez's book is coming out, and I am in a position to help him. I must remain in journalism if for no other reason."

" Are you free to write what you like ? " Michel asked.

" As one is, when one is indispensable," Lucien replied with false modesty.

It was nearly midnight when they sat down to supper, and the party began to grow wild. Speech was freer at Lucien's party than it had been at Matifat's, for nobody suspected that there was any difference of opinion as between the three deputies from the Rue des Quatre-Vents and the journalists present. These young wits, demoralised by the habit of writing indifferently for or against, came to grips with one another and gave utterance to fearful axioms of journalistic jurisprudence, then in its infancy. Claude Vignon, who was anxious to uphold the dignity of criticism, inveighed against the tendency of the smaller newspapers to descend to personalities, and said that sooner or later writers would bring themselves into disrepute. Lousteau, Merlin and Finot openly defended the system, known in journalistic slang as *humbug*, maintaining that it was a sort of probe for testing talent.

" Anyone who can stand that test is a really first-rate man," said Lousteau.

" I would go further," said Merlin. " When a great man is being praised, there ought to be a chorus of insults at the same time, as there was in a Roman triumph."

" Oh! " said Lucien. " Then everyone who is held up to ridicule will fancy that he is having a triumph! "

" You have not a personal interest in the matter, by any chance?" said Finot.

" What about our sonnets ? " said Michel Chrestien. " Don't they deserve the triumph of Petrarch ? "

" *L'or* (Laure) counts for something already in their fame," said Dauriat, whose pun was universally acclaimed.

" *Faciamus experimentum in anima vili,*" Lucien retorted with a smile.

" And woe betide those whom the press never attacks, and to whom it throws bouquets when their first books appear! Such men will be relegated to their niches like saints, and no one will take any further notice of them," said Vernou.

" ' Pass on, my friend, you have had her already,' as Champcenetz said to the Marquis de Genlis who looked too covetously at his wife," said Blondet.

" In France success kills," said Finot. " We are all too jealous of one another here, and we soon forget one another's triumphs and try to make the world forget them."

" In fact it is attacks that give a work a long lease of life," said Claude Vignon.

" As in nature, it is the result of the conflict of two opposite principles ; if either triumphs, the result is fatal," said Fulgence.

" The same thing is true in politics," added Michel Chrestien.

" We are just going to see the proof of it," said Lousteau ; " Dauriat will have sold six thousand copies of Nathan's book by the end of the week. And why ? The book that has been attacked is about to be brilliantly defended."

" An article like this," said Merlin, producing the proofs of the next day's paper, " cannot fail to sell out an edition."

" Read me the article," said Dauriat ; " I am a publisher before everything, even at supper."

Merlin read Lucien's triumphant article, which was applauded by the whole assembly.

" Could that article ever have been written without the first ? " Lousteau demanded.

Dauriat drew the proofs of the third article from his pocket and read it. Finot listened attentively as this article, destined for the second number of his weekly, was read aloud ; and, in his capacity of editor of the paper, he exaggerated his enthusiasm.

" Gentlemen," he said, " if Bossuet had been alive today he could not have done better."

" I entirely agree," said Merlin. " Bossuet today would have been a journalist."

" To the second Bossuet! " Claude Vignon exclaimed, raising his glass, with an ironical bow to Lucien.

" To my Christopher Columbus! " Lucien replied, drinking to Dauriat.

" Bravo! " cried Nathan.

" Is it a nickname ? " Merlin inquired maliciously, looking enquiringly at Finot and Lucien.

" If you go on like this, we shall not be able to keep up with you," said Dauriat, " and these gentlemen "—indicating Matifat and Camusot—" won't understand you. Wit is like a thread ; spin it too fine and it will break, as Bonaparte said."

" Gentlemen," said Lousteau, " we are the witnesses of an unbelievable, inconceivable, utterly unheard-of, and truly surprising phenomenon. Is it not astonishing to contemplate the rapidity with which our friend has been transformed from a provincial to a journalist ? "

" He was born a journalist," said Dauriat.

" My children," said Finot, rising to his feet, a bottle of champagne in his hand, " we have all encouraged and watched over our amphytrion in his entry upon a career in which he has surpassed all our hopes. In two months he has proved himself in the brilliant articles that we have all read : I propose to baptise him, formally, as a journalist."

" A crown of roses, to mark his double triumph! " cried Bixiou, with a glance at Coralie.

Coralie beckoned to Bérénice. The portly maid soon came back with some boxes of old artificial flowers from the actress's dressing-room, and with these the more tipsy members of the party bedecked themselves, while a crown of roses was woven. The high priest sprinkled a few drops of champagne on Lucien's beautiful golden hair and pronounced with delicious gravity these sacramental words:

" In the name of the Inland Revenue, the Caution Money and the Fine, I baptise thee journalist. May thy articles weigh lightly upon thee! "

" And no deductions for blanks! " Merlin put in.

At this moment Lucien noticed the sad faces of Michel Chrestien, Joseph Bridau and Fulgence Ridal,who took their hats and went out, amid a burst of ironical cheering.

" Very odd Christians, these! " said Merlin.

" Fulgence used to be a good fellow," said Lousteau, " but the other have corrupted his morals."

" Who ? " asked Claude Vignon.

" Some very serious-minded young men who meet at a philosophical-religious society in the Rue des Quatre-Vents, where they rack their brains over the meaning of human life," said Blondet.

" Oh Lord! "

" They are trying to find out whether it goes round in a circle," Blondet went on, " or if it progresses. They have been at great pains to decide between the circle and the straight line ; the Biblical triangle seemed to them nonsense, but now some prophet or other has pronounced in favour of the spiral."

" Men might meet to invent more dangerous ideas than that," Lucien exclaimed, attempting to defend his old friends.

" You may think theories of that kind are empty words," said Félicien Vernou, " but the day comes when they are transformed into bullets and the guillotine."

" That hasn't happened yet," said Bixiou. " They are still trying to discover the purposes of Providence behind the invention of champagne, the humanitarian significance of trousers, and the little monster who makes the world go round. They pick up fallen great men like Vico, Saint-Simon, and Fourier. I am very much afraid that they will turn the head of my poor friend, Joseph Bridau."

" My old school-friend Bianchon gives me the cold shoulder," said Lousteau, " and it is all their doing."

" Do they give lessons in intellectual gymnastics and orthopedics ? " Merlin inquired.

" More than likely," replied Finot, " if Bianchon has a hand in their theories."

" All the same," said Lousteau, " he will be a great physician one day."

" Isn't d'Arthez their visible head ? " Nathan asked. " That little fellow who is going to make a meal of all of us ? "

" He is a genius ! " cried Lucien.

" I would rather have a glass of sherry ! " said Vignon with a smile.

At this point everyone began to explain his character for the benefit of whoever was sitting next to him. When intelligent men reach the stage of feeling that it is necessary to explain themselves, and give away the key to their hearts, it is a sure sign that the wine has gone to their heads. An hour later all the guests, who by that time had become the best friends in the world, were all telling one another what great men they were, first-rate men, men who held the future in their hands. Lucien, as host, had managed to remain tolerably clear-headed ; he listened to all this sophistry and was impressed. His demoralisation was complete.

" My children," said Finot, " the Liberal party is compelled to start up a controversy, because at the present moment there is nothing to be said against the Government, and that puts the Opposition in a very awkward situation, as you will understand. Which of you would like to write a pamphlet demanding the restitution of the rights of primogeniture, to raise an outcry against the secret designs of the Court ? It will be well paid."

"A crown of roses, to mark his double triumph!"

" I will," said Hector Merlin ; " those are my own views."

" Your party will complain that you are compromising them," Finot retorted. " Félicien, you must write the pamphlet, Dauriat will publish it, and we will all keep the secret."

" How much shall I be paid ? "

" Six hundred francs. You can sign it ' Count C——' "

" Good enough," said Vernou.

" So you are bringing the *canard* into politics ? " said Lousteau.

" It is simply the Chabot case transposed into the realm of ideas," said Finot. " You attribute intentions to the Government in order to arouse public opinion against them."

" It always seems to me a most astonishing thing," said Claude Vignon, " that the Government leaves the dissemination of ideas in the hands of such a pack of scoundrels as ourselves."

" If the Ministry commits the blunder of coming down into the arena," said Finot, " we can beat them hands down ; if they persist, we can poison the issue and turn the public against them. The press risks nothing, and the authorities have always everything to lose."

" France will be paralysed," said Claude Vignon, " until the day that newspapers are made illegal. You are growing more powerful every day," he said to Finot ; " you will be the new Jesuits, but without the faith, the fixed policy, the discipline, or the unity."

They went back to the card-tables ; and soon the light of dawn made the candles grow pale.

" Your friends from the Rue des Quatre-Vents looked as sad as criminals condemned to death," Coralie said to her lover.

" They were the judges, not the criminals," the poet replied.

" Judges are more amusing than that," said Coralie.

During the next month Lucien's time was taken up with suppers, dinners, lunches, and evening parties, and he was swept by an irresistible current into a whirl of pleasures and easy work. He no longer looked ahead. The power of maintaining a fixed purpose in the midst of the distractions of life is the mark of a strong will—a quality that poets, weak characters, and those who live a purely spiritual life, can never imitate. Like most journalists, Lucien lived from one day to the next, spending money as quickly as he earned it, not giving a thought to those days of reckoning that recur with such cruel regularity in the Bohemian life of Paris.

In dress and appearance he rivalled the most celebrated dandies of the day. Coralie, like all devoted worshippers, loved to adorn her idol; she ruined herself in order to give her beloved poet all those elegant accessories that he had so much coveted on the occasion of his first walk in the Tuileries. Lucien now had beautiful walking-sticks, a charming monocle, diamond studs, rings for his morning cravats, signet rings, and waistcoats marvellous to behold, in every colour to match his various suits. He soon became an acknowledged dandy. On the day when he accepted the German diplomat's invitation, his metamorphosis created an unspoken envy among the young men present on that occasion, men who were leaders in the world of fashion, like de Marsay, Vandenesse, Ajuda-Pinto, Maxime de Trailles, Rastignac, the Duke de Maufrigneuse, Beaudenord, Manerville, and the rest. Men of fashion are just as jealous of one another as woman are. Lucien was seated between the Countess Montcornet and the Marquise d'Espard, the guests of honour at the dinner, and both ladies overwhelmed him with flatteries.

"But why have you left society," the Marquise asked him, "when you would have been so well received, and been such a success? I have a quarrel with you—you were going to come and see me, and I am still waiting for your visit! I saw you the other day at the Opéra, and you did not deign to pay me a visit or take any notice of me!"

"Your cousin, madame, dismissed me so unmistakably. . . ."

"You do not understand women!" said the Marquise, interrupting Lucien. "You have wounded the most angelic heart, the noblest nature that I know. You have no idea of all the things that Louise wanted to do for you, and how cleverly she had planned it all! And she would have succeeded"—she went on in answer to Lucien's unspoken incredulity. "Her husband has died, as he was bound to die sooner or later, from an attack of indigestion—he was bound to leave her free in the end. You don't imagine that she would have liked to be Madame Chardon? The title of Countess de Rubempré would have been worth some trouble. Love, don't you see, is a great vanity that must correspond, especially in marriage, with all the other vanities. I might love you to distraction, that is to say enough to marry you, but I should find it very hard to be called Mme Chardon. You can see that! And now that you have seen the difficulties of Paris life, you can understand all the roundabout ways that one has to take to reach one's end ; and you must admit that, considering that you were unknown and had no fortune, Louise was aspiring to an almost impossible favour, and that she was bound to proceed with great caution. You are very brilliant ; but when we are in love we are cleverer than the cleverest man. My cousin wanted to make use of that ridiculous Châtelet. . . . I am indebted to you for a great deal of amusement," she said, changing the subject ; " your articles against him have made me laugh so much."

Lucien no longer knew what to think. He had been initiated into the treachery and perfidies of journalism, but those of the world were unknown to him ; and so, for all his perspicacity, there were some hard lessons in store for him.

" You surprise me," said the poet, all his curiosity aroused ; " I thought that the Heron was under your protection."

" But, in society, one is obliged to be polite to one's worst enemies," she said, " to seem to be amused by bores, and often to appear to sacrifice one's friends in order to help them. You are still a novice, I see! Come, now, you want to write books, and you don't know the current deceptions of present-day society ? If my cousin seemed to be giving you up for the Heron, it was for no othe reason than to make use of his influence on your behalf—he stands very well with the present Ministry, you know, and we have pointed out to him that, up to a point, your attacks are to his advantage—because we want you to make it up one of these days. They have compensated Châtelet for your persecutions, because, as des Lupeaulx said to the Minister, ' so long as the newspapers are ridiculing Châtelet, they will leave the Ministry alone '."

" M. Blondet tells me that I may hope to have the pleasure of seeing you at my house," said the Marquise de Montcornet during the pause that followed—for the Marquise had left Lucien to his own reflections. " You will meet several artists there, and

He soon became an acknowledged dandy

writers, and a lady who is longing to meet you—Mlle des Touches, who has a talent that is rare among our sex, and who will certainly ask you to go and see her. Mlle des Touches—Camille Maupin, if you prefer it—has one of the most interesting salons in Paris. She is immensely rich; she has heard that you are as handsome as you are brilliant, and she is dying to meet you."

Lucien could only stammer out incoherent thanks and glance enviously at Blondet. There is as much difference between a woman of breeding, like the Countess de Montcornet, and a Coralie, as between Coralie and a common prostitute. This countess, young, beautiful, and intelligent, was remarkable for that extreme fairness of northern women; her mother was the Princess Sherbellof, and so the Minister, before dinner, had treated her with marked attention. The Marquise was now toying disdainfully with a chicken-wing.

"Poor darling Louise," she resumed, "was so fond of you! She confided to me the great future that she was planning for you; she could have borne a great deal, but she was terribly hurt by the scornful way in which you returned her letters! We can endure cruelty—those who hurt us must still have some faith in us—but not indifference! Indifference is like the ice-cap, it freezes all life. Come now, you must admit that you have lost a wonderful treasure through your own fault. Why did you break with her? Even if you disdained her, you still had your way to make, your name to be restored. Louise thought of all that."

"Why did she never send me a word?" said Lucien.

"Well, as a matter of fact it was I who advised her not to take you into her confidence. Between ourselves, seeing that you were not accustomed to the world, I was afraid; I was afraid on account of your inexperience; your rash enthusiasm might have wrecked, or at all events interfered with, her schemes and our carefully laid plans. Can you remember what you were like? You must admit, if you could see your old self today, that you would have done the same. You are a different person. That was our one mistake. But would one find one man in a thousand as brilliant as yourself with so much social sense? I never dreamed that you would prove the astonishing exception. You underwent such a rapid metamorphosis, and fell so easily into Paris ways, that when I saw you in the Bois de Boulogne a month ago I did not recognise you."

Lucien listened to the great lady with inexpressible pleasure. She spoke her flattering phrases with such a confiding, childish, roguish air; she seemed so deeply interested in him that he began to believe that another miracle was about to happen, like that on his first night at the Panorama-Dramatique. Ever since that happy evening the world had smiled on him, and be believed that his youth possessed a kind of talismanic charm. He decided, without committing himself, to sound the Marquise.

"Then what were those plans that have now become chimeras?"

"Louise wanted to obtain a patent of nobility from the King, allowing you to use the name and title of de Rubempré. She wanted to consign Chardon to oblivion. It would have been relatively easy then, but now, of course, your political opinions make it impossible. That success, at the outset, would have been worth a fortune to you. You think these ideas are just idle notions; but you don't know very much of the world yet and we all know that the title of Count is worth something to an elegant and attractive young man. If you announce, at a reception where there are English girls worth millions, or wealthy heiresses, '*M. Chardon*', that is one thing, but '*M. le Comte de Rubempré*' is quite another matter. If he is in debt, a count finds everyone willing to help him, and his good looks are brought out like a diamond in a rich setting. M. Chardon would not even be noticed. We did not invent these ideas, we found them in force everywhere, even among the middle classes. Take that good-looking young man Félix de Vandenesse, he is one of the King's two private secretaries. The King takes an interest in young men of talent.... When that young man came up from the country his luggage was no heavier than yours, and you have a thousand times more talent; but do you belong to a great family? Have you a name? You know des Lupeaulx—his name is very much like yours, he is called Chardin; but he would not part with his little farm of Lupeaulx for a million; he will be Count des Lupeaulx one day, and his grandson may become a Duke, who knows? You have made a false start; and if you go on as you are you are lost.

That is where M. Émile Blondet is wiser than you! He is on a Government newspaper, and he is in the good graces of all the powers that be. He can afford to mix with the Liberals, because he is known to be sound. He is bound to succeed, sooner or later, but he has been wise in his choice of his opinions, and his protectors.

" Your pretty neighbour on your left is a de Troisville, and there are two Peers of the Realm and two Deputies in her family ; she made a wealthy marriage because of her name ; she entertains a great deal ; she has influence, and will shake the political world on behalf of that young man, M. Émile Blondet. What can Coralie do for you ? a few years from now you will be up to your ears in debts and tired of a life of pleasure. You have made a mistake in love, and you are making a mistake in your career. That is what the woman whom you take so much pleasure in wounding said to me the other day at the Opéra. She was deploring the way you are wasting your talent, and your good looks, and she was only thinking of you, not of herself."

" If only I could believe you, madame! " said Lucien.

" What motive could I have for telling lies ? " said the Marquise, annihilating Lucien once more with a glance of cold disdain.

Lucien, thus rebuffed, did not dare to resume the conversation ; the Marquise had taken offence and did not address him again. He was piqued, but he realised that he had been tactless, and made up his mind that he would put it right. He turned towards Mme de Montcornet and talked to her about Blondet, praising that young writer's talents to the skies. This was well received by the Countess who invited him, at a sign from Mme d'Espard, to her next soirée ; she asked him if he would not like to meet Mme de Bargeton again, who would be there, although she was in mourning. It would be quite an informal evening, just a few friends.

" Mme la Marquise tells me that the faults were all on my side," said Lucien. " It is surely for her cousin to decide whether she is prepared to forgive me."

" Stop those ridiculous attacks, of which she is the victim, and which, besides, are compromising her very strongly with a man whom she despises, and you will soon make peace. You thought that she had treated you badly, I hear; but I have seen with my own eyes how sad she was because you had deserted her. Is it really true that she left Angoulême for your sake and in your company?"

Lucien smiled at the Countess, but did not dare to answer her question.

"How did you ever come to doubt a woman who had made such sacrifices for you!—and she is so beautiful and brilliant, besides, she would deserve to be loved whatever she had done. Mme de Bargeton put your career even before her wish to see you. I assure you that women love men more for their talent than for their good looks," she said, with a surreptitious glance at Émile Blondet.

Lucien realised, at the Minister's house, the great difference that exists between the world of high society and the Bohemian world in which he had been living for some time. There was nothing in common between these two kinds of magnificence, not a single point of resemblance. The height and spaciousness of these rooms (it was one of the best houses of the Faubourg Saint-Germain), the antique gilding, the scale of the decorative conceptions, the subdued richness of the furnishings, were all new and strange to him; but we very quickly become accustomed to luxury, and no trace of surprise escaped him. Lucien's expression was as far removed from fatuity and self-assurance as it was from complaisance and servility. The poet had naturally good manners, and had the gift of pleasing those who had no reason to be hostile to him—as had the young men who found occasion for jealousy at his sudden appearance in society, his success, and his good looks.

As they left the table he offered his arm to Mme d'Espard, and she accepted it.

Noticing that the Marquise d'Espard was being so attentive to to Lucien, Rastignac came over and introduced himself as a compatriot, reminding the poet that they had met once before, at Mme de Val-Noble's party. The young patrician seemed eager to make friends with the great man from his own province and asked Lucien if he would lunch with him one day, offering to introduce him to some of the younger set. Lucien accepted this invitation.

" I will ask our friend Blondet," Rastignac added.

The Minister came over and joined the little group made up of the Marquis de Ronquerolles, the Duke de Rhétoré, de Marsay, General de Montriveau, Rastignac, and Lucien.

" Very good," he said to Lucien, with that German heartiness that concealed his redoubtable subtlety. " So you have made peace with Mme d'Espard. She is enchanted with you, and we all know," he said, looking round the group of men, " that she is very difficult to please."

" Yes, but she adores talent," said Rastignac, " and my illustrious compatriot deals in that commodity."

" He will soon realise that he has made a bad bargain," said Blondet quickly ; " he will come over to us, he will be one of us before long."

There was a chorus around Lucien on this theme. The older men let fall a few weighty phrases, in tones of authority ; and the younger men made fun of the Liberal party.

" I am sure he tossed up to decide whether to be Left or Right," remarked Blondet, " but he will choose for himself now."

Lucien laughed aloud, remembering the scene in the Luxembourg Gardens with Lousteau.

" He has put himself under the wing of one Étienne Lousteau," Blondet continued, " a newspaper gangster for whom a column means five francs and whose politics consist of believing that Napoleon will come back, and what seems to me still more far-fetched, in the patriotism of the Deputies of the Left. As a Rubempré, Lucien's sympathies ought to be with the nobility ; as a journalist, he ought to be on the side of authority, or he will never be de Rubempré or a Secretary General either."

The Minister invited Lucien to take a hand at whist ; Lucien had to admit that he could not play—much to everyone's surprise.

" My dear fellow, come to my house early on the day you are coming to eat a very bad lunch there and I will teach you to play whist ; you will bring dishonour on our royal city of Angoulême—you know what M. de Talleyrand said, ' If you don't know how to play whist you are laying up for yourself a desolate old age '."

Des Lupeaulx was announced—a Master of Requests much in favour, who had rendered secret services to the Ministry, a scheming and ambitious man who moved in all circles. He greeted Lucien, whom he had already met at Mme de Val-Noble's house, and in his manner there was an appearance of friendship that quite took Lucien in. On seeing the young journalist there, this man, who made a point of making friends with everyone who might conceivably be of use to him at some time or another, guessed that Lucien would make as great a success in society as he had already done in journalism. He recognised the poet's ambition, and he overwhelmed him with protestations, and expressions of friendship and interest, as if they were old friends. Lucien was easily taken in by his promises and empty phrases. Des Lupeaulx was always at pains to get to know well anyone whom he had reason to fear, or who might prove to be a rival. So that Lucien was well received in the social world. He realised how much he owed to the Duke de Rhétoré, to the German Minister, to Mme d'Espard, to Mme de Montcornet. He went over and spoke to each of these ladies for a moment before taking his leave, and was at his most brilliant, for their benefit.

" What a conceited ass! " des Lupeaulx remarked to the Marquise after Lucien had gone.

" He will be rotten before he is ripe," de Marsay said with a smile. " You must have reason of your own for turning his head like this."

Lucien found Coralie waiting in her carriage in the court ; she had come to fetch him. He was touched by this attention and gave her an account of his evening. To his great surprise, the actress fully approved of the new ideas that were taking shape in Lucien's mind, and strongly urged him to enlist under the Ministerialist banner.

" As a Liberal you can expect nothing but hard knocks. They are always plotting ; they murdered the Duke de Berri. Are they likely to overthrow the Government ? Never! You will never gain anything through them ; whereas, on the other side, you will become Count de Rubempré. You can render them services, and be made a Peer of France, and marry a rich woman. Be an Ultra. Besides, the best people are all Ministerialists," she added. This, for Coralie, was the last word on all subjects. " I dined with the Val-Noble and she told me that Théodore Gaillard was definitely going to start his little Royalist newspaper, *Le Réveil*, to reply to your attacks and those in the *Miroir*. According to them, de Villèle's party will be in office before the year is out. Try to take advantage of the change by joining them while they are still obscure ; but don't say a word to Étienne or your other friends, who are quite capable of doing you a bad turn."

A week later Lucien went to Mme de Montcornet's house, and there he was deeply moved at seeing again the woman whom he had loved so much and had afterwards wounded to the heart with a jest. Louise, too, had been transformed! She had become what she would have been long ago but for her exile in the country, a great lady. There was a grace and an elegance in her mourning that suggested a happy widowhood. Lucien fancied that this coquetry was to some extent meant for him, nor was he mistaken ; but, like an ogre, he had tasted human flesh—beautiful, youthful flesh—and all that evening he remained undecided between the beautiful, amorous, voluptuous Coralie, and the dry, haughty, cruel Louise. He could not make up his mind to sacrifice the actress to the great lady. Mme de Bargeton, whose old love for Lucien had revived, on seeing him so brilliant and so handsome, waited all the evening for that sacrifice ; but for all her insinuating words, her display of charm, he gave her nothing for her pains, and she left the room burning with an irrevocable desire for revenge.

" Well, dear Lucien," she began, with a kindness full of generosity and Parisian grace, " you were to have been my pride, and instead I have been your first victim. But I have forgiven you, dear child, because I fancied that there must be some trace of love left in such a revenge."

With those words, and the queenly air with which they were spoken, Mme de Bargeton regained her ascendency. Lucien, who had thought himself a thousand times in the right, felt himself utterly in the wrong. There was no mention either of the terrible farewell letter with which he had broken with her, nor of the reasons

Louise, too, had been transformed!

for that break. Women of the best society have a wonderful gift of making their faults seem mere trifles. They know how to wipe out everything with a smile, or a light phrase, or a question of feigned surprise. They remember nothing; they have an explanation for everything, they express astonishment, they are incredulous, they explain, amplify, and quarrel with you, and in the end, they have wiped out their fault like a stain by the application of a little soap and water; you know them to be black, and in a moment, behold, they are white and innocent. As for you, you are very lucky if you do not find that you have been guilty of some irreparable crime!

In a moment, old illusions regained their power over Lucien and Louise, and they talked like friends, as before; but Lucien, intoxicated with gratified vanity, intoxicated by Coralie, who, it must be said, made life very easy for him, could not bring himself, when Louise, after an eloquent pause, asked him with a sigh, " Are you happy? " to give a direct answer. A melancholy " No " would have made his fortune. But he decided to be clever and to justify his relationship with Coralie. He loved her for herself, he said, and went on to expatiate on their relationship with all the imbecility of a man in love. Mme de Bargeton bit her lip. There was no more to be said.

Mme d'Espard came over and joined her cousin, Mme de Montcornet with her. Lucien saw himself as the hero, so to speak, of the evening; he was the centre of attention, flattered, and made much of by the three ladies, who wove around him the webs of their subtle arts. His success in this exalted and brilliant world was no less than it had been in journalism. The beautiful Mlle des Touches, famous under the pseudonym of Camille Maupin, to whom Mme d'Espard and Mme de Bargeton introduced him, invited him to dinner on one of her Wednesday evenings, and seemed charmed by his good looks, so justly famous. Lucien set out to prove that his brilliance was even greater than his beauty. Mlle des Touches expressed her admiration with that mock-naïveté and that charming gush of superficial friendship that takes in anyone who does not know Paris life inside out, and who has never encountered that thirst for novelty that is bred by the habit of wanting to be perpetually amused.

"If she liked me as much as I like her," Lucien confided to Rastignac and de Marsay, "it would be a rapid romance. . . ."

"You are both much too good at writing romances ever to want to act one," said Rastignac. "Can writers ever fall in love with each other? There would always come a moment when they would say clever cutting things to one another."

"Very nice for you," said de Marsay with a laugh. "That charming girl is thirty, to be sure; but she is worth nearly eighty thousand francs a year. She is adorably capricious, and her beauty is of the kind that will not age quickly. Coralie is a little fool, my dear fellow. Good enough for a start; no good-looking young man ought to be without a mistress, but if you don't succeed in making a good match in society you will get bored with your actress sooner or later. Well, why not, my dear boy—go and cut out Conti, who is just going to sing with Camille Maupin. From time immemorial poetry has taken precedence over music."

But when Lucien heard Mlle des Touches singing with Conti his hopes faded.

"Conti sings too well," he remarked to des Lupeaulx.

Lucien rejoined Mme de Bargeton, who led him into the drawing-room where the Marquise d'Espard was sitting.

"Well, now, will you not interest yourself in him?" Mme de Bargeton asked her cousin.

"First of all," the Marquise replied in tones of honeyed insolence, "let M. Chardon place himself in a position in which his patrons will not be compromised. If he wants to obtain permission to exchange his father's unfortunate name for that of his mother, surely the least he can do is to belong to our party?"

"I can arrange that within two months," said Lucien.

"In that case," said the Marquise, "I will speak to my father and my uncle, who are attached to the Palace, and they will mention you to the Chancellor."

The Diplomat and these two women had observed where Lucien's weak spot lay. The poet, under the spell of all this aristocratic splendour, suffered inexpressible mortification on hearing himself addressed as Chardon; for every man who entered these apartments bore a high-sounding name, set off with a brilliant title. This humiliation he experienced everywhere he went during the next few days. And what was more, he experienced the most disagreeable sensation when he had to descend once again to his professional duties, after an evening spent in high society, where he appeared in state in Coralie's coach and attended by Coralie's servants. He took riding lessons in order to canter beside the carriages of Mme d'Espard, Mlle des Touches, and Countess Montcornet, a privilege he had so greatly envied during his early days in Paris. Finot was delighted to obtain for his right-hand man a press pass to the Opéra, and Lucien wasted many evenings there; and from this time he belonged to the little world of the smart set of the day.

The poet returned Rastignac's invitation and gave a splendid lunch party for that gentleman and his friends, but he made the fatal mistake of giving it at Coralie's flat. He was too young, too much a poet, and too guileless to be aware of certain fine shades of social convention; and how could a young actress, a good-hearted girl, but without any education, be expected to know such things? It seemed abundantly clear to these young men, who were by no means well disposed towards him, that there was a collusion of interests between Lucien and the actress; they all openly condemned, but secretly envied his relationship with Coralie. The one who that very evening said the cruellest things on that subject was Rastignac, although he himself had kept himself afloat in the world by similar means; but he had kept up appearances so well that he was able to treat gossip as slander.

Lucien had quickly learned whist, and gambling became a passion with him. Coralie, far from discouraging Lucien, encouraged all his dissipations with the blind devotion that is the mark of that absolute passion that sees only the present, and which is prepared to sacrifice everything, even the future, to the pleasure of the moment. Besides, she feared rivals. True love is in many ways like childhood; it has the same heedless, careless dissipation of energies and the child's ready laughter and ready tears.

At that time there flourished a circle of young men, some rich, others poor, all equally idle, known as *viveurs*—and indeed their lives were carefree to a degree ; they ate intrepidly, drank still more intrepidly. They were all wildly extravagant and fond of playing crude practical jokes. They were not merely foolish, they were mad; they drew back before no impossibility, and gloried in their misdeeds—which, however, they kept within certain limits ; and there was so much wit and originality in their escapades that it was impossible not to forgive them.

The Restoration had condemned its young men to the idleness of helots, and this fashion was symptomatic. There was so much wasted energy and ability allowed to go to seed among the youth of France that young men, with no outlet for their energies, threw themselves not only into journalism and conspiracies, literature and the arts, but into the most extravagant excesses and dissipations. Those who were by nature cut out to be men of energy and hard work wanted power and pleasure. Those with a natural love of the arts wanted money ; and the idle wanted sensation ; they all wanted something to do, and the political situation gave them no opening.

Nearly all the *viveurs* were men of outstanding abilities ; some of them were ruined by this enervating life, others held out against it. The most notorious of the *viveurs* as well as the most intelligent was Rastignac, who in the end, through de Marsay's influence, embarked upon a serious and distinguished career. The practical jokes played by these young men have become so famous that they have provided material for more than one vaudeville programme. Blondet introduced Lucien into this dissolute set, and in it he shone, along with Bixiou, as one of the most daring and indefatigable wits of the day. So that all through that winter Lucien's life was one long intoxication, broken only by intervals of the easy work of journalism ; he went on with his series of Paris sketches, and from time to time made an enormous effort and produced a few fine pages of more serious criticism. But serious work was the exception, and the poet only resorted to it when it was absolutely necessary ; lunches, dinners, parties, evenings in society, and gambling, took up most of his time, and Coralie devoured the rest. Lucien did not allow himself to think of the future. And, besides, he saw all his so-called friends behaving in exactly the same way, meeting their expenses by writing highly paid puffs for publishers, and on the proceeds of articles commissioned by speculators, spending as they earned, and giving no thought to the morrow. Lucien had been admitted into the ranks of literary journalism on terms of equality, and he now began to realise that enormous difficulties would be in his way if he were to attempt to rise higher; everyone was willing to accept him as an equal, but no one wanted him as a superior. So that he insensibly renounced his ideas of literary glory and began to think that it would be easier to make his fortune in politics.

"Intrigue arouses less opposition than talent; its underground methods pass unnoticed," Châtelet remarked to him one day (for he and Lucien had made friends again). "Intrigue, therefore, has the advantage over talent—it makes something out of nothing; whereas, for the most part, the immense resources of talent only serve to bring misfortunes upon their possessor."

So although the work he intended to do was never done, Lucien still pursued his main purpose, in the course of that life, in which each morning dawned upon the heels of the previous night's dissipation. But he was assiduous in the social world, he paid his court to Mme de Bargeton, the Marquise d'Espard, and Countess Montcornet, and never missed one of Mlle des Touches' parties; he called on these great ladies on his way to a party, or after some dinner given by an author or a publisher; he left their drawing-rooms to go on to a supper-party, the fruit of some wager; the demands of Paris conversation, and gambling, absorbed the dwindling stock of ideas and energy left him by his dissipations.

The poet was no longer sufficiently clear-headed, no longer had the lucidity of mind to notice what was going on around him, and to use that extreme tact that social climbers need to employ at every moment; he did not realise how again and again Mme de Bargeton turned to him, only to withdraw with wounded feelings; how she alternately forgave him, and again condemned him. Châtelet saw that his rival still had a chance. He made friends with Lucien, in order to encourage him in the dissipations that wasted his energies. Rastignac, jealous of his compatriot, and realising, besides, that the Baron would be a more reliable and useful ally than Lucien, took up the Baron's cause. So, a few days after the meeting between the Petrarch of Angoulême and his Laura, Rastignac had made peace between the poet and the old beau of the Empire, at a magnificent supper at the Rocher de Cancale.

Lucien never returned home before morning or rose earlier than midday ; he could not resist Coralie's domestic love, always beside him. So little by little his character was undermined by idleness that rendered him day by day more indifferent to the good resolutions he made in those moments when he saw his position in its true light. His will became slack and no longer responded even to the strong pressure of necessity.

At first Coralie had been delighted to see Lucien enjoying himself, and encouraged him, for she thought that these dissipations would bind her lover to her, that luxurious habits would make her necessary to him ; but as time went on, the gentle, tender Coralie summoned up courage to say to her lover that he must not neglect his work altogether, and more than once she had to remind him that he had earned very little that month. Lover and mistress both ran up debts at an alarming rate. The fifteen hundred francs that remained from the price of the *Marguerites* and the first five hundred francs of Lucien's earnings were soon gone. In three months he only earned a thousand francs by writing articles, and yet he thought he had been working tremendously hard. But Lucien had already adopted the *viveur's* comforting theory of debts. Debts are becoming to a young man of twenty-five ; later, they are inexcusable. It is noticeable that some characters, genuinely poetic, but lacking in will-power, give themselves up to feeling, in order to reproduce their feelings in images. Such men are completely wanting in that moral sense that ought to accompany the power of observation. Poets are more apt to receive sensations themselves than to enter into the experiences of others, or to study the mechanism of sensation. And so Lucien never inquired after the *viveurs* who disappeared from time to time ; he did not look into the futures of these pretended friends of his, some of whom were heirs to large estates, or had certain prospects, others talents already recognised, and others again an intrepid faith in their destiny, or the deliberate intention of circumventing the law. Lucien believed in his future, and put his faith in certain profound sayings of Blondet's —that everything works out in the end; that those who have nothing have nothing to lose; that we can only lose the fortune we aim at; that if you keep in the swim it will take you somewhere; and that an intelligent man with a footing in the world can make a fortune any time he wants to.

That winter, taken up by so many pleasures, was spent by Théodore Gaillard and Hector Merlin in finding the necessary capital for starting the *Réveil*, whose first number did not appear until March 1822. The matter was arranged in Mme du Val-Noble's flat. That elegant and intelligent courtesan, who used to say as she showed friends her magnificent rooms, "My house comes straight from the Arabian Nights!"—had a certain amount of influence over the financiers, writers, and nobility of the Royalist party. They used to meet in her drawing-room to discuss matters that could not well be discussed elsewhere. The assistant editorship of the *Réveil* had been promised to Hector Merlin, and he was sure to take on Lucien—who had become his particular friend—as his right-hand man; Lucien had also been promised a page in one of the Ministerialist dailies. Lucien was secretly preparing for this change of front all through that winter of dissipations. Child that he was, he fancied himself a deep politician, because he had kept his forthcoming transformation a complete secret. He was counting on Ministerial largesse to settle his debts and to dissipate Coralie's secret worries.

The actress, always smiling, concealed her anxiety; but Bérénice, with greater boldness, told Lucien how things stood. Like all poets, this budding great man was moved, for the moment, by the tale of disaster, and resolved to work; but he forgot his resolution, and drowned this fleeting worry in renewed dissipations. And the moment Coralie saw clouds on her lover's brow, she scolded Bérénice and told her poet that everything was going to be all right.

Mme d'Espard and Mme de Bargeton were waiting for Lucien's change of front before asking the Ministry, through Châtelet, so they told him, for the permission to change his name, upon which he had set his heart. Lucien proposed to dedicate the *Marguerites* to the Marquise d'Espard, who seemed enchanted at an honour that has become rare since authors have become powerful. When Lucien called on Dauriat one evening to ask how his book was getting on, the publisher gave him excellent reasons for holding back its publication for the moment. Dauriat had this and that project in hand, that was taking up his time, a new volume by de Canalis was out, and it would be better if the *Marguerites* did not appear at the same time, M. de Lamartine's second series of *Méditations* were in the press, and two important volumes ought not to appear together; the author must trust his publisher's knowledge of the book-market.

But for all that, Lucien's difficulties became so pressing that he had recourse to Finot, who gave him an advance on his articles. At supper one evening the poet-journalist confided his situation to his friends the *viveurs*, but they drowned his scruples in champagne, iced with wit. Debts! First-rate men always had debts! Debts represented the satisfaction of needs, the gratification of vices! No one would ever get on unless urged by the sharp goad of necessity.

" The pawn-brokers owe a lot to great men! " Blondet declared.

" If you want everything, you must owe for everything," said Bixiou.

" On the contrary, to owe for everything means that you have had everything! " retorted des Lupeaulx.

The *viveurs* found no difficulty in proving to our simple Lucien that debts are the golden spurs with which he could urge on the horses harnessed to his chariot of fortune. And of course they brought out the old story of Caesar's debt of forty millions, and Frederic II whose father only allowed him a ducat a month—the corrupting examples of the vices of famous men, but no mention of their indomitable courage, or the greatness of their projects. At last Coralie's carriage, horses, and furniture were seized by various creditors for sums amounting to a total of four thousand francs. When Lucien went round to Lousteau to ask him to return the thousand francs that he had borrowed, Lousteau showed him some pieces of stamped paper which proved that Florine was in much the same situation as Coralie ; but Lousteau, out of gratitude, offered to help him to find a publisher for *An Archer of Charles IX*.

"How did Florine get into this situation ?" Lucien asked.

"The Matifat took fright," Lousteau told him, "we have lost him ; but if Florine will agree, he shall pay dearly for his betrayal! I will tell you all about it."

Three days after Lucien's unsuccessful appeal to Lousteau, the two lovers were lunching sadly beside the fire in their pretty bedroom, Bérénice had cooked them some eggs over the fire, for the cook, the coachman, and the other servants had left. They could not sell the furniture, which was under distraint. There was not a single object of any intrinsic value left in the flat, nothing made of gold or silver ; but instead, a very instructive little octavo volume of pawn-tickets. Bérénice had kept back enough cutlery for two. The little newspaper was of some small use to Lucien and Coralie, for the tailor, the dressmaker and the milliner were all afraid to give offence to a journalist in a position to cry down their establishment. Lousteau burst in on them half-way through breakfast.

"Hurrah!" he cried. "Long live *An Archer of Charles IX*! I have sold a hundred francs' worth of books, children ; we'll go shares!"

He handed Coralie fifty francs, and sent Bérénice off in search of a more substantial lunch.

"Well, Hector Merlin and I were at a publisher's dinner, and we prepared the way for selling your book by a few tactful insinuations. Dauriat has made you an offer, but he is haggling over the price ; he does not want to give more than four thousand francs for an edition of two thousand, and you are asking for six thousand francs. We have made you out to be twice as great as Walter Scott! Yes, you have it in you to write novels the like of which have never been seen! It is not a matter of selling a book, but big business! You are not merely the author of one more or less ingenious novel, you are working on a series. That word *series* works wonders! So don't forget, you are planning to write *La Grande Mademoiselle, or France in the Days of Louis XIV* ; *Cotillon I, or The Early Days of Louis XV* ; *The Queen and the Cardinal, or Paris under the Fronde* ; *A Son of the Concini*, or *An Intrigue of Richelieu*! These novels will be announced on the cover. That is what we call giving success a boost on the dust-jacket! You advertise books on the cover until they become well-known, and then you are more famous for the books you have not written than for those you have! 'In Preparation' is the great hypothetical phrase of literature! Now, cheer up! Here comes some champagne. And believe me, Lucien, our men opened their eyes as wide as saucers—have you any saucers left, by the way?"

"The bailiffs have taken them," said Coralie.

"I see; well, to continue: the publishers will believe in all your manuscripts if you show them only one. Publishers always ask to see the manuscript, and they make a great show of reading it. Let them keep up their pretences—they never read them; otherwise they would never publish the rubbish one sees! Hector and I dropped a hint that for five thousand francs you might consider two editions of three thousand copies. Give me the manuscript of the *Archer*, and the day after tomorrow we will have breakfast with the publishers and put the deal across."

"Who is the publisher?" Lucien asked.

"Two partners, called Fendant and Cavalier, good chaps, quite straightforward in business. One of them was with Vidal and Porchon, and the other used to be the cleverest traveller in books on the Quai des Augustins. They have been established for just over a year. They lost a little at first on some English translations, and now my customers want to exploit the native product. There is a rumour that these two dealers in spoilt paper are not risking any of their own capital, but I don't suppose it matters to you whether the money they pay you is their own or somebody else's."

Two days later, the two journalists were duly invited to breakfast in the Rue Serpente, in Lucien's old quarter, where Lousteau still kept his room in the Rue de la Harpe; Lucien went to call for his friend there, and found it in the same condition as it had been on the evening of his introduction into the literary world. He was no longer surprised; for his education had initiated him into the vicissitudes of the life of journalists; he knew all about it now. The great man from the provinces had received and gambled away the proceeds of more than one article, and lost also the desire to write ; he had filled many a column according to the ingenious procedures that Lousteau had described to him as they walked down the Rue de la Harpe to the Palais-Royal. He had come to depend on Barbet and Braulard, and traded in review copies and theatre tickets ; and, in the end, he no longer drew back from writing up any book, or attacking it, as circumstances required. And at this very moment he was taking a perverse pleasure in getting as much as he could out of Lousteau before turning his back on the Liberals ; he would be able to attack them all the better because he had known them so well. Lousteau, on his part, was being paid five hundred francs cash down by Fendant and Cavalier—his so-called commission—for having procured this future Scott for the two publishers in search of a French Sir Walter.

Fendant and Cavalier's was one of those publishing houses founded without capital of any kind, that were springing up in great numbers at that time, and that will continue to spring up as long as paper manufacturers and printers give credit to the publishing trade for terms long enough to enable them to venture upon seven or eight of those gambles called publications. Then, as now, authors were paid in cheques post-dated at six, nine, or twelve months, a form of payment based on the nature of the sales, for in the book trade itself accounts are settled by cheques made out at still longer terms. Paper manufacturers and printers are paid in the same way, so that publishers have anything from twelve to twenty works at their disposal, gratis, for a whole year. Supposing that only two or three succeed, the profits on those that sell covers the losses on those that do not, and the publishers pay their way by grafting, as it were, one book on another. If these ventures all turn out badly, or if, by some misfortune, they find themselves burdened with good books that will only sell when a taste for them has been created, and a serious public has come to appreciate them ; or if the depreciation in value on his books becomes too great, then the mushroom publisher calmly closes his business, without another thought, for he was prepared in advance for this possibility.

All the odds, therefore, are in their favour; they are risking other people's money, not their own, on the gaming-tables of business speculation.

Fendant and Cavalier were in this position. Cavalier brought to the business his experience of the trade, Fendant his industry. Their joint capital consisted of a few thousand francs, scraped together by their mistresses out of their savings. Out of this, they paid one another liberal allowances for expenses, which they laid out scrupulously on dinners for journalists and authors, and tickets for the theatres where, they said, they made useful contacts. This shady pair passed for clever business men; but Fendant was up to more tricks than Cavalier. True to his name, Cavalier travelled for the firm, and Fendant looked after the Paris end of the business. This partnership was, like any other partnership in the publishing trade, a duel.

The partners had an office on the ground floor of one of the old houses in the Rue Serpente, hidden away behind what had once been great drawing-rooms, now converted into business premises. They had published a number of novels already, like *La Tour du Nord*, *Le Marchand de Bénarès*, *La Fontaine du Sepulcre*, *Tekeli*, translations of the novels of Galt, an English author who had not proved popular in France. The success of Walter Scott had made such an impression in the publishing world that publishers all had their eyes on England and were all busy, like true Normans, planning an English conquest. They prospected for Walter Scotts just as later prospectors went on expeditions in search of asphalt in desert regions, or bitumen in marshes, or speculated in railway shares. One of the greatest fallacies of the Paris business world is to imagine that success ever comes by doing the same thing a second time; success goes not by analogies but by contraries. In Paris, above all, success kills success. And so, on the title-page of *Strelitz, or Russia a Hundred Years Ago*, Fendant and Cavalier boldly printed, in large letters, "in the style of Walter Scott". Fendant and Cavalier were badly in need of a success; a good book might float their sunken merchandise, and they were tempted by the prospect of articles in the newspapers, on which sales were so largely dependent at that time; rarely indeed is a book bought on its merits—nearly always it is bought for quite other reasons. Fendant and Cavalier knew that Lucien was a journalist, and saw his book as a manufactured commodity whose rapid sales would tide them over a monthly settlement.

The journalists found the partners in their office, the contract already made out, and the cheque signed. This promptness astonished Lucien. Fendant was a little thin man with a sinister face. He looked like a Tartar, with his broad narrow forehead, squat nose, tight lips, and his restless little black eyes. His worried expression, harsh complexion, and his voice that sounded like a cracked bell, in fact his whole appearance, plainly declared him to be a consummate rascal; but he made up for these shortcomings by the honeyed tones of his conversation. Cavalier was a stout individual who looked more like a cabby than a publisher; he had the fairish hair, red face, heavy build, and ready tongue of the commercial traveller of all times.

" There is nothing to discuss," said Fendant, addressing Lucien and Lousteau. " I have read the work; it is very literary, just the sort of thing we want. I have sent the manuscript to the printers already, and we have made out the contract on the terms we agreed upon; our terms are always the same—the cheques fall due in six, nine, and twelve months respectively; you won't have any difficulty in cashing them, and we will refund you the discount. We reserve the right to give the book another title. We don't like *An Archer of Charles IX*, it does not stimulate the reader's interest. There are too many kings called Charles, and there were so many archers in the Middle Ages! Now if you were to say *A Soldier of Napoleon*! but *An Archer of Charles IX*!—Cavalier would have to give lessons in history before he could sell a single copy in the provinces."

" If you knew the sort of people we have to deal with! " said Cavalier.

" *Saint-Bartholomew* would go down better," Fendant suggested.

" *Catherine de Medici*, or *France under Charles IX* would sound more like Walter Scott," said Cavalier.

" We can settle it when the book is printed," said Fendant.

" I don't mind so long as I approve of the title," said Lucien.

Lucien read through the contract, signed it in duplicate, and put the cheques in his pocket with unutterable satisfaction. Then all four went upstairs to Fendant's flat, where they ate that vulgarest of all lunches—oysters, beefsteaks and kidneys, with champagne and Brie cheese; but these dishes were accompanied by exquisite wines, for Cavalier knew a man who travelled in wines. Just as they were sitting down to lunch the printer to whom the novel had been sent came in, to Lucien's surprise, with the first two proof-sheets of his book.

" We want to get on with the job quickly," Fendant explained to Lucien; " we are relying on your book, and we are pretty desperately in need of a success."

The lunch began at noon and went on until five.

" Where shall we get cash for these things ? " said Lucien.

" Let us go and see Barbet."

The two friends, a little heated and flushed with wine, set off in the direction of the Quai des Augustins.

" Coralie could hardly believe it when she heard of Florine's loss," said Lucien ; " Florine only told her about it yesterday. She blamed it on you, and seemed so bitter about it that she even talked of leaving you."

" It is true," said Lousteau ; and, throwing caution to the winds, he opened his heart to Lucien. " My dear friend—because you are my friend—you, Lucien, lent me a thousand francs, and you have only once asked me to return it—beware of gambling! If I had never touched a card, I should have been a happy man today. I am in debt all round. The bailiffs are on my tracks at this very moment ; and I have to double several dangerous capes every time I go to the Palais-Royal.

In the language of the smart set " doubling a cape " in Paris means either to go a long way round to dodge a creditor, or to keep out of his vicinity. Lucien, who was keeping away from certain streets himself, knew the manœuvre, but had not heard its name before.

"Do you owe a lot then?"

"A mere trifle!" said Lousteau. "A thousand crowns would put me straight. I have decided to go steady and to give up play, and I have even been doing a little blackmail to tide me over."

"What is blackmail?" Lucien asked. The word was new to him.

"It is an invention of the English press, recently imported into France. Blackmailers are individuals with some sort of influence with the press—never an owner or editor, they don't mix themselves up in such things—they have their Giroudeaus and Philippe Bridaus. These gangsters ask for an interview with some personage who for one reason or another is anxious to avoid publicity. There are plenty of people with sins, more or less original, on their consciences. There are any number of fortunes in Paris that have been made by means that will not bear looking into, often by crime, and that would make very good stories—like the one about Fouché's police encircling the spies of the Prefect of Police, who, not having been let into the secret of the forging of false English bank-notes, were just about to seize the clandestine printing-press that was under the Minister's protection; then there was the story of Prince Galathione's diamonds, and the Maubreuil case, the affair of the Pombreton succession, and so on. The blackmailer manages to get hold of some piece of evidence, some important document, and he goes to see the man that made the money. If the individual who is compromised does not hand over a certain sum, the blackmailer paints a picture of the press ready to take the matter up and uncover all his secrets. The rich man is scared, and he pays up. That is all there is to it.

"Or you are involved in some risky undertaking, that would be ruined by a series of articles; a blackmailer comes along and offers to arrange for you to buy back the articles. Blackmailers are sent to certain Ministers, who come to terms with them on the agreement that the newspaper may attack their political activities, but not their private lives; or they consent to be attacked on condition that their mistresses are spared. Des Lupeaulx, that good-looking Master of Requests who is a friend of yours, is perpetually busy with negotiations of that kind with the newspapers. That scoundrel has made a wonderful position for himself as a sort of centre of power; he is both a go-between for the press and an ambassador for Ministers; he mediates on behalf of self-respect. He even extends this commerce into political fields, and arranges for the newspapers to remain silent on certain loans, or concessions, granted without the public consent, and the jackals of the Liberal bank get their share. You indulged in a little blackmail yourself, with Dauriat; he gave you three thousand francs to stop you from attacking Nathan. In the eighteenth century, when journalism was still in its infancy, blackmail was done by means of pamphlets, and favourites and great lords used to pay to have them destroyed. Aretino was the first blackmailer—the famous Italian. He made kings pay, in much the same way as newspapers blackmail actors in our own days."

"What have you done to the Matifat to get three thousand francs?"

"I had Florine attacked in six newspapers, and Florine complained to Matifat. Matifat begged Braulard to find out the reason for these attacks. Braulard was put on the wrong scent by Finot (I was working the blackmail for Finot's benefit), and Finot told the druggist that you were demolishing Florine in the interests of Coralie. Giroudeau went along and told Matifat in confidence that everything could be arranged if he would agree to sell his sixth share in Finot's weekly for ten thousand francs. Finot promised me three thousand francs if the thing succeeded. Matifat was only too glad to conclude the deal and to get back ten thousand francs of the thirty thousand he had invested in what he thought was an unsound speculation; because for some time past Florine had been telling him that Finot's review was not taking on; instead of paying a dividend, there was talk of raising more capital. Meanwhile the manager of the Panorama-Dramatique was just about to file his petition, and he was very anxious to negotiate one or two bills; and in order to induce Matifat to help him out, he dropped a hint about the trick Finot was playing on him. Matifat, like a shrewd business man, has left Florine, kept his sixth share, and seen through our game. Finot and I are howling in despair. We were unlucky enough to pick on a man who did not care about his mistress, a heartless unfeeling wretch. Matifat's business is not within the reach of the press, worse luck ; we cannot attack his interests. One cannot criticise a druggist as one can criticise a milliner or a dressmaker, or theatres or works of art. One cannot attack cocoa and pepper and dyes and pigments and opium! Florine is at her wits' end—the Panorama closes down tomorrow, and she does not know what she is going to do."

" As the theatre is closing, Coralie is going to the Gymnase in a few days," said Lucien ; " she might help Florine."

" Never! " said Lousteau. " Coralie may not have very many brains, but she is not such a fool as to help a rival! Our affairs are in a hopeless state! But Finot was so anxious to buy back his sixth! "

" Why ? "

" Business is going well, dear boy. There is a chance of selling the paper for three hundred thousand francs. Then Finot would get a third, plus a commission paid by his partners to be shared with des Lupeaulx. So I am going to propose another bit of blackmail."

" So blackmail means ' your money or your life ' ? "

" It goes one better," said Lousteau. " It is your money or your character. Two days ago the proprietor of a small newspaper who had been refused credit published a statement to the effect that a repeater watch set with diamonds, belonging to a personage well known in Paris, had in a most curious way come into the possession of a private in the Royal Guard, and he promised to give a full account of this story, which is worthy of the *Arabian Nights*. The personage in question lost no time in inviting the editor to dinner. The editor certainly profited, but contemporary history has lost the story of the watch. Whenever you see the press out for the blood of some powerful figure, you will not be far wrong in concluding that behind the attacks there is the story of a refusal to pay or to render some service or other. Blackmail arising out of their private lives is the special terror of rich Englishmen, and it is a major source of secret revenue for the English press, which is far more depraved than our own. We are children in comparison! In England they will pay five or six thousand francs for a compromising letter to sell again."

"What means have you found of getting Matifat into your power?"

"My dear boy, that low shopkeeper wrote the most curious letters to Florine; you never saw anything so funny in your life—handwriting, style, and sentiments, everything about them. Matifat goes in terror of his wife; and without naming him, so that he cannot protest, we can reach him in the bosom of his family, where he thinks himself safe. Imagine his fury when he reads the first instalment of a little modern novel entitled *The Loves of a Druggist* in which he will be fairly warned of the dangers of allowing letters in which he speaks of the little love-god to fall into the hands of the editors of a certain newspaper—letters in which he has written *gamet* for *jamais*, and in which he tells Florine that she has helped him to cross the desert of life—as if she was a camel. There is enough material in that highly entertaining correspondence to send the circulation soaring up for the next fortnight. We will put the fear of death into him by threatening an anonymous letter to his wife, letting her into the secret. But will Florine consent to lend herself to the persecution of Matifat? She still has some principles left, that is to say, some hopes. She may want to keep the letters for her own use, to make something out of them. She is clever—as befits my pupil. But when she realises that the bailiffs are in earnest and if Finot gives her a suitable present, or holds out the hope of an engagement, she will hand over the letters to me, and I will let Finot have them, at a price. Finot will give the correspondence to his uncle, and Giroudeau will make the druggist come to terms."

These confidences sobered Lucien. His first thought was that he had extremely dangerous friends; then it crossed his mind that it would be as well not to break with them, because he might need to make use of their terrible influence to bring pressure to bear on Mme d'Espard, Mme de Bargeton, and Châtelet, if they failed to keep their promises. Étienne and Lucien by this time had reached Barbet's squalid little bookshop on the Quai.

Étienne acted as spokesman. " Barbet," he said, " we have cheques for five thousand francs from Fendant and Cavalier, post-dated at six, nine, and twelve months ; will you cash them for us ? "

" I will take them for three thousand francs," said Barbet with imperturbable coolness.

" Three thousand francs ! " Lucien repeated.

" Not many people would give you that," said the bookseller. " These gentlemen will be bankrupt in three months. But I happen to know they have some good books in stock that will be sure to sell. They can't wait, and I shall buy them up, and pay them with their own cheques ; I shall get the books at two thousand francs discount in that way."

" Are you prepared to lose two thousand francs ? " Étienne asked Lucien.

" No ! " Lucien declared emphatically, dismayed by this first rebuff.

" You are making a mistake," said Étienne.

" You won't find anyone else to honour their cheques," said Barbet. "Your book is their last hope, sir. They won't even be able to print it, except by leaving the copies in the hands of their printer, and a success would only keep them going for another six months—sooner or later they will go up in smoke ! Messrs. Fendant and Cavalier dispose of more brandies than books ! In my case, their cheques represent business, and so I can afford to offer you more than an ordinary discounter would, who only considers what a signature is worth. The discounter's business is to know if three signatures will be worth thirty per cent each in case of bankruptcy. And in the first place, you only offer two signatures, neither of them worth more than ten per cent."

The two friends looked at one another, amazed to hear this concise analysis of the whole business of discounting coming from the mouth of this journalist's gyp.

" That's enough, Barbet," said Lousteau ; " what discounters can we try ? "

" Well, there is old Chaboisseau, Quai Saint-Michel—he tided

Fendant over his last monthly settlement, you know. If you won't take my offer, you might try him; but you will come back to me, and next time I shall only offer you two thousand five hundred."

Étienne and Lucien made their way to the Quai Saint-Michel, where Chaboisseau lived in a little house down an alley; they found him in a room furnished in the most original style. This discounter of the book trade was a minor figure in the world of finance, but, even so, he was a millionaire, and his passion was the Greek classical style. The cornice was in a Greek pattern; the bed, of the purest Greek design, dated from the Empire, when this style was fashionable, and the purple wall hangings were disposed behind it in Grecian style, just like the background of a painting by David. The chairs and tables, the lamps and sconces, everything down to the smallest accessories, had obviously been chosen at second-hand furniture dealers, with the greatest care, and all breathed the fine and fragile grace of antiquity. This elegant and mythological setting contrasted strangely with the habits of its occupant. It is a remarkable fact that men of the most fantastic taste are very often to be found among bankers and others who trade in money. Such men are the libertines of ideas. They are able to buy anything, and are therefore bored; and so they make enormous efforts to overcome their indifference. If you study their character, you will always find, in a corner of their hearts, some hobby through which they are accessible. Chaboisseau seemed to have entrenched himself in antiquity as in an impenetrable fortress.

"He must match his setting," Étienne remarked with a smile. Chaboisseau was a little man with powdered hair, a greenish coat, nut-brown waistcoat, black breeches, ribbed stockings and shoes that squeaked. He took the cheques and examined them, and then handed them back to Lucien gravely.

"Messrs. Fendant and Cavalier are two charming gentlemen, young men with plenty of ideas, but unfortunately I have no money at the moment," he said in honeyed tones.

"My friend would meet you in the matter of discount," said Étienne.

"I cannot take these cheques on any consideration," said the little man, his words cutting short Étienne's proposal like the knife of a guillotine cutting off a man's head.

The two friends withdrew. Chaboisseau prudently accompanied them as far as the outer office, and on their way out Lucien noticed a pile of books that the discounter had bought. He had once been a bookseller ; among these one leaped to the eyes of our novelist—Ducereau's work on the royal houses and châteaux of France, in which their plans and designs are given with great exactitude.

" Would you sell me that book ? " Lucien asked.

" Yes," said Chaboisseau, the discounter reverting to the bookseller.

" How much ? "

" Fifty francs."

" It is dear, but I must have it ; and I have no money with me, only the cheques that you don't want."

" You have one there for five hundred francs at six months—I will take that," said Chaboisseau ; an equivalent sum must have been carried over to the credit of Fendent and Cavalier at the last settlement.

The two friends returned to the Greek room, where Chaboisseau wrote out a little calculation, six per cent interest and six per cent commission, which came to thirty francs deduction ; he added the fifty francs for the Ducereau to this total, and took from his cash-box, which was full of shining coins, four hundred and twenty francs.

" But look here, Monsieur Chaboisseau, either none of the cheques are good, or all of them are ; why will you not cash the others ? "

" I am not chasing them ; I am paying myself for a sale," the old man replied.

Étienne and Lucien were still laughing at Chaboisseau, whose methods remained a mystery to them, when they arrived at Dauriat's book-shop, where Lousteau asked Gabusson to recommend them a discounter. The two friends took a cab and drove to the Boulevard Poissonnière, armed with a letter of introduction that Gabusson had given them, telling them as he did so that they would find " a very odd queer fish ", to use his own expression.

A minor figure in the world of finance

"If Samanon won't take your cheques," said Gabusson, "nobody will."

Samanon was a bookseller on the ground floor, a wardrobe dealer on the first, a vendor of indecent prints on the second; he was also a money-lender. No character from Hoffmann's tales, no sinister miser from Sir Walter Scott, could compare with the individual that the mysterious laws that govern society, and Paris society in particular, had made of this man—if Samanon could be called a man. Lucien involuntarily drew back in alarm at the sight of this little dried-up old creature, whose bones seemed almost to be coming through his tanned leather skin, spotted with countless green and yellow patches, exactly like a canvas by Titian or Veronese seen close up. One of Samanon's eyes was glazed and immobile, the other bright and sharp. The miser seemed to use the blind eye in his discount business, and the good one when he sold pornographic prints. He wore a small smooth black wig, rusty with age, and straggling wisps of white hair escaped from under it. His yellow forehead seemed to threaten one; his cheeks were so hollow that you could see the outline of his jaws; his teeth, which were still white, seemed to draw back his lips, giving him the expression of a yawning horse. His two contrasting eyes and that grimacing mouth combined to give him a decidedly ferocious expression, and the stiff, pointed hairs of his beard looked as sharp as pins.

To judge by his clothes, he had no wish to redeem this sinister appearance by a careful toilet. His threadbare jacket looked ready to drop to pieces; his black cravat, covered with stains, and worn by the bristles of his beard, revealed a throat as wrinkled as a turkey's.

The two journalists found this man sitting in his filthy little counting-house, engaged in sticking labels on the backs of some old books bought at an auction. Lucien and Lousteau exchanged a glance that asked the thousand and one unspoken questions raised by the existence of such a being. They then addressed him, and handed him Gabusson's letter and Fendant and Cavalier's cheques. While Samanon read the letter, a man of great brilliance came into that obscure den, dressed in a short jacket so solidly encrusted with a thousand kinds of dirt and grime that it looked as if it had been cut out of zinc.

" I need my coat, black trousers, and satin waistcoat," he said to Samanon, handing him a card with a number on it.

Samanon pulled the brass handle of a bell, and a woman, a Norman to judge by her fresh colouring, came down from an upper floor.

" Give this gentleman his clothes," he said, pointing to the author. " It is a pleasure to do business with you," he said, " but one of your friends brought a young fellow along who took me in badly."

" Took him in ! " said the man of letters, turning to the two journalists with an expression of comic incredulity.

That man of genius counted thirty sous into the money-lender's yellow wrinkled hand, for all the world like an Italian beggar getting his Sunday suit out of pawn for one day.

" What on earth are you doing here ? " Lousteau asked that great writer, an opium addict, who, under the spell of the enchantment of the magic palaces of his dreams, could not, or would not, accomplish any creative work.

" He lends much more than the pawnbrokers on anything you pledge, and, besides, he is appallingly charitable, and allows you to take out your clothes for special occasions when you have to be dressed," he said. " I am going to dinner with the Kellers tonight with my mistress. It is easier to raise thirty sous than two hundred francs, and I have come to fetch my suit, which has been worth a hundred francs to this charitable usurer during the last six months. Samanon has already devoured my library, volume by volume " (*livre à livre*).

" And sou by sou," said Lousteau with a laugh.

" I will give you fifteen hundred francs," Samanon said to Lucien.

Lucien jumped as if the discounter had plunged a red-hot iron into his heart. Samanon looked over the cheques again carefully, examining the dates.

" Even then," said the money-lender, " I should have to see Fendant, who would have to deposit some books with me. You are not worth much," he said to Lucien. " You are living with Coralie, and your furniture is under distraint."

Lousteau looked at Lucien, who took back his cheques, and fled from the shop into the boulevard.

" Is he the devil ? " he asked.

The poet stood for a moment looking at that little shop, the shabby dirty little piles of second-hand books were so pitiful that passers-by could not see them without a smile, and might well wonder how anyone could make a living there.

A few moments later the great man who ten years later was to play a part in the widespread but ill-founded Saint-Simonian movement, walked out very well dressed, smiled at the two journalists, and walked with them as far as the Passage des Panoramas, where he completed his toilet by having his boots blacked.

" When you see Samanon going into a book-shop, or a paper merchant's, or a printer's, they are lost," he said to the two journalists. " Samanon is like the undertaker going to measure the body for the coffin."

" You won't be able to change your cheques now," said Étienne.

" What Samanon refuses, no one will accept," said the unknown writer ; " he is the *ultima ratio*! He is a decoy for Gigonnet, de Palma, Werbrust, Gobseck, and the rest of the crocodiles of the Place de Paris ; every man with a fortune to make or lose comes across one or other of them sooner or later."

" If you can't cash your cheques at fifty per cent, you must turn them into hard cash," Étienne continued.

" How ? "

" Give them to Coralie, and she will get Camusot to cash them. You don't like the idea ? " Lousteau added, as Lucien cut him short with a gesture. " Don't be childish! You cannot afford to allow silly scruples to stand in your way when your future is at stake! "

" In any case I am going to give Coralie this money," said Lucien.

" That is silly, too," said Lousteau. " Four hundred francs won't help you when you need four thousand! Keep enough to get drunk on in case we lose, and use the rest to gamble with! "

"Very sound advice," said the great man. These words, spoken four paces from Frascati's, had a magnetic effect. The two friends dismissed their cab and went upstairs to the gaming tables. To begin with they won three thousand francs, then lost all except a hundred. Then their winnings rose to three thousand seven hundred, then they lost all but a five-franc piece; they won again, and made two thousand francs, which they staked on an even number, hoping to double it at a single stake; for the last five stakes odd numbers had come up, and they punted the whole amount. Another odd number came up. Lucien and Lousteau fled down the stairs of that celebrated casino, having spent two hours in a state of frenzied emotion. They had kept back a hundred francs. On the steps of the diminutive peristyle with the two pillars that support the little corrugated iron verandah that so many eyes have contemplated in rapture or despair, Lousteau looked at Lucien's flushed face.

"Just fifty francs," said Lousteau.

The two journalists went upstairs once again. An hour later they had won three thousand francs; black had come up five times in succession. Putting their faith in the form of luck that had brought about their downfall earlier in the evening, they staked the whole three thousand on the red. Black turned up. It was now six o'clock.

"Only twenty-five francs," said Lucien.

This new venture did not take long; the twenty-five francs were lost in ten stakes. Lucien, in a frenzy, staked his last twenty-five francs on the number of his age, and won. His hand trembled as he raked in the coins that the bank paid him one by one. He gave two hundred francs to Lousteau, and said: "Run! Wait for me at Véry's!"

Lousteau understood, and went off to order dinner.

Lucien, left alone, staked his six hundred francs on the red, and won. Emboldened by that secret voice that sometimes inspires gamblers, he left everything on the red, and won again. There was a furnace raging within him. He disregarded the voice, and staked his two thousand four hundred francs on the black, and lost. Then he experienced the sense of lightness that succeeds their anxious torments, when, having no more to lose, gamblers leave the burning palace where their fleeting dreams have melted away. He rejoined Lousteau at Vérys, where, to use La Fontaine's expression, he fell upon the food and drowned his cares in wine. By nine o'clock he was so completely drunk that he was unable to understand why the porter at the Rue de Vendôme was trying to send him to the Rue de la Lune.

" Mlle Coralie has left her flat. She has written down her new address on this piece of paper."

Lucien was too drunk to be surprised at anything. He got back into the cab that had brought him and drove to the Rue de la Lune, making puns to himself the while on the name of the street.

That morning the Panorama-Dramatique had been declared bankrupt. The actress had taken fright and had made haste to sell all her furniture, with the bailiff's consent, to old Cardot. So as not to change the character of the flat, he installed Florentine there. Coralie had paid all the bills, sold up everything, and settled her account with the landlord. During the time taken up by these operations—Coralie called it a " spring-cleaning "—Bérénice had furnished a little three-roomed flat on the fourth floor of a house in the Rue de la Lune, just by the Gymnase, with a few indispensable pieces of furniture bought second-hand; Coralie was waiting there for Lucien; for she had saved her love, unspotted, from the general wreck, together with a little store of twelve hundred francs. Lucien, still drunk, told his troubles to Coralie and Bérénice.

" You did quite right, dearest angel," the actress said to him, clasping him in her arms. " Bérénice can easily go and cash your cheques for you with Braulard."

The next morning Lucien awoke to the magic world of happiness with which Coralie surrounded him. The actress redoubled her love and tenderness, as if to compensate, by the rich treasures of her heart, for the poverty of their new household. She had never been so beautiful; her hair escaped from under a twisted scarf, white and fresh, her eyes were full of laughter, and her talk as gay as the morning sunshine that streamed in through the window and poured its gold upon such charming poverty

The room itself was far from sordid. It was papered with a sea-green wallpaper with a red border, and adorned with two mirrors, one over the mantelpiece, the other over the chest of drawers. The cold bare boards were covered by a second-hand carpet, that Bérénice had paid for out of her savings, against Coralie's orders. The clothes of the two lovers were neatly put away in a wardrobe with a mirror, and in the chest of drawers. The mahogany furniture was upholstered in a blue cotton material. Bérénice had saved from the disaster a clock and two porcelain vases, four silver spoons and forks, and six teaspoons. The bedroom was reached through a dining-room that might have been that of a clerk earning twelve hundred francs a year. The kitchen was on the other side of the landing, and Bérénice slept in an attic above. The rent was only three hundred francs.

This ugly block of flats had a sham carriage entrance. The porter's lodge was behind one of the blocked-up wings of the gate in which a sash-window had been made, through which he kept watch over the seventeen families. This bee-hive was of the kind known in house-agents parlance as *profitable premises*. Lucien noticed a desk, armchair, ink, pens and paper. Bérénice was cheerful, for she was counting on Coralie's appearance at the Gymnase ; the actress was cheerful, as she learned her part from a paper-covered exercise book tied with a blue ribbon. The sight of them drove away all the worries and cares of the sobered poet.

" So long as nobody hears about this come-down, we shall pull through," he said. " After all, we have four thousand five hundred francs in prospect! I shall make use of my new position in the Royalist press. The *Réveil* is coming out tomorrow ; I have a name in journalism now, and I shall get on."

Coralie, who saw only love in those words, kissed the lips that had spoken them. Bérénice by this time had laid the table, in front of the fire, and prepared a modest lunch of boiled eggs, two cutlets and coffee. There was a knock at the door. Lucien was astonished to behold three true friends, d'Arthez, Léon Giraud, and Michel Chrestien, and, deeply touched, he invited them to share his lunch.

" No," said d'Arthez. " We have come about something much more serious than just to offer you our sympathies. We know everything, because we have just come from the Rue de Vendôme. You know my views, Lucien. Under other circumstances I should have been delighted to see you adopting my own political convictions, but in your present position as a writer for the Liberal newspapers you cannot go over to the ranks of the Ultras without leaving a permanent stain on your character and disgracing yourself. We have come to intreat you, in the name of our friendship—however much that friendship may have been weakened—not to dishonour yourself in this way. You have attacked the Romantics, the Right and the Government ; you cannot now turn round and defend the Government, the Right, and the Romantics."

" My reasons for doing so are determined by lofty motives, and the end will justify the means," said Lucien.

" Perhaps you do not understand our position," said Léon Giraud. " The Government, the Court, the Bourbons, the Absolutist party, which, if you like to sum it up in a single phrase, means the system opposed to constitutional government, and which is divided into a number of divergent factions on the issue of the best method of extinguishing the Revolution, is unanimous at least on one question—the necessity for suppressing the newspapers. The *Réveil*, the *Foudre* and the *Drapeau blanc* are all papers whose express purpose is to reply to the calumnies, insults, and gibes of the Liberal press, and for that reason I do not approve of them. It is precisely this failure to understand the dignity and sanctity of the writer's function that has induced us to publish a serious and honourable periodical, whose influence will in time be felt, and respected, and carry weight," he added in parenthesis. " But to return ; this Royalist and Ministerialist artillery is a first attempt at reprisals, undertaken in order to pay back the Liberals in their own coin, blow for blow. What good do you imagine will come of it, Lucien ? Most of the readers belong to the Left. In the press, as in war, victory always goes to the side with the big battalions! You will be blackguards, liars, enemies of the people ; the others will be honourable men, and martyrs, even though they may be more hypocritical and treacherous than you are. This means will only serve to increase the pernicious influence of the press, by legitimising and sanctioning journalism of the most odious kind. Insult and slander will become one of its acknowledged privileges; it was resorted to in the first place to increase circulations, but when both sides use the same method it becomes an accepted thing. When the full extent of the evil becomes clear the restrictions and prohibitions of censorship—introduced at the time of the assassination of the Duke de Berri, and lifted again since the opening of the Chambers—will be imposed once more. Do you realise what conclusion the French nation will draw? They will believe all the insinuations of the Liberal press, they will think that the Bourbons want to take away all the material advantages and concessions gained by the Revolution, and one fine day they will rise and throw out the Bourbons. You will not only be damaging your reputation; you will find yourself, sooner or later, on the losing side. You are young, you still don't know all the ways of the press; you do not know even now all its secret motives and tricks! You have aroused too much jealousy to escape the hue and cry that will be raised against you in the Liberal press. You will be caught up in violent party conflict, which is still at fever-heat; the only difference is that the brutal acts of 1815 and 1816 have passed into the sphere of ideas, into the verbal warfare of the Chambers and newspaper polemics."

"I am not the poetic simpleton you take me for," said Lucien. "Whatever may happen, I shall have gained one advantage that a Liberal victory could never give me. By the time you win your victory, I shall have got what I want."

"We will cut off—your hair," said Michel Chrestien, laughing.

"I shall have heirs by that time," said Lucien; "and even if you cut off my head, it won't make any difference."

The three friends could not understand Lucien, whose relations with the social world had developed in him to the highest degree pride of family and all the other aristocratic vanities. The poet imagined, and with good reason, that his good looks, combined with his brilliance and the title of Count de Rubempré, were worth a fortune. Mme d'Espard, Mme de Bargeton, and Mme de Montcornet held him by that thread as easily as a child holds a cockchafer. Lucien could only move within a limited circle. The words "He is one of us—he is a sound man! " spoken three days ago in Mlle des Touches' drawing-room, had gone to his head, and so had the congratulations he had received from the Dukes of Lenoncourt, de Navarreins, and de Grandlieu; from de Rastignac, and Blondet, from the beautiful Duchess de Maufrigneuse, Count d'Esgrignon, des Lupeaulx, and from all the most influential and prominent members of the Royalist party.

" Well, there is no more to be said," said d'Arthez. " You will find it harder than most men to keep your hands clean and not to compromise your self-respect. I know you, and know that you will suffer enormously when you find yourself despised by the very people to whom you have offered yourself."

The three friends took their leave of Lucien without shaking hands with him. Lucien remained thoughful and sad until Coralie came and sat on his knees and threw her beautiful young arms round his neck.

" Oh, never mind those ninnies! " she said. " They take life much too seriously, and life is not meant to be serious. And what does it matter, so long as you are Count Lucien de Rubempré? I shall flirt with the *Chancellerie*, if that will help. I know how to get round that libertine des Lupeaulx, who will arrange to have your patent signed. Did I not tell you that if you were ever almost within reach of your goal, you should have my body to climb on? "

On the following day Lucien allowed his name to appear in the list of contributors to the *Réveil.* This name was announced as a conversion in the prospectus, of which, with the backing of the Ministry, a hundred thousand copies were distributed. Lucien went to the inaugural dinner, which lasted nine hours, at Robert's, only a few yards away from Frascati's, and all the pillars of the Royalist press were present: Martainville, Auger, Destains, and a host of writers who are still living, and who, in those days, had " taken up Monarchy and Religion".

" We'll let the Liberals have it! " said Hector Merlin.

" Gentlemen," replied Nathan (who had enrolled under the Royalist banner, for he had rightly decided that it would be more to his interest to have the authorities for him than against him if he wished to succeed as a playwright, as he was hoping to do), " if we make war on them, let us make it in good earnest. Do not let us simply amuse ourselves by scoring points off them! Let us attack all classical and Liberal authors, without distinction of age or sex, hold them up to ridicule, and allow no quarter! "

" Let us be honourable in our methods—no profiting by selling copies, no presents, or bribes from the publishers! We must undertake the reformation of journalism! "

" Good! " said Martainville. " *Justum et tenacem propositi virum!* Let us be scathing and implacable! I shall paint la Fayette as the clown that he is! "

" You can leave the heroes of the *Constitutionnel* to me," said Lucien, " and Sergeant Mercier, and the *Complete Works of M. de Jouy*, and the illustrious orators of the Left! "

At one in the morning a resolution for war to the death was put to the vote and passed unanimously by all the journalists, whose differences of opinion, together with their other ideas, had been drowned in a flaming bowl of punch.

" Well, we have helped ourselves to a jolly good slice of Church and Monarchy! " one of the most celebrated writers of the Romantic School remarked as he left.

This famous remark, passed on by a publisher who had been present at the dinner, duly appeared in the next day's *Miroir* ; but it was attributed to Lucien. This defection was the signal for an outburst of abuse in the Liberal newspapers; Lucien became their *bête noire*, and was hounded down ruthlessly ; the unfortunate story of his sonnets was told, and the public informed that Dauriat would rather lose three thousand francs than print them. He was called " the poet without sonnets ".

One morning, in the very newspaper in which Lucien had made such a brilliant beginning, he read the following lines, written expressly for his own perusal, for the public could not possibly have seen the point of them :

⁂ " If Dauriat persists in withholding the sonnets of the future Petrarch of France, we will act like generous enemies and open our columns to these poems, which must be amusing, to judge from the specimen that has been communicated to us by a friend of the author." The poem was entitled *The Thistle* (Le Chardon).

And, beneath that terrible announcement, the poet read the following sonnet, which made him shed hot tears :

"A Plant of dubious and mean aspect
Grew up one morning in a garden gay
Boasting the splendid colours that one day
Would spring from noble and illustrious seed.

They let it stay ; instead of gratitude
With insults its fair sisters 'gan repay
Who, grown indignant at its proud display
Now bid it prove its ancestry indeed.

It flowered! But never mountebank or clown
Was louder mocked than was this vulgar bloom ;
For seeing it, all the flowers began to laugh,
And soon the gardener, passing, lopped it down
Remorseless, and a donkey o'er its tomb
Brayed the ignoble thistle's epitaph."

Vernou wrote of Lucien's passion for gambling, and spoke of the forthcoming *Archer* as an anti-national work in which the author took the side of the Catholic cut-throats against their Calvinist victims. Within a week the quarrel became yet more venomous. Lucien had counted on his friend Lousteau, who owed him a thousand francs, and with whom he had a private understanding ; but Lousteau had become his sworn enemy, in the following manner.

For the past three months Nathan had been in love with Florine, but could find no way of getting rid of Lousteau to whom Florine was, be it said, very useful. Florine was in distress and despair when she found herself without an engagement, and Nathan exerted himself to get an engagement at the Gymnase for the young actress without a theatre. Nathan (as Lucien's colleague) went to see Coralie and begged her to ask for a part for Florine in his new play, which was about to be put on at the Gymnase. Florine, who was wildly ambitious, did not hesitate. She had had time to get to know Lousteau well. Nathan was an ambitious author and political journalist, a man with enough energy to accomplish his ambitions; whereas Lousteau's vices were stronger than his will. The actress, determined to make a new and brilliant appearance on the stage gave the druggist's letters to Nathan, and Nathan sold them back to Matifat in return for the sixth share in Finot's weekly. Florine was, forthwith installed in a luxurious flat in the Rue Hauteville, and took Nathan as her protector, in the face of the journalists and the theatrical world.

Lousteau was dreadfully upset by this incident. He shed tears after a dinner, given by his friends in order to console him. In the course of this party the guests decided that Nathan's behaviour had been perfectly straightforward. Several of the writers present—Finot and Vernou, for example—had known about the dramatist's love for Florine; but it was unanimously agreed that Lucien, in aiding and abetting the affair, had broken the most elementary rules of friendship. Motivated by party spirit, and the desire to be of service to his new friends, the new Royalist had behaved inexcusably.

" Nathan obeyed the logic of passion ; but the provincial great man, as Blondet says, is simply scheming for his own ends ! " Bixiou declared.

And so Lucien's ruin—the downfall of this upstart, this little nobody who wanted to climb on everybody's shoulders—was unanimously agreed upon and carefully planned. Vernou, who hated Lucien, undertook to pursue him ruthlessly. Finot, anxious to get out of paying three thousand francs to Lousteau, accused Lucien of having let Nathan into the secret of the plot against Matifat and thereby of having cheated him (Finot) out of fifty thousand francs. As a matter of fact, Nathan, on Florine's advice, came to terms with Finot and sold him his " little sixth " for fifteen thousand francs. Lousteau, who had lost his three thousand francs, could not forgive Lucien for this tremendous blow to his interests. The wounds of pride become incurable when they come into contact with the oxygen of money.

No words, no description, can depict the rage of an author when his vanity is wounded, or the access of energy that comes to him when he feels himself pricked by the poisoned darts of satire. But those whose energy and resistance is stimulated by attack soon give in. The men of real literary courage are the calm minds who put their trust in the oblivion into which injurious articles soon fall. And so it is that the weaklings at first sight seem the stronger ; but their resistance soon reaches its limits.

For the first fortnight Lucien, furious, poured out a storm of articles in the Royalist newspapers in which he shared with Hector Merlin the responsibility for the criticism. Every day he returned to the attack in the *Réveil* and fired off all his artillery, seconded by Martainville, the only one of his associates who stood by him without any ulterior motive, and the only one who was not let into the secret of the agreements that were reached in the course of pleasant chats over drinks, and in the Wooden Galleries, at Dauriat's, and in the green-rooms, between journalists of both parties, between whom existed a secret bond of friendship. When Lucien went into the Vaudeville foyer he was no longer treated as a friend, and only members of his own party offered to shake hands with him ; whereas Nathan, Hector Merlin, and Théodore Gaillard fraternised shamelessly with Finot, Lousteau, Vernou, and a number of other journalists known to be " good chaps ".

At that time the Vaudeville bar was the headquarters of literary scandal, neutral ground where men of all parties, even political men and magistrates, used to meet. On one occasion after a sharp exchange in a court of law, in which the President had accused one of his colleagues of " Sweeping the green-rooms with his gown ", the President and the reprimanded colleague found themselves gown to gown in the bar of the Vaudeville. Lousteau in the end consented to shake hands with Nathan. Finot was there almost every evening. When time permitted, Lucien went there to study the disposition of his enemies, and the unfortunate boy found them always distant and cold.

In those days party hatred was much more bitter than it is at the present time. Everything is rendered less intense nowadays by the strain under which we all live. Now, the critic who has just demolished an author's book shakes hands with him. The victim cannot refuse to take the sacrificial hand, on pain of being subjected to a scathing series of jibes. If he refuses, a writer gets the reputation of being unsociable, disagreeable, abominably conceited, standoffish, ill-natured and vindictive. Nowadays, when an author has been lucky enough not to be killed by treacherous attacks, and has managed to avoid snares spread with shameful hypocrisy, or swallowed the grossest injuries, he hears his assassins wishing him good day and showing that they expect to be treated with esteem, not to say friendship. There is an excuse and a justification for everything in an age that has transformed virtue into vice and set up certain vices as virtues. Good fellowship has become the most sacred of our liberties. The leaders of the most opposite schools of thought temper their phrases and fence with blunt weapons. But in those days, if I remember aright, it required some courage for certain Royalist writers, and for certain Liberal writers, to set foot in the same theatre. One heard provocations of the ugliest kind. Looks were like loaded pistols, and the smallest spark was enough to start a quarrel. Which of us has not overheard the man next to him muttering imprecations on seeing some individual, some special *bête noire* of one or other of the opposing factions, come in? In those days there were only two parties, Royalists and Liberals, Romantics and Classicists—the same hatred under different names, a hatred that made one understand the scaffolds of the Convention.

Lucien, who had been a furious Liberal and Voltairean, had become a rabid Royalist and a Romantic; De Martainville, the only man who stood by him, was the man best hated by the Liberals in those days; and Lucien shared, therefore, the full weight of the hatred that descended on the head of his only friend. This friendship did Lucien a great deal of harm. Parties are ungrateful to their lonely sentinels, and abandon their casualties without a thought.

In politics, especially, those who want to succeed must keep with the main body of the army. The malice of the small Liberal newspapers coupled the name of Lucien with that of Martainville; and by so doing they succeeded in throwing them together. This friendship, real or imaginary, brought upon both of them venomous articles written by Félicien, who could not endure the thought of Lucien's social success, and who believed, as did all the poet's late companions, that he would soon be granted a title. The poet's alleged betrayal was accordingly embellished with the most aggravating circumstances. Lucien was called Judas the Less, and Martainville Judas the Greater, for Martainville, rightly or wrongly, was held to have been responsible for allowing the bridge at Pecq to fall into enemy hands. Lucien admitted, laughing, to des Lupeaulx, that he, for his part, had undoubtedly handed over the Pons Asinorum.

Lucien's luxurious existence, hollow as it was, and based only on expectations, was more than his friends could bear ; they could not forgive him his carriage—for them it was still driving in the Bois de Boulogne—nor the late splendours of the Rue de Vendôme. They all instinctively felt that a handsome young man whom they themselves had corrupted would get on in the world ; and so they used every means in their power to ruin him.

A few days before Coralie's first appearance at the Gymnase, Lucien strolled into the Vaudeville bar, arm in arm with Hector Merlin. Merlin was scolding his friend for having helped Nathan over Florine.

" You made two mortal enemies for yourself—Lousteau and Nathan. I gave you good advice, but you disregarded it. You have praised Nathan and helped Lousteau financially, and you will be cruelly punished for your good deeds. Florine and Coralie will never be able to remain on friendly terms on the same stage ; they will be bitter rivals. You can only defend Coralie in our newspapers; but Nathan, besides the advantage of being a playwright, has the Liberal papers at his disposal as well when it comes to theatre notices ; he has been in journalism longer than you have."

These words found an echo in Lucien's secret fears ; he found neither Nathan nor Gaillard as open with him as he felt they ought to be ; but he could not complain, he was such a recent convert! Gaillard poured cold water on Lucien by saying to him that newcomers had to prove their good faith for a long time before their party could place any reliance on them. The poet encountered jealousies that he had little expected, among journalists of Royalist and Ministerialist circles—the inevitable jealousy that breaks out whenever there is a cake to be shared out, and that makes men behave like dogs fighting over a bone ; they even growl and show their teeth and snarl at one another in the same way. These writers played any number of underhand bad turns to lessen one another's power ; they accused each other of political indifference ; and in order to steal a march on a rival, resorted to the basest kind of plotting and scheming. The Liberals had no motive for internal contentions, because they were not in power, and could not hope for official favours. As he became aware of the inextricable network of conflicting ambitions, Lucien had not the courage to take a sword and cut the knots, and he lacked the patience to untie them ; he had not got it in him to become the Aretino or the Beaumarchais, or the Fréron of his day. He clung to his one desire—to be granted his patent of nobility—in the belief that this restitution would be worth a distinguished marriage to him ; so that his fortune now depended on nothing but chance, aided by his good looks. Lousteau, who had been in his confidence, knew his secret, and that journalist knew where the poet from Angoulême was most vulnerable. On the same day that Merlin spoke to him in the bar of the Vaudeville, Étienne had laid a horrible trap for Lucien, into which, child as he was, the poet was sure to fall.

" Why, there is our handsome Lucien," said Finot. He had been talking to des Lupeaulx a few feet away from Lucien ; and now the two came over to the poet, and Finot shook hands with him, with all the smooth semblances of friendship. " I have never known anyone get on as quickly as he has," said Finot, turning towards the Master of Requests. " In Paris there are two kinds of success—material success, money, that anyone can pile up ; and social success, position, connection, the right of entry into a world closed for ever to certain persons, however great their material success ; and my friend. . . . "

" Our friend," des Lupeaulx interrupted, smiling at Lucien in the most friendly manner.

"Our friend," Finot continued, patting Lucien's hand, "has made a brilliant success of the second kind. The fact is that Lucien has more ability, more talent, and more brains than the people who envy him, and he is marvellously good-looking into the bargain; his old friends cannot forgive him for his success—they call it luck!"

"That kind of luck never comes to fools or incapables," said des Lupeaulx. "You cannot call Bonaparte's story a case of luck. There were twenty generals with better chances than he had of getting the command of the armies in Italy, just as there are a hundred young men at this moment who would like to get to know Mlle des Touches—her name is coupled with yours already, my boy!" said des Lupeaulx, slapping Lucien on the shoulder. "Yes, you are in high favour! Mme d'Espard and Mme de Bargeton and Mme de Montcornet are wild about you! You are going to Mme Firmiani's reception this evening, aren't you, and tomorrow to the Duchesse de Grandlieu's party?"

"Yes," said Lucien.

"Allow me to introduce you to a young banker, M. du Tillet, whom you ought to know—he managed to make a splendid fortune in a very short time."

Lucien and du Tillet bowed to one another, fell into conversation, and the banker invited Lucien to dinner. Finot and des Lupeaulx, two deep schemers who knew one another well enough to remain on good terms, appeared to be continuing their conversation as they strolled over towards one of the divans, leaving Lucien, Merlin, du Tillet and Nathan talking together.

"By the way," said Finot to des Lupeaulx, "tell me, is it true that Lucien has powerful backing? Because he has become my staff's *bête noire*; and before I favour their conspiracy, I should like your advice—would it be better to call it off, and to be on good terms with him?"

The Master of Requests and Finot looked at one another attentively.

"My dear fellow," said des Lupeaulx after a pause. "You don't suppose, do you, that the Marquise d'Espard, or Châtelet, or Mme de Bargeton, who has obtained the Baron's nomination as Prefect of the Charente, and the rank of Count, so as to return in triumph to Angoulême, will ever forgive Lucien for his attacks? They have pitched him into the Royalist camp in order to crush him. At this very moment they are all trying to find some excuse for refusing to give this boy what they have promised him. If you can find one for them, you will be doing these two ladies the greatest possible service! If you do, they will show their gratitude one day. I happen to know that they both hate that little upstart—I was surprised when I discovered how much! This Lucien might have rid himself of his worst enemy—Mme de Bargeton—by ceasing his attacks on conditions which all women love to grant, if you follow me. He is young and handsome; he might have drowned that hate in torrents of love, and then he would have been Count de Rubempré. The Cuttle-bone would have obtained a sinecure for him in the Royal Household! Lucien would have made a charming lector to Louis XVIII, or he might have been made librarian, or Heaven knows what, or Master of Requests for a joke, or Master of Revels, or some thing. The little fool has missed his chance. That is probably what they won't forgive. Instead of imposing conditions, he has accepted them. The day on which Lucien allowed himself to be caught with the bait of a patent of nobility was a lucky one for Châtelet. Coralie has been that boy's undoing. If he had not had the actress as his mistress he would have gone back to the Cuttle-bone, and she would have taken him."

"Then we can finish him off."

"How?" des Lupeaulx asked negligently; he was anxious to be of service to the Marquise d'Espard.

"He is under contract to write for Lousteau's little paper; he will be all the more easily persuaded to do so, because he hasn't a sou. If we can irritate the Keeper of the Seals with a facetious article, and then prove that Lucien wrote it, he will regard him as a man unworthy of the Royal favour. Just to make our distinguished provincial lose his head a little, we have arranged the ruin Coralie's career. He will see his mistress hissed off the stage and offered no parts. Once the patent is indefinitely suspended, we can ridicule our man on the subject of his aristocratic pretensions, and mention that his mother was a midwife and his father a chemist. Lucien's courage is only skin-deep ; he will go to pieces, and we can send him back to where he came from. Nathan arranged through Florine for me to buy back Matifat's sixth share in the newspaper, and I have managed to buy the paper merchant's share as well. Dauriat and I are the only shareholders ; you and I might arrange to have the newspaper taken over by the Royalists. I only agreed to protect Florine and Nathan on condition that I got back my sixth—they have sold it to me, and I owe them a good turn ; but first I wanted to know how Lucien stood. . . . "

" You deserve your name," said des Lupeaulx, laughing. " You are the kind of man I like."

" Very well ; can you arrange for Florine to have a definite engagement ? "

" Yes ; but you must get rid of Lucien for us ; Rastignac and de Marsay would be glad to see the last of him."

" You may sleep soundly," said Finot. " Nathan and Merlin will always have articles ready that Gaillard will promise to put in ; Lucien will not be able to get a line into the paper—we will cut off his supplies. He will only have de Martainville's paper to defend Coralie and himself—one newspaper against all the rest cannot do very much."

" I will tell you the weak spots in the Ministry ; but let me have the manuscript of the article you are going to get Lucien to write," said des Lupeaulx, who took good care not to tell Finot that the promise of a patent of nobility to Lucien was nothing but a joke.

Des Lupeaulx left the bar. Finot strolled over to Lucien, and in that tone of familiarity that took in so many people, he explained that he could not allow Lucien to break his contract. Finot did not want to bring in a law-suit, which would ruin his friend's prospects with the Royalist party. Finot liked a man who had the courage to come out into the open with a change of opinion. But he and Lucien would be sure to come across one another, and they could do one another quite a number of small services. Lucien would need a friend in the Liberal camp to attack Ministerialists or Ultras who refused to help him.

" What will you do if they double cross you ? " Finot concluded. " If some Minister who fancies that your hands are tied by your change of front, refuses to trust you, and shows you the door, you would find it useful to be able to unleash a few dogs to snap at his heels. Very well, you have broken with Lousteau, who is out for your blood. You and Félicien will never be on speaking terms again. I am the only friend you have left! It is one of the rules of my profession to keep on good terms with really first-rate men. You will be able to do as much for me, in the circles you move in now, if I help you in the press. But to return to business—let me have some purely literary articles, they will not compromise you, and you can fulfil your contract in that way."

Lucien saw no other motives than those of friendship behind these calculated proposals ; Finot's flattery and des Lupeaulx' had put him in a good humour, and he thanked Finot!

In the lives of all ambitious men who can only succeed by the help of other people, and circumstances, and by some plan of conduct, more or less well prepared, adhered to, and carried out, there comes a cruel moment when some unknown power tests them to the utmost ; everything fails at once, all the threads break or become entangled, and misfortune threatens them from every side. When a man loses his head in the midst of this confusion of mind he is lost. The really strong men are those who are able to resist this first revolt of circumstances, who can stand firm until the ordeal passes, or who can escape by climbing, with a supreme effort, into a higher sphere. Every man—or at least every man who is not born rich—has, sooner or later, what one may call his fatal week. For Napoleon that week was the retreat from Moscow. The moment had come for Lucien. Everything had come to him too easily in the world of journalism, and in society ; he had been too happy, and he was about to see men and events turn against him.

The first sorrow was the most painful and cruel of all, for it touched him where he thought that he was invulnerable, in his affections, and in his love. Coralie may not have been clever ; but, gifted with a fine and sensitive nature, she had the faculty possessed by some great actresses, of suddenly surpassing herself. This remarkable phenomenon, until it has become a habit by long practice, is subject to passing moods, and sometimes, in young actresses, to a modesty admirable in itself. Coralie might appear to have the confidence and smartness of the theatre, but inwardly she was simple, and timid ; what was more, she was in love, and her woman's heart reacted against her comedienne's mask. The art of impersonating feelings, that sublime falsehood, had not yet triumphed, in her, over nature. She was ashamed to give to the public that which belonged only to love. She had another weakness, of a very womanly kind. Even though she knew, in her heart of hearts, that she was born to be a great actress, she needed success. She could not face an audience with whom she was out of sympathy, and she never went onto the stage without suffering the most acute nervousness ; a cold reception paralysed her completely. This agonising emotion made every new part as great a strain on her as a first appearance. Applause was a kind of intoxication that she needed, not out of vanity, but in order to give her courage. A murmur of disapprobation, or silence from the audience, paralysed her ; but a full and attentive house, giving her admiration and sympathy, electrified her ; she seemed to establish a kind of communication with the noblest qualities in the minds of every member of the audience, and then she felt herself capable of carrying them away, of swaying their emotions.

This combination of qualities gave proof of the highly strung constitution of genius ; but it also betrayed the poor girl's sensitive, fine nature. Lucien had learned to value the rare treasures of her heart ; and he had also come to realise that his mistress was still only a girl. She was incapable of the deceptions practised by so many actresses, and quite unable to protect herself against the rivalries and green-room intrigues in which Florine was in her element. Florine was already as depraved and dangerous as her friend was simple and generous. Parts must come in search of Coralie—she was too proud to beg authors for parts, or to accept them on dishonourable conditions, or to give herself to the first journalist who threatened her with his love or his pen.

Talent is rare enough in the extraordinary art of acting; but it is only one of the conditions necessary to success. It may remain useless for a long time unless a talent for intrigue goes with it; and this quality Coralie entirely lacked. Foreseeing the sufferings that awaited his mistress at her first appearance at the Gymnase, Lucien was eager, at all costs, to ensure her a triumph. All the money that remained from the sale of the furniture, and Lucien's earnings, had been spent on costumes, on fitting up Coralie's dressing-room, and on all the other expenses of a first appearance at a new theatre. A few days before the play was to come on Lucien took a humiliating step, for the sake of his love. He took Fendant and Cavalier's cheques, and went to the Golden Cocoon, in the Rue des Bourdonnais, to ask Camusot to cash them.

The poet was not yet so corrupt that he could do this in cold blood. He suffered deeply as he went, and the way was paved with terrible misgivings, as he said to himself alternately, "Yes" and "No". But all the same, he found himself in the cold dark little office, lit only from an inner court, where he found gravely seated no longer Coralie's lover, the debonair, happy libertine, the simple-minded Camusot whom he knew; but the responsible father of a family, a shopkeeper grown grey in business methods and respectability, wearing a mask of judicial hypocrisy as befitted a magistrate of the Commercial Court. It was not easy to approach this personage, who as the head of a large business maintained a cold formality, surrounded as he was by salesmen, clerks, cardboard boxes, invoices, and samples, with his wife, accompanied by a plainly dressed daughter, hovering in the background. Lucien was trembling from head to foot as he addressed him, for this respectable business man gave him the same look of insolent indifference that he had already seen in the eyes of the discounters.

"These are some cheques; I would really be most grateful if you would take them from me," he said, standing opposite the shopkeeper, who remained seated.

"You have taken something from me," said Camusot, "that I do not forget."

Lucien thereupon gave an account of Coralie's situation, speaking in a low voice so that he should not be overheard. The silk merchant could hear the beating of the poet's humiliated heart.

It was no part of Camusot's plan to allow Coralie to suffer a serious setback. As he listened to Lucien, he looked at the signatures on the cheques, and smiled to himself, for as a magistrate of the Commercial Court, he knew the situation of the publishers. He gave Lucien four thousand five hundred francs, on the understanding that he should enter the transaction in his books as "value received in silks".

Lucien went straight to Braulard and paid him handsomely to make sure that he would make arrangements for a first-class reception. Braulard promised to come to the dress rehearsal, in order to see for himself where his "Romans" could best employ their fleshy paws and start the general applause; and he did so. Lucien handed over the rest of the money to Coralie, but he did not tell her that he had been to see Camusot; he calmed her anxieties and those of Bérénice, who were already beginning to wonder how the household bills were to be paid. Martainville, one of the men of that time who knew most about the theatre, came two or three times to see Coralie rehearse. Several Royalist journalists had promised favourable notices, and Lucien had no suspicion of impending disaster.

On the evening before Coralie's first night a fatal event befell Lucien. D'Arthez's book had just come out, and the editor of Hector Merlin's paper asked Lucien to review it, he being the member of the staff best able to do so; he owed his fatal reputation for writing articles of this kind to his reviews of Nathan's novel. There were a number of people in the office, and all the newspaper staff was present. Martainville had come to discuss a point of general policy to be adopted by the Royalist newspapers against the Liberal press. Nathan, Merlin, and the rest of the staff of the *Réveil* had begun to realise the influence of Léon Giraud's bi-weekly newspaper whose influence was all the more dangerous because its language was moderate, prudent, and carefully weighed. People were beginning to talk of the circle in the Rue des Quatre-Vents as a second Convention. It had been decided that the Royalist newspapers must carry on a systematic war to the death against these dangerous adversaries, who were, indeed, responsible for sowing the seed from which the Doctrine later sprang, that sect fated to overthrow the Bourbons, with the help of the most brilliant of the Royalist writers, who joined them for the sake of a mean revenge.

D'Arthez, whose absolutist opinions were not known, was included in the general anathema pronounced on his circle, and he was to be the first victim. His book was to be given a " slashing review ", according to the time-honoured formula.

Lucien refused to write the article. His refusal aroused violent indignation among the eminent supporters of the Royalist party, who had come to the meeting. Lucien was bluntly told that a new recruit could not say what he would and would not do ; if he was not prepared to stand by the Monarchy and the Church, he could go back where he came from. Merlin and Martainville took him aside and pointed out to him in the most friendly way that he had exposed Coralie to the hatred of the Liberal papers, and that she had only the Royalist and Ministerialist press to support her. Coralie was sure to arouse fierce controversy, the kind of notoriety that all actresses long for.

" You know nothing about it," Martainville told him. " She will play for the next three months, exposed to the cross-fire of articles, and she will make thirty thousand francs in the provinces if she goes on tour at the end of the season. Just because of one of those scruples that will prevent you from ever becoming a politician, and that you ought to make an effort to overcome, you will ruin Coralie and your own career. You are throwing away your bread and butter."

Lucien found himself forced to choose between d'Arthez and Coralie ; if he refused to demolish d'Arthez's book in the leading Royalist newspaper and in the *Réveil*, his mistress would suffer. The poor poet returned home, death in his soul ; he sat down by the fire in his room, and read that book, one of the finest works of modern literature. His tears fell on page after page, and for a long time he hesitated ; but in the end he wrote a contemptuous article, as he could do so well; he treated the book as boys treat some beautiful bird, pulling out its feathers and tormenting it. His terrible sarcasm was enough to ruin the book.

He read it through a second time ; and as he did so, all Lucien's better nature awoke in him ; he crossed Paris, although it was midnight, and stood outside d'Arthez's lodgings. He saw the pure faint light shining in his window, the light he had watched so many times, with the deep sense of admiration merited by the noble constancy of that truly great man. He could not bring himself to go up those stairs, and for a while he stood irresolute on the pavement. At last, impelled by his good angel, he knocked at d'Arthez's door. D'Arthez was reading ; he had no fire.

" What has happened ? " the young writer asked when he saw Lucien, for he guessed that only some great disaster could have brought him.

" Your book is sublime," Lucien began, his eyes filling with tears, " and they have ordered me to attack it."

" Poor child, you are eating hard-earned bread," said d'Arthez.

" I ask you only one thing—don't tell a soul that I have been here, leave me to my hell, and my occupations of the damned. Perhaps no one can ever succeed until his heart has become utterly callous in its most sensitive parts."

" Still the same! " said d'Arthez.

" Do you think I am an utter cad ? No, d'Arthez, that is not true; I am only a child, madly in love."

And he explained his situation.

" Let me see the article," said d'Arthez, moved by what Lucien had told him about Coralie.

Lucien handed him the manuscript. D'Arthez, as he read it, could not help smiling.

" What a waste of talent! " he exclaimed. But when he looked at Lucien, sitting in an armchair, overcome with grief, he said no more.

" Will you leave it with me to correct ? I will let you have it back tomorrow," he said. " Flippancy dishonours a work, but serious criticism is sometimes a compliment. I will make your article more honourable for both of us. And besides, nobody knows my faults as well as I know them myself."

" When you are climbing a bare mountainside, you sometimes find fruit to quench the torments of thirst ; this is such a fruit! " said Lucien, throwing himself into d'Arthez's arms and bursting into tears. " I seem to have put my conscience into your keeping, to return it to me one day."

" I regard periodical repentance as great hypocrisy," said d'Arthez solemnly. " Such repentance is a sort of tax levied on wrongdoing. Repentance is a virginity that the soul owes to God ; a man who repents twice is a horrible sycophant. I am very much afraid that you only repent in the hope of absolution! "

These words shattered Lucien. He walked slowly back to the Rue de la Lune. The next day he handed in his article, which d'Arthez had corrected and returned ; but from that time he sank into a melancholy that he did not always succeed in disguising.

That evening, when he saw the house full at the Gymnase, he experienced the agonising emotions to which a first performance gives rise, augmented, in his case, by the strength of his love. All his vanity was at stake and he scanned the rows of faces as an accused man scans the faces of the jury and the court ; a murmur made him tremble ; every little incident on the stage, Coralie's entrances and exits, the smallest inflexions of her voice, agitated him beyond measure. The play in which Coralie was appearing was of the kind that often falls flat at first, but which afterwards has an immense success ; it did fall flat. When she came on, Coralie got no applause, and was struck by the coldness of the house. The only applause in the boxes came from Camusot. Certain individuals in the upper circle and in the gallery silenced the shopkeeper with repeated cries of " Hush! " The gallery silenced the claque when they delivered salvoes of obviously exaggerated applause. Martainville applauded courageously, and the hypocritical Florine, Nathan, and Merlin followed suit. The play was clearly a failure. There was a crowd in Coralie's dressing-room, but that crowd only aggravated the disaster with their commiserations. The actress returned home in despair, not so much on her own account as on Lucien's.

" Braulard has let us down! " he said.

Coralie was heartbroken. The next day she was in a high fever, utterly unable to play ; she saw her career ruined. Lucien kept the papers from her, but in the dining-room he opened them and read them. Every newspaper without exception attributed the failure of the play to Coralie. She had over-estimated her capacities ; she was charming in the Boulevards, but had not the stature for the Gymnase ; she had been driven on by a laudable ambition, but she had misjudged her powers, she had attempted a part for which she was not naturally fitted. Lucien now read paragraphs on Coralie composed according to the treacherous formulæ of his own articles on Nathan. Lucien raged like Milo of Crotona when he found his hands made fast in the oak that he himself had cleft. He grew white with anger. His friends gave Coralie the benefit of their generosity in the form of advice, uttered in tones of friendship, but treacherous in its intent. She ought, they said, to play parts that the perfidious authors of these shameful reviews knew to be entirely contrary to her talent. This was the line taken by the Royalist newspapers ; no doubt Nathan had told them what to say. As for the Liberal press and the smaller newspapers, they employed all the perfidies, all the clever sarcasm, that Lucien himself had once practised. Coralie heard sobs and leaped from her bed to comfort Lucien. She saw the newspapers, and was anxious to know what they said. She read them all, and then she went back to bed, where she lay in silence.

Florine was in the conspiracy ; she had been prepared for the result, and had learned Coralie's part—she had rehearsed it with Nathan. The management, who believed in the play, was willing to give Coralie's part to Florine. The manager came to see the poor actress ; she was in tears and utterly downcast. But when he told her, in front of Lucien, that Florine had learned her part and that it was impossible not to put on the play that evening, she sat up and sprang out of bed.

" I will play! " she exclaimed, and then fainted.

So Florine was given Coralie's part, and in it she made a name for herself and saved the play. She was praised to the skies in all the newspapers, and that was the beginning of her career as the great actress you all know. Florine's triumph infuriated Lucien beyond all bounds.

" A wretched girl whom you rescued from want! If they like, the Gymnase can cancel your engagement! I shall be Count de Rubempré—I shall make a fortune and marry you! "

" What nonsense! " said Coralie, looking at him with a wan smile.

" Nonsense ? " said Lucien. " Just wait a few days, and you shall have a beautiful house, and a carriage, and I will write a play for you! "

He took two thousand francs and made for Frascati's. The unhappy poet remained there for seven hours, inwardly devoured by the furies, but his expression calm and cool. During that day, and part of the evening, his luck varied between the two extremes. At one moment, he possessed as much as thirty thousand francs ; but he left without a sou. When he got back, he found Finot, who had come to see him about " his little articles ". Lucien made the mistake of complaining.

" Oh, life is not all rosy," said Finot. " You made your right-about-face so abruptly that you were bound to lose the support of the Liberal newspapers, which are much more powerful than the Ministerialist and Royalist press. You should never go from one camp to another without first preparing a good berth for yourself to make up for the losses that you are bound to suffer ; but, in any case, the sensible thing to do is to go and see your friends, explain your reasons, and get their advice on your change of front ; then they are in your confidence, and they will defend you, and the upshot is that you remain on good terms with your old colleagues, like Nathan and Merlin, and do one another services. Wolves do not eat wolves. You have behaved with lamb-like innocence over this affair. You will have to show your teeth to your new party if you hope to get any of the pickings. And so you have, quite naturally, been sacrificed to Nathan. I will not conceal from you that your article against d'Arthez has caused a great deal of talk, in fact quite an outcry. Marat is a saint in comparison with you. Attacks are being prepared against you, and your book will never survive. What stage has it reached, by the way, your novel ? "

" There are the final proofs," said Lucien.

" All the unsigned articles against this young d'Arthez in the Ministerialist and Ultra newspapers are attributed to you. All the pinpricks in the *Réveil* are directed against the group in the Rue des Quatre-Vents these days. The hits are all the more telling because they are funny. There is a very serious and responsible political group behind Léon Giraud's newspaper, a group that will come into power sooner or later."

" I have not set foot inside the *Réveil* offices for the last week."

" Well, don't forget my little articles. Write fifty of them straight off if you like, and I will pay you for the lot ; but mind they are the right colour! " And Finot, with seeming carelessness, suggested the subject of an amusing article against the Keeper of the Seals, and told Lucien a little story against him that was, so he said, going round Paris.

Anxious to make good his losses at play, Lucien overcame his depression, summoned up his youthful energy and brilliance, and composed thirty articles of two columns each. This done, he went to Dauriat's, where he was sure of finding Finot, to whom he wanted to hand them over secretly ; he also wanted to have a word with the publisher on the subject of the non-appearance of the *Marguerites*. He found the bookshop full of his enemies. All conversation stopped when he appeared and there was a dead silence. Seeing himself cut by all the journalists, Lucien's courage was redoubled, and he said to himself, as he had said in the avenue in the Luxembourg gardens, " I will triumph! "

Dauriat was neither friendly nor helpful. He was sarcastic and pointed out that, according to the terms of the contract, the publication date of the *Marguerites* was left entirely to his discretion. He was waiting until Lucien's position was such as to ensure the book's success, and he reminded the poet that he had purchased the manuscript outright. When Lucien objected that Dauriat was bound to publish the *Marguerites* by the very nature of the contract, and the relative professions of the contracting parties, the publisher replied that, on the contrary, he was in no way bound to publish at a loss, and he was the sole judge of the expediency of bringing the book out. There was, of course, a solution in which the law always took the part of the author: Lucien was perfectly free to return the three thousand francs, to take back his manuscript, and to place it with a Royalist publisher.

Lucien retired, more exasperated by Dauriat's moderate tones than he had been by his autocratic arrogance at his first interview. And so it seemed that the *Marguerites* would not be published until Lucien had the backing of powerful friends, or until he himself became a power to be reckoned with. The poet went home slowly, in a state of depression that would have led him to suicide if action had followed thought. He found Coralie in bed, pale and ill.

"She must have a part or she will die," Bérénice said to him, as Lucien dressed to go to a party given by Mlle des Touches, where he would be meeting des Lupeaulx, Vignon, Blondet, Mme d'Espard and Mme de Bargeton.

The party was being given for Conti, the composer, who possessed one of the most beautiful voices off the stage, not excepting Cinti, la Pasta, Garcia, Levasseur and two or three of the most celebrated amateurs of the day. Lucien slipped across to where the Marquise and her cousin were sitting with Mme de Montcornet. The unhappy boy assumed a light-hearted, happy and confident manner; he was witty, and behaved as he had done in the days of his splendour; he was anxious on no account to allow these people to see that he was in need of their help. He expatiated on the services that he was rendering to the Royalist party, pointing out, by way of proof, the outcry against him in the Liberal press.

"You will be well rewarded," Mme de Bargeton said to him with a gracious smile. "Go to the Chancellory the day after tomorrow, with the Héron and des Lupeaulx, and you will be given your patent, signed by the King. The Keeper of the Seals will be taking it to the Palace tomorrow; but there is to be a meeting of the Council, and he won't be back until late; but if I hear the result during the evening I will send you a message. Where are you living?"

"I will call," said Lucien, ashamed to admit that he was living in the Rue de la Lune.

"The Duke de Lenoncourt and the Duke de Navarreins have spoken to the King on your behalf," said the Marquise, "and they have mentioned your absolute and entire devotion, which deserves a high recompense to compensate for the persecutions of the Liberal party. And you will add lustre to the name and title of De Rubempré, to which you have a claim through your mother. The King commanded His Excellency this evening to draw up a patent authorising Lucien Chardon Esquire, as the grandson of the last Count, on his Mother's side, to bear the name and title of the Count de Rubempré.

"My cousin had the happy thought of sending him, through the Duke, your sonnet on the Lily, and when he had read it, His Majesty said, 'We must favour the songsters (Chardonnerets) of Pindus'—and M. de Navarreins replied, 'Especially when the King can work the miracle of turning them into eagles'."

Lucien's effusion of gratitude would have softened the heart of any woman whose feelings had been less deeply wounded than had those of Louise d'Espard de Nègrepelisse.

Her desire for vengeance was great in proportion to Lucien's good looks. Des Lupeaulx was right, Lucien had no tact; he had no suspicion that the patent was only one of those chimeras for which Mme d'Espard was famous. Made bold by this success, and by the flattering attentions shown him by Mlle des Touches, he stayed on until two in the morning in order to be able to speak to her privately. Lucien had heard, in a Royalist newspaper office, that Mlle des Touches had secretly collaborated in writing a play in which the marvel of the moment, *la petite Fay*, was to appear. When the drawing-rooms had emptied, he drew Mlle des Touches onto a sofa in her boudoir and told her the story of Coralie's misfortunes and his own in so touching a fashion that the illustrious hermaphrodite promised to give Coralie the principal part.

The next day Coralie, cheered by Mlle des Touches' promise to Lucien, got up, and was sitting at breakfast with her poet, who was reading Lousteau's newspaper. In it he found his amusing account of the story that had been invented against the Keeper of the Seals and his wife. The blackest malice was concealed beneath the most telling strokes of wit; Louis XVIII himself was brought into the picture and made to look ridiculous, but in such a way that prosecution was impossible. This is the story, which the Liberal party gave out as true, but which only added to the number of their clever calumnies.

It was said that Louis XVIII's passion for sentimental correspondence, scented notes full of stars and madrigals, was the last expression of his love, which had become purely theoretical; he had passed, so it was said, from the real to the ideal. The illustrious mistress, so cruelly attacked by Béranger under the name of Octavia, had become seriously alarmed. Correspondence was languishing. The more Octavia displayed her wit, the cooler and shorter grew her lover's replies. At last Octavia discovered the cause of her fall into disfavour; her power was being threatened by the sweets and spices of a new correspondence between the Royal scribe and the wife of the Keeper of the Seals. This excellent lady was said to be incapable of writing even a short note, and it was concluded that she was purely and simply the editor responsible for the productions of a bold ambition. Who could be concealed underneath her petticoats? After making her own observations, Octavia came to the conclusion that the King was carrying on a correspondence with his Minister.

Her plans were quickly made. With the help of a faithful friend, she arranged that the Minister should be kept in the Chamber by a stormy discussion, and she contrived a private interview with the King, in which she told him the secret of this deception. Louis XVIII flew into a royal and truly Bourbon passion; the storm broke on Octavia's head; he refused to believe her. Octavia offered to prove it to him forthwith, and begged him to write a note requiring an immediate reply. The unlucky wife, taken by surprise, sent for her husband to come at once from the Chamber; but everything had been planned in advance, and at that very moment he was making a speech. His wife sweated blood, racked her brains, and replied as best she could.

" Your Chancellor will tell you the rest," said Octavia, laughing at the King's discomfiture.

Although this story was utterly untrue, the article infuriated the Keeper of the Seals, his wife, and the King. Des Lupeaulx was said to have been the inventor of the story, but Finot never gave him away. This witty and scurrilous article was a source of great delight to Liberals and Royalists alike. Lucien thought it amusing, and saw it as nothing more than a good story. He went, next day, to pick up des Lupeaulx and Baron du Châtelet. The Baron was going to offer his thanks to His Excellency, for Châtelet had been made a Councillor of State Extraordinary, and promoted to the title of Count, with the promise of the Prefecture of the Charente in a few months' time, when the present Prefect should have completed his term of office in order to receive the maximum retiring pension. Count du Châtelet (for the *du* had found its way into the patent) took Lucien in his carriage and treated him as an equal. But for Lucien's articles, he might not have risen so quickly; the Liberal persecution had served him as a stepping-stone. Des Lupeaulx was already at the Ministry, in the Secretary-General's office. On seeing Lucien, that functionary gave a start of surprise and looked at des Lupeaulx.

" What! You dare to come here? " said the Secretary-General, to Lucien's utter astonishment. " His Excellency has torn up the patent that was prepared for you—here it is! " (He held up the first torn sheet of paper that came to hand.) " The Minister was determined to find out who was the author of the abominable article that appeared yesterday—here is a copy of the newspaper," said the Secretary-General, handing Lucien his own article. " You call yourself a Royalist, and yet you write for this scurrilous newspaper, that turns the hair of the Ministers white, that is a constant source of worry to the Centre, and that wants to drag the country headlong into ruin! You lunch with the *Corsaire* and the *Miroir* and the *Constitutionnel*, and the *Courier*, and then you go on to dine with the *Quotidienne* and the *Réveil*, and sup with Martainville, the sworn enemy of the Ministry, who is driving the King towards absolutism, and who is doing more to precipitate a revolution than if he belonged to the extreme Left! You are a very clever journalist, but you will never be a politician! The Minister denounced you to the King as the author of this article, and the King was so angry that he severely reprimanded the Duke de Navarreins, his First Gentleman of the Bedchamber. You have made enemies who will be all the more formidable because they have shown you favour in the past! Conduct that one expects from an enemy is monstrous in a friend! "

" But, my dear fellow, are you a child ? " said des Lupeaulx. " You have compromised me. Mme d'Espard and Mme de Bargeton and Mme de Montcornet must be furious. The Duke is bound to vent his annoyance on the Marquise, and the Marquise will blame her cousin! Keep away from them—wait! "

" Here is His Excellency—go! " said the Secretary-General.

Lucien found himself in the Place Vendôme, stunned like a man who has been knocked on the head with a club. He made his way home, walking along the boulevards, and trying to think clearly. He saw himself as the plaything of envious, grasping, and treacherous men. What could he do in that world of contending ambitions ? He was a child running after the pleasures and gratifications of vanity, and losing them all ; a poet incapable of deep-laid plans, flying like a moth from one candle-flame to another ; the slave of circumstance, thinking nobly and acting badly. His conscience was a pitiless executioner. And what was more, he had no money left, and he was exhausted with work and misery. His articles took third place after Merlin's and Nathan's.

Sunk in these thoughts, he did not notice where he was going. As he walked he noticed, in some of the reading rooms, which were beginning at that time to lend books as well as newspapers, a poster, upon which, under a most odd title, quite unknown to him, he read his own name : " By Lucien Chardon de Rubempré." His book had come out, and he had not even heard about it! The newspapers had not so much as mentioned it. He stood there, his arms hanging at his sides, motionless, and did not even notice a group of elegant young men, including Rastignac and de Marsay and others of his acquaintance. Nor did he notice Michel Chrestien and Léon Giraud, who were walking towards him.

" You are Chardon ? " Michel said to him in a voice that set Lucien's nerves vibrating like struck strings.

"Don't you know me?" he asked, turning pale. Michel spat in his face.

"Take that for your articles against d'Arthez. If everyone was true to his cause and to his friends, as I am, the press would be what it ought to be—a sacred office, honoured and honourable!"

Lucien had staggered back; he fell against Rastignac and appealed to him and to de Marsay:

"Gentlemen, you cannot refuse to be my seconds. But first of all I want to make matters even, and withdrawal out of the question."

Lucien struck Michel a blow in the face, for which he was not prepared. The others threw themselves between the Republican and the Royalist, to prevent the dispute from developing into a street brawl. Rastignac seized Lucien and took him to his flat in the Rue Taitbout, which was only a few steps away from the scene of this incident, which took place on the Boulevard du Gand, just at dinner-time; thanks to this circumstance, the crowd that usually gathers on such occasions, did not appear. De Marsay came to fetch Lucien, and the two young dandies, in the best of spirits, led him off to dine with them at the Café Anglais, where they made him drunk.

"Are you a good swordsman?" De Marsay asked him.

"I have never had a foil in my hand."

"Pistols, then?" said Rastignac.

"I have never fired a pistol in my life."

"Then you will have luck on your side. I would not like to have to fight against you; you will probably kill your man," said de Marsay.

Fortunately Lucien found Coralie in bed and asleep.

She had acted, at short notice, in a one-act play, and had had her revenge; for she was applauded legitimately, not by a hired claque. Her enemies had been taken unprepared, and this evening the manager of the theatre decided to give her the leading part in Camille Maupin's play. He had discovered, by this time, the reason for Coralie's failure in her first part. He was indignant when he learned of Florine's and Nathan's intrigues to bring about the downfall of an actress in whom he believed, and promised Coralie the protection of the management.

At five o'clock Rastignac came to fetch Lucien.

" The name of your street is most appropriate, my dear fellow," he said by way of greeting. " Let us be the first on the field, on the Clinancourt road—it is good form, and we ought to set them an example."

" I will tell you the form," said de Marsay, as the cab drove along the Faubourg Saint-Denis. " You are given your pistols at twenty-five paces, and then you walk towards one another as far as you like, up to a distance of fifteen paces. Then you may each take five steps, and fire three shots, not more. Whatever happens, that is the end of the matter. We load your adversary's pistols, and his seconds load yours. The weapons were chosen by the four seconds, jointly, at the gunsmith's. I give you my word that we have increased the element of luck—they are cavalry pistols."

Lucien's life had become a nightmare ; he did not care whether he lived or died. The courage of the suicide stood him in good stead, for it enabled him to carry the affair off with an air of bravado in the presence of the onlookers. He remained where he was, without taking a single step forward. This indifference passed for calculated coolness, and they all thought the more of the poet's courage. Michel Chrestien advanced up to his limit. The two adversaries fired simultaneously, for the insults had been judged to be equal.

At the first shot, Chrestien's bullet grazed Lucien's chin, and Lucien's passed ten feet above the head of his adversary. Michel's second bullet lodged in the collar of the poet's great-coat, which, fortunately for its wearer, was padded with buckram. The third bullet struck Lucien in the chest, and he fell.

" Is he dead ? " Michel asked.

" No," said the surgeon, " he will pull through."

" So much the worse ! " said Michel.

" Yes, indeed, so much the worse ! " Lucien repeated, and he wept.

By midday the wretched boy was in his own room, and in bed ; it had taken five hours, and infinite pains, to move him. His wound was not dangerous in itself, but great precautions were necessary in case fever should set in and cause troublesome complications.

Coralie fought back her despair and grief. All the time that her lover was in danger, she spent the evenings saying over her parts with Bérénice. Lucien was not out of danger for two months; and the poor girl sometimes had to act parts in which she had to seem gay and light-hearted, while all the time she was thinking:

"My beloved Lucien may be dying at this very moment."

During this time, Lucien was attended by Bianchon; he owed his life to the devotion of this friend whom he had so deeply injured; but d'Arthez had told him the story of Lucien's secret visit in an attempt to vindicate the unfortunate poet. In a period of lucidity—for Lucien had developed a very severe attack of brain-fever—Bianchon, who suspected d'Arthez of having made up the story out of generosity, questioned the invalid; Lucien assured him that he had written only one article on d'Arthez's book, the serious piece of criticism that had appeared in Hector Merlin's newspaper.

At the end of the first month Fendant and Cavalier went bankrupt. Bianchon told Coralie to keep this fearful blow from Lucien. The famous *An Archer of Charles IX*, published under a fantastic title, had no success whatever. In order to raise what money he could before filing his petition, Fendant (unknown to Cavalier) had sold the edition outright to a firm of grocers, who hawked it at a cheap rate. At this moment Lucien's book was adorning the parapets of the bridges and Quais of Paris. The bookstalls on the Quai des Augustins, who had taken a small number of copies from the publishers, therefore found themselves seriously out of pocket as a result of this sudden remaindering of the edition; the four duodecimo volumes that they had bought at four francs fifty were being sold for fifty sous. The booksellers raised a great outcry; but the newspapers maintained an absolute silence.

Barbet had not expected this book to be remaindered; he believed in Lucien's talent. Contrary to his habits, he had bought two hundred copies, and the prospect of losing his money drove him to distraction. He called Lucien every name he could think of. But then Barbet made a heroic decision; he put away his copies in a corner of his shop and waited, with the stubbornness peculiar to misers, until his competitors had sold out their stock at cheap rates. Later, in 1824,

An air of bravado in the presence of the onlookers

when, thanks to d'Arthez's fine preface, the merit of the book and two articles by Léon Giraud, the novel was sought after, Barbet sold all his stock, one by one, at ten francs a copy.

The precautions of Bérénice and Coralie notwithstanding, it was impossible to prevent Hector Merlin from coming to see his dying friend; and he made him drink, drop by drop, the bitter draught of the story of Fendant and Cavalier, made bankrupt by the publication of an unknown author's first book. Only Martainville stood by Lucien and wrote a fine article in favour of his novel; but the editor of *Aristarque,* the *Oriflamme* and the *Drapeau Blanc* was so well hated by Liberals and Ministerialists alike that the courageous efforts of this fighter, who never failed to repay the Liberal insults tenfold, did Lucien nothing but harm. Not a single newspaper took up the critical challenge, in spite of all the attacks of the Royalist swash-buckler.

Coralie, Bérénice and Bianchon shut the door on all Lucien's so-called friends, who raised cries of indignation. But it was impossible to keep out the bailiffs. Fendant and Cavalier's bankruptcy rendered their cheques exigible according to a ruling of the Commercial Court that hits third parties extremely hard, for they are thus deprived of the advantage of deferred payments. Lucien learned that Camusot was prosecuting him vigorously. When she saw his name, the actress guessed the disgraceful and humiliating step that her poet had taken; but in her eyes it was an angelic sacrifice; she loved him more than ever, and was determined not to approach Camusot.

When the bailiffs, armed with a warrant, came to arrest their prisoner, they found him in bed, and were reluctant at the idea of taking a sick man to prison. They went off to consult Camusot before applying to the President of the Commercial Court for an order to take the debtor to a hospital. Camusot hurried round to the Rue de la Lune. Coralie went downstairs, and came up again, with the warrants, in which Lucien was described as a tradesman, in her hands. How had she obtained these papers from Camusot? What had she promised him? She maintained a mournful silence; but she came upstairs looking like death.

Coralie acted in Camille Maupin's play, and helped to make the name of that distinguished literary hermaphrodite. The creation of that part was the last flicker of Coralie's bright flame. After the twentieth performance, just when Lucien was beginning to recover and go about again, and eat, and to talk about returning to work, Coralie fell ill. A secret sorrow was preying on her. Bérénice always believed that, in order to save Lucien, she had promised to go back to Camusot. The actress had the mortification of seeing her part given to Florine. Nathan had declared war on the Gymnase unless Florine was allowed to be Coralie's successor.

Coralie, in her anxiety not to see her part given to her rival, went on acting until she was at the end of her strength ; the Gymnase had made her several advances during Lucien's illness, so that she could not ask them to help her again. With the best will in the world, Lucien was not yet well enough to work, but he helped to nurse Coralie, in order to give Bérénice a little respite. This poor little household had reached a condition of absolute penury ; but they were fortunate enough to have, in Bianchon, a skilful and devoted doctor, who arranged with a chemist to give them credit.

The situation of the two lovers soon became known to the tradesmen and the landlord. The furniture was seized ; the tailor and the dressmaker, who were no longer afraid of the journalist, pursued Coralie and Lucien relentlessly. At last, only the chemist and the pork-butcher would give credit to these two unlucky children. For a whole week Lucien, Bérénice, and the invalid had nothing to eat except pork in the various ingenious disguises devised by pork-butchers ; and this diet, indigestible at any time, made the actress worse. Lucien was forced by poverty to go in search of Lousteau to ask his late friend once again for the thousand francs owed him by that traitor. This, of all the steps that he was compelled to take in his desperation, was the one that he found the hardest of all.

Lousteau no longer dared to go back to the Rue de la Harpe ; he was sleeping in his friends' rooms in turn, for he was being pursued, tracked like a hare. Lucien at last succeeded in finding the fatal mentor who had initiated him into the world of letters at Flicoteaux. Lousteau was dining at the old table at which he had sat on the evening when Lucien, to his eternal misfortune, had left d'Arthez in order to join him. Lousteau offered to pay for his dinner, and Lucien accepted! They left Flicoteaux along with Claude Vignon, who was also dining there that day, and the great unknown author who kept his wardrobe at Samanons; but they could not raise enough among the four of them to pay for a cup of coffee at the Café Voltaire; their combined resources amounted to less than thirty sous. They strolled into the Luxembourg Gardens, in the hope of meeting a publisher, and they were lucky enough to meet one of the most famous printers of that time. Lousteau asked him for a loan of forty francs, which he gave him.

Lousteau divided the sum into four equal portions and gave one to each of the authors. Poverty had extinguished all Lucien's pride, along with every other sentiment: he shed tears as he described his situation to the three writers; but each of them had a story just as cruel to tell, and when each had told his tale of woe it seemed to the poet that he was the least unfortunate of the four. So that they all needed to forget their misfortunes and their painful thoughts, which redoubled their misfortunes. Lousteau made for the Palais Royal to gamble with what remained of his ten francs. The great nameless author, although he had the most heavenly mistress, went to a vile and sinister house there to sink into the mire of perilous delights. Vignon betook himself to the Petit Rocher de Cancale where he proposed to drown memory and thought by drinking two bottles of Bordeaux. Lucien parted from Claude Vignon at the door of the restaurant, declining to join him in that supper. The great poet of Angoulême took his leave of the only journalist who had not been hostile to him with fearful misgivings in his heart.

"What shall I do?" he asked him.

"It's the way of the world," said the eminent critic. "Your book is very good, but you have made enemies, and you must expect a long uphill fight. Genius is a painful malady. Every writer goes about with a parasite in his heart, a sort of tape-worm that eats up his feelings as they hatch. Which will survive, the parasite or the man? The fact is, it takes a very great man to hold the balance between genius and character. As talent increases, the heart dries up. Any man who is not a colossus, or who has not, at least, the shoulders of a Hercules, is left, in the end, either without heart or without talent. You are fragile and delicate; it will break you," he added, as he turned to go into the restaurant.

Lucien walked home, turning over in his mind that terrible verdict, whose profound truth seemed to him to throw light on the literary profession.

"Money!" a voice kept crying.

He made out, payable to himself, three cheques for a thousand francs, payable in one, two, and three months respectively, signing them with a perfect imitation of David Séchard's signature. He took them to Métivier, the paper-merchant in the Rue Serpente, who cashed them without raising the slightest difficulty. Lucien wrote a few lines to his brother-in-law to give him warning of this raid on his cash-box, promising him, as men in such circumstances usually do, to meet the bills when they fell due. When he had paid his own and Coralie's debts, there were three hundred francs left, which the poet handed over to Bérénice, telling her not to give him any money if he should ask for it. He was afraid that he might yield to the impulse to go and gamble. Lucien, animated by a sombre, taciturn inward rage, set to work to write his most brilliant series of articles, working by lamplight as he watched by Coralie's bedside. When he ran short of ideas, he looked at his adored mistress, pale as porcelain, beautiful with the beauty of the dying, and she smiled at him with her wan lips, her eyes burning with a fever more of the mind than of the body. Lucien sent his articles to the papers; but as he was unable to go in person, and bully the editors, the articles were rejected. When he did finally go to the office, Théodore Gaillard, who had formerly advanced him money and who later made capital out of these literary jewels, gave him a cool reception.

"You must be careful, my dear fellow; you are not as witty as you used to be—you must not let yourself down. Your work lacks *verve*!" he said.

"That young Lucien has written himself out with his novel and his first few articles," was the verdict of Félicien Vernou, Merlin, and all the journalists who had envied him, when his name happened to be mentioned at Dauriat's or at the Vaudeville. " He is sending in very poor stuff now."

To have written yourself out, to use a phrase current among journalists, is a sentence against which it is difficult to appeal once it has been passed. This verdict, which was repeated everywhere, was, unknown to himself, the ruin of Lucien, who already had more than enough to bear. Exhausted by the strain of work, he was sued for the bills he had made out in David Séchard's name, and in desperation he asked Camusot for advice. Coralie's rejected lover was so generous as to help Lucien. This dreadful situation went on for two months punctuated by any number of writs, which, on Camusot's advice, Lucien put in the hands of Desroches, a friend of Bixiou, Blondet, and des Lupeaulx.

At the beginning of August Bianchon told the poet that Coralie could not recover and had only a few days to live. Bérénice and Lucien spent those fateful days in weeping. They could not hide their tears from the poor girl, who was in despair at the thought of dying, because of Lucien. She was strangely altered, and begged Lucien to send for a priest. The actress desired to be reconciled with the Church and to die in peace. She died as a Christian, in sincere repentance.

The anguish of these days, and Coralie's death, broke down Lucien's courage. The poet was overwhelmed with grief and sat in a chair at the foot of Coralie's bed, not taking his eyes off her until he saw the actress's eyes dimmed by the hand of death.

It was five o'clock in the morning. A bird flew against the flower-pots that stood on the window-sill and twittered a few notes of song. Bérénice was on her knees, kissing Coralie's dead hand, that grew cold under her tears. At eleven Lucien went out, driven by his despair, to try to raise enough money to bury his mistress, ready to throw himself on the mercy of the Marquise d'Espard, or Count du Châtelet, or Mme de Bargeton, or Mlle des Touches, or that terrible dandy, de Marsay ; he no longer had either pride or strength left. He would have enlisted as a soldier to raise a little money. He walked on, bowed down and distraught with grief, and scarcely noticing where he was going, to Camille Maupin's house. He went

She died as a Christian, in sincere repentance

in, without giving a thought to the state of his clothes, and asked if she would see him.

" Mademoiselle did not go to bed until three," he was told, " and we dare not disturb her before she rings."

" What time does she ring ? "

" Never before ten."

Lucien thereupon wrote one of those terrible letters in which destitute elegance no longer attempts to conceal anything. There had been a day when he had wondered how such self-abasements could be possible, when Lousteau had told him of the appeals made by young men of talent to Finot, and now his pen surpassed, perhaps, the limits to which misfortune had driven his predecessors. He returned by the boulevards, crazed and delirious, without suspecting that despair had dictated to him a terrible masterpiece. On the way he met Barbet.

" Barbet," he begged, holding out his hand to him, " five hundred francs! "

" No, two hundred," replied the bookseller.

" Ah, then you have a heart! "

" Yes, but I have a business as well. I have lost a lot of money through you," he added, and gave Lucien an account of the bankruptcy of Fendant and Cavalier. " Can you put me in the way of making some ? "

Lucien shuddered.

" You are a poet, I suppose you can write all kinds of verses," the bookseller continued. " I am looking for some songs just now to go into a collection of popular songs by various authors, so that I can get round the copyright regulations. I want a nice collection to sell on the streets at ten sous. If you like to let me have ten good drinking songs, something with a bit of smut—you know—by tomorrow evening, I will let you have two hundred francs."

Lucien returned home. He saw Coralie lying stiff and straight on a camp-bed, wrapped in an old sheet that Bérénice had sewn with tears. She had lighted four candles at the four corners of the bed. Coralie's face was radiant with that flower of beauty that speaks so eloquently to the living of perfect calm. She looked like a pale girl in a decline ; and it seemed almost as if her two violet lips were about to murmur the name of Lucien, that, together with the name of God, she had spoken with her last breath.

Lucien sent Bérénice to order a funeral that would not cost more than two hundred francs, including a service at the poor little church of Bonne-Nouvelle. As soon as she had gone, the poet sat down at his table, beside the body of his dead love, and composed the ten street-songs to fit popular tunes. It cost him an untold effort to force himself to work ; but in the end inspiration came at the bidding of necessity, as if he had never suffered. He was already learning to put into practice the terrible divorce between heart and mind, of which Claude Vignon had spoken. What a night the poor child spent, composing by the light of the wax candles, in the company of the priest who was praying for Coralie, songs to be sung in public houses. By the next morning Lucien had written the last of the songs, and was trying it out to a popular tune ; Bérénice and the priest thought that he was out of his mind when they heard him singing :

Away with morality,
   Cares and pretence,
Why should servants of folly
   Call upon sense ?
Any words that are jolly
   Will serve for a song,
Philosophers sage do attest,
   So away with Apollo,
   His music is hollow,
   For Bacchus is lord
   Of drinking and jest!
Laugh and be merry!
And the devil may care for the rest!

Every good drinker,
   Hippocrates says,
Lives ninety-nine years,
   And what does it matter

If he's weak at the knees
  And the girls cannot please
So long as the flagon is filled!
  So long as the elbow
  Can lift up a glass
  We'll laugh with the best
  With drinking and jest.
Laugh and be merry!
And the devil may care for the rest!

Where we have come from
  We know very well,
But where we are going
  There's no man can tell,
But whate'er may come after
  With song and with laughter
We'll drink to the end of our days.
  It's sure we will die,
  Let us live while we may,
  Turn night into day
  With drinking and jest.
Laugh and be merry!
And the devil may care for the rest!

The poet was singing the last terrible couplet when Bianchon and d'Arthez came in and found him in a paroxysm of despair and exhaustion. He burst into a storm of tears, and had not enough strength left to make a fair copy of his verses. When, through his tears, he had given an account of his situation, there were tears in the eyes of his friends as well.

" This wipes out many sins," said d'Arthez.

" Happy are those who suffer their hell in this life," said the priest gravely.

The aspect of that beautiful dead face smiling at eternity ; the spectacle of her lover buying her a grave by writing street songs ; the coffin paid for by Barbet ; the four candles burning round the actress of the basquina and the red stockings with green clocks who had once thrilled a packed house; and in the doorway the priest who had reconciled her to God, and who was now going back to his church to say a Mass for the girl who had loved much—these grandeurs and infamies, these sorrows crushed under the weight of necessity, left the great writer and the great doctor speechless, and they sat down without being able to utter a word.

A servant appeared, and announced Mlle des Touches. That beautiful and high-minded girl took in the situation at a glance. She hurried over to Lucien and pressed two thousand-franc notes into his hand.

" It is too late," he said, looking at her with lifeless eyes.

D'Arthez, Bianchon and Mlle des Touches stayed with Lucien and tried to comfort his despair with kind words, but all the springs of life seemed to be broken in him. At noon all the circle of friends except Michel Chrestien—who had, however, learned the truth about the extent of Lucien's culpability—came to the little church of Bonne-Nouvelle; Bérénice and Mlle des Touches, two fellow-actors from the Gymnase, Coralie's dresser, and poor Camusot were also there. The men accompanied the actress to the cemetery of Père-Lachaise. Camusot shed hot tears, and gave Lucien his solemn word that he would buy the grave-plot in perpetuity, and erect a tombstone with the words CORALIE and beneath it,

Aged nineteen years
August 1822.

Lucien remained alone until night fell, on that hill from which he could see all Paris below him.

" Who will ever love me now ? " he wondered. " My real friends despise me. Whatever I may have done, everything about me seemed noble and beautiful to the girl who lies here! I have no one left in the world except my sister and David and my mother! What can they be thinking of me, I wonder ? "

The poor provincial celebrity went back to the Rue de la Lune. He could not endure the sight of the empty room, so he went and slept in a cheap hotel in the same street. Mlle des Touches' two thousand francs, and the proceeds of the sale of the furniture, paid all his debts. Bérénice and Lucien had a hundred francs left between them, on which they lived for two months, during which time Lucien remained in a state of morbid dejection. Bérénice took pity on him.

" If you were to go back to your home, how would you go ? " she said, in response to an exclamation of Lucien's. He was thinking of his sister and his mother and David Séchard.

" On foot," he said.

" Even so, you would have to buy food on the way. Even if you were to walk twelve leagues a day, you would need twenty francs at least."

" I will raise them somehow."

He collected all his clothes, and his beautiful linen, keeping only what was absolutely indispensable. He went to Samanon, who offered him fifteen francs for his entire wardrobe. He begged the money-lender to let him have enough to pay for his journey, but he could not move him. In his rage Lucien hastened hot-foot to Frascati's, staked his whole fortune, and returned without a sou. When he got back to the dreary room in the Rue de la Lune, he asked Bérénice for Coralie's shawl. The good-hearted girl quickly realised what the poor poet in despair meant to do, for Lucien told her that he had lost his money. He was going to hang himself.

" Are you mad, sir ? " she said. " Go out for a walk, and don't come back before midnight ; I will get the money for you ; but go by the boulevards, don't go down to the quais."

Lucien went and walked along the boulevards, beside himself with grief ; he watched the carriages and the passers-by and he felt utterly alone, a tiny particle in that great crowd in which ebbed and flowed the thousand currents of Paris life. In his fancy he could see the banks of the Charente and he longed for the happiness of being with his family. He experienced one of those sudden bursts of courage that are so deceptive in feminine natures, like Lucien's, and he resolved not to give up until he had confided everything to David Séchard and sought the advice of those three good angels that were left to him. As he walked, he saw Bérénice, dressed in her best clothes. She had taken her stand on the muddy pavement of the Boulevard Bonne-Nouvelle at the corner of the Rue de la Lune, and she was talking to a man.

" What are you doing here ? " Lucien asked her, appalled by the suspicion that arose in him.

" Here are twenty francs that may cost dear, but now you can go," she said, and slipped four coins into the poet's hand.

Bérénice left him, and Lucien lost sight of her, for, in justice to him it must be said that those four coins burned his hand, and he would gladly have returned them ; but he was obliged to keep them, as a last stigma set upon him by Paris life.

PART THREE

The Sufferings of an Inventor

Three kinds of greed

PART THREE

The Sufferings of an Inventor

THE NEXT day Lucien obtained a visa for his passport, bought a holly-wood walking-stick and took a place in a coach that left the square at the corner of the Rue de l'Enfer. For the sum of ten sous, the coach took him as far as Longjumeau. His first night on the road he slept in the stable of a farm two leagues beyond Arpajon. By the time he reached Orleans he was already thoroughly weary and exhausted, but a boatman, for three francs, agreed to take him down the river to Tours ; he only spent two francs on food on the journey. Five days' walking took Lucien from Tours to Poitiers. Some way beyond Poitiers, he found that he had only five francs left, but he summoned up his remaining strength in order to complete his journey. One evening, night overtook Lucien in the middle of open country, and he had just made up his mind to sleep in the open, when, looking down into a valley, he saw a carriage climbing the hill towards him. He managed to climb up behind and to squeeze himself between two travelling trunks without being seen by the postillion, the travellers, and a servant perched on the back seat. He succeeded in making himself comfortable enough to fall asleep in spite of the jolts. In the morning he was awakened by the sun shining on his face and by the sound of voices. He recognised Mansle, the little town where, eighteen months before, he had waited for Mme de Bargeton, his heart overflowing with love, hope, and joy. He realised that he was the centre of a little group of postillions and onlookers, and that, covered with dust, dirty and travel-stained as he was, he was bound to be an object of suspicion. He jumped down, and was about to speak, when two travellers got out of the carriage. He remained speechless, for he recognised the new Prefect of the Charente, Count Sixte du Châtelet, and his wife, Louise de Negrèpelisse.

"If only we had known whom chance had given us as a travelling companion!" said the Countess. "Won't you come inside with us?"

Lucien bowed to the pair with a look at once humble and hostile, and slipped away down a side road leading out of Mansle, intending to find some farm where he could buy milk and bread for his breakfast, rest, and think quietly about his future. He still had three francs left.

The author of *Marguerites* walked on and on in feverish haste. He followed the course of the river, noticing the features of the landscape, that became more and more beautiful as he went on. Towards midday he reached a place where a still expanse of water, bordered with willows, spread into a kind of lake. He stopped to contemplate this fresh and leafy grove, whose rural grace stirred him deeply. A house, belonging to a mill built on a turn of the river, was visible through the treetops, houseleeks growing on its thatched roof. The front of the house had no other ornament besides a few plants of jasmin, honeysuckle, and hops, and the garden plot was bright with phloxes and magnificent succulent plants. On the stone embankment, supported on roughly constructed piles that raised the foundations of the house above the level of the highest floods, he noticed nets spread out in the sun. Some ducks were swimming about in the clear pool between the two currents of rushing water from the mill-wheels, and the creaking noise of the mill was audible above the roar of the water. On a rustic bench, the poet saw a stout, good-natured housewife knitting as she watched a small child, who was chasing chickens.

"My good woman," said Lucien, advancing towards her, "I am quite exhausted—I have a touch of fever, and I have only three francs; will you give me a little brown bread and milk, and allow me to sleep on the straw for a week? That will give me time to write to my family, who will either send me some money or come here and fetch me."

"Willingly," she said, "if my husband has no objection, that is. Hey! Good man!"

The miller appeared, looked at Lucien, took his pipe from his mouth, and remarked :

" Three francs for a week ? We might as well let you stay for nothing."

" Perhaps I shall end as a miller's man," the poet reflected, as his eyes wandered over that delightful landscape, while the miller's wife prepared a bed for him ; there he slept on so long that the miller and his wife became alarmed.

" Courtois, go and see whether that young man is dead or alive ; he has been asleep fourteen hours now. I don't like to go in," said the miller's wife at midday the next day.

" It's my belief," said the miller to his wife, as he finished spreading out his nets and his fishing tackle, " that that handsome young fellow is some strolling actor, without a shirt to his back or a penny in his purse."

" What makes you think that, good man ? " asked his wife.

" Well, he is not a prince, or a minister, or a member of parliament, or a bishop ; so why are his hands white, like those of a man who does no work ? "

" It is surprising that hunger does not wake him," said the woman, who had just prepared some breakfast for the guest whom chance had sent them the previous day. " An actor ? " she went on thoughtfully. " Where would he be going ? This isn't the time of the Angoulême fair."

How could the miller and his wife know that, besides actors, princes and bishops, there is another kind of man, a man at once actor and prince, and a high priest by right of birth—the poet, who seems to do nothing, and who, when he has learned to paint humanity, is yet a ruler over humanity ?

" Who can he be then ? " said Courtois to his wife.

" Do you think it is dangerous to keep him ? " asked his wife.

" Oh, thieves are more wide awake than this fellow ; we should have been robbed already," said the miller.

" I am neither a prince nor a thief nor a bishop nor an actor," said Lucien sadly ; he had appeared suddenly, and had evidently overheard, through the window the discussion between husband and wife. " I am poor, and quite worn out, and I have walked all the way from Paris. My name is Lucien de Rubempré, and I am the son of M. Chardon, who had the chemist's shop in l'Houmeau that now belongs to M. Postel. My sister is married to David Séchard, the printer in the Place du Mûrier, in Angoulême."

" Wait a moment! " said the miller. " That printer, now, isn't he the son of that old skinflint who is making such a good thing out of his land at Marsac? "

" The very man," said Lucien.

" A nice father he is, upon my word! " said Courtois. " They say he has sold his son up and yet he's worth well over two hundred thousand francs without counting his savings."

When body and soul have been broken in a long and bitter struggle, the moment when breaking point is reached is succeeded either by death or by a state of complete collapse, not unlike death, but in which those natures capable of resisting summon up their strength once more. Lucien was going through a crisis of this kind, and on hearing the rumour, vague as it was, that a disaster had befallen David Séchard, his brother-in-law, he seemed on the point of breaking down altogether.

" Oh! My sister! " he cried. " My God, what have I done? I am an utter wretch! "—and he sank down on a wooden bench, as pale as death and as weak as a dying man. The miller's wife hurriedly brought him a bowl of milk, which she tried to force him to drink; but he begged the miller to help him to his bed, begging his pardon for giving him the inconvenience of his death, for he thought that his last hour had come. As the spectre of death rose before his mind, that charming poet turned his thoughts to religion; he desired to see a priest, confess, and receive the sacraments. These sentiments, spoken in a scarcely audible voice by a young man with Lucien's beautiful face and handsome figure, touched Mme Courtois to the heart.

" Come, good man, take the horse and go and fetch M. Marron, the doctor at Marsac; he will see what is the matter with this young man, who seems to me to be in a bad way, and you can bring the curé at the same time. Perhaps they would know more than you do about what has happened to that printer in the Place du Mûrier, because Postel is M. Marron's son-in-law."

Courtois departed, and the miller's wife, who firmly believed, like all country people, that the sick need building up, tried to make Lucien eat; but he took no notice of her, and gave way to an outburst of violent remorse; the reaction produced by this psychological mustard-plaster roused him from his lethargy.

Courtois' mill was a league outside Marsac, the chief town of the Canton, lying half-way between Mansle and Angoulême; and the good miller soon returned with the doctor and the curé of Marsac. These two individuals had both heard rumours of Lucien's escapade with Mme de Bargeton, and as the chief topic of conversation at the moment was that lady's marriage and her return to Angoulême with the new Prefect, Count Sixte du Châtelet, both the doctor and the curé were possessed with the most violent curiosity to know the reasons that had prevented M. de Bargeton's widow from marrying the young poet with whom she had eloped; and to know whether he had returned in order to help his brother-in-law, David Séchard. Curiosity and humanity alike impelled them to hasten to the aid of the dying poet. And so, two hours after Courtois' departure, Lucien heard the rattle of the wheels of the country doctor's old trap on the stony causeway of the mill. The two Marrons appeared together, for the doctor was the curé's nephew. The two men who now came to Lucien's bedside were as well acquainted with David Séchard's father as neighbours usually are in a little vine-growing town. When the doctor had examined the dying man, felt his purse and looked at his tongue, he turned to the miller's wife and smiled in a most reassuring way.

"Madame Courtois," he said, "I dare say you have a good bottle of wine in your cellar, and a good eel in your larder; give them to your invalid—there is nothing wrong with him except exhaustion That will soon put our great man on his feet again."

"Oh, sir," said Lucien, "my sickness is not of the body, but of the soul, and these good people said something that nearly killed me—they spoke of disasters happening to my sister, Mme Séchard! Mme Courtois tells me that your daughter has married Postel; for

Heaven's sake, do you know anything about David Séchard's affairs?"

"Well, he must be in prison I suppose," said the doctor, "for his father refused to help him."

"In prison!" Lucien repeated. "But why?"

"Because of some bills that came through from Paris, which he must have overlooked—they say he scarcely knows what he is doing these days," said M. Marron.

"Please leave me with M. le Curé," said the poet, whose face expressed the gravest dismay.

The doctor, the miller and his wife left the room. When Lucien was alone with the old priest, he exclaimed:

"I deserve the death that I feel approaching, and I am a miserable sinner who can only throw myself upon the mercy of the Church. I am responsible for the ruin of my sister and brother—for David Séchard has been a brother to me! I signed the bills that David could not meet. . . . I have ruined him! In my terrible misery, I had forgotten that crime. A millionaire intervened and put a stop to the proceedings over these bills, and I quite thought that he had paid them. It seems that he did nothing of the kind!"

And Lucien told the story of his misfortunes. His feverish narration was indeed a theme worthy of a poet. He ended it by begging the curé to go to Angoulême and to make enquiries from his sister, Eve, and his mother, Mme Chardon, about the present state of affairs, and to let him know whether there was anything he could do to remedy it.

"I shall live until you come back," he said, weeping hot tears. "If my mother, and my sister, and David do not cast me off, I shall not die."

Lucien's Parisian eloquence, the tears of his bitter repentance, the beauty of this young man, pale with suffering, almost dying of despair, the story of misfortunes almost beyond human endurance, all combined to arouse the curé's pity and interest.

"It is the same in the provinces as in Paris," he said; "you cannot believe half you hear. You must not allow yourself to be so distressed by a rumour that is almost sure to be greatly exaggerated, three leagues from Angoulême. Old Séchard, our neighbour, left Marsac a few days ago; so he is probably busy putting his son's affairs in order. I shall go to Angoulême, and come back and tell you whether you can return to your family; your confession and your repentance make it easier for me to plead your cause."

The curé did not know that Lucien, during the past eighteen months, had repented so often, that his repentance, however violent, had no value beyond that of a scene perfectly acted, and acted, what is more, in all good faith! After the curé had gone, the doctor came in. He recognised in his patient the symptoms of a nervous crisis whose danger was beginning to subside. The nephew was no less consoling than his uncle had been, and succeeded in persuading the invalid to take some nourishment.

The curé, who knew the ways of the district, had gone meanwhile to Mansle, where he managed to get a seat in the coach from Ruffec to Angoulême which passed at that time. The old priest was relying on learning news about David Séchard from his grand-nephew, Postel, the chemist of l'Houmeau—the printer's old rival for pretty Eve. Anyone seeing the assiduity with which the little chemist helped him down from the rickety old coach that plied in those days between Ruffec and Angoulême might have guessed that M. and Mme Postel were basing their hopes on the old man's will.

" Have you had any lunch? Can we get you anything? We had no idea that you were coming—this is a pleasant surprise"—Postel asked a dozen questions at once.

Mme Postel might have been born to be the wife of the chemist of l'Houmeau. She was about the same height as little Postel, with the rosy face of a country girl; her features were common enough, and her only beauty was her air of wholesome freshness. Her red hair grew low over her forehead, and her conversation and manners were in accordance with the simple stupidity of her round face and greenish-yellow eyes. She was very obviously the kind of woman who is married only for her expectations. But after a year of marriage, she was already wearing the trousers, and Postel, only too delighted to have found this heiress, was obviously completely under her thumb. Mme Léonie Postel, *née* Marron, was already the mother of a little Postel, the apple of the old curé's eye, a repulsive child who took after both his parents.

"Well, Uncle, and what are you doing in Angoulême?" Léonie asked. "Since you won't take anything, and talk of going when you have only just arrived?"

No sooner had the worthy priest spoken the names of Eve and David Séchard than Postel blushed pink, and Léonie turned on the little man the look of jealousy with which a woman who has her husband completely under her thumb inevitably reproaches him for the past by way of a warning for the future.

"What have those people to do with you, Uncle, that you should concern yourself with their affairs?" Léonie enquired, with noticeable ill-humour.

"They are in distress, my child," the curé replied, and described to Postel the state in which he had found Lucien at the Courtois' mill.

"Ah! So that is how he has come back from Paris!" Postel exclaimed. "Poor lad! He had brains all the same, and he was ambitious! He went to look for corn in Egypt and he comes back sleeping on straw! But what will he do here? His sister has not a penny, because none of these geniuses—David is no better than Lucien—know anything about business. His case came up before the Tribunal, and as a magistrate I had to sign the warrant against him. . . . I did not like having to do it! I don't see how Lucien can go to his sister's, as things are at present; but in any case, the little room he used to have here is empty, and he is very welcome to use it."

"Thank you, Postel," said the priest, putting on his tricorne hat and preparing to leave the shop, having first bestowed a kiss on the baby asleep in Léonie's arms.

"You will have dinner with us, won't you, Uncle?" said Mme Postel, "because if you are interfering in those people's affairs it will be some time before you are finished! My husband will drive you back in his pony trap."

Husband and wife watched their valued great-uncle as he set off in the direction of Angoulême.

"He carries himself well for his age all the same," said the chemist.

While the venerable clergyman is climbing the steps up to Angoulême, it will be as well to say something of the network of intrigues in which he is about to become involved.

After Lucien's departure for Paris, David Séchard (who had all the courage and sagacity of the ox represented by painters as the companion of the Evangelist) made up his mind to make the large fortune based on the project that he had outlined to Eve, one evening, as they sat together on the weir, by the Charente—that evening when Eve had given David her hand and her heart. This fortune he desired less for himself than for Eve's sake and for Lucien's. David's ambition was written before his eyes, in letters of fire—he would give his wife the life of elegance and comfort that she deserved; and he would sustain, with his strong arm, his brother's ambition.

Political journalism, the immense expansion of literature and the book trade, as well as of the sciences, the movement towards public discussion of all affairs of national importance—in fact, the whole tendency of society during the years when the Restoration seemed secure, had created a demand for paper nearly ten times as great a the quantity envisaged by Ouvrard, whose speculations, in the early days of the Revolution, were based on similar considerations. Ouvrard had gained control of all the principal paper-mills of France and obtained a monopoly in their products, but by 1821 there were too many factories in existence for any speculator to hope to do the same; nor had David either the audacity or the capital to envisage any such project.

At about this time machinery for making paper in lengths was coming into use in England; and one of the most pressing needs in France, where discussion was threatening to extend to every subject, and whose culture was coming more and more to be based on the perpetual expression of individual opinion (a serious evil, for nations that are for ever discussing issues, never act) was to find some means of meeting the ever-increasing demand for paper. And so, by a strange coincidence, while Lucien was caught up in the machinery of journalism, where he seemed likely to leave his honour and his intelligence torn to shreds in its vast mechanism, David Séchard, at the back of his printing house, was confronting the material aspect of the phenomenon of newspapers and periodicals. It was his ambition to find means in harmony with the ends towards which the spirit of the age was tending.

The soundness of his foresight and judgment,—that there was a fortune to be made by the manufacture of cheap paper—has been borne out by the event. During the past fifteen years the Patents Office has received more than a hundred applications based on claims of discoveries of new materials to be employed in the manufacture of paper. More certain than ever of the practical importance of this discovery, that would not bring him fame, but which might well be worth a fortune, David, after his brother-in-law's departure for Paris, became increasingly preoccupied by the problem that he had set himself to solve.

He had used up all his savings on his marriage and on meeting the expenses of Lucien's departure for Paris; and so he found himself embarking upon married life in a state of extreme poverty. He had kept back a thousand francs for the running expenses of his printing business, and he owed another thousand to Postel, the chemist; David's problem was therefore a double one—he must invent a cheap paper, and he must invent it quickly, for he needed the profits of his discovery for the expenses of his household and his business.

What man of exceptional intelligence is capable of contending with the cruel anxieties occasioned by secret poverty, the thought of a family without bread, and the daily exigencies of a profession as exacting as that of printing, and at the same time of devoting himself to speculations in an unknown field, with all the ardour and concentration of a student in pursuit of a secret that perpetually eludes the most subtle researches? Alas, as we shall see, inventors have many troubles to endure—besides the ingratitude of the public, who are informed, by the idle and incapable, that a man of genius was born to become an inventor, for he was not fit for anything else; and that we have no more reason to feel indebted to him for his discovery than we have to a man for being born a prince. He is merely making use of his natural aptitudes, and therefore he is sufficiently recompensed by the work itself!

Marriage causes profound psychological and physical disturbances in a young girl; but under the conditions of middle-class marriage, she has, besides, to turn her attention to new interests and to learn her new responsibilities; and so the young wife must have a period during which she can observe before she needs to take an active part. Unfortunately David's love for his wife retarded her education, for he did not dare to tell her the true state of affairs immediately after the wedding or for some time to come. In spite of the financial straits to which his father's avarice had reduced him, he could not bring himself to spoil the honeymoon by initiating his young wife into his laborious profession, and the knowledge necessary to the wife of a tradesman. So the thousand francs—David's only resources—were taken up by the household expenses instead of going into the business. David's carelessness and his wife's ignorance of their true situation lasted for four months; and the awakening was a rude one.

When the post-dated cheque that David had made out to Postel fell due, there was no money in the house; Eve knew the reason for that debt very well, and so she sacrificed her dowry, her marriage jewellery, and her silver.

On the evening of the day on which this bill was paid Eve made up her mind to speak to David about the state of his affairs, for she had noticed that he was neglecting the printing business and giving more and more of his attention to the problem that he had explained to her. Ever since the second month of their married life David had been spending the greater part of the day in the shed at the end of the courtyard, in the little room where the rollers were moulded. Three months after his arrival in Angoulême David had substituted an ink-table and rollers for the old ink-balls; by this method the ink was applied and spread evenly by means of rollers made of glue and treacle. The advantages of this latest improvement in printing was so obvious that as soon as they had seen its results the Cointet brothers adopted the new method. David had built a kind of kitchen in a lean-to shed against the dividing wall, with a grate and a copper pan, in order to use less coal, so he said, for melting down the rollers. But the rusty moulds stood ranged along the wall ; the rollers were never cast a second time. He built into this room a door of heavy oak, lined with sheet-iron, and, as a further precaution, replaced the dirty window-panes with grooved glass, to prevent anyone from seeing, from outside, what he was doing in that room.

At the first word that Eve spoke to David on the subject of their future he looked at her with a troubled expression and cut her short.

" My dear child," he said, " I know what you must be thinking, when you see a deserted workshop and the state of commercial paralysis in which I exist ; but you see," he continued, leading her to the window of their living-room and pointing to the mysterious workshop, " our fortune lies there. We shall still have to go through a few months of hardship ; but let us bear it in patience ; leave me to solve the industrial problem about which I told you, and then we shall see the end of all our troubles."

David was so good, his devotion was so patently sincere, that his poor wife, whose mind, like that of other wives, turned naturally to household expenses, set herself the task of sparing her husband all domestic worries ; so she left her pretty blue and white room where she had been happy sewing and chatting with her mother, and installed herself in one of the two wooden offices at the back of the workshop, there to learn the printing trade. A heroic step in a wife already pregnant!

During these early months, the workmen, who no longer had work enough to occupy them, had drifted away from David's idle workshop ; they had departed, one by one. Snowed under with orders, the Cointet brothers had not only taken on all the workmen of the Department, attracted by the prospect of high wages, but already several workmen had come from Bordeaux, most of them apprentices who thought themselves clever enough to break their contracts of apprenticeship.

Eve found that the only remaining resources of the Séchard printing business consisted of three persons. First of all there was Cérizet, the apprentice whom David had taken under his wing when he was with the Didots. Nearly all foremen single out in this way one or two of the large number of workmen under them. David had brought this apprentice, Cérizet, to Angoulême with him and had there completed his training. The second was Marion, who was as devoted to the household as a watchdog ; and lastly there was Kolb, an Alsatian, who had formerly been a porter at the Didots'. Kolb had been called up for military service, and chance brought him to Angoulême, where David recognised him during a military revue, just before he was due to be discharged. Kolb came to see David and took a great fancy to the sturdy Marion, in whom he divined all the qualities that a man of his class desires in a wife—the rude health that glowed in her brown skin, the masculine strength that enabled her to lift a forme of type with perfect ease, and that scrupulous honesty by which Alsatians set such great store. Her devotion to her masters gave proof of the integrity of her character, and she had, besides, managed to save a little store of a thousand francs, besides linen, clothes, and household gear, neat and well cared-for, as such things are in the provinces. Marion, who was both tall and stout, and thirty-six years of age, was not a little flattered at finding herself the object of the attentions of a cavalry-man standing five-foot seven, well built, and strong as a fort, and she very naturally suggested to him the idea of becoming a printer. So when the Alsatian received his discharge, Marion and David made a very tolerable *bear* of him, although he could neither read nor write.

The compositing of the " town work ", as it was called, had been light enough during the past three months for Cérizet to manage single-handed. Compositor, foreman, and lay-out man all in one, Cérizet realised in his person what Kant calls the " phenomenal triplicity " ; he set up the type, corrected the proofs, took the orders, and made out the bills ; even so, he had a great deal of time on his hands, and he used to sit reading novels in his office at the far end of the workshop, waiting for an order to come in for a printed notice or a handbill. Marion, who had been trained by old Séchard, prepared the paper, damped it down, and helped Kolb to print, stretch it out to dry, trim it, and still had time to act as cook and to do the marketing first thing in the morning.

Eve asked Cérizet for a balance sheet of the last six months. She discovered that the receipts had amounted to eight hundred francs. The running expenses including the three francs a day paid in wages to Cérizet and Kolb (Cérizet was paid two francs, Kolb one franc a day) amounted to six hundred francs ; and since the cost of materials for work carried out and delivered amounted to over a hundred francs, it was clear to Eve that during the first six months of her marriage David had been running the business at a loss. David had not paid the rent, the interest of the capital represented by his plant and his printing-licence, or Marion's wages, ink, or all the necessary outlay comprised under the heading " wear and tear ", an expression taken from the cloths and silks used to save the type from being worn by the pressure of the vice ; a layer of material (the " blanket") is laid between the platen of the press and the paper to be printed. A rough comparison of the expenses of the business with the profits made it clear to Eve that the old printing house, its business increasingly diverted by the all-devouring industry of the Cointet brothers, who were at once paper manufacturers, newspaper publishers, licensed printers to the Diocese, the Municipality, and the Prefecture, had very little chance. The newspaper that the Séchards, father and son, had sold two years ago for twenty-two thousand francs was now bringing in eighteen thousand francs a year. Eve recognised the calculations of self-interest that had underlain the apparent generosity of the Cointet brothers ; they were leaving the Séchard business just enough work to enable it to subsist, but not enough to threaten them with competition.

As a first step in taking over the running of the business, Eve had an exact inventory drawn up of all the stock. She set Kolb, Marion and Cérizet to work to set the workshop in order. Then, one evening when David had come in from a long walk in the fields, followed by an old woman carrying an enormous bundle tied up in linen, Eve asked his advice about how to turn the junk that old Séchard had left them to some profit, promising him to make herself entirely responsible.

On her husband's advice Mme Séchard took all the remainders of paper stock that she could find, arranged them according to quality, and used them for printing, double columns and on one side of the paper only, those popular coloured broadsheet ballads that peasants stick up on the walls of their cottages—the story of the *Wandering Jew*, *Robert the Devil*, *La Belle Maguelonne*, and the stories of several miracles. Eve sent Kolb out to hawk them. Cérizet did not waste a minute, and set up those naïve broadsheets, with their crude illustrations, from morning till night. Marion printed them off single-handed. Mme Chardon undertook all the housework, while Eve coloured the woodcuts. In two months, thanks to Kolb's industry and honesty, Mme Séchard had sold, within an area of twelve leagues round Angoulême, three thousand broadsheets, that had cost thirty francs to produce, at two sous apiece, bringing in a profit of three hundred francs. But when all the cottages and country inns had been papered with these ballads, it became necessary to think of some new means of raising money, for the good Alsatian was not permitted to travel outside the Department.

Eve, who had gone through everything in the workshop, had found a collection of the figures necessary for the printing of a so-called *Shepherd's Calendar*, in which everything was represented by signs and pictures, figures printed in red, black, and blue. Old Séchard, who could neither read nor write, had at one time made a great deal of money out of this book designed for men who could not read. This calendar, sold for one sou, consists of a single sheet folded six times, so as to produce a volume of a hundred and twenty-eight pages.

Delighted by the success of her broadsheets—an industry common among small country printers—Madame Séchard set to work to produce the *Shepherd's Calendar*, on a large scale, and devoted her profits to the undertaking. Hundreds of thousands of copies of this work are sold in France every year. The paper used for the *Shepherd's Calendar* is coarser than that used for the *Liége Calendar*, and costs about four francs a ream. After printing, therefore, a ream of paper consisting of five hundred sheets, sold at the rate of one sou a sheet, brings in twenty-five francs. Mme Séchard planned a first printing of a hundred reams, fifty thousand calendars, representing two thousand francs profit. Preoccupied as he was with his own thoughts, and apt not to notice things, David was surprised, onl ooking into his workshop, to hear the press groan, and to see Cérizet busily occupied setting up type under the direction of Mme Séchard. The day he came in to see what Eve had been doing was a triumph for his wife, for her husband gave his full approval to the projected calendar. He thought it an excellent idea. David promised to advice her on the coloured inks for the designs of the calendar, whose appeal is to the eye. He even offered to re-cast the ink-rollers himself, in his mysterious laboratory, so as to help his wife, to the best of his ability, in her small but important enterprise.

While all this strenuous activity was still in its early stages, heartbreaking letters arrived from Lucien, in which he told his mother, sister, and brother-in-law of his failure and distress in Paris. It is not difficult to understand, therefore, that in sending their spoilt darling three hundred francs, Eve, Mme Chardon and David were each in their different ways giving the poet their heart's blood. Overcome by this sad news, and in despair at earning so little for all her courageous work, Eve looked forward with some dismay to an event which ought to be the crowning happiness of a young marriage. She would soon be a mother, and she thought, " If my dear David has not made his discovery by the time of my confinement, what will become of us ? And who will watch over the work in our poor printing house, that is just beginning to go so well? "

The *Shepherd's Calendar* should have been ready well before the first of January ; but Cérizet, on whom Eve was dependent for the setting of the type, was working unaccountably slowly. This delay was the more distressing because Eve did not know enough about the work of printing to make any protest ; and she had to be content with watching the young Parisian. Cérizet, an orphan from one of the big orphanages of Paris, had been apprenticed to the Didots. Between the ages of fourteen and seventeen he had been Séchard's satellite ; David had put him under one of the best workmen, and this urchin had been his copy-holder and devoted page. David took a very natural interest in Cérizet, for he found him intelligent ; he won his affection by giving him small treats and presents that, poor as he was, were beyond the lad's means. His little weasel-face was not unattractive, with his red hair and his hazy blue eyes ; but he brought the ways of the Paris street-arab to the ancient city of Angoulême. His sharp unkind wit, and his spitefulness, made him feared there. Less under David's eye than he had been in Paris—partly because, being older, his mentor placed more trust in him, and partly because David counted on the good influence of provincial life—Cérizet had become, unknown to his tutor, the little Don Juan of three or four young working girls, and he had gone completely to the bad. His morality, picked up in the cabarets of Paris, knew only one law—self-interest. Besides this, Cérizet was due for his call-up the following year, and his career would be cut short ; so he ran up debts, reflecting that in six months' time he would be a soldier, and that then none of his creditors would be able to get at him. David still had some influence over this lad, not because he was his master and not because he had been kind to him, but because the ex-Paris street-arab recognised David's great intelligence. Before long Cérizet began to fraternise with the Cointet's workmen, drawn into their circle by the attraction of the printer's jacket and overall—in other words, by a sense of professional solidarity, a sentiment even stronger among the lower than among the higher classes. In their company Cérizet forgot the few sound precepts that David had instilled into him ; but all the same, when anyone teased him about the " old clogs " in his workshop—the scornful epithet by which the *bears* described the Séchards' old printing-presses, as they showed him splendid cast-iron presses, twelve in number, in use in the Cointets' immense workshop, where the one wooden press was used only for rough proofs, he still took David's part and used to retort with pride to the boasters, " My boss with his old clogs will go further than yours all the same ; they are only job-printers, after all, for all their cast-iron contrivances they produce nothing but prayer-books! All the printers in France and Navarre will be queueing up for the discovery that he is working on! "

" In the meantime your boss is a washer-woman, you miserable twopenny halfpenny foreman! " was the retort.

" Never mind that, she's very pretty—I would rather look at her than at your two bosses' ugly mugs! "

" Does the sight of a pretty face pay for your bacon ? "

From the lower regions of the café and the door of the workshop where these amicable disputes took place some echoes of the state of affairs at the Séchards' workshop reached the ears of the Cointet brothers ; they found out about Eve's speculation, and judged it necessary to nip in the bud an enterprise that might possibly set the poor girl on the way to prosperity.

" Give her a rap over the knuckles, to discourage her," said the two brothers.

The Cointet in charge of the workshop encountered Cérizet, as if by chance, and suggested that he should read proofs for them, at so much a sheet, to help out their own proof-reader who could not cope with the work. By working for a few hours in the evenings, Cérizet was earning more with the Cointet brothers than his days' wages with David Séchard. By this means relations were established between the Cointets and Cérizet ; the brothers praised his abilities, and commiserated with him for being in a job so unfavourable to his interests.

" You could become foreman of a big printing business where you would earn six francs a day. With your brains you might have a share in the business yourself one day," one of the Cointet brothers remarked to him one day.

" Being a good foreman will never get me anywhere," Cérizet replied. " I am an orphan, and I am due to be called up next year, and if I draw an unlucky number who is going to pay for a substitute ? "

" If you make yourself useful," replied the rich printer, " why shouldn't someone buy you a discharge ? "

" You don't know my boss ! " said Cérizet.

" Why! He may have found the secret he is looking for by that time! "

This phrase was spoken in a way that awakened the worst thoughts in the man who heard it ; and Cérizet darted a searching look at the paper merchant. But the business man said nothing.

" I have no idea what he is working on," he replied prudently, " but he is not the man to look for capitals in the lower case! "

" Look here, my friend," said the printer, handing Cérizet six proof-sheets of the Diocesan prayer-book, " if you can get these corrected by tomorrow I will let you have eighteen francs. After all, we are not shabby—we are putting our competitor's foreman in the way of earning a little money!—The fact is, we might have let Mme Séchard go on with her *Shepherd's Calendar* and ruin herself over it—but between ourselves, you have my permission to tell her that we are printing a *Shepherd's Calendar,* and you can drop her a hint that she won't be the first in the field. . . . "

It is now easy enough to see why Cérizet was working so slowly on the composition of the calendar.

When she discovered that the Cointets were putting obstacles in the way of her poor little speculation, Eve was seized with panic and tried to see in the warning that Cérizet so hypocritically delivered, of the competition that was awaiting her, a proof of his attachment ; but on more than one occasion she noticed, in their single compositor, traces of too eager a curiosity, which she tried to put down to his age.

" Cérizet," she said to him one morning, " you are always hanging about outside the door and waiting for M. Séchard in the passage to see what he is doing, and you look out into the yard every time he leaves the workshop where the rollers are melted, instead of getting on with the setting up of our calendar. That is not right—especially when you see that even I, his wife, respect his secrets, and that I am taking so much trouble to leave him free to continue with his work. If you had not wasted so much time, the calendar would have been finished by now and Kolb would have been selling it, and the Cointets could not have done anything to us."

" Well, ma'am," Cérizet replied, " for the forty sous a day I earn here, don't you think it's good enough, if I do a hundred sous' worth of compositing ? If I hadn't the Cointet brothers' proofs to read in the evening I should be living on bran."

" You have soon learned to be ungrateful; you will get on! " said Eve cut to the quick, not so much by Cérizet's words as by his impertinent manner, his aggressive attitude, and insolent stare.

" Then it won't be while I have a woman for a boss because blue moons don't often come round when that is the case."

Her womanly pride thus wounded, Eve turned a withering look on Cérizet and went up to her own room. " Are you sure you can trust that little scamp Cérizet ? " she asked David when he came in for dinner.

" Cérizet ! " he replied. " Why, he was my apprentice, I trained him as a compositor—he owes everything to me ! You might as well ask a father if he can trust his son ! "

Eve told her husband that Cérizet was reading proofs for the Cointets.

" Poor boy ! He's got to live ! " David replied, with the humility of a master who feels himself to blame.

" Yes, my dear, but look at the difference between Kolb and Cérizet ! Kolb walks twenty leagues every day, spends fifteen or twenty sous, and brings us back seven, eight or nine francs from the sales of the broadsheets, and never asks me for more than his twenty sous and his expenses. Kolb would cut off his right hand before he would work a press for the Cointets, and he would never think of looking at anything you may happen to drop in the court, not if they offered him a thousand pounds ! But Cérizet is always picking things up and examining them."

Noble minds find it difficult to believe in wickedness or ingratitude, and it needs hard lessons to make them recognise the extent of human corruption ; and even then, when they have received their education in this respect, they rise to those heights of magnanimity, that are, as a matter of fact, the most extreme form of contempt.

" Nonsense ! Just the curiosity of a Paris street-boy," David exclaimed.

" Very well, my dear, but just to please me do come down into the workshop and see how much your street-boy has set up in a month, and tell me whether, in that month, he ought not to have been able to finish our Calendar."

After dinner David at once saw that the calendar could have been set up in a week ; and when he heard that the Cointets were also preparing one, he came to the aid of his wife. He took charge in the workshop himself and stopped Kolb from going out to sell the broad sheets.

He prepared one forme so that Kolb and Marion could start printing, and he worked on the other with Cérizet, supervising the printing of the colour blocks himself. Each colour necessitated a separate process. Four inks of different colours required four separate impressions. In fact the *Shepherd's Calendar*, which requires four printings instead of one, costs so much to produce that it is printed only in provincial printing-houses, where the cost of labour and overhead expenses are almost negligible. This work, crude as it is, is therefore too expensive to be worth producing by printers of fine work.

For the first time since old Séchard's retirement the presses were rolling again in the old workshop.

But even though the calendar was, in its way, a work of art, Eve was forced to sell it for next to nothing, because the Cointet brothers were selling their calendar to the hawkers at three centimes a copy ; she just covered her costs on the copies taken by hawkers, and she made a small profit on the copies sold directly by Kolb ; but the speculation was a failure.

Cérizet realised that his beautiful mistress did not trust him ; in his secret heart he vowed enmity, and said to himself, " If you suspect me, I will have my revenge." That is the way the Paris guttersnipe's mind works. Cérizet therefore accepted from the Cointet brothers payment that was obviously too high for reading the proofs that he collected at their office every evening, and returned first thing every morning. By talking to them every day, he got onto familiar terms with them, and finally saw how he might get out of his military service—the proffered bait ; and far from having to corrupt him, the Cointet brothers heard the first words on the subject of spying on David and exploiting his secret spoken by Cérizet.

Eve, troubled by the realisation that she could place very little reliance on Cérizet, and that she could not hope to find a second Kolb, made up her mind to dismiss their one compositor ; with the second-sight of a woman in love, she recognised him for a traitor. But as this would mean a death-blow to the business, she took a manly resolution ; she wrote a letter to M. Métivier, with whom

David Séchard, the Cointets and nearly all the paper manufacturers of the Department were in correspondence, asking him to put the following advertisement in the *Publisher's Journal* in Paris:

"For sale, a printing establishment, a going concern, with license and plant situated in Angoulême. For particulars, write to M. Métivier, Rue Serpente."

When they saw this advertisement in the *Journal* the Cointets thought to themselves:

"That little woman is no fool; we had better get control of her business by allowing her enough to live on; otherwise David's successor might be a serious competitor, and it is in our interest to keep an eye on that business."

Activated by this reflection, the Cointet brothers came to see David Séchard. Eve, who received them, was greatly delighted to see that her ruse had had such a rapid effect, for they made no secret of their intention of offering to give M. Séchard work to do for them. They were snowed under with orders, they had not enough presses to cope with the work that came in, they had had to get workmen from Bordeaux, and would be very glad to make use of David's three presses.

While Cérizet went to inform David of his colleagues' visit, Eve reminded the brothers that her husband had known many excellent and enterprising printers while he was with the Didots in Paris. "No doubt he will sell the business to one of them," she said. "Would it not be much better to sell his business for something like twenty thousand francs, which would give us an income of a thousand francs, than to lose a thousand francs a year on the work you allow us to do? Why did you envy such a poor little speculation as our calendar, which in any case this house has always brought out?"

"Why, you should have let us know, then we should never have stood in your way," said the brother, who was always known as the tall Cointet, gallantly.

"Oh come! You did not begin your calendar until you had heard from Cérizet that I was bringing one out." She spoke these words with emphasis, and looked at the tall Cointet as she did so.

He lowered his eyes. This gave her proof positive of Cérizet's treachery.

This brother, who was the manager of the paper-mill and the business side, was a much cleverer business man than his brother, Jean ; Jean ran the printing business with great intelligence, but his capabilities were those of a colonel rather than a general. Boniface was the general to whom Jean deferred, as commander-in-chief.

Boniface was a thin dry man with a mottled face as yellow as a wax candle, a tight mouth, and eyes like a cat's. He never lost his temper ; he would listen with pious serenity to the grossest insults, and reply to them in a smooth voice. He went without fail to Mass and confession, and was a regular communicant. Beneath a smooth manner, and an almost soft exterior, he concealed the tenacity and ambition of a priest and the avidity of a business man consumed with the thirst for riches and honours. Ever since 1820 the tall Cointet had hoped for everything that the middle classes finally obtained by the revolution of 1830. Full of hatred for the aristocracy, and indifferent to the essentials of religion, he was pious for the same reasons as Bonaparte was a member of the *Mountain*. His dorsal vertebrae inclined with marvellous flexibility before the powers that be, and before them he was servile, humble, and obsequious. And, to describe the man by means of a trait whose significance will be well appreciated by those accustomed to conducting business, he wore dark-blue glasses, which concealed the expression of his eyes, on the pretext of protecting his eyes from the brilliant light of a town where the ground and the buildings are of a dazzling whiteness ; for the brightness of the sunlight is increased by the town's high altitude. He was of little more than middle height, but he looked taller, because he was thin, as men are who are overworked, and whose thoughts are in a continual ferment. His lank and sleek grey hair, cut in ecclesiastical fashion, and his dress, which for the last seven years had consisted of black breeches and stockings, a black waistcoat, and a snuff-coloured frock-coat (called a *lévite* in the south of France), made him look more than ever like a Jesuit. He was called the tall Cointet in order to distinguish him from his brother, who was known as the fat Cointet.

The epithet described the contrast between the respective mental capacities of these two brothers no less than between their physical appearances ; but both alike were redoubtable business men.

Jean Cointet was a stout, stolid individual with a face that might have come from a Flemish painting, sunburned by the sun of Angoulême, small, short and as pot-bellied as Sancho Panza. With his perpetual smile and his broad shoulders, he was in striking contrast to his elder brother. Not only did Jean differ from his brother in features and cast of mind ; he professed political opinions that were almost liberal, he was Left Centre, and only went to Mass on Sundays ; he got on wonderfully well with the Liberal customers. There were certain tradesmen in l'Houmeau who maintained that this divergence of opinion was a part played by the two brothers for reasons of their own. The tall Cointet knew well how to exploit the apparent good nature of his brother and used Jean as a bludgeon. It was Jean who took upon himself to say the hard words, to do the unpleasant tasks that were uncongenial to his meek brother. Jean was responsible for producing the displays of anger, the bursts of temper ; it was he who made unacceptable propositions, that made those of his brother seem sweeter by contrast ; and by these means the pair always, sooner or later, gained their ends.

Eve, with feminine intuition, had soon divined the character of the two brothers ; she was on her guard in the presence of adversaries so dangerous. David, who had already been forewarned by his wife, listened to his enemies' propositions with a distracted air.

" Arrange everything with my wife," he said to the two Cointets, as he turned to leave the office and go back to his little laboratory ; " she knows more about my printing business than I do myself. I am occupied in a matter that will be more profitable than this poor little business, and by means of which I shall make good the losses I have suffered through you. . . ."

" Really ? What is that ? " asked the fat Cointet, smiling.

Eve, with a look, warned her husband to be careful.

" You will be my tributaries, you and all consumers of paper," David replied.

"What are you working on, then?" asked Benoit-Boniface Cointet.

When Boniface had asked this question, in affable and insinuating tones, Eve once more looked at her husband, beseeching him not to answer, or to be entirely non-committal in his reply.

"I am working on a process for manufacturing paper at fifty per cent less than the present cost."

And he went out without noticing the glance that the two brothers exchanged. "This man must be an inventor; no one with a headpiece like that was ever an idler! We must exploit him!" was the meaning of Boniface's look. "How can we do it?" was Jean's rejoinder.

"David tells me no more than he has told you," said Mme Séchard. "When I am curious, he no doubt remembers my name, and puts me off with what he has just told you—which, after all, is only a programme."

"If your husband is able to realise that programme, he will certainly make a fortune more rapidly than in the printing trade, and I am not surprised that he has been letting his business go," replied Boniface, looking in the direction of the deserted workshop where Kolb was sitting on a bench rubbing his bread with a clove of garlic, "but it wouldn't suit us to see this business fall into the hands of an active printing competitor, an ambitious man, and so perhaps we can come to an understanding. You might, for example, agree to rent us your plant and we would put in one of our workmen to work for us, but in your name. It is done in Paris—we could give him enough work to enable him to pay you a very good rent, and still make a small profit."

"That would depend on the sum," replied Eve Séchard. "What is your offer?" she added, looking at Boniface in a way that made it perfectly clear to him that she completely understood his scheme.

"What would you suggest yourself?" Jean Cointet retorted quickly.

"Three thousand francs for six months," she said.

"Oh! My dear young lady, you talk of selling your printing business for twenty thousand francs," Boniface replied with the utmost affability, " the interest on twenty thousand francs at six per cent is only twelve hundred francs."

Eve could not immediately think of a reply, and realised, in that moment, the need for discretion in business.

" You would be using our presses and our type, and I have proved to you that I can still do little pieces of printing," she replied. " And we have rent to pay to M. Séchard senior, who does not overwhelm us with his generosity."

After two hours of fighting, Eve obtained a promise of two thousand francs for six months, a thousand payable in advance. When everything had been arranged, the two brothers informed her that they intended to rent the workshop and printing presses to Cérizet. Eve could not conceal a look of surprise.

" It is surely best to take on someone who knows the workshop ? " said the fat Cointet.

Eve took leave of the two brothers without answering, and promised herself to keep a careful watch on Cérizet.

She gave David the agreement to sign when he came in for dinner.

" Well, so our enemies are installed! " said David to his wife, laughing.

" Nonsense! " she said. " I will answer for the loyalty of Kolb and Marion ; these two will watch over everything. And what is more, we shall have an income of four thousand francs from business premises that we were running at a loss, and now you have a year before you in which you may realise your hopes! "

" You were born to be an inventor's wife—as you said yourself by the weir! " said Séchard, pressing his wife's hand tenderly.

David's household now had enough money to see them through the winter ; but they were under the observation of Cérizet, and, without realising it, in the hands of the tall Cointet.

" We've got them! " said the manager of the paper-mill to his brother the printer, as they left. " They will become accustomed to living on the rent of their printing-house, they will count on it, and they will get into debt ; in six months we will not renew the agreement, and then we will see what this man of genius has up his sleeve; then we will propose to get him out of his difficulties by taking him into partnership, and we will exploit his discovery."

If any shrewd business man had seen the tall Cointet as he spoke the words "take him into partnership" he would have reflected that partnerships entered into at the Tribunal of Commerce are even more hazardous than those embarked upon at the Registry Office. Was it not bad enough already that these fierce hunters were already on the scent? Were David and his wife, with only Kolb and Marion to help them, in any position to stand out against the schemes of a Boniface Cointet?

When the time of Mme Séchard's confinement came, the cheque for five hundred francs from Lucien, together with Cérizet's second payment, were enough to cover all the expenses. Eve, her mother, and David, who thought that Lucien had forgotten them, were delighted by this token of attention, as they were by the first successes of the poet, whose first triumphs in journalism were making even more stir in Angoulême than in Paris.

Lulled into false security, David was staggered to receive a cruel letter from Lucien:

"My dear David,

"I have cashed three cheques with Métivier, on your account, made out to me, to fall due in one, two, and three months' time respectively. I had to choose between this terrible alternative and suicide, even though I know that it will place you in difficulties.

"Burn my letter, and please say nothing to my mother or to Eve, because the fact is, I am counting on your heroism, which I know so well.

"Your despairing brother,
"Lucien de Rubempré."

"Your poor brother is in desperate straits and I have sent him three cheques for a thousand francs, to be cashed in one, two and three months' time. Will you make a note of it?" David told his wife, who was just getting up after her confinement.

And he went for a walk in the fields to avoid having to go into explanations with Eve. Eve, already alarmed by the fact that Lucien had not written for six months, talked over this ominous announcement with her mother; and she made up her mind to a desperate step, that would put an end to their anxiety. Young M. de Rastignac had come down on a short visit to his family, and he had said things about Lucien that had set Paris gossip circulating in Angoulême; these rumours, exaggerated at every telling, had at last reached the ears of the journalist's mother and sister. Eve called on Mme de Rastignac and asked the favour of an interview with her son, to whom she confided her fears, and begged him to tell her the truth about Lucien's situation in Paris. Eve was promptly informed that her brother was living with Coralie, and heard the story of his duel with Michel Chrestien, the result of his betrayal of d'Arthez—in fact, the full story of Lucien's life. The clever young man of fashion gave the story a malicious turn; he knew well how to give his personal antagonism and envy the semblance of sympathy, and the false colours of local patriotism worried as to the future of a great man, and of the alarm that he felt at seeing a native of Angoulême, whose talent he sincerely admired, seriously compromised. He spoke of the blunders that Lucien had made, that had lost him the protection of several highly placed persons; so much so that a patent of nobility conferring on him the name and arms of de Rubempré had been torn up.

"If your brother had listened to good advice, he would have been on the highroad to fame by this time, and married to Mme de Bargeton; but there you are! He deserted her, and insulted her; and she, with infinite regret—for she was in love with Lucien—has become Countess Sixte du Châtelet."

"Is it possible!" exclaimed Mme Séchard.

"Your brother is an eagle, blinded by the first rays of luxury and fame. When an eagle falls, who can say down how deep a precipice he may drop? A fall is always in proportion to the height that a man has attained."

Eve went home, appalled by that last phrase, that had pierced her heart like an arrow. She had been wounded to the quick, and she said not a word; but more than once tears rolled down her cheeks and fell onto the head of her baby as she nursed him. It is so hard to give up those illusions, cherished in the heart of the family, that begin with life itself, that Eve refused to believe the word of Eugène de Rastignac, and was determined to hear the verdict of a real friend. So she wrote a touching letter to d'Arthez, whose address Lucien had given her, at the time when he was an enthusiastic member of d'Arthez's circle; and she received the following reply:

"Madame,

"You ask me to tell you the truth about the life that your brother is leading in Paris; you want to know what his prospects are, and in order to induce me to reply candidly, you tell me what M. de Rastignac has told you, and ask me whether this is the truth.

"As to the story concerning myself, M. de Rastignac's account must be corrected, in Lucien's favour. Your brother, in a fit of remorse, brought his critical attack on my book and showed it to me; he told me that he could not bring himself to publish it, although by disobeying his orders he was endangering the woman he loved. Alas, a writer has to understand all passions; after all, his fame depends upon his ability to describe them. So I understood that, when there is a choice between a friend and a mistress, it is the friend who is bound to be sacrificed. I made your brother's crime easier for him by correcting the murderous article myself, and it had my full approval.

"You ask me whether Lucien has kept my esteem and friendship. That question I find it more difficult to answer. Your brother is well on the way to ruining himself. At the present moment I am still very sorry; but before long I shall be glad to forget him, not because of what he has already done, but because of what he is bound to do. Your Lucien is very poetic, but he is not a poet; he dreams, but he does not think, he acts but does not create. In short he is, if I may say so, an effeminate young man who loves to be admired—the besetting sin of the French character. Lucien would always sacrifice his best friend for the sake of being witty. He would gladly sign a pact with the devil, for the sake of a few years of a life of brilliance and luxury. Has he not already done worse, in bartering his future for the fleeting pleasures of living openly with an actress? At present, his youth and good looks, and the devotion of this girl—for she adores him—blind him to the dangers of a situation that neither fame, fortune, nor success can make acceptable in the eyes of the world. Well, at every new temptation, it will be the same—your brother will see only the immediate pleasures.

" You need not fear that Lucien will go so far as to commit a crime—he is took weak a character; but he would accept the fruits of a crime already committed, and share the profits without having shared the danger—a trait that everybody is bound to despise, even the criminals themselves. And he would despise himself, and even repent; but if the same situation were to arise again, he would act in exactly the same way, because he is weak, and can never resist the temptations of pleasure, or let pass any opportunity of satisfying even his most trivial ambitions. Like all poetic natures, he is lazy, and he uses his wits to get out of difficulties, instead of overcoming them. He may show courage at one moment, but at another he will give way completely; and it would be as wrong to admire him for his courage as to blame him for his cowardice. Lucien is a harp, whose strings tighten or slacken according to the variations in the atmosphere. He might very well write a fine book in a mood of anger or happiness, and then care nothing for the success he had once set his heart on. Soon after his arrival in Paris, he came under the influence of a young man who has no principles, but who made a great impression on Lucien because of his experience and talent for coping with the difficulties of literary life. This mountebank bewitched Lucien completely and led him into a way of life entirely lacking in dignity, and, unfortunately, the beguilements of love led him along the same path. To give one's admiration so readily is a sign of weakness—one does not pay a tightrope-dancer in the same coin as a poet. We were all very much hurt by the fact that Lucien preferred intrigue and superficial literary success, to the courage and honour of the friends who advised him to face the struggle instead of snatching at a cheap success, to jump into the arena, instead of helping to blow the trumpets in the orchestra.

" Society, strangely enough, is wonderfully tolerant of people like Lucien ; people love men of his type, excuse all their errors, give them all the benefits of privileged natures, and turn a blind eye to their faults. They are always spoiled. Strong and independent characters, on the other hand, can expect nothing but boundless hostility. But society is perhaps wiser, in this flagrant injustice, than might appear. She asks of her comedians nothing more than to be amusing, and quickly forgets them ; while, before doing homage to genius, she demands proof of superhuman greatness. Every order of being has its own laws. The immortal diamond must be flawless, but the ephemeral creations of fashion have every right to be flimsy and amusing and superficial.

" All the same, in spite of his faults Lucien might succeed in spite of himself if he could only take advantage of a good vein, or if he happens to get into good company ; but if he meets a bad angel, he will go down to the depths of hell. He has many brilliant and good qualities, embroidered, as it were, on a flimsy foundation. These flowers will fade with age, and then only the foundation will be left ; and if that is poor, there will be only a rag at the end. While Lucien is young, everybody will like him ; but what will become of him at thirty ? That is the question that his true friends are bound to ask themselves. If this had been only my own opinion, perhaps I might have hesitated to give you so much pain for the sake of being honest ; but—apart from the fact that to answer your questions, asked in so much anxiety, evasively or with banalities, would be unworthy of you (for your letter was a cry from the heart), and of myself as well, since you are good enough to have a high opinion of me . . . those of my friends who knew Lucien are unanimous in agreeing with my judgment of him. I have therefore thought it my duty to tell you the truth, painful as it may be. Lucien might do anything, good or bad. That, in a word, is what we think of him, and that is the essence of this letter. If by some chance he should return to you—and his life at the moment is very unhappy, very insecure—use your influence to keep him with his family ; for, until his character has become more stable, Paris is the worst place in the world for him. He used to speak of you and your husband as his guardian angels ; he has most likely forgotten you, but he will remember you again when he is so battered by the storm that he has no one to turn to except his family ; so keep a place for him in your heart—he will need it.

" Permit me, madame, to offer you the sincere homage of one to whom your rare qualities are known, and who respects your womanly solicitude too much to sign himself otherwise than as your humble servant,

" d'Arthez."

Two days after receiving his reply, Eve was obliged to find a nurse, for her milk dried up. She had worshipped her brother ; and now she saw that, through the exercise of his best talents, he had become corrupted. Her idol had fallen into the mire at last! She, noble creature that she was, could never have swerved from the standards of integrity, and delicacy of feeling, from the religion of domestic virtues that is still cultivated in all its purity, that still throws out its clear beams from the hearths of country homes. David's fears, then, had been justified! Eve at last confided to her husband the trouble that had overcast her clear brow with leaden hues. They talked the matter over candidly, as young couples in love with each other do, telling one another everything ; and David found words to console her. Although there were tears in his eyes when he realised that grief had dried up his wife's lovely breasts, and that this young mother was too much shattered by the blow to nurse her baby any longer, he reassured her, and held out some hopes.

" You see, dear child, your brother's imagination has carried him away. It is so natural for a poet to want his mantle of purple and azure, and to find the temptation of going to parties almost irresistible. Such birds fly after bright things, and luxury, in all good faith, and God forgives them if the world does not! "

" But he is ruining us! " exclaimed the poor girl.

" He is ruining us at the moment, but he saved us a few months ago, when he sent us the first-fruits of his earnings," replied David, in the goodness of his heart ; he had the good sense to realise that his wife was carried away by despair, and that her love for Lucien would presently return. " Mercier wrote fifty years ago in his *Tableau de Paris* that no man can hope to live by literature and poetry, by writing or by science, in fact, by the creatures of his brain ; and Lucien, like all poets, has refused to believe the experience of five centuries. Harvests watered with ink are only reaped ten or twelve years after the sowing, if they are reaped at all ; and Lucien has mistaken the sprouting crop for the harvest. He must have learned something about life, anyway ; he was bound to be taken in by the world, and by false friends. He has paid dearly for his experience, that is all. Our ancestors had a saying that so long as the son of the house returns with both ears and his honour intact, all is well! "

" Honour! " poor Eve exclaimed. " Oh, dear, Lucien has behaved badly in so many ways! To attack his best friend, and write against his conscience! And he has accepted money from an actress, and gone about openly with her! And he is taking our last penny! "

" Oh, that—that is nothing," said David, and then stopped short. He had almost let slip the secret of Lucien's forgery, and Eve, unfortunately, noticed that David had kept something back, and was vaguely uneasy.

" What do you mean by nothing ? " she said. " And where are we going to find the money to pay three thousand francs ? "

" Well, to begin with," said David, " we will renew the lease of the workshop with Cérizet. The fifteen per cent the Cointets allow him on the work he does for them has brought him in six hundred francs during the last six months, and he has managed to make another five hundred by job printing."

" If the Cointets knew that perhaps they would not renew the lease—they might be afraid of him," said Eve, " because Cérizet is a dangerous man."

" Well, what does it matter ? " said Séchard. " We will be rich very soon now! And if Lucien is rich, my angel, he will be a pattern of all the virtues! "

" Ah, David, my dear, darling David, what are you saying! So you admit that if Lucien is poor, that he cannot resist temptation!

Then you think exactly the same of him as M. d'Arthez does! No weak character can be a great man, and Lucien is weak. . . . What is the use of an angel that cannot resist temptation! "

" Why, there are natures that only shine in their proper setting, in the right surroundings, in their own sphere. Lucien is not by nature a fighter, and I will spare him the need to fight! Look at this —I am so near to success now that I can tell you about my experiments."

He drew from his pocket several octavo sheets of white paper, brandished them triumphantly, and laid them in his wife's lap.

" A ream of this paper, in royal size, would cost under five francs," he said, and made Eve examine the specimens ; she looked at them in childish astonishment.

" Well, tell me how you made these samples ? "

" With an old hair-sieve I borrowed from Marion."

" And are you still not satisfied ? "

" The difficulty is not in the process, it is in the initial cost of the pulp. The trouble is, dear child, that I am a late-comer in this difficult field. Mme Masson, in 1794, attempted to reconstitute printed paper ; she succeeded—but at what a price! The Marquis of Salisbury in England, in the year 1800, and Séguin in France the following year, tried to find a method of using straw as a raw material. The sheets you are holding were made from the common rush, *arundo phragmitis* ; but I shall experiment with nettles and thistles ; for if the price of the raw material is to be kept down, one must make use of vegetable substances that can be grown in swamps and waste ground. They must be very cheap. The secret lies entirely in the preparation of the stems. At the present moment, my process is not yet simple enough ; but in spite of the difficulty, I am certain that I shall be able to give the French paper industry the privileged position enjoyed by our literature and make it a national monopoly—as England has a monopoly in iron and coal and cheap pottery. I want to be the Jacquart of paper manufacture."

Eve stood up, moved to enthusiasm and admiration by David's simplicity ; she opened her arms to him, and held him close to her, drawing down his head on her shoulder.

" You are rewarding me as if I had succeeded already," he said.

Eve's only reply was to raise her beautiful tear-wet face to him ; it was some time before she was able to speak.

" That kiss is not for the man of genius, but for my comforter! One glory has set, but instead, yours is rising. You give me a husband's greatness to console me for the decline and fall of a brother. Yes, you will be as great as Graindorge or Rouvet or van Robia, like the Persian who discovered madder, like all the men you have told me about, whose names remain obscure ; nobody ever hears the names of the men whose contribution to humanity takes the form of inventing industrial processes. They do good without seeking glory."

. . . . .

" What are they doing at this moment ? " Boniface asked.

The tall Cointet was walking across the Place du Mûrier with Cérizet, watching the shadows of husband and wife outlined on the muslin curtains ; he always came at midnight, to have a word with Cérizet, who was instructed to spy on his old master's every movement.

" He must be showing her the samples of paper he made this morning."

" What materials did he use ? " asked the paper manufacturer.

" Impossible to say," said Cérizet. " I have made a hole in the roof, and I climbed up there last night and watched my boss boiling his pulp in a copper pan. I had a good look at a pile of stuff in a corner ; it looked like a heap of flax, so far as I could make out."

" Don't go any farther," said Boniface Cointet to his spy in unctuous tones ; " it would be dishonest. Mme Séchard will offer to renew your lease of the workshop ; tell her that you are thinking of setting up on your own, and offer her half the value of the lease and the plant. If she agrees, come and see me. In any case, spin it out. Haven't they any money ? "

" Not a sou! " said Cérizet.

" Not a sou! " repeated the tall Cointet. " I've got them! " he thought to himself.

Métivier, wholesale paper merchant, and Cointet brothers, printers and paper manufacturers, also transacted a considerable amount of banking business ; they took good care, however, not to do so nominally, so as to avoid paying for a banker's licence. The Inland Revenue Department has not yet found any means of controlling commercial transactions that will oblige all the businesses that conduct banking business behind the scenes to take out bankers' licences—which, in Paris, cost five hundred francs. But although Cointet Brothers and Métivier were what on the Stock Exahange are called unlicensed brokers, between them they could, nevertheless, set several hundred thousand francs moving every quarter, in the markets of Paris, Bordeaux, and Angoulême. That very evening Cointet Brothers had received from Paris Lucien's three thousand-franc forged cheques. The tall Cointet lost no time in constructing from that debt a formidable machine, directed, as we shall see, against the poor long-suffering inventor.

At seven o'clock next morning Boniface Cointet was walking along the mill-stream that produced the power for his vast paper-mill. The noise of the water prevented his words from being overheard. With him was a young man of twenty-nine or thereabouts, who just six weeks previously had been appointed attorney to the Lower Court of Angoulême. His name was Pierre Petit-Claud, and he had lost no time in answering the rich manufacturer's request that he would go and see him.

" Weren't you at the Angoulême Grammar-school at the same time as David Séchard ? " he asked.

" Yes, sir," said Petit-Claud, falling into step with the tall Cointet.

" Have you renewed the acquaintance ? "

" We have only met once or twice at most since he came back. It was bound to be like that—I was up to the ears in work, or at the Courts on weekdays ; and on Sundays and holidays I was working for my examinations ; you see, I have only myself to rely on."

The tall Cointet nodded approvingly.

" When David and I met again, he asked me what I was doing. I told him that when I had finished my course in law at Poitiers, I had become M. Olivet's chief clerk, and that I was hoping to be his successor some time or another. I knew Lucien Chardon much better—he calls himself de Rubempré now—Mme de Bargeton's lover, our great poet, David Séchard's brother-in-law."

"Then you could go and tell David about your appointment and offer him your services," said the tall Cointet.

"That isn't done," said the young lawyer.

"He has never had a lawsuit, and he has no lawyer, so I don't see why not," said Cointet, taking the measure of the little solicitor from behind his dark glasses.

Petit-Claud was the son of a tailor in l'Houmeau, and he had been looked down on at school. He seemed to have an admixture of gall in his blood, for his complexion was of that muddy and bilious hue that comes from a long record of bad health, late hours, and poverty, and that is nearly always the sign of a bad-tempered nature. To be perfectly frank, he was a curt and irritable young man. His cracked voice was in harmony with his pinched face, his meagre look, and the nondescript colour of his magpie's eyes. Magpie's eyes, according to Napoleon, are a sure sign of dishonesty. "Look at So-and-so," he once said to Las Casas at Saint-Helena, referring to a member of his staff whom he had had to dismiss for corrupt administration, "I cannot think why I trusted him for so long—he has eyes like a magpie." The tall Cointet looked this seedy little lawyer up and down. His face was pitted with small-pox, his thin hair was already receding at the temples ; he noticed, too, the way he rested his hand on his hip, like a man whose health is already feeble ; and he said to himself, "This is my man."

As a matter of fact Petit-Claud, who had been forced to swallow so much contempt, was eaten up with a burning desire to get on ; he had had the audacity, although he had no fortune, to buy up his employer's connection for thirty thousand francs, and was counting on a wealthy marriage to get him out of his financial difficulties ; and, according to the usual custom, he was counting on his employer to find him a wife. (It is always in the interests of a solicitor, on his retirement, to find a good match for his successor, so as to get his own money back.) But Petit-Claud was placing even more reliance in himself, for he had more ability than one usually finds in the provinces, even though its driving principle was his hatred. The greater the hate, the greater the energy.

There is a great difference between Paris solicitors and those of the provinces, and the tall Cointet was much too clever not to take advantage of the small-town passions that move small-town lawyers. A distinguished Paris solicitor—and there are many such—possesses qualities rather like those that mark the diplomat. The large number of cases with which they deal, the large scale of the interests involved, the wide import of the questions submitted to them, are such that Paris solicitors do not look upon a case as a means of making money. The law, for an eminent Paris solicitor, is a weapon of offence or defence, and no longer, as it used to be, simply a lucrative profession. But in the provinces solicitors practise what in Paris is called " trifling "—the art of totalling up that multitude of small items that crowd the columns of lawyer's bills and use up so much stamped paper.

These small items are a major concern of country lawyers, who think in terms of their expense-sheets where Paris solicitors think in terms of their fees. Lawyer's fees over and above the costs are paid by the client to his lawyer for his more or less able conduct of the case. The Revenue Department collects a good half of the costs of the case, whereas the whole of the fees go to the lawyer. Let us admit it frankly—the honorarium actually paid seldom corresponds to the honorarium asked for, and indeed due, to an able solicitor for his services. Solicitors, doctors and barristers in Paris are like courtesans with their casual lovers, very much on their guard against the ingratitude of their clients. The client, before the case and after, would make a good pair of *genre* pictures in the style of Meissonier, and would certainly be much sought after by lawyers depending upon their fees.

But there is another difference between the Paris solicitor and his provincial counterpart. The Paris solicitor very seldom appears in court, although he occasionally speaks at a trial, as an arbitrator; there are swarms of barristers in the provinces nowadays, but in 1822, in most country districts solicitors acted as barristers as well and pleaded their own causes. This double function created in country lawyers the intellectual vices of the barrister, without lessening the solicitor's heavy burden of hard work. The country solicitor is liable, in acquiring the gift of fluency, to lose that lucidity of judgment so necessary in his profession ; and in doubling his functions in this way, a man of good abilities is liable to turn himself into two mediocrities. In Paris the solicitor who does not waste himself in words at the courts, and who seldom has to plead, indifferently, for and against, can conserve a degree of rectitude in his ideas. It is true that he prepares the artillery of the law, and hunts through the arsenal of weapons presented by the contradictions of jurisprudence ; but he keeps his own opinion of the case for whose successful outcome he is obliged to work. In short, thoughts do not turn a man's head so completely as words. By the force of his own eloquence a man comes to believe what he says, whereas one may act against one's convictions without altering them, and win a shady lawsuit without persuading oneself that it is an honourable one, as the barrister must do. For this reason, a retired Paris solicitor is much more likely than a retired barrister to make a good judge.

A country solicitor is liable, then, for many reasons, to be a mediocrity ; he espouses the causes of petty passions, he conducts petty cases, he lives by charging up petty expenses, he abuses the Code of Procedure, and pleads in Court. In short, he has many weak points. And if, among country solicitors, you find a man of outstanding abilities, he is undoubtedly an exception.

" I thought, sir, that you had sent for me on your own account," replied Petit-Claud, giving epigrammatic point to his remark by means of a glance that he directed upon the tall Cointet's impenetrable glasses.

" No beating about the bush," said Boniface Cointet. " Listen to me."

After this opening, big with unspoken confidences, Cointet seated himself on a bench and motioned Petit-Claud to do the same.

" When M. du Hautoy passed through Angoulême in 1804 on his way to take up his consulship in Valencia, he made the acquaintance of Mme de Senonches—Mlle Zéphirine she was then—and he had a daughter by her." Cointet spoke these words to his companion in a confidential whisper. " Yes," he went on, seeing Petit-Claud's start of surprise, "Mlle Zéphirine's marriage with M. de Senonches took place very soon after the birth of that child, which was kept secret. The girl was brought up in the country by my mother; she is Mlle Françoise de la Haye, who lives with Mme de Senonches—she passes for her goddaughter. My mother has the home farm belonging to old Mme de Cardanet, Mlle Zéphirine's grandmother, and she knows the secret of the only heiress of the Cardanets and the elder branch of the Senonches, and she asked me to invest the little sum which M. Francis de Hautoy set aside for his daughter's fortune. I made my own fortune with that ten thousand francs, which has increased to thirty thousand by this time. Mme de Senonches is sure to give her goddaughter the trousseau, and silver, and a certain amount of furniture; and I, my boy, can arrange for you to marry the girl," said Cointet, slapping Petit-Claud on the knee. " If you marry Françoise de la Haye, you will have more than half the aristocracy of Angoulême for your clients. This left-handed marriage will open up a magnificent prospect for you. The status of a solicitor and barrister is good enough—they will ask nothing better, I assure you."

" What do you want me to do?" Petit-Claud enquired avidly. " M. Cachan is your lawyer, is he not?"

" Yes, and I am not going to leave Cachan for you in a hurry—I shall not be your client until later on," said the tall Cointet significantly. " What do I want you to do, my friend? Why, I want you to act for David Séchard. Poor devil, he has got to meet bills for three thousand francs, and he will never do it; and you will defend him when the case comes up, but at the same time see that you run up an enormous bill for costs. Don't worry, go ahead, and pile on the incidental expenses. Doublon, my bailiff, who will be acting for me, under Cachan's directions, will not pull his punches—a word to the wise is enough. So that's the situation, young man."

There was an eloquent pause, and the two men looked at one another.

"We have not seen one another," Cointet resumed; "I have said nothing to you, you know nothing about M. du Hautoy or Mme de Senonches, or Mlle de la Haye; only, when the time comes, say in two months' time—you will ask for that young lady in marriage. If there is anything to discuss, come here, in the evening. We will put nothing in writing."

"You want to ruin Séchard?" asked Petit-Claud.

"Not exactly; but he must be sent to gaol for a time."

"For what object?"

"Do you think I am such a fool as to tell you that? If you are clever enough to guess, you will be clever enough to hold your tongue."

"Old Séchard is a wealthy man," said Petit-Claud, who was already beginning to enter into Boniface Cointet's schemes and who saw in this fact a possible cause of failure.

"So long as the old man is alive he won't give a penny to his son; and the old ex-typographer has no intention of ordering his funeral cards just yet."

"Then that is agreed!" said Petit-Claud, making up his mind promptly. "I am a solicitor, so I won't ask you for guarantees. But if anyone tries to cheat me, there will be an account to settle between us."

"That scoundrel will go far," Cointet thought to himself as Petit-Claud took his leave.

The day after this conversation was the thirtieth of April, and Cointet Brothers sent in the first of Lucien's forged bills. As ill luck would have it, it was handed to poor Mme Séchard, who recognised Lucien's imitation of her husband's signature as a forgery. She called David and asked him point blank whether he had signed the money order.

"No," he said, "your brother needed the money at once, and so he signed for me."

Eve returned the cheque to the boy from Cointet's banking department.

"We cannot pay it," she said. Then, feeling her strength failing her, she went upstairs to her room, David following her.

" My dear," said Eve in mournful tones, " go at once to the Cointets—they will show you some consideration ; ask them to wait. And while you are there you might just mention that when Cérizet's lease is renewed they will owe you a thousand francs."

David went immediately to his enemies. Any foreman can become a master-printer, but there is many a skilled typographer who will never make a business man, and David had no business ability. His heart beating fast, and tight at the throat, he mumbled his excuses and brought out his request clumsily. He was cut short by the tall Cointet's reply.

" This has nothing to do with us, the cheque was sent us by Métivier ; Métivier will pay us. You will have to write to Métivier."

" Oh! " said Eve when she heard this reply. " The moment the cheque is returned to M. Métivier we can stop worrying."

At two o'clock the following day, the time when the Place du Mûrier is always full of people, Victor-Ange-Herménégilde Doublon brought the protest for David's signature. Although he was careful to go round to the back door and speak to Marion and Kolb, the news was known to every tradesman in Angoulême by the evening. And in any case, how could Doublon's hypocritical tact, that the tall Cointet had insisted upon most emphatically, save Eve and David from the commercial disgrace of a suspension of payment ? It is not to be imagined! One might digress endlessly at this point, and still not cover the complexities of the situation ; and ninety-nine readers out of a hundred will devour the details that follow as most exciting and novel—which all goes to show the truth of the axiom that the subject about which least is known is the one that everybody is supposed to know—the Law!

In fact, to the immense majority of Frenchmen, a detailed description of the mechanism of one particular branch of banking will have all the fascination of a chapter in a book of foreign travel. When a tradesman sends a money order from the town in which he has his place of business, to some other town, as David was supposed to have done to oblige Lucien, the simple transaction of giving a promissory note, as from one tradesman to another, in the same town, becomes something in the nature of a letter of exchange, drawn at one place, met at another. Therefore, when he accepted Lucien's three cheques, Métivier, in order to collect his money, was obliged to send them to Cointet Brothers, his agents in Angoulême. This represented an initial deduction from the amount paid to Lucien, under the heading of *commission for change of place*, in the form of a percentage on each cheque, over and above the fee for discounting. In this way Séchard's bills had passed into the category of a banking transaction. The extent to which the title of banker, united with the august name of " creditor ", changes the situation of the debtor is scarcely to be believed. For example, in *banking* (note well that word!), if a draft is sent from the Paris exchange to the exchange of Angoulême, and that draft is protested, the bankers have the right to draw up, on their own account, an expenses account for presenting the protested cheque. Joking apart, romance has never invented a more improbable sequence of events. Countless ingenious jokes in the style of Mascarille are authorised by one particular article of the Commercial Code. You will see, from the practical application of this article that follows, how many atrocities are concealed behind that terrible word *legality*.

As soon as Doublon had received the signed protest, he took it back, himself, to Cointet Brothers. The bailiff had a standing account with these lynxes of Angoulême and gave them six months' credit, which the tall Cointet managed to stretch out to a year, by the way in which he settled it; every month he would say to the under-lynx, " Are you needing any money, Doublon ? " Nor was that all! Doublon favoured that powerful business establishment with a discount, and in this way they saved a little on each process served—a mere trifle, next to nothing, something like one franc fifty on a protest, for example. The tall Cointet sat down at his desk in the best of humours and took a small sheet of paper bearing a thirty-five-centime stamp, chatting with Doublon the while, in such a way as to extract from him information about the true state of various local tradesmen.

" Well, how do you think young Gannerac is doing ? "

" Not so badly. A carrier jolly well ought to be doing well."

" Yes. But the fact is that he has heavy expenses. I hear that his wife spends a lot of money."

" Of *his* money ? " Doublon asked with a sneer.

The lynx, who had now finished ruling out his sheet, proceeded to write out in a round hand the following sinister account :

" *ACCOUNT OF EXPENSES FOR PROTEST AND RETURN*

" To one draft for one thousand francs, dated February the tenth, eighteen hundred and twenty-two, signed by Séchard junior, Angoulême, to be paid to Lucien Chardon, known as de Rubempré, endorsed to the order of Métivier, and to the order of the undersigned, expiring on the thirtieth of April last, protested by Doublon, process-server, the first of May, eighteen hundred and twenty-two.

	francs	*centimes*
Principal	1,000	—
Protest	12	35
Bank charges, at one-half per cent	5	—
Brokerage charge, at one-quarter per cent	2	50
Stamp on the draft and present account	1	35
Interest and postage	3	—
	1,024	20
Exchange at one and a quarter per cent on 1,024fr. 20c.	13	25
Total	1,037	45

One thousand and thirty-seven francs forty-five centimes, on which we reimburse ourselves by our draft at sight on M. Métivier, Rue Serpente, Paris, by the order of M. Gannerac, of l'Houmeau.

Angoulême, the second of May, eighteen hundred and twenty-two.

Cointet Brothers."

At the foot of this little memorandum, made out with the facility that comes from long practice (for he was talking to Doublon all the time he was writing), the tall Cointet added the following memorandum :

" We the undersigned, Postel, licensed chemist of l'Houmeau, and Gannerac, haulage contractor, tradesmen of this town, certify that the current rate of exchange as between Angoulême and Paris is one and one-quarter per cent.

Angoulême, May 2nd, 1822."

" Here, Doublon, do you mind calling on Postel and Gannerac and asking them to sign this declaration ? Let me have it tomorrow morning."

So Doublon, who was familiar with these instruments of torture, went off for all the world as if it was the simplest thing imaginable. Obviously even if the protest had been sent by post, as in Paris, all Angoulême would still have known about the desperate state of poor Séchard's affairs. And everybody blamed his want of initiative! Some said his excessive love for his wife had been his undoing ; others blamed him for showing too much affection for his brother-in-law. And from these premises they drew the worst conclusions! No one should ever espouse the interests of near relations! And old Séchard's hardness towards his son met with unanimous approval!

Meanwhile, all those of you who, for whatever reason, may fail to " honour your engagements ", take careful note of the proceedings —all perfectly legal—which, in banking, bring in twenty-eight francs' interest on capital of a thousand francs!

The first item in the above " Account of Expenses " is the only one that is not open to question.

The second item is shared between the bailiff and the Inland Revenue Department. The six francs that goes to the State, for registering the debtor's deep regrets on a piece of stamped paper, will ensure the long continuance of this abuse! And, I would remind you, this item put one franc fifty into the banker's pockets in the form of Doublon's discount.

The one-half per cent " bank charges ", referred to in the third item, is made on the ingenious pretext that if a banker has not received payment, that he has, in effect, discounted a bill. This is the very opposite of the truth, but it seems that not to have received a thousand francs is equivalent to having paid them out. Everyone who has ever cashed a bill with a discounter knows that, besides the six per cent fixed by law, the discounter charges, under the humble heading of " commission ", a certain percentage which represents the interest that his genius for increasing his capital brings him in, over and above the legal tax. The more money he makes out of you, the more he asks—so that it would be cheaper, if it were possible, to cash your cheques with a fool. But then, are there any fools in banking?

The law obliges the banker to obtain a certificate from a stock-broker for the rate of exchange. In towns that are not fortunate enough to have a stock-exchange, the signature of two shopkeepers is accepted instead. The so-called brokerage charge, due to the stockbroker, is fixed at a quarter of one per cent of the sum involved in the protested cheque. By courtesy this commission is regarded as being paid to the shopkeepers who act instead of a stockbroker, and the banker quietly pockets the amount. So much for the third item of this interesting account.

The fourth item represents the cost of the sheet of stamped paper on which the " Account of Expenses " is written, and that of the stamp so ingeniously called the " re-draft ", that is to say, the new draft drawn by the banker on his colleague in order to reimburse himself.

The fifth item comprises the cost of postage, and the legal interest on the sum during such time as it may be absent from the banker's cash-box.

The final charge, for the exchange, is for the sending of money from one place to another—for which very purpose banks exist!

And now analyse this account carefully. The method would seem to be very similar to that employed by Polichinelle in the Neapolitan song that Lablache used to sing so delightfully, by which fifteen and five make twenty-two! Obviously Postel and Gannerac affixed their signatures to oblige a business colleague; the Cointets would do the same for Gannerac if occasion were to arise, according to the proverb about " you scratch my back and I'll scratch yours ". Cointet Brothers, who had a current account with Métivier, had no occasion to make out a re-draft, for between them a returned cheque represented simply one item more or less on the *debit* or *credit* side.

What this fantastic account really amounted to was the thousand francs owed, thirteen francs for the protest, and about one-half per cent interest for the month's delay—perhaps one thousand and eighteen francs all told.

If a large banking house receives once a day, on an average, a protest on a sum of a thousand francs, the bank daily makes a profit of twenty-eight francs, by the grace of God and the constitution of the bank, that formidable power invented by the Jews of the twelfth century, which today controls both kings and their subjects. In other words, a thousand francs brings into the bank twenty-eight francs a day, or ten thousand two hundred and twenty francs a year. Treble the average of protested cheques, and you will have a revenue of thirty thousand francs, raised on purely fictitious capital. So that nothing is cultivated more lovingly than expense accounts. David Séchard might have gone to pay his bill on May 3rd, or on the very day after the protest, and Cointet Brothers would have said, " We have returned your cheque to M. Métivier ", although the cheque would still in fact have been lying on their desk. The account for expenses is made out on the day of the protest; and this, in the language of provincial banking, is what is known as " sweating one's sovereigns ". Postage charges alone bring in twenty thousand francs a year to the Kellers, who transact business all over the world, and the Nucingen's expense accounts pay for boxes at the Italiens, and the Baroness' dress-bill and her carriage. The postage charge is an abuse all the more shocking because bankers always deal with a dozen items at once in a dozen lines of a single letter. And, strange to relate, the Government takes its share of this harvest wrung from misfortune, and the

Treasury funds are swelled by this tax on commercial adversity. The bank, meanwhile, from the heights of her counters, flings this unanswerable question at the debtor : " Why could you not meet your bills ? "—to which question, unfortunately, there is no answer. Those of you who are debtors would do well to think over these instructive pages ; for the story of the expenses account is one whose monstrous fictions may well make you shudder!

On May 5th Métivier received the account from Cointet Brothers with instructions to prosecute M. Lucien Chardon, *alias* Rubempré, in Paris, with the utmost rigour of the law.

A few days later Eve received, in reply to the letter that she had written to M. Métivier, the following brief note, which completely reassured her.

" To M. Séchard, Junior, Printer, Angoulême :

" I have duly received your esteemed communication of the 5th inst. I understand from your explanations relating to the cheque unpaid on the 30th April last that you had obliged your brother-in-law M. de Rubempré, who is spending so much money that it will be doing you a service to make him pay : he is so placed that he is not likely to delay payment for long. If your esteemed brother-in-law does not pay, I shall rely upon the credit of your long-established house, and sign myself, now as always,

" Your obedient servant,

" Métivier."

" Well," said Eve to David, " my brother will realise when they summons him that we could not pay."

What a change in Eve was expressed in those words! The growing love that she felt for David, as she had come, little by little, to know him better, was taking the place, in her heart, of her old love for her brother. But to how many illusions had she not said goodbye!

Let us now follow the tracks of the re-draft in the exchanges of Paris. A third holder, the commercial term for any third party into whose hands a cheque passes, is at liberty, according to the law, to pursue only that one, among a number of debtors, by whom he thinks he has the best chance of being paid promptly. By virtue of this right, Lucien was pursued by Métivier's bailiff. There followed the successive phases of this action, which, as it transpired, was entirely without result. Métivier, behind whom the Cointets were concealed, knew of Lucien's insolvency; but, in the eyes of the law, insolvency *de facto* is not recognised by the law until it has been formally proved.

Formal proof of Lucien's inability to meet the cheque was obtained as follows:

On May 5th Métivier's bailiff informed Lucian that the cheque had been protested in Angoulême, and handed him the account of expenses; he summoned Lucien to attend the Tribunal of Commerce in Paris in order to listen to a whole series of items, including the fact that he was liable to be sentenced to prison, as a tradesman. By the time that Lucien, hunted down and on the run, had brought himself to read this abracadabra, he had received notice that a judgment had been obtained against him, in default, at the Tribunal of Commerce. Coralie, his mistress, who had no idea what it was all about, imagined that Lucien must have come to the rescue of his brother-in-law; she gave him all these papers at the same time—and too late. An actress sees too many stage bailiffs on the music-halls to believe in a piece of stamped paper!

Tears came into Lucien's eyes, and his heart bled for Séchard. He was ashamed of what he had done, and he wanted to pay. Naturally he consulted his friends as to the best way to gain time. But by the time Lousteau, Blondet, Bixion and Nathan had assured Lucien that a poet ought to pay no attention to a Tribunal of Commerce, a Court set up for shopkeepers, the bailiffs were already in possession. He saw on his door that little yellow notice whose colour is reflected in the jaundiced eyes of porters, that has such an astringent effect on credit, that strikes alarm into the hearts even of the humblest shopkeepers, and that strikes a chill of terror, above all, into the veins of poets who have enough feeling to be attached to pieces of wood, scraps of silk, and lengths of woollen material—all those odds and ends we call furniture.

When the men arrived to remove Coralie's furniture, the author of *Marguerites* went in search of a friend of Bixiou's, a barrister called Desroches, who burst out laughing when he saw Lucien in such a state of terror over such a trifling matter.

"That is nothing, my dear fellow.... You want to gain time?"

"As much as possible."

"Very well, appeal against the execution of judgment. Go and see my friend Masson, a solicitor at the Tribunal of Commerce, take your documents along to him and he will ask for the case to be re-heard, appear for you, and appeal against the verdict of the Court. That will present no difficulty at all—you are a well-known journalist. If your case comes up for trial before a civil court, come and see me, that will be my affair. I promise you that I will soon send anybody about his business who attempts to annoy the fair Coralie!"

On May 28th Lucien's case came up before a civil court, and he was condemned more promptly than Desroches had expected, for Lucien's creditors were out for his blood. When a new warrant was issued, and the yellow notice once again gilded Coralie's door-posts, and the men came to take away the furniture, Desroches, who felt rather a fool for having been caught napping by a colleague (as he put it), opposed the warrant, on the grounds (perfectly just, what was more) that the furniture belonged to Mlle Coralie, and he demanded an enquiry. The Judge, on the findings of the enquiry, dismissed the case, in which the furniture was adjudged to the actress, and a judgment made out to that effect. Métivier, who appealed against this decision, had his appeal dismissed in Court on July 30th.

On August 7th Maître Cachan received, by parcel post, an enormous dossier, headed *Métivier versus Séchard and Lucien Chardon.*

The first item was the following nice little bill, for whose accuracy I vouch, for it is copied from the original document:

"Bill due on 30th April last, drawn by Séchard junior, to order of Lucien de Rubempré (May 2nd), protest and return . . . 1,037. 45

May	5th	Serving notice of protest and return, with summons to appear before Paris Tribunal of Commerce on May 7th .	8.	75
May	7th	Judgment by default and warrant of arrest	35.	00
May	10th	Notification of judgment	8.	50
May	12th	Warrant	5.	50
May	14th	Cost of Inventory...............	16.	00
May	18th	Cost of placards................	15.	25
May	19th	Insertion of notification in journal..	4.	00
May	24th	Cost of Re-examination and verification of inventory, including application for stay of execution by the said M. Lucien de Rubempré..........	12.	00
May	27th	Order of the Court on application being duly repeated, and transfer of the case to the Civil Court........	35.	00
May	28th	Notice of summary proceedings before the Civil Court, by Métivier represented by Counsel..........	6.	50
June	2nd	Judgment ordering Lucien Chardon to pay costs of protest and return, and assigning to the plaintiff costs of case brought before the Tribunal of Commerce	150.	00
June	6th	Notification of aforesaid..........	10.	00
June	15th	Warrant of execution............	5.	50
June	19th	Inventory and valuation preparatory to execution, and appeal against said execution by Mlle Coralie, on grounds that furniture is her property, requesting immediate special enquiry before further proceedings be taken...	20.	00
,,	,,	Order from Judge, referring parties to Registrar for special enquiry....	40.	00

June 19th	Judgment in favour of the said Mlle Coralie	250.	00
June 20th	Appeal by Métivier	17.	00
June 30th	Confirmation of judgment	250.	00
	Total	1,926.	45
	Cheque due May 31st, protest and return	1,037.	45
	Serving notice of protest on Lucien .	8.	75
	Total	1,046.	20
	Cheque due June 30th, protest and return, serving notice of protest on Lucien	8.	75
	Total	1,046.	20

These documents were accompanied by a letter in which Métivier instructed Maître Cachan, solicitor, of Angoulême, to proceed against David Séchard with the utmost rigour of the law. So Maître Victor-Ange-Herménégilde Doublon summoned David Séchard to appear before the Angoulême Tribunal of Commerce for the sum-total of four thousand and eighteen francs, eighty-five centimes, including the three cheques and the expenses already involved. On the same day that Doublon handed the writ to Eve in person, ordering the payment of this sum—enormous in her eyes—she had received a shattering letter from Métivier by the morning's post:

" To M. Séchard, Junior, Printer, Angoulême.

" Your brother-in-law, M. Chardon, has had the shameless dishonesty to declare his furniture to be the property of an actress with whom he is living, and you ought in all fairness to have informed me honestly of these circumstances and so saved me from pursuing a useless law-suit; instead of which you sent no reply to my letter of May 10th. Please do not take it amiss, therefore, if I ask you for immediate repayment of the three cheques and the expenses in which I have been involved.

"I am, Yours, etc.,

"Métivier."

As she had heard nothing more of the matter, Eve, who knew nothing of commercial law, had thought that her brother had made reparation for his crime by meeting the forged bills.

"Go at once to Petit-Claud, my dear," she said to her husband, "explain our situation to him, and take his advice."

David hurried round to his old schoolfellow's office.

"I never dreamed, when you came and told me of your appointment and offered me your services, that I should need them so soon," he began.

Petit-Claud studied the fine intellectual face of the man sitting in the chair opposite to him. He did not listen to the details of the case, for he knew more about these than did the man who was explaining them to him. As soon as he had seen Séchard come in, obviously worried, he had said to himself, "The thing is done!"

Situations of this kind are very common in solicitors' offices.

"Why are the Cointets persecuting him?" he wondered. It is the way of lawyers to use their wits to penetrate the minds of their clients, just as they do those of their opponents; they have to know the seamy side, as well as the upper surface, of the judicial web.

"You want to gain time," Petit-Claud observed at last, when Séchard came to a pause. "How long do you want? Something like three or four months?"

"Oh! Four months would save me!" exclaimed David, who saw Petit-Claud as an angel of light.

"Very well, no one shall lay a finger on any of your furniture, and no one shall arrest you for four months. . . . But it will be an expensive business," said Petit-Claud.

"Oh! That does not matter to me!" exclaimed Séchard.

"You are expecting some money then—are you sure of it?"

asked the lawyer, almost surprised by the way in which his client was walking into the trap set for him.

" In three months' time I shall be a rich man," replied the inventor, with all an inventor's assurance.

" Your father is still above ground," retorted Petit-Claud, " and he means to stay among his vines."

" You surely don't imagine that I am counting on my father's death ? " David replied. " I am on the tracks of an industrial secret that will enable me to manufacture, without a thread of cotton, a paper as strong as Dutch paper, and at fifty per cent less than the price of cotton pulp! "

" That would be worth a fortune! " exclaimed Petit-Claud, who now understood tall Cointet's project.

" A very large fortune, because ten years from now the demand for paper will be ten times as great as it is today. Journalism is going to be the particular folly of our time! "

" Nobody knows your secret ? "

" No one except my wife."

" You have not said anything about your plans to anyone—to the Cointets, for example ? "

" I did mention it, I believe, but very vaguely."

A generous impulse flashed through Petit-Claud's embittered mind ; it seemed to him that he might reconcile everyone's interests, the Cointets, Séchard's, and his own.

" Listen to me, David. You and I were at school together, and I will defend you ; but I warn you—this defence, which will run counter to the law, will cost you five or six thousand francs! Don't compromise your future! In my opinion you would be well advised to share the profits of your invention with some local paper manufacturer. Look at it in this way. You would have to think twice before buying or building a paper mill, and besides that, there will be the patent. All these things will take time, and they will take money. The bailiffs will be down on you perhaps before you are ready, in spite of everything I can do to prevent them."

" I shall keep my secret! " David replied, with all the simplicity of a student.

" Well, in that case your secret is your only hope," said Petit-Claud, repulsed in his first, and honourable, attempt to avoid the law-suit by a compromise. " I don't want to know what it is ; but mark my words—work in the depths of the earth, if you can, so that nobody can see what you are doing, or get any suspicion of the means that you are employing, or your safety-plank will be snatched from under you! An inventor is often a simpleton as well. You spend too much thought on your research to think of other things. Sooner or later the object of your research will leak out. This town is full of paper manufacturers—and every paper manufacturer is a potential enemy! You remind me of an otter surrounded by the hunt—don't let them get your skin! "

" I don't know how to thank you, my dear fellow—all these things had occurred to me," said Séchard, " but I am very grateful to you for advising me to be careful! I do not really mind for myself. I could live very happily on twelve hundred francs a year and my father is bound to leave me at least three times that sum sooner or later. I live for my work, and for those I love . . . a heavenly life . . . I am thinking of Lucien and my wife—it is for them that I am working."

" Well, then—sign this Power of Attorney for me, and you need not think about anything except your invention. If there should be a warrant for your arrest, I will give you warning in advance—we must think of all possibilities. And let me advise you not to allow anyone inside your house of whom you are not as sure as you are of yourself."

" Cérizet has decided not to renew the lease of my printing house —that is why we are in money difficulties for the moment. I have only Marion and Kolb with me now—Kolb is an Alsatian who is as devoted as a watchdog—besides my wife and my mother-in-law."

" A word of advice," said Petit-Claud ; " watch the watchdog! "

" You don't know Kolb! " exclaimed David. " I would no more doubt him than I would doubt myself! "

" Would you like me to try him ? "

" Yes," said Séchard.

" Very well, goodbye for now ; but send your wife along to see me, because I shall require her signature. And bear in mind that a fire has started in your hay-rick," Petit-Claud observed to his companion, by way of warning him of the judical disasters that were about to descend upon him. " Here I am with one foot in Burgundy and the other in Champagne," Petit-Claud thought to himself, as he saw David Séchard to the door of his office.

Worried by money troubles, worried by the state of his wife's health, wounded to the quick by Lucien's shameful behaviour, David still carried on with his experiments ; and as he walked from his own house to Petit-Claud's office, he had absent-mindedly chewed as he went a nettle-stalk that he had been steeping in water. He was trying to find some method of maceration of the vegetable fibres employed in the composition of his paste, some single process that would replace the repeated operations of pounding involved in the maceration of cotton and linen rags of all kinds. As he returned home, reasonably satisfied at the result of his interview with his friend Petit-Claud, he found a pellet of paste sticking between his teeth. He examined it, stretched it, and saw that he had a paste far superior to any that he had yet made ; for the principal drawback of vegetable pastes is want of cohesion. Straw, for example, produces a brittle paper, almost metallic, that rustles loudly. Accidents of this kind only happen to audacious investigators of the laws of nature!

" I must find a way of carrying out by means of a machine and a chemical agent the process that I have just performed absent-mindedly," he reflected.

He greeted his wife in all the joy of his belief in his triumph.

" Oh, my angel, you must not worry! " said David to his wife, who had obviously been crying. " Petit-Claud has undertaken to see that we are left in peace for the next few months. It will be expensive, but as he said as he saw me out, ' Every Frenchman has the right to make his creditors wait, so long as, in the end, he pays them capital, interest, and expenses.' Well, we shall pay."

" And how are we going to live meanwhile ? " said poor Eve, who thought of everything.

" Yes, that is true," said David, raising his hand to his ear, with that unaccountable gesture used by nearly all mortals when they are in great perplexity.

" My mother can look after little Lucien, and I can go back to work," she said.

" Eve, my darling Eve! " David exclaimed, taking his wife in his arms and drawing her close to him. " Eve, at Saintes, not far from here, in the sixteenth century, lived one of the greatest men that France has ever produced—he was not only the inventor of enamel, but the glorious precursor of Buffon and Cuvier, and he studied geology long before they did, that old simpleton! Bernard Palissy was a prey to his passion for experimental research, but his wife, his children, and all his neighbours were against him. His wife sold his instruments, and he wandered about the countryside, misunderstood, hunted down, and jeered at. . . . But I am loved! "

" You are indeed! " Eve replied with the serenity of a love sure of itself.

" I may have to suffer all that poor Bernard Palissy suffered—he was the inventor of Écouen ware, and Charles IX ordered him to be spared on the day of St. Bartholomew ; and in his later years he was rich and honoured, and gave his public lectures on the ' Science of Earths ' in the face of the whole of Europe."

" So long as my hands can hold an iron, you shall not want for anything! " said his poor wife, in tones of heartfelt devotion. " When I was Mme Prieur's forewoman I made friends with one of the girls—a good girl, Postel's cousin, Basine Clerget ; Well, Basine told me a little while ago, when she brought my laundry, that she was taking over Mme Prieur's business, and I shall go and work for her."

" Ah! You shall not work there for long! " said David. " I have discovered . . ."

For the first time Eve responded to the sublime belief in success that sustains inventors and gives them the courage to go on into the virgin forests of unexplored continents, with a sad smile ; and David bowed his head sadly.

" Oh, my dear, I was not laughing at you, I am not making fun of you, I have no doubts," cried Eve, going down on her knees before her husband. " But I do realise how right you were not to talk about your experiments and your hopes. Yes, my dear, inventors must conceal the painful labours of bringing their fame to birth, even from their wives! A wife is still only a woman. Your own Eve could not repress a smile when you said 'I have discovered' for the seventeenth time this month."

David laughed so wholeheartedly at his own expense that Eve took his hand and kissed it tenderly. It was a heavenly moment; one of those roses of love and tenderness that flourish by the barest roadsides of poverty, and sometimes even at the bottom of the deepest precipices.

Eve met the redoubled fury of the storm of misfortune with redoubled courage. Her husband's greatness, the inventor's simplicity, the tears that she sometimes saw, unawares, in the eyes of this man of feeling and poetry, all gave birth in her to an undreamed-of power of endurance. She once again had recourse to a means that had on a former occasion served her so well. She wrote to M. Métivier asking him to advertise the printing business for sale, offering to pay him out of the price obtained, and begging him not to ruin David with useless expenses. Métivier responded to that heroic letter by shamming dead. His chief clerk replied that in M. Métivier's absence he could not take it upon himself to stop the proceedings, because this was not his employer's usual practice in business matters. Eve suggested renewing the bills, and paying the costs, and the chief clerk agreed to this, on condition that David's father would guarantee payment by endorsing the bills. So Eve walked all the way to Marsac, taking with her Kolb and her old mother. She braved the old vine-grower, and she was so charming that she succeeded in making his old face relax; but when, with inward trepidation, she broached the subject of the endorsement, she beheld a sudden and complete change in his topographic features.

" If I allowed my son to dip into the mouth of my cash-box, he would plunge in his arm and tear out all its innards and leave it empty! " said he. " Children are all alike—they eat up their fathers' savings! What did I do myself, eh? I never cost my father a penny! Now your printing house is standing idle. The only printing done in it is done by the mice and rats. . . . You are very pretty, and I am very fond of you; you are a hard-working and economical wife; but as for my son—do you know what David is? I'll tell you—he's a scholar and a good-for-nothing! If I had reared him, as I was reared, without knowing how to read or write, and if I had made him into a bear like his old father, he would have had interest coming in on his money by now! Ah, that son of mine is my cross, and that's a fact! And he's the only son I'm likely to have, worse luck; there won't ever be a second edition now! And he makes you unhappy, what is more. . . ."

Eve protested with a gesture of absolute denial.

"Yes, he does," the old man said, in answer to that gesture; "you had to find a nurse, because worry dried up your milk. Why, I know how things stand—you have received a summons, and the whole town is talking about you. I was only a bear, I'm not educated, I was never foreman at Messrs. Didot's, the best typographers in the world! But I never had a writ served on me! Do you know what I say to myself as I go up and down among my vines, tending them and harvesting the grapes, and doing my little bits of business? I say to myself, 'Poor old chap, you are taking a lot of trouble, you are piling up the sovereigns, and you will leave a nice little bit of property, and the bailiffs and the lawyers will get it all—or else it will go on fancy notions—some wild idea or other.' You listen to me, my dear, you have that little youngster of yours to think about, and it struck me when I held him at his christening with Mme Chardon that he has his grandfather's truffle-nose in the middle of his face—well, think less about Séchard and more about that little fellow. . . . You are the only one I trust. . . . You will see to it that he doesn't waste my property . . . my poor property!"

"But dear Papa Séchard, you will have reason to be proud of your son, and he will be rich by his own efforts one day, you will see, and have the cross of the Legion of Honour in his button-hole. . . ."

"What's he going to do for that, eh?" asked the old vine-grower.

" You will see! But meanwhile, would three thousand francs ruin you ? Three thousand francs would put a stop to the proceedings. Well, if you don't trust David, lend them to me, and I will pay you back ; you can rely on my marriage settlement, and on my work. . . ."

" So it is true that David Séchard has been summonsed ? " exclaimed the vine-grower, greatly surprised to discover that what he had taken to be malicious gossip was in fact true. " That's what comes of knowing how to sign your name! And what about my rent ? Yes, my dear girl, I shall have to go to Angoulême and look into this and consult Cachan, my solicitor. You did quite right to come and see me! Forewarned is forearmed! "

After two hours of argument, Eve left, defeated by the unanswerable argument that " women understand nothing about business ". There was no more to be said. She had come with some faint hope of success, but she walked back along the road from Marsac to Angoulême almost heartbroken. She arrived home just in time to receive notice of the judgment ordering Séchard to pay Métivier the full amount. In the provinces, a bailiff at the door is an event ; and Doublon had appeared so often lately that everybody was talking about it. Eve no longer dared to leave her own house for fear of hearing her neighbours whispering.

" Oh, Lucien, Lucien! " Eve said aloud as she hurried into the passage and up the stairs. " I shall never be able to forgive you unless it was . . ."

" Yes," said David, who had followed her, " it was that or suicide, I am afraid."

" Do not let us ever mention it again," she answered gently. " The woman who led him into the depths of Paris has much to answer for! And your father, David, is quite heartless . . . we must suffer in silence."

David was about to reply with some loving word, when a discreet knock cut him short, and Marion appeared, with Kolb's tall stalwart figure in tow.

" Please, ma'am," she began, " Kolb and I, we know that you and the master have been in difficulties, and as between us we have eleven hundred francs in savings, we thought that the best thing we could do with them was to offer them to you, ma'am."

" To de mistress! " echoed Kolb, with enthusiasm.

" Kolb," exclaimed David Séchard, " you and I will always stand by one another! Take a thousand francs on account to Cachan, the solicitor, and ask for a receipt; we will keep the rest. And Kolb, let no power on earth draw one word from you about what I am doing, about when I am away, or anything you may see me bring back, and when I send you to collect plants, you know, do not let a living soul see you. . . . They will try to bribe you, Kolb, and they may very well offer you a thousand or even ten thousand francs for information. . . ."

" Dey may offer me pillions, but dey hear not ein vort from me! Have I not peen in de army? I know how to opey orders! "

" Well, I have warned you—go now, and ask M. Petit-Claud to go with you when you pay the money to M. Cachan."

" Yes," said the Alsatian. " One day I shall pe rich enough to settle de accounts with dat man of law! I like not his face! "

" He is such a good man, ma'am! " exclaimed the stout Marion. " He is as strong as a Turk and as gentle as a lamb! That's the sort of man to make a woman happy! And it was him who had the idea of investing our savings in this way—' safings ' he calls them! Poor man, he may not speak very well, but his heart is in the right place, and I can understand him just the same! He had the idea of going to work for the others so as not to cost us anything . . ."

" We must become rich if only to repay these good friends! " said Séchard, looking at his wife.

Eve took the whole thing very simply. It did not surprise her to find other human beings as noble as herself. Her behaviour on this occasion would have revealed all the beauty of her character to the stupidest, the most indifferent observer.

" But you will be rich, sir, one day. Your bread is ready baked," said Marion, " your father has just bought a farm, he is laying money by for you, and that's a fact."

Under the circumstances, for Marion to say this, as if to belittle, as it were, the merit of her action, surely showed a most exquisite delicacy!

Like all things human, French legal procedure has its defects; but being a two-edged weapon, it serves as well in defence as in attack. It has, besides, this amusing feature—that if two lawyers come to an understanding (and they can come to an understanding without so much as exchanging a single word, for their manner of conducting a case makes their intentions plain to one another) a lawsuit comes to resemble war as it was waged by the elder Marshal Biron, whose son suggested, at the siege of Rouen, a means by which the town might be captured in two days. "You must be in a great hurry to go and plant cabbages," was his father's reply. Two generals can spin a war out for ever by always sparing their troops after the manner of the Austrian General Staff who are never reprimanded by the Aulic council for having failed to make a combination on the grounds that their soldiers needed plenty of time to eat their soup. Cachan, Petit-Claud, and Doublon did even better: they followed the example of that Austrian of antiquity, Fabius *Cunctator*!

Petit-Claud, malevolent as a mule, had been quick to recognise all the advantages of his position. From the moment the tall Cointet had guaranteed his expenses, he promised himself to lead Cachan a dance, and to dazzle the paper manufacturer with a display of his genius by creating incidental expenses to be charged to Métivier's account. But, unfortunately for the glory of this Figaro of the bench, the historian must pass over the terrain of his exploits with the haste of a man walking on burning coals. But a single bill of costs, on the lines of the one sent from Paris, will no doubt suffice to illustrate this history of contemporary manners. We will therefore imitate the style of the dispatches of the Grande Armée; and in any case, the more brief and concise the summary of Petit-Claud's exploits and achievements in the field of pure law, the better they will be understood.

David Séchard was summoned before the Tribunal of Commerce of Angoulême on July 3rd, and defaulted; judgment was passed on the 8th. On the 10th Doublon obtained a warrant and on the 12th attempted to put it into execution; Petit-Claud opposed this by an inter-pleader summons against Métivier, in fifteen days.

Métivier, on his side, judged this delay too long, and applied for a hearing without delay; accordingly on the 19th Séchard's plea was dismissed. A ratification of this verdict was passed on the 21st, authorising the issue of an execution warrant on the 22nd, a warrant of arrest on the 23rd, and the bailiff's inventory prior to execution on the 24th. This storm of warrants was stayed by Petit-Claud, who arrested it by lodging an appeal with the Royal Court. This appeal, reiterated on July 25th, drew off M. Métivier to Poitiers.

"Good," Petit-Claud thought to himself. "That will bring things to a standstill for some time to come."

No sooner had the storm been diverted to Poitiers, and Petit-Claud given instructions to a barrister of the Royal Court, than this double-faced defender applied, in the name of Mme Séchard, for an immediate separation of her estate from that of her husband. According to the legal phrase, he used "all diligence" and accordingly obtained an order of separation on July 28th, which he inserted in the *Charente Courier*, duly notified, and on August 1st drew up before a notary a statement of Mme Séchard's claims upon her husband's estate. These claims amounted to the modest sum of ten thousand francs, which David, in the days of his courtship, had settled on Eve as her dowry in the marriage contract. In payment of this sum, David now made over to his wife, as his creditor, the plant of his printing establishment.

While Petit-Claud was busy securing the household goods in this way, he was also successful in winning the case at Poitiers. He had based his appeal on the claim that David could not be held liable to pay the expenses occasioned in Paris by the case against Lucien de Rubempré, since the Civil Court of the Seine had ordered Métivier to pay costs. The Court took this view of the case, and a judgment was entered accordingly; the judgment of the Angoulême Commercial Court against David Séchard was confirmed, less the sum of six hundred francs expenses incurred in Paris, which was assigned to Métivier. The Court, having regard to the principle upon which the plaintiff based his claims, ordered each side to pay its own cost. David Séchard was given notice of this judgment on August 17th, and on the 18th the judgment was translated into action, and David received an order to pay the capital, interest, and costs forthwith. On the 20th came the notice of execution of judgment. At this point Petit-Claud produced old Séchard, who had become his client in the following manner.

The day after his daughter-in-law's visit, the vine-grower had gone to see Maître Cachan, his lawyer in Angoulême, to consult him as to the best means of retrieving the rent due to him, which was compromised in the general scrimmage in which his son was engaged.

" I cannot act for the father at the same time as I am suing the son," Cachan told him, " but go and see Petit-Claud, he is a very able man, and perhaps he will be able to help you even better than I could."

In the Courts Cachan said to Petit-Claud, " I have sent old Séchard to you; take him on for me—one good turn deserves another."

Lawyers do one another services of this kind in the provinces, just as they do in Paris.

The day after old Séchard had taken Petit-Claud into his confidence, the tall Cointet paid a visit to his accomplice.

" Try to teach old Séchard a lesson! He's the sort of man who would never forgive his son if he cost him a thousand francs. If he had to fork out that sum, it would dry up any generous impulse he may ever have had! "

" Go back to your vines," Petit-Claud advised his new client. " Your son is on the rocks, so don't eat him out of house and home by staying with him. I will send for you when the time comes."

So, in the name of Séchard senior, Petit-Claud claimed that the presses, which were fixtures, ought to be regarded as implements of trade, the more so in that the house had been used as a printing-press ever since the reign of Louis XIV. Cachan waxed indignant on behalf of Métivier; for, having been informed in Paris that Lucien's furniture was Coralie's property, he was now told, in Angoulême, that David's goods belonged to his wife and to his father. (Here followed some sharp exchanges in Court. Father and son were summoned, for such untenable claims could not be allowed to stand.) " We are determined," he said, " to unmask the frauds of these men who are entrenched behind such redoubtable fortifications of bad faith ; who from the most innocent and plainest articles of the law, have constructed an all but unassailable defensive position! And for what purpose ? In order to avoid paying three thousand francs! Where did these three thousand francs come from ? From the pocket of the unfortunate Métivier. And yet there are those who dare to speak against discounters! What times we live in! . . . Finally, I should like to put it to you—is not this plain robbery ? . . . You will surely not sanction a claim that would introduce immorality into the very heart of the law! " The Court of Angoulême was impressed by Cachan's forensic eloquence, and brought in a divided verdict, allowing Mme Séchard's claim to the ownership of the household goods, but rejecting the plea of Séchard senior, and ordering him to pay forthwith costs amounting to four hundred and thirty-four francs sixty-five centimes.

" Very good for old Séchard! " the lawyers remarked, laughing ; " he would have a finger in the pie, so let him pay! "

Notice of judgment was given on August 26th, and the presses and plant of the printing-house were liable to be seized on the 28th. The bailiff's placards were posted! An order was issued, on application, empowering the bailiff to sell the plant on the spot. The announcement of this sale appeared in the local papers, and Doublon flattered himself that he would be able to proceed with the inventory and that the sale would take place on September 2nd. David Séchard by this time owed Métivier, by formal judgment confirmed by appeal, the sum of five thousand two hundred and sixty-five francs twenty-five centimes, not counting the interest that was accumulating. He owed Petit-Claud two hundred francs and the fees, which were left with that noble confidence of cab-drivers who have taken their fare a long way round, to David's generosity. Mme Séchard owed Petit-Claud about three hundred and fifty francs, and fees. Old Séchard owed his four hundred and thirty-four francs sixty-five centimes, and Petit-Claud asked for a fee of three hundred francs. The total amounted to something like ten thousand francs. Quite apart from the usefulness of these documents to foreign countries, who can study in them the play of the French judicial artillery, those responsible for legislation ought to know the lengths to which abuses of procedure can be carried—always supposing, that is, that legislators have time to read. Could not some small law be devised by which, in certain cases, lawyers would be forbidden to allow the expenses to exceed the sum involved in the case? Surely there is something ridiculous in allowing a property of a square yard to involve a client in expenses of the same order as an estate of thousands of acres? These bare outlines of the various phases through which a lawsuit passed lends meaning to the phrase " formalities, justice, and costs ", little guessed by the immense majority of Frenchmen. That is what is known, in the slang of the Courts, as setting fire to a man's business.

The type of the printing house, weighing five thousand pounds, was valued at two thousand francs as scrap metal; the three presses at six hundred francs. The rest of the plant was to be sold as old iron and firewood. The household furniture would have brought in a thousand francs at most. So that the entire property of Séchard junior, represented a sum of about four thousand francs; and Cachan and Petit-Claud had made it the pretext for a claim of seven thousand francs costs, not counting the future, whose green blades already promised a rich harvest, as we shall see. Members of the legal profession of France and Navarre, and even of Normandy, ought indeed to accord their esteem and admiration to Petit-Claud; but surely the kind-hearted will spare a tear of sympathy for Kolb and Marion?

Throughout the course of this war Kolb, seated at the door of the passage on a chair that David did not need, acted as watchdog. He received the notifications, and he himself was under the observation of one of Petit-Claud's clerks. No sooner were the placards announcing the sale of the printing plant put up than Kolb tore them down; he ran up and down the town tearing them down, and exclaiming:

" Ze scountrels, to torment ein so goot man! And zey call dat justice! "

Marion worked during the mornings as a machine-tender in a

paper-mill, and her earnings of ten sous a day served for the daily household expenses. Mme Chardon had gone back, without a murmur, to her tiring vigils as a nurse, and she brought her daughter her earnings at the end of every week. She had already made two *novenas*, and could not understand why God was deaf to her prayers and blind to the light of the candles she lit for the intention of those she loved.

On September 2nd, Eve received the only letter that Lucien had written since the one in which he had told David of the forgery of the three bills ; David had concealed this letter from his wife.

"The third letter I have had from him since he went away!" thought Lucien's poor sister, scarcely daring to open the fatal envelope.

She was feeding her baby when the letter came, for she had been forced to give up the wet-nurse, whom she could no longer afford. It is easy to imagine the state of mind into which she was thrown when she read the following letter, and David, too, for Eve called him. David, who had been up all night, working on his invention, had only gone to bed at daybreak.

"My dear Sister,

"Two days ago, at five o'clock in the morning, one of the loveliest beings God ever made died in my arms—the only woman who could ever have cared for me as you, David, and Mother love me. But she gave me more besides than this disinterested affection felt by a mother and a sister—all the bliss of love! Coralie gave up everything for my sake, and she died for my sake, it may be—for me, who at this moment have not even the means to bury her! She would have been my life's consolation ; but only you, my good angels, can console me for her death. I believe that God has forgiven that innocent girl, for she died as a Christian. Oh, Paris! My dear Eve, Paris is the glory and the shame of France, and I have already lost many illusions here, and I shall soon lose still more, now that I must beg for the little money that I need in order to lay the beloved body of my angel in consecrated ground!

"Your heartbroken brother,

Lucien.

"P.S. I must have given you a great deal of worry by my feckless-ness, but some day I will tell you the whole story, and you will forgive me. Meanwhile, do not worry: a shopkeeper, called Camusot, a good sort, whose feelings I hurt very much at one time, seeing Coralie and myself in such distress, has promised to arrange everything."

"The page is still damp with his tears!" she said to David, looking at the letter; she felt such an access of pity that some of her old affection for Lucien shone in her eyes.

"Poor boy, what he must have gone through, if she loved him as he says!" exclaimed Eve's husband, so happy in his marriage.

Wife and husband both forgot all their own troubles, in the face of that cry of supreme sorrow.

At this moment Marion burst into the room. "They are here, ma'am, they are here!" she exclaimed.

"Who is here?"

"Doublon and his men, the Devil take him! Kolb is keeping them out—they have come to sell us up!"

"No, no," said a voice in the next room. "They won't sell you up, don't you worry!" and Petit-Claud arrived on the scene. "I have just lodged an appeal. We cannot accept the onus of a judg-ment that attaches to us the stigma of bad faith. I thought it was best not to fight the case at this stage. I let Cachan talk, so as to gain time for you, and I am convinced that we shall win the day again at Poitiers——"

"But what will it cost to win the day?" asked Mme Séchard.

"Fees if you win, and a thousand francs if we lose!"

"Oh dear!" cried poor Eve. "Surely the remedy is worse than the disease!"

Petit-Claud was at a loss to find an answer to this cry of inno-cence, enlightened by the mounting flames of the judicial confla-gration; for he thought Eve a very beautiful woman. Meanwhile old Séchard arrived on the scene, summoned by Petit-Claud. The old man's presence in the bedroom of his son and daughter-in-law, where his grandson lay in his cradle smiling at misfortune completed the tableau.

" You owe me seven hundred francs for the intervention, Papa Séchard," said the young lawyer, " but you can charge it to your son, along with the arrears of rent."

The old vine-tender did not miss the sting of sarcasm in Petit-Claud's voice and manner.

" It would have cost you less to give security for your son in the first place," said Eve, coming over from the cradle to greet her father-in-law.

David was quite overcome by the sight of a small crowd that had gathered outside his house, where the argument between Kolb and Doublon's men had attracted quite a number of onlookers. He shook hands with his father without a word.

" How do you make out that I owe you seven hundred francs ? " the old man demanded, addressing Petit-Claud.

" In the first place, because I am acting on your behalf; as your rent is in question, you are, so far as I am concerned, identical with your debtor. If your son does not pay me these costs, why then, you will pay me—but that is not important—they want to put David in prison a few hours from now—are you going to let him go ? "

" How much does he owe ? "

" Why, something like five or six thousand francs, not counting what he owes you and his wife."

The old man, thoroughly on his guard, looked from one to another of the pathetic little group in the blue and white bedroom; a beautiful woman in tears beside a cradle; David bowed at last beneath the weight of his troubles, and the lawyer who had, in all probability, trapped him into the situation; the old bear suspected that they were trying to play on his paternal feelings. At the thought that they might be taking advantage of him, he took fright. He crossed the room to look at the baby and play with him, and the little fellow stretched out his hands to the old man.

In the midst of so much distress, the baby was cared for as if he had been the heir of an English peer. He was wearing a little embroidered bonnet with a pink lining.

"Eh! Let David get out of it as best he can; I am only thinking of this little fellow here," said the old grandfather, "and his mother will approve of that. David, with all his education, ought to be able to find a way of paying his debts."

"I will translate your meaning into plain French," said the lawyer ironically. "The fact is, Papa Séchard, that you are jealous of your son. I will be perfectly frank with you! You have forced David into this situation by selling him the printing business for three times its value, and then by ruining him in order to reimburse yourself for the extortionate price you demanded. No, it's no use shaking your head; the price of the newspaper that you sold to the Cointets, and pocketed yourself, was all the printing business was worth. You have a grievance against your son, not only because you have swindled him, but also because you have made him a better man than you are. All this pretence of loving your grandson so much is simply in order to disguise the bankruptcy of your feelings for your own son and your daughter-in-law, which would cost you money *hic et nunc*, whereas you need not give any proof of affection to your grandson until after you are dead. You make a show of affection for the little fellow for the sake of appearances—to show that you have some feelings for some member of your family, or you might be taxed with insensibility, you know. And that's the long and the short of the matter, Papa Séchard."

"Did you bring me here to listen to all this?" said the old man in threatening tones, looking in turn at the lawyer, his daughter-in-law, and his son.

"Oh, you must have vowed to ruin us!" exclaimed poor Eve, addressing Petit-Claud. "My husband has never uttered a word against his father—never!"

The old bear looked at her suspiciously.

"He has said to me time and again that you loved him in your own way," she said, turning to the old man and guessing his suspicions.

Petit-Claud was acting on the tall Cointet's instructions, which were to make trouble between father and son, in case the father should help David out of his cruel predicament.

" The day we have David in prison, you shall be introduced to Mme de Senonches," the tall Cointet had said to Petit-Claud the previous evening.

Mme Séchard, with the clear insight of love, had divined that concealed hostility, just as she had previously suspected Cérizet's betrayal. David's expression of astonishment can be easily imagined, for he had never suspected that Petit-Claud knew so much about his father's character and his own affairs. Honourable man that he was, he had no inkling of the understanding between his own lawyer and the Cointet brothers ; and still less did he suspect that the Cointets were using Métivier as a cat's-paw. The old vine-grower, meanwhile, interpreted his son's silence as an insult ; and the lawyer took advantage of his client's consternation to beat a retreat.

" Goodbye, my dear David ; you have been warned—the order for arrest is not invalidated by the appeal ; it is the only course now open to your creditors, and they will take it. So make your escape! . . . Or, better still, if you will take my advice, why not go and see the Cointets ; they have capital ; and if your invention comes off, and does what you claim for it, go into partnership with them. They are very good sorts, after all. . . . "

" What invention ? " put in old Séchard.

" You surely did not suppose that your son was so foolish as to give up his printing business without having anything else in mind?" said the lawyer. " He tells me he is on the track of a process for manufacturing paper for three francs a ream that at present costs ten."

" Another dodge for taking me in ! " said old Séchard. " You are all playing up to each other ; you are as thick as thieves! If David has found how to do that, he doesn't need any help from me, because he will be a millionaire! Goodbye, my dears, good evening" —and the old man disappeared down the staircase.

" Think of some way of hiding yourself," said Petit-Claud, turning to David, as he hurried off after old Séchard, with the intention of exasperating him still further.

The little lawyer found old Séchard grumbling to himself in the Place du Mûrier, and walked with him as far as l'Houmeau. There he left him, with the threat of putting in an order for execution if the expenses due to him were not paid within the week.

" I will pay you if you will find me a way of disinheriting my son without injuring my grandson or my daughter-in-law! " said old Séchard bluntly, and went his way.

" Tall Cointet knows the people he is dealing with all right! . . . He made no mistake when he said to me, ' those seven hundred francs will be enough to stop the father from paying his son's seven thousand.' " So the little lawyer reflected as he climbed up the steps to Angoulême. " All the same, I don't intend to be made a fool of by that swindler of a paper manufacturer—it is time to ask him for something better than words."

" Well, David, my dear, what do you propose to do ? " Eve asked her husband as soon as old Séchard and the lawyer had gone.

" Put your biggest pot on the fire, my girl," David called to Marion, " I must press on with my work."

At these words, Eve put on her hat, shawl, and walking shoes in feverish haste.

" Get your hat, Kolb," she said, " you must come with me, because I must see if there is any way out of this Hell."

" Oh, sir," Marion began, when Eve had gone out, " do be reasonable, or the mistress will break her heart worrying. Make a little money to pay off your debts, and after that you can take your time looking for treasures."

" Don't talk, Marion. I am going to solve my last problem," David replied. " I want to take out a patent for the invention and the improvement at the same time."

In France the patent for improvement of an invention is the greatest worry to inventors. A man may spend ten years of his life in working on an industrial process, a machine, or some discovery, and he takes out a patent in the belief that he is master of his own invention ; then comes a competitor, and, unless the original inventor has foreseen every possibility, " improves " his invention by adding a single screw and takes it out of his hands. Therefore the discovery of a method of manufacturing a cheap paper was not the whole story! Some rival might improve upon the process. David

Séchard was determined to envisage every possibility, lest he should see the fortune that he had worked for in the face of so many difficulties snatched from him. Dutch paper (as paper made from linen pulp is still called, although it is no longer manufactured in Holland) is slightly sized ; but it is sized one sheet at a time, by hand, and this adds to the cost. If David could find a process for glazing the paper in the pulping-trough, by means of an inexpensive size (like that in use today, although even now the process is not entirely satisfactory), no improvement would remain to be discovered. For the past month, therefore, he had been working on a method for sizing his paper in the pulping-trough. He was working, in fact, on two inventions.

Eve went to see her mother. By a lucky chance, Mme Chardon was nursing the wife of the Deputy Magistrate, who had just presented an heir presumptive to the Milauds of Nevers. Eve, in the face of all the powers of the law, had had the idea of asking the legal defender of widows and orphans to advise her on her position, and to tell her whether she could possibly set David at liberty by taking his liabilities on herself and selling her claims on the estate. She also hoped to discover what lay behind Petit-Claud's ambiguous conduct. The magistrate, struck by Mme Séchard's beauty, received her not only with the consideration due to a woman, but with a kind of courtesy to which Eve was little accustomed. She saw in the magistrate's eyes an expression which, since her marriage, she had no longer seen in any eyes but Kolb's—an expression which, for beautiful women like Eve, is the criterion by which they judge men. The light of an unconditional homage kindles in the eyes of a young man at the sight of a beautiful woman ; and when some passion, self-interest, or age, extinguishes that light, a woman is at once on her guard and begins to watch a man critically. The Cointets, Petit-Claud, Cérizet, all the men whom Eve had suspected of being enemies had looked at her with cold indifferent eyes ; and so it was that she felt at her ease with the Deputy Magistrate ; but although he received her graciously he quickly shattered her hopes.

" It is by no means certain," he began, " that the Royal Court will reverse the judgment overruling your claim on your husband's property, and your husband's handing over to you all his goods and chattels in payment for the settlement due to you in the terms of your marriage contract. Your privileged position ought not to be made use of in order to cover a fraud. But, as a creditor, you are entitled to a proportion of the proceeds of the sale of the property, and your father-in-law is also a privileged creditor for the arrears of rent due to him. When the Court has issued the order, various points will no doubt be raised on the question of other claims, as to the 'contribution', as it is called in legal language, to which each of the various creditors is entitled."

"Then M. Petit-Claud is in fact ruining us!" she exclaimed.

"M. Petit-Claud is carrying out your husband's instructions," said the magistrate. "He is anxious, so his lawyer tells me, to gain time. My personal opinion is that he would be well advised to drop the appeal, and that you and your father-in-law should buy back what you can at the sale; the bare essentials for carrying on—you to the extent of the sum due to be refunded to you, and your father-in-law for the amount due to him in rent. But that would settle the matter too quickly—the lawyers are eating you out of house and home."

"In that case, I shall be entirely in the hands of old M. Séchard; I should owe him rent for the machinery as well as for the house, and my husband would still be liable to further proceedings by M. Métivier, who would have got almost nothing!"

"That is so."

"Well, then, our situation would be even worse than it is at present...."

"The power of the law, *madame*, is undoubtedly exercised on behalf of the creditor. You have received three thousand francs, and you must certainly pay them back."

"Oh, sir, you surely cannot think that we are capable of——" She stopped short, suddenly realising that if she were to attempt to justify herself she would involve her brother.

"Oh, I know very well that this is a very obscure affair," said the magistrate. "The debtors, on their side, are people of integrity and feeling, I might even say behaving with some dignity; and on the other hand, the creditor, who is only a cat's-paw...."

Eve, aghast, looked at the magistrate in bewilderment.

"You must understand," he continued, looking at her with an expression of honest shrewdness, "that we magistrates have plenty of time to reflect on what goes on under our noses while we sit listening to the lawyers arguing with one another."

Eve went home in despair at her own uselessness.

At seven o'clock that evening Doublon arrived with the warrant of imprisonment for debt. The affair had now reached its crisis.

"From tomorrow I shall no longer be able to go out except at night," said David.

Eve and Mme Chardon burst into tears. For them, to go into hiding meant disgrace. When Kolb and Marion knew that their master's liberty was threatened, they were the more alarmed because they had realised that his nature was utterly guileless. They were so anxious on his account that they came to look for Mme Chardon, Eve, and David, to ask whether anything they could do would be of any use. They found those three good people, whose lives had hitherto been so simple, weeping at the thought that David would have to go into hiding. But how were they to escape from the hidden spies who from now onwards were bound to watch his every movement, and he so unfortunately absent-minded?

"If montame vill vait ein leetle kvarter of an hour, I vill make ein reconnaizance of der enemy's camp," said Kolb. "I shall see vot I can do, although I look like ein German; but I am a true Frenchman, and vat is more, I am ver' cunning."

"Oh, do let him go!" Marion begged. "He has only one thought, and that is the master's safety—that is all he cares about. Kolb is no Alsatian—he is—he's more like a Newfoundland if you ask me...."

"Go, Kolb, by all means," said David; "we have still time to do something."

Kolb hurried off to the bailiff's office, where David's enemies were holding a council of war as to the best means of securing their man.

The arrest of a debtor is an unheard-of thing in the provinces, something altogether abnormal, if it ever occurs. In the first place, everybody knows everybody else far too well ever to put into effect such an odious course. One often finds debtor and creditor meeting every day of their lives. Besides, when a bankrupt intends—to use the provincial expression, for they do not mince matters in the country on the subject of this form of legalised theft—to default on a large scale, he takes refuge in Paris. Paris is a kind of sanctuary for provincial bankrupts, an almost impenetrable retreat, for the bailiff's writ is invalid outside the area of his jurisdiction. There are other obstacles, too, which render it virtually null and void. For example, the law that respects the inviolability of the home holds good everywhere in the provinces; the bailiff has not the right, as he has in Paris, to enter the house of a third party in order to arrest a debtor. The law no doubt made an exception of Paris in this respect because there it is usual for several families to live in the same house. But, in the provinces, the bailiff cannot even enter the debtor's own house without an order from a Justice of the Peace; and as the Justice of the Peace has it in his power to give or withhold his consent, at his discretion, the bailiffs are, virtually, in his power. To the credit of Justices of the Peace, it must be said that this responsibility is one that they dislike; they are unwilling to be the servants of blind passions or the desire for revenge.

There are other serious difficulties that serve to modify the futile cruelty of the law of arrest for debt—public opinion, which often modifies laws to the point of annulling them. In any large city there are enough degraded types, down-and-outs, the dregs of society, who are willing enough to act as spies; but in small towns everybody is too well known to take the pay of a bailiff. Anyone, even in the lowest stratum of society, who lent himself to this form of degradation, would be forced to leave the town.

The arrest of a debtor is not, therefore, as it is in Paris or in any large centre of population, a privileged industry, protected by the Commercial Courts; in fact, it is an extremely difficult matter, a battle of wits between debtor and bailiff, that often provides amusing anecdotes for the Paris newspapers.

The elder Cointet was unwilling to be mixed up in the matter; but the fat Cointet, on the pretext that Métivier had entrusted the case to him, had gone to Doublon, taking with him Cérizet, who was now his foreman, and whose co-operation he had secured at the price of a thousand-franc note. Doublon could count on two of his men ; so the Cointets had already three bloodhounds on the track of their victim. For the actual arrest, Doublon could, moreover, call upon the police, who are bound, if so required, to assist a bailiff in the performance of his duty. These five individuals were now laying their heads together in Doublon's private office, on the ground floor of his house, behind his public office.

The public office lay at the end of a fairly wide paved passage, a kind of corridor. The gilded scutcheons of the Court hung on either side of a door on which you read, in black letters, the word "Bailiff". The two windows of the office looking out on to the road were protected by heavy iron bars. The private office looked out onto the garden, where the bailiff, whose hobby was apples, grew espaliers, with remarkable success. The kitchen was opposite, and the staircase that led up to the first floor was beyond the kitchen. The house stood in a narrow street behind the new Courts of Law, then in process of construction, which were not in fact completed until after 1830. These details are necessary if the reader is to understand Kolb's subsequent adventures.

The Alsatian's idea was to go and see the bailiff on the pretext of being prepared to sell his master ; in this way he hoped to learn what traps were being set, and to warn David against them. The cook came to the door, and Kolb told her that he wished to speak to M. Doublon on business. The cook was busy doing the washing-up, and not too well pleased at the interruption. She opened the door of the office and told Kolb—whom she did not know—to wait, for M. Doublon was engaged in his private office ; she then went off to tell her master that a man wished to speak to him. This expression "a man" nearly always means a peasant, and so Doublon merely said, "Tell him to wait."

Kolb seated himself close to the door of the inner office.

"By the way, what plans have you got in mind?" the fat Cointet was saying, "because, if we can lay hands on him tomorrow morning it will be so much time saved."

" Nothing easier, with a simpleton like my late boss," put in Cérizet.

Kolb recognised the fat Cointet's voice, and when he heard those two remarks, he guessed at once that they were talking about his master ; great was his astonishment when he heard Cérizet speak. " Ein poy vot has eaten his pread ! " he thought, horrified.

" Boys," said Doublon, " we must go about it this way. We will post our men at wide intervals, between the Rue de Beaulieu and the Place du Mûrier, in every direction, so that we can follow the simpleton—a good name for him—without his knowing it ; we will not leave him until he is inside the house where he is planning to hide ; we will leave him in peace for a few days, and then one fine day we will run into him, first thing in the morning, or after sunset."

" But what is he doing at the present moment ? " said the fat Cointet. " He may give us the slip."

" He's at home," said Doublon ; " if he goes out, I shall know it. One of my assistants is in the Place du Mûrier, another at the corner by the Law Courts, and another only thirty paces from this house. If our man goes out, they will whistle ; and I shall know it by this kind of telegraphy before he has taken three steps."

Bailiffs refer to their men by the euphemistic name of "assistants".

Kolb had not hoped for such a piece of luck. He went out quietly, saying to the cook that, as Monsieur Doublon appeared to be engaged for some time, he would call early next morning.

The good Alsatian, who had served in a cavalry regiment, was struck with an idea which he immediately proceeded to put into execution. He hurried off to see a livery stable keeper of his acquaintance, selected a horse, had it saddled, and hurried back to his master's house, where he found Eve in the depths of despondency.

" What is it, Kolb ? " the printer asked, for the Alsatian's expression was one of mingled alarm and exultation.

" You are surrounded by scountrels. De best vill be to hide mein master. Has montame thought of anyvheres to send de master ? "

When the good Kolb had told them about Cérizet's treachery, the encirclement of the house, about the fat Cointet's share in the business, and had given them some idea of the schemes that these men were planning against his master, they realised David's position with deadly clarity.

" It is the Cointets who are persecuting you ! " exclaimed poor Eve, appalled at the thought. " And that is why Métivier is so hard. . . . They are paper manufacturers—they want your secret."

" But what can we do to escape them ? " exclaimed Mme Chardon.

" If montame vas to find some leetle place vhere de master can go," said Kolb, "I gif you mein vort I vill take him zere so dat no one knows vhere he is."

" Wait until after dark, and then go to Basine Clerget's," said Eve. " I will go now and arrange everything with her. Basine will do anything for me, in this emergency."

" The spies will follow you," said David, who had recovered some of his presence of mind. " We must find some way of letting Basine know without any of us going to see her ourselves."

" Montame can go," said Kolb. " Here is my plan—I vill go out with de master, and ve vill draw de vhistlers on our tracks. And then, montame can go to Mlle Clerget, she vill not be followed. I haf ein horse, I take de master up behind, and der teufel is in it i. zey catch us! "

" Very well—goodbye, my darling," poor Eve exclaimed, throwing herself into her husband's arms ; " none of us can come and see you, or we may lead to your being discovered. We must say goodbye for as long as this voluntary imprisonment lasts. We will write to one another—Basine will post your letters, and I will write to you under cover to her."

No sooner had they left the house than David and Kolb heard the whistles, and they led the spies down to the Porte Palet, where the livery-stable keeper lived. There Kolb took his master up behind, telling him to hold on tight.

" Vhistle, vhistle, mein goot friends! I care not for you! " said Kolb. " You vill never catch an old trooper "—and the old cavalryman clapped both spurs to the horse, and rode off into the country at a speed that left the spies far behind, unable to follow them or even to discover which way they had gone.

Eve went to see Postel, on the reasonably convincing pretext of asking his advice. She remained, for a while, submitting to the insults of the kind of sympathy that expresses itself only in words, and then slipped away, unseen, to see Basine Clerget, to whom she confided her troubles, and asked for her advice and help. Basine, for greater safety, had taken Eve into her bedroom ; she opened the door of a little adjoining room, lighted only by a skylight, into which no curious eye could possibly look. The two women unstopped the flue which opened into the chimney of the workroom where the girls kept a fire burning to heat their irons. Eve and Basine spread some old blankets over the floor to deaden the sound, if David were to make a noise, unintentionally ; they made up a camp bed for him, and put in a stove for his experiments, and a table and chair. Basine promised to bring him food late at night ; no one should ever set foot in his room, so that David could defy all his enemies, and the police into the bargain.

" At last," said Eve, throwing her arms round her friend, " he is safe."

Eve went back to Postel, with one other doubt that, so she said, had occurred to her, and brought her back to consult such a learned member of the Tribunal of Commerce. She succeeded in making him walk home with her, and she listened patiently to his condolences.

" This would not have happened if you had married me, would it ? "

This was the burden of all the little chemist's observations. When he got home, Postel found his wife in a pet of jealousy ; she was furious with her husband for his polite attention to beautiful Mme Séchard. Léonie was only appeased when her husband assured her that he preferred little red-haired women to tall dark ones, who were, in his opinion, like fire horses, always in the stable. He must have given proofs of his sincerity, for Mme Postel was very sweet to him the next day.

" We need not worry any more," Eve told her mother and Marion, whom she found, as Marion would have put it, still " taking on something terrible ".

"Oh yes, they have gone," said Marion, as Eve looked round the room mechanically.

"Vitch vay shall we go?" Kolb enquired, when they had ridden about a league along the main road to Paris.

"To Marsac," said David. "Since you have brought me so far, I would like to make one last appeal to my father's kindness of heart."

"I vould rather mount to der assault of a battery, pecause your fader haf no heart." The old bear had no belief in his son; he judged, as men of the people always judge, by results. It never entered his head that he had fleeced David; and, since he made no allowance for the changed circumstances, he said to himself, "I set him up in a printing business, just as I started myself; and he, with a far better education than I had, couldn't make it pay!"

Incapable of understanding his son, he blamed him, and even prided himself on his superiority to that man of outstanding talent, for he said to himself, "I am saving him enough to live on."

Moralists will never succeed in making us realise the extent of the influence of sentiment on self-interest. This influence is just as powerful as that of self-interest on sentiment, for every law of nature works in two opposite ways. So it was that David, on his side, understood his father, and had the sublime charity to forgive him.

Kolb and David reached Marsac at eight o'clock, just as the old man was finishing his dinner, which, naturally, meant that it was very nearly his bed time.

"I will see you, from a sense of duty," said the father to his son with a sour smile.

"And how else should you meet mein master?" put in Kolb indignantly. "He soars in ze skies, and you are always among your vines. You must pay, you must pay! Zat is vot you are a fader for!"

"That's enough, Kolb, off with you; take the horse round to Mme Courtois, so that it will not be in my father's way, and remember that fathers are always in the right."

Kolb went off, growling like a dog whose master has rebuked him for doing his duty, obedient but protesting. David, while not giving away his secrets, then offered to give his father clear proof of his discovery, and offered him a share of the proceeds, in exchange for the money that he needed in order to free himself; or, if he liked, enough to finance the exploitation of the secret.

" How are you going to prove to me that you can make good paper that costs nothing, out of nothing, eh?" asked the old typographer, looking at his son with a bleary eye, but an eye in which shone cunning, curiosity, and greed—a look like a beam of light from a sodden cloud; for the old bear, faithful to his custom, never went to bed without his night-cap, which consisted of two bottles of the best wine, over which, as he said, he liked to take his time.

" Nothing easier," David replied. " I have no paper with me—I came this way to escape Doublon; and as I was on the Marsac road, it occurred to me that I might as well ask for your help as borrow from a money-lender. I have nothing with me but my clothes. Shut me up in some place where no one can come in or see what I am doing, and . . ."

" What's that?" said the old man, with a look of displeasure. " So you won't let me see what you are doing?"

" Father," said David, " you yourself have taught me that there is no question of father and son in business."

" Ah! So you distrust the father who gave you life!"

" No—the father who has deprived me of the means of living."

" Each for himself—you are right," said the old man. " Very well, I will put you in the cellar."

" I shall go there, with Kolb; if you will just give me a cauldron to make my pulp," David went on, not noticing the look his father gave him, " and then go and fetch me some stems of artichoke, and asparagus, and stinging-nettles, and rushes, that you can cut down by your little stream. Tomorrow morning I will come out of your cellar with a beautiful sample of paper."

" If you can do that . . .!" the bear exclaimed, with a hiccough, " I might give you—well, I shall think over what I might give you . . . why, twenty-five thousand francs, on condition you pay me that amount each year."

"Put me to the test," said David. "I agree to that. Kolb, take the horse and go to Mansle—buy a large hair-sieve at the cooper's, and some glue at a grocer's, and come back as quickly as you can."

"Here—have something to drink," said the father, and he set before his son a bottle of wine, some bread, and the remains of some cold meat. "You will need all your strength, and I will go and collect your green-stuff for you—green rags you use—a bit too green for my liking."

Two hours later, at about eleven o'clock, the old man locked Kolb and his son into a little room adjoining the wine-cellar. The floor was paved with runnel tiles, and it was provided with all the utensils necessary for distilling the wines of Angoulême, from which, as is well known, all kinds of cognac brandy are made.

"Why, this is as good as a factory!" David exclaimed. "Look at the pans and the firewood!"

"Very well, I will see you tomorrow," said old Séchard. "I am going to lock you in, and I will loose my two dogs, and I am sure nobody will bring you any paper. Show me the samples tomorrow, and I promise to go into partnership with you, and the business will be straightened up and properly run."

Kolb and David, locked in the distillery, spent about two hours in crushing and macerating the stems, pounding them with two logs. The fire burned up, the water came to the boil. At about two in the morning Kolb heard a sound like the hiccough of a drunken man (David was too busy to notice) and, taking one of the two candles, he set out to look everywhere; he soon discovered old Séchard's purple visage pressed against a little square aperture above a door leading from the cellar into the distillery, concealed by a pile of empty casks. The cunning old fellow had let his son and Kolb into the distillery by the outer door through which the full casks were carted away. This other inner door was used for rolling barrels into the distillery without taking them through the yard.

"Ah! Papa Séchard, you do not play fair, you vant to svindle your son. . . . Do you know vat you do, ven you trink ein bottle of goot vine? You gif goot vine to ein scountrel!"

" Oh, Father! " said David.

" I came to see if there was anything you wanted," said the old toper, half sober by this time.

" And it vos for de interest dat you takes in us dat you brought ein leetle ladder ? " said Kolb. He had moved the barrels out of the way and opened the door, and there he discovered the old man in his nightgown, standing on a step-ladder.

" Risking your health! " said David.

" I must have been walking in my sleep," said old Séchard, as he descended from his ladder, in confusion. " Your want of confidence in your father set me dreaming, and I dreamed that you had made a pact with the Devil, to do the impossible."

" Der Teufel! dot is your own passion for zie leetle yellow boys," said Kolb.

" Go back to bed, Father," said David ; " lock us in if you like, but don't trouble to come back. Kolb will keep watch."

At four o'clock the next morning David emerged from the distillery, having disposed of all traces of the operation he had completed, and presented his father with thirty sheets of paper which, for fineness, whiteness, texture, and strength, left nothing to be desired, bearing by way of water-mark the pattern of the uneven hairs of the sieve. The old man took these samples, and put his tongue to them with the life-long habit of a bear who from his earliest youth has used his palate as a test for paper ; he felt them between his finger and thumb, creased them, folded them, and tested them in every way known to typographers who are accustomed to examining samples of paper and judging their quality ; he had no criticism to make of David's samples, but he did not want to admit himself beaten.

" We still do not know how it would take an impression," he said, in order to avoid congratulating his son.

" Fonny man! " said Kolb.

The old man, recovering his presence of mind, tried to dignify his assumed irresolution under the guise of paternal dignity.

" I have no wish to deceive you, Father ; this paper still seems to me to be too expensive, and I want to find a process for sizing it in the trough. . . . That is the only problem that remains to be solved."

"Ah! So you were trying to deceive me!"

"But am I not telling you? I am sizing the paper in the pulp, only, at the moment, the size does not combine evenly with my pulp, and the paper is as rough as a brush."

"All right, find your method of sizing your pulp in the trough, and you shall have my money."

"Nefer vill mein master see ze colour of your money!"

Clearly the old man wanted to pay David out for the humiliation of the previous night; and so he was excessively cold.

David sent Kolb away. "Father," said David, "I have never reproached you for selling me your printing business at an exorbitant price, or of having made me take it at your own estimate; I have always seen you as a father, and I have always said to myself, 'Let an old man who has worked hard, and who has certainly brought me up better than I had any right to expect, enjoy the fruits of his labours in peace.' I even let you keep my mother's legacy, and I have never grumbled at the burdens you laid upon me at the start of my career. I made up my mind to make money without putting you to any trouble. Well, with no bread in the house, and my feet in the flames already, burdened with debts that were not of my making, I have discovered this secret. Yes, I have worked on, patiently, to the limits of my strength. Perhaps it is your duty to help me—but I don't want you to think about me—think of my wife and the little boy"—David could not keep back the tears as he said this—"and give them your help and protection. Will you refuse to do as much as Marion and Kolb, who have lent me their savings?" exclaimed the son, seeing that the father remained as cold as an impression-stone.

"And wasn't that enough for you?" exclaimed the old man, without a blush. "You would eat up the Bank of France, you would! No thank you! I am too ignorant to let myself in for exploitations when I'm the only one to be exploited! A monkey can't eat up a bear," he said, alluding to his name in the trade slang. "I am only a vine-grower, I am not a banker. . . . And what is more, business between father and son never turns out well. You had better stay for dinner as you are here ; you shan't say that you came for nothing! "

David was one of those men of deep feeling who can repress their sufferings and keep them hidden from those who are closest to them ; with such men, when feeling breaks out, it is a shattering experience ; and David broke down now.

Eve had completely understood her husband's fine character. But the father took the flood of grief that burst from the bottom of David's heart for the vulgar outpourings of sons who want to " take advantage " of their fathers, and his son's extreme dejection for mortification on account of his failure. Father and son parted in anger.

David and Kolb re-entered Angoulême at about midnight. They entered the town on foot, with all the precautions of thieves planning a burglary. By one o'clock David had been installed, without anyone having seen him, in the impenetrable hiding-place prepared for him by his wife in Basine Clerget's attic. When he set foot in that house, he entered the protection of the most resourceful of all kinds of compassion—that of a working-girl. Kolb, next morning, went about boasting that he had saved his master, on horseback, and had only left him when he had found a van that would take him as far as Limoges.

A good supply of raw materials had been laid up in Basine's cellar, so that it would not be necessary for Kolb, Marion, Eve or her mother to have any communication with Basine Clerget.

Two days after this scene with his son, old Séchard, who found himself with twenty clear days in front of him, before he need begin work on the vintage, hurried up to see his daughter-in-law. Avarice brought him. He had not been able to sleep for wondering whether there was really a fortune in David's invention, and he wanted to keep an eye on things, as he said. He moved into one of the two attics above his daughter-in-law's rooms, that he had reserved for himself in the terms of the lease, and there he lived, shutting his eyes to the financial straits in which his son's family were living. They owed him rent ; they could at least feed him! It was nothing new to him to eat off an enamel plate!

" I began like this," he said, when his daughter-in-law apologised for the absence of silver cutlery.

Marion had to run up credit with all the tradespeople for the food they ate. Kolb worked as a mason, for twenty sous a day. At last, poor Eve, who, in the interests of David and her little son, had sacrificed her last remaining resources in order to entertain the old man, discovered that she had only ten francs left. She went on hoping that her patience, and her respectful affection, and her coaxing, would soften the miser's heart; but they found him obdurate as ever. Then she noticed that he, too, turned on her the same cold eye as the Cointets, Petit-Claud, and Cérizet; and she made up her mind to study him, and to fathom his motives; but it was trouble thrown away! Old Séchard, never quite drunk, never quite sober, remained impenetrable. Intoxication is a double veil. With the help of his drunkenness, assumed as often as it was real, the old man tried to induce Eve to give away David's secrets. Sometimes he cajoled his daughter-in-law, sometimes he threatened. When Eve told him that she knew absolutely nothing, he said:

" I shall drink my fortune, *I shall buy an annuity*."

These dishonourable battles of will wore out the poor victim, who, so as not to show any disrespect towards her father-in-law, finally took refuge in silence. One day, driven to extremes, she said to him:

" But, Father, there is one very simple way for you to find out everything: pay David's debts, then he will come home, and you can discuss everything with him."

" Ah! So that's what you want to get out of me! " he exclaimed. " It's as well to know."

Old Séchard had no faith in his son, but he had great faith in the Cointets. He went off to consult them, and they purposely gave him a dazzling account, assuring him that his son's invention would be worth millions.

" If David can prove that he has succeeded, I should not hesitate to take him into partnership, and count your son's discovery as half the firm's capital," said the tall Cointet.

The suspicious old bear picked up pieces of information, here and there, by drinking nips of brandy with the workmen, and he managed, by pretending to be stupid, to get enough out of Petit-Claud to convince him that the Cointets were behind Métivier; they were plotting, he decided, to ruin the Séchard printing business and to get the money out of him, using David's invention as a bait to make him pay up—for the old man never suspected that Petit-Claud was in the plot, or that snares had been spread to capture, sooner or later, a valuable industrial secret.

At last, one day, the old man, exasperated at his failure to break down his daughter-in-law's silence, and at not even having been able to persuade her to tell him where David was hidden, decided to force the door of the lean-to shack where the rollers were melted down; for he had discovered, at last, where his son had carried out his experiments. He went down, very early in the morning, and set to work on the lock.

"Why, what are you doing there, Papa Séchard?" Marion called to him. She had got up, at daybreak, to go to her factory, and now she hurried down to the work-shop.

"This is my own house, isn't it, Marion?" said the old man in confusion.

"And so you are turning thief in your old age, are you? And you're not drunk, either. . . . I'm going straight away to tell the mistress."

"Don't say anything, Marion," said the old man, drawing two six-franc pieces from his pocket. "Here. . . ."

"Very well, I won't say anything, but don't you come here again," said Marion, shaking her finger at him, "or I will tell all Angoulême."

No sooner had the old man gone out than Marion went up to her mistress.

"Look, ma'am, I managed to get twelve francs out of your father-in-law—here they are."

"How did you manage to do that?"

"What should he be doing, if you please, but trying to look at all the pots and pans and stuff that the master had, so as to find out the secret. I knew quite well that there is nothing left in the little workshop now, but I gave him a fright, just as if he had been going to rob his son, and he gave me two crowns not to say anything."

At this point Basine came in, her face radiant, bringing her friend a letter from David, written on magnificent paper, which she handed to Eve when they were alone.

" My beloved Eve," it read, " I am writing to you on the first sheet of paper obtained by my process. I have succeeded in solving the problem of sizing the paper in the trough! Even supposing the raw materials I use are specially cultivated on good soil, a pound of pulp will cost about five sous. Therefore a ream, weighing twelve pounds, will take three francs' worth of sized paste. I am sure that I can reduce the weight of books by one half. The envelope, the letter, and the samples enclosed are all made by different methods. I send you all my love—we shall have money, now, to add to our good fortune—the only thing we lacked."

" There," said Eve, as she handed the specimens to her father-in-law, " if you will give your son the profits of your vintage and let him make his fortune, he will pay you back ten times what you will have given him, because he has succeeded! "

Old Séchard hurried off to the Cointets. There, every specimen was tested and examined minutely. Some were sized, others unsized; the costs were estimated at prices varying from three to ten francs a ream; some were of a metallic purity, others as soft as Chinese paper, and of every shade of whiteness. Never did the eyes of Jews examining diamonds glisten with more eagerness than did those of the Cointets and old Séchard.

" Your son is on to something," said the fat Cointet.

" All right, pay his debts for him," said the old printer.

" By all means, if he will take us into partnership," retorted the tall Cointet.

" You are bandits! " the old bear exclaimed. " You have been suing my son under cover of Métivier's name, and you expect me to pay, that's about it. No, sirs, I'm not such a fool! "

The brothers looked at one another, but they managed to conceal their surprise at the old miser's astuteness.

" We are not multi-millionaires," replied the fat Cointet. " We don't discount bills just for the fun of the things. We should think ourselves lucky if we could pay for our rags in cash—we still pay our dealer with bills."

" The experiment ought to be tried out on a large scale," the tall Cointet observed coldly, " because a process that succeeds in a saucepan might fail altogether in bulk. You should get your son out of his difficulties."

" Yes, but when my son was at liberty, would he take me on as his partner ? " said old Séchard.

" That's no business of ours," said the fat Cointet. " You don't suppose, do you, my good friend, that when you have given your son ten thousand francs that will be the end of it ? An inventor's patent costs two thousand francs, and there will be visits to Paris, too. Before going in for anything on a big scale, it would be prudent to do as my brother suggested just now—manufacture a thousand reams or so ; try out several batches to make sure. You mark my words, you can't be too careful in your dealings where inventors are concerned."

" I like my bread ready buttered," remarked the tall Cointet.

The old man spent the night thinking the matter over.

" If I pay David's debts, he will be free, and once he is free he won't need me for a partner. He knows quite well that I cheated him over our first partnership, and he won't want to enter into a second. The best thing for me is to keep him shut up, drat him."

The Cointets knew old Séchard well enough to realise that he and they would do well to hunt in couples. All three, in fact, were saying to themselves :

" Before starting a company based on the discovery, experiments should be tried ; and in order to make the experiments, David Séchard must be set free. But if David is freed, he will slip through our fingers."

Each of the men involved had, besides, his own afterthought.

Petit-Claud thought to himself, " As soon as I am married, I shall slip my neck out of the Cointets' yoke ; but until then, I'll hang on."

The tall Cointet thought, " I would rather have David under lock and key, then I would have the upper hand."

And old Séchard thought, " If I pay his debts for him, all I shall get from my son will be his thanks."

Eve, hard pressed—for the old man was holding out the threat of turning her out of the house—would neither reveal her husband's place of hiding, nor even agree to suggest to him that he should accept a safe conduct. She did not feel at all certain that she could succeed a second time in hiding David as well as he was hidden now, and so she said to her father-in-law :

" Set your son free, and you shall know everything."

The four interested parties sat, as it were, before a well-spread table which not one of them dared to touch, in case one of the others should steal a march on him ; so they all sat and watched one another suspiciously.

A few days after David had gone into hiding Petit-Claud had gone to see the tall Cointet at the paper mill.

" I have done all I could," he said ; " David has gone into voluntary seclusion, we don't know where, and he is working quietly on improving his invention. If you have not succeeded in gaining your end, it is no fault of mine. Are you going to keep your promise ? "

" Yes, if we succeed," said the tall Cointet. " Old Séchard has been here for the last few days, and he has been round asking questions about the manufacture of paper ; the old miser has got on to his son's invention, and he wants to make capital out of it, so there is just a chance that we may be able to come to terms. You are acting for the father and the son. . . . "

" Be the Third Person of the trinity and set them free," said Petit-Claud with a smile.

" Yes," said Cointet. " If you can succeed either in getting David into prison, or in putting him in our hands by means of a deed of partnership, you shall marry Mlle de la Haye."

" Is that your *ultimatum* ? "

" Since we are speaking in foreign languages," said Cointet, " Ja ! "

"All right, here is mine in plain French," returned Petit-Claud dryly.

"Oh? Really?" Cointet enquired in some curiosity.

"Introduce me tomorrow to Mme de Senonches, do something definite for me—in a word, keep your promise—or I shall pay Séchard's debt myself, sell my practice, and go into partnership with him. I don't intend to be cheated. You have spoken plainly, so I propose to do the same. I have given proofs of good faith; it's your turn now. You have all the cards in your hands, I have none. But unless I have some proof of your good faith, I shall play your game myself."

The tall Cointet put on his hat and his jesuitical expression, took up his umbrella, and, telling Petit-Claud to follow him, led the way out of the office.

"My good friend, you shall see for yourself whether or not I have prepared the ground for you," said the business man to the lawyer.

The shrewd and quick-witted paper manufacturer had instantly perceived the danger of his position, and he recognised in Petit-Claud a man with whom it would pay him to be straightforward. Partly so as to be prepared, in advance, partly to satisfy his conscience, he had already, on the pretext of giving a report on the financial situation of Mlle de la Haye, said a few words to the ex-Consul-General.

"I have just the party for Françoise—because, you know, a girl with thirty thousand francs as a dowry cannot be too particular these days," he had remarked, smiling.

"We will talk about it later," Francis du Hautoy had replied. "Since Mme de Bargeton left, you know, Mme de Senonches is in a very different position; we could marry Françoise to some worthy old country gentleman."

"And then she would misbehave herself," said the paper manufacturer, putting on his puritanical manner. "No, far better marry her to some capable young man, who, with your influence behind him, could give his wife a good position."

"I will think it over," Francis had said. "In any case, her godmother would have to be consulted first."

After M. de Bargeton's death, Louise de Nègrepelisse had sold the house in the Rue du Minage. Mme de Senonches, who considered that her own house was much too small for her, had persuaded M. de Senonches to buy that house, the cradle of Lucien's ambitions, and the scene in which this history opened. Zéphirine de Senonches had made up her mind to succeed Mme de Bargeton in the all but royal powers that she had exercised—she, too, would have a salon and become a great lady.

Ever since the duel between M. de Bargeton and M. de Chandour there had been a schism in Angoulême society. One faction maintained the innocence of Louise de Nègrepelisse, the other believed the calumnies of Stanislas de Chandour. Mme de Senonches had declared for the Bargetons and began by winning over all the members of that party. Later, when she had moved into her new house, the habits formed by the visitors who had played cards there every evening for years gave her the advantage over Amélie de Chandour. She was at home every evening, and she carried the day against her professed rival. Francis du Hautoy, who now found himself in the inner circle of aristocratic Angoulême, even went so far as to contemplate a marriage between Françoise and old M. de Sévérac, whom Mme de Brossard had failed to catch for her daughter. Mme de Bargeton's return, as wife of the Prefect, only served to to increase Zéphirine's ambitions for her dear goddaughter, for she argued that Countess Sixte du Châtelet would use her influence on behalf of the friend who had constituted herself her champion.

Boniface Cointet, who knew his Angoulême from A to Z, instantly appreciated all these difficulties ; but he made up his mind to sweep them aside by a bold stroke worthy of Tartuffe. The young lawyer was not a little surprised to find that his fellow-conspirator was keeping his word ; he had plenty of time for reflection as they walked from the paper-mill to the house in the Rue du Minage. At the door their progress was arrested by the words :

" Monsieur and madame are at lunch."

" Take in our names all the same," said Cointet ; and that assiduous business man was soon introducing the lawyer to the affected Zéphirine, who was lunching alone with M. Francis du

Hautoy and Mlle de la Haye. M. de Senonches had gone, as he usually did for the opening of the shooting season, to M. de Pimentel's estate.

" This is the young lawyer of whom I spoke," he said, addressing Mme de Senonches, " who is willing to take over the affairs of your fair ward."

The ex-diplomat looked Petit-Claud over, and the lawyer, for his part, stole a furtive look at the " fair ward ". Zéphirine's surprise was such—for neither Cointet nor Francis had said a word to her on the subject—that she dropped her fork. Mlle de la Haye was a thin, bad-tempered Miss with a sullen expression, a bad figure and colourless fair hair ; she was, in spite of her aristocratic airs, an excessively difficult girl to marry. The words " Parentage unknown " on her birth certificate closed to her the sphere into which the affection of her godmother and of Francis would have liked to place her. Mlle de la Haye, ignorant of her true position, was hard to please ; she had already refused to marry the richest business man in l'Houmeau. Mlle de la Haye's expression, at the sight of the weedy little lawyer, spoke plainly enough ; and, turning to his companion, Cointet saw exactly the same expression on the face of Petit-Claud. Mme de Senonches and Francis looked at one another as if to find some excuse for getting rid of Cointet and his protégé. Cointet, taking in the whole situation, asked M. du Hautoy if he would see him alone for a moment, and accompanied the diplomat into the drawing-room.

" Sir," he began point-blank, " paternity blinds you. You won't find it easy to marry your daughter ; and in the interests of everyone concerned, I have taken it upon myself to commit you—because, you know, I am fond of Françoise myself—she is my ward, after all. Well, Petit-Claud knows the whole story! His extreme ambition is the guarantee of your daughter's happiness. In the first place Françoise will do as she likes with her husband ; and you will have no difficulty in using your influence with the Prefect, who is due to arrive, to get him the place of Crown Attorney. M. Milaud's nomination for Nevers is quite definite, Petit-Claud can sell his practice, and you can easily get him appointed Deputy Public Prosecutor, with a good chance of becoming Crown Attorney, and then President of the Court, Deputy, anything you like. . . . "

"This is the young lawyer of whom I spoke"

They returned to the dining-room and Francis made himself most agreeable to his daughter's suitor. He gave Mme de Senonches a significant look, and concluded the interview by inviting Petit-Claud to dinner the following evening to discuss the business in hand. He saw the business man and the lawyer into the court, and took the opportunity of saying to Petit-Claud that, on Cointet's recommendation, he and Mme de Senonches were prepared to agree to whatever Mlle de la Haye's trustee might see fit to arrange for the happiness of that little angel.

" Oh! " exclaimed Petit-Claud. " What a plain girl! I have been taken in! "

" She is a lady," replied Cointet, " and you don't suppose they would have given her to you if she had been pretty, do you ? After all, my boy, thirty thousand francs will buy a nice little place, and with the protection of Mme de Senonches and Countess du Châtelet, you will get on!—and, what is more, M. Francis du Hautoy will never marry, and his daughter is his heir. . . . Your marriage is as good as settled."

" What do you mean ? "

" I was just coming to that," said Cointet, and gave the lawyer a brief outline of his private interview.

" They say that M. Milaud is sure to be nominated as Crown Attorney at Nevers. Sell your connection, my boy, and ten years from now you will be Keeper of the Seals. You are not the kind of man to think twice about doing anything the Court might ask you to do."

" All right, be in the Place du Mûrier at half-past four tomorrow afternoon," said the lawyer. These future probabilities had gone to his head. " By that time I shall have seen old Séchard, and we will draw up a deed of partnership that will put the father and the son into the power of the Third Person of the Trinity—the Cointets."

So it came about that as the old Curé of Marsac was climbing the steps to Angoulême to tell Eve of her brother's desperate straits, David had been in hiding for eleven days, only two doors away from the house that the old priest had just left.

When the Abbé Marron reached the Place du Mûrier, he saw there the three men—each remarkable in his own way—who were bringing all their weight to bear on the present and the future of the poor voluntary prisoner—old Séchard, Boniface Cointet, and the puny little lawyer. These three men represented three kinds of greed, each as different as were the men themselves. The one was prepared to sell his own son, the other his client; while the tall Cointet was preparing to buy both these infamies, and congratulating himself that he would not have to pay a penny for either. It was now almost five, and most of the passers-by on their way home to dinner stopped for a moment to look at the group.

"What the deuce can old Séchard and the tall Cointet find to say to one another?" the more curious asked.

"It must have something to do with that wretched fellow who has left his wife, his mother-in-law and his child to starve," others suggested.

"That's what comes of sending your son to Paris to learn a trade!" observed a provincial pundit.

"Monsieur le Curé, what brings you here, eh?" exclaimed the old vine-grower, who recognised Abbé Marron as soon as he appeared.

"I have come on account of your family," said the Curé.

"Here's another of my son's notions!" said old Séchard.

"It would cost you very little to make everybody happy," said the priest, indicating the windows, at one of which Mme Séchard's beautiful head could be seen between the curtains.

Eve was quieting her baby by singing to him, and dandling him in her arms.

"Are you bringing news of my son?" asked old Séchard. "Or money, which would be better still?"

"No," said M. the Abbé Marron, "I am bringing your son's wife news of her brother."

"Of Lucien?" Petit-Claud exclaimed.

"Yes. The poor young man has walked all the way from Paris. I found him at the Courtois', half dead with exhaustion and destitute," the priest continued. "Oh, he's very much to be pitied."

Petit-Claud took his leave of the priest, and, taking Cointet by the arm, said aloud, " We are dining with Mme de Senonches—it is time we were getting along."

When they were out of earshot, he said :

" If you can take the young, you can often take the mother. We have a hold on David. . . . "

" I have found you a partner, find one for me," said Cointet with a hypocritical smile.

" Lucien was at school with me—we were *chums*! A week from now I shall know a thing or two about him. If you can arrange for the banns to be read, I will guarantee to get David into prison. And when he is under lock and key, I shall have done my share in the matter."

" Oh! " Cointet exclaimed under his breath. " If only we could take out the patent in our name! "

When he heard these words, the miserable little lawyer shuddered.

Meanwhile Eve saw her father-in-law come in with the Abbé Marron, who had just spoken the few words that were to bring the whole judicial drama to its conclusion.

" Look, here is our Curé, Mme Séchard," said the old bear. " It seems he has some fine story or other to tell about your brother."

" Oh! " poor Eve exclaimed, cut to the quick. " What can have happened to him now! "

That exclamation was eloquent of so many sorrows, so many anxieties and dreads, that the old Abbé hastened to add :

" Do not be alarmed, madam, he is alive."

" Please be so kind as to fetch my mother," Eve said to the old bear. " She must hear whatever it is that this gentleman has to tell us about Lucien."

The old fellow went off to look for Mme Chardon, to whom he remarked, " Go and have it out with Abbé Marron ; he is a good sort, although he's a parson. I suppose dinner will be late, so I shall go out for an hour." And the old man, insensible to everything that had not the clink or the shine of gold, left the old lady without so much as noticing the effect that this blow produced on her.

The misfortunes hanging over both her children, the downfall of the hopes she had built on Lucien, the unlooked-for change in a character she had believed to possess both ability and integrity, in fact, the whole course of events during the last eighteen months had wrought a great change in Mme Chardon. She was no longer the same woman. Not only was she noble by birth, she was noble, also, in her nature, and she adored her children ; so that she had suffered more during the last six months than in the whole of her widowhood. Lucien had had the chance of becoming Count de Rubempré, by Royal patent ; he might have founded the family again, revived its titles and arms, and become a great man! And he had fallen into the mud! She was more severe in her judgment of him than was his sister, and she had regarded Lucien as lost on the day she heard the story of the forged bills. Mothers may sometimes try to deceive themselves ; but they always know very well the children they have nursed and brought up, who have spent so many years of their lives with them ; and in the discussions that Eve and David had so often had on the subject of Lucien's chances in Paris, Mme Chardon, while seeming to share Eve's illusions about her brother, had inward misgivings, and feared that David was right, for he put into words what her mother's intuition so greatly feared. She understood her daughter's sensitive nature too well ever to be able to share with Eve the anxieties that preyed on her in silence—a silence of which only mothers who love their children are capable. Eve, for her part, saw with deep dismay the ravages that sorrow wrought in her mother ; she saw her declining from old age into decrepitude, from day to day! So that mother and daughter acted towards one another those generous lies that deceive no one. For that mother, the heartless remark of the brutal old man was the last drop that filled to the brim the cup of her afflictions. She felt that her heart would break.

So when Eve said to the old priest, " This is my mother," and he saw her face, lined and worn like that of an old nun, framed in hair that had become quite white, but made beautiful by the expression of calm sweetness and resignation that comes to women who walk, as the saying is, by the will of God, he understood the lives of these two women. He no longer felt any sympathy for Lucien, who had inflicted so much suffering, and he shuddered to think what griefs the victims must have endured.

"Mother," said Eve, drying her eyes, "poor Lucien is not far away—he is at Marsac."

"And why not here?"

Abbé Marron repeated to them Lucien's account of the sufferings of his journey and the misfortunes of his last days in Paris. He described the agonies of mind that the poet had so lately undergone, on learning of the results that his imprudence had brought upon his family, and his misgivings as to the reception that might await him in Angoulême.

"He doubts us? Has it come to that?" said Mme Chardon.

"Poor fellow, he has returned to you on foot, enduring the most dreadful hardships on the way, and he has come back prepared to enter the humblest walks of life . . . to make reparation for what he has done."

"Oh, sir," said Lucien's sister, "whatever he may have done to us, I love my brother as one loves the body of someone who has died; and even that is more than many sisters love their brothers. He has reduced us to poverty, but let him come to us, and we shall share our last crust, which is all that he has left us. Oh, if only he had never left us, we should never have lost everything that we valued most."

"And it was the carriage of the woman who took him away that brought him back!" Mme Chardon exclaimed. "He left in Mme de Bargeton's calèche, travelling beside her, and he came back behind!"

"Is there anything that I can do to help you?" asked the good Curé, looking for an excuse for going.

"Money complaints are not fatal, so they say," said Mme Chardon, "but the patient must cure himself."

"If you have sufficient influence over my father-in-law to induce him to help his son, you would save a whole family," said Eve.

"He has no faith in you, and he seemed to me to be very much exasperated against your husband," said the Abbé; he had gathered from the old vine-grower the impression that the affairs of the

Séchards were a kind of wasp's nest that it would be as well not to meddle with.

His mission performed, the old priest went back to dine with his great-nephew Postel, who dissipated whatever good-will his old uncle may still have retained, for, like everyone else in Angoulême, he took the father's side against the son.

" One can do something with wasters," Postel concluded, " but when it comes to inventors, they will ruin you."

The Curé went home to Marsac, his curiosity entirely satisfied—and that, in all the French provinces, is the chief end of the excessive interest taken in other people's affairs. That very evening he told the poet how things stood at the Séchards, and gave him to understand that his journey had been in the nature of a mission undertaken from motives of the purest charity.

" You have involved your sister and your brother-in-law in debts amounting to ten or twelve thousand francs," he concluded, " and, my dear sir, nobody hereabouts can lend that trifling amount to a neighbour. We are not rich in Angoumois. I understood when you spoke to me of your bills, that the sum involved was much smaller."

The poet thanked the old man for his kindness. " The message of forgiveness that you have brought me is a treasure beyond price."

Lucien set off from Marsac first thing the next morning and reached Angoulême at about nine o'clock, stick in hand, and wearing a short jacket, a good deal the worse for his journey, and black trousers, whitened with dust. His worn boots were enough in themselves to declare him one of the luckless class of pedestrians. He did not try to disguise from himself the fact that the contrast between his departure and his return was bound to strike his fellow-townsmen. But, with his heart still throbbing with the remorse occasioned by the old priest's story, he accepted his punishment, for the time being, and made up his mind to brave the glances of people he knew. " I am behaving heroically," he said to himself.

Poetic temperaments like Lucien's always begin by deceiving themselves. As he walked through l'Houmeau, his soul was torn between the shame of his return, and the poetry of his memories. His heart beat fast as he passed Postel's door—where, fortunately for himself, only Léonie Marron and her baby were in the shop. He noticed, with pleasure (for vanity was still strong within him), that his father's name had been painted out. After his marriage Postel had had his shop redecorated, and the one word, " Pharmacy ", was now displayed above the door, in the best Paris style. As he climbed up the steps to the Porte Palet, and Lucien breathed his native air once more, he no longer felt weighed down by his misfortunes. " I am really going to see them again," he thought to himself rapturously.

He reached the Place du Mûrier without having met anyone he knew—a piece of unhoped-for good luck for the young man who had once carried his head so high in his native city! Marion and Kolb, keeping watch at the door, rushed up the stairs, exclaiming :

" Here he is! "

Once more Lucien saw the old workshop and the old courtyard, and on the stairs he met his sister and his mother, and as they embraced one another, they forgot, for the moment, all their troubles in one another's arms. Inside the family circle, we can nearly always come to terms with misfortune ; we make it a kind of bed, whose hardness is made tolerable by hope. Lucien was the very picture of despair, but he was also the picture of poetry. He was sunburned from his long days on the open road ; an expression of melancholy had settled on his features and laid its shadows on the poet's brow. This change in him told of so much suffering that at the sight of the lines that misfortune had traced upon his features it was impossible to feel anything but pity for him. The man of imagination who had left the bosom of his family found there, on his return, sad realities. Eve, in her joy, had the smile of a martyred saint. Sorrow had rendered her young face sublimely beautiful. The grave expression that had replaced the look of complete innocence he had seen in it on the day of his departure for Paris was eloquent, and Lucien grieved to see it. So that the first effusion of affection, so natural and spontaneous, was quickly followed, in all three, by a reaction, and each was afraid to speak. But Lucien almost involuntarily looked round for the fourth who should have been present at that meeting. At that look, well understood, Eve burst into tears, and Lucien did the same. Only Mme Chardon's worn face remained impassive. Eve got up and went downstairs so that her brother should be spared any word of reproach and said to Marion :

" Lucien is so fond of strawberries, we must find some for him! "

" Oh, I was sure you would want to give M. Lucien a welcome! Don't you worry, ma'am, you are going to have a nice little lunch and a good dinner as well."

" Lucien," Mme Chardon said to her son, " you have a great deal to repair here. You left to do something to make us all proud of you, and you have involved us in ruin. You have all but ruined David's chances of making a fortune, and he was working only for the sake of his new family. And that is not the only thing you have destroyed," she added. There was a dreadful pause, and Lucien's silence implied his acceptance of his mother's reproaches.

" Now you must work," Mme Chardon continued gently. " I do not blame you for attempting to revive the fortunes of my noble family ; but in order to do that, you needed money, and a sense of pride—and you had neither. We have lost our faith in you. You have wrecked the peace of the quiet, hard-working little family that had difficulties enough to contend with here. A first offence may be forgiven—but let it be the last. We are in great difficulties at the moment, so do nothing rash, and do whatever your sister advises. Misfortune is a hard teacher, but its lessons have born fruit in her. She has become very responsible—she is a mother, and she carries the whole burden of the household, in her devotion to our dear David. Indeed, since you have failed us, she has become my only comfort."

" You might have been still more severe," said Lucien. " I accept your forgiveness, because I shall never need to ask for it again."

Eve came into the room ; she saw, from her brother's chastened aspect, that her mother had been talking to him. She smiled at him, out of kindness, and, in response, his eyes filled with tears. There is something magical in a living presence ; whether between lovers, or between members of a family, the bitterest hostility, however justly grounded, melts away. Perhaps affection traces roads in our hearts, into which it always tends to return—it may be that this phenomenon belongs to the science of magnetism. Or does reason tell us that we must either forgive, or never see one another again ? For whatever reason, whether the cause be physical, mental, or spiritual, we all of us know that the looks, the gestures, the actions of a being once loved, always reawaken, even in those whom they have most bitterly offended, some vestiges of tenderness. The mind may find it hard to forget, we may still be suffering the consequences of the injury, and yet the heart, in spite of everything, still returns to its old allegiance. And so Lucien's poor sister, as she listened until lunch-time to her brother's confidences, could not keep back the tears from her eyes when she looked at him, or keep her voice steady when she spoke what was in her heart. When she heard the truth about literary life in Paris, she realised why Lucien had found the struggle too much for him. The poet's delight as he held his sister's little son in his arms, his old childish ways, his happiness at seeing his family and his native place once more, mingled as it was with deep distress when he learned that David was in hiding ; the melancholy story that he had to tell them, his deep emotion to see, when Marion brought in the strawberries, that in the midst of her troubles his sister had remembered his favourite dessert ; indeed everything, even the fact that Eve had now to take in a prodigal brother and occupy herself with his affairs, combined to make the day a festival. It was a kind of truce with misfortune. Old Séchard rubbed the two women's feelings the wrong way, by remarking, " You are making as much of him as if he had brought you any amount of money."

" And what has my brother done that we should not celebrate his return ? " Eve asked, anxious to cover up Lucien's disgrace.

All the same, when the emotion of the first meeting was over, the darker shades of truth became clear. Lucien soon noticed, in Eve, the difference between her present affection and the affection of the old days. David was deeply respected, whereas Lucien was loved " in spite of everything ", as a man loves a mistress in spite of the disasters she has brought upon him. Respect—so necessary as the foundation of our affections—is the solid stuff that gives them the sureness, the certainty by which we live. This was lacking in the relationship between mother and son, between sister and brother. Lucien was no longer given their entire confidence, as he would have been if he had not sacrificed his honour ; and he felt this. His sister had come to hold the same opinion of him as d'Arthez had expressed in his letter, and she could not help letting it be seen, in her expression, her tone of voice, and her way of looking at him. Lucien was pitied, to be sure!—but as to the glory, the pride of the family, the hero of the home circle—all those bright hopes had faded for ever. They were too much afraid of his unreliability to tell him where David was hidden. Eve, paying no attention to the endearments with which Lucien, in his curiosity, plied her—for he was eager to see his brother-in-law—was no longer the Eve of l'Houmeau, to whom, in the old days, a single look from Lucien had been an order that she would not have dreamed of disobeying. Lucien talked of making good his misdeeds, and spoke as though he would be able to save David, but Eve only answered :

" Don't interfere—we have enemies who are both treacherous and extremely clever."

Lucien tossed his head, as much as to say, " I have coped with Parisians " ; but his sister replied with a look that meant, " Yes, but you were defeated."

" They don't love me any more," Lucien thought to himself. " Families are like the world—they only admire success."

By the second day the poet was trying to explain away their lack of confidence in him, and a thought took possession of him that was not so much bitter as irritating. He compared that simple provincial life with Paris standards, forgetting that the patient mediocrity of that household, so courageous in its endurance, was his own doing.

" They are bourgeois ; they are incapable of understanding me," he thought to himself, setting himself apart from his mother and sister and David, who could no longer deceive themselves either as to his character or his future.

Eve and Mme Chardon, whose intuitive perceptions had been

quickened by the shock of so many misfortunes, guessed at Lucien's secret thoughts and felt that he had withdrawn himself from them and that he looked down on them.

" How Paris has changed him! " they thought.

The truth of the matter was that they were reaping the fruits of the egoism that they themselves had fostered. It was inevitable that this ferment should work in all three, as in fact it did; but chiefly in Lucien, because he knew that he was to blame. As for Eve, she was one of those sisters who know how to say, to a brother who is in the wrong, " forgive me for *your* trespasses." But when the sympathy between two souls has been as perfect as Eve's and Lucien's had been from their earliest childhood, any flaw in an understanding so perfect is fatal. Rogues can make up a quarrel after blows have been given and received, but lovers will part for ever because of a look or a word. The secret of many an inexplicable separation is to be found in some such memory of an all but perfect understanding that existed once. We can come to terms with a certain mistrust, so long as the past presents no picture of a pure and unclouded affection; but two beings, who have once known a perfect understanding, can never endure a relationship in which every look and every word must be carefully watched. And so it is that a great poet has made Paul and Virginie die at the end of their youth. Who can conceive Paul and Virginie estranged? It must be said, in all honour both to Eve and to Lucien, that it was not the injury, grave as it was, that Lucien had done his sister, that caused this painful wound; with the blameworthy poet and the irreproachable sister alike, it was entirely a matter of feeling; so that the smallest misunderstanding, the least quarrel, or any fresh reason for thinking ill of Lucien, would have been enough to produce a complete estrangement, or a breach in the family that would never be healed. Matters of money can always be put right, but feelings are inexorable.

Next day, Lucien received a copy of the Angoulême local paper, and he turned pale with pleasure when he saw that he was the subject of a modest " first leader ". That respectable journal, like our provincial universities, compared by Voltaire to well-bred young ladies, never got itself talked about.

" Let Franche-Comté boast that it was there that Victor Hugo, Charles Nodier, and Cuvier first saw the light, Brittany, of Chateaubriand and Lammenais; Normandy of Casimir Delavigne, and Touraine of the author of *Eloa*. Today Angoulême, that in the reign of Louis XIII gave birth to the illustrious Guez, better known under the name of Balzac, has no longer cause to envy the province of Limousin, that produced Dupuytren, nor Auvergne, the birthplace of Montlosier, nor Bordeaux, the cradle of so many great men; for we also have our poet! The author of the beatiful sonnets entitled *Marguerites* is likewise the author of a fine novel, *An Archer of Charles IX*. Our nephews will be proud to claim as compatriot Lucien Chardon, of the tribe of Petrarch!!! "

(The provincial newspapers of those days were sown thick with exclamation marks, like the " cheers " in reports of speeches at English public meetings.)

" In spite of his brilliant success in Paris, our young poet has not forgotten that Bargeton House was the cradle of his triumphs, or that the Angoulême aristocratic circle was the first to applaud his poetry; or that the wife of Count du Châtelet, Prefect of the Department, encouraged his first steps in the paths of the Muses. He has come back to us once more! All l'Houmeau was in a state of excitement yesterday when our Lucien de Rubempré made his appearance. The news of his return has produced a sensation in all quarters. It is certain that the City of Angoulême will not allow l'Houmeau to be the first to do honour to the author who, both in journalism and in literature, has represented our city so gloriously in Paris. Lucien, who is both a religious and a Royalist poet, has braved the fury of party factions; he has come, we understand, to take a holiday after the fatigues of a struggle that might well try the strength of an even greater intellectual athlete than a poet and a dreamer.

" There is some talk of restoring to our famous poet the name and titles of the illustrious family of de Rubempré, of which his mother, Mme Chardon, is the last survivor, and it is said that Countess du Châtelet was the first to suggest this eminently politic course, which has our entire support. Thus to renew, through fresh talents and fresh fame, the glories of ancient families on the verge of extinction, is another proof that the immortal author of the Charter still cherishes the desire expressed by the words: '*Union and oblivion*.'

"Our poet is at present staying with his sister, Mme Séchard."

The following items appeared in the Angoulême news column:

"Our Prefect, Count du Châtelet, Gentleman in Ordinary to His Majesty, has been appointed Councillor of State Extraordinary.

"All the authorities called on the Prefect yesterday.

"Countess Sixte du Châtelet will receive on Thursdays.

"The Mayor of Escarbas, M. de Nègrepelisse, representing the younger branch of the d'Espard family, and father of Mme du Châtelet, recently raised to the rank of Count and Peer of France, and Commander of the Royal Order of Saint-Louis, has been nominated for the Presidency of the Electoral College of Angoulême at the forthcoming elections."

"Read this," said Lucien, handing the newspaper to his sister.

Eve read the article carefully, and then handed the paper back to Lucien with a thoughtful air.

"What do you say to that?" Lucien asked, astonished at a caution that seemed to him little better than indifference.

"The Cointets are the proprietors of that paper," she said. "They can put into it absolutely any articles they like—the only people who could force their hands are the Prefecture or the Diocese. You surely do not suppose that your old rival, now that he is Prefect, is generous enough to sing your praises in this way? Don't forget that the Cointets are suing us, under Métivier's name, and there is little doubt that they are trying to induce David to allow them to make capital out of his inventions. Whoever put in this article, it worries me. You aroused nothing but jealousies and hatred here, and they slandered you, according to the proverb that a prophet is without honour in his own country; and now, suddenly, all that is changed!"

" You don't know the vanity of country towns," retorted Lucien. " A whole town in the south turned out not so long ago to meet a young man who had won a prize in some competition or other—they hailed him as a budding great man."

" Listen to me, my dear Lucien—I don't want to preach at you, but I must say just this—you must suspect even the smallest things here."

" You are quite right," said Lucien, surprised at his sister's lack of enthusiasm. The poet was overjoyed to find his shameful and humiliating return to Angoulême turned into a triumph.

" You don't even believe in the small amout of glory that has cost so dear," Lucien exclaimed an hour later. He had been silent, meanwhile, a storm gathering in his heart.

Eve's only reply was a look, that made Lucien ashamed of his accusation.

Just after dinner a messenger from the Prefecture office called with a letter addressed to M. Lucien Chardon, which in this conflict between the world and the family, seemed to carry the day for the poet's vanity. The letter contained the following invitation :

" Count and Countess du Châtelet request the honour of M. Lucien Chardon's company at dinner on September 15th.

RSVP."

A visiting-card was enclosed :

" *Count Sixte du Châtelet*

Gentleman in Ordinary of the Bedchamber,
Prefect of Charente, Councillor of State."

You are in favour," remarked old Séchard. " They are talking about you in the town as if you were somebody. Angoulême and l'Houmeau are disputing the honour of twisting wreaths for you."

" My dear Eve," Lucien whispered to his sister, " I am in exactly the same position as I was at l'Houmeau on the day I had to go to see Mme de Bargeton—I haven't a dress suit to dine with the Prefect! "

" Then are you thinking of accepting the invitation ? " Eve asked in dismay.

There followed an argument between brother and sister as to whether or not Lucien should dine with the Prefect. Eve's provincial common sense told her that if you appear in society it must be with a smiling face and irreproachably dressed ; but she concealed her real thought, which was : " Where will the Prefect's dinner lead him ? What can Angoulême society possibly do for Lucien ? Is there not some plot against him ? "

Lucien said the last word as he got up to go to bed :

" You do not know how much influence I have! The Prefect's wife is afraid of a journalist ; and, besides, Countess du Châtelet is still Louise de Nègrepelisse! A woman in her position can surely save David! I will tell her about the invention, and it will be a simple matter for her to ask the Ministry for a grant of ten thousand francs."

At eleven o'clock that night Lucien, his sister, his mother, old Séchard, Marion and Kolb, were all awakened by the town-band, reinforced by the military band from the Garrison. The Place du Mûrier was full of people. The young men of Angoulême had come to serenade Lucien Chardon de Rubempré. Lucien appeared at his sister's window, and there was immediate silence. " I would like to thank you, my fellow townsmen, for the great honour you have done me, and which I will strive to deserve. I must ask you to forgive me if I say no more—I am so deeply moved that I cannot speak."

" Long live the author of *The Archer of Charles IX* ; Long live the author of *Marguerites*! Long live Lucien de Rubempré! " Three cheers followed and three wreaths and several bouquets were adroitly thrown in through the open window. Ten minutes later the Place du Mûrier was empty and silence reigned.

" I would sooner have ten thousand francs myself," old Séchard remarked, turning the wreaths and bouquets over with an air of profound disgust. " You gave them marguerites, and they give you bunches of flowers—flowers are your line of business."

" So that is your opinion of the honours paid me by my fellow-townsmen, is it ? " said Lucien, whose expression had lost every trace of melancholy and who was positively beaming with satisfaction. " If you understood human nature, Papa Séchard, you would realise that this is one of those moments that do not come twice in a lifetime. A triumph like this comes only from genuine enthusiasm! My dearest mother and wonderful sister, this makes up for many troubles! "

Lucien kissed his sister and his mother as men do when their joy overflows in such great waves that they must pour it into the heart of some friend. " If there is no friend about, an author drunk with success will kiss his porter," according to Bixiou.

" Why, darling Eve, why are you crying ? " he exclaimed. " Oh! I see, they are tears of joy! "

" Oh dear! " said Eve to her mother, when they were alone, " I am afraid that there is a vain woman of the worst kind in every poet! "

" You are right! " said her mother, shaking her head. " Lucien has forgotten everything already, not only his own troubles, but ours as well."

Mother and daughter separated. Neither dared to utter all her thoughts.

In a country taken up by the attitude of social insubordination disguised by the word *equality*, every triumph is one of those miracles that do not happen (like certain miracles of an earlier age) without the co-operation of an adroit stage-manager. Nine out of ten ovations given to a living man, singled out for distinction by his compatriots, are brought about for reasons unguessed by the applauded hero. What was Voltaire's triumph at the Théâtre-Française but the triumph of the philosophy of his age ? In France there is no triumph, unless the public, in crowning its idol, is crowning itself. So that the two women might well be anxious. The public applause of our provincial great man was foreign to the conservative habits of Angoulême ; it must have been engineered by some enthusiastic intriguer or by interested parties—in either case, it was highly suspect. Eve—like most women for that matter—was mistrustful by intuition, and without being able to find any justification of her suspicions, she asked herself, before she went to sleep :

" Who is there here who is sufficiently fond of my brother to organise a public welcome for him? The *Marguerites* have not even been published yet, and how can they fête him for a future success?"

As a matter of fact, the reception was the work of Petit-Claud. On the day that the Curé of Marsac had brought the news of Lucien's return, the lawyer had dined with Mme de Senonches for the first time, and she received his formal offer for the hand of her goddaughter. It was one of those family dinners whose solemnity is marked not so much by the number of the guests as by the formality of their dress. Although it is a family affair, everybody is acutely conscious of the part that they are playing, and every face wears an expression of set purpose. Françoise was on display, like goods in a shop-window. Mme de Senconches was in full feather for the occasion. M. du Hautoy wore a black coat; and M. de Senonches, to whom his wife had written to tell him of Mme du Châtelet's arrival—she was expected to make her first visit that evening—and that a suitor for Françoise was to be officially introduced, had cut short his visit to M. de Pimentel in order to return. Cointet, in his best maroon-coloured coat of clerical cut, wore in his necktie, for all to see, a diamond worth six thousand francs—the wealthy business man's revenge on an impoverished aristocracy. Petit-Claud, fresh from the barber's, scrubbed, combed, and brushed, had not been able to scrub away that harsh manner of his. One could not look at the puny little lawyer, tightly buttoned into his clothes, without thinking of a hibernating viper; but hope shone so bright in his magpie's eyes, his face was frozen into such icy rigidity, and he behaved with such stiff formality, that he managed to achieve all the dignity of an ambitious little Public Prosecutor.

Mme de Senonches had begged her friends not to say a word on the subject of the formal introduction of a suitor for her goddaughter, or about the arrival of the Prefect, and, accordingly, she fully expected her drawing-room to be crowded that evening. The Prefect and his lady had left their cards, by way of official visits, reserving the honour of personal visits as acts of policy. All Angoulême society was, therefore, filled with a curiosity so great that quite a number of adherents of the Chandour faction proposed to visit Bargeton House that evening—for they obstinately refused to call it by the name of its new occupants. Proofs of the Countess's influence in Paris had reawakened more than one sleeping ambition, and, moreover, it was said that the lady herself had changed so much for the better that everyone was eager to see for themselves. When he learned from Cointet, on the way, the great news that Zéphirine had obtained from the Prefect the great honour of introducing to him her dear Françoise's husband-to-be, Petit-Claud made up his mind to take advantage of the false position in which Lucien's return placed Louise de Nègrepelisse.

M. and Mme de Senonches had undertaken such heavy commitments in order to buy their house that, after the manner of country gentry, they had decided to change absolutely nothing. And so Zéphirine's first words to Louise, when she hurried out to meet her on her arrival, were:

" My dear Louise, you see, you are still in your own house! "—and she pointed to the little lustre chandeliers, the panelling and the furniture that had charmed Lucien so long ago.

" That is the last thing, my dear, that I wish to remember," the Countess had replied graciously, allowing her eye to stray over the faces gathered there.

Everyone was agreed that Louise de Nègrepelisse had changed beyond all recognition. The Paris world in which she had moved during the past eighteen months (for the happiness of the first months of marriage had transformed the woman as completely as Paris had transformed the provincial lady), the air of dignity that power confers, had all combined to make Countess du Châtelet seem a younger version of Mme de Bargeton—like her only as a girl of twenty is like her mother. She wore a charming hat of lace and flowers, negligently pinned with a diamond pin. Her English side-curls became her, and made her face look younger, by concealing its contours. Her foulard dress, by Victorine, with its pointed bodice, exquisitely trimmed, set off her figure. Her shoulders were concealed by a light-coloured scarf whose delicate gauze was cleverly arranged to soften the line of her too thin neck. She toyed with those trifles that women carry with an ease that is the despair of provincial ladies. A charming scent-bottle hung from her bracelet by a chain; and she carried her fan and her handkerchief with consummate negligence. The perfect taste of all these small details, the poise and manner (copied from Mme d'Espard), showed that Louise was a profound student of the ways of the Faubourg Saint-Germain.

The elderly beau of the Empire, on the other hand, had, since his marriage, lost his youth—not unlike those melons that turn from green to yellow overnight. Everybody noticed that his wife's face was radiant with all the youth that the Sixte had lost, and broad provincial jokes passed from ear to ear, which circulated the more readily because all the women were furious at the new superiority of the one-time queen of Angoulême; the tenacious climber was made to pay for his wife.

The rooms were almost as full as on the memorable day of Lucien's reading; Chandour and his wife were not present, nor was M. de Pimentel, or the Rastignacs, or, of course, the late M. de Bargeton. But the Bishop arrived, with his vicars in train. Petit-Claud was deeply impressed by the spectacle of the fine flower of Angoulême; four months ago he had never dreamed that he would find himself among them; and he felt his hatred of the upper classes greatly diminished. He thought Countess du Châtelet a most fascinating woman. "That is the woman who can get me appointed as Public Prosecutor," he thought to himself.

Half-way through the evening, after chatting for the same length of time with each of the women (varying her tone and manner according to the importance of the person addressed, and her behaviour over the matter of her flight with Lucien), Louise withdrew into the boudoir with the Bishop. Zéphirine thereupon took Petit-Claud by the arm and led him, his heart beating fast, into that boudoir where Lucien's misfortunes had begun and in which they were soon to be completed.

"My dear, this is M. Petit-Claud; I can recommend him to you the more warmly, because anything that you can do for him will be in the interests of my god-daughter."

"You are a lawyer?" asked the proud Nègrepelisse, scanning Petit-Claud.

"Yes, unfortunately, *Madame la Comtesse*."

The son of the tailor of l'Houmeau had never, in all his life, on so much as a single occasion, had occasion to speak those three words; and so he spoke as if his mouth was full.

"But it rests with you, *Madame la Comtesse*," he continued, "to place me at the Bar. I understand that M. Milaud is going to Nevers. . . ."

"But it is usual to be Second Deputy, then First Deputy, is it not? I would like to see you made First Deputy at once. But if I am to exert myself on your behalf, I would like some proof of your devotion to the cause of Royalism, and the Church, and, above all, to Monsieur de Villèle."

"I am the man, madam, to obey the King absolutely," he said, coming nearer.

"That is just what *we* want today," she replied, drawing back a little, so as to make him understand that she had no wish for a confidential discussion. "If you continue to satisfy Mme de Senonches, you may count upon me," she concluded, with a royal gesture of her fan.

Petit-Claud saw that Cointet was just coming into the boudoir. "Madam," he said hurriedly, "Lucien is here."

"Well, sir?" the Countess retorted, in tones that would have made the words die on the lips of any ordinary man.

"*Madame la Comtesse*, you do not understand me," Petit-Claud continued, using the more respectful form of address. "I wish to give some proof of my personal devotion to you. How would you wish the author whom you protected to be received in Angoulême? There can be no middle course—he must either be an object of scorn or a celebrity."

Louise de Nègrepelisse had not thought of this dilemma, but clearly it was important to her, though rather because of the past than of the present; and upon that lady's present feelings towards Lucien depended the success of the plan that the lawyer had made for David's arrest.

" You wish for a Government appointment, M. Petit-Claud," she said, assuming an air of haughty dignity. " You must know that the first principle of government is never to have been wrong; and women have, even more than governments, the instinct for power and a sense of their own dignity."

" That is exactly what I thought, madam," he replied eagerly, observing the Countess with an attention that she did not observe. " Lucien arrived here virtually destitute. But if he is to receive an ovation, I can perfectly well manage things so that he is forced for that very reason to leave Angoulême. His sister and his brother-in-law, David Séchard, are being hard pressed by the law."

Louise de Nègrepelisse allowed a barely perceptible change of expression—the result of the attempt not to allow her pleasure to appear—to pass into her face. She was surprised to find herself so well understood, and she looked at him as she opened her fan; Françoise de la Haye came up at this moment, giving her time to find an answer.

" You will very soon be Public Prosecutor," she said, with a significant smile. Did not those words, while not compromising her in any way, promise everything?

" Oh, madam," exclaimed Françoise, coming forward to thank the Countess, " then I shall owe my life's happiness to you! " She bent towards her protectress with a girlish gesture and added in a whisper, " I should die by inches as the wife of a country lawyer! "

It was Francis, who had a certain amount of knowledge of the bureaucratic world, who had urged on Zéphirine to make this set at Louise.

" Just after a promotion, everybody, be it prefect, royalty, or mining-engineer, is always longing to do services to friends; but they soon discover the drawbacks, and then they become extremely cold. At this moment Louise will agree to do more for Petit-Claud than she would do for your husband, three months from now."

" You realise, *Madame la Comtesse*, all the obligations that our poet's triumph will entail? " said Petit-Claud. " You will have to receive Lucien during our nine days' wonder."

The Countess terminated the interview with a bow, as she rose to go and talk to Mme de Pimentel, who put her head round the door of the boudoir at this moment. The news of old de Nègrepelisse's elevation to the peerage had impressed that lady, and the Marquise had judged it expedient to pay her respects to a woman who had been clever enough to make use of a lapse to improve her position. " Tell me, my dear, why did you go to the trouble of putting your father into the House of Peers ? " the Marquise asked her, in the course of a confidential conversation, in which she bowed to the superiority of her " dear Louise ".

" My dear, they were all the more ready to accord that favour because my father has no heir, and will always vote for the Crown, but if I have sons I fully expect that the eldest will succeed to the name, title, and arms."

Mme de Pimentel saw, with annoyance, that she could not hope to realise her own designs to see M. de Pimental raised to the peerage through the influence of a woman who was already ambitious for her unborn children.

" The Prefect's wife is willing to play," Petit-Claud remarked to Cointet as they left. " I can promise you your deed of partnership. A month from now I shall be Deputy Public Prosecutor, and you will have David Séchard in your power. Meanwhile try to find me a purchaser for my connection ; in five months I have made it the best in Angoulême."

" One only needs to put you on horseback," said Cointet, almost jealous of his own work.

The causes of Lucien's triumphant reception in his native city must now be clear to everybody. Louise was following the example of the King of France who refrained from taking revenge for offences against the Duke of Orléans ; she was willing to forget injuries done to Mme de Bargeton in Paris. She would patronise Lucien, overwhelm him with her protection, and get rid of him *by fair means*. Petit-Claud had formed a pretty clear idea, from gossip, of the intrigues that had gone on in Paris, and had made a shrewd guess at the bitter hatred that a woman was bound to feel towards a man who had refused her when she had wanted him to love her.

On the day following the serenade, designed to justify the past of Louise de Nègrepelisse, Petit-Claud, in order to complete Lucien's intoxication, and to get him into his power, called on Mme Séchard, accompanied by six young men of the town, all old school-fellows of Lucien's from the Angoulême Grammar School.

This deputation had been organised on behalf of his old school, to invite Lucien to be the guest at a dinner that they wished to give, in honour of the great man who had risen from their ranks.

"Why, this must be your doing, Petit-Claud!" Lucien exclaimed.

"Your return has been a challenge to our local pride—we feel that it is a point of honour to get up a subscription for a grand banquet. The headmaster and the staff will be present; and as things seem to be going at present, we shall have all the authorities."

"For what day?" asked Lucien.

"Next Sunday."

"I'm afraid I can't possibly manage it," said the poet, "I cannot accept any invitations for the next ten days . . . but after that, I should be delighted."

"Very well, so be it," said Petit-Claud. "In ten days, then."

Lucien was perfectly charming to his old schoolfellows, who behaved towards him with almost respectful admiration. He talked for about half an hour, quite brilliantly, for, finding himself on a pedestal, he was anxious to justify the high opinion of his fellow-townsmen. He stood with his hands in his pockets, and spoke with the air of a man who sees everything from the high eminence on which his fellow-citizens have placed him. He was modest and affable, as became a genius on an informal occasion. He spoke as an athlete wearied by the struggles of Paris, and, above all, disillusioned; he congratulated his old friends on never having left their native city, and so on and so forth. They were quite delighted with him. After a while he took Petit-Claud aside and asked him for the real truth about David's affairs, blaming him for having ever allowed his old friend to go into hiding. Lucien tried to match his wits against those of Petit-Claud, who, for his part (with some effort), forced himself to confess to his old schoolfellow that he, Petit-Claud, was only a poor country lawyer without a trace of the finer subtleties of his profession.

The whole machinery of modern societies is infinitely more complex than it was in more primitive times, and its result has been specialisation. In the ancient world outstanding men, universal in their field of knowledge and activity, appeared from time to time, like bright torches to illuminate the nations of antiquity. Later, even though the faculties of knowledge became more specialised, any eminent man could still retain some grasp of every branch of knowledge. Louis XIth, for example, that " rich and cautelous " man, could employ his cunning in many directions. But nowadays even the upper strata of society are sub-divided. Every profession, for example, has its own brand of cunning. A wily diplomat could easily be taken in, in some business affair in the depths of the country, by a second-rate lawyer, or by a peasant for that matter. The cleverest journalist can be made a fool of in business matters, and Lucien might well be—and was—a puppet in the hands of Petit-Claud.

That malicious lawyer himself had, of course, written the article which had committed Angoulême and l'Houmeau to fêting Lucien. The fellow-townsmen who had gathered in the Place du Mûrier were hands from the Cointets' printing-works and paper mills, the clerks from Petit-Claud's office, Cachan, and one or two old school friends. The lawyer, who had now once more become the school " chum ", thought—and rightly—that his friend would sooner or later give way the secret of David's retreat ; and that if David came to grief through Lucien, Angoulême would be too hot to hold him. The better to assure his influence, Petit-Claud posed as Lucien's inferior.

" What more could I have done ? " he said to Lucien. " It is true that my school-friend's sister was involved, but there are some cases that one is bound to lose. David asked me, on the first of June, to see that he was left alone for three months ; he was left in peace until September, and even now I have not let his creditors touch his property—because I will win his case for him at the Royal Court. I shall argue that the wife is a privileged creditor, and that her claim is absolute, unless there is the intent to conceal a fraud. As for yourself, you have come back in straits, but of course you are a genius." (Lucien made a deprecating gesture, as of a man when a censer is swung too near his face.) "Yes, my dear fellow," Petit-Claud continued, "I have read *An Archer of Charles IX*—it is more than a novel, it is literature! The preface could only have been written by one of two men—Chateaubriand and yourself."

Lucien accepted the compliment; he did not feel called upon to mention that the preface had been written by d'Arthez. Out of a hundred French authors, ninety-nine would have done the same.

"Well, nobody here seemed to have heard of you," Petit-Claud continued, feigning indignation. "When I saw the general indifference, I made up my mind to wake them up. I wrote the article you read."

"Really? It was you then?" said Lucien.

"None other. Angoulême and l'Houmeau were provoked to rivalry, and I collected the young men—your old school-friends—and organised last night's serenade; then, the enthusiasm fairly started, we opened a subscription list for the dinner. 'David may be in hiding, but at least we can crown Lucien!' I said to myself; and I have done even better," Petit-Claud went on, "I have seen Countess du Châtelet, and I have told her that she owes it to herself to get David out of his difficulties—she can do it, and she must do it. If David has really discovered the secret he described to me, the Government would not be ruined, and what a feather in the cap of any Prefect, to earn some of the credit for such a discovery, by having given timely help to the inventor! They say he is a very enlightened administrator. Your sister is frightened by the noise of our judicial artillery—she was afraid of the smoke! Warfare in the courts is as expensive as it is on the battlefield; but David has stood by his guns, he has kept his secret; they have not managed to arrest him, and he won't be arrested."

"Thank you. I see that I may tell you my plan—you will help me to realise it."

Petit-Claud looked at Lucien; and his gimlet-nose might have been a question-mark.

"I mean to save Séchard," said Lucien, with a certain importance. "I caused his misfortune, and I intend to repair it. I have more influence over Louise . . ."

"Who is Louise?"

"Countess du Châtelet!"

Petit-Claud started.

"I have more influence over her than she herself realises," Lucien went on, "only, my dear fellow, whatever power I may have over your local government, I have no clothes. . . ."

Petit-Claud made as if to offer Lucien his purse.

"Thank you!" said Lucien, pressing Petit-Claud's hand. "Ten days from now I shall call on the Prefect's wife, and return your call."

They parted, shaking hands like old friends.

"He must be a poet," Petit-Claud thought to himself, "for he is quite mad."

"It is a true saying that there are no friends like one's school-friends," Lucien reflected as he walked back to his sister's house.

"Lucien, what has Petit-Claud promised to do for you, that you are so friendly with him?" Eve asked. "Don't trust him too far!"

"Him!" Lucien exclaimed. "Listen, Eve," he continued, as if a thought had just struck him. "You have no faith in me any more, you don't trust me, so you may well distrust Petit-Claud; but within a fortnight you will change your mind," he added, with a rather fatuous air.

Lucien went upstairs to his bedroom, and there he wrote the following letter.

"Dear Lousteau,

"Of the two of us, I am the only one who is likely to remember the thousand-franc note I once lent you; and—alas—I know only too well the situation you are bound to be in when you get this letter; so I will add at once that I am not going to ask you to repay it in the form of gold or silver ; no, I am going to ask you to let me have it in the form of credit—as one would ask Florine for a thousand francs' worth of pleasure. We both go to the same tailor, and so you can ask him to make up for me, as quickly as possible, a complete outfit. I may not be precisely in the state of Adam, but all the same, I cannot go anywhere. The Departmental honours reserved for distinguished Parisians are being paid me here—much to my surprise. I am to be the hero of a dinner, for all the world as if I were a Deputy of the Left. Now do you see why I simply must have a black suit ? Promise to pay ; put it down to your account—in fact, invent an unpublished scene between Don Juan and Monsieur Dimanche, because I must have a Sunday-best suit at all costs! I am in rags—start from there! It is August, and the weather is magnificent ; *ergo* see that I receive, by the end of this week, a charming morning-suit, a dark bronze-green jacket, three waistcoats, one pale yellow, another in a pattern (a plaid), and the third plain white. I also want three pairs of trousers (*to take the ladies!*), one in white English material, one nankeen, and the third in a thin black cashmere ; and lastly, a black evening-suit with a black satin waistcoat to go with it. If you have a Florine with you, may I beg her to buy me one or two fancy ties ? But all that is easy—I rely on you, you are good at these things—I am not worrying about the tailor! My dear Lousteau, as you and I have often had cause to deplore, the intelligence of the hard-up is the most active poison known to the human species in its most typical manifestation—to wit, the Parisian! But even that intelligence, capable of outwitting Satan himself, has not yet discovered a means of obtaining a hat on credit! When we have created a fashion for hats that cost a thousand francs, my dear boy, then, and not until then, we shall be able to wear them! But until that day comes, we shall always have to have enough money in our pockets to pay cash for a hat! What a lot of harm the Comédie-Française has done us, with its line, 'Lafleur! You will put money in our purses!'

"I do realise all the difficulties involved by this request—especially as I want a pair of boots, a pair of evening-shoes, a hat, and six pairs of gloves sent with the things from the tailor! It is asking the impossible, I know. But what is literary life but the perpetual recurrence of the impossible? All I can say is this—work this miracle somehow, write a long article, or do some small piece of blackmail, and I will discharge you from your debt. Don't forget it is a debt of honour, my boy, and it has been owing for twelve months. You ought to be ashamed of yourself, if you had any shame left.

"But joking apart, my dear Lousteau, I am in a pretty serious mess, as you may guess when I tell you that the Cuttlebone is thriving mightily; she has married the Heron, and the Heron is Prefect of Angoulême. That fearful pair are in a position to do a great deal for my brother-in-law, who is in a desperate situation, thanks to those bills I cashed; he is under warrant of arrest, and in hiding. And so I simply must see the Prefect's wife again, and try to regain some of my old influence over her. It is a terrible reflection, is it not, that David Séchard's fortunes depend on a pair of well-cut boots, grey silk stockings (don't forget these) and a new hat! I shall say that I am ill, and cannot go out, and take to my bed, like Duvicquet, so as to avoid having to accept the pressing invitations to my fellow-townsmen. My fellow-townsmen, my dear boy, gave me a beautiful serenade. I sometimes wonder how many fools go to make up that word *fellow-townsmen*, since I discovered that it was one or two of my old schoolfriends who worked up the capital of Angoumois to such a pitch of enthusiasm. If you could put a line or two about my reception in the Paris gossip-columns, I should grow in stature here by several inches. Besides, I should like the Cuttle bone to be made to realise that I have, if not friends, at least a certain amount of credit with the Paris press. As I have not given up any of my hopes, I will repay you for that. If you want any solid articles for any of the magazines, I have time on my hands at the moment to think up something. I will say no more, only that I count on you, and that you may count on the friend who signs himself,

"Yours ever,

"Lucien de R.

"P.S. Send me everything to the coach-office, Poste Restante."

As he wrote this letter, in which Lucien assumed once more the accent of superiority—his self-esteem had returned with success—he thought, once again, of Paris. He had for the last six days been lulled in the absolute calm of provincial life, but now his thoughts turned back to those wonderful sufferings, and he experienced a vague sense of regret. For a whole week he thought of nothing but Countess du Châtelet, and in the end he had come to attach so much importance to his reappearance, that when at last, after dark, he went down to l'Houmeau to see whether the parcels he was expecting from Paris had arrived at the coach-office, he suffered all the tortures of suspense, like a woman who has set her last hopes on a dress, and despairs of ever possessing it.

" Lousteau! I forgive you everything! " he exclaimed under his breath, as he realised, from the shape of the parcels, that they must contain everything he had asked for.

In the hat-box he found this letter :

" Florine's Drawing-room.

" My dear boy,

" The tailor behaved very well ; but as your penetrating retrospective glance led you to foresee, the ties, hat, and silk stockings, set us all racking our brains, because there was nothing to rack in our purses. As Blondet says, there is a fortune to be made by a shop that will supply young men on credit with inexpensive articles—because we pay dear in the end when we can't pay. And as the great Napoleon said when his advance towards India was arrested for want of a pair of boots, ' If a thing is easy, it is never done! ' So everything went well, except for the boots. I had a picture of you, dressed but hatless, waistcoated but shoeless, and I was even thinking of sending you a pair of mocassins that an American gave Florine as a curiosity. Then Florine offered us the enormous sum of forty francs, to gamble for you ; and Nathan, Blondet and I were so lucky (as we were not playing for ourselves) that we had enough over to invite La Torpille (des Lupeaulx's one-time ballet-dancer) to supper. Frascati certainly owed us that much. Florine undertook the shopping, and she has added three beautiful shirts. Nathan sends you a walking-stick. Blondet, who won three hundred francs, sends you a gold watch-chain. The ballet-dancer adds a gold watch, the size of a forty-franc piece, that some fool gave her, and that does not go. 'Worthless trash; like the man who gave it to me,' she says. Bixiou, who joined us at the Rocher de Cancale, wanted to include a bottle of Eau de Portugal in the parcel that Paris was making up for you. 'If it will make him happy, let the dear boy have it,' he said, in his famous bass-baritone imitation of the pompous pater familias. All of which, my boy, only goes to show that we love our friends when they are in trouble. Florine, whom I have been fool enough to forgive, asks me to ask you for an article on Nathan's new book. Goodbye, my dear boy! I can only offer you my sympathy for finding yourself back in the same goldfish bowl you had just left when you met

"Your old friend

"Étienne L."

"Poor fellows! They gambled for me!" he exclaimed, deeply touched. A gust of air from an unhealthy country, or from the one where one has suffered most, can seem like a breath from Paradise; and into a colourless existence, the memories of past sufferings bring an indefinable joy. Eve was speechless with amazement when her brother came downstairs in his new clothes; she did not recognise him.

"Now I can walk in Beaulieu," he exclaimed, "and nobody can say of me, 'He has come back in rags!' Here, take this watch—I owe it to you, and it is really mine; and besides, it resembles its owner, it is most erratic."

"What a child you are!" said Eve. "It is really impossible to be angry with you."

"You surely don't imagine, my dear girl, that I would have sent for all this simply for the idiotic pleasure of shining in the eyes of Angoulême? I don't give *that* for Angoulême!" he declared (twirling his cane with its engraved gold knob). "No—I want to repair the harm I have done, and this is my battle-dress."

Lucien's success as a young man of fashion was the only real success he ever achieved ; but it was immense. Admiration may freeze some tongues, but envy unlooses as many more. If women lost their heads over him, and men slandered him, he could say, in the words of the song, " Oh Coat, I have you to thank for this! " He left two cards at the Prefecture, and called also on Petit-Claud, who was not in. The next day, the day of the banquet, the Paris newspapers all carried the following paragraph :

" *Angoulême.* The return of the young poet who made such brilliant beginnings, has been marked by an ovation that does as much honour to the city of Angoulême as it does to M. Lucien de Rubempré. His first novel *An Archer of Charles IX* is the only historical romance written in France that is not an imitation of Sir Walter Scott, and its preface is a literary event. The city has lost no time in arranging a civic banquet in his honour. The new Prefect, only recently installed, is attending the public celebration organised in honour of the author of *Marguerites*, whose talent was so actively encouraged, in his early years, by Countess du Châtelet."

In France, when once something has been set in motion, nobody can stop it. The Colonel of the regiment stationed at the garrison offered his band. The landlord of the Bell—whose magnificent porcelain jars of truffled turkeys are exported to the uttermost ends of the earth—the famous innkeeper of l'Houmeau, who was providing the banquet, decorated his largest room with flags, garlanded with laurel-wreaths and bouquets of flowers. The effect was superb. At five, some forty persons arrived, all in full dress. A crowd of over a hundred onlookers (attracted principally by the presence of the military band in the yard) represented the citizens of Angoulême.

" The whole of Angoulême is there! " said Petit-Claud, looking out of the window.

" It beats me," Postel remarked to his wife (they had come out to listen to the band). " Why, the Prefect, and the Receiver-General, and the Colonel, the Superintendent of the Arsenal, and the Deputy and our Mayor, the Headmaster of the Grammar School, and the Manager of the Foundry at Ruelle, and M. Milaud the Public Prosecutor—all the authorities have just arrived! "

As they sat down to table the military band struck up with a suite of variations on the tune of *Vive le Roi, Vive la France,* a tune that has never become popular. It was five in the evening when the banquet commenced, and at eight a dessert consisting of sixty-five dishes, notable amongst which was an Olympus made of sugar, and surmounted by a figure of France, in chocolate, gave the signal for the toasts.

" Gentlemen," said the Prefect, rising, " the King! The rightful ruler of France! The years of peace that have produced the generation of poets and thinkers who maintain the sceptre of letters in the hands of France—to whom do we owe these years, but to the Bourbons ? "

" Long live the King," cried the guests—the majority of whom were Ministerialists.

The old Headmaster rose to his feet. " To the hero of the day," he began, " to the young poet, who combines the poetic gift of Petrarch, the mastery of the sonnet-form that Boileau declared to be so difficult, with the talents of a writer of prose! "

" Bravo! Bravo! "

The Colonel rose.

" Gentlemen, to the Royalist! For the hero of this evening has had the courage to stand by his principles ! "

" Bravo," cried the Prefect, leading the applause.

Petit-Claud rose.

" To all Lucien's school-fellows, to the pride of the Angoulême Grammar school, and to our revered Headmaster, who is so dear to us all, and to whom our thanks is due for the part that he has played in our subsequent success! "

The old Headmaster dried his eyes ; he had not expected this toast. Lucien rose to his feet ; there was immediate silence, and the poet turned pale. His old Headmaster, who was seated on his left, crowned his head with a laurel-wreath. Everybody applauded. When Lucien began to speak it was with tears in his eyes, and his voice was unsteady with emotion.

" He is drunk," the Attorney-General-Designate of Nevers remarked to Petit-Claud.

" But not with wine," retorted the lawyer.

" My dear fellow-countrymen, my dear friends," Lucien began at last, " I could wish that all France might be the witness of this scene. It is thus that men are raised to greatness, it is thus that great works and great deeds for our country are brought into being. But, when I consider how little I have done, and this great honour that you have shown to me today, I am covered with confusion, and I can only dedicate my future to the task of justifying your reception of me. The memory of this evening will give me strength to go forward with renewed courage. And permit me to indicate, as worthy of your homage, the lady who was my first muse and protectress, and to associate her name with that of my native city. I propose the toast of the beautiful Countess Sixte du Châtelet and the noble city of Angoulême! "

" He came out of that pretty well," said the Public Prosecutor, nodding approvingly; " our speeches were prepared, he spoke without notes."

At ten, the guests began to drift away in twos and threes. David Séchard, when he heard these unusual strain of music, asked Basine what could possibly be going on in l'Houmeau.

" They are giving a dinner in honour of your brother-in-law, Lucien."

" I am sure he must have been sorry that I was not there," said David.

At midnight Petit-Claud was seeing Lucien home through the Place du Mûrier. There, Lucien turned to the lawyer:

" My dear fellow, you and I are friends, through thick and thin," he remarked.

" My marriage-contract is being signed tomorrow at Mme de Senonches', with Mlle Françoise to la Haye, her god-daughter; it would give me great pleasure if you would come—Mme de Senonches has asked me to bring you, and you will meet Countess du Châtelet there. She will be delighted when she hears about your speech, as no doubt she will."

" I had my reasons," said Lucien.

" Oh! You are going to save David! "

" I am sure I shall."

At this moment, as if by magic, David himself appeared. This is how it happened.

David was in a difficult position. His wife absolutely forbade him to see Lucien, or to let him know where he was hidden ; Lucien, on the other hand, was writing him most affectionate letters, assuring him that within a few days he would have repaired the harm he had done ; and Mlle Clerget had brought David two letters telling him about the celebration whose music had reached his ears.

Eve had written :

" My dear, behave as if Lucien were not here, and engrave these words on your dear brain : our only safety depends on the impossibility of your enemies discovering where you are. I am sorry to say that I have more confidence in Kolb, Marion, and Basine than in my brother. Poor Lucien, I am sorry to say, is no longer the open, sensitive poet we used to know ; and it is just because he wants to interfere in your affairs, and has the presumption to imagine that he can settle your debts for you (out of vanity, be it said!), that I am afraid of him. He has just had a lot of beautiful clothes sent from Paris, and five gold pieces in an expensive purse. He has given me the money, and that is what we are living on.

" We have one enemy the less—your father has left us, and for that we have to thank Petit-Claud. Petit-Claud managed to get to the bottom of his designs, and put an end to them once and for all by telling him that you would do nothing without consulting him; and that he, Petit-Claud, would not hear of your giving away any part of your secret until you were paid an initial sum of thirty thousand francs, fifteen at once, to clear your debts, and another fifteen thousand to be paid to you whether or not your invention succeeds. I cannot understand Petit-Claud at all.

" I send you all the love a wife feels for a husband in misfortune. Our little Lucien is well. It is wonderful to see how the little blossom grows and blooms in spite of all our domestic storms! My mother, as always, prays for you, and sends you almost as much love as " Your own

" Eve."

(Petit-Claud and the Cointets had taken fright at old Séchard's peasant cunning, and they had got rid of him, as we see—the more easily because he was now anxious to get back to his vines at Marsac in time for the vintage.)

Lucien's letter, enclosed with Eve's was as follows :

" My dear David, all goes well. I am armed from head to foot, and today I am beginning the campaign. Two days from now I shall have made some headway. How I look forward to meeting you, when you are free, and clear of *my* debts! But I am deeply and painfully wounded by Eve's and my mother's continued want of confidence in me—as if I did not already know that you are in hiding at Basine's. Whenever Basine has called, I have news of you, and replies to my letters, and, besides, it is very obvious that there was no one except her old workroom friend that she could have trusted. Today I shall be very near you, and terribly distressed that you cannot come to the dinner they are giving in my honour. Angoulême's civic vanity has meant quite a little triumph for me—it will all be forgotten again in a few days ; you are the only person whose pleasure in it would have been sincere. But before long now you will forgive everything to the friend who counts it worth more than all the glories in the world that he is,

" Your brother,

" Lucien."

David was terribly torn between two conflicting forces, even though they were not of equal force ; for he adored his wife, and his friendship for Lucien no longer included respect. But when a man is alone, feelings become strong out of all due proportion. A man alone with his preoccupations, as David was, will give way to devouring thoughts against which he has defences in the ordinary course of life. And so, as he read Lucien's letter to the sound of the fanfares of this unexpected triumph, he was deeply moved to find expressed in it the regret that he had been so sure that Lucien would feel. Those who feel deeply are always touched by these small expressions of affection, which they assume to mean as much, from others, as they would from themselves. What else can such things be than the overflowing of the full cup? And at midnight not all Basine's entreaties could prevent David from going to see Lucien.

"No one is ever about in the streets of Angoulême at this hour," he argued; "I shall not be seen, they cannot arrest me at night; and even if I am seen, I can always get back to my hide-out by Kolb's method. And it is so long since I have seen my wife and my little boy!"

Basine gave way before all these plausible reasons and let David go out. Petit-Claud was just saying good night to the poet when David, with a cry of "Lucien!" flung himself into his friend's arms. Both were moved to tears.

Such moments come seldom in any lifetime. Lucien experienced the warm outpouring of a friendship that had persisted in spite of everything, never counting the cost. To have betrayed such a friendship filled him with self-reproach. The inventor, in his noble generosity, wanted, above all, to read Lucien a lecture, and to dissipate the cloud that divided the affections of brother and sister. Before these human considerations, all the dangers created by want of money had faded from his mind.

"Now that you are here you had better take advantage of your imprudence," said Petit-Claud. "Go home and see your wife and baby—and do not let anybody see you!" "Most unfortunate," he said to himself, left alone in the Place du Mûrier. "Now if only I had Cérizet here."

The lawyer muttered these words to himself as he walked along beside the hoardings that had been erected about the site of the building that today is so proudly styled the Law Courts. He heard a tap on the boards close behind him, like someone knocking on a door.

"I'm here"—Cérizet's voice came from the crack between two planks. "I saw David coming up from l'Houmeau. I had begun to have a suspicion of where he was hidden, and now I am sure, and I know where we can get him any time; but if we are going to set a trap, I should like to know something about Lucien's plans, and here you are sending them into the house! But at least find some excuse for stopping here. When David and Lucien come out, send them round this way ; they will think that they are alone, and I shall hear what they say when they say goodnight."

" You are the very devil," said Petit-Claud under his breath.

" Well, upon my word, what wouldn't a man do for what you promised me! " said Cérizet.

Petit-Claud walked away from the hoardings and walked up and down the Place du Mûrier, to keep up his courage, as he watched the windows of the room where the family were sitting together, and thinking of his future, for, thanks to Cérizet's cleverness, he was now in a position to strike the final blow. Petit-Claud was one of those deep and treacherous double-dealers who is never caught by the bait of an immediate advantage, nor by the snares of any friendship ; for he had observed the fickleness of the human heart, and the strategies of self-interest. So at first he had not placed any great reliance on Cointet. If the plans for his marriage had fallen through, without his actually having been able to accuse Cointet of treachery, he had made plans of his own to annoy the Cointets. But since things had gone so well at Bargeton House, Petit-Claud had been above-board in his actions. His sub-plot had become useless, and indeed might endanger the political position to which he aspired. He had laid the foundations of his future importance in the following manner :

Gannerac and several other wealthy business-men of l'Houmeau had founded a Liberal committee, which kept in touch with the leaders of the Opposition through commercial channels. The advent of the Villèle ministry, accepted by the dying Louis XVIII, was the signal for a change of tactics by the Opposition, who, since the death of Napoleon, had renounced the dangerous methods of conspiracy. The Liberal Party was organising a system of lawful resistance throughout the provinces, and aiming at a majority in the next elections, by propaganda among the masses. Petit-Claud was a man of l'Houmeau and a rabid radical, and he was the instigator, organiser, and moving spirit of the Opposition in the Lower Town, downtrodden by the aristocracy of the city of Angoulême. He was the first to perceive the danger of leaving the entire press in the

Department of Charente in the control of the Cointets: the Opposition must have its organ, if it was not to fall behind other towns.

" If each of us was to give five hundred francs to Gannerac, that would come to well over twenty thousand francs, and we could buy the Séchard printing-business. We could control it if we gave a loan to the nominal proprietor," said Petit-Claud.

The lawyer had argued the meeting into accepting this idea, which had the advantage of strengthening his ambiguous position in relation of Cointet and Séchard; and, looking round for a man who might thus be made a devoted tool of the Liberal Party, he very naturally thought of that rogue Cérizet.

" If you can discover where your old boss is, and hand him over to me," he said to David's one-time apprentice, " I can get you a loan of twenty thousand francs to buy his printing establishment, and it would probably mean that you would be in control of a newpaper. So let us see what you can do."

Petit-Claud had more faith in the activity of a man like Cérizet than in all the Doublons in the world; and that was why he had ventured to promise the Cointets that David should be arrested. But since Petit-Claud had begun to cherish hopes of a Government appointment, he had foreseen the necessity of turning his back on the Liberals; and he had already stirred up so much enthusiasm in l'Houmeau that the funds necessary for the purchase of the printing business had been collected. Petit-Claud made up his mind to let things take their natural course.

" What does it matter? " he thought. " Cérizet will soon get into trouble with his newspaper, and I shall take the opportunity of displaying my talents."

He crossed over to the door of the printing house and spoke to Kolb, who was acting as sentinel.

" Go up and warn David that he had better leave now—and take every precaution: I am going;—it is one o'clock."

When Kolb left his post at the door, Marion came to take his place. Lucien and David came down together, and Kolb walked a hundred paces in front of them, Marion a hundred paces behind. As the two friends walked along by the hoardings, Lucien was talking to David in animated tones.

" My plan is extremely simple," he said, " but it is quite impossible to discuss it in front of Eve, who would never understand the means. I am certain that Louise, at the bottom of her heart, still cherishes feelings that I could reawaken ; I would like to do it, if only to have my revenge on that fool of a Prefect. Even if we were lovers only for a week, I could get her to ask the Ministry to make you a research grant of twenty thousand francs. I shall see the lady tomorrow, in the very same little boudoir where our love began—Petit-Claud says that nothing in it has been changed. I shall act a part! And by the day after tomorrow I shall send you a note by Basine to tell you whether I was hissed off the stage! Who knows, perhaps you will be free by that time! Now do you see why I had to have Paris clothes ? One cannot act the *jeune premier* in rags! "

At six in the morning Cérizet went to see Petit-Claud.

" Doublon can be ready to make his arrest at midday tomorrow ; he will get his man—I will guarantee that," he told the lawyer. " One of Mlle Clerget's girls will do anything for me, if you take my meaning."

Petit-Claud listened to Cérizet's plan ; then he hurried to see Cointet.

" If you can persuade Monsieur du Hautroy to settle his property on Françoise, you shall sign a deed of partnership with Séchard two days from now. I shall not be married until a week after the contract, so we shall both have kept within the terms of our agreement—one good turn deserves another. But we must keep our eyes open this evening, at Mme de Senonches's party, to see what Lucien and Countess du Châtelet have to say to one another, because it all turns on that. If Lucien is hoping to succeed through his influence over the Prefect's wife, then I've got David."

" You will be Keeper of the Seals one day, it is my belief."

" And why not, if M. de Peyronnet can be ? " (Petit-Claud had not quite sloughed his skin of Liberalism.)

The ambiguous status of Mlle de la Haye brought most of the nobility of Angoulême to the signing of her marriage-contract.

The poverty of the young people, the absence of wedding presents, quickened the interest that the social world always likes to display; for in matters of benevolence, as with ovations, everybody loves a charity that is flattering to self-esteem. So the Marquise de Pimentel, Countess du Châtelet, M. de Senonches and two or three of the more constant visitors to the house gave Francoise a few wedding presents, which were talked of in the town. These pretty trifles, together with the trousseau that Zéphirine had been preparing for the past year, the jewels from her godfather, and the usual wedding gifts, consoled Françoise, and aroused the curiosity of one or two mothers who came accompanied by daughters.

Petit-Claud and Cointet had already noticed that the nobility of Angoulême only tolerated their presence on their Olympus as a necessary evil. Cointet was Françoise's trustee and guardian; and Petit-Claud's presence was as indispensable at the signing of the contract, as that of the condemned man at an execution. But on the day after her marriage, Mme Petit-Claud might still have the right of entry to her god-mother's house, but her husband would not find it so simple a matter; Petit-Claud made up his mind to impose himself upon that proud world. The lawyer, blushing for his obscure parents, had persuaded his mother to remain at Mansle, where she was living in retirement, and had asked her to say that she was ill, and to give her consent in writing. Ashamed as he was to appear without any relations or protectors or witnesses to his signature, Petit-Claud was delighted to be able to bring a presentable friend, in the person of a celebrity whom the Countess wanted to meet again. So he called for Lucien in a cab.

For that memorable evening the poet had dressed in such a way as to outshine, beyond all question, every other man present. Mme de Senonches had already told everyone that the hero of the hour was to be present; and a meeting between the two estranged lovers was just the kind of situation that country society most enjoys. Lucien had risen to the status of lion. He was said to be so handsome, so completely transformed, so marvellous, that the noble ladies of Angoulême were all dying to see him again. He was dressed, according to the fashion of the transition period between the eighteenth-century tight-fitting breeches and the ignoble trousers of the present day, in tight-fitting black trousers. Men still displayed their figures in those days, to the great despair of the thin and the misshapen ; and Lucien had the figure of an Apollo. His open-work grey silk stockings, his neat evening shoes, his black satin waistcoat, and his cravat, were all without a crease or a wrinkle, and seemed moulded to his figure. The luxurious golden waves of his hair set off the whiteness of his brow, about which its curls were arranged with studied grace. His eyes shone with pride. His hands, small and fine as a woman's, looked so exquisite in gloves that one fancied that he must wear gloves always. He had copied his deportment from de Marsay, the famous Parisian dandy, holding his stick and hat in one hand, and using the other for those occasional gestures with which he illustrated his conversation.

Lucien would have liked to slip into the drawing-room unobserved, in the way of those celebrities, who, out of false modesty, bow their heads as they pass through the Porte Saint-Denis. But Petit-Claud, who had only one friend, made full use of him. He led Lucien up to Mme de Senonches, in the middle of the party, with something like pomp. As he passed through the crowded drawing-room, the poet heard the whisperings that had made his lose his head in the old days, but now they left him cold. He was quite sure that he himself was worth more than the whole Olympus of Angoulême put together.

" Madame," he said to Mme de Senonches, " I have already congratulated my friend Petit-Claud, who has in him the makings of a future Keeper of the Seals, on his good fortune in forming this connection with you—however slight may be the ties that unite godmother and god-daughter" (this phase he spoke with an epigrammatic air that was not lost on any of the ladies present, who were all listening without appearing to do so) " and I am most happy to have this opportunity of paying my respects to you."

Lucien spoke with the easy grace of a young duke or an earl, paying a visit to his social inferiors. As he listened to Zéphirine's involved reply, he let his eye travel round the room, so as to get his bearings and to make his plan of action. He greeted both Francis du Hautoy and the Prefect, to both of whom he bowed, with a perceptible shade of difference; and at last he went over to Mme du Châtelet, pretending that he had only just seen her. That meeting was the real event of the evening; the marriage contract lying in the adjoining bedroom, whither Françoise or the lawyer led various important people, to affix their signatures, was entirely forgotten. Lucien took a few steps towards Louise de Nègrepelisse; he addressed her with that Parisian grace that had become a mere memory for her since her arrival in Angoulême.

"Do I owe to you, *madame*, the pleasure of an invitation to dine at the Prefecture the day after tomorrow?"

"You owe it solely to your fame, *monsieur*," Louise retorted dryly, somewhat taken aback by the premeditated unkindness of a phrase in which Lucien had deliberately sought to wound the pride of his former patron.

"Ah! *Madame la Comtesse*," said Lucien with an expression of pointed affectation, "I cannot bring you a guest who is in disgrace." Without waiting for her reply, he turned away to speak to the Bishop, to whom he bowed with grave dignity.

"Your Grace's prophecy has been partly fulfilled," he said in charming tones, "and I shall endeavour to fulfil it to the letter. I count myself the more fortunate in being here this evening, because it enables me to pay my respects to you."

Lucien drew the Bishop into a conversation that lasted for ten minutes. All the women looked at Lucien as if he were something phenomenal. His unexpected insolence had left Mme du Châtelet speechless. Seeing Lucien the centre of admiration of every woman in the room, and watching how everyone was repeating, in whispers from group to group, the exchange of phrases in which Lucien had crushed her with seeming disdain, her heart contracted with a spasm of wounded pride.

"If he does not come to the Prefecture after that, it will create a scandal!" she thought. "How did he come by such pride? Has Mlle des Touches fallen in love with him? He is so handsome! They say that she hurried round to see him in Paris, the day after that actress died. Perhaps he came to Angoulême to save his brother-in-law, and it was only by chance that he happened to be riding behind our calèche, at Mansle. Lucien looked at Sixte and myself very strangely that morning."

A crowd of thoughts passed though her mind ; and, unluckily for Louise, she gave way to them as she watched Lucien talking to the Bishop, for all the world as if he were king of the drawing-room. He spoke to no one, but waited until they came and spoke to him, looking round the room with varying expression, with an air of ease worthy of de Marsay, his model. He did not leave the Bishop in order to speak to M. de Senonches, who was hovering close by.

By the end of ten minutes Louise could bear it no longer. She got up, went over to the Bishop, and said :

" What are you hearing about, your Grace, to make you smile so often ? "

Lucien withdrew discreetly, to allow Mme du Chatelet to talk to the Prelate.

" You know, *Madame la Comtesse*, that is a very brilliant young man. He has just been telling me that he owes everything to you."

" I am not ungrateful, madam," Lucien put in, with a look of reproach that charmed the Countess.

" We must talk things over," she said, and beckoning Lucien with her fan. " His lordship shall judge between us."

She led the way to the boudoir, the Bishop in tow.

" She has cast His Lordship for a strange part! " remarked one of the ladies of the Chandour faction, in a voice loud enough to be audible.

" Judge between us? " Lucien repeated, looking at the Prelate and the Prefect's lady in turn. " Then is one of us to blame ? "

Louise de Nègrepelisse seated herself on the sofa of her old boudoir. She made Lucien sit down on one side of her, and the Bishop on the other, then she began to speak. To the surprise and delight of his old love, Lucien did her the honour of hearing nothing that she said. He adopted the pose and the gestures of la Pasta in Tancredi, when she is about to say *O Patria*. All the feelings expressed in the famous cavatina *dell Rizzo* were written on his face,

"His Lordship shall judge between us!"

and Coralie's pupil even succeeded in bringing a few tears to his eyes.

"Oh, Louise! How I loved you!" he murmured, regardless alike of the Bishop's presence and of what his old love was saying, as soon as he saw that the Countess had noticed the tears.

"Dry your eyes, or I shall lose my heart to you in this room, for a second time!" she said, turning to him, in an aside that shocked the Bishop to the core.

"Once is enough," Lucien responded eagerly. "That, from Mme d'Espard's cousin, would be enough to dry the tears of a Magdalene. Oh, for a moment it all comes back to me, my illusions, my twentieth year, and you have ..."

His Lordship at this point beat a hasty retreat into the drawing-room, for it seemed clear to him that his dignity would be compromised by these two old lovers. Everyone made a point of leaving Lucien and Countess du Châtelet alone in the boudoir. But at the end of a quarter of an hour Sixte, who did not like the way people were laughing and talking, and constantly going up to the door of the boudoir, came in, looking distinctly annoyed; he found Lucien and Louise talking excitedly.

"You know Angoulême better than I do," Sixte whispered to his wife; "ought you not to think of your position as the Prefect's wife, and of the Government?"

"My dear," said Louise, scanning her lord and master with a look of haughtiness that made him tremble. "I was just talking with M. de Rubempré about a matter that concerns you. It is a question of rescuing an inventor who is about to become the victim of intrigues of the basest kind, and you can help us. As to the opinion these ladies may hold of me, you shall see how I shall freeze the venom of their tongues."

She came out of the boudoir, leaning on Lucien's arm, and led him with her to sign the contract, parading him with all the audacity of a great lady.

"We will sign it together," she said, handing the pen to Lucien.

Lucien signed his name obediently below hers, in the place she indicated, so that their signatures appeared together.

" M. de Senonches, would you have recognised M. de Rubempré ? " said the Countess, forcing that insolent sportsman to greet Lucien.

She led Lucien back into the drawing-room and made him sit between herself and Zéphirine on the redoubtable sofa in the middle of the room. Then, like a queen enthroned, she began, in a low voice at first, a conversation, evidently full of epigrams, in which some of her old friends, and various ladies who were paying court to her, gradually joined. Lucien soon became the hero of a little circle, and the Countess drew him out on the subject of Paris life ; he talked on, with incisive wit and dazzling brilliance, interspersing his talk with amusing stories about well-known people—the kind of conversational luxury that people long for in the provinces. They admired his wit as much as they had admired his good looks. And Countess Sixte du Châtelet meekly smoothed the way for his triumph ; she played the part of a woman delighted with her instrument ; she gave him openings for repartee, she looked round the circle, inviting approbation for him with looks so compromising that some of the ladies present begant to suspect that there was something more than coincidence in the simultaneous return of Louise and Lucien, and that two devoted lovers had been divided by some double misunderstanding. Perhaps she had made an unfortunate marriage with Châtelet out of pique ; there was a general reaction against the Prefect.

At one o'clock in the morning Louise got ready to leave. " Well," she said in a low voice to Lucien, " I shall expect you the day after tomorrow—come early."

She left Lucien with the friendliest little nod and went over to say a few words to Sixte, who was looking for his hat.

" If what Mme du Châtelet has just told me is true, my dear Lucien, you may count on me," said the Prefect, as he hurried after his wife, who was leaving without him, as in Paris. " Your brother-in-law may consider that his troubles are at an end."

" You owe me that much," said Lucien with a smile.

Cointet and Petit-Claud heard these parting speeches.

"Well, now we are done for!" Cointet remarked to his companion.

Petit-Claud was thunderstruck by Lucien's success, dumbfounded by the brilliance of his wit and the display of his charm. He looked at Françoise de la Haye, in whose face admiration for Lucien was plainly written, and her expression, as she looked at her fiancé, seemed to say, "Be like your friend!"

A gleam of hope passed across Petit-Claud's face.

"The Prefect's dinner-party is not until the day after tomorrow—we have still a whole day in front of us. I will answer for everything."

At two in the morning Lucien and Petit-Claud walked home together.

"Well, old boy, *I came, I saw, I conquered!* Séchard will be very happy in a few hours' time!"

"That is all I wanted to know!" Petit-Claud thought to himself. Aloud he said, "I thought you were only a poet, but you are a Lauzum as well—a poet twice over." He shook hands with Lucien—for the last time, as it proved.

"I have good news, dear Eve!" said Lucien, who went in to wake his sister. "David will be clear of his debts in a month!"

"How so?"

"Well, Mme du Châtelet is still my Louise of old days; she loves me more than ever, and she is going to get her husband to send in a report to the Minister of the Interior about our discovery! So our sufferings will be over in less than a month—during which time I shall take my revenge on the Prefect and make him the happiest of men."

Eve thought she must still be dreaming.

"When I saw the little grey drawing-room again, where I trembled like a child two years ago, and looking at the furniture and the pictures and the faces, scales seemed to fall from my eyes! How Paris changes one's ideas!"

"Is that a good thing?" Eve asked, understanding her brother at last.

"You are half asleep—we will talk about it after breakfast," said Lucien.

Cérizet's plan was exceedingly simple. Although it is a well-known dodge among provincial bailiffs, its success depends upon circumstances. In this case it was bound to succeed, because it was built upon a knowledge of the characters of Lucien, and David, and of their hopes. Cérizet, while he was still a supernumerary foreman at the Cointets, was, besides, a Don Juan among the work-girls of the town, whom he played off one against the other. At that time he had become involved with one of Basine Clerget's work-girls, a girl called Henriette Signol, almost as pretty as Mme Séchard, whose parents owned a small vineyard a few miles outside Angoulême, in the direction of Saintes. The Signols, like other country people, were too poor to keep their only daughter at home, and so they planned that she should go into service as a housemaid. In the country a housemaid must know how to wash and iron fine linen. Such was the reputation of Mme Prieur, Basine's predecessor, that the Signols had sent their daughter there as an apprentice and paid for her board and lodging.

Mme Prieur had been one of those old-fashioned mistresses that one finds in the country, who look upon themselves as filling a parent's place. She treated her apprentices like a family, took them to church with her, and kept careful watch over them. Henriette Signol was a dark, fine-looking girl with a bold eye, long thick black hair, and the pale complexion of the South, a skin white as a magnolia flower. So that Henriette was one of the first on whom Cérizet cast his eye; but as she came of respectable farming stock, she only finally yielded when she had been undermined by jealousy, bad example, and by those deceptive words, "I will marry you." Cérizet was by then second foreman at the Cointets. When he discovered that the Signols owned a vineyard worth ten or twelve thousand francs, and a very comfortable cottage, he lost no time in making it impossible for Henriette to marry anybody else.

This was how things stood between pretty Henriette and little Cérizet when Petit-Claud had broached to him the possibility of being in charge of Séchard's printing business, and the loan of twenty-thousand francs, that was to give the Liberals a hold over him. This prospect quite dazzled the Cointets' foreman and turned his head ; Mlle Signol was now only an obstacle to his ambitions, and he neglected the poor girl. Henriette, in despair now that he was trying to shake her off, clung all the more desperately to the Cointets' foreman. When he discovered that David was hidden in Mlle Clerget's house, Cérizet changed his plans with regard to Henriette, but not his conduct, for he proposed to take advantage of the madness that works in a girl's mind when she must marry her seducer in order to conceal her dishonour.

On the morning of the day on which Lucien was to reconquer his Louise, Cérizet confided Basine's secret to Henriette, and told her that their marriage and their future depended upon the discovery of David's hiding-place. Thus instructed, Henriette quickly realised that the only place where the printer could be hidden was in Mlle Clerget's dressing-room ; she thought no harm in acting as a spy in this way, but Cérizet, by this first step, had already implicated her in the guilty betrayal.

Lucien was still asleep as Cérizet, who had gone to Petit-Claud's office to hear the results of the previous evening, listened to the story of the insignificant yet significant events which were soon to be the talk of Angoulême.

Cérizet gave a nod of satisfaction as Petit-Claud came to an end. " Has Lucien written you any little note since he has been back ? " he asked.

" This is the only one I have," said the lawyer, handing him a short note from Lucien on a sheet of his sister's notepaper.

" All right," said Cérizet, " ten minutes before sunset let Doublon set a watch at the Porte Palet, post his gendarmes, and have his assistants ready, and you shall have your man."

" Are you sure of *your* side of the business ? " Petit-Claud asked, scrutinising Cérizet.

" I am trusting to luck," said the Paris guttersnipe, " but luck is a funny business—it doesn't come to honest folk."

" We have got to succeed," said the lawyer sharply.

"I will succeed all right," said Cérizet. " It's you who have pushed me into this dirty business ; you might at least let me have a few banknotes, to clean off some of the mud. And if you think you can double-cross me, sir," he added, seeing an expression that he did not like on the lawyer's face, " if you have not bought the printing office for me within a week—well, you will leave a young widow," the foreman concluded, in a low voice, with an ugly look at the lawyer.

" If we have David under lock and key by six o'clock, come round to M. Gannerac's at nine, and we will settle your affair," answered the lawyer dryly.

" Very good ; at your service, governor! " said Cérizet.

Cérizet had already mastered the art of washing paper, that has since proved such a danger to the Treasury. He washed out the four lines that Lucien had written, and replaced them by the following, written in an imitation of Lucien's hand, whose perfection boded ill for the foreman's future :

" My dear David,

" You can come to see the Prefect without any fear ; your affair is settled ; and what is more, you can come at once. I shall be waiting for you to tell you what you had better say to the Prefect.

Your friend,

Lucien."

At noon, Lucien wrote to David, telling him of his success of the previous evening, and assuring him that the Prefect would use his influence on his behalf—he was writing to the Ministry about the discovery that very day, he was so enthusiastic about it. Petit-Claud had warned Cérizet that there probably would be such a letter ; and so the foreman had called for Mlle Signol and taken her for a walk beside the Charente. Henriette's integrity must have held out for a long time, for the walk lasted for two hours. Not only was the interest of a child at stake, but a whole future of happiness, a fortune; and what Cérizet asked her to do was a mere nothing—for he took good care not to say what the consequences would be. It was the greatness of the reward for such a trifle that alarmed Henriette. But in the end Cérizet succeeded in making his mistress consent to help him in his stratagem. At five o'clock Henriette was to go out, come back, and tell Mlle Clerget that Mme Séchard wanted to see her at once. Then, a quarter of an hour after Basine had left, she was to go upstairs, knock at the door of the dressing-room, and give David the forged letter from Lucien. That done, Cérizet was relying entirely on chance.

For the first time for over a year Eve felt that the iron grip of necessity had relaxed a little. At last she had begun to hope. She, too, wanted to enjoy her brother's visit, and to be seen walking with a young man fêted by his native town, the idol of the women, and loved by the proud Countess du Châtelet. She dressed herself in her best clothes, and suggested a walk in Beaulieu after dinner. At that time, in September, everyone in Angoulême goes out to enjoy the evening air.

" Look there is pretty Mme Séchard," several people remarked, when they saw Eve.

" I should never have thought it of her! " said one woman.

" The husband hides, the wife shows herself off," said Mme Postel, loud enough for poor Eve to hear.

" Oh! we must go home—I did wrong to come," Eve said to her brother.

A few minutes before sunset, the sound of a crowd rose from the steps that lead down to l'Houmeau. Curiosity drew Lucien and his sister towards the steps, for they heard several people coming from the direction of l'Houmeau talking to one another as if some crime had been committed.

" It's probably a thief that they have just arrested. . . . He looks as pale as death," a passer-by told Eve and Lucien, as they hurried towards the growing crowd.

Neither Lucien nor his sister had the slightest misgivings. They saw some thirty children and old women and workmen going home from work, walking in front of the gendarmes whose embroidered hats were conspicuous in the centre of the crowd. About a hundred people followed behind, in procession, like a gathering thunder-cloud.

" Oh! " cried Eve. "It is my husband! "

" David! " Lucien exclaimed.

" It is his wife! "—the rumour spread, and people made way.

"What induced you to come out?" Lucien asked.

"Your letter," said David, white and haggard.

"I knew it!" said Eve, and fell in a dead faint.

Lucien lifted up his sister and, with the help of two strangers, carried her home, and Marion put her to bed. Kolb hurried off to fetch a doctor.

Eve was still unconscious when the doctor arrived, and Lucien had to admit to his mother that he was to blame for David's arrest; for he had no idea that a misunderstanding had been produced by the forged letter. Lucien, struck dumb by a look from his mother, fraught with malediction, went upstairs to his room and shut himself in.

In the middle of the night he wrote one last letter; again and again he broke off, and began again, and from the disjointed sentences that he wrote, one by one, disconnectedly, the reader can guess at Lucien's agony of mind as he wrote:

"My dearly loved sister,

"We have looked upon one another for the last time. My resolution is final. The reason is this. In many families there is a member who carries with him a fatal ill-luck—he is a sort of disease. That is what I am for you. This is not something that I have thought of myself, but the observation of a man who has seen a great deal of the world. I was dining with some friends one evening at the Rocher de Cancale, and among all the brilliant nonsense that was being talked, this diplomat suddenly said that a certain young lady who, to everybody's surprise, persistently remained unmarried was 'suffering from her father'. And he went on to expand his theory on the maladies of the family. He explained to us how, but for a certain mother, a certain household would have prospered, how in one case a son had ruined his father, in another how a father had destroyed the future and the social status of his children. Although it was all said in joke, this social theory was applied to so many examples in ten minutes that I was deeply struck by it. It was a truth worth something more than the usual witty paradoxes, cleverly sustained, that journalists bandy about among themselves, when there is nobody else there to mystify. Well, I am the fatal member of our family. With my heart full of love for you, I have injured you like an enemy. For all your devotion, I have rewarded you with injuries. Although it was quite involuntary, the last blow has been the cruellest of all.

" While I was in Paris, living a life devoid of all dignity, a life of pleasures and miseries, mistaking social acquaintances for friends, deserting my real friends for people who only wanted to exploit me —and did—forgetting you, and only remembering you in order to bring trouble upon you—you were living here, following the humble path of hard work, proceeding laboriously but surely to win that fortune that I so foolishly attempted to take by storm. While you became better people, I allowed a deadly poison to infect my life. Yes, I have boundless ambitions that will not allow me to accept an obscure life. I have tastes, and remembrances of past pleasures whose memory poisons for me the happiness that is within my reach, and that would once have satisfied me. Oh, my dearest Eve, no one could judge me more severely than I judge myself, because I condemn myself absolutely and without any mercy. The struggle in Paris needs a steady effort, and my will-power only operates by fits and starts, my brain works intermittently. The future is so appalling to me that I cannot bear to face it, and the present I cannot endure.

" I wanted to see you again ; but it would have been better if I had stayed in exile for ever. But exile, without any means of support, would be madness ; and I shall not add it to all the rest. Death is better than an incomplete life ; and I can imagine no situation in which my excessive vanity would not lead me into some sort of folly.

" Some beings are zeros, they need a figure to precede them, and then their negative existence gains a tenfold value. I could only have acquired any value if I had been married to a woman with a strong will, with no weakness in her character. Mme de Bargeton would have been the right wife for me—I ruined my life when I refused to leave Coralie for her. David and you might have steered me admirably ; but you are not strong enough to manage my weakness, which always tries to escape from domination. I like an easy life, with no troubles; and in order to get out of a difficulty I would stoop to almost anything. I am a born prince.

"I have more than enough talent to succeed, but it only functions spasmodically, and the prizes in a career overcrowded by so many ambitious competitors go to those who know how to conserve their strength and still have some reserves left at the end of the day. With the best intentions in the world I shall always do the wrong thing—as I have done here. Some men are like oaks, and at most I am an elegant shrub—and I aspire to be a cedar! That is the plain truth. There is an utter disproportion between my capacities and my desires, and that want of equilibrium will annul all my efforts. There are plenty of others like me in the literary world who lack the necessary balance between intellect and character, or whose will is disproportionate to their desires. What will become of me? I can see in advance what it will be, when I think of more than one brilliant Paris reputation that I have seen forgotten. On the threshold of old age, I shall be prematurely old, without position or reputation. My whole being revolts against such an old age as that—I will not live to be a social rag.

"My darling sister, whom I love as much for your recent severities as for your old affection, even though we have paid dearly for the pleasure I had in seeing you again, you and David, someday perhaps you will think that no price was too high for the last happy moments of a poor soul who loved you! Do not try to find out anything either about myself, or my fate—at least my intelligence will have served me sufficiently well to enable me to do what I want to do. Resignation, my angel, is a daily suicide; but I have only resignation enough to serve me for one day, and I am going to make use of it today. . . .

"Two o'clock.

"Yes, I have made up my mind. Goodbye, then, for always, my dearest Eve. There is some consolation in the thought that I shall continue to live only in your hearts. There shall be my grave, and I would have no other. Again, goodbye! That is the last word of your brother,

"Lucien."

Lucien crept downstairs without making any noise and left the letter in his nephew's cradle. He printed a kiss on the brow of his sleeping sister, a last kiss, mingled with tears, and left the house. He put out his candle in the morning dusk, and, looking for the last time at the old house, he opened the door at the end of the passage softly. But in spite of his precautions, he woke Kolb, who was sleeping on a mattress on the floor of the workshop.

" Who goes dere ? " Kolb exclaimed.

" It is Lucien. I am going away, Kolb."

" You vould haf done better if you had nefer kom," Kolb muttered to himself, but loud enough for Lucien to hear.

" I would have done better never to have come into the world," Lucien replied. " Goodbye, Kolb ; I bear you no grudge for thinking as I do myself. Tell David that my last thought was regret that I could not say goodbye to him."

By the time the Alsatian was up and dressed, Lucien had closed the house door and was on his way down to the Charente. He went by Beaulieu, and he might have been going to a party, for he had put on his Paris clothes and all his dandy's trappings, to be his winding-sheet. Kolb had been struck by something in Lucien's tone of voice, and he was anxious to know whether his mistress knew that her brother was leaving, and whether he had said goodbye to her ; but when he found that the whole house was quiet, he decided that Lucien's departure must have been arranged beforehand, so he went back to bed again.

When we consider the seriousness of the question, it is surprising that so little has been written about suicide, and that so little attention has been paid to it. Perhaps this malady cannot be observed. Suicide is the result of a sentiment that we may call *self-esteem*, not to be confused with the concept of *honour*. On the day when a man despises himself, and feels himself despised, when he sees that the reality of his life bears no relation to his hopes, he takes his life, and in so doing pays homage to society ; for he is unwilling to appear before the world, stripped of his virtues, or his glory. For the Christian there can be no question of suicide, but whatever may be said to the contrary, among atheists only the cowardly can consent to live a dishonoured life.

There are three kinds of suicide : the first is only the final stage of a long illness and belongs unquestionably to the sphere of pathology ; the second is the suicide of despair ; and the third is suicide based on a process of reasoning. Lucien wanted to kill himself both from despair, and on rational grounds,—both of which motives still permit a man to change his mind ; for the only irrevocable suicide is the pathological kind. But very often the three causes all act in combination, as with Jean-Jacques Rousseau.

His resolution once taken, Lucien fell to considering ways and means ; for the poet wanted to die a poetic death. At first he had thought of simply going and throwing himself into the Charente ; but as he descended the steps from Beaulieu for the last time, he heard in advance the talk there would be about his suicide, he saw the horrible spectacle of his own dead body dragged up from the water, deformed, the object of an inquest ; like some other suicides, he felt a posthumous self-respect.

On the day he had gone to the Courtois' mill he had walked along the river, and had particularly noticed, not far from the mill, one of those round pools that are often seen in small streams, a pool whose smooth surface conceals great depths beneath. The water is neither green, nor blue, neither clear, nor turbid ; it is like a mirror of polished steel ; no flag-irises, or blue forget-me-nots, fringe its banks, nor the broad leaves of the water-lily. The grass on its margin is short and close, and the weeping willows that droop over its brim all grow picturesquely enough. It is easy to divine there a precipice filled with water. Any man with the courage to fill his pockets with stones would find there certain death and never be seen thereafter.

" There," the poet had thought, as he admired the beauty of that scene, " is a spot to make one long to drown."

This memory flashed into his mind just as he reached l'Houmeau; so, the prey of his last sombre thoughts, he firmly resolved to conceal, in this way, the secret of his death, not to be the object of an inquest, not to be buried, not to be seen in the loathsome condition in which the bodies of the drowned float up to the surface of the water. Soon, as he walked on, he came to one of those steep hills that one finds so often on French roads, and especially between Angoulême and Poitiers. The stage-coach from Bordeaux to Paris was overtaking him rapidly, and the passengers would no doubt have to get out and walk up the long hill. Lucien did not want to be seen, and so he turned off into a lane and began to pick flowers in a vineyard. When he returned to the main road, he was carrying in his hand a big bunch of the yellow stonecrop that grows in the stony soil of vineyards; and he came out into the road just behind a traveller dressed all in black, with powdered hair, shoes of Orleans leather with silver buckles, a dark complexion, and scars on his face as if he had fallen into the fire when a child. This traveller, so evidently clerical, was walking slowly, and smoking a cigar. When he heard Lucien, who jumped down from the vineyard on to the road, and seemed to be struck by the deeply melancholy beauty of the poet, his symbolic flowers, and his elegant dress. His expression was that of a hunter who has sighted his quarry at last after a long and fruitless search. He allowed Lucien to catch up with him, slowing his walk, and turning to look down to the bottom of the hill. Lucien followed his glance, and there he saw a small carriage with two horses, and a postillion walking beside it.

"You have allowed the stage-coach to pass you, sir; you will lose your seat unless you would care to get into my carriage until we overtake it, for it is quicker travelling post than by stage-coach," said the traveller to Lucien, speaking with a very marked Spanish accent, and making his offer with extreme politeness.

Without waiting for a reply, the Spaniard drew a cigar-case from his pocket, opened it, and offered it to Lucien.

"I am not travelling," said Lucien, "and I am too near the end of my journey to enjoy the pleasure of smoking."

"You are very severe with yourself," returned the Spaniard. "I myself am an Honorary Canon of the Cathedral of Toledo, but I allow myself a small cigar from time to time. God gave us tobacco to dull our passions and our pains. . . . You seem distressed—at all events, you carry the emblem of sorrow in your hand, like the

His expression was that of a hunter who has sighted his quarry at last

mournful god Hymen. Take one—your troubles will vanish with the smoke."

The priest held out his straw case ; there was something seductive in his manner, and his features were lit up with kindness as he looked at Lucien.

" You must excuse me, Father," Lucien retorted curtly. " No cigars in the world can dispel my troubles." Tears dimmed the poet's eyes as he spoke.

" Then perhaps it was Divine Providence, young man, that prompted me to take a little exercise to shake off the drowsiness that overcomes travellers in the morning—so that, by consoling you, I can fulfil my mission here on earth ? But what great troubles can you have at your age ? "

" Your consolations can do nothing to help me, Father ; you are Spanish, I am French ; you believe the teachings of the Church ; I am an atheist."

" *Santa Virgen del Pilar!* You are an atheist ! " cried the priest, putting his arm through Lucien's with maternal solicitude. " And so you are one of those curiosities that I promised myself to see in Paris. In Spain we do not believe in atheists. France is the only country in which one can have such opinions, at nineteen."

" Oh, I assure you I am a perfect atheist—I believe neither in God, nor in society, nor in happiness. Look at me well, Father, because in a few hours I shall no longer exist. This is my last sunrise ! " said Lucien, somewhat dramatically, pointing to the sky.

" Is that so ! And what have you done that you must die ? Who has condemned you to die ? "

" A judge against whom there is no appeal : myself ! "

" What a child ! " exclaimed the priest. " Have you killed a man ? Is the scaffold waiting for you ? Let us talk about it a little. If you wish to return, as you say, into nothingness, everything on earth is indifferent to you, then ? "

Lucien inclined his head in assent.

" Very well, perhaps you can tell me about your troubles ? Some little love-affair has gone badly, no doubt ? "

Lucien shrugged his shoulders significantly.

" Do you want to kill yourself to escape dishonour, or because you despair of life? Very well, you can kill yourself just as well at Poitiers as at Angoulême, or at Tours just as well as at Poitiers. The shifting sands of the Loire never give up their prey."

" No, Father," said Lucien, " I have made up my mind. Three weeks ago I saw the most charming road that ever led a man utterly weary of this world into another."

" Another world ? Then you are not an atheist."

" Oh, when I say another world, I mean my future transformation into animal or plant."

" Have you some incurable disease ? "

" Yes, Father."

" Ah! So that is it," said the priest, " and what is it ? "

" Poverty."

The priest looked at Lucien. " The diamond does not know its own value." There was an inexpressible charm, something almost like irony in his smile as he spoke.

" Only a priest could flatter a poor man about to die," Lucien exclaimed.

"You are not going to die!" said the Spaniard in a tone of authority.

" I have often heard of men being robbed on the road," said Lucien, " but I have never heard of anyone becoming rich there."

" You shall hear of one now," said the priest, glancing towards the carriage, to see how far they still had to walk alone together. " Listen to me," he said, biting the end of his cigar. " Your poverty is no reason for dying. I need a secretary—mine died in Barcelona. I find myself in the same position as the famous Baron de Göertz, Charles XII's Minister, who arrived in a little town on his way to Sweden, as I am now on my way to Paris, without a secretary. There the Baron met the son of a goldsmith, a remarkably beautiful youth—but not more beautiful than you are. Baron de Göertz recognised him as a young man of great intelligence—just as I see poetry written on your brow ; he took him into his carriage, just as I am going to take you into mine ; and that boy, destined to spend his days burnishing cutlery, and making jewellery, in a little provincial town much like Angoulême, became his favourite, as you are going to be mine.

" When he reached Stockholm, he installed his secretary and overwhelmed him with work. The young secretary spent whole nights in writing, and, like all great workers, he contracted a habit—he began to chew paper. The late M. de Malesherbes used to blow smoke-rings—and once, by the way, he did this in the face of some important personage, I forget who it was, on whose favourable report the case depended. Well, our handsome young man began with blank paper, but as the habit gained a hold on him, he went on to manuscripts, which had more flavour. Smoking had not come into fashion in those days, as it has now. And so the little secretary proceeded, by degrees, to chewing and eating parchments.

" Now they were engaged at that time on the treaty between Russia and Sweden that his Parliament imposed on Charles XII, just as the States-General tried to force Napoleon to sue for peace in 1814. The basis of the negotiations was the treaty that had been made between these two nations on the Finnish question. Göertz entrusted the original to his secretary ; but when the time came for submitting the draft to Parliament, a small difficulty arose—the treaty could not be found. Parliament imagined that the Minister, to serve the passions of the King, had hit upon the idea of losing this document ; Baron de Göertz was accused, and his secretary then confessed that he had eaten the manuscript. He was tried, found guilty, and condemned to death—which has not yet happened to you, so take a cigar and smoke it while we are waiting for our carriage."

Lucien took the cigar and lit it, in the Spanish fashion, from that of the priest. " He is right," Lucien thought ; " there is plenty of time to kill myself."

" It often happens," the Spaniard continued, " that it is at the very moment when a young man has touched the depths of despair of his future, that his fortunes begin to improve. That is what I wanted to say to you, but I preferred to prove it by an example. This handsome secretary, under sentence of death, was in a seemingly desperate situation, for since the sentence had been passed on him by the Swedish Parliament, the King could not give him a pardon. But he shut his eyes to an escape. The pretty little secretary escaped in a ship, with a few gold pieces in his pocket, and came to the court of Courland, armed with a letter of recommendation to the Duke from Göertz, who explained the situation and his protégé's unfortunate habit. The Duke made this handsome child secretary to his steward. The Duke was a spendthrift, he had a pretty wife, and he had a steward—three causes of ruin ! If you imagine that this handsome young man, condemned to death for eating a Finnish treaty, had been cured of his depraved taste, you know nothing of the hold that a bad habit has over a man. The fear of death itself will not stop a man from indulging in some pleasures of his own invention. How is it that a depraved habit has this power? Is it the innate power of vice, or is it the weakness of human nature ? Are there certain practices that should be regarded as verging on insanity ? I myself cannot help laughing at moralists who think that one can combat such perversions with fine phrases ! Well, in course of time, the steward refused the Duke when he asked for money, and the Duke asked to see the accounts—a pure piece of folly! Nothing in the world is easier than to write out a balance sheet—the trouble never lies there! The steward gave the secretary all the documents necessary for compiling a civil list of Courland. He had nearly finished it, when, late at night, our little paper-eater suddenly realised that he was chewing up a receipt from the Duke for a considerable sum. Horrified, he put down his pen in the middle of the word he was writing, fled to the Duchess, threw himself at her feet, told her of his strange habit, and implored her sovereign protection—and implored it in the middle of the night! The young clerk's beauty made such an impression on the lady that she married him when she was left a widow. And so, in the middle of the eighteenth century, and in a country where a coat-of-arms means so much, the son of a goldsmith became a sovereign prince! He became more than that—he became regent after the death of Catherine I ; he ruled the Empress Anne, and tried to be the Richelieu of Russia. Very well, young man, be sure of one thing : you may be handsomer than Biron ; but I, although I am only a simple canon, am worth more than Baron de Göertz. So get in! We will find you a Duchy of Courland in Paris, and, if not a Duchy, at least a Duchess! "

The Spaniard took Lucien's arm, and literally forced him to get into the carriage, and the postillion shut the door.

" Now tell me everything—I am listening," said the Canon of Toledo, to Lucien's utter bewilderment. " I am an old priest, and you can tell me everything, without danger. I don't suppose you have done anything worse than squandering your patrimony, or spending all your mother's money. We are running away from our creditors, no doubt, and we are the soul of honour down to the tips of our exquisite little boots. Come now, confess boldly—it will be exactly as if you were talking to yourself."

Lucien felt like the fisherman in the *Arabian Nights* who, when he tried to drown himself in mid-ocean, sank down into a country under the sea and there became a king. The Spanish priest seemed so really affectionate that the poet did not hesitate to open his heart to him ; and so, between Angoulême and Ruffec, he told the story of his whole life, extenuating none of his faults, and concluding with the disaster that he had just caused. Just as he came to the end of the story—which lost nothing in poetic effect for being told for the third time during the past fortnight—they reached the stretch of road, just outside Ruffec, that passes through the Rastignacs' estate. When Lucien had mentioned Rastignac for the first time, in his story, the priest had started at the name.

" That is the house that young Rastignac came from—he is certainly not my equal, but he has been luckier than I."

" Ah! "

" Yes, that quaint little family seat belongs to his father. He, as I told you, is now Mme de Nucingen's lover—the wife of the famous banker. I let myself drift into poetry. He was cleverer, and more practical."

The priest stopped the carriage, and, from curiosity, walked down the little avenue that led from the road to the house. He looked at everything with rather more interest than Lucien would have expected from a Spanish priest.

" Do you know the Rastignacs, then ? " Lucien asked him.

"That quaint little family seat belongs to his father"

" I know everyone in Paris," said the Spaniard, as he got back into the carriage. " And so, for want of ten or twelve thousand francs, you were going to kill yourself! You are a child, you know nothing either of men or things. A destiny is worth whatever value a man likes to set upon it—and you only valued yours at twelve thousand francs ! Very well, I will buy it from you, presently, for more than that. As for your brother-in-law's imprisonment, it is a trifle. If the worthy M. Séchard has made a discovery he will be a rich man. Rich men have never been sent to prison for debts. You do not seem to be very strong in history. There are two kinds of history —the official kind, full of lies, which is taught in schools—history *ad usum delphini* ; and then there is secret history—in which we learn the real causes of events—a shameful chronicle. Allow me to tell you, in three words, another little story that you have not heard. A certain ambitious young priest wanted to enter politics, and so he fawned on a favourite—a queen's favourite ; the favourite took an interest in this young priest, and obtained a place for him as a Minister with a seat in Council. One evening one of those people who think they are doing a kindness (never do kindnesses without being asked!) wrote and told this ambitious young man that the life of his benefactor was in danger. The King had become extremely angry at having a rival, and the next day, the favourite would be killed if he went to the palace. Well, young man, what would you have done if you had received that letter ? "

" I would have gone at once to warn my benefactor! " Lucien exclaimed without hesitation.

" You are even more of a child than I had already concluded from the story of your life," said the priest. " No, our man said to himself: ' If the King is prepared to go to the length of committing a crime, my benefactor is as good as dead ; I must have received this letter too late! ' —and he went to sleep, until the favourite was stabbed."

" He was a monster! " said Lucien, who suspected that the priest was trying to sound him.

" All great men are monsters ; this one was Cardinal de Richelieu," the Canon retorted, " and his benefactor was Marshal d'Ancre. You see, you don't know your French history. Am I not right in saying to you that the history taught in schools is a collection of dates and events—exceedingly doubtful, at that—without the least relevance? What good does it do you to know that such a person as Joan of Arc existed? Have you ever gone on to consider that if France had accepted the Angevin dynasty of the Plantaganets at that time, the two nations that would have been thus united would have been ruling the world today, and that the two islands that brew most of the troubles of the continent would have been two French provinces? And have you studied the means by which the Medicis, simple merchants, became Grand Dukes of Tuscany?"

"A poet in France is not bound to be as learned as a Benedictine," said Lucien.

"Well, they became Grand Dukes in the same way as Richelieu became a Minister. If you had studied history in order to discover the human causes of events, instead of learning lists by heart, you would have found precepts for the conduct of your life. I have just taken a few examples, at random, from the existing facts, and from these you may deduce this rule: Never regard men, still less women, otherwise than as instruments; but don't let them see it. Adore the man who is more highly placed than you are, and who is in a position to help you, as if he were God himself, and do not leave him until you have made him pay a high price for your servility. In your dealings with the world, in fact, be as grasping as a Jew, and as unscrupulous: do for power what the Jew does for money. But when a man has fallen from power, give him no more thought than if he had never existed. Do you know why you must do these things? You want to rule the world, do you not? Then you must begin by serving the world, and studying it well. Scholars study books, but politicians study men, their interests, and the causes from which their actions spring. Now, the world—society—mankind taken as a whole—is fatalistic; the world adores the accomplished fact. Do you know why I am giving you this little history lesson? It is because I suspect that your ambition is boundless."

"Yes, Father."

"I could see that for myself," the Canon continued; "but at this moment, you are thinking, 'This Spanish Canon is inventing anecdotes and quoting history to prove to me that I have been too virtuous.' "

Lucien could not help smiling, for the Canon had read his thoughts correctly.

" Very well, young man, let us take facts that are matters of common knowledge," said the priest. " One day, France was almost conquered by the English ; the King had only one Province left. From among the people, two figures arose—that same Joan of Arc of whom we have just been speaking ; and a burgher called Jacques Coeur. One brought the strength of her arm and the prestige of her virginity ; and the other gave his gold. The kingdom was saved ; but the young girl was taken prisoner. The King could have ransomed her, but he allowed her to be burned ; and as for the heroic burgher, the King allowed his courtiers to accuse him of capital crimes and divide his goods among themselves. The spoils of an innocent man, hunted down, brought to bay, and ruined by the law, went to enrich five noble families ; and the father of the Archbishop of Bourges went into exile, never to return, without a penny of all his wealth in France, without any resources except money that he had remitted to Arabs and Saracens, in Egypt. Of course, you can still say that these examples are very old ; that three centuries of public education have elapsed since these instances of ingratitude ; or that the skeletons of that time are mere fables. Very well, young man, do you believe in France's latest demigod, Napoleon? He kept one of his generals in lifelong disgrace, and only very reluctantly made him a marshal ; never, if he could avoid it, did he make use of his services—I am speaking of Marshal Kellermann. Do you know why ? Kellermann had saved France, and the First Consul at Marengo, in a brilliant charge, applauded by the troops in the face of fire and slaughter. There was not even a mention of that heroic charge in the despatches. The reason for Napoleon's coldness towards Kellermann is the same as that of Fouché's disgrace, and that of Talleyrand ; the one was the ingratitude of Charles VII, the other the ingratitude of Richelieu—ingratitude."

"But, Father, supposing that you save my life and make my

fortune," said Lucien, " You are making it very easy for me to be ungrateful."

" Little rogue," said the Canon, smiling and pinching Lucien's ear with almost royal familiarity. " If you are ungrateful to me, it will be because you are a strong man, and I shall bend before you; but you are not that yet, because, simple schoolboy that you are, you have wanted to be the master too soon. It is the great fault of Frenchmen of your generation. You have all been spoiled by the example of Napoleon. You hand in your resignation because you have not managed to win the epaulettes you had set your heart on. But have you ever attempted to concentrate all your will, all your actions, upon a single idea? "

" No, alas! " said Lucien.

" You have been what the English call *inconsistent*," said the Canon, smiling.

" What does it matter what I have been, if I can no longer be anything! " Lucien replied.

" Behind all your good qualities there must be a force *semper virens*," said the priest, anxious to show that he knew a little Latin, " and then nothing in the world will be able to resist you. I am fond enough of you already. . . . "

Lucien smiled incredulously.

" Yes," replied the stranger, responding to Lucien's smile, " I feel for you as if you were my own son, and I am powerful enough to be able to afford to speak to you openly, as you have just been speaking to me. Do you know what it is that I like about you? You have made of yourself a sort of *tabula rasa* and so you can listen to a discourse on morality that you will hear nowhere else; because men, in the mass, are even more hypocritical than they are when self-interest makes some piece of dissimulation necessary. And so we pass a good part of our lives in ridding our minds of the notions that have grown up there during our adolescence. That operation is known as *acquiring experience*."

Lucien, as he listened to the priest, said to himself:

" This is some old diplomat, pleased to have the chance of amusing himself on his journey. It amuses him to make a poor boy on the point of suicide change his mind, and he will leave when he is tired of the joke. But he understands paradox ; he seems quite up to the standard of Blondet or Lousteau."

In spite of this sage reflection, however, the corruption that the diplomat was attempting had entered deeply into that impressionable mind, and the havoc was all the greater, because the Spaniard built up his case on such illustrious examples. Captivated by the charm of this cynical discourse, Lucien clung the more willingly to life, because he felt that the arm that was drawing him up from his suicidal depths was a strong one.

In this respect the priest evidently was winning. And from time to time a malicious smile accompanied his historical sarcasms.

" If you deal with moral questions in the same way as you envisage history," said Lucien, " I would very much like to know the motive of your present apparent charity."

" That, young man, shall be the last point of my sermon ; and you must permit me to reserve it, because then we shall not part company today," he said, with the finesse of a priest who sees that his trick has succeeded.

" Very well, talk morality," said Lucien. " I will draw him out," he thought to himself.

" Morality, young man, begins with the law," said the priest. " If it were a question only of religion laws would be superfluous ; religious races have few laws. The laws of politics are above the civil law. Very well, would you like to know what a politician may read on the brow of our nineteenth century ? The French in 1793 invented the idea of popular sovereignty, and it ended in the absolute rule of an Emperor. So much for your national history. As to private morals—Mme Tallien and Mme de Beauharnais both acted in the same way. Napoleon married the one and made her your Empress, but the other he would not even receive, although she was a princess. Napoleon was a sans-culotte in 1793, and donned the iron crown in 1804. The fierce fanatics of Equality or Death in 1792, in 1806 conspired with the Legitimist aristocracy for the restoration of Louis XVIII. And that same aristocracy, the men who today hold their heads so high in the Faubourg Saint-Germain, did worse abroad—they became usurers, and shopkeepers, pastry-cooks, farm-hands, shepherds. So that in France, in politics, and in morals alike we see that every one, without exception, has ended in a position that is a denial of their first principles; their conduct has been a betrayal of their beliefs, or *vice versa*. There has been no logical consistency either in government or in the conduct of individual lives. In fact, you no longer have any morality. In France today success is the supreme justification of any action whatsoever. The act is nothing in itself; all that matters is what other people think about it. And that, young man, brings us to our second precept—have a fair exterior! Conceal the shady side of your life, and present a brilliant façade to the world! Discretion must be the guiding principle of any ambitious man—it is that of our Order, let it be yours! The great commit almost as many shameful acts as the outcasts of society, but they commit them in the dark, and make a parade of their virtues—and so they remain great! The little men hide their virtues, and expose their miseries for all to see—and so they are despised. You have hidden your greatness, and exposed your sores. You went about openly with an actress, you lived with her, under her roof; you were not in any way blameworthy, anyone would admit that you were both perfectly at liberty to do as you pleased; but you acted in defiance of the social conventions, and therefore you were not accorded the respect that society reserves for those who obey its code. If you had left Coralie with her M. Camusot, if you had kept your relations with her secret, you might have married Mme de Bargeton, and you would have been Prefect of Angoulême and Marquis de Rubempré. Reverse your conduct—present to the world your goodlooks, your charm, your intelligence and your poetry. If you permit yourself small lapses, let it be within four walls; then you will not any longer be guilty of smirching the scenery of this great theatre we call the world. Napoleon used to say that we should 'never wash our dirty linen in public'. Upon this second precept depends a corollary—everything is a matter of good form. Try to grasp the full significance of that word *form*. There are people who know no better who, under the pressure of necessity, take another man's goods, by violence ; such individuals are called criminals, and they are called to account by the law. A poor man of genius makes a discovery, and the exploitation of his secret is worth a fortune, and you lend him three thousand francs (that is how the Cointets see it, at all events, because they have your three thousand francs in their hands, and they are going to rob your brother-in-law) and then torment him until he gives away his secret, or a part of it, and you are answerable to no one except your conscience ; and your conscience does not lead you into a Court of Law. Enemies of the social order make this contrast an excuse for yapping at the heels of the law, and fulminating in the name of the people, against those who send a pickpocket or a poor man who has stolen a few chickens from a back garden at night to the hulk, while a man who has ruined whole families by a fraudulent bankruptcy is, at most, sent to prison for a few months ; but these hypocritical judges know very well what they are doing in punishing the thief—they are maintaining the barrier between the rich and the poor, which, if it were to be overturned, would mean the end of social order ; whereas the bankrupt, the man who is clever enough to steal an inheritance, the banker who ruins a business for his own profit, produces nothing more than a displacement of wealth. So you see, my son, society is bound to make the same kind of distinction, for its own advantage, as I am advising you to make, for yours. The essential thing is to be a match for society. Napoleon, Richelieu, and the Medicis were all a match for society in their day. And as for you—you value yourself at twelve thousand francs ! Your society no longer worships the true God, but the golden calf! That is the religion of your Charter, which in politics, recognises only one thing—property. That amounts to the same thing as issuing an order to all its members, ' Try to become rich! ' When you have discovered some means, within the law, of coming by a fortune, you will be a rich man, and Marquis de Rubempré—then you can allow yourself the luxury of a sense of honour! Then you can profess so much delicacy that no one will dare to suggest that you ever showed any lack of it, least of all in coming by a fortune—which, indeed, I should never advise," said the priest, patting Lucien's hand. " So what must you get into that handsome head of yours? Just this—set yourself a brilliant goal, and conceal the means by which you arrive at it, conceal every step you take towards it. You have behaved like a child—now be a man, be a hunter, get into the swim, lie in ambush in the world of Paris, wait until chance brings the quarry within your reach and do not worry too much about your personal integrity and your so-called dignity—because we are all more or less in the power of something—a vice, or a failing ; but keep the one supreme law—that of secrecy! "

" Father, you frighten me! " Lucien exclaimed. " This seems to me to be a brigand's philosophy! "

" You are quite right! " said the Canon. " But I did not invent it. That is how *parvenus* have always argued, Hapsburgs and Bourbons alike. You have nothing ; then you are in precisely the same situation as the Medicis, Richelieu, and Napoleon at the beginning of their careers. These men, my dear child, set a price on their future in terms of ingratitude, treachery, and the most flagrant betrayals. To win everything you must risk everything. Look at it in this way. When you sit down to play *bouillotte*, do you call the rules of the game in question ? The rules are there, and you accept them."

" Come," Lucien thought, " he knows the rules of *bouillotte*."

" Well, how do you behave when you play *bouillotte* ? " the priest continued. " Do you practise that fairest of all virtues, openness ? Not only do you conceal your hand, but you attempt to make others believe, when you are sure to win, that you are going to lose—in other words, you dissimulate, do you not ? You lie, for the sake of winning five sovereigns! What would you think of a gambler who was generous enough to warn the other players that he held all the royal trumps ? Very well then ; the ambitious man who proposes to gamble according to the precepts of virtue, when his antagonists have discarded them, is a child to whom an old politician like myself would say just what any gambler would say to a player who refrained from using his trumps. 'Sir, you ought never to play *bouillotte*.' Did you make the rules in the game of ambition ? Why do you suppose I have just told you that you must be a match for society ? It is because in these days, my young friend, society has abrogated to itself, little by little, so many of the rights of the individual that the individual is forced to take up arms against society. There are no more laws, only customs, that is to say, posturings—it is all a matter of form."

Lucien's astonishment was plain to see.

The priest was afraid that he had shocked Lucien's innocence. " Ah, my child! " he said. " Do you expect to find an Abbé loaded with all the inquities of the diplomatic exchanges between two great kings, talking like the angel Gabriel ? (I am the intermediary between Ferdinand VII and Louis XVIII, two great kings who owe their respective crowns to profound—shall we say—adjustments ?) I believe in God, but I believe even more firmly in our Order, and our Order believes only in temporal power. In order to strengthen temporal power, our Order upholds the Catholic, Roman, and Apostolic Church, that is to say, a combination of ideas that keeps the people in a state of obedience. We are the Templars of the modern world ; we have a doctrine of our own. Like the Templars, our Order has been dispersed—and for the same reasons : we were a match for the world. If you want to be a soldier, I will be your captain. Obey me, as a wife obeys her husband, or as a child obeys his mother, and I give you my word that within three years you shall be Marquis de Rubempré, married to the daughter of one of the noblest families of the Faubourg Saint-Germain, and that some day you will have a seat in the House of Peers. At this very moment, if I had not amused you by my conversation, what would you be ? A corpse, lost for ever in a bed of slime ; very well, now make an effort of imagination!

" The young man who is at present sitting in this carriage beside Abbé Carlos Herrera, Honorary Canon of the Chapter of Toledo, secret envoy of His Majesty Ferdinand VII to His Majesty the King of France, who is the bearer of a dispatch which possibly reads, ' When you have delivered me, hang all those whom I favour at this moment, but in particular my Secret Envoy, to ensure his secrecy '. This young man," the Canon continued, " no longer has anything in common with the poet who has just died. I have fished you up, restored you to life, and you belong to me as the creature belongs to the creator, or as the afrits in the fairy-tales belong to the genii, or the Icolgan to the Sultan, or the body to the soul! I, for my part, will sustain you, on the road to power, with a strong arm, and I promise you, at the same time, a life of pleasure, honours, and perpetual enjoyment. You shall never be short of money. You shall shine, you shall be in the public eye, while I, crouching in the mud, lay the foundations of the brilliant edifice of your fortune. I love power for its own sake. I shall be happy in your enjoyments, which are forbidden to me. In fact, I shall live through you! Very well—on the day when this pact between man and devil, or child and diplomat, no longer suits you, you can always go and find some picturesque spot, like the one you have just described, and drown yourself: you will be a little more, or a little less, wretched and dishonoured than you are at this moment, that is all."

" This is not a sermon in the style of the Archbishop of Granada!' said Lucien, as the carriage drew up at a posting-stage.

" Call this intensive course of instruction what you like, my son —for you are my son, I adopt you, and you shall be my heir ; but it is the code of ambition. God's elect are few in number. There are only two alternatives : either you must bury yourself in some cloister—and the chances are that you would only find there the world in miniature—or you must accept this code."

" Perhaps it would be better to know less," said Lucien, making an effort to fathom the soul of this terrible priest.

" Come, now," said the Canon, " first you play without knowing the rules of the game, and then you throw your hand in just when you begin to be in a strong position, and you have a godfather of substance to back you! Do you not even want to have your revenge ? Come, now, would you not like to be even with the people who drove you out of Paris ? "

Lucien shuddered as if the sound of some bronze instrument, some Chinese gong, had vibrated through every nerve.

"I am only a humble priest," the Canon continued, and an expression terrible to behold appeared for a moment on his face, bronzed by the sun of Spain. " But if I had been humiliated, vexed, tormented, betrayed, and sold, as you have been by the individuals of whom you have told me, I should be like the Arabs of the desert—I should devote myself, body and soul, to vengeance. What would I care if I were to end my life dangling from a gibbet, or garrotted, or impaled, or guillotined in your French style; but they should not have my head until after I had ground my enemies beneath my heel!"

Lucien was silent. He no longer felt any wish to draw this priest out.

"Some men are descended from Abel, others from Cain," said the Canon in conclusion; "I, for my part, am of mixed blood: Cain for my enemies, Abel for my friends—and woe betide those who awaken Cain! You, after all, are a Frenchman; but I am a Spaniard, and, what is more, a Canon."

"What a man!" Lucien thought to himself, as he looked at the protector that Heaven had just sent him.

Abbé Carlos Herrera had nothing of the Jesuit about him, nor even of the priest. He was thick-set, with large hands, powerful chest, and Herculean strength. His look was naturally terrible, but softened by a mildness that he could assume at will; his bronzed, inscrutable features, which revealed nothing of what was passing in his mind, were repellent rather than attractive. His long thick hair, powdered in the style of Prince de Talleyrand, gave this strange diplomat something of the air of a bishop, and from a blue ribbon, bordered with white, hung a gold cross that suggested high ecclesiastical rank. His black silk stockings covered leg muscles that might have belonged to an athlete. His clothes were of exquisite neatness and revealed a personal fastidiousness not often met with among simple priests, especially among Spanish priests. A tricorne hat lay on the front seat of the carriage, which bore the arms of Spain. But although there was so much that was repulsive about the man, his manner, which was at once violent and ingratiating, did much to diminish the effect of his appearance; and the priest was evidently laying himself out to charm Lucien, flattering him, almost fawning on him. Lucien observed all these things with some uneasiness. He felt that the moment had come when he must make his choice between life and death. They had now reached the second posting stage beyond Ruffec.

The last words spoken by the Spanish priest had stirred many chords in his heart; and to the shame both of Lucien and of the priest, who had studied the poet's handsome face with a shrewd eye, it must be said that the worst in Lucien responded to an appeal to all that was most depraved in his nature. Lucien remembered Paris, he grasped once more at the reins of domination, that had slipped from his unskilful hands, and he pictured his vengeance! The comparison between provincial life and the life of Paris, that he had so lately had occasion to make, and the strong motives for suicide that had but now impelled him, faded from his mind, he would go back to his natural element, but protected, this time, by a diplomat as profoundly unscrupulous as Cromwell himself.

"I was alone, but now there will be two of us," he thought.

The more guilt he had confessed to in his past conduct, the more interest this man in holy orders had shown in him. The priest's charity had grown greater in proportion to his calamities, and nothing seemed to surprise him. Nevertheless, Lucien asked himself what motives could possibly activate this negotiator of royal intrigues. He told himself, at first, that it was Spanish generosity—a superficial answer! All Spaniards are generous, just as Italians are poisoners and liable to jealousy, the French are fickle, the Germans honest, the Jews ignoble and the English noble. If we reverse these propositions we shall be nearer the truth. The Jews have monopolised the gold of the world; Jews have played *Phèdre*, sung William Tell, written *Robert the Devil*, *Reisebilder*, and much fine poetry, and are today more powerful than they have ever been; their religion is tolerated, and they lend money to the Pope himself! In Germany dishonest dealings are so common that even in the smallest matters they will always ask a foreigner if he has a written agreement. In France, the nation has been applauding its own national stupidities for the past fifty years; we continue to wear inexplicable hats, and changes in the government are only tolerated on the understanding that everything is to remain just as it is. England flaunts in the face of the whole world perfidies whose baseness is equalled only by her greed. Spain, who once had the gold of the two Indies, no longer has any wealth. In no country in the world are there fewer cases of poisoning than in Italy, where manners are more easy and courteous than elsewhere; as for the Spanish, they have existed for a long time on the reputation of the Moors.

As the Spaniard climbed back into the carriage, he told the postillion to drive at full speed, promising him a three-franc tip. Lucien hesitated; but when the priest urged him to get in, he obeyed, telling himself that the time had come to have the matter out with the priest in an argument *ad hominem*.

"Father," he said, "a man who has just expounded with the most perfect coolness a series of maxims that most people would consider profoundly immoral——"

"And so they are," said the priest. "That is why Jesus Christ said that it needs must be that offences come, my son; and that is why the world displays such a great horror of offences."

"I hope that a man of your stamp will not be surprised by the question that I am about to ask?"

"Come, my son," said Carlos Herrera, "you do not know me. Do you suppose that I should engage a secretary without first knowing whether I could depend upon him not to steal from me? I am quite satisfied with your principles—you have all the innocence of a twenty-year-old suicide. What is your question?"

"Why are you interested in me? What is the price of my obedience? Why do you want to give me everything? What is your share in the bargain?"

The Spaniard looked at Lucien and smiled.

"Wait until we come to a hill, and we will walk up it and talk in the open air. One must be discreet in a carriage."

They were both silent for some time, and the speed at which they were driving aided what one may call Lucien's moral intoxication.

"Here is a hill, Father," said Lucien, waking from a kind of dream.

"Very well, let us walk," said the priest, and he called to the postillion to stop the carriage. The two men jumped down on to the road.

" My child," said the Spaniard, taking Lucien's arm, " have you ever thought about Otway's *Venice Preserved*? Do you understand the significance of that deep friendship between two men, that united Pierre and Jaffier so closely that women meant nothing to them, so that between them all the social terms were changed ? Well —so much for the poet."

" So the Canon knows something about the theatre as well," Lucien thought to himself. " Have you read Voltaire ? " he said aloud.

" I have done better, I have put him into practice," said the Canon.

" Do you not believe in God ? "

" Come, it is I who am the atheist, then ? " said the priest with a smile. " Let us come to the point, my child," he continued, putting his arm round Lucien's waist. " I am forty-six years old, and as I am the natural son of a noble lord, I have no family ; but I have a heart. . . . But let me tell you this, engrave this on that still impressionable brain of yours ; man dreads solitude. And of all the kinds of solitude, mental solitude is the most appalling. The early anchorites lived with God—they lived in the most populous world of all, the spiritual world. Misers live in a world of fantasy and imaginary enjoyments. For the miser, everything, even his sex-life, goes on in his head. A man's first thought, whether he be leper or criminal, sick or in disgrace, is to find a companion to share his destiny. To satisfy that longing—which is life itself—he will exert all his powers, all his vital energy. Without this overriding desire, would Satan have found companions ? There is a poem to be written on that theme, a prelude to *Paradise Lost* ; Milton's poem is only the apology for the revolt."

" That would be the *Iliad* of corruption ! " said Lucien.

" Well, I am alone, I live alone. I may wear a priest's habit, but I have not a priest's heart. I like to devote myself to someone—that is my vice, if you like. That devotion is my life—that is why I became a priest. I am not afraid of ingratitude, and I myself am not ungrateful. The Church is nothing to me—it is only an idea. I serve the King of Spain ; but one cannot feel affection for the

King of Spain ; he is my protector, he is too high above me. I want someone to love, someone to mould and fashion to my use, to love as a father loves a child. I shall drive in your Tilbury, my boy, I shall enjoy your success with women, and I shall say to myself, ' This handsome young man is part of myself! I created this Marquis de Rubempré, and raised him into the aristocratic world ; his greatness is my work, he speaks or is silent as I bid him, he consults me in everything.' The Abbé de Vermont was all that for Marie-Antoinette."

" He led her to the scaffold! "

" He did not love the Queen! " said the priest. " He loved only the Abbé de Vermont! "

" And must I leave desolation behind me ? " said Lucien.

" I have money, and it is at your disposal."

" I would give a great deal, at this moment, to set Séchard free," said Lucien in the voice of a man who has no longer any thought of suicide.

" You have only to say the word, my son, and he shall receive the sum necessary for his liberation tomorrow morning."

" What! Would you give me twelve thousand francs ? "

" Why, what a child you are! Don't you see that we are travelling at twelve leagues an hour? We shall reach Poitiers by dinner-time. And there, if you are willing to sign the pact, and give me just one proof of your obedience—and it is a great proof that I shall ask—why, then, your sister shall receive fifteen thousand francs by the Bordeaux stage-coach."

" Where is the money ? "

The Spanish priest returned no answer, and Lucien thought to himself :

" That has caught him—he was only making fun of me."

A moment later, the Spaniard and poet took their places again in the coach, in silence. Silently, the priest put his hand into the pocket of the coach, and drew out a leather pouch, with three compartments, of the kind used by travellers ; he plunged in his large hand three times, bringing it out each time filled with gold pieces, until he had produced a hundred Portuguese moidores.

" Father, I will do anything you like ! " Lucien exclaimed, dazzled by this stream of gold.

" Child! " said the priest. He kissed Lucien's brow tenderly. " There is twice as much gold left in this bag, thirty thousand francs, besides the money for travelling expenses."

" And you are travelling alone ? " said Lucien.

" What does it matter ? " said the Spaniard. " I have over a hundred thousand crowns in drafts in Paris. A diplomat without money is no better off than you yourself were this morning—a poet without will-power! "

While Lucien was stepping into the carriage with the man who called himself a Spanish diplomat, Eve was getting up to give her son his morning feed, and in his cradle she found the fatal letter. As she read it a cold sweat chilled her, and her senses swam. She called Marion and Kolb.

" Has my brother gone out ? " she asked.

" Yes, montame, first ting dis morgen," said Kolb.

" Do not say a word to anyone," Eve said to the two servants, " but my brother has almost certainly gone out to end his life. Go, both of you, and make inquiries without arousing suspicion, and look along by the river! "

Eve remained alone in a state of utter stupefaction, pitiful to see. It was in this state that Petit-Claud found her, when at about seven in the morning he called to discuss the situation with her. At such times we will listen to advice from anyone.

" Our poor dear David is in prison," the lawyer began ; " I foresaw from the beginning that it would come to that in the end. I advised him from the first to go into partnership with his rivals, the Cointets ; because, whereas your husband has only the idea, the Cointets have the means of exploiting the discovery in a practical way. And so yesterday evening, as soon as I heard of the arrest, I went along to see the Cointets to find out if I could obtain concessions from them that would satisfy you. If you go on trying to keep the secret of this discovery, your life will continue to be what it is now—a series of endless shifts, at the end of which, when you are exhausted and at your wits' end, you are bound to be driven into making a bad bargain with some man with capital—but I should like to see you make a good bargain here and now, with the Cointet brothers. If you do, you will spare yourself the privations and the endless hardships of the inventor's struggle against the greed of the capitalists and the indifference of society. Now look at it in this way! If the Cointet brothers pay your debts—and if, in addition, they pay you another sum, unconditionally, whether or not the discovery proves successful and practicable ; and if, furthermore, they agree to pay you a proportion of the profits of the exploitation of the process, would you not be satisfied ? You yourself would then be the proprietor of the printing house, and no doubt you would wish to sell it—it is certainly worth twenty thousand francs, and I will guarantee to find you a purchaser at that price. If you realise fifteen thousand francs, by signing a deed of partnership with the Cointets, you will have thirty-five thousand francs in hand, and at the current rate of interest, that would bring you in two thousand francs a year. In the country one can live on two thousand francs a year. And you must consider, besides, that you would still have the possibility of the proceeds of your partnership with the Cointet brothers. I say possibility, because we must always bear in mind that the process might prove a failure.

"Very well; now I am in a position to obtain the following terms : firstly, David's unconditional liberation ; fifteen thousand francs premium paid on his discovery, and not returnable, even if the discovery proves to be economically impracticable; and, thirdly, a deed of partnership between David and Cointet Brothers for the exploitation of the patent to be taken out, after a trial made jointly and in secret, of his process. The terms would be these : the Cointets would agree to bear all expenses—David's contribution would be the costs of the patent, and he would be entitled to twenty-five per cent of the profits. You are a clear-headed and extremely sensible woman, qualities which are not often found together with great beauty ; think over these proposals, and you will see that they are very reasonable."

Poor Eve, in despair, burst into tears. " Oh, why did you not come and make me this proposal last night ?" she exclaimed. "Then we would have avoided disgrace, and . . . worse than disgrace. . . ."

"I was talking with the Cointets until midnight—they, as you must have suspected, have been behind Métivier. But what can have happened since yesterday evening worse than poor David's arrest?"

"This is the terrible news that I found first thing this morning," she said, handing Lucien's letter to Petit-Claud. "I believe now that you want to help us, and you were at school with David and Lucien, so I do not need to ask you to keep this secret."

"You need not worry," said Petit-Claud, handing back the letter after reading it. "Lucien will not kill himself; after being responsible for his brother-in-law's arrest, he was bound to find some excuse for leaving, and so far as I can see, this letter is simply a piece of melodrama, a theatrical exit."

The Cointets had got what they wanted. They had tormented the inventor and his family, until they could seize the moment when, worn out by prolonged torture, the victims longed only for respite. Not every inventor is a bulldog ready to die rather than give up the prey into which he has fastened his teeth, and the Cointets had studied the characters of their victims with some attention. For the tall Cointet, David's arrest was the last scene of the first act of this drama. The second act opened with the proposal just made by Petit-Claud. The lawyer, that masterly schemer, realised that Lucien's headstrong behaviour was an unhoped-for piece of good luck, which would turn the tables in favour of a decision. He realised that Eve was so completely broken by this event, that he made up his mind to profit by the occasion to gain her confidence —for he had come to realise the extent of Eve's influence over her husband. Therefore, instead of plunging Mme Séchard deeper into despair, he tried to reassure her, and in her present state of mind he found it easy to direct her thoughts to the prison—for then, he thought, she would advise David to go into partnership with the Cointets.

"David told me," he began, "that he only wanted to make a fortune for your sake, and your brother's; but you must have realised that it would be folly to try to keep Lucien—that boy would run through three fortunes ! "

Eve's attitude told him plainly enough that her last illusions with regard to her brother had faded ; and so the lawyer paused for long enough to allow his client's silence to become a tacit assent.

" In that case," he continued, " we have only to consider yourself and your child. It is for you to decide whether you can live happily on two thousand francs a year—quite apart from what you will inherit from old Séchard. Your father-in-law's income has amounted to seven or eight thousand francs for a long time past, not counting the interest on his capital ; so that you have, after all, a very comfortable future before you. So why torment yourselves ? "

The lawyer left Mme Séchard to think over these propositions, which had been prepared by the tall Cointet, with some skill, the previous evening.

" Hold out to them the possibility of a lump sum," this local lynx had said, when the lawyer had brought him the news of the arrest, " and when they have got used to the idea of cash in hand, they will be ours—then we can drive a bargain, and little by little we shall bring them down to letting us have the secret, at our own price."

The second act of this drama of commerce is, in fact, summed up in these words. By the time Mme Séchard, heartbroken and full of misgivings for her brother's fate, had dressed and come downstairs, ready to visit the prison, she was suffering agonies at the thought of walking through the streets of Angoulême, alone. Petit-Claud cared nothing for his client's anguish of mind ; but he came back and offered to go with her, from a more Machiavellian motive. Eve gave him the credit for a delicate consideration that she greatly appreciated ; and he allowed her to thank him without disillusioning her. This small attention at such a moment from this hard, curt little man modified the opinion that Mme Séchard had hitherto held of Petit-Claud.

" I will take you the longest way round, so that we won't meet anyone," he said.

" This is the first time," she said, " that I have not had the right to hold my head high! Yesterday's lesson was a hard one! "

" It shall be the first and the last."

" Oh, I shall never be able to go on living in this town! "

" If your husband accepts the proposals that were to all intents and purposes agreed upon between the Cointets and myself, let me know," said Petit-Claud, as he left Eve at the door of the prison, " and I will go at once to Cachan and ask for an authorisation for David's release; then, in all likelihood, he will not go back to prison."

These words, spoken just outside the gaol, were what the Italians call a " conbinazione "—a word that expresses a certain indefinable blend of truth and perfidy, characteristic of a kind of fraud, carefully planned, and within the letter of the law; they would call, for instance, the Eve of St. Bartholomew a political " conbinazione ".

For reasons already explained, imprisonment for debts is a judicial event so rare in the provinces that in most French towns there is no accommodation for debtors. When this is the case, the debtor is locked up in gaol with the accused, convicted and condemned—for such are the successive names that the law affixes to that class of persons generically known as *criminals*. David, therefore, was, for the time being, put in one of the prison cells which, perhaps, had been lately vacated by some prisoner who had served his sentence. When he had been entered in the gaol-book, for the sum set down by the law for a prisoner's board for one month, David found himself face to face with a big man, a personage who in the eyes of prisoners soon becomes a power greater than the king himself—the gaoler, in fact. There is no such thing, in the provinces, as a thin gaoler. In the first place, the gaoler's appointment is virtually a sinecure; besides, a gaoler is a kind of innkeeper who has no rent to pay for his house, and he lives very well, while his prisoners, for whom he caters, live very badly. None the less, he treats them, as do other innkeepers, according to their means. He knew David by name, chiefly because of his father, and he took the risk of giving him a good room for one night, although David in fact had not a sou.

The prison of Angoulême dates from the Middle Ages, and, like the Cathedral, it has changed little. It adjoins the ancient Presidiae and it is still known as the Maison de Justice. The doorway is the typical solid, nail-studded, mediaeval prison door, under a low, wellworn archway, like the entrance to the Cyclop's cave—the more so from the fact that, in the centre of the door, there is, like a single eye, the *Judas*, through which the gaoler looks to see who is there before he opens the door. A corridor runs the whole length of the building, on the ground floor, and out of this corridor a number of cells open, whose high, barred windows are lighted from the prison yard. The gaoler led David to the cell next to the archway, opposite his own lodge, thinking that it would help to pass the time pleasantly to have a man in David's predicament for company.

" This is the best room," he said, seeing that David was appalled at its aspect.

The stone walls of the cell were decidedly damp. The windows were very high and heavily barred. The stone flags struck an icy chill. The measured tread of the warder as he walked up and down the corridor was as monotonous as the sound of waves breaking on the shore, and seemed to say to the prisoners every moment, " You are under guard! You are not free any more! " All these details, taken together, have a prodigious effect upon the minds of honest people. David noticed the squalid bed ; but a prisoner is always in such a violent state of agitation on the first night that he does not realise the hardness of his bed until the second.

The gaoler was most agreeable, and suggested of his own accord that his prisoner might like to walk in the yard until nightfall.

David's anguish only began when he lay down on his bed. Prisoners are not allowed to have lights, except by a special permit issued by the Public Prosecutor, excepting the prisoner from rules obviously made for the punishment of criminals. The gaoler, it is true, allowed David to sit by his fire, but he had to lock him in his cell at nightfall. Then, and only then, did Eve's poor husband experience the full horror of prison, and at the coarse brutality of the place he was overcome with revulsion. But, with a kind of reaction usual enough with intellectuals, he performed an act of mental detachment, and, in the solitude of his cell, escaped into one of those day-dreams that poetic natures can always create, even in broad daylight. Finally he brought his thoughts to bear on his situation. Prison incites men strongly to an examination of conscience ; and David began to ask himself whether he had fulfilled his duties as the head of a family. What must his wife be suffering at this moment ! Why had he not followed Marion's advice and earned enough money to enable him to make his discovery afterwards, at leisure ?

" How can I stay in Angoulême after such a public disgrace ? If I ever get out of prison, what are we going to do ? Where shall we go ? "

He began to have one or two doubts about his processes—a kind of mental torment that can only be understood by inventors ! Passing from doubt to doubt, David began to see his situation more clearly, and he began to ask himself the question that the Cointets had asked old Séchard, and Petit-Claud had just asked Eve:

" Even supposing that all goes well, what are the practical facts of the situation ? I must have a patent, and for that I need money! I must find a factory where my experiments can be tried out on a large scale, and that means giving up my secret. Oh, how right Petit-Claud was! "

A very clear light sometimes shines even into the darkest prisons.

David turned to sleep on the dirty mattress of the camp bed, covered with the coarsest kind of brown blanket. " Never mind," he reflected. " No doubt I shall see Petit-Claud in the morning."

So David, too, was quite prepared to listen to the proposals that his wife brought him, on behalf of his enemies. After she had kissed her husband, she sat down on the edge of the bed (for there was only one wooden chair, of the commonest and worst kind). Her eye fell on the odious bucket in one corner, and on the walls, scrawled over with names and inscriptions left by David's predecessors. Her eyes were red with weeping, but now she began to cry again. She had shed tears enough already, but at the sight of her husband in the situation of a criminal, she wept afresh.

" To think that the desire for fame may lead one to this ! " she exclaimed. " Oh, my angel, give up this career! Let us go, side by side, along the beaten track, and give up trying to make a fortune overnight! I could be happy on so very little, especially after all that we have been through! And if you only knew! This shameful arrest is not the worst thing that has happened to us—read this! "

And she handed David Lucien's letter ; when he had read it, the only consolation he had to offer was Petit-Claud's bitter comment.

" If Lucien has killed himself, he is already dead at this moment," said David, " and if he is not already dead, he will not kill himself—because, as he himself says, he has only enough courage for one morning."

" But the suspense! " said Eve, who had forgiven almost everything at the thought of Lucien's possible death.

She then told her husband of the proposals that Petit-Claud said that he had obtained from the Cointets ; David accepted them at once, with evident pleasure.

" We shall have enough to live on in a village outside l'Houmeau, not too far from the Cointets' paper mill, and all I ask for now is a quiet life," said the inventor. " If Lucien has punished himself by death, we shall have enough to live on for the time being, until we inherit my father's estate ; and if he is still alive, the poor boy will just have to adapt himself to our modest position in the world. The Cointets will certainly profit by my discovery ; but, after all, what am I, in comparison with my country ? Only one man! If my discovery increases the general good, I shall be quite satisfied. The fact is, my dear Eve, that neither you nor I were ever cut out to be successful in business. We neither of us have that love of making profits, or that unwillingness to part with money in any shape or form, even when it is legally owing, that may possibly be virtues in a business man, because these two forms of avarice are called prudence and business ability! "

They were delighted to find that they thought alike—for like-mindedness is one of love's sweetest flowers,—two people who love one another do not necessarily share the same intellectual tastes.

Eve asked the gaoler to send a note to Petit-Claud, asking him to come and set David free, and saying that they both agreed to the general terms of the scheme that he had outlined. Ten minutes later Petit-Claud appeared in David's loathsome cell. He told Eve to go home, promising to follow presently with David.

" Well, old man," Petit-Claud said to David, " so you got yourself caught! How did you come to make such a blunder ? Why did you come out ? "

" Well, how could I have done otherwise ? This is the note that Lucien sent me."

David handed Cérizet's letter to Petit-Claud, who took it, read it, examined the paper, and, as he talked of other things, folded the letter, as if absent-mindedly, and put it in his pocket. Presently the lawyer took David's arm, and they left the prison together, for the bailiff's discharge was brought to the gaoler while they were talking.

It was like being in Heaven to David to be home again.

He cried like a child as he took little Lucien in his arms and kissed him ; now he would sleep in his own bed again after three weeks as a prisoner, and the disgrace, according to provincial ideas, of the last few hours. Kolb and Marion had come back. Marion had heard, in l'Houmeau, that Lucien had been seen walking along the Paris road, beyond Marsac. His elegant appearance had struck some peasants on their way to market. Kolb had set out on horseback along the Paris road, and had heard, at Mansle, that Lucien had been seen travelling post—Monsieur Marron had recognised him.

" What did I tell you ? " said Petit-Claud. " That boy is not a poet, he is a serial romance ! "

" Travelling post ! " Eve exclaimed. " Where can he be going this time ? "

" Well, now," Petit-Claud said to David, " come and see the Cointets ; they are expecting you."

" Oh, please do your best for us," said pretty Mme Séchard, " because our whole future is in your hands."

" Would you rather discuss the matter here, in your own house?" Petit-Claud said to Mme Séchard, " because in that case I will leave David with you, and ask the Cointets to come here this evening—then you shall see for yourself whether I can defend your interests."

"Oh, that would give me great pleasure!" said Eve.

"Very well, this evening, here, at seven o'clock," said Petit-Claud.

"Thank you," said Eve, and her look and tone of voice told Petit-Claud that he had made great progress in the confidence of his client's wife.

"Don't worry. You see I was right!" he said as he turned to leave. "Your brother is nowhere near suicide. And perhaps by this evening you will have quite a little fortune. A man has turned up who is seriously interested in buying your printing business."

"In that case," said Eve, "perhaps we ought to wait before going into partnership with the Cointets."

Petit-Claud saw the danger.

"You are forgetting," he said, "that you will not be free to sell the business until you have paid M. Métivier, because the plant is still under distraint."

When Petit-Claud reached home he sent for Cérizet. When the foreman appeared in his office, he led him into the bay of a window.

"By tomorrow evening you will be the proprietor of the Séchard printing business, and you will have strong enough backing to get the transfer of the licence," said the lawyer, "but I suppose you do not want to end your days in the hulks?" he added in a low voice.

"What's that? What's that? The hulks?" Cérizet repeated.

"Your letter to David is a forgery, and it is in my possession. If Henriette were to be cross-questioned, what would she have to say? Oh, I don't want to ruin you," Petit-Claud hastened to add, for Cérizet had turned pale.

"Is there something else you want me to do?" said Cérizet.

"I will tell you what I want you to do," Petit-Claud resumed. "And you had better pay attention to what I say. Two months from now you will be a licensed printer in Angoulême, but it will take you a good ten years to pay off the loan on your business. You will work for a long time to come for the men who are lending you the money. And, what is more, you will take your orders from the Liberal party. I shall make out your agreement with Gannerac myself, and I shall word it in such a way that you will have the business in your own hands one of these days. But if they decide to bring out a newspaper, and you are the publisher, and I am Deputy Public Prosecutor here, you must come to an understanding with the Cointets to print in your newspaper articles of such a nature that the paper will be seized and suppressed. The Cointets will pay you well for doing them that service. I realise that you will be sentenced, and have to do time in prison, but you will get a reputation as a man who has been persecuted—you will be quite a hero with the Liberal party, a Sergeant Mercier, or a Paul-Louis Courier, or a Manuel, in a small way. I will see to it that they do not take away your printing licence. And on the day when the newspaper is suppressed, I shall burn this letter, in your presence. Your fortune will be cheap at the price."

A working man has only very inaccurate ideas on the laws of forgery, and Cérizet, who already saw himself in the dock, breathed again.

"Three years from now I shall be Public Prosecutor in Angoulême," Petit-Claud continued. "And you may need my help, don't forget that!"

"All right, it's agreed," said Cérizet. "But you don't know me. Burn that letter now, and trust to my gratitude."

Petit-Claud looked at Cérizet. It was one of those battles of will in which one man's eye is like a scalpel with which he attempts to lay bare the soul of his antagonist, and the other attempts to summon up into his eyes all his virtues, displaying them there, as on the stage of a theatre.

Petit-Claud said nothing; he lit a candle and burned the letter.

"He has his way to make," he said to himself.

"I would damn myself for your sake," said the foreman.

David awaited the interview with the Cointets in a state of vague uneasiness. It was not the question of his interests that worried him, or the deed of partnership that was to be made out; what troubled him was his anxiety over their opinion of his work.

He felt just as the author of a play feels before the critics. The inventor's pride and his misgivings were such at that moment that they overshadowed all other considerations.

At last, at seven o'clock that evening—at which hour Countess du Châtelet went to lie down, saying that she had a headache, leaving her husband to play the host at dinner, so distressed was she by the contradictory rumours that she had heard about Lucien—the Cointets, the tall and the fat, along with Petit-Claud, entered the house of the rival who had delivered himself up to them, bound hand and foot.

A difficulty arose at the outset : how could a deed of partnership be drawn up unless they knew David's secret ? And once David had divulged his secret he would be at the mercy of the Cointets. Petit-Claud obtained, as a concession, that the deed of partnership should be drawn up first. The tall Cointet thereupon asked David to show them some of his specimens, whereupon the inventor produced his most recent samples and guaranteed the economy of production.

" Well, here you have the essentials of the agreement ready made ; you can safely go into partnership on the strength of these samples, and introduce a clause allowing for dissolution of the agreement in case the conditions of the patent are not fulfilled in the manufacturing process."

" It is one thing to make samples of paper, on a small scale, in your room with a small mould," the tall Cointet remarked to David, " but it is another thing altogether to undertake manufacture on a large scale. I will give you an example! We manufacture coloured papers and we buy, for dyeing purposes, lots of colour that are absolutely identical. The indigo we use to blue our demi-octavo is taken from a batch of cakes that all come from the same factory. Well, and good ; but we have never been able to obtain two batches of paper of exactly the same shade. Phenomena occur in the process of manufacture that we have not been able to trace down to any known cause. The quantity and the quality of the pulp introduce variations in several respects simultaneously. When you have, in a cauldron, a sample of certain ingredients (mind you, I am not asking what those ingredients are!) you are in control of the experiment, you can mix and pound and knead the sample as you like, until it is homogeneous. But what guarantee have you got that in a batch of five hundred reams it will behave in the same way—that your process will succeed?"

David, Eve, and Petit-Claud looked at one another, and their eyes said many things.

"Take a somewhat similar case," the tall Cointet continued after a pause. "You cut two or three trusses of hay in a meadow, and you pack it away tightly in a hay-loft 'before the heat is out of the grass', as the farmers say; the hay ferments, but it does not cause an accident. Now what if you were to rely on that experience to stack two thousand trusses in a wooden barn? I don't need to tell you that the hay would catch fire, and your barn would go up in flames like a lighted match. Now you are an educated man," Cointet continued, addressing David. "This is how I see it—you have, at this moment, cut two trusses of hay, and we don't feel inclined to set fire to our paper mill by stacking two thousand. In other words, we stand to lose several batches, lose over it, and then, after laying out a lot of money, find ourselves no better off at the end, than we were at the beginning."

David was quite crushed by this argument, for the practical man spoke the language of common sense to the theorist, who speaks always in terms of the future.

"I'll be damned if I'm going to sign a deed of partnership like that!" the fat Cointet exclaimed bluntly. "You can throw your own money away if you like, Boniface; but I shall hold on to mine. What I offer is this—to pay M. Séchard's debts and six thousand francs, and another three thousand francs in twelve or fifteen months' time—that is quite enough to risk. We shall be twelve thousand francs to the bad over our account with Métivier. That brings it up to fifteen thousand francs—I would not pay more than that for the secret if I were buying it outright. So this is the gold-mine you told me about, Boniface! Thank you very much; I thought you had more sense. No, you cannot call this doing business!"

" The question for you," said Petit-Claud, undismayed by this outburst, " reduces itself to this : are you prepared to risk twenty thousand francs to buy a secret which may bring you in a fortune? Well, gentlemen, the risk is usually in proportion to the profit. You are staking twenty thousand francs against a possible fortune. A gambler will risk a sovereign at roulette for the chance of winning thirty-six, but he knows that his louis is lost. Do the same."

" I must think it over," said the fat Cointet ; " I'm not clever like my brother. I am just an ordinary sort of fat chap who is only good for printing prayer-books at twenty sous and selling them at forty. I see nothing but ruin in an invention that has not been tried out. You might be successful with the first batch, then lose the second, and then you try again, and so it would go on, and once your arm gets caught in that kind of machinery, the body follows."

He then told the story of a tradesman in Bordeaux who was ruined by following the advice of a scientist and trying to bring the sand-dunes under cultivation ; he could point to half a dozen examples known to him personally, in the Charente and the Dordogne, in industry and in agriculture ; he was carried away by this theme and would not listen to another word. Petit-Claud's attempts to pacify him only served to increase his irritation.

" I would rather pay more for a certainty even if it brought in only a small profit than for this discovery," he said, looking at his brother. " My view is, that it is all far too much in the air for talking business," he declared, in conclusion.

" Still, you had a proposal in mind when you came here," said Petit-Claud. " What is your offer ? "

" To free M. Séchard from his debts, and to guarantee him, in case of success, thirty per cent of the profits," said the fat Cointet promptly.

" But what should we have to live on while the experiments were being carried out ? " said Eve. " My husband has had the disgrace of being arrested, and he may as well go back to prison—it can make no difference now—and we shall pay our own debts."

Petit-Claud made a sign to Eve to keep quiet.

" You are unreasonable," he said to the two brothers. " You have seen the paper ; old M. Séchard has told you that his son, whom he locked in, produced excellent samples of paper in a single night from raw materials that must have cost next to nothing. You come here as prospective purchasers. Do you wish to make an offer ? Yes or no ? "

" Look here," said the tall Cointet, " whether my brother is willing or not, I am willing to risk, on my own account, paying M. Séchard's debts. I will pay six thousand francs down over and above the debts, and M. Séchard shall have thirty per cent of the profits ; but I should like to make this clear—if within a year he has not fulfilled the conditions which he himself will lay down in the deed of partnership he is to return us the six thousand francs, and we will keep the patent and get out of it as best we can."

" Are you sure of yourself ? " Petit-Claud asked David, drawing him aside.

" Yes," said David. He was deceived by the tactics of the two brothers, and was only afraid that the fat Cointet would break off the negotiations on which his future depended.

" Very well, I shall go home and draw up the agreement," said Petit-Claud to Eve and the Cointets ; " you shall each have a duplicate copy by this evening, and you can have all tomorrow to think it over. Then, tomorrow evening, you can sign it. You, gentlemen, will withdraw Métivier's suit, I will write to stop the case at the Royal Court, and we will notify one another officially that proceedings have been stopped on both sides."

David Séchard's undertakings were set forth as follows :

" Between the undersigned, etc. . . .

" M. David Séchard, junior, printer, of Angoulême, affirming that he has discovered a method of sizing paper pulp evenly in the vat, and a method of reducing the cost of manufacture of paper of all descriptions by more than fifty per cent by the introduction of vegetable substances into the pulp, either in combination with rags as at present employed, or without any admixture of rags ; a partnership for the exploitation of the patent applied for in respect of this invention is hereby formed between M. David Séchard junior and the firm of Cointet Brothers, subject to the clauses and conditions hereinafter appended."

One of these clauses stipulated that David Séchard should forfeit completely all his rights if he failed to fulfil his undertakings as set forth in the agreement, carefully worded by the tall Cointet, and passed by David.

When Petit-Claud brought this draft at half-past seven next morning, he told David and his wife at the same time that Cérizet was prepared to offer twenty-two thousand francs for the printing business. The sale could be completed that very evening.

" But if the Cointets were to hear about the sale, they are quite capable of refusing to sign your agreement, of persecuting you, and selling you up."

" Are you sure of payment ? " said Eve, astonished to see an affair settled that she had despaired of, and that would have saved her three months earlier.

" The money is in my hands," said Petit-Claud briefly.

" But this is magic," said David, and asked Petit-Claud for some explanation of this piece of good fortune.

" It is very simple," said Petit-Claud ; " the tradespeople of l'Houmeau want to establish a newspaper."

" But I have undertaken not to publish a paper," David exclaimed.

" You may have done so—but not your successor. . . . In any case," he went on, " don't worry about it, sell the business and pocket the money, and leave Cérizet to disentangle the conditions of the sale ; he knows how to take care of himself."

" He does indeed ! " said Eve.

" If you are forbidden to publish a paper in Angoulême," the lawyer continued, " Cérizet's backers will transfer it to l'Houmeau."

Eve was so dazzled at the prospect of possessing thirty thousand francs, of being free from want, that she saw the deed of partnership as of only secondary importance. And so it came about that M. and Mme Séchard conceded a further point that was raised at a second discussion. The tall Cointet insisted that the patent should be taken out in his name. He managed to establish that, since

David's rights were perfectly clearly defined in the deed of partnership, it made no difference which name appeared on the patent. His brother clinched the matter by saying :

" He is putting up the money for the patent, and paying the travelling expenses, another two thousand francs! Either he takes it out in his name or we drop the matter altogether."

The lynx won the discussion on every single point in turn. The agreement was signed at half-past four. The tall Cointet gallantly presented Mme Séchard with a dozen rat-tailed spoons and forks and a beautiful Ternaux shawl, by way of pin-money, so he said, to make her forget any unpleasantness there might have been during the discussion! Scarcely had the duplicate agreement been exchanged, Cachan had no sooner handed over to Petit-Claud the discharge and all the documents, including the three disastrous bills that Lucien had forged, than a deafening rumble was heard as a heavy carrier's van drew up at the door ; Kolb's voice was heard on the stairs.

" Montame! montame! fifteen tausand francs! " he cried. " Dey come from Poitiers, in goot gold, from meinherr Lucien! "

" Fifteen thousand francs! " Eve repeated, throwing up her hands.

" Yes, ma'am," said the carrier, who appeared behind Kolb, " fifteen thousand francs sent by the Bordeaux coach, and no carriage to pay either! I have two men down there bringing up the bags. The name of the sender is M. Lucien Chardon de Rubempré. I have brought up a small leather bag, in which there is five hundred francs for you, in gold pieces, and I think there is a letter as well."

Eve thought she must be dreaming as she read :

" My dear Sister,

"Here are fifteen thousand francs. Instead of killing myself I have sold myself. I am no longer my own master. I am the secretary of a Spanish diplomat, and something more than a secretary. I belong to him body and soul.

" I am entering upon a terrible existence. Perhaps I would have done better to drown myself.

" Goodbye. David will be free, and with the extra four thousand francs you can buy a little paper mill, and make a fortune.

" I ask you only to forget

Your unhappy brother,

Lucien."

" It seems to be fated that my poor son must always bring disaster upon us, as he himself said—even in doing good," said Mme Chardon.

" We have had a lucky escape! " said the tall Cointet, as the brothers walked back across the Place du Mûrier. " An hour later and the shine of gold would have thrown its light on the deed of partnership, and our man would have taken fright. Now he has promised us, and in three months' time we shall know what to do."

At seven the same evening Cérizet bought the printing business and paid for it, undertaking to pay rent for the last quarter. The next day Eve sent forty thousand francs to the Receiver General, to invest in her husband's name, so as to bring in an income of two thousand five hundred francs. She then wrote to her father-in-law, asking him to find a small estate at Marsac, for ten thousand francs, in which to invest her personal property.

Boniface Cointet's plan was alarmingly simple. From the outset he had come to the conclusion that the sizing of the pulp in the vat was impracticable. The addition of inexpensive vegetable products to the linen pulp was, as he at once saw, the real and essential means of making a fortune. He therefore proposed to make little of the cheapness of the pulp, and to lay great stress on the sizing process, on the following plausible grounds. The Angoulême paper mills were engaged almost exclusively, at that time, in the manufacture of writing-papers—crown, foolscap, post-demy, and note-papers, which, of course, are all sized. These papers had long been the special pride of the Angoulême paper industry; the fact that sized papers had long been the speciality, the monopoly of the Angoulême manufacturers, gave weight to the Cointets' insistence on this point; although, as a matter of fact, the sizing process counted for nothing in their speculation.

The market for writing-papers is very limited; whereas that for unsized papers, for printing purposes, is practically unlimited. During his visit to Paris, to take out the patent in his own name, the tall Cointet planned various business deals that were to revolutionise completely the output of his factory. Cointet stayed with Métivier in Paris and instructed him to obtain the custom of as many newspapers as he could. Cointet proposed to undercut the current prices of paper to such an extent that no other manufacturer would be able to compete, and he promised the newspapers at the same time white paper of better quality than the best samples then available.

Since existing contracts with paper retailers would take some time to expire, the realisation of this monopoly meant a certain period of subterranean negotiations with the proprietors of newspapers; Cointet calculated that he would have time to get rid of Séchard while Métivier was obtaining orders from the principal Paris newspapers, whose paper consumption had at that time risen to two hundred reams a day. Cointet naturally offered Métivier a commission on these orders on a percentage basis; he was anxious to have an able representative on the spot, in Paris, so as not to have to spend time in travelling. This was the beginning of Métivier's fortune—one of the largest in the paper-trade. For ten years he held contracts from all the Paris newspapers without any fear of competition.

The tall Cointet went back to Angoulême with his mind at rest as to the future. He arrived just in time for Petit-Claud's marriage. Petit-Claud had sold his connection, and was only waiting for his successor to be appointed in order to take Monsieur Milaud's place, which had been promised to Countess du Châtelet's protégé. The Second Deputy Prosecutor of Angoulême was promoted to the post of First Deputy at Limoges, and the Keeper of the Seals sent a man of his own to Angoulême, where the post of First Deputy was kept vacant for two months. This interval was Petit-Claud's honeymoon.

In the tall Cointet's absence, David had made a first experimental batch of unsized paper, far superior to the paper then used by the newspapers, and then a second batch of beautiful vellum paper, intended for fine printing. The Cointets used this paper for a new edition of the Diocesan Prayer-book. The material was prepared, in secret, by David himself, assisted only by Kolb and Marion.

But when Boniface Cointet returned from Paris things took on a different aspect. He looked at the samples of paper, and he was moderately satisfied.

" My dear friend," he said to David, " the trade of Angoulême is in crown paper. First of all, we must produce the best quality crown paper at fifty per cent less than the present cost."

David tried out a batch of sized pulp for crown paper, but the surface was rough, and the size formed grains on its surface. On the day this experiment was made, David took one of the sheets of paper and went into a quiet corner to devour his disappointment in solitude ; but the tall Cointet sought him out and was most amiable to him. He tried to comfort his partner.

" Don't be discouraged," he said, " keep on trying! I am not a bad sort, I understand you, and I will stand by you to the last! "

" Really," David said to his wife when he went home to dinner, " our partners are very good people, I never should have expected the tall Cointet to be so generous! " And he told her of his conversation with his treacherous associate.

David spent three months in making a series of experiments. He slept at the paper mill and studied the results of various compositions of his pulp. At one time he attributed his failure to the admixture of rags in his raw materials, and he made a batch entirely composed of vegetable ingredients. Then he tried to size a pulp composed entirely of rags ; and so he proceeded with his experiments, under the eye of the tall Cointet, whom he had ceased to mistrust, using first one compound and then another until he had tried every possible combination of raw materials with every kind of size.

During the first six months of the year 1823 David Séchard lived at the paper mill, with Kolb—if living it can be called, when a man scarcely takes time to eat, and ceases to pay any attention to his dress or personal appearance. He struggled so desperately with difficulties that any men but the Cointets would have recognised the sublimity of the single-minded devotion of this man who laboured at his task without any thought of self-interest. For by now, his one thought was to conquer his problem.

He observed, with deep insight, the behaviour of substances synthesised by man into products for his own purposes, in which the secret resistances of nature are, as it were, overcome ; and he deduced more than one conclusion of great importance to industry ; he observed that one could only create synthetic products of this kind by observing the innate affinities of things—what he himself called the " secondary nature " of substances.

At last, in August, he succeeded in obtaining a paper, sized in the vat, indistinguishable from the paper used at the present time for proofs in printing-houses, a paper not uniform in quality, for the sizing itself is unreliable. This result, which was a triumph in 1823 in the existing state of the paper trade, had cost ten thousand francs, and David had hopes of solving the last difficulties of the problem. But there were strange rumours circulating in Angoulême and l'Houmeau. David Séchard was ruining the Cointet brothers! He had devoured thirty thousand francs in experiments, and he had finally produced, so it was said, only very poor paper. Other manufacturers, taking fright, congratulated themselves on having kept to the old methods ; and, jealous of the Cointets, they spread the rumour that that ambitious firm was on the verge of ruin. Tall Cointet, meanwhile, had ordered machines for manufacturing paper in continuous lengths, giving out, however, that these machines were being bought for David Séchard's experiments. But that Jesuit mixed his pulp according to David's formula ; and while he was urging David to direct all his efforts to the question of sizing in the vat, he was already despatching thousands of reams of paper to Métivier.

One day in September the tall Cointet took David aside ; when David told him that he was contemplating an experiment that he believed would prove finally successful, he dissuaded him from continuing the struggle.

" My dear David, go down to Marsac and see your wife, and take a holiday after your exertions—we don't want to be ruined," said Cointet in the friendliest way imaginable. " What you see as a final success, after all, is only a beginning. We must wait a bit before undertaking any new experiments. Be reasonable! The results have not amounted to much! We are not only paper manufacturers, we are printers and bankers as well, and people are beginning to talk. They say you are ruining us."

David Séchard, in the simplicity of his heart, was about to protest his good faith.

"Oh, fifty thousand francs thrown into the Charente would not ruin us," the tall Cointet continued, waving aside David's gesture; "but we do not want to be obliged to pay cash for everything because our credit is suffering through current rumours; that would bring our business to a standstill. The year of our agreement is up, and we shall both have to think it over."

"He is right!" David thought, for, immersed in his own large-scale experiments, he had not given a thought to the output of the factory.

He went home to Marsac, where, during the last six months, he had spent only his week-ends, from Saturday evening to Tuesday morning. Eve, acting upon her father-in-law's good advice, had bought a house called la Verberie, immediately adjoining the old man's vineyard. There were three acres of garden, and a vine-close dovetailed into the old man's vineyard. She lived very simply, with her mother and Marion, for she still owed five thousand francs on the purchase of this charming little estate, the prettiest in Marsac. The house lay between a court and the garden, and was built of white tufa stone, with a slate roof, and freely decorated with carvings, which, as tufa is a soft stone, cost very little. The pretty furniture from Angoulême looked even prettier in Eve's new house, for in those days nobody thought of living in luxury in the country. On the garden side stood a row of oranges, pomegranates and rare shrubs, planted by the previous owner, an old General, who had died at the hands of Marron.

David was sitting with his wife, his father and little Lucien under an orange tree, when the bailiff from Mansle appeared, bringing a formal notice from the Cointet brothers requesting their partner to appoint an arbitrator to settle disputes arising from the terms of

A house called la Verberie

their agreement. Cointet Brothers were demanding the restitution of six thousand francs and the surrender of all David's rights in the patent as indemnity for the exorbitant outlay made by them to no purpose.

" They say you are ruining them! " said the old bear to his son. " Well, if that is so, it is the first thing you have ever done that has given me real pleasure."

At nine o'clock next morning Eve and David were sitting in the waiting-room of M. Petit-Claud who had by now become the defender of widows, and guardian of orphans ; he was the only person who seemed likely to be able to advise them.

The magistrate received his old clients most warmly and absolutely insisted that they should lunch with him.

" So the Cointets are claiming six thousand francs! " he said, smiling. " How much do you still owe on the purchase of la Verberie ? "

" Five thousand francs, but I have two thousand already," said Eve.

" Keep your two thousand," said Petit-Claud. " Five thousand is not much! You could do with another ten thousand to settle you in comfortably there. All right, in two hours' time the Cointets shall present you with fifteen thousand francs."

Eve's astonishment was plain to see.

" In return for your renunciation of all claims to the profits arising from the partnership, which you will agree to relinquish in an amicable settlement," said the magistrate. " How will that suit you ? "

" Would it really be legally ours ? " Eve asked.

" No doubt about that," said the magistrate, smiling. " The Cointets have caused you enough troubles, and I should like to put an end to their pretensions. Listen to me. I am a magistrate now, and I owe it to you to tell you the truth ; very well, the Cointets are playing you false at this moment, but you are in their hands. You might win the case that they intend to bring against you if you decide to fight it. Do you want to find yourselves exactly where you are now, after ten years' litigation ? Experts' fees and arbitration can be multiplied indefinitely, and contradictory opinions will be given —it is a toss-up whether you would win the case. And besides," he added with a smile, " I don't know where you would find a lawyer here capable of defending you. My successor is certainly not equal to it. Come, now, an unsatisfactory settlement would be better than a successful lawsuit."

" Any arrangement that will allow us to live in peace will satisfy me," said David.

" Paul! " Petit-Claud called his servant. " Go and fetch M. Ségaud, my successor! He will go and see the Cointets while we have lunch," he added, turning to his old clients, " and in a few hours' time you can go back to Marsac, ruined, but with nothing further to worry about. With ten thousand francs you can purchase another five hundred francs' income, and you can live at peace on your pretty little property."

Two hours later, just as Petit-Claud had promised, M. Ségaud came back, with an agreement duly signed by the Cointets and fifteen thousand-franc notes.

" We owe you a great deal," said David to Petit-Claud.

" But I have just ruined you," said Petit-Claud, to the great astonishment of his former clients. " I tell you once more, I have ruined you, as you will see as time goes on ; but knowing you as I do, I believe you would rather be ruined than wait for a fortune that might come too late."

" We don't care about money," said Eve, " and we can only thank you for having given us the means of happiness. We shall always be deeply grateful to you."

" Gracious heavens! Don't thank me! " said Petit-Claud. " It puts me to shame ; but I think that today I have made up for everything. If I am a magistrate, it is thanks to you, and if anyone ought to be grateful, it is I. Goodbye! "

As time went on, Kolb modified his opinion of old Séchard, who, for his part, took a liking to the Alsatian when he found that, like himself, he could neither read nor write, and that it was easy to make him a little drunk. The old bear taught the ex-cavalryman the art of vine-tending and the sale of the vintage ; he trained him with the idea of leaving a responsible man in charge of his children, for, in his later years, he grew childishly anxious about the fate of his property. He had taken Courtois the miller into his confidence.

" You will see how things will go with my children when I am underground," he used to say. " Eh, dear! I don't like to think about what will become of them! "

Old Séchard died in the March of 1829, leaving real estate to the value of two hundred thousand francs. His land, added to la Verberie, made a very fine property, which for the last two years had been managed admirably by Kolb.

David and his wife discovered about a hundred thousand gold crowns in the old man's house. Public opinion, as usual, had exaggerated old Séchard's wealth, which was given out in the Department of the Charente to be in the region of a million. Eve and David's income, when their inheritance was added to their little fortune—for they waited for some time before investing their capital, with which they bought Government bonds after the July Revolution—amounted to about thirty thousand francs a year.

Only then did the Department of the Charente and David Séchard come to have any idea of the wealth of the tall Cointet. A multimillionaire, and a Deputy, Boniface Cointet has become a Peer of France, and it is rumoured that he will be Minister of Commerce in the next Government. In 1842 he married the daughter of one of the most influential statesmen of the day, Mlle Popinot, daughter of M. Anselme Popinot, a Deputy for Paris, and Mayor of an *arrondissement.*

David Séchard's discovery has been assimilated into French industry, as food is assimilated into a great body. Thanks to the introduction of materials other than rags, French factories today manufacture paper more cheaply than do those of any other country in Europe. Dutch paper, as David Séchard foresaw, no longer exists. Sooner or later it will no doubt be necessary to establish a Royal Paper Manufactury, like the Gobelins, Sèvres, the Savonnerie, and the Imprimerie Royale, which have hitherto survived the attacks made upon them by bourgeois vandalism.

David Séchard, happy in his marriage, and the father of two sons and a daughter, has the tact never to talk about his experiments. Eve had the good sense to persuade him to give up the terrible vocation of the inventor, that Moses consumed by his own burning bush. He takes an interest in literature, by way of relaxation, and lives the happy indolent life of a landowner managing his own estate. He has said goodbye for ever to dreams of fame, and taken his place, with a good grace, in the class of dreamers and collectors ; he has taken up entomology, and is at present engaged on investigating the metamorphoses of certain insects, hitherto known to science only in their final stages.

Petit-Claud's success as Attorney-General is a matter of common knowledge ; he is the rival of that famous man, Vinet of Provins, and it is his ambition to become President of the Royal Court at Poitiers.

Cérizet has been condemned so frequently for political offences that he has been a good deal talked about ; as one of the most incorrigible radical agitators, he is widely known as the " brave Cérizet ". When Petit-Claud's successor compelled him to sell his printing-house in Angoulême, he found a new outlet for his talents on the provincial stage, where his gift for acting a part seemed to promise him a brilliant future. But on account of a certain leading lady he was forced to go to Paris to find a cure for love in the resources of science, and there he tried to curry favour with the Liberal party.

As for Lucien, his return to Paris belongs to the *Scènes de la vie Parisienne*.

ABOUT THE AUTHOR

HONRE DE BALZAC, often said to be the greatest of French novelists, was born in 1799. His novels, taken together, form what he called "The Human Comedy." His purpose in this monumental undertaking was to make an inventory of all the vices and virtues, the manners and customs, of Nineteenth Century French Society. Among the most outstanding in this series of novels are *Eugenie Grandet* (1834), *Père Goriot* (1834) and *Cousine Bette* (1846).

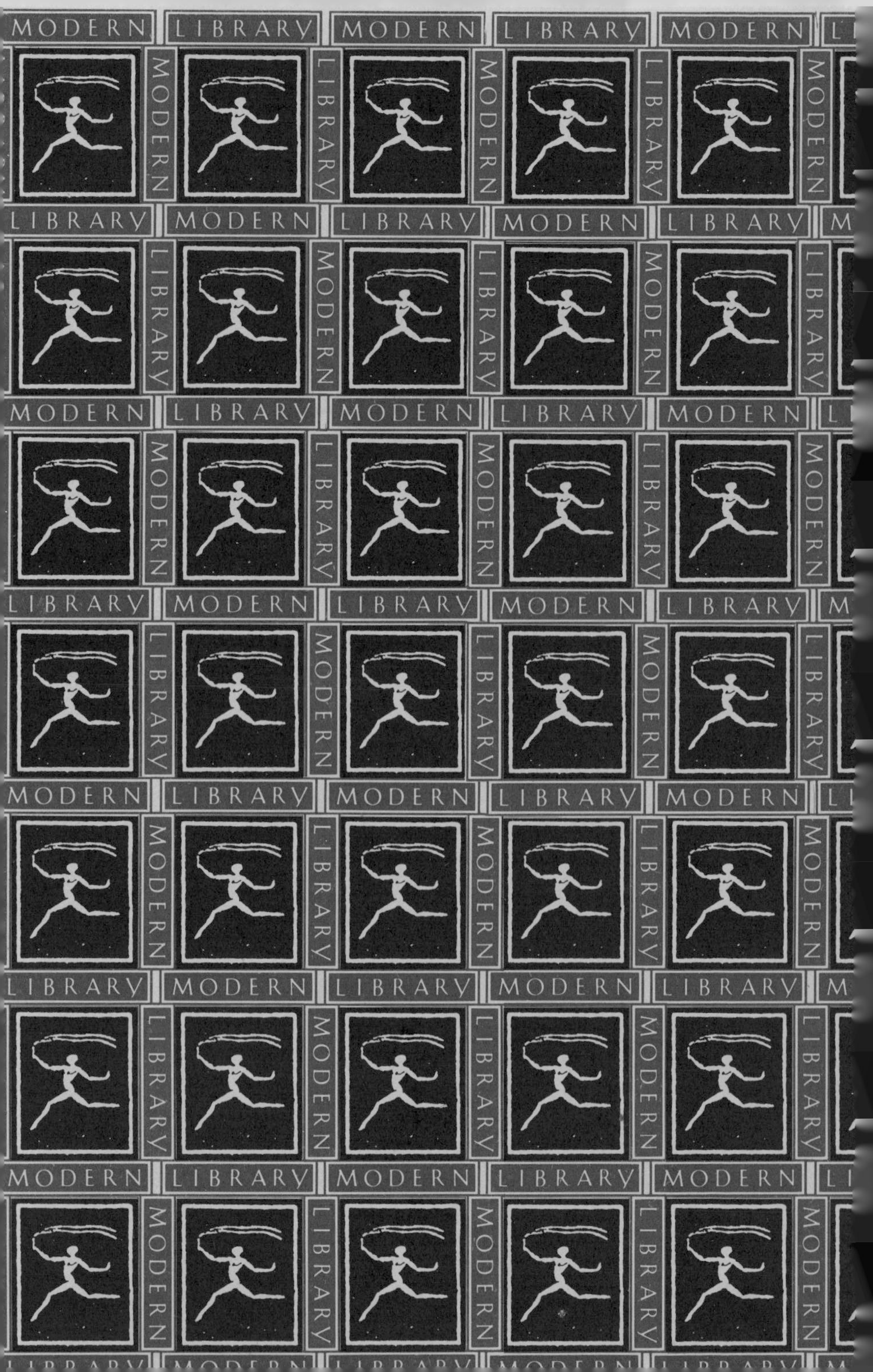
MODERN LIBRARY